PENGUIN BOOKS

The Plutonium Factor

Michael Bagley was born in London in 1947. He is now a lecturer in Teachers' Education at a College of Further Education in Hampshire, where he lives with his wife and two children. This is his first novel, which he wrote in his spare time, and he hopes to follow it with more fact-based thrillers on politically contentious themes.

Michael Bagley

THE PLUTONIUM FACTOR

Penguin Books

For my wife

Penguin Books Ltd, Harmondsworth, Middlesex, England
Penguin Books, 40 West 23rd Street, New York, New York 10010, U.S.A.
Penguin Books Australia Ltd, Ringwood, Victoria, Australia
Penguin Books Canada Ltd, 2801 John Street, Markham, Ontario, Canada L3R 1B4
Penguin Books (N.Z.) Ltd, 182–190 Wairau Road, Auckland 10, New Zealand

First published by Allison and Busby Ltd 1982
Published in Penguin Books 1983

Copyright © Michael Bagley, 1982

Made and printed in Great Britain by
Richard Clay (The Chaucer Press) Ltd,
Bungay, Suffolk

Set in 9 on 10½ Monophoto Sabon

FAUST: Go bear these tidings to great Lucifer:
Seeing Faustus hath incurr'd eternal death
By desperate thoughts against Jove's deity,
Say, he surrenders up to him his soul,
So he will spare him four-and-twenty years,
Letting him live in all voluptuousness;
Having thee ever to attend on me,
To give me whatsoever I shall ask,
To tell me whatsoever I demand,
To slay mine enemies, and aid my friends,
And always be obedient to my will.
Go and return to mighty Lucifer.

Christopher Marlowe, *The Tragical History of*
Doctor Faustus (1604)

Plutonium has a half-life of 24,000 years.

MEPHISTOPHELES: A task that gives me little cause to shrink,
I'll readily oblige you with such treasures.
But now, my friend, the time is ripe, I think,
For relishing in peace some tasty pleasures.

FAUST: If I be quieted with a bed of ease,
Then let that moment be the end of me!
If ever flattering lies of yours can please
And soothe my soul to self-sufficiency,
And make me one of pleasure's devotees,
Then take my soul, for I desire to die:
And that's a wager!

MEPHISTOPHELES: Done!

Goethe, *Faust* (1805)

Contents

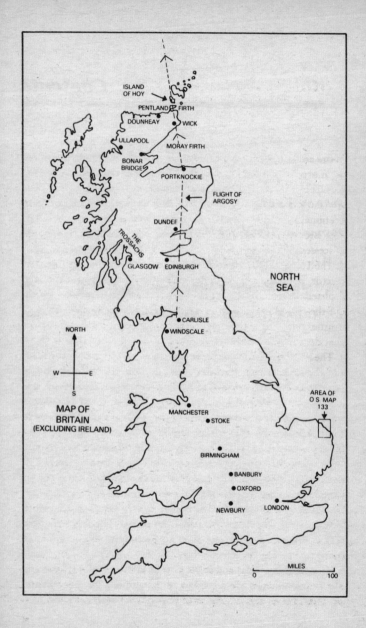

ISLAND
OF HOY
PENTLAND FIRTH
DOUNREAY
WICK
ULLAPOOL
MORAY FIRTH
BONAR
BRIDGE
PORTKNOCKIE
FLIGHT OF
ARGOSY
DUNDEE
THE
TROSSACHS
GLASGOW EDINBURGH
NORTH
SEA
CARLISLE
WINDSCALE
NORTH

W——E

S

MAP OF
BRITAIN
(EXCLUDING IRELAND)

AREA OF
O S MAP
133

MANCHESTER
STOKE

BIRMINGHAM

BANBURY
OXFORD
NEWBURY LONDON

MILES
0   100

Author's Note

There are four main types of nuclear reactor in operation in Britain, or in process of construction: the Magnox Reactor, the Advanced Gas-Cooled Reactor (AGR), the Pressurized Water Reactor (PWR) and the Fast Breeder Reactor. The first three are thermal or 'conventional' reactors – that is they use *uranium* as their fuel. The Fast Breeder, on the other hand, uses *plutonium*, or, rather, reprocessed plutonium oxide.

The Department of Energy says: 'The case for the fast (breeder) reactor rests on its ability to make use of the plutonium and depleted uranium which are by-products of thermal reactors. Without the fast reactor, shortages of natural uranium could begin to constrain nuclear power station ordering beyond the end of the next decade' (21 December 1979).

The Fast Breeder has been in development in Britain since the 1950s and the experience gained has given the country an international position as one of the world leaders in Fast Reactor technology. It is seen by many as *the* energy development of the future. At the moment we have one experimental Fast Breeder at Dounreay on the north coast of Scotland and two reprocessing plants which can supply the plutonium fuel – one at Dounreay and one at Windscale in Cumbria.

The author is convinced that what follows is possible. Indeed, it is that conviction which led him to write this book. But it is not his intention to provide a blueprint for any criminal mind so inclined. He has therefore not only deleted one or two key facts (the word 'deleted' will appear in the text), but also deliberately changed others, because he does not wish to precipitate the events he is trying to avoid by writing the book.

However, the places and statements of fact are real and accurate. The people, though, are a product of the author's imagination and any reference to individuals, alive or dead, is purely coincidental.

9

Prologue

The town had about three dozen small houses and four or five larger buildings. They formed two rows on either side of a dusty road, ending in a square, in the centre of which stood the church and, beside it, a well. The buildings were all made of white stone, with black holes for windows and doors, all shutters closed against the heat of the day.

The cantina, like all the dwellings, was flat-topped and flat-sided. The owner had rigged a large canvas awning outside, that had faded a dull, yellow-green colour, with several battered tables and chairs scattered around underneath. At this time of the day it was seldom used, his customers preferring the cooler air inside. But yesterday the two strangers had arrived by helicopter – an Englishman and an American.

As he stopped at the door the owner saw them, out there sipping their beer and watching the road. They had shown everyone the photograph, but no one had seen the man. They had been insistent that he might have passed through. But no one passes through San Claro. There is nowhere to go. No one ever comes to San Claro. There is nothing to do. Yet there they were, waiting and looking down the road, dressed in stupid clothes, the sweat pouring off them. Still, who was he to complain? They had paid handsomely for the room, they drank beer (which was expensive) continuously, and they provided a ready topic of conversation inside, which kept people drinking.

He continued his journey with the two beers and put them gently on the table beside the two men. As he did so, one of them stiffened. It was so out of character with the general malaise that had overcome them that the innkeeper was momentarily captivated by the slight movement. Then the blond American kicked his companion awake and they both stared down the road. The Mexican turned his head and there, just entering the gap between the houses, was a man on horseback. The rider was wearing a white and brown patterned poncho and a straw hat left the face in shadow.

As he approached, the Englishman withdrew the photograph.

'What do you think?' he asked.

'It's gotta be him,' answered the blond man. 'Too much of a coincidence. Anyway, you heard Slim,' flicking his thumb at the owner. 'No one ever comes here – only mad dogs and Englishmen.'

The other smiled. The rider dismounted from his sweating horse at the well and removed his hat.

'The beard changes his whole appearance,' said the Englishman.

There was still some water in the bucket from the last time someone had drawn water. The rider poured it into an old trough near by and allowed his horse to drink. When he considered that she had taken enough, he tethered her to one of the well stanchions and stroked her head for some time. Then he walked over to the cantina.

By now most of the inhabitants had come out to watch. The man stopped in the shade of the awning and eyed the onlookers. He seemed unsurprised by the interest shown in him. No one spoke.

What they saw was a tanned Caucasian, in his late twenties, with brown hair bleached by the sun in streaks. He had a nose that was a little too flat, a generous mouth and a wide jaw. The latter was covered by a thick, but trimmed, black beard. He was about six feet tall, must have weighed about thirteen stone and, Striker thought, in that get-up he looked the image of a nineteenth-century Mexican bandit. The only thing missing was a crossbelt of bullets.

The rider's gaze lingered on the two strangers as they found themselves unable to speak. Then he looked at the owner of the cantina – his position in the group obvious from his apron and rotund figure. Only the innkeepers could afford to eat well in that part of the world.

'*Dos cervezas, por favor, Señor,*' said the rider.

This time it was the owner's turn to jump, as if being awoken from a dream. '*Si, Señor,*' and he hurried inside.

The rider walked slowly to a table and sat down. Then he eyed the onlookers again. Most averted their faces as his gaze alighted upon them and some went inside. As his look took in the two obvious strangers for the second time, Striker began to feel distinctly uncomfortable. The rider looked away to his horse.

'Mr Calder?' ventured the American.

The rider's expression didn't alter. Then he laughed. It was a full deep-throated laugh.

'This has got to go down in my memoirs,' he said, and threw his head back and roared again.

The other two men looked at each other, got up and walked over.

'My name is Peter Striker,' said the American. 'This is Tony Fox.'

Calder looked up at them and, now that they were standing, took them in quickly. They were both in their mid twenties and very fit, especially the fair-haired American, although, judging by the way their shirts were plastered to their bodies, they weren't prepared for this sort of temperature. By the colour of their skin they hadn't been in Mexico more than a day or two.

'Sit down, and bring your beer – it's precious out here.'

Fox walked back for it, and the owner arrived with Calder's two bottled lagers and a glass. With a sigh and a quick *'gracias'* he reached out and started to pour one, very slowly.

'I'm intrigued to hear what's brought you all the way out here to find me, but just at this moment even that must take second place to this beer, even if it is American.'

With the froth at the top of the glass, he raised it to his lips and, with eyes closed, drained it. He filled it again with the remainder of the bottle and drained that too. A low sigh emerged from his throat and between slitted eyes he stared at the empty glass.

'There are some moments in life,' he said, 'some pleasures, that must be savoured above most others. And that was one of them.'

For a few moments more he gazed at the glass, then swivelled his eyes to look at Striker. They were grey, the latter decided, and the most piercing he had ever seen.

'You had us fooled for a moment,' said Fox. 'The beard . . .'

'I've got rather fond of it,' said Calder, stroking the result of two months in Central America.

'General Stoddard,' said Striker. 'He wants to see you urgently.' The eyes swung back again, boring into him this time.

'Why?' asked Calder in a low voice, still glaring at Striker. The blond man was determined not to look away, but blinked instead under the steady gaze.

'We don't know exactly,' said Striker, glancing at Fox. 'But the General did say to tell you that something you told him would happen, has.'

Calder looked away for several seconds. He then filled his glass from the second bottle and drank it slowly.

'Have you made transport arrangements?' he asked.

'We've got a helicopter just outside the village,' answered Striker. 'We picked it up from Mexico City, but it's probably better to head north, across the US–Mexican border and catch a direct flight back. We could be in London by tomorrow morning.'

Calder grimaced. 'Then we don't have time to waste,' he said. 'If I were you, while you're settling up with the owner, I'd buy some food and beer for the journey. How much money do you have?'

Striker was a little taken aback. 'Enough.'

'Good. Then when I've found an honest man to look after my horse until I return, you can pay him what he asks.'

He drained his glass and stood up.

'There is one other thing. Do you think I could see your IDs?'

Striker had asked Stoddard what they should do if Calder refused to come. The General had just smiled and said that the question would not arise. It had struck him at the time that the Old Man must really have something going with this guy. Now, with Calder smiling at him, he thought he understood.

I HIJACK

Monday, 5 May (three days earlier)

Chapter 1

It can be very cold at dawn in early May at Carlisle Airport. The sun had not yet risen but a delicate glistening of frost could be seen in the slowly gathering light. It was also very quiet, so when the curlew called across the flats, a stark and eerie sound, the man in the thicket, on the west border of the airfield, came fully awake.

Not that he had been sleeping. The biting cold had seen to that. But he had become drowsy as the heat from his body had slowly dissipated into the night. He began to beat his arms across the front of his body, trying to be as silent as possible. As the blood started to circulate he began to shiver. He was still some way from dying of exposure, he thought, but pneumonia was a distinct possibility. Gradually, he explored the sensations of his body. They weren't many. He had spent the night standing against a sapling, clothed in fur-lined anorak, hands in pockets. His hands were not too cold but his feet weren't there at all. He wanted to walk, to get some life back into them, but knew he couldn't. So he began to stretch on to his toes, breathing deeply, his breath visible in the chill, still air. After a few minutes he stopped, conscious of how his back ached. He still couldn't feel his feet. God, he was cold.

Carefully, he stalked forward and, crouching down, emerged from the copse behind some low bushes. From anywhere but the air, he reasoned, he was totally invisible, even if you could see in the near-dark.

Looking to the east, as he was, the man could dimly discern a control-tower against the lightening horizon. Behind it were two large hangars and beside these, across the entrance road, were the various ancillary buildings, stretching in line about a hundred yards or so along the perimeter. Electric light shone through some of the windows. There was a large concrete space outside the two hangars, which came towards him in two tarmac roads. These led to the east–west runway, stretching into the distance to his right, and the north–south runway, which ran across in front of him. Neither could have been more than half a mile long.

Carlisle Airport, the man thought, was not a major international air terminal. Indeed, now that the sharply rising hills were coming into focus against the brighter sky to the east and with the first beams of light touching the still snow-capped mountains to the south, glistening spectre-like against the darker sky, the airport looked more like an almost forgotten Andes staging post in some South American dictatorship. This impression was added to when the fence which surrounded part of the field was taken into account. It could not have been designed to keep out people, being the sort of obstruction you normally see around a field to retain cattle. But even that was a flattery. In parts the fence had broken down and for most of the perimeter a holey hedge was the only obstacle. Last night the man had simply walked through one of the open boundary gates behind the coppice in which he now knelt.

The sound of a fast-moving car on the secondary road less than a mile away reminded him of his task. Scuffling to his left made him also realize that he was not the only fauna in the little copse. Suddenly, a rabbit popped out from behind a bush. Instinctively, he remained completely still, just as Brown had taught him, but the rabbit sensed something was wrong and scampered back. A curlew called again. The man looked at his watch. The luminous hands said 5.10. He would have sold his soul for a good, stiff brandy.

Instead, Martin the Lookout slowly crept back to the nearest tree, stood up, hunched his shoulders against the cold and stared at the second hangar across the airfield, now coming more into vision as the horizon began to streak in yellow and pink.

Inside the hangar, Brown also looked at his watch. He too was cold, but at least he wasn't shivering. He looked round into the blackness beside him – at the five others who were huddled there. He still couldn't see them. The light from the small office, to the side and in the middle of the hangar, created a shadow behind the boxes and chests where they hid at the back. He knew they weren't asleep. Occasionally one would stir, but that wasn't the reason, he knew. Perhaps within minutes, certainly within the hour, the months, for him years, of planning would be put into practice, and they were apprehensive.

He, though, was more excited than uneasy. This tension was what he lived for. To him the quintessence of existence was planning an 'operation', for every contingency, and then executing it. It was a test of his own abilities. Anyone foolish enough to get in the way would probably be killed. Had he lived in medieval times he would have been called 'evil', but he wasn't born bad.

He took a quick look over the boxes. The two men were still inside the glass office, working on something probably. They certainly weren't talking, as the sound would have carried in the stillness of the morning.

Out in the centre of the hangar stood the Hawker Siddeley Argosy 220, wraith-like in the shadows. It looked like a rather portly, yet ghostly, albatross, its bulbous belly supported by a large wing and square tailplane section. This last feature of the aircraft made it resemble the rear end of the original Second World War Mosquito. But that was the only similarity between the two planes. The Mosquito was a fast, wooden-built fighter-bomber. The Argosy is a large, four-engined, short-range freighter with a wingspan of 115 feet and a maximum payload of 32,000 lb, about 14,545 kilos. With the 12,000 lb of freight and a third of the potential fuel capacity on board, Brown knew that she had a maximum range of about 750 miles. He knew how much was on board because he had watched it being loaded the night before.

The fork-lift that had come with the cargo on the lorry had worked well as it seemingly struggled to cope with the weight of each hexagonally shaped fuel assembly. Each was twelve feet long and about six inches across between the diagonals, and the lifter had been especially adapted to cope with this odd shape. Each assembly, he knew, weighed about 1,000 lb – about 450 kilos – and he had counted twelve trips from the truck to the cargo hold of the Argosy. The rear-loading capability of the plane made it a comparatively easy job. The loader simply drove into the cargo hold and stacked the assemblies in the prepared racks.

The job had been done inside an hour. The fork-lift was secured away aboard the lorry and it had left, leaving the Austin, plus its two passengers – security officers, both in plain clothes and both, Brown knew, armed.

Getting into the hangar had been child's play. He still couldn't believe how easy. Hiding behind the east hedge after dark, they had waited for the big, articulated lorry to arrive, plus the Austin Princess which followed at a discreet distance. They waited a further thirty minutes, while the transport was backed into the hangar and in order to allow the security team time to search the place. Then seven people had simply walked through the hedge, past the fuel store and straight to the back of the hangar. Brown was glad there had been no moon. They would have been forced to crawl and, with the packages they had carried, that would have proved difficult, although quite possible.

Brown had opened the padlock guarding the small, rear door of the hangar with a key, the impression of which one of his men had obtained on a previous trip; and, under cover of the noise of the fork-lift truck being started up, the six had entered to hide behind the boxes at the rear.

What to do with the padlock at this stage was a problem that had occupied a lot of thought. Brown's instincts told him he should have an escape route. But that meant retaining the padlock, which in turn meant that anyone testing locks wouldn't take very long to tumble to the fact that it was missing and their discovery would then be immediate. Brown had no doubt about their ability to escape, but the operation would be blown. He didn't think anyone was likely to be testing locks but he couldn't take the chance. So Martin had simply locked the door from the outside and walked off the airfield the way they had come.

There was no way out now except forward. But although his instincts rebelled, rational thought told him that it had to be this way. Whether they succeeded or failed, this was the last job that any of them would pull, therefore they had to commit themselves totally. He also knew that he would not fail.

As a young army officer he had realized very quickly that a life in the service of Her Majesty was not an attractive one. He had resolved that at the end of his short-service commission he would be out and away, to make a great deal of money. But how?

The answer had come to him one night while he lay in bed, and he had never changed it. He would have to steal. He wondered why he hadn't thought of it before. It seemed to him the most natural thing in the world. If the legitimate means of achieving wealth were not available, then he would have to use the illegitimate ones. Any scruples that he might have had before entering the Army, it soon beat out of him. The subservience to discipline created its own values, where survival, the Army's way, was the only route.

He had soon learnt, however, that the Army could teach a good deal and discovered that he had a talent for many things. He practised on the rifle-range until he could split an orange at two hundred yards, with a standard-issue rifle, ten times out of ten. But what he really liked was 'war games', as he called them. On manoeuvres his platoon always performed impressively. This was mainly because Brown could lead men.

He had an excited and at times animated personality, and could tell tales round the camp-fire until the early hours. But above all, when he gave orders they were firm and explicit, and his men obeyed them to the letter – not because he was an officer, but because he was Lieutenant Brown. Like all great leaders, he had that indefinable quality of being able to be 'one of the boys' yet somehow remain above them.

The final years of his commission had been spent waiting and planning. He talked more intimately to the non-commissioned officers and the men of his company, probing unobtrusively about their motives, their fears and their needs. He had also found out what they were prepared to do for money. When the time came for him to leave the Army he was a captain. He was also ready.

He had begun with a few petty thefts from houses, on his own, to provide enough working capital. It had been magnificently sensuous at first – observing the house from afar with binoculars for a few days and then, on a moonless night, silently drifting over the dewy turf, forcing the lock on the French windows, or using a glass-cutter and plunger, and looting the lower rooms, knowing that if he made a sound he might be discovered. It was a test of his competence and that was how he liked it. If he were disturbed, there was the knife in his belt. Then he would be gone the same way he had come – across the lawn at the rear and the fields beyond.

Eventually, though, the excitement began to go from houses, so he gathered his band together and robbed a few banks. They were more difficult but, provided you had enough imagination and thought of every contingency beforehand, it worked. Those who worked for him stayed, and all the time he was waiting and planning the big one – this one.

He glanced at his watch again. 5.33. Things would be happening soon. The most hazardous part of the operation was about to begin. The problem was crossing those forty yards of open concrete to the office without being seen. What's more, he had to wait until the flight crew arrived. He didn't want to repeat requests to the tower that had already been made.

He couldn't take any chances, so he reached down to his right and found a small, cold hand.

'Now,' he whispered.

Rustling movements in the dark told him that his command was being obeyed. Not that he expected anything else – it was just reassuring. Within minutes he knew that she would be naked but for a T-shirt, a very short skirt, stockings and a pair of high-heeled shoes. A somewhat incongruous get-up but, with a figure like Judy's, one designed to have the maximum effect on the men in the office. She would be cold for a while, but that was unavoidable. He probably wouldn't use her anyway, but he wanted every possibility at his disposal when the moment came.

He became aware of noises outside the hangar doors – the scuff of boot on stony concrete and the low murmurings that men reverently make at dawn. He really should have got Judy changed earlier. Still, she must be nearly ready.

There were three short raps. The noise reverberated around the confined area almost as one continuous sound. The two men in the office had heard them too and had been ready when the knocks came. It took the bigger of the two about twenty-five seconds to walk to the small inset in the huge, sliding doors, but no further sound was heard. The other was by the door of the office, gun in hand.

Brown could watch everything. With all attention riveted on the front of the hangar, neither security guard was going to turn to the back.

'Who is it?' shouted the guard at the door.

There was a short, guttural exclamation from outside.

'It's your pilot,' replied an Australian voice. 'Who the hell else do you think would be out here in this Godforsaken cold at this hour of the bloody morning?'

Brown noticed that the guard seemed to hesitate, but he stuck to his task.

'Name?'

'Oh, blimey, mate! You'll be asking for a password next. Greenfield. Now for God's sake, Rufus, open this bloody door.'

The door was opened and two men, clad in heavy leather flying gear, entered. One laughed and clapped the guard on the back.

'You know your trouble, Rufus?' said the Australian. 'You have no faith in people.'

Brown did not catch Rufus's reply, even if there was one. He had ducked down as they began to walk towards the glass office. The tension was building in him and he smiled in the dark.

'Take-off in thirty minutes,' called the pilot, apparently determined not to be disheartened by Rufus's sullen disposition. 'The wind is light, north to south, and the morning is fair.'

Brown could imagine him smiling into the face of the man by the office door. He looked at his watch again. 5.39. He peeped over the boxes. They were all inside the office and he knew instinctively that this was the right moment. With the four men in one place and blinded by the light of their own room, the chance was too good to miss.

'Wait,' he whispered, as he slipped a balaclava mask over his head. On rubber-soled shoes he rose from his hiding place. He was committed.

He slid along the wall and within thirty seconds was beside the office, crouching down to below glass level. He moved to the door, which was facing out into the hangar, and beckoned to his team. The next moment he was standing in the doorway.

The four men, all standing in the ten-by-ten feet space, made the place look very small. The pilot and the senior of the two security officers had their backs to Brown, bending over a desk situated against the wall. Rufus stood in the far right corner looking at them, and the co-pilot was looking out of the door at the plane, three feet from the nozzle of Brown's automatic carbine.

The man in the balaclava mask wished he had more time to study the expression on the co-pilot's face, but he was blocking the field of fire. Quickly, before the man knew what was happening, Brown took one step forward, swung the butt of the carbine and struck the co-pilot on the cheek. There was a sharp crack as the jaw broke. The automatic was back in position long before the man collapsed to the floor, unconscious. It happened so fast, and Rufus was so surprised, that his hand hadn't even reached the lapel of his jacket before he was staring into the snub nose of the Schmeisser. The others hadn't even begun to turn.

'The first one to move gets a bullet in the head,' said Brown.

The two at the desk began to straighten.

'I said, don't move,' Brown insisted fiercely and they both stood still. 'Now, very slowly, raise your hands above your head.'

The two with their backs to Brown didn't react, but Rufus, who could see the weapon, raised his arms.

'I said raise your hands, now.' The last word was shouted.

Gradually, with their heads turned towards Rufus, they complied.

'All right,' said Brown, 'now you two, turn round slowly until you're facing me.'

They did that too. The pilot had a look of wide-eyed, open-mouthed astonishment imprinted upon his face. He stared first at Brown's mask and then at his mate, lying unconscious on the floor. From then on his terrified gaze focused on the carbine. The other took one look at the weapon, then looked into Brown's mask with an expression of thoughtful hostility. Aged about thirty-five, he was of medium height and build, with dark hair and blue eyes that didn't once turn to the man on the floor. He also seemed to be unafraid and that didn't suit Brown's purpose. Rufus was clenching his fists nervously.

'This,' said Brown, raising his weapon a little, 'is a Schmeisser automatic carbine. It was made during the Second World War. That makes it a bit dated. But as a killing machine, at this range, it's not bettered by anything manufactured today. Make one move without my permission and it will scythe you down within one second.'

He paused for effect.

'Besides, there are three identical weapons also pointing at you through the glass.'

Rufus and the Australian turned their heads, straining to see through their own reflections. Brown addressed himself to the calm security officer, whose head hadn't moved.

'You have probably worked out that it would not suit my purpose to fire. Too much noise. But we are going to take that plane, and if one of you does anything to jeopardize that, I shall shoot you all down without a moment's hesitation, because I shall then have nothing to lose. I shall also be very annoyed. Believe me.'

They believed him. Even the calm one began to look worried.

'Now, I want you all, one at a time, to follow me. Remember those other carbines and keep your hands above your heads. You first, then you, then you last. Come.'

They came – first the calm one, then the pilot, then Rufus, stepping over the co-pilot on the way, until they were all lined up outside.

'Tom?' called Brown.

A small, chunky figure detached itself from the group of armed men. He had been a corporal in one of Brown's platoons. Not possessed of a first-class brain, he made up for it in natural cunning. He was also as tough as old boots, as skilful with a knife as anyone Brown had seen and thoroughly dishonest. But due to some paradox of character that Brown had given up trying to fathom, he was devoted to his leader. On leaving the Army he had been dumped on the unemployment heap and when the chance had come to join Brown's band he had jumped at it. As the workhorse of the team, he was invaluable.

'Watch him,' said Brown to Tom, pointing to the fallen co-pilot. 'He may regain consciousness.'

He turned to his prisoners. 'You three walk over to that wall and put your hands up against it.'

There were three of them covering now and there was no resistance. All the same, Brown kept fairly close to the calm one while he was being searched. When two guns had been removed and their faces were still towards the wall, Brown spoke again, in a matter-of-fact voice, as if he were a bored schoolteacher addressing an obedient and unresponsive class.

'You now have two choices. You can remain absolutely still while my colleague injects you with a substance that will put you out for four to five hours – the only effect you will suffer is a thundering headache when you wake up – or you can resist and die with either a knife or bullet in your back.'

There was a short silence.

'Mac,' said Brown, motioning the Scotsman to get on with it.

The calm one spoke. 'How do we know the stuff won't kill us?'

'You don't,' answered Brown, signalling to Wilson at the same time. 'But we would hardly bother to wear masks if we were going to kill you.'

'He's right,' shouted the Australian. 'Let him do it and get it over with.'

The calm one was looking at Brown now, still unhappy, but then Wilson was there on his blind side, with one arm wrapped around his neck and a knife between the eyes. Wilson had been a sergeant and Brown had fought tooth and nail to get him into his platoon. Finally, he had managed it, with a little subtle blackmail on a brother officer, and neither man had looked back since. Wilson had no desire to be a 'bourgeois' officer, yet Brown knew that he had more insight than any officer he had known. On an operation, he was Brown's right-hand man and usually anticipated his next move. No one knew his first name, except Brown.

Any resistance that might have been anticipated from the security officer disappeared. Mac followed in with a syringe to the man's neck, and within a minute he was limp. There was no trouble from the other two.

'Don't forget the co-pilot,' said Brown casually, as the Scotsman was injecting Rufus, and then he walked off to inspect the door inset.

'No. OK,' answered Mac, but he had forgotten. He arrested the downward plunge of the syringe immediately, withdrew it and inspected the amount remaining by the office light. Nearly all the serum was gone. He walked over to the fallen figure and, with Tom's help, removed the heavy sheepskin jacket. He then rolled up a shirt-sleeve and injected what was left into the main vein, hoping that, as with the others, it would be enough to kill him.

Brown was pulling off his mask and anorak, and speaking at the same time, his voice raised so that it could be heard at the back of the huge hangar.

'Sash, don your 'chute and make sure the plane is OK. Judy, come here. Tom, front door.'

He waited for the girl.

'Judy, collect Mac's syringe, all these masks and anoraks, put them in the disposable bag, take them on to the plane and get into your wet-suit. Mac, Wilson, let's get the heavy gear on to the plane.'

As they walked to the rear of the hangar, the co-pilot became semi-conscious. He had the worst toothache he had ever known. He tried to move a hand to his face, but his arm wouldn't work. He just couldn't feel it. He thrashed his whole body in panic and the sudden, violent movement threw him from his side on to his stomach. The mist in front of his eyes momentarily cleared and he saw a pair of woman's legs, in high-heeled shoes, walking across the hangar. Then the fog came back, covering his mind as well as his sight, and he sank into oblivion.

Within five minutes, Brown, Wilson and Mac had transported all the bags from behind the boxes into the front of the main hold of the plane, out of the way of the fuel assemblies.

'OK,' said Brown; 'Mac, you're the nearest in size to that security officer.'

'I was hoping you were going to say that,' smiled the Scotsman. 'The North Sea I can do without.'

He began to undress immediately and Judy put his clothes in the disposable bag. Brown and Wilson jumped down from the aircraft and trotted over to the three bodies. Within minutes the calm one was stripped and Mac, his bare limbs shaking from cold, gratefully put on the shirt, tie, trousers, jacket and overcoat. They weren't a perfect fit, but the coat would hide everything, and, with a cap on his head – Brown's idea of what smart security officers were wearing these days – he would pass muster. Brown removed the pilot's jacket and boots, and put them on himself, over his wet-suit. The boots were tight, but he wouldn't have to wear them for long. They then dragged the four bodies behind the boxes.

Brown looked at his watch. 5.55 exactly. Not bad. Fifteen minutes to take-off.

'Wilson, on to the plane. Make sure everyone's got a parachute on and then give Sash a hand with the checks. Mac, back that pulling trolley into position and couple it up to the plane – and don't prang the Princess while you're doing it. I'll give you a hand with the doors in a moment.'

Mac was laughing.

'Donna worry,' he replied. 'I would na damage ma own transport,' and he trudged off happily across the hangar.

Brown treated himself to a growing feeling of inner satisfaction, although he wouldn't have dreamt of showing it. But that was as far as it went. Things had gone well up to now, but the next stage was a tricky one. When they opened the doors and pulled the plane out on to the dawn-splashed tarmac, they would be in full view of anyone looking their way. But it would still be fairly dim outside, if not dark, and it was unlikely that anyone would notice the difference between himself and the co-pilot. His wet-suit was jet-black, without a stripe, he had a flying-jacket and boots on and the colour of their hair wasn't all that different in the dark. His height was the only problem. No one would notice the change, he was sure, between Mac and the security officer. The other, Rufus, would simply have travelled with the plane. All this, of course, was assuming that anyone was up at this hour. A man in the control-tower, yes, but the front of the hangar was not visible from there and he would be surprised if there was anyone else about.

He signalled Tom to come over from the door and get on to the plane. Then he climbed aboard himself and helped Tom put on his parachute, which, like those of the others, had an attached life-jacket. Brown began to walk to the front of the hold and caught sight of Judy, seated on the heavy bags, her arms crossed in front of her in a futile attempt to keep warm.

'Cold, isn't it?' she called. 'Is it going to be worse up there?'

He stopped and looked at her, wondering how she would react if she knew how cold she was going to be in about an hour's time. A wet-suit was no real protection against the cold of prolonged immersion in the North Sea at that time of the year.

'Yes,' he answered, 'I'm afraid it is.'

He heard the trolley starting up and turned, climbing up to the cockpit where Sash and Wilson were seated, checking the aircraft. Sash looked around as he entered. Despite the cold there were beads of perspiration on his forehead and he hadn't been doing any of the heavy work.

'I hope these engines start,' he said. 'It's been a cold night.'

'They have to start,' replied Brown.

But he didn't like the negative attitude of the pilot. Sash could fly the plane blindfolded if necessary. He wouldn't have been chosen otherwise. He would be all right when they were on the runway, but he was nervous now and nervousness is infectious.

'Can you handle it?' asked Brown.

The implied criticism was not lost on the pilot and his hands gripped the stick tightly for a few moments. When he turned round to face his leader, everything except his eyes looked angry.

What Sash saw was a man six feet two inches tall and very slightly underweight. He had a pale, unimaginative face, with full lips and a stubby nose, all framed by raven-black hair. Brown's small brown eyes were now looking at him inquiringly. The one thing which he had in common with the others was a bushy beard. To Sash he had always been an imposing figure, but absolutely no one criticized his flying abilities.

'Don't you worry. I can handle it.'

Wilson glanced wryly at Brown, who placed a hand on the pilot's shoulder and said:

'OK. We're pulling her out now.'

Chapter 2

The short, round figure in a brown trilby ascended the last dozen steps to the door of the control-tower, and reflected that the climb became more of an effort every time he did it. It fitted into his general mood – tired depression.

Not that he disliked his job. On the contrary, he enjoyed the power and responsibility, and the perfection of it. It was firm and tangible, and he could see the end product. Every plane that took off gave him personal satisfaction. True, there weren't many aircraft these days to fill his day, but that usually meant that he concentrated more on each one. No, the job was suffering, but it wasn't the cause of his malaise.

He unlocked the door and walked in. He didn't bother to close it quickly to keep the cold out, but took his time, knowing from experience that the temperature inside would not be very different from that outside. The thermometer hung on one of the window uprights showed that it was only just above freezing point. He plugged in the two rather primitive, electric-bar fires and, reluctantly, the two extractor fans. The windows of an airport control-tower are one place where condensation must not be allowed to form.

The man removed his hat to reveal the classic bald head, with a band of hair running around the base of the skull. The thick overcoat he kept on. He sat down on his stool and looked out, under paradoxically bushy eyebrows, at the orange sky.

No, the job was suffering, but it wasn't the cause. The truth was, the job was the only thing he was good at. He certainly wasn't any good at holding his marriage together. If only they could have had children. He had been in favour, but she had always won the argument. They had either needed a new carpet for the hall, or a new bedroom unit in the spare room so that she would not be ashamed to invite her mother to stay again. How could they afford children? He knew there was another reason, but hadn't been able to work it out. At one time he thought it was because she didn't want any rivals for his affections, but that couldn't be it – theirs wasn't exactly an affectionate relationship at the best of times.

Now it was too late. They were both past forty and sex was regarded as a treat on birthdays and bank holidays, except, of course, Christmas Day, which was sacred. She had become more withdrawn than even her introverted character allowed and conversation between them centred on the shopping or the state of the weather. He had his work and she had her garden – the onions and lettuces in neat little rows, like sentries guarding her chastity. She said she did it to save them money, but he knew different. They were very alike really – both very orderly and pedantic – yet somehow they didn't meet.

Last night, things had seemed to come to a head. He'd told her there was a dawn flight and that it would probably be more convenient for him to sleep at the airfield. It was an exaggeration and she'd sensed it, accusing him of not loving her any more and only being interested in his work. What she said didn't hurt him these days, but he had left puzzled. He finally concluded that she hadn't wanted him to go, not because she wanted him at home, but because she didn't want *him* to enjoy himself when *she* couldn't. She always was perceptive about his moods.

Then he had lost heavily in a bridge game he had played until midnight, partnering the airfield cook, who lived in, against the two pilots of the special flight that morning. He should have known better than to gamble in his state of mind, but then George Grimble was everyone's fool. The cook, who had learnt the game in a Liverpool Salvation Army hostel, was a poor player and the cards had been against him. The slump had begun when, being dealt a quite miraculous fistful of picture cards, he had bid for a small slam. The cook mixed up the replies, they were doubled and went down by four tricks, vulnerable. From then on they couldn't get it together. When it finally looked as if the cards might be changing, the Australian had smilingly said that he must get his beauty sleep, and George had reluctantly paid up, double, since the cook was broke until pay-day.

He had gone to bed, but hadn't slept.

The warden's car, returning from checking the runways, brought him back to reality. He looked at his watch. Three minutes to six. Then he thought he heard the pulling trolley being started up in Number 2 hangar.

These BNFL people were always the same. Anyone else would be content to leave their aircraft on the apron overnight, but not these bastards. They had to pull it into the hangar so that they could load in secret. And why was everyone so close-mouthed about it? British Nuclear Fuels Limited, he was told it meant, but that didn't help him much. What was so damned secretive about a load of uranium anyway? He should be told. After all, he was the air-traffic controller.

The plane emerged at no more than a snail's pace, as the trolley struggled with the weight. A solid plane – Grimble liked it. An aircraft in the classic mould.

The 220 version, as this was, was powered by four Rolls-Royce Dart turboprops, each developing 2,230 h.p. With her maximum payload, she could climb at 900 feet a minute and, flying at her economic cruising speed of 280 m.p.h., she could cover 485 miles with a 230-mile diversion and forty-five minutes' reserve. But such were the economics of flying that if you reduced the payload to 18,000 lb, about 8,200 kilos, she could fly no less than 1,760 miles, with the same allowances. Grimble knew that she wouldn't be fully loaded, otherwise she wouldn't get off the short runway, and she was only going to Wick, a distance of about 250 miles, so she wouldn't be fully fuelled either.

The disgruntled man realized that he had better warm up and check his equipment. The place felt less cold now, but he kept his coat on.

He watched as the engines started up. One engine seemed to cough a little, but eventually all the propellers were turning satisfactorily. The sort of car that he could never afford cruised out of the hangar and stopped on the apron, behind the aircraft. He couldn't see whether anyone had closed the hangar doors.

In a few minutes the Argosy began to move out on to the taxiroad. Grimble began to imagine what the pilot was going to say when he called up. 'Morning, George. Thanks for the beer money.' Well, that was one possibility. The man in the tower set his face in a resigned grimace.

Suddenly, he realized why he hated the Australian so much. He envied him. He was jealous of his carefree, bachelor ways and his roguish good looks. Quite unexpectedly he felt a lump in his throat, as he wished and imagined himself the man in the aeroplane, flying into the blue, with a red-headed lass and a bottle of good malt waiting in the Highlands. Then, just as suddenly, he realized it wasn't to be. He gazed unseeingly at the chart-board and felt his eyes begin to water.

On the plane, Brown was with Sash and Wilson in the cockpit. The vibration and noise were worse than he had expected and he had to raise his voice to make himself heard.

'Sash, can you do an Australian accent?'

The pilot, his confidence returned after the heart-stopping hesitation of the near-port engine, looked quizzically at Wilson, sitting beside him. Then comprehension dawned.

'Sorry, old boy,' he replied, looking back at his leader. 'Not one of my specialities.'

'Never mind,' shouted Brown. 'When you're due to get through to the tower, pass the earphones and mike to me.'

It was essential that, even at this late stage, there was no hint of suspicion.

Back in the control-tower, Grimble watched the plane reach the southern end of the north–south runway and wheel round to face north. The balloon was just beginning to lift off the vertical as a northerly breeze began to blow, gently. There was a crackle of static and the loudspeaker barked at him.

'This is BNFL Special Flight to Wick. Permission to take off. Over.'

Grimble was slightly disappointed. The Australian seemed subdued. He blew his nose quickly and switched to transmit.

'Tower to BNFL. Permission granted. Wind still light, nor'-nor'-east. Over.'

'Thank you, sport. See you again.'

'Good-bye,' said Grimble, 'and take care,' he added as an afterthought, regretting it immediately. It sounded silly. There was no reply.

He watched the plane's engines work up the revolutions and, as the pilot released the brakes, she began to move, gathering speed as both pilots pushed the throttles forward to maximum. As she passed

33

the tower though, she was still on the tarmac, hurtling towards the fence. Incredibly, the pilot seemed to have left it too late. Then, seconds before the end of the runway, the nose lifted and the great bird inched off the ground, missing the boundary fence by what seemed like a whisker. Grimble could see the limp wire vibrating.

Just like the Australian, he thought, and watched the plane climb steadily out of sight as it headed due north, without deviation. With the sunrise to its right, it had to be a marvellous sight up there.

Across his line of vision, the Austin Princess passed under the path the aircraft had just taken, as it travelled around the airfield on the boundary road. He watched it dazedly as it continued its journey, briefly disappearing behind some trees to the west, then emerging, more slowly, as it headed for Carlisle. Probably braked to avoid a rabbit, Grimble thought. Soft, these city folk.

Martin began to swear at the cold as soon as he got inside the car.

'Is that heater on, you Scots bastard?'

Mac turned briefly to smile at him.

'Aye, but try a drop o' this,' he replied, reaching inside his coat. 'I hid it in ma underpants.'

A small metal flask emerged and Martin grabbed it eagerly.

'You crafty bugger,' he said, 'but I love you,' as he brought the flask to his lips.

After a couple of grateful swigs, Martin felt much better and he settled back comfortably. Compared to the way he had spent the night, the car seats were luxurious. Mac turned right on to the B6264, en route for the M6. Martin suddenly realized that the Scotsman was chuckling.

'It went well?' inquired Martin, a little suspiciously.

Mac didn't look round.

'Aye, it went bloody well,' and he continued laughing.

Martin gazed through the windscreen. Then the relief rushed over him as well and, with the whisky doing its work on an empty stomach, he too began to laugh.

'And I'll tell ye what, ye Sassenach bastard,' said Mac, attempting to control his laughter, 'you may have been a wee bit cold last night, but by the Christ ye were not as cold as they're goin' to be in aboat an hour, when they take their wee dip.'

Both men looked at each other and laughed uproariously.

Chapter 3

As the Argosy transport rose into the clearing sky, Sasha Goodwin-Smith was in his element. Even though he'd been to a good school, his masters had never been able to give him a formal education. He'd only been interested in one thing – flying. He didn't actually get to do it until his middle teens, but by that time he knew more about aircraft than his contemporaries knew about Latin, Greek, history, English and mathematics put together. The local airfield was his classroom. He read everything about aircraft that he could lay his hands on and virtually nothing about anything else.

He scraped through O levels by the skin of his teeth, but he was not recommended to continue for A levels, 'not because he lacks ability, but due to an almost total lack of motivation'. The school was immensely relieved when his father finally gave in to his son's repeated pleas and withdrew him for flying lessons.

Sasha had no trouble qualifying as a pilot, but found that he couldn't get a job with any of the reputable companies, due to his lack of formal academic qualifications and a bad report from his school. Moreover, his father had no contacts in the aviation industry. Still, he told the young Sasha, he had made the choice himself, against advice, and he must therefore make his own way in the world.

But Sasha wasn't worried. He packed his bags for the Middle-East and was soon flying ageing transports from one Arab sheikdom to another. Since then he had flown everything, from two-seater mail planes in Australia to freighters and airliners in a number of the developing countries of Asia and Africa. The fact

35

that he had no future had not concerned him. His fair hair always seemed to attract the African and Asian women and he was never far from a cockpit. It was the way he liked to live.

He glanced at the altimeter. 4,300 feet. It should take about six to seven minutes to reach 10,000, when he'd level off. She could climb faster, but this was the way Brown wanted it. Crossing the Scottish border now, course due north. He liked the Argosy. Fully loaded she was a little underpowered and could be a real bitch when taking off from mountain airfields. But being only a third loaded and with a third of the possible fuel, she handled excellently for a heavy freighter. This was a milk run and he was as happy as a king.

Sasha was also a little naive. Indeed, that was one of the reasons why Brown had chosen him. He was not part of the regular team as this was a one-off job requiring a pilot, and he had been told just enough to keep him happy. But he wasn't really interested in the cargo anyway, or the fate of the four men they had left in the hangar. His job was to fly the plane. Nothing more. The fact that Brown had promised him £100,000 at the end was also not far from the front of his mind and had helped him turn a blind eye to a lot of things. Had he known his fellow pilots were dead he would certainly have regretted it, but done nothing. Sasha was going to retire. He was also a coward.

In his ear, Brown shouted, 'OK, Sash?'

The pilot looked up, smiling. 'So when do you want the somersaults?' he asked.

Brown grinned before replying.

'You know what to do. Keep her on this bearing until we reach Portknockie. I should be back by then. If I'm not, send Judy for me.'

Sash nodded.

'In precisely three minutes from my "execute",' continued Brown, 'take her into the steepest climb that you can manage for fifteen seconds, then put her back on the normal climb level. OK?'

Again Sash nodded, looking at his watch. Brown was doing the same.

'Execute,' said Brown, then left.

Sash noted the position of the sweep second-hand and glanced down at the open map on his lap. In a little under fifteen minutes they should be over the Borders and passing fourteen miles east of Edinburgh. Then it was across the Firth of Forth and, in less than another ten minutes, they would pass to the east of Dundee by a mere five miles. Then it was on over the Sidlaw Hills and Forfar to the distant Grampians.

As Brown entered the hold, he signalled the others to join him. He glanced at his watch as Judy struggled up.

'Go and strap yourself in beside Sash,' he said and she left immediately.

He pulled the two men closer so that he could be heard.

'We have about thirty-five minutes to Portknockie. Perhaps less. There's a slight head-wind, but it shouldn't affect us very much at all. We must work on thirty minutes to be sure.'

He looked hard at both of them before continuing. 'That means only two minutes per rod. No more.'

They both nodded and Brown looked at Wilson.

'Got the magnet?' he asked.

Wilson handed it to him.

'Right, let's get into position.'

Brown led the way to the rear of the plane, glancing at his watch as he walked. The lights, which had been switched on soon after take-off, helped a lot, making the alloy fuel assemblies shine silver in their racks. When he reached the first port-side assembly he turned round to face it, so that he was now facing the front of the plane. Tom came round on his left and clasped the rack with his left hand. Wilson was already on his right, clutching the rack with his right fist. He felt their free hands lock together behind him and leant back to test the bond.

Again he looked at his watch. Less than thirty seconds to go. He reached out and released the retaining clip on the end of the hexagonal fuel assembly. Slowly, it swung open and he felt a tightening in his stomach as he saw the ends of the fourteen stainless-steel fuel rods, lying flush with the assembly. Each was twelve feet long and half an inch in diameter, and each nestled snugly in its own half-inch hole. He knew that a quarter-inch hole ran down each rod and that it was filled with half-inch-long plutonium oxide pellets. The combined weight of each rod and the oxide within it was just over 30 kilos. If you multiplied that by fourteen and added the weight of the, admittedly light, magnesium fuel assembly of 25 kilos, you had a combined weight per assembly of close on 450 kilos, or 1,000 pounds.

He drew the huge round magnet to his chest, already feeling the strong pull from the steel bars and the rack. Then he heard the engines beginning to whine as their power increased, and the deck tilted quite sharply as the Argosy clawed higher.

Slowly, but as quickly as he could, he allowed the magnet to close on the rods. When it was just under a foot away, the pull became too strong for him to reverse and the magnet slammed on to the end of the assembly, the noise echoing around the hold. With the deck canting now at over 35 degrees, he pulled with all his strength and felt the rods sliding out.

He let out his breath and sucked in some air. Wilson was grinning broadly. Brown had been a little worried about this part and Wilson knew it. The rods would probably have come out without the extra angle, but it was best not to take chances. The deck began to return to its normal level and the engine note decreased.

'Right,' said Brown, still panting slightly, 'let's get this thing off.'

All three men grasped one half of the magnet edge.

'Ready,' said Brown. 'Now!'

He didn't need to say it. The swing of his body told them exactly when they should pull and, with a sideways and outward jerk, the magnet came free. Brown retained his hold and handed it to Tom.

'Disposable bag and let's go. You both know the routine.'

Tom and Wilson moved to the front of the hold, while Brown began to slide the first rod from its container. The job was easy now that he could grip it. After six feet had been extracted, he grasped it with both hands and walked along until it was totally removed.

Wilson and Tom arrived with large bags in their grip. Each unzipped one and began to extract bright, orange, inflatable rafts, together with parachutes. One of the specially made rafts, with attached carbon dioxide gas cylinder, was fitted around the rod and zipped up. Then a parachute was attached and the whole lot, now a dead weight of something like 55 kilos, was moved to the rear of the plane. Another cylinder was then prepared. The same operation had to be repeated thirteen times.

Each member of the team, except Sash and Judy, had practised this so often that it was second nature to them, and Brown knew that this part of the operation could be completed in under fifteen minutes, if they really pushed it. But that was at ground level. As the plane reached its cruising height of 10,000 feet, the hard, heavy work became progressively more difficult in the oxygen-lacking air. Brown knew that for men not used to it, sustained or sudden, violent exercise at 10,000 feet could be crippling, but, this time, he'd had to take the chance. There was nowhere in Britain where they could have obtained the sort of training needed, and he had had to make do with severe physical exercise for the whole team.

He was glad he had, for as more cylinders were dragged to the rear of the hold, his breath began to come in short gasps and he felt the sweat breaking out under his wet-suit, despite the cold. The weight of the 'chute strapped to his back with the attached life-jacket made the task worse, and he wondered whether they should have put them on later.

He looked at Tom and Wilson, who seemed to be having similar trouble. The last meal they had eaten, apart from a few glucose tablets, was at lunchtime yesterday in a motorway restaurant. They had spent a sleepless night and now this crippling physical task. He hadn't known it would be quite so bad.

As he zipped up the eighth cylinder, he glanced at his watch. They were only just on schedule and he knew it would get worse.

'Come on, lads,' he shouted, 'we've got to work faster.'

Wilson showed his teeth as he fought for breath and switched his eyes towards Tom. Brown did too and saw that the little man was already in a bad way. His face had lost its usual rosy glow and the way he lifted his feet made Brown doubt whether he would last. That meant that he and Wilson had to work harder.

He took a 'chute from Tom and buckled it to the next raft. There were no seconds to waste and he quickly jumped up to extract the next cylinder.

As he worked, his feet became more leaden, a pain in his back stabbed at him every time he straightened up and sweat began to run into his eyes, blurring his vision. He was also, apparently, becoming light-headed, for, as he glanced up, Tom appeared to vibrate like a man working a pneumatic drill.

After what seemed an age, the last cylinder was dragged to the rear cargo-door. Brown turned round, expecting to see Judy attempting to gain his attention, but she wasn't there. Wilson was propping himself up against one of the racks, his head low as he gasped for breath. Tom, miraculously, was still on his feet, tottering slightly, but showing a smile to Brown, his arms hanging vertically from his sloping shoulders. He looked like an ape.

Brown forced himself to move.

'Well done,' he gasped, but doubted whether they had heard what to him sounded like a whisper in the din of the hold. He paused for several seconds while he regained some more breath, but his voice still sounded weak as he shouted: 'Just the disposable bag now and we're set.'

Wilson would see to it.

He clapped them both on their bowed shoulders as he passed and walked uncertainly towards the ladder to the cockpit. As he placed a heavy leg on the bottom rung, he glanced up and saw Judy, framed in the entrance at the top. She retreated as he came up. The climb was easier than he anticipated, but, even so, Judy's mouth dropped open as she saw him.

'Christ, John!' she exclaimed. 'Are you all right?'

Sash swung round and said, 'You don't look too good, old boy,' a look of genuine concern on his face.

Brown, still breathing fairly deeply, ignored them. He could see the coastline approaching and the Moray Firth beyond.

'Portknockie?' asked Brown.

'You guessed it,' answered Sash, still glancing at his leader.

'You know the flight plan. The second we pass over the coast, alter course to Wick Airport. The boat should be exactly twenty-five miles along that line.'

There was silence for a while. Brown retrieved some more breath and looked out of the window as Judy stared at him. Sash concentrated on the coming turn. He had known exactly when the turn had to be made and had planned the angle beforehand.

With one final glance at the map, he turned the aircraft fractionally to port and settled her down on that compass bearing.

'Wind going to give you any trouble?' asked Brown.

'No.' Then after a pause, 'Oxygen masks would have made it worse, you know.'

Brown remembered that it was Sash who had advised him against using oxygen. He hadn't intended to anyway – the altitude was far too low and the masks would have been cumbersome – but the pilot needed praise.

'I know,' said Brown, and smiled.

The grin was returned and Judy joined in. She had found a blanket from somewhere and had it wrapped around her like a cocoon. Suddenly, Brown became aware again of how much everything depended on him and his smile disappeared.

'How long?' he asked.

Sash looked through the window. 'About six minutes.' Then he bent down to his left and, straightening up, proferred some binoculars.

Brown braced himself against the bulkhead and raised the lenses to his eyes. The image was completely blurred. He adjusted the screw and the distant sea sprang into focus. It appeared as if the surface was hardly rippled. It probably was a calm sea, with such a light wind. All right for ditching, but not too good for sailing away. Slowly, he scanned the empty horizon, moving his body to left and right to see past the window uprights. Nothing. His arms were tired and he found it increasingly difficult to hold the glasses still.

'You should be able to see it now,' said Sash, as Brown lowered the binoculars.

While his arms rested, Brown gazed out of the window, as if trying to see the yacht with his bare eyes. That it would be where it was supposed to be, he had no doubt. If there had been cloud they would have jumped and dropped through it, blind, at the planned rendezvous point, trusting that it would be there. Radio, or radio direction-finders, would have been a dead giveaway – if not now, then later.

He lifted the binoculars again and saw it immediately. In the upper left radius of the circle there was a minute orange dot.

'I've got it,' he said, matter-of-factly, lowering his binoculars to fix its position. 'Fine on the port bow.'

Sash smiled, both with relief and at Brown's nautical expression.

'Shall I alter course?' he asked.

'No. We may be out of sight of land, but they may have us on radar at Wick. Besides, if we go slightly past then the breeze will drift us down to the boat.'

Looking through the glasses again, Brown was glad that he had decided on the orange sails – well worth the expense. They were beginning to take form now. Jerry had the Main and Number 1 Genoa up, sailing west on a reach so that Brown could see them more easily. He lowered the binoculars again.

Judy was still hunched in the blanket and Brown felt suddenly chill. The sweat inside his wet-suit was turning cold and, although the sea looked inviting in the bright, morning sun, he knew that at 7 a.m. in early May, the North Sea is far from warm. He turned his mind away from the unpleasant thought. It was inevitable and that was all there was to it.

He spoke to Sash: 'Open the rear cargo-door.'

Sash pulled a switch.

Brown focused on the yacht again until it disappeared from sight below the level of the console. It would be directly under the plane soon.

'You might as well put her on auto-pilot now,' said Brown, 'and switch out the cargo-hold lights. Your job is over, Sash. Let's go.'

He unstrapped Judy and ushered her out of the cabin. He waited for the pilot and then followed, his face a mask of concentration.

They were waiting for him by the open freight doors. Wilson and Judy were looking at him and Tom was looking out of the door and the big drop beyond.

He estimated that they had just passed over the boat. This was not a moment for hesitation. In one sudden and continuous movement, he launched the binoculars out of the plane, jumped towards the raft nearest the door and pressed a button on the side of his wristwatch.

'Right, let's get these out,' he shouted and they were spurred into action.

Wilson swiftly clipped the 'chute-lines, attached to each raft, to the nearest plutonium rack, so that the parachutes would open immediately. Tom quickly walked along the row, turning each CO_2 gas valve to inflate the rafts and, as he did so, Brown pushed them out. The last half-dozen took longer because they were further back, but in forty-five seconds they were all clear, including the disposable bag.

Brown flashed a look at Sash. 'Any not open?'

He saw a quick shake of the head before he stood back and shouted: 'OK, then jump! And don't forget to open your 'chute as soon as you're clear.'

Before the last words were spoken, Wilson had jumped, and Tom and Sash followed at two-second intervals. During that time period, Brown had gathered up the trailing 'chute-lines and began to tie them in a rough knot around the rack. On finishing he turned round to find Judy still hesitating on the brink, despite her six training jumps.

It was so imperative that she jump quickly that time seemed to stop. She was standing on the edge of the cargo floor, looking back at him, and he couldn't move. It was as if there was some bond between them that would be broken if she jumped. He wanted to shout at her, to push her – do anything to get her off the plane. But he made no move. Then she turned and disappeared, as if there hadn't been a problem at all. Suddenly he too felt released. He counted two seconds, pressed the button on his watch and jumped into space.

A few seconds after he pulled the cord the straps bit into his life-jacket as the opening parachute brought him up with a jerk. He glanced at his watch. His finger had stopped the second hand at sixty-three seconds. Their immobility must have been more imagined than real. With a bit of luck the whole lot would be strung out over no more than three miles of the Moray Firth.

He looked down at the floating white puffs, but didn't think to glance back at the plane. If he had, he would have seen an almost indistinguishable black shape, winging its undeviating way to the tip of Scotland.

Chapter 4

Troutman stared at the telephone. It was quite an aesthetic instrument really, for what it was: a jumble of wires and diaphragms, or whatever. The shell was so constructed that it seemed to blend in with man's idea of natural acceptability. There were no corners, for instance – just gentle curves. Other things that man makes, like buildings, consist almost entirely of straight lines, perpendiculars and angles. And then, when you wanted to dial your number, you put your finger in a hole and twisted your hand in a circle several times, until a bell rang and you obtained your reward. Yes, definitely an interesting, possibly even erotic, artefact, the humble telephone.

Erotic! He slapped his thigh and admonished himself at his thoughts. But, at the same time, he realized that it was a subconscious form of escapism, so that his mind didn't have to grapple with the problem that was presenting itself. A telephone was undoubtedly an inanimate object and, what was more, the one he was looking at refused, obstinately, to ring.

He looked at his watch yet again. 6.49. Drake knew the plan and he had rung on all previous occasions. Their plane was due to leave at 6.10. There could have been a little delay, but not *so* long, and anyway Drake would have let him know.

Troutman reached into his deep mackintosh pocket and extracted cigarettes and lighter. As he lit up, he made his decision. He picked up the telephone receiver and dialled the operator. If the phone was engaged when his deputy called, he would just have to call again. After only one ring a male voice answered.

'Is there any way you can check whether this phone is working properly?' asked Troutman. Hearing his own voice he realized how worried he was and hurried on. 'I'm expecting an incoming call which has not arrived.'

'Well, sir, I can phone you back. If you don't hear the telephone ring in thirty seconds, pick it up anyway and we can speak to each other.'

The operator sounded bored and tired. Troutman wondered whether it was because he was coming to the end of a long shift or because he had heard the same sort of inane request many times before from distraught wives and mothers.

'Will it give us the answer? I mean, if *you* can get through then anyone can?' asked Troutman.

'Yes, sir,' replied the operator, kindly.

Troutman was about to replace the phone when the operator said:

'Can I have your number?'

He gave it and put the receiver down more heavily then he had intended. He *was* on edge. He took another, longer drag on his cigarette and tried to relax. The sound of the telephone bell made him jump and he answered it before it could ring again.

'Operator?'

Strange how he had unconsciously assumed that Drake would not be phoning.

'Yes. It appears, sir, that your phone is in order.'

Why was it only now that he realized the man did not have a Scottish accent?

'Thank you,' he replied calmly, and replaced the receiver.

He took another long pull on his cigarette and forced himself to think. He could phone Carlisle, but Drake would not be by the public telephone that they used, for the obvious reason that if he were he would have used it. And anyway, they could cross calls. The plane was either delayed for some reason or it had taken off on time. Either way, Drake should have phoned. The best way to find out was by going to the control-tower. They would most likely have it on radar by now, if it had taken off on time, and he could use their phone to rouse control at Carlisle if necessary.

In the meantime he didn't want to leave his present phone un-guarded, just in case. He cast his eyes round desperately, but there was no one in the lobby. Wick Airport, he reflected, was not busy at the worst of times. At 6.55 a.m. it was almost deserted. Then he saw a mechanic, in stained, blue overalls, walking past one of the windows, an open tin of tobacco in his hands. Troutman rushed to the door and ran after him.

The man heard him coming and turned round suspiciously. He was young — about nineteen or twenty — with red hair and a short moustache. The sad, blue eyes looked Troutman over as he approached, then he looked down at his cold hands. With the taciturn disposition of the working man the world over, he concentrated on rolling his cigarette.

Troutman was conscious of the condensation of his breath on the still, cold air as it rasped in his lungs. He paused for a few moments, deciding how to put it to this young man, who seemed interested in nothing but his tobacco.

'Would you do me a great favour?' he asked, pointing through one of the windows. 'Guard that telephone until I return. I shouldn't be away long. I've just got to go up to the control-tower.'

It sounded like a desperate plea and the mechanic's apparent concentration on his roll-up had not wavered. On an impulse Troutman withdrew his wallet and extracted a five-pound note.

'Take any message for me and bring it to the tower, and don't let anyone else use the phone.'

The mechanic had finished the construction of his cigarette. He popped it in his mouth, shut the tin with a loud click and raised his head. He looked first at the fiver in Troutman's outstretched hand and then into his face. He appeared to make up his mind.

'Well, if it means that much to ye, I daresay I could do it for nothin',' he said in broad Scots and ambled towards the door.

Troutman looked after him, convinced that the assertion of the tight-fistedness of the Scots must be a myth. He replaced the note in his wallet and began to run towards the control-tower.

As he reached the bottom of the stairs, he slowed. It occurred to him that it must be very cold, if he could put his mind to thinking about it. He didn't want to burst in if all was well, so he climbed the stairs at what he considered to be a respectable speed.

When he reached the top, his thighs aching, he stopped at the door. The two occupants were looking at him through the glass. They had obviously heard him clanging up the iron steps in his policeman's boots. Embarrassed, he threw away his cigarette and went in.

The heat hit him immediately and he quickly closed the door. A slight, grey-haired man of about sixty stood perfectly relaxed, his hands at his sides, in the middle of the room. He wore an overcoat, but no gloves. Behind him, seated at two emerald-green screens, was a man in his mid twenties, who was perhaps less appropriately dressed in a green anorak. Both were staring at Troutman. The grey-haired man spoke first.

'Can I help you?' he asked in a home-counties accent, and then, more forcefully, 'The public are not allowed in here,' fixing the newcomer with a piercing look.

It occurred to Troutman that there weren't many Scotsmen around.

'My name is Troutman. I'm Chief Security Officer for BNFL.'

'Aah! So that's it,' said the controller, and then: 'I suppose you have proof of that?'

'Yes, of course.' Troutman reached for his wallet again. As he handed the card over, trying to keep his voice as calm as possible, he said, 'I'm a little worried about my plane.'

'Needn't be,' answered the controller immediately. He handed the card back. 'We've just got her on the radar,' pointing at the anoraked figure. Troutman felt relief flooding through him.

'How do you know it's the BNFL flight from Carlisle?' he asked, a little hesitantly.

The controller turned on a condescending smile. Troutman knew the type. Supremely self-confident in his technical expertise, but with about as much general awareness as a Yorkshire pudding. He would make few mistakes, but when they did come, they would be big ones.

'Because,' said the controller, as if Troutman were a retarded child, 'the blip should be exactly where it is and we are not expecting any other aircraft at this time.'

He smiled at Troutman again before continuing, making the security man realize that he had rather unfairly maligned that venerable pudding.

'The plane crossed into the Moray Firth at Portknockie, which is exactly what it should do, and it is bang on time for a 6.10 lift-off, given a slight northerly. What's more, it has altered course very slightly and is now heading straight for where we are standing. In addition, it is at the correct height and Jamie here says that the blip corresponds to the size of the aircraft – an Argosy, I believe?'

Troutman nodded absently. He had been worried unduly. His policeman's training had taken over from reason. What could possibly go wrong anyway? Here it was, on route and on schedule. There had obviously been some sort of technical hitch in communication. Well, at least the controller hadn't asked him to leave, but then he'd want him to stay, to show Troutman how good he was.

As if in answer to his thought the controller said: 'You can stay if you like.'

He then walked towards the screens, picked up a microphone and flicked a switch.

'This is Wick control calling BNFL Special Flight.'

He waited several seconds. There was no reply.

'This is Wick control calling BNFL. Do you read? Over.' And again, the wait.

Troutman felt a tightening in his throat.

'Why aren't they answering?' he questioned.

The controller just repeated the message.

'BNFL, this is Wick control. Come in.'

The silence was almost overpowering. The controller gazed out of the window towards the south, as if he could see the plane. Troutman stared at the microphone. The radar man peered myopically at his equipment. Interference began to develop behind the plane on both screens, but that often happened. The pilot wasn't answering, but at least they had radar, and the operator knew that his job was now becoming more important. He looked first at the left screen, that gave distance, and then at the one on the right, which gave height. Apart from that interference, which was now beginning to go, both screens were working well. The young man was new at his job. Radar operators didn't stay long at Wick Airport.

'Perhaps he hasn't switched his set on,' ventured Troutman.

The little man turned round and gave him a long withering look.

'No,' said the controller at last, 'there must be something wrong with his set.'

But he called up again, just to make sure.

Troutman was very worried now. First, the lack of a phone call. Now this. Too much coincidence, surely? And there was something at the back of his brain.

'Does this often happen?' he asked, braving the controller's wrath and hoping to stimulate his own mind.

'Sometimes,' replied the older man, in what Troutman regarded as being a fairly reasonable tone. 'There is often interference of some kind, but not on a day like this. Technical faults do occur in the pilot's radio but they are usually spotted before take-off.'

'That's it,' said Troutman suddenly.

Both men turned round to look at him.

'When he took off,' continued Troutman, 'wouldn't he call up the control-tower at Carlisle, to get clearance of some kind?'

Both men now looked at each other as if Troutman ought to be committed.

'Yes,' said the controller, as if humouring a child, 'he would.'

'Then the fault would have been noticed when he was still on the ground,' said Troutman. 'The controller at Carlisle would surely have called through to let you know that the plane had no radio.'

The little grey man opened his mouth to speak, but Troutman didn't give him a chance.

'So the fault must have developed during the flight. What chance would you say there was of that happening, Mr Controller, with a clear sky, no wind and on a straight, one-hour milk-run?'

The radar operator was standing as well now, looking at Troutman. The controller looked puzzled and perhaps a little worried.

'What's on that plane?' he asked suddenly.

The question caught Troutman by surprise.

'Never you mind,' he said, waving an arm in dismissal. What was he arguing with this little man for anyway? But it was a lame reply and the controller stepped forward with triumphant gait.

'What are you afraid of?' he asked, boring his eyes into Troutman's. 'A hijack?'

The security officer looked back into the red rims. Of course it was obvious. He had stupidly given it away by his insane behaviour. Well, perhaps he would get some authority if he told. The controller was still glaring up at him, waiting for an answer.

'Yes,' said Troutman, trying to keep his voice as level as possible.

But the controller continued to leer at him.

'Then tell me this, Mr Chief Security Officer. Why is it that the aircraft is on course and on schedule for Wick? Why is it that it's not half-way across the North Sea by now?'

A good point. It might be a ruse on the part of the hijackers to fool him, but that would sound far too weak for this upstart of an idiot controller. He felt so frustrated that he wanted to hit the man, and was about to explode the tension inside him by shouting when the radar man spoke for the first time.

'We'll know in a wee while anyway,' he said. 'He's due to begin his descent about now.'

Troutman wondered whether the controller was going to ask him to leave. He was still squinting up at him. Instead, he pivoted round like a ballet dancer and strutted over to the mike.

'Is he still on course?' he asked.

Troutman had to admire his control.

'Aye,' replied the radar man, now seated again, his eyes on the right-hand screen.

There was the flick of a switch.

'This is Wick control calling BNFL. Over.'

There were several seconds of silence before he spoke again.

'BNFL. This is Wick control. We are assuming that you cannot transmit, but there should be no difficulty. We have you on our screens and you are cleared for landing. You are dead on line for Wick airport, but you must begin to lose height now.'

He looked at the right screen.

'BNFL, you are approximately six miles from north–south runway. Wind is light, northerly, backing slightly to the east. It's as clear as a bell here and you should have no difficulty with visual landing.'

He flicked the switch again, just in case, and they all stared at the right-hand screen.

Thirty seconds went by.

'He's no' coming down,' said the radar operator, a little incredulously.

A crease appeared between the eyes of the controller. He continued to watch the screen as he flicked the switch again.

'BNFL, this is Wick control. You must reduce height to approach from the south.'

The blip remained perfectly steady on both screens and, for the first time, the controller began to realize that something was very wrong. He moved his gaze to the security man.

Troutman's mouth was now completely dry and he also became conscious of the sweat breaking out all over his body. *My God, a hijack.* He had been convinced it would never happen. But why was the plane coming on?

'Can we see it yet?' he asked.

The controller walked over to a desk top and lifted some binoculars to his eyes. Troutman stood mesmerized by the sweeping green arms of the radar screens.

'There she is,' said the controller, 'coming straight for us.'

Troutman moved over quickly and the little grey man handed him the glasses, pointing. The plane came into view at once, as Troutman didn't have to refocus at all. It galled him to realize that the sod of a controller had the same strength eyesight as himself. Strange how totally irrational thoughts impinge upon your reality in these situations. Then he was searching the aircraft for any telltale signs. But there was nothing to see – just an Argosy, flying in orderly fashion at 10,000 feet. He knew it wasn't going to stop, but he followed it until it was nearly overhead.

As the controller began to call up again, he moved outside, not bothering to close the door this time. He could hear the four Rolls-Royce engines clearly and he could see with the binoculars that all the propellers were turning. As the plane passed him he saw that the rear part of the cargo section looked odd. It took him fully five seconds to realize that the rear door was wide open. He watched it for a few more moments with the naked eye, then moved back inside.

This was the moment he had dreaded happening, the moment that he was sure couldn't or wouldn't happen. Yet he now had to make that phone call. The two occupants were looking at him.

'Any response or change of course?' he asked.

'No,' answered the controller.

The hostility was still in his voice – probably more because he had been proved wrong than anything else, thought Troutman.

'Do you mind if I use your phone?' he asked briskly, clearly not expecting a negative reply as he walked towards it.

He reached for his wallet for the third time in half an hour and extracted a piece of rather crumpled paper. It was odd, but although he was acting quickly he felt like taking his time, as if what he did now didn't matter. He turned to the two technicians. The scene had changed completely. *They* were now the onlookers.

'What you have seen and heard this morning comes under the Official Secrets Act. So does what I am about to say on this phone. I would advise you to go outside while I make the call.'

The young man started to move, but the older one motioned him back. The latter then thrust his chin out and folded his hands across his chest, defiantly.

Troutman shrugged, picked up the receiver and dialled the numbers backwards. There was a long pause before the bell rang. After the second ring it was answered.

'I'd like to speak to the Director,' said Troutman.

'What director is that, sir?' replied the voice.

Troutman envisaged a long, pointless conversation with this minion and time was of the essence.

'Look here, sonny,' he growled, 'my name is Troutman. I'm Chief Security Officer for British Nuclear Fuels Limited. I have reason to believe there has been a hijack of plutonium and I need air surveillance immediately. I don't care where the Director is, or whether he's still having his beauty sleep, but get him now, d'ya hear.'

The man at the other end appeared to hesitate, before saying:

'Could you give me your number, sir?'

He gave it. Then he had a sudden thought and gave the public telephone number as well, just in case the Director couldn't get through. The phone went dead. He replaced the receiver and slowly walked over to the radar screens.

'Is it still at the same course and height?' he asked, not really expecting that it wasn't.

The radar man, who was still staring open-mouthed at Troutman, came out of his reverie. He turned, scanned the screens and nodded his head.

'Write down his course for me, will you?' said Troutman.

He felt wretched and gazed forlornly out of the window. Even the controller had ceased to exist within his thoughts. He lit up a cigarette and just sat, staring at the 'No Smoking' sign. Then the phone rang and he rushed to it.

'Troutman,' he said tightly.

'This is the Director. What's happened?'

It was a voice you obeyed instantly and Troutman explained as succinctly as he could. But he felt some urgency creeping into his voice and at times he had to pause to run his tongue over dry lips.

'Have you been on to Carlisle?' asked the Director, when he had finished.

'No, I phoned you the moment the plane flew over.'

'Good. Anything else that you think I should know?'

'No,' replied Troutman again, thinking furiously. 'I think the open freight-door must be significant.'

'Yes. I'll handle things from now on. It's become a matter of state security. I'll be in touch, so stay available, where you are.'

And with that the phone went dead in Troutman's hand again.

Well, it was out of his control now. He'd passed the buck. He licked his lips again and turned, looking the controller straight in the eye as he spoke. He felt strangely buoyant.

'If either of you two breathe a word of what you've heard here today, you'll be slapped in irons so quickly your teeth will rattle.'

It gave him some small pleasure to see a nerve twitch in the controller's face. But the feeling was short-lived as he suddenly and belatedly focused on the fact that he'd had two men and two pilots at Carlisle, and he hadn't heard from any of them.

Chapter 5

Judy was the last person to break the surface of the sea. The first panic-stricken thought that registered on her already numb brain was that she was drowning. When you hit water travelling at over twenty miles an hour, even wearing a life-jacket, your body totally submerges for a few seconds. Long enough for you to realize that you are under.

She thought of her father, a merchant seaman whom she hadn't seen for eight years. As a child she used to dream that he would die like this, his mouth open, calling her name and the frothing sea filling him up. It was that, really, which had made her give in to the neighbourhood boys when she was fourteen. She had developed early and been attractive even then. Later, her fair hair had curled naturally at the shoulder, framing big, green eyes and high cheek-bones on a rosebud skin. She had what novelists call 'natural' beauty, ostensibly because it needed no help from make-up, but really because the loveliness held an essence which defied description.

She threshed her arms and legs to get to the surface. The legs worked, but the arms kept getting caught up. She opened her eyes as little as she could and discovered, to her horror, that she was still under. She tried to thrust her body upwards again in renewed panic, her feet kicking wildly and her hands beating imaginary drums in front of her. But still the darkness. Why wasn't the life-jacket working? She wanted to breathe.

When Judy had reached puberty, she remembered, her mother had become hostile to her, entertaining her men from the textile factory where she worked while her husband was at sea, and threatening her daughter with all sorts of dire consequences if she told. On leaving school at sixteen, Judy had run away from Manchester, to London. She had seen neither parent in the five years since then. Too curvy for modelling and her deportment all wrong, she had undressed on film and made a mint. When she'd blown the money, a prominent politician, with a wife and four kids in the provinces, had supported her in a flat in Chelsea. That had cost her an abortion. Her general melancholy and a search for some sort of fulfilment had eventually led her to the French Mediterranean coast.

Now terrified and unable to hold her breath any longer, she opened her eyes wide and, with a relief that can only come to those who believe they are about to die, realized that she *was* on the surface. The trapped air in the 'chute had formed a canopy above her head, shielding the sun and creating a cocoon of darkness. She gulped great mouthfuls of air, breathing deeply. But the relief was soon to go, for as she relaxed she felt the cold penetrating her wet-suit – sudden, shocking, unbelievable cold. John. She thought of him, as she always did in times of stress.

They had met in Cannes. It had been the classic situation. She, the penniless nymph, lounging on the beach in seductive pose and he, the rich playboy, flicking sand off her excuse for a bikini. But she hadn't cared. He had provided her with the strength she didn't have. The blind persistence that she had acquired for finding something unseen and unknown, she also saw in him. It bound her to him. He had sent the crew of his yacht back to Britain by plane and the two of them had sailed it all the way back on their own. Those had been the most blissful four weeks of her life . . .

What was it about him she had sensed up there at 10,000 feet that had frightened her? What was it he had said? *Keep your body moving. Move your arms and your legs to keep the circulation going.* The darkness. She must move out of the darkness.

As quickly as she could with frozen hands, she unbuckled the harness and swam to the edge of the canopy, which was now collapsing on top of her. She had to pull her head under the water again to escape, her motions slow and laboured. She felt strangely colder in the sun.

Her limbs ached and her brain wasn't functioning too well either. She gazed towards the east searching for her rescuers. It did not occur to her that it was the wrong direction. The arm movements became more laboured as the blood flowed less and less fast and the brain ceased to send messages of instruction. Her head dropped back as consciousness began to leave her. All bodily feeling had gone. In less than another minute her heart would have stopped. Then, through a silent haze, she heard Brown's voice.

'An armpit each, quickly.'

Then he started asking stupid questions.

'Judy,' he said anxiously, 'can you hear me?' A pause, and then, 'Can you move your legs?'

Stupid man. Of course she couldn't move her legs. She couldn't even feel them.

'Is she . . .?' someone shouted before he was dug in the ribs.

At that Judy opened her eyes and saw Brown's face. She dropped her lids against the brightness and tried to smile.

'No,' said Brown, 'but almost. We'll take a limb each and massage like hell.'

The big rubber dinghy skimmed across the water and keeping balance was difficult when you couldn't use your hands. Besides, Brown thought that he ought to be directing operations. Sash, Wilson and Tom were rubbing furiously. He called over the second of the two-man dinghy team and told him to take over Judy's right leg. This enabled him to crawl up to the bows, two or three feet above the water. They were heading straight for the yacht which, its sails down, lay motionless. Far over on the starboard bow, he spotted the other inflatable, stopped in the water as it picked up another rod.

The operation was going well, but they had to move faster. The authorities would take some time to get organized. He would guess at at least half an hour after the plane flew over Wick. But when someone started to make decisions, everything in a line from Carlisle to the tip of Scotland and beyond would be surveyed. He wanted to be well away by the time they got around to the Moray Firth. The likelihood was that they would be slow to react, and a thorough air-to-ground/air-to-sea search would be difficult to mount at short notice. Anyway, they would concentrate on the Argosy. Eventually they would figure a parachute jump, but would be unlikely to give priority to the sea areas. He also reckoned that coordination would be bad. The people who understood the details of the plutonium shipments, and therefore how, when and where the plutonium was hijacked, were unlikely to be the same people who would lead the search. They would also have to find out what had happened at Carlisle in order to get some insight into what, exactly, had occurred, and that, too, would take time, especially since they would need to keep things quiet. And, anyway, Carlisle would compound their problems. Brown didn't envy them. Of course, there was always the possibility that he would be discovered by pure luck, but that was one chance you always took.

The yacht was fast approaching now and he signalled to the helmsman to slow down. The inflatable was skilfully glided to the yacht's stern cockpit and Irma, the only person left on board, secured the painter that Brown handed her.

There would be a tendency now to become lethargic, Brown knew. The immediate danger was over and relief would flood through the body like a tide, washing away the adrenalin. Reaction would set in. That must not happen. There was still a lot to do. Without greeting her, Brown called to the woman on deck.

'Irma, Judy is literally dying from cold. Take her into the peak cabin, strip her off and dry her.'

Wilson and Tom, having secured the dinghy aft, were already beginning to lift the girl.

'Paul, George, get her into the cabin,' said Brown. 'Then get the white sails ready to hoist. Light-weather Main and Number 1 Genny. Got that?'

They both answered in the affirmative and jumped on deck. Judy was passed to them and they disappeared into the cabin. Tom was looking at him and Brown flicked his thumb towards the boat. With a remarkable degree of speed, considering what he had been through, Tom vaulted off the dinghy and quickly cast off fore and aft.

Brown settled down in the bows as Wilson gunned the engine and steered a north-westerly course in search of the other dinghy. He forced himself not to think of the cold that was creeping into his bones and slowing his actions.

As they approached the other inflatable, which was again stopped in the water, one of the two-man crew looked up. Brown cupped hands to mouth and the engine died to a murmur.

'How many?' shouted Brown.

'Twelve,' came the instant reply.

Brown had already spotted two rods, nestling in their rafts, as they had approached. He cupped his hands again.

'Get those back to the boat. We'll get the other two,' and Wilson accelerated again as Brown pointed.

Each rod-raft had had a stainless-steel ring fitted and reinforced into each end, and it was simplicity itself to cleat the rings on to the many ropes that Brown had fitted to the dinghy's rim. Then they were heading back at a much reduced speed. Even so, they managed to overtake Jerry's inflatable.

Back at the yacht, both rod-rafts were hauled aboard the dinghy and the stainless-steel rods extracted. Brown and Wilson handed them up to Sash and Tom, both in a dry set of clothing, who took them into the main cabin. There they were fitted into a cavity that was skilfully cut out of the top of the fibre-glass keel. The other inflatable arrived, and Brown and Wilson jumped aboard the yacht to supervise the loading of the rods. All fourteen were soon in the cavity. The top of the keel was then slotted back into place above them and, apart from a hairline crack, which they would temporarily seal in transit, the rods were undetectable. The duckboards and cabin floor were then replaced.

'Well,' said Brown, emerging from the cabin into the sunlight, 'she'll ride a little lower in the water, but with an extra 900 pounds of ballast, she'll stand upright in a Force 10.'

He was glowing now and it was infectious. With the exception of Wilson and the two men puncturing the rod-rafts to a watery grave, everyone was laughing.

The two puncture experts finished and quickly moved to one of the inflatable dinghies. They removed the engine and, with everyone working with excited alacrity, it was moved, hand over hand, to Brown and Wilson, who stowed it. The inflatable itself followed, was deflated and stuffed in a large aft locker. Men were laughing and joking the whole time. Brown let it continue. The release of tension was practical now and he could always bring them back to a fast-moving team when he wanted. He would be expected to join in. No sour-faced leader, he.

With a joyous leer on his face he put his right foot on the starboard aft locker, looked down at the remaining inflatable, turned his head to his men and shouted:

'Where's the pigsticker?'

Some loud cheers went up and someone darted into the cabin. A stiletto knife, strapped to a four-foot length of bamboo, emerged and was passed, carefully, from hand to hand, to Brown. He grasped it with obvious glee, leant over the rail and carefully punctured all the air compartments of the inflatable. With the engine to weigh it down, it sank like a stone. There were some more cheers and some laughter.

Brown didn't feel cold any longer. He looked up at the burgee and raised his voice.

'Jerry, I do believe the wind is freshening. Let's have those sails up. Then put her over on the port tack. I want to sail sixty miles due east into the North Sea before we turn south.'

He was above to give a hand with the mainsail when it occurred to him that there was something he should have remembered. Judy.

He walked through the main cabin and opened the for'ard doors. A somewhat bedraggled female, draped in several blankets, was propped up against the bulkhead. Irma, appearing the more flushed of the two, was sitting in front of her with a large glass of brandy in her hand. They both looked up as he came in. Irma glanced back at the other woman and Judy fixed her eye on Brown. It was several seconds before he spoke.

'How are you?'

There was another pause.

'I'm fine,' she eventually replied in a husky voice. It was also a little restrained. She cleared her throat.

'Has she drunk some yet?' he asked Irma.

The woman nodded. 'A little.'

He turned back to Judy and said with a smile, 'Try some more. It'll do you good.'

With that he left, shutting the door quietly behind him. Wilson was looking at him rather absently as he exited the aft cabin.

'Towel yourself down and get some clothes on,' Brown said to him, and there was an immediate response.

The leader sat back against the pulpit and relaxed as he watched his team at work, getting the fast boat underway. He had been foolish to bring Judy along. In the event, she hadn't been needed and had almost died. That would have been bad for morale. What was more, he didn't like making mistakes.

Chapter 6

Standing in the centrally heated hall of his London flat, General Sir Giles Stoddard replaced the telephone receiver and looked at his watch. 7.29. He picked up the phone again to make his third call in ten minutes, dialling a Scotland number.

The bell rang once before a harsh voice barked, 'Amis.'

'Clive, Giles Stoddard.'

Amis said: 'Hello, Giles, how's tricks? Dashed time to ring, old boy. Haven't even . . .'

'Listen, Clive,' interrupted Stoddard brusquely, 'this is not a social call, I'm afraid. I'm at home, so I can't go through official communication channels. An Argosy plane that flew over Wick Airport about twenty minutes ago, heading approximately nor'-nor'-west, is full of plutonium and I've reason to believe it's been hijacked. It should have landed at Wick. Can you get some of your jets on to it as soon as poss? Wick still have it on radar.'

There was a small pause.

'Can do,' answered Amis. 'Where do I get in touch?'

'You have the Control number?'

'Yes.'

'I'll be there in twenty minutes or so. I'll phone you then. All right?'

'Just a minute,' said Amis.

There was a pause of about five seconds.

'Who was best man at my wedding?'

Stoddard couldn't help smiling at the caution.

'How could I ever forget,' he replied. 'Making a speech about how wonderful you are is not my favourite pastime.'

There was a short laugh at the other end. 'Fine. Anything else?'

'No. I'll be in touch,' said Stoddard and hung up.

He then immediately dialled Control.

'Pomfret?'

'Yes.'

'This is Sir Giles. I've requested an immediate Fireball Alert. The aircraft that Troutman told you of is being taken care of. When I arrive I want all the communication networks manned. Is that clear?'

'Er, yes, sir.'

Stoddard would have to have been totally insensitive not to feel the insecurity of the other man.

'This is urgent, Pomfret. You have my personal authority to draft anyone until I get there. Do your best. Any new developments?'

'No, sir.'

'Good,' and with that he put the phone down, grabbed his coat and left.

It was 8 a.m. when he pushed open the door of Communications Control. Everyone looked up as he entered. What they saw was a man in his middle fifties, about five feet eight in height, with a thick-set figure. Sparklingly clear blue eyes shone against a mildly florid complexion and short, grey hair covered the squarish head in tight curls. A pipe protruded from a corner of his mouth, but everyone in the room knew that he never lit it until midday. The smart, grey suit was the same one he always wore. There would have been speculation that he went to bed in it if it didn't look so well-pressed every morning.

On the frustrating car journey over, Stoddard had listed in his mind the things he had to do and shuffled them into an order of priority. But he had to be here to do it. The reason why, in a war, your enemy invariably aims to destroy your command headquarters is because you are virtually lost without a centre of communications. From this hub, Stoddard could, in theory, control the rim. He had decided that he would be his own Director of Operations, when the holder of the office had retired, as well as being Head of the Department.

Pomfret, who, Stoddard knew, was supposed to go off duty at 8.00, was still manning the console. He'd done a good job in getting everyone together, especially since it was so early in the morning. Most of the equipment had an operator in front of it and the place was filling with more people, all looking to him for direction. He removed his pipe.

'Any new developments?' he asked Pomfret.

'No urgent ones, sir. Mr Jensen will be arriving shortly.'

The voice was more confident now, but Stoddard noticed beads of sweat on Pomfret's brow.

The older man nodded and said, 'Can you stay on for a bit?' knowing that Pomfret wouldn't have left now for anything. Before he could reply, Stoddard turned to his replacement, a man called Deansworthy.

'Give him a hand and get me General Amis in Scotland, immediately,' he ordered.

'Sir,' said Pomfret, 'perhaps I ought to say that Air Commodore James wants to know what the flap's about. I said you'd call him back. And General Jacks is on at the moment, demanding to know why his whole unit is about to besiege Heathrow.'

Stoddard suppressed a groan. At least his request for a Fireball Alert had been granted. But these sorts of questions were bound to come up and there would be many more. He turned to Deansworthy, who was holding a phone towards him. Stoddard took it and said:

'Take over the console. Pomfret, try and quieten down General Jacks and deal with any other similar inquiries. I am not available.'

Looking up, he saw his Intelligence Director, Jensen, coming in by the other door and put the speaker to his mouth.

'General Amis? What's happening?'

'We're in pursuit, but we don't have radar contact yet,' answered the ebullient Amis.

'Let me know when you do. I shall also want helicopters and troops for an air-to-ground search soon, General. Can you manage that?'

'Thought you might ask,' said Amis modestly. 'I have five on stand-by, and some more coming.'

'Good man. We'll link up by radio from now on. Also, if you don't mind, I'd like to be in direct hearing of your jets when they catch the Argosy.'

'Can do,' replied Amis.

Stoddard replaced the receiver and turned to Jensen, who had been listening.

'I'll tell you all about it in a second, Bill. For the moment, can you see to the radio contact – with Amis in Scotland?'

With what Stoddard thought was commendable restraint, his deputy hesitated, nodded and turned towards the radio operators. One of the console assistants, wearing tinted glasses, was looking at him, and before he could turn his head away Stoddard spoke.

'Get me the Chief Constable for Cumbria on the phone, now.'

The young man turned at once to a book fixed to the desk in front of him.

'Try his home first,' said Stoddard, as an afterthought. Chief Constables didn't usually begin their working day before 9 a.m. at the earliest. He glanced at his watch. 8.06. Nearly an hour had passed since the plane had flown over Wick and the doubts were beginning to multiply in his mind. Turning, he stopped a passing controller.

'Turf out all the maps between Carlisle and Wick.' Then another afterthought: 'Plus the Admiralty charts to the north of Wick, clear to the Pole.'

Jensen was returning. He had a forceful face, the nose long and narrow, the jaw large and dark, and the eyebrows black and bushy. This was topped by contrasting reddish brown hair. He was of normal build, although he had a substantial paunch, which was catered for by the immaculately tailored, Savile Row, double-breasted, pin-stripe suit. He was what socialists see as a typical product of the English upper-middle classes – public school, fashionable Cambridge college and a career civil servant. He was more than a little pompous, but Stoddard had a grudging respect for him. Respect because he had a good brain, grudging because he didn't like him. He recognized him as a necessary evil, whose connections, through what was euphemistically called the 'old-boy network', were greater than his own. He himself had been down a similar route: prep school, Eton, Oxford, Sandhurst Military Academy, then into the Guards. He'd had a heavy Etonian accent at one time, which he now played down. Jensen didn't, and Stoddard had always thought it odd that he insisted on being called Bill. He had an infuriating habit of screwing up his eyes and grinning after almost every utterance.

'We have the radio link-up,' said Jensen, and then, not being able to restrain himself any longer, 'what's all this about?'

'Plutonium hijack. I'm going to explain it to the Chief Constable for Cumbria in a minute, so hang on.'

'Mr Phillipson, sir,' called the young man with the tinted glasses, holding out the phone, and then he realized that Stoddard probably hadn't a clue who Phillipson was. He reddened and added quickly, 'The Chief Constable for Cumbria.'

Stoddard took the phone and paused while Jensen linked himself into the same line.

'Mr Phillipson?' asked Stoddard politely.

'That's right. And who may you be?' answered the policeman in a northern accent.

Stoddard decided it was no time for modesty.

'My name is Stoddard. I'm the Head of MI5.'

It wasn't strictly true. 'Internal Security' was split up into so many horizontal sections now that it was difficult to know who was actually in charge. But he didn't think Phillipson would know that and it might impress him. In any case, his real position in the hierarchy would take far too long to explain.

'Oh, yes,' came the non-committal reply.

The Chief Constable appeared to be unmoved. Stoddard took a deep breath and decided to be honest.

'I need your help urgently. An aircraft – a Hawker-Siddeley Argosy – has been hijacked. It contained plutonium from the re-processing plant at Windscale. The plane took off from Carlisle Airport early this morning for Wick. As yet I have no idea where the hijack took place. I want that information. I must, therefore, know what happened, if anything, at Carlisle Airport. I'm phoning you because it's your patch and I need the information urgently. I should be obliged if you would take personal charge.'

He paused, but Phillipson said nothing. Stoddard wasn't noted for his tact and Chief Constables needed to be handled with kid gloves. Phillipson, he thought, might think it was one big hoax, but he would still be curious.

'If you wish to verify my authority, Mr Phillipson, I'm sure you know how, but it would waste valuable time.'

It was another five seconds before Phillipson said, 'Do what I can,' in a voice which implied that he hadn't actually made up his mind.

Stoddard nevertheless breathed a silent sigh of relief and continued.

'We won't be able to keep this out of the media eventually, but I'd rather it was later than sooner.'

'Of course.' Phillipson sounded more sure now. 'Anything else?'

'Perhaps you could ring me here as soon as you have the information?' said Stoddard and he gave the number.

'I'll see to it myself,' replied Phillipson and hung up.

Stoddard had wanted to impress upon the Chief Constable how desperately urgent it was to have the information, but he knew he couldn't. The policeman would be expected to work that out for himself. And Stoddard had to rely on Phillipson's quick organization in the area. A radio operator was signalling him and he walked over. Jensen followed him, looking worried.

'Sorry, sir,' said the operator, 'I didn't want to disturb your call. The jets have had the Argosy on radar for a couple of minutes. They should have her on visual any second.'

He looked closely at Stoddard to gauge his mood. He knew from experience that the Old Man had a genuine manner and an almost lovable character, provided you were on his side. His face held an almost perpetual frown and he lost his temper frequently, but this acted as a sort of release valve for letting off tension and he was quickly back to normal. He also smiled a lot. What the radio operator didn't know, though he would have believed it if he had, was that, as a man of extremes, Stoddard was often quoted at mess parties as saying, 'There is nothing worse than mediocrity,' which would be followed by bouts of affectionate laughter. Seeing no hostility, the man replaced the headphones.

Stoddard bent down to the other operator who he knew was monitoring communications between ground and air. Transferring his pipe to his left hand he wrote on a pad, 'Switch to loudspeaker.' The operator immediately flicked a switch and removed his headphones. He realized there was no sound and turned a knob. The room was instantly filled with static.

'They haven't spotted it yet, sir,' ventured someone.

Stoddard said, 'Thank you,' and smiled.

The pause gave him time to think and he sucked on his empty pipe.

There were things he wanted to know about the plane, yes, but more than anything else he wanted to know how the hijack took place and how they could have done it. He needed to know more about the transportation arrangements. Jensen broke into his thoughts.

'Do we know enough about this plutonium?'

'No, we don't,' answered Stoddard churlishly, but Jensen was persistent.

'What happens if the plane crashes, for instance? Is it dangerous? Could we have a contamination problem as well?'

Stoddard realized that that was a very good question.

'I don't know, Bill,' he replied, running fingers through his short grey hair, 'but see if you can get me Troutman, BNFL Chief Security Officer. He's at this number.' He wrote it down on the pad. 'There are one or two other questions I want to ask Mr Troutman.'

Jensen grinned thinly and walked away. Through the arch in the next room, Stoddard watched several people laying out large maps on the briefing table. Suddenly the static became a voice.

'*This is Red Leader to Base. We have target on visual. Height is ten-thou'. Speed 270. Course steady. Request instructions, over.*'

Stoddard tapped one of the radio operators on the shoulder and held out his hand. The shirt-sleeved man passed over the earphones and mike. Before he could speak Stoddard heard:

'*Stand by, Red Leader.*'

'This is General Stoddard. Get me General Amis.'

Amis must have been about to call up, because he was on within two seconds.

'General, we are under your instructions.'

Despite the situation, Stoddard couldn't help smiling.

'Request you ascertain whether there is anyone flying the plane or whether it is on automatic pilot,' said Stoddard.

'Wilco, out,' replied Amis.

It occurred to Stoddard that Amis's operation was working well and he immediately heard instructions being given to the jets. Jensen spoke at his shoulder.

'Troutman's on.'

Stoddard turned and called, 'Pomfret, link into my call,' and he walked over to the phone.

As he waited for Jensen to listen in, he was struck by a feeling of loss. That somehow this was all a waste of time. That he would be far too late. So far he knew virtually nothing. He mentally shook himself and none of the defeatist attitude showed in his voice.

'Mr Troutman?'

'Yes?' The voice was faint.

'This is the Director. There are a number of questions I wish to ask you, and when you answer I must ask you to speak up because the line is a bad one.'

There was no reply.

'Can you hear me, Mr Troutman?'

'Er, perfectly. The bad line seems to be only one way,' replied Troutman in a clearer voice.

'Where was the plutonium stored last night?' asked Stoddard quickly, to forestall any more trivial conversation.

'It would have arrived at the airport about 10 or 11 last night, by lorry, and then been loaded on to the plane immediately. So the plutonium would have been on the aircraft overnight.'

The voice was still faint, but Troutman was obviously taking great care to speak clearly. Stoddard crushed his impatience to hurry.

'Can you be a little more specific, Mr Troutman, about the time of arrival of the plutonium at Carlisle and, indeed, whether it did arrive at all?'

There was a pause of several seconds. Stoddard forced himself to remain silent.

'No,' came the eventual reply, 'I'm afraid I can't.' Another slight pause. 'I haven't been in touch with my deputy since yesterday morning. He was my man at the airport. But he would certainly have phoned me if the cargo had not arrived at all.'

Stoddard let that one go. There was no point in phoning Windscale to find out whether the shipment was delivered to Carlisle. They would probably say yes because their records said yes, but that didn't make the records correct. He knew enough about bureaucracy to know that you had to actually go to the horse's mouth to be sure of your information, and by the time he could institute that sort of inquiry he would probably have the facts anyway. Moreover, the same sort of investigation at the airport would pre-empt Phillipson's arrival. The Chief Constable wouldn't be too pleased about that and the press would probably get to know of it more quickly. He would just have to wait. The feeling of surrealism increased. There was still so little he knew.

'Mr Troutman, what form is the plutonium in?'

'It's in the form of plutonium oxide pellets, reprocessed and ready for immersion into the Fast Breeder Reactor at Dounreay. These are contained in stainless-steel rods in a fuel assembly, which is designed to fit straight into the reactor. There would have been twelve assemblies in all. They're each twelve feet long, about six inches across and they weigh close on a thousand pounds each.'

Stoddard staggered a bit at that. He knew they were heavy, but 1,000 lbs! That raised an enormous logistical problem for the hijackers and pointed forcefully at a ground hijack. Now he had something to work on. But he wasn't finished with Troutman yet.

'One final question, Mr Troutman. How dangerous is it if the plane crashes?'

Again there was a long pause. It was as if Troutman were expecting the question but hadn't made up his mind how to answer it. When he spoke, his voice was so faint that it was almost inaudible.

'We have considered this possibility and tests have been carried out with successful results.'

Stoddard glanced at Jensen and pulled a face. The latter, his ear to the extension phone, did the same.

'You mean there is no contamination problem?' persisted Stoddard.

He was fairly sure that Troutman said, 'That is what our tests have shown.'

'Does that apply if the aircraft catches fire and explodes on impact?'

The answer came back immediately, in a much clearer and firmer voice: 'Since the aircraft is now flying over nothing but open sea, I wouldn't have thought that applied.'

Troutman was beginning to bristle. Jensen pulled another face. Suddenly someone shouted.

'Sir. The loudspeaker!'

'. . . Control. There is no one flying aircraft. Cockpit deserted. Over.'

Stoddard's thoughts were racing. So, either the plutonium was thrown out and the crew baled out, or the plutonium was hijacked on the ground and the plane was a decoy.

'*Will attempt search of cargo hold through open rear cargo-door. Over.*'

The pilot then baled out after setting the automatic pilot.

'*Proceed, Red Leader. But don't get too close.*'

Given the weight problem, the latter possibility was almost certainly the case. But if the plutonium arrived at Carlisle before midnight it could be anywhere in the country by now. It could even be in London with a fast lorry! Road blocks would be pointless. The surrealism became reality as he focused upon the enormity of the problem and, just as swiftly, he knew what must be done. The pilot would have to be found. He lifted the phone.

'Are you still there, Mr Troutman?'

'Yes, what's happening?'

Troutman, Stoddard reflected, must have been able to hear the radio and general commotion, although probably not the words. He ignored the question.

'Was the route the Argosy took a straight one?' he asked.

'No,' answered Troutman, to Stoddard's relief. 'It was due to fly due north to Portknockie on the Moray Firth and then turn slightly westward to Wick.'

Stoddard signalled an aide to come over while Troutman continued.

'The air-traffic controller here confirms that it was at least on route from Portknockie. Before that I can't say.' Troutman was far more cautious in his answers now.

'Thank you,' said Stoddard, really meaning it. 'Stay on the line would you,' and he put the phone down.

He turned to the aide, who was standing faithfully at semi-attention.

'Get me a map covering the whole of Scotland – a contour map with roads.' And to Tinted-Glasses, 'See if Phillipson's arrived at Carlisle Airport yet.'

'He's on now, sir. Been waiting about half a minute,' replied the operator.

The Chief Constable had worked quickly. As he was handed the phone, Stoddard became aware of the loudspeaker.

'*Red Leader to Base Control. Cargo hold too dark. Repeat, too dark. Also, angle of sight obstructs most of hold. Over.*'

There was a slight pause.

'*Roger, Red Leader. Stand by.*'

Stoddard handed the phone back to Tinted-Glasses and walked over to the radio. He wanted to know how many of the assemblies were missing. He wrote a message on the operator's pad: 'Did the pilot see anything?' Amis might think it a stupid question, but he didn't care now. The odds were getting longer and longer.

He walked back across the room, passing Jensen studying a map of Scotland. He signalled him to listen in again and picked up the phone.

'Mr Phillipson?'

'Yes, Mr Stoddard?'

'Sorry to keep you waiting. What's the score?'

'Well, don't know whether this is going to come as good or bad news to you, but the 'ijack certainly took place 'ere, in one of the 'angars. Found three bodies behind some boxes at the back. One's already been visually identified as the pilot. T'other two 'ave papers saying they are security officers for British Nuclear Fuels Limited. Co-pilot appears to be alive, barely. Odd thing is, 'e's the only one with any physical signs of injury. My guess would be that t'others were injected with a drug of some kind. It's nice and quiet. Suit their purpose down t'd ground I should think. But can't say for sure until doctor gets 'ere. That what you wanted to know?'

Phillipson sounded quite pleased with himself and certainly more forthcoming than during their last conversation.

'Yes, you've been extremely helpful. There are two further questions. First, I'd like the take-off time and the heading. And . . .'

'Just a minute,' interrupted Phillipson. Then, after about five seconds: 'Carry on.'

'And second,' continued Stoddard, 'the time of death.'

'Thought you might ask me that,' replied the Chief Constable. 'Can't say definitely until doctor arrives, of course, but I 'ave been giving it some thought. Don't know what temperature was down in London last night, Mr Stoddard – quite mild, I shouldn't wonder

– but there was a frost up 'ere. The 'angar, of course, 'ad no 'eating, and in my experience, bodies left in freezing conditions not only mask the exact time of death, but the approximate time as well. I've touched one o' them – 'e was like ice. Now . . .'

There was a slight pause and a mutter. Stoddard did not interrupt. Phillipson was obviously enjoying himself.

'I've just been 'anded information, Mr Stoddard, which says that the plane left at exactly 6.10, 'eading due north, by the way. That means that, at a minimum, they 'ave been dead two and a half hours, and in my experience the maximum that doctor will judge is considerably more. 'E'll probably say from one and a half to eight hours, but I've been known to be wrong.'

There was another slight pause.

'Can you 'old on a moment please, Mr Stoddard?' and there was some more muttering.

Stoddard had that feeling of unreality again.

'Mr Stoddard?'

'Yes, Mr Phillipson.'

'I've got some new information 'ere which 'elps us quite a lot.' The Chief Constable obviously now considered himself part of the case. 'The Warden of the airfield says that 'e saw the pilot and co-pilot walking towards the 'angar at about 5.45, just as 'e was going to check the runway. Now, if it was them, that means they were probably killed, or rather the pilot was killed, between two and a half and three hours ago. However . . .'

Stoddard waited for Phillipson's slow, but deadly, logic.

' . . . the Warden also says that the BNFL lorry, which presumably was carrying the plutonium for transfer to the plane, arrived 'ere at approximately 10.15 and left at approx 11.50. During that time it was inside the 'angar and the doors were closed. So, although the killings didn't occur until much later, the 'ijack could 'ave taken place earlier, about 10.30. The plutonium needn't have been transferred to the plane at all.'

Of course Phillipson was right. Although Stoddard had arrived at the same conclusion he felt no feeling of elation at having his deduction confirmed. The plutonium could be anywhere in the country by now. Then, for a sudden, shocking moment, he realized that it could even be out of the country. They had at least seven clear hours before anyone knew there was anything wrong, and nearly nine hours before he was in a position to do anything about it. The hijack had probably taken place just after the lorry arrived. The two security officers had been killed and dumped out of the way at the back of the hangar, and the drivers of the lorry similarly killed and thrown in the vehicle. The hijackers had then simply waited an hour or so, the time any onlookers would expect it to take for the plutonium to be transferred to the plane, and had driven the lorry out, with the plutonium still inside. The fact that the driver and his mate were not lying on the floor with the two security officers was an attempt to fool him into thinking that the hijack had taken place later. The rest of the hijackers had then simply waited for the flight crew to arrive, and killed them. A substitute pilot had then flown the empty aircraft to Wick, while the others left by another route. The security officers must have had a car if they weren't due to fly with the plane, and if there were more than two hijackers left, then they could have lain below the level of the seats until they were out of the aerodrome. They could even have delayed killing the security guards until the time they killed the crew, just to confuse. The plane was not just a decoy, it was part of a brilliantly conceived plan to give the hijackers a few extra hours. Why? He filed that away because Phillipson was speaking to him.

'. . . Mr Stoddard, are you still there?'

The Chief Constable sounded worried.

'Thank you, Mr Phillipson. I am very grateful. Some of my people will be coming up shortly. I should appreciate it if you would hand over the investigation to them.'

'I understand,' replied Phillipson.

'In the meantime,' said Stoddard, 'I wonder whether you can do me one last favour? Find out the description of the BNFL lorry and the car belonging to the security officers. Then put out an all-points alert.'

'Already done it for the lorry, but not the car. I'll find out about that,' replied the Chief Constable.

'They are both probably still on your patch,' continued Stoddard as if Phillipson had not spoken, 'having transferred the goods and themselves to other vehicles. You have my number if anything develops.'

'Yes.'

'Thank you once again, Mr Phillipson. Good-bye.'

As he hung up, a very tall controller, who was standing beside Stoddard, said, 'The pilot could see nothing in the hold, sir.' On receiving no reply, he asked, 'Where do we set up the road-blocks, sir?' and waited patiently.

'Everywhere,' came the sudden, rather gruff statement. 'I want every lorry capable of carrying a ton or more stopped and searched, anywhere and everywhere in the country. See to it.'

Stoddard walked over to Pomfret, leaving the lanky controller rooted to the spot, open-mouthed. He made to call after Stoddard, thought better of it and walked off, scratching his head.

'Did you get all that, Pomfret?' asked the General.

'Yes, sir,' came the confident reply.

Jensen looked up from the Scotland map as Stoddard approached, sensed his mood and asked quickly, 'Are we talking about a one-man bale-out?'

Stoddard nodded curtly. So his deputy had come to the same conclusion. Well, it *was* rather obvious. He bent down to the map.

'In that case,' said Jensen, 'there are only three areas where he could have jumped. We know it must have been after Portknockie because he made a course alteration there. That's on the coast here, so the first possibility is into the sea.'

The eyes narrowed and the lips stretched into a grin as he continued.

'I suggest that is unlikely. It would be cold and uncomfortable, and it would need a boat to pick him up. Also to be borne in mind, of course, is the fact that it's rather difficult to search a boat from a helicopter; and even if we did have a ship in the area, which I doubt, stopping a foreign vessel on the high seas is still piracy.'

The grin became longer.

'The next and most likely possibility, in my view, is the small spit of land beyond Wick, before the Pentland Firth. It's about seven miles across and could be searched quite quickly. If he had a car hidden he could get out of the Highlands by only two routes: the A9 from Wick, or around to the north on to the A835 at Ullapool.'

Jensen paused and looked at Stoddard again.

'What time would he have dropped here?' He pointed to the peninsula.

Stoddard thought for a moment.

'About 7.15. Say 7.00 for safety.'

They both glanced at their watches. 8.48.

'So's he's got an hour and a half on us,' continued Jensen. 'If we set up road-blocks at Bonar Bridge and horizontally at Ullapool, we must have him.'

Jensen narrowed his eyes again. The inane grin was still there. Listening to him, Stoddard could see the reasoning, but he had a feeling it was too obvious. These boys were as sharp as needles and must have foreseen the possibility. Nevertheless, there didn't seem to be any harm in setting up the barricades.

'Do that,' he said.

Suddenly the room was filled with static again. The radio operator had obviously previously switched the air-to-base link off the loudspeaker so as not to disturb everyone.

'. . . *Repeat. Argosy is diving uncontrollably. Am following down.*'

There was nothing but static for about thirty seconds, while most people looked at Stoddard. The General was apparently assiduously studying the map.

'*Aircraft broke up on impact. No explosion. Over.*'

No one moved or spoke for a further five seconds. Stoddard turned and began to walk through to the chart room.

'*Stand by, Red Leader.*'

O'Conner, one of the Chief Assistants, saw Stoddard coming.

'Get the coordinates, will you, O'Conner? And pinpoint it on one of those Admiralty charts you turfed out,' said Stoddard, pointing his pipe at the table.

He then returned to Jensen, noting that one or two in the room were averting their eyes as he walked.

'What was the third possibility?' he asked his deputy.

Jensen resumed his survey, while Stoddard made vulgar sucking noises on his pipe.

'If you draw a line from Portknockie to Wick and continue it, you'll see that it goes over the Orkneys, touching the island of Hoy very briefly. Rough terrain, but a good place for a lonely parachute landing. The apparent problem then for him is that he has to get off the island, but he would have made prior arrangements. A small, fast boat after dark and he could be through the Skagerrak before we knew it.'

That seemed to Stoddard to be the most likely possibility of the three, but he still wasn't hopeful. He walked over to the radio, noting that O'Conner was still hunting through the charts. Whatever happened, he had learnt from this. He switched the link to loudspeaker and picked up the microphone.

'This is General Stoddard. Get me General Amis immediately.'

Amis answered in a few moments.

'What do you want me to do with my jets?'

It sounded as if he had expected Stoddard to come through earlier, but the latter was in no mood for truculence.

'I want some aerial cover of the crash area until the Navy gets there, General. How you handle that is up to you.' He paused, thinking. 'In the meantime, how many helicopters can you let me have?'

'Seven,' replied Amis, 'four of which are long-range and can carry troops.'

'Good. I'd like two of the troop-carriers and one of the other 'copters to the island of Hoy. The whole island should be searched from the air and the ground. You're looking for one parachutist. No, possibly more than one. I'm sorry I can't be more specific than that. I want the other two big ones and a small one to search the whole peninsula from Reiss to Castletown. Get as many troops as you can to both locations, General. Another possibility is that he dropped into the Moray Firth, although, for obvious reasons, we think this is unlikely. But the remaining small 'copter is to search the area, including outward into the North Sea. If he dropped there, he will almost certainly have been picked up. Make a note of all shipping, including small boats. Try and get some assistance there if you can. All sightings to be reported to this control.'

If there is one thing you never tell a General it's how to deploy his own troops. Stoddard realized that he had done just that. It was a long time since he had been used to an Army chain of command, and the strain of the moment had to be getting to him. What he should have done was explain the situation to Amis and let him take over. He could imagine the man at the other end fighting down his anger.

'I'm sorry, General,' continued Stoddard, 'but the situation is urgent. The aircraft was flying in a straight line from Portknockie to Wick and, as you know, did not deviate until it ran out of fuel.

Deploy any other troops and equipment that become available as you see fit. You have the full authority of a Fireball Alert.'

'Yes, *sir*,' answered Amis and the line went dead.

Stoddard returned to Jensen, where O'Conner was pointing at a map. They both looked up as he approached.

'We've found it, sir,' said O'Conner excitedly. About 120 miles north-east of the Faeroes and about 380 east-south-east of Iceland.'

He paused and pointed.

'Here, sir.'

'What's the depth, man?' asked Stoddard impatiently.

'Twelve hundred fathoms, sir,' answered O'Conner with a smile.

Stoddard was stunned.

'Seven thousand feet!' he exclaimed.

'Yes, sir,' replied O'Conner, completely unabashed. 'A bit o'luck, really. Another sixty miles and she'd be down another four thou'.'

He looked up. The Old Man was looking at him as if he'd stolen his whisky. There had been a tentative suggestion from one of the lads the other day that the General wore a girdle or belt of some kind to keep his stomach in, since in all other respects he cut a rather robust figure. Looking back into the angry blue eyes he could now see what a stupid idea that had been.

'O'Conner,' said Stoddard in a rather strangled voice, 'go back into the other room, will you?'

He knew that it would take the Navy days, perhaps a week or more, to get the equipment needed to dive to 7,000 feet to that exact spot, and then make the dive itself, even if the weather held. It just got worse every minute. As yet he had no evidence that any plutonium was even missing. It could still all be down in that plane. It was always possible that it was a gigantic hoax, to demonstrate the possibility of a hijack, and that all twelve assemblies were lying at the bottom of the Norwegian Sea. But somehow, he didn't think so. He felt sure the aircraft was empty, but there was only one way of finding out. He leant forward, both hands on the table, and thought.

'Bill, take some notes.'

He waited while Jensen dutifully picked up a pad and a pen.

'Troutman is still on the phone at Wick. Give him my condolences and tell him that his two security officers and *both* pilots are dead. Then tell him to stand by for a jet to bring him to London. I need him down here as soon as possible. Arrange it with Amis, will you, and make the transport arrangements this end. Then brief half a dozen of our boys and get them to Carlisle and Wick, fast. We also need a naval vessel over the crash area as soon as poss' and a naval diving team with deep-water equipment. I don't even know if they have it. Then we need as many vessels in the Moray Firth and North Sea area as we can.'

He paused.

'On second thoughts, I'd better see to the Navy side of things.'

He turned and called to the console operator.

'Get me the Admiralty.' And turning back to his deputy, 'See to that now, will you, Bill.' It was a statement, not a question.

Stoddard unconsciously struck the classic pose, with pipe held in mouth, and looked at his watch. 9.04. The morning had only just begun, yet he felt ready for bed. He knew that he would be up till midnight at least, because he also knew that the search was going to fail. He would do everything he could – ritually make the right moves – but the battle was lost before it had begun. He didn't know how much, if any, plutonium was missing. He didn't have a clue where it was. It could be anywhere in the country or already on some foreign ship at sea. He didn't know where the hijackers were. He didn't even know where the pilot-hijacker was and, even if he did catch him, that provided no guarantee of finding the plutonium. He was concentrating a lot of resources on finding one man who might know virtually nothing.

The search would have to be stepped up at goods yards, sea and airports. You cannot put a twelve-foot package in your pocket. Already the Fireball Alert would mean that troops would have moved into all goods transit areas. Passengers at the UK's major air-terminals would be thinking that there had been a revolution. That was to say nothing of the massive troop movements that would be taking place all over the country, to scour deserted coasts and airfields. Late breakfasters would be hearing it on the radio over their Shredded Wheat. It wouldn't be long before a smart reporter put it all together. As time went on, too, he would have to speak to the Prime Minister again and that would be painful. He was surprised that he hadn't been on already.

Then Stoddard thought of the weekend just gone, that he'd spent at his family estate in Hertfordshire, just as he did most weekends – riding horses, playing the piano, enjoying good food and wine, and drinking malt whisky. It was his form of escapism and he often thought of it in moments of tension. He was regarded as something of a squire in the county, although he refused to join the local hunt, and really lived for his job since his wife's death. There were no children. Somehow he sensed that he wasn't going to be able to get up to the country for some time.

'The Admiralty, sir,' called Tinted-Glasses.

With the force of mind that had helped him be good at his job, Stoddard pushed the doubts out of his mind, rose from his chair and, with a smile on his face, walked over to the telephone.

The electrical instrument panel above the cabin hatch glowed green in the dark. Beyond that Brown could see the dark outline of the sails against the star-spotted sky, but not the riding lights which were shielded from the cockpit. It was indeed a dark night. But quiet it wasn't as he listened to the sleek craft sliding into the swell. The water rippled down the hull and gurgled at his back in the boat's wake. Occasionally, the mast or a shroud creaked. Brown lay on one of the aft lockers, a coffee in one hand, wrapped up against the cold. The helmsman, steering by compass, tried to ignore him.

Late in the morning the helicopter had buzzed them and come down very low for an inspection. It had played havoc with the wind and the boat had rocked uncontrollably. They had shouted their outraged shouts at the pilot and shaken their justified fists, and he had gone away. All afternoon they had seen nothing. At 5.30 they had turned south and, a few hours later, night had come to mask their passage.

Then they had all got busy, peeling off the red plastic from gunwale to waterline, revealing the gleaming royal blue below. *Nessy* had become *The Gorgon* as the names were changed. It had been difficult work in the dark, with only torches for light, but worth it.

The wind had continued its move towards the east all day, until backing to the north again at dusk. Now it was blowing a steady Force 4 out of the north-east and *The Gorgon* was slightly back of a broad-reach – her fastest point of sailing.

Brown sipped his coffee, content.

2   *BOMB*

Chapter 7

'No. It would not, in my view, be possible for a terrorist group to make a bomb from fast-reactor fuel,' said the tall, slight, black-haired man seated across the desk from Stoddard. His suit and shoes were also black. Indeed, the only bit of colour on his entire frame were the minute sky-blue dots on the inevitable black tie, set against the white shirt. Even his eyes seemed colourless. He sat with one long leg crossed over the other, hands in lap, perfectly relaxed, the small, clipped moustache refusing to move any more. He was a very high Scientific Officer in the Department of Energy and not pleased at being taken from his valuable work to give answers to questions from a 'security man'.

Stoddard gazed over his pipe at the third man in the room. Although by far the youngest there, he was almost completely bald. He was also much smaller and rounder in appearance than the other and wore a bright green tweed suit. The shoes were of fashionable design, made of brown leather. He was from the Atomic Weapons Research Establishment (AWRE) at Aldermaston, and so far he hadn't said a word. As Stoddard looked at him, he took out a large, green and yellow handkerchief and blew his nose.

When the handkerchief had disappeared, it became clear that neither man was going to continue the conversation. Stoddard said:

'Would you like to explain that to me, Dr Pond?'

The tall man sighed audibly.

'Well, what you have to do is highly complex. You have first to remove the oxygen from the plutonium oxide and then separate out the plutonium, which is a tremendously difficult operation. And don't forget,' he bent forward to give weight to his words, 'that this all has to be done under conditions of great care because of the problem of radioactivity from the plutonium. A large well-equipped science firm might be able to do it and one or two educational establishments like Queen Mary College, London. And, of course,' glancing under furrowed brows to the man on his left, 'AWRE. But I don't think any smaller group could do it, and I don't believe it could be done without people finding out.'

Stoddard, who had been watching the smaller man's nervous glances at Pond, removed his pipe and opened his mouth to speak, but, having been reluctantly prodded into verbal action, the man from the Ministry wasn't going to stop now until he was finished.

'I would therefore regard it as an extremely tricky operation. If I felt I had to have a bomb, I'd go and steal one from some military establishment. I'd regard that as being more worthwhile, and certainly less dangerous, than trying to make fast-reactor fuel into a bomb.'

As Pond sat back, now purse-lipped, Stoddard refrained from mentioning that the security surrounding military bases was a great deal more effective than that guarding reprocessed reactor fuel. He turned to the smaller of the duo, who seemed to be expecting it, because the points of his shoes had begun rubbing together on the floor.

'Dr Ogilvie,' said Stoddard gently, 'how do you feel on this?'

Ogilvie shot a quick glance at Pond. 'Well, um, this is not exactly my line of work at all,' he replied in a Welsh accent, 'but I would say that what Dr Pond has said is essentially true.'

He stopped and looked at the ground. When he began again his head was still lowered.

'It *is* an extremely difficult operation, even if you do have the knowledge. But,' he looked up and attempted to smile at Stoddard, 'who knows?'

It was a stupid thing to say and he realized it. His face flushed and he looked at his feet again. Stoddard felt sorry for him.

Pond gave him a withering look of absolute disdain, stood up, and said, 'Will that be all, Sir Giles?'

He wasn't expecting a negative reply and Stoddard certainly wasn't going to give one.

'Yes, of course, Dr Pond. Thank you very much for coming.' He didn't bother to shake his hand, just stood up and smiled benignly. The tall man turned and left without ceremony.

Ogilvie had made no movement. He was still bent over his knees, too embarrassed to look up. Stoddard walked over to the window and looked down at the milling traffic, his right hand holding the pipe and his left in a trouser pocket.

He had seen Ogilvie's file before he had come in. Once into his PhD in some obscure branch of nuclear technology, he hadn't needed to apply for a job. The government had recruited him for Aldermaston. They had known he was homosexual and the British security services were very sensitive about that sort of thing since the Vassall scandal. But homosexuality was no longer a crime, the social norms regarding it had considerably changed and, anyway, Owen Ogilvie was too good to pass up.

Stoddard turned to look at him, wondering about the best way to tackle it. The General had reached the top of the tree partly because he had the right background (of which he was quite well aware), partly because he had a much better brain than the normal commissioned officer, but mainly because he understood men, their motives and desires. He removed his pipe.

'Ever met Dr Pond before?' he ventured.

Ogilvie looked up with a brave smile. 'No. 'Fraid not.'

'Me neither, and frankly I hope I never shall again,' Stoddard added feelingly.

Ogilvie laughed slightly and looked into Stoddard's eyes. The General smiled too and hoped the little man saw no hostility there. He decided to push on while the going was good.

'Your record says that you are good at your job. Is that true?'

'That's for other people to judge,' replied Ogilvie immediately.

There was a small silence. Stoddard decided to try again.

'Someone told me once that Einstein did most of his original thinking before he was twenty-three. Is *that* true?'

Ogilvie laughed again. 'I don't know. Probably. It certainly seems logical.'

'Oh, why's that?' asked Stoddard.

'Well, after the early to mid twenties the brain deteriorates physically. A man can still increase his knowledge and, indeed, his adaptive thinking; but his capacity for, as you rightly put it, "original thinking", actually lessens. There are exceptions, of course.'

Stoddard, who knew all this, replied with a smile, 'I promise I won't tell A WR E that you're over the hill.'

Ogilvie laughed fully this time.

Stoddard looked away. He wasn't too concerned with amateur bomb-making, because he was pretty sure that the stuff was already out of the country, or certainly destined for overseas, but he didn't like uncertainties. He sat on the corner of the desk and looked down at Ogilvie, seriously.

'I need to know whether Pond is right. Can you tell me?'

Ogilvie began fidgeting again.

'I'd like to, Sir Giles, I really would. But I honestly don't know. I certainly wouldn't be as definite as Dr Pond.'

He looked worriedly down at his hands again. 'You see, I've never made one out of this sort of material. I can see that it's possible, given the right sort of information.'

The Welsh accent was strong now as he struggled to continue.

'You see, I've led – I lead – a rather sheltered existence. If I want something I just have to ask for it. I would think that the availability of this sort of information on the open market was nil. On the other hand, a government scientist, or even *ex*-government scientist, would surely be discovered before he completed the process, even if he did know how to, which I doubt. We don't make bombs from this sort of material, Sir Giles. I doubt whether there is anyone in the country who ever has done. But the real answer is, I simply don't know.'

He looked at Stoddard more confidently.

'There is one other thing too. In my opinion, Dr Pond understated the difficulties. He only mentioned the chemical process. There are far more techniques involved in making an atomic bomb, I can assure you. You need a high degree of sophistication in metal-working and electronics – neither of which I have.'

'I see,' said Stoddard. He stood up and smiled. 'In that case I won't detain you any further.'

Ogilvie stood up immediately and Stoddard showed him to the door.

'Can you make your own way back to Aldermaston?'

'Yes, of course,' answered Oglivie. 'I'm sorry I couldn't help you further.'

'You have been a help.'

The little man nodded to himself and scuttled away. Stoddard was left wondering at the thought that if it was not possible to make a bomb out of the stuff, then why steal it?

The basement workshop was twenty-four feet by twenty. At strategic positions against the walls stood three Calor-gas heaters, as the place was cold and damp. Stacked against three walls were metal shelves, stretching right up to the ceiling. On two of these series of shelves were various kinds of machine tools, bottles and gas cylinders. The other one was half filled with files and books.

Against the far wall – the wall opposite the door above the corner stairs – stood what appeared to be a large, transparent, plastic bag, that almost reached to the ceiling. It was about eight feet wide and ten feet long when fully extended and it was, in fact, an adapted oxygen tent. A variety of objects could be seen inside and a number of electronic leads led from it.

The big, low, metal workbench was sited off-centre in the room, due to the protrusion of the tent. On one side of it was placed an oblong of slotted angle iron, three feet long, two feet wide and eighteen inches deep. Attached to one inside corner of the frame were two square boxes. Many electronic leads ran from these boxes to a panel across the width of the frame, on which were scores of electronic connections. There were a number of small cylinders in the frame and on top of the upper box was a switch. Even more electronic leads wound from the assembly to a mechanism called a double-beam oscilloscope with long-stay traces, and to a digital timer.

There were two men in the room. The one who was bending over the assembly was called Caren Macdonald, a twenty-four-year-old graduate in cybernetics. He had orange hair and freckly skin and was rather plump. With his fingernails bitten down to the quick, he worked with a fanaticism which almost rivalled that of the other man. He was Keith Vaisey, of medium height and build, with dark-brown hair. But there the normality stopped. A plane crash at fifteen had left him badly disfigured about the face and he had false legs. He had managed, through tremendous motivation and no little ability, to get to university and graduate in physics.

Now forty-two, he had been unemployed for two years. During that time he had researched, in his own home, in nuclear physics.

He was impressed with Caren's work. He liked professionalism and admired his skill. Once he had explained to the young man what was required he went and did it and, indeed, they had just more or less completed the construction of a simultaneous detonation system, or at least as much of it as they could without the other 'parts'.

The problem was to achieve detonation of all the explosive lenses at the same time – in fact, in less than a nano-second after the plutonium hemispheres had been brought together. Detonators were notoriously inconsistent and there weren't any on the market which had this degree of accuracy. So it necessitated building high-quality electronic control units to enable synchronization to occur. The metering equipment and the oscilloscope had shown a quite remarkable degree of simultaneity.

Vaisey sat back, pleased. This was a vital stage in the construction. No matter how well he handled the plutonium side of things, if the lenses did not explode simultaneously, the resulting explosion would be less than the maximum possible, and the device might even fail to go off altogether.

Thinking of the plutonium side, he began to worry again about the time limit. He had told Brown that he needed more time for the construction of the rest of the mechanism, so that all they would have to do after the hijack would be concerned with the plutonium itself. But a delivery was being made and Brown couldn't wait. Apparently only seven or eight deliveries were made a year, and if they didn't take this one they might have had to wait another six to eight weeks. And that, Brown had said, was too long. Vaisey didn't know why, but that was that. He would just have to work harder and faster. The plutonium would be coming soon and they had only just begun.

Anyway, for the moment, he was satisfied. As the scientist in charge, it was his responsibility if the bomb failed to work. He didn't expect it to be used, Brown had said, but he wanted those pompous cretins in Whitehall to know that it would have worked. Besides, it might well have to.

Caren stopped what he was doing and put down the screwdriver. He looked at Vaisey and nodded.

'I'll away an' make supper. Cheese and pickle?'

'Fine,' answered Vaisey, looking at Caren intently. He watched him climb the stone steps. So far he hadn't been able to reach him. He'd thought that the week of confinement would lead to certain developments, but the red-haired man had stayed distant, Vaisey's one advance being repulsed with an indignant expletive.

He levered himself on to his feet with powerful arms and walked, stiff-legged, to the other end of the bench. He sat down on the stool and resumed reading where he had left off. The book was *The Plutonium Handbook*, Volume 2, published by Gordon and Breach. He had bought it, together with Volume 1, in London, over the counter of a perfectly respectable bookshop in Charing Cross Road.

Scattered around the worktop were a number of other volumes, all American and bought quite openly. The most well-thumbed among them were: *The Los Alamos Primer* by the Atomic Energy Commission, declassified in 1964; *Manhattan District History: Project Y, the Los Alamos Project* by the Office of Technical Services, US Department of Commerce, declassified in 1961; *Source Book on Atomic Energy* by Samuel Glasstone; *Rare Metals Handbook*; *The Reactor Handbook* (four volumes); and *The Curve of Binding Energy*.

Together, they contained all the information he needed

Chapter 8

Ann Stuart looked at her watch. 5 p.m. Her normal time for leaving the office, providing there was nothing urgent on, which at the moment there wasn't. She hesitated. That Romeo from down the corridor would be waiting at the lift for her to appear. She had finally given in last week to his repeated requests to go out, mainly because she was bored. Now she regretted it. After dinner and two bottles of wine he had put his hand on her thigh. She had liked it and allowed him to keep it there. It was naughty really, because she had no intention of letting it go any further. In the taxi, she had thanked him for a wonderful evening and suggested that they were not suited. But he wouldn't take no for an answer. She was going to have to be cruel and she didn't like that, especially since it was partly her fault.

Having been educated at private all-girls schools until the age of eighteen, she had been taught rather traditional values and they had stuck. Those who were unaware of the devotion she gave to her job often called her old-fashioned, because she believed that women should be women and men, men, although she found great difficulty when asked to explain what this meant. She was devoted to the classical novelists and loved the theatre, going at least once a fortnight, if possible. Secretly, she read romantic novelettes and, despite the tragedy of her marriage, which had ended in divorce two years earlier, she wanted to marry again and live a simple life in rural England, bringing up children. But she was aware that if she didn't remarry soon, she'd become wedded to her desk. She loved her job and there were scores of women in the building who existed in a semi-nun-like state. She was also aware that she was already on that slippery slope of self-sacrifice, as she now seemed incapable of forming close relationships with men.

She knew that men found her attractive, though. She had light skin colouring, contrasting with raven hair. The lips were generous, slightly pouting, and her eyes were brown. She always thought that her features were too big – her hips, breasts and mouth in particular – but she hadn't found them a handicap. She knew she was pretty, but certainly not beautiful.

Then, quite suddenly, she was angry with herself. There was only one reason for her delayed departure. This man, Matthew Calder, was due to meet the General and she wanted to meet him in the flesh. She had read his file when Sir Giles had finished with it, and had had a good look at the photograph. She knew that she was stupidly romanticizing about a man she had never met, like a frustrated schoolgirl. But Calder intrigued her.

Peter Striker had been in that morning, exhausted and very disorientated from lack of sleep. He said they had finally picked Calder up in Mexico. Apparently he'd ridden out of the desert on horseback, looking like a bandit, and they'd whisked him away so fast that he hadn't had time to pick up his normal clothes. He had travelled all the way to London in jeans, riding boots and poncho. Striker had said that people kept giving the man suspicious glances, expecting that they were going to be hijacked. At one point the Captain had come back to have a look and Striker had had to show his identity card. Calder, with straw hat over his face, hadn't moved the whole trip.

He had refused to see Sir Giles until he had 'slept off his jet lag', so Striker had come in to report on his own, before he himself went to bed. With some quip about her joining him, he had left, crashing into the door-jamb on his way out.

As she followed her thought by looking at the door, there was a knock on it and it opened before she could answer. She wondered who he was as the man walked in. Then it struck her that photographs could be very deceptive. True, he now had a black beard, a dark-brown tan that looked incongruous in May London, and his brown hair had contracted fair streaks – from the sun, she reasoned, not from the hairdressers. He was tall and dressed casually in white polo-necked sweater, red leather jacket and brown trousers. Not the usual sort of get-up she saw in the building and he looked at variance with his surroundings, although, strangely, not out of place.

She took all this in very quickly as he approached the desk, but she must have been staring for too long, because he began to smile. It was odd, but it wasn't the teeth that shone against the darkness of the face, but the eyes. She should have said something by now.

'My name is Calder. I'm here to see General Stoddard.'

She managed to speak. 'He's expecting you,' and she flicked a switch on her intercom.

'Sir Giles, Mr Calder is here.'

'Ah, good. Send him in.'

She flicked the switch back and looked at Calder again.

'Through the door,' she said, pointing.

He walked towards it and, his hand on the door knob, looked back at her for a few moments. She smiled. He did the same, turned and went in.

Stoddard walked round from behind his desk and considered the man he had met once only, seven months previously, at a controversial lecture given by Calder at the In-service Training Centre of the Ministry of Defence. It had included a warning about the dangers apparent in unlawful possession of fast-reactor fuel. Stoddard had invited him to lunch afterwards and been impressed by his knowledge and by the man himself. He had recognized in Calder a kindred spirit and felt that the younger man sensed it too.

Now, his presence in the room was immense. Perhaps it was more imagined than real – an old man's last, desperate clutch at a straw of hope, that became bigger than it really was. Both men grinned and shook hands.

'It's good of you to come,' said Stoddard.

'You've got to be joking,' answered Calder. 'After the trouble and expense you've been to to find me I dread to think what would have happened if I'd refused.'

Stoddard smiled. 'Scotch?' he asked.

'I have a feeling I'm going to need one.'

Stoddard walked over to a filing cabinet, unlocked it and withdrew a bottle of good blend, together with two glasses. To Calder, the General looked older and more strained. There was some dark around the eyes and he was a little thinner.

'No water, I'm afraid,' said Stoddard.

'That's fine.'

The General handed Calder the thick glass, one-third full.

'Apparently you caused quite a stir on the flight from the States.'

Calder smiled. 'I felt sorry for your two messengers who were sitting next to me. I was badly in need of a bath.'

Stoddard also smiled, though hesitantly, as if his mind were on something else. The small-talk had finished.

'Striker and the press were a little vague,' said Calder. 'What's happened, exactly?'

Stoddard looked at the leather of his desk-top, motioned Calder to sit down and told him everything. He was a good teller. He knew which points to emphasize and which not. What's more, he did it in sequence, which made it interesting, only summarizing towards the end. As an ex-professional in the art of oral communication, Calder was impressed.

The General paused when he'd finished and lit his pipe. A cloud drifted across to Calder until the fire got going. Stoddard stuck it in the corner of his mouth, held on to it and puffed between sentences.

'My biggest mistake, of course, was not realizing that the rods could be removed from the assembly. I didn't know that until Troutman told me later. If I had known, I could have seen the possibility of an air-drop and intensified the search over the flight-path. I could have set up road-blocks in strategic positions. Instead of having about eight hours' start, as I had thought, they had only about two.'

Calder sensed the anger and frustration that had built up in Stoddard.

'It wasn't your fault,' said the younger man. 'If anything it was Troutman's for not telling you early enough.'

Stoddard was standing at the window, nodding slowly.

'Perhaps,' he replied, 'but the point is that it happened and it shouldn't have.'

Calder knew that it was self-recrimination, not self-pity.

'I don't think it would have made any difference,' he said.

Stoddard swung round from the window as Calder continued. The pipe was pointing out of the mouth like a weapon.

'The man who masterminded this operation is no fool. He must have foreseen the possibility that you might think it was a parachute drop and he would have made plans accordingly. He would also think it likely that you would make the mistake you did, because he must know the scattered nature of the security concerning plutonium oxide. That would give him extra time for the getaway. But he could not possibly have afforded to take the chance, especially after the thought and investment that he must have put in.'

Calder paused. 'He would have got away even if you had known.'

Stoddard looked away. When he turned back there was a grim smile on his face. A pigeon fluttered silently down on to the ledge behind him.

'Perhaps I needed someone else to say that,' he said.

Calder waited a few moments.

'I take it they were standard fuel assemblies,' he asked, 'with fourteen twelve-foot rods in each one?'

'Yes.'

'Then they probably denuded one assembly.'

'Why?' asked Stoddard quickly, but removing his pipe slowly.

'Because that's how much plutonium they'd need to make a reasonable-sized bomb.'

Stoddard stared at Calder for a number of seconds. He didn't know whether to be glad or sorry that he'd sent for him.

'I've been told by experts that it's impossible to make a bomb from fast-reactor fuel,' said the General.

Behind him the pigeon began to groom its feathers. Calder pulled a face and his voice took on a resigned tone.

'I'm not surprised. They either have an economic axe to grind or they lack overview. Probably both.'

Stoddard thought of Pond and Ogilvie.

Calder said, 'No, that's too simplistic.'

He drained his glass before continuing.

'The hoverfly beats its wings 175 times a second. According to the experts it's impossible. When Galileo said that the sun did not revolve around the earth, he was branded as a heretic. It wasn't just that the experts of the time didn't want to believe it; as far as they were concerned it was simply impossible.'

The bird arched its wings to clean underneath.

'Man establishes laws of nature or contrivance,' Calder went on, 'that are essential to his survival and progression, at every stage of history. He needs them like he needs food, as a foundation – a raft of sanity on an unsteady sea. He cannot accept that *they* are not true, because that would erode the very basis of the justification of his existence. But they invariably are untrue. Almost every law or rule that we have ever established can be, or has been, questioned or disproved. I've heard too many so-called experts claim that something cannot be done, and, quite frankly, I'm pissed off with it.'

He switched his gaze from bird to man. When he spoke again his voice was steadier.

'It can be done, General, believe me.'

Stoddard was strangely pleased at the emotional outburst. It was reassuring to know that Calder was capable of strong emotions like everyone else. Silly, really. As he looked into the steady eyes, he had no doubt that the man behind them was right.

'I believe you,' he said seriously. 'Have some more Scotch.'

'Thanks,' replied Calder, holding out his glass. 'It might be worth considering the implications of a bomb later on, but for the moment I want to ask you some questions.'

'Fire away,' said Stoddard, refilling his glasses.

'Have you any clues at all as to where they dropped?'

'Clues, no,' said Stoddard immediately. 'My own view is that the jump area was over the sea, or the Moray Firth to be exact. They could have kept to their flight path and still been out of sight of land. Difficult and bloody cold, but not impossible if you are determined enough, and we know they are that. The fact that we haven't found any evidence at all – not even a piece of parachute cloth – again points to the sea. And, of course, a boat is an ideal vessel for carrying twelve-foot rods. They wouldn't need to enter Britain again. With the start they had, they could have sailed for almost any foreign port. Once in the open sea the chances of detection are slim, even if we did have a blanket search of the area, which we didn't until later. It takes time and all this is with the benefit of hindsight.'

Stoddard sucked vigorously on his pipe to keep it alight and continued in a less bitter tone.

'It would have needed split-second timing to land in the sea, but it's possible. It would also explain why we didn't find a trace of the pilot. He would already have completed his last course alteration at Portknockie. All he had to do then was set the automatic-pilot and jump out with the rest of them. It would also explain why the rear cargo-door was open. If the pilot was still on board at Wick, he would almost certainly have closed it.'

Stoddard sat down slowly and glared at Calder before continuing.

'Funny how one works it out when it's too late. I must be getting old.' He smiled. 'Of course, I could be completely wrong – about the sea, I mean, not about getting old.'

Calder, already having decided that Stoddard, among other things, had one of the finest analytical minds he had come across, thought, again, that it probably wouldn't have made any difference if the General had worked it out at once. But this time he considered it polite not to say so. Instead, he asked:

'You said you had some helicopters in the air. What about shipping?'

Stoddard continued looking at Calder for a few seconds, before reaching for a file on his desk.

'Four vessels were seen. Two we have found and cleared. One of the others was a foreign fishing vessel; Polish. We're following that up, but so far all we've got is a flat denial. I must confess I'm inclined to believe it. I can't see any reason why the Poles should get involved in this sort of thing. The other was a sailing vessel, a yacht, about forty feet or so according to the pilot. One mast, red hull, with the name of *Nessy*. Seems unlikely, but we checked it out. Can't find it. Lloyds have no trace of it and it's not registered anywhere, it seems. That in itself is not unusual. Owners are always changing the names of their boats and not telling even their insurance companies. We're still looking for it. We've given up the air-to-sea search now. No vessel of any kind, though, is allowed off our shores without a thorough search. And that goes for aircraft as well.'

Again Stoddard paused and looked at Calder intently before continuing.

'As you can imagine, the manpower usage, not to mention the

possible diplomatic repercussions, are immense. But that's not what bothers me. It's good training for the men involved, and I couldn't care a monkey's toss about diplomatic bloody problems. The thing that worries me is not finding it. And I don't think I'm going to, not the way I've been trying. In fact, I'd be very surprised if it isn't already in another country.'

Calder looked out of the window again. The bird's head had completely disappeared under a wing. Beyond it the sky was mauve and cold.

'The Navy presumably is still diving?'

'Yes,' answered Stoddard, his voice returning to normal. 'They say it will probably take at least another couple of days. But those are rough seas and if it gets too choppy they will have to suspend activities. Theoretically, it could be weeks.'

Stoddard compressed his lips and his voice became bitter.

'The more I think about the plan – the hijackers' plan – the more I realize how good it was.'

'How did they know when and how the shipment was going to be made?' asked Calder quickly.

'Ah, yes, I wondered about that. They had to have someone inside the security set-up itself, because the transit security boys are not told until three days in advance when a delivery is going to be made. What's more, they don't know before then whether the shipment is going by road or by air. We discovered that only guards who have been with BNFL for two years or more are chosen for the transit jobs, which tends to rule out anything but a long-term infiltration. That's most unlikely and, anyway, risky from the point of view of the hijackers; there was no guarantee that their man would get a transit security clearance. So, there was only one guaranteed way they could have known.'

He stopped to see if Calder could fill in the answer. The younger man suitably obliged.

'Threats of violence on the family of one of the guards. "No harm will come to them if you give us the when, where and how of the next shipment."'

'You guessed it,' said Stoddard heavily. 'We checked all the families. One of the wives had a broken arm and looked very ill. She said she had fallen by the coal bunker, so we knocked up a few of the neighbours. Apparently, she and her seven-year-old son had been away for about three weeks. It took some time to extract a confession. They were terrified. Three heavies had broken her arm in the husband's presence to demonstrate their genuine intent.'

Stoddard's voice was even more bitter now and he had let his pipe go out.

'It's the worst kind of human activity and a policeman's nightmare. There's virtually nothing one can do to prevent it – not while there is just a glimmer of hope that the man's family is going to be returned in one piece.'

'I don't think they were being humanitarian by returning them,' said Calder, in a voice that, in contrast to Stoddard's, was totally devoid of emotion. 'They killed at the airport quickly enough. I'm sure they would have preferred to kill the wife and child as well, but they might want to use the trick again and we'll know that they keep their word.'

Stoddard noticed that Calder's eyes shifted rapidly when he thought hard.

'Indeed,' continued the younger man, 'it seems to me that the fact that they did release them indicates that we *will* hear from them again. No clues from the woman, I suppose?'

For the second time since their conversation had begun, Stoddard became vaguely uneasy. He still clung to what he considered was the well-reasoned belief that, if the plutonium was not out of the country by now, then it soon would be. To him, it all pointed very strongly to a foreign terrorist group.

'No,' he said, placing his pipe on the blotter and picking up the file again, 'no real clues. They wore masks, only one of them ever spoke, in a "foreign" accent, and anyway they kept the woman and boy in one room. She had no idea where. Food and water were pushed through the door. She overheard one sentence in the whole three weeks, through the door, in an "English" accent. I quote: "Get that off to Paddington," unquote. She didn't know what it was. If that's a clue it's a pretty vague one.'

Calder was thinking, chin in hand.

'There's one thing,' he said. 'The *Guardian* said that four men were killed at the airport. You said that the co-pilot lived.'

Again Stoddard hesitated before replying.

'We lied about that because we thought the co-pilot might give us a clue. But again, it came to nothing. The man who hit him wore a balaclava mask and he heard nothing said.'

The General opened the report again.

'He came round for a few moments. All he saw,' said Stoddard looking up, 'this is what he claims, was a woman walking across the hangar. Then he blacked out again.'

Stoddard folded the file.

'Is that all?' said Calder in disbelief.

'No,' answered the General, without taking his eyes off Calder.

'He said that she had the most fantastic pair of legs that he had ever seen.'

Both men stared at each other for a few moments in silence. Then they laughed. Stoddard picked up his pipe and placed it in his mouth without bothering to relight it.

'One thing, though,' he said. 'He was injected with the drug too, so they obviously intended to kill him. But they didn't. A mistake. I find that a little comforting. Unless, of course, they just wanted us to think they intended to kill him.'

Calder stood up and walked over to the window. The bird didn't see him, its head tucked under the other wing, and he stood perfectly still, looking at the lights of the city beginning to show.

'I don't really know why I sent for you,' said Stoddard behind him. 'All the foreign departments are making inquiries abroad, where I believe the plutonium is, or shortly will be.'

He looked hard at Calder's back, expecting argument, but none came.

'Also, of course, I have my own department, and almost the entire armed forces, to say nothing of the police, working around the clock searching for the bloody stuff.'

He tapped out the contents of his pipe into a large glass tray. 'But, as I've already said, I don't think we're going to find it, or them.'

There was silence for about five seconds, then Calder turned away from the window and walked slowly over to the chair in front of the desk. Stoddard noticed the calm way in which he settled, arms perfectly relaxed along the arms of the chair, eyes gazing back openly.

The General busied himself in refilling his pipe. During their previous meeting, he had discovered that Calder had four major interests in life: environmentalism, women, chess and sports, in descending order of importance. He played most sports, especially rugby union and cricket. He was also a keep-fit fiend, although health foods were strictly out. He ate well, drank most alcohol moderately, but didn't smoke. His environmentalist views were closely connected with his view of the world and his idealism, and Stoddard judged them to be the major source of his motivation. He held life and the development of social and cultural existence as being distinct from, and more important than, economic goals. That, unfortunately, technology is seen as the god and man as its tool, instead of the other way around. It was these views which had forced him to resign his post at the In-service Training Centre for top security and military personnel. At that time he had been involved in doing a special study, in his own time, on environmental pollution, especially the nuclear variety. On looking at Calder's file, Stoddard had discovered that, although his first degree was in physics, he had an M A in International Relations.

As he continued to fill his pipe, the older man thought, too, of the quick, concise way in which Calder had asked the right questions. This business had to some extent damaged his confidence in his own ability, but if there was one thing he felt that he did know about, it was men. And the man sitting calmly in front of him was definitely someone he wanted on his side, especially when one considered that there was probably someone very much like him on the other side.

Calder heard the rasp of a Swan Vesta being scraped along sand-paper and watched the General lighting his pipe. A cloud drifted across again and Stoddard began to talk at the same time as he was sucking, between words, as only the real practitioners can do.

'I wanted to talk to you, but that isn't all, I know now. You said it yourself, partly. I distrust experts as well. Yet I'm surrounded by them.' He grinned. 'I'm one myself.'

Calder smiled too.

'Don't get me wrong,' continued the General, examining the glowing bole with satisfaction. 'I believe in organizations, up to a point. They can be extremely *efficient* and I think mine is, but on certain investigations they can be *ineffective*. It's well over four days since the hijack – nearly five – and we have got absolutely nowhere. I can't allow that state of affairs to continue.'

Calder suddenly realized the terrifying responsibility that Stoddard had. Whatever happened in the field, whatever he asked anyone to do, it was Stoddard who was to blame if anything went wrong, or if the results were not achieved. It also occurred to him that the pipe was finally failing to fulfil part of its unconscious purpose, and that the General was going to lose his temper. He was surprised that he had held it for so long.

'You warned me it would happen,' said Stoddard, 'and I know you have certain specialized knowledge. What's more, I have no way of knowing whether or not Mr Hijack knows every move we are going to make. He seems to have allowed for all contingencies and I have no intention of taking for granted the assumption that he could not possibly have infiltrated my organization.'

Calder was nodding slowly. 'You want me to operate on the outside,' he said.

'Exactly. But I want more. Above all else, what I need is a fresh mind. Someone whose outlook is not narrowed by technique. Christ!' he crashed his left hand down on the desk, 'what I need are new ideas, because I don't have any more.'

Calder was smiling. 'You know, General, for one awful, terrifying moment, I thought you were going to let me go without asking me to do anything.'

He got up and walked to the window again. The pigeon was still concerned only with its grooming. He placed a hand low down on the pane and it flew away. He wondered whether its brain would work out which feather it had got up to. Stoddard couldn't hold himself back any longer.

'Do you have any ideas?'

The younger man turned. 'At the moment, just one or two vague glimmers, but I'd rather follow them up first, if that's all right with you?'

'Perfectly,' said Stoddard. Calder was obviously going to be cautious before presenting anything.

'I will say this, though, General. I've a feeling the plutonium is going to remain in this country.'

Stoddard nodded. 'Perhaps you're right.'

There was a pause before Calder spoke.

'I'll need an assistant, someone to do some legwork. He has to be the sort of person who has access to police information and knows what to do with it.'

Stoddard didn't hesitate.

'I can give you Striker. He had a year's training with Special Branch before he came to me. What's more, he's an American on loan to us for a few years and unlikely to be involved. One of our boys is over there.'

Calder thought for a moment.

'Has he been involved in the investigation at all?'

'No. He was looking for you from Monday afternoon. I expect he's still in bed.'

'Fine. Then Peter Striker will do.'

Stoddard baulked slightly at the somewhat casual way in which Calder appeared to accept the services of a highly trained agent.

'When do you want to see Striker?' asked Stoddard.

'I'd be obliged if you could tell him to come round to my place at 8.30 tomorrow morning.'

Stoddard placed his pipe on the blotter and walked over to an old combination safe crouched in a corner of the room. Calder watched as he turned the knob several times, opened the door and extracted a thick pile of £5 notes. He walked over to Calder and held them out to him.

'Five hundred pounds. Operating expenses. You'll need it. Let me know if you want any more.'

Calder hesitated momentarily. Then he took the money and placed it in the inside pocket of his jacket.

They walked to the door together.

'I hope you're not right about it being an internal hijack,' said Stoddard, 'but either way I'll give you all the help I can, although essentially you're on your own.'

The General opened the door.

'Ann! You're still here,' he said, surprised.

'Yes, sir. I thought you might need me,' she answered, smiling uncertainly.

Stoddard looked at his watch, then at his secretary in a familiar, speculative sort of way and she, unaccountably, looked down at her desk. He was always able to read her like a book. Of all the men that had been through that office, he thought, but he'd known that it would happen one day. She was too damned good-looking.

The trend away from attractive secretaries that had swept through Whitehall recently had not affected him. He saw no point in attempting an outward demonstration of chastity and lack of interest in things of the flesh, merely to fall in with a hypocritical, probably transient and anyway dubious notion of piety, the main reason for which was to impress superiors. Well, he had no one above him to impress, and Ann did give him little interludes of self-indulgent pleasure when, at various times during the day, she came into his room.

'Well, perhaps you'd better show Mr Calder out,' he said, then turned and shook the younger man's hand.

Calder smiled at him and he wondered whether anyone could get used to those eyes. Then he closed his door, sighed and walked back for the solace of his pipe.

Chapter 9

Calder woke instantly, without any movement or disturbance in his breathing. His eyes were open in the near-dark, but that was the only overt difference between sleep and wakefulness. Several times in the past he had awoken like this and had learned to listen to his instincts. His brain was working furiously, trying to fathom the reason for his disturbed repose – what sound he had heard, or what thought had subconsciously occurred to him like a flash of inspiration in his slumber. He could remember nothing. He listened, every muscle ready to move immediately. But again, there was nothing.

He had woken like this two days ago in the Mexican desert. That time he had identified the sound in his memory: an almost human scream as the natural selection of the desert had worked to the detriment of some creature or other. He had found it difficult to return to sleep and knew it would be the same now.

He swung his legs out of bed and switched on the bedside lamp, his eyes immediately sweeping the strange room. After all, something had stirred him. He measured the trip to the door, extinguished the lamp, stood up slowly so as not to make the bedsprings creak, and moved silently across the room. Then he swiftly opened the door and pounced through, crouching. He waited a full minute, until the muscles of his thighs protested, but the only sound was from his own breathing.

Feeling rather silly, he looked at his watch. The luminous hands said 1.15 a.m. He switched on the lights and systematically searched the obviously female flat. Nothing. He even checked that the windows were locked and that the front door was fixed from the inside.

Restlessly he returned to the bedroom and, in the light from the front room, took in the sleeping Ann on the double bed. Like him she was naked, but unlike him she was a picture of beauty as she slept. He remembered the night before and the suppressed passion with which she had made love. Quickly but noiselessly he dressed, then looked at her again before leaving, her heavy breasts lying across her chest, her arms outstretched and the concave of her stomach disappearing into the sheet. He looked for a long time, then let himself out.

On the parapet outside the bedroom window, the cat continued his journey. His passage had disturbed the sleeping bird and it had fluttered away into the night. Some lights had gone on, but no one seemed to have noticed him.

The gloved hands inside the adapted oxygen tent worked like automatons, the man manipulating them almost lost in the folds of translucent plastic, as he sat as close as he could to his materials. These included an electric induction furnace, hydrofluoric acid, metallic calcium flake, nitric acid, crystalline iodine, quartz glassware, magnesium oxide, a cylinder of argon gas and high-temperature crucibles. Brown's men had bought them at various retail outlets, on the open market.

Vaisey was very tired. He had been working on the chemical process almost continuously since very early on Friday morning, and it was now the late, small hours of Saturday morning. He found that he didn't need much sleep these days, but he needed to take a break soon.

He had just completed the first stage of a highly complex process that he had copied many times in the last twenty-four hours. This first stage had converted a fairly small quantity of raw plutonium oxide into concentrated plutonium nitrate.

He now finished measuring a litre of hydrofluoric acid and poured it into a quartz flask. Then he led a rubber tube from the furnace, that contained the plutonium nitrate, to the flask and placed it on a burner. Soon, hydrogen fluoride gas began to fume. He then switched on the furnace, watched the temperature rise to 524 degrees centigrade and steadied it. He then waited for about twenty minutes until the conversion to plutonium fluoride had been made, then switched off the furnace.

Vaisey now prepared a graphite crucible by lining it with a thick magnesium oxide paste. Then, using no more than the steel calipers on the end of the heat-resistant gloves, he removed the ceramic crucible containing the plutonium fluoride from the furnace and replaced it with the magnesium oxide crucible. The oven was switched on and the paste dried.

While the crucible was returning to something like room temperature, Vaisey withdrew his arms from the gloves. He removed the black-rimmed spectacles from his Halloween face and rubbed his eyes. Yes, this would definitely be the last one. If he slept for the rest of the morning he could be back on it that afternoon. Then he should have enough plutonium 239 that night or the following morning. It never occurred to him that he might be working too hard. The job simply had to be finished quickly. His amazingly strong will would see that it was.

The spectacles went back on the stump of a nose and the arms filled the gloves out once more. The cooled magnesium crucible was packed with measured quantities of metallic calcium, crystals of iodine and the plutonium fluoride. The specially adapted crucible lid was sealed and the interior filled with argon gas. It was then placed into the furnace and heated to 700 degrees centigrade. The temperature was steadied and Vaisey waited for about sixteen minutes, until a violent reaction occurred in the crucible and its temperature rose very quickly to 1,630 degrees centigrade. At this point the furnace was switched off, the crucible removed and cooled.

Vaisey had puzzled for some time over how to speed up the cooling period. He had finally decided that most attempts to artificially impose cold to the degree of sophistication that he could manage might damage the natural chemical process, but he had eventually hit upon the idea of using an ordinary, small household freezer, turned up to maximum. It was a little slower than he would have liked, but once he had worked out exactly how long it took to cool to room temperature, he was able to use the time usefully.

Extracting himself from the tent again, he used the stool on which he was seated to lever himself on to his legs. He waddled to the workbench and began to study a computer print-out.

In order to prevent the danger of accidentally assembling a critical mass, and therefore creating an explosion somewhat prematurely, the plutonium oxide had to be converted in small quantities. But when he had enough plutonium 239 it had to be cast into two identical hemispheres, the dimensions of which had to be exact. So, he had hired computer time. All the computer programmer saw was a set of, to him, meaningless differential equations and one of Brown's men.

After about fifteen minutes, Vaisey returned to the tent.

DELETED

It was a lump of P-239. He put it with the others and sat perfectly still for a moment or two, doing nothing. He liked being in his converted glove-box. With the mechanical arms added to his mechanical legs he felt more machine than man and the thought did not displease him.

Then he left for the stairs. Using his arms only, he pulled himself up by transferring his weight from one arm to the other on the iron railings. Even at his age, he could make any gymnast look pretty sick for upper-arm strength.

At the top, he switched off all the electricity and looked back to make sure that nothing but the Calor-gas heaters glowed in the dark. Satisfied, he closed and locked the door.

When the front door-bell rang, Calder, dressed in denim shirt and jeans, had a piece of toast in his left hand and Striker's file in the other. He just managed to stop himself from turning his left wrist to look at his watch, in case the thick marmalade fell off. Instead, he transferred the toast to the plate. 8.30 a.m. on the nose. He got up and walked to the door.

Standing there was Peter Striker in a smart blue suit and tie to match, looking like a Pan-Am commercial. With his straight blond hair and moustache, thin nose and the best-looking teeth that money could buy, when he smiled, which he did as often as he could, he also looked like a Hollywood mogul's dream. Calder wouldn't have been surprised to hear that he had a haircut and manicure once a fortnight. But Calder also knew that this smooth exterior hid a very hard man indeed. His file had said that he had been educated at private schools in the United States and at an Ivy League University, and that he was super-fit, having no surplus fat whatever. His sporting interests included jogging, pistol shooting and the martial arts. In this latter skill he was proficient enough to be an unarmed-combat instructor.

'Come in,' said Calder and led the American into the front room of the small flat. Striker was taken by its neatness. Two whole walls, from floor to ceiling, were given over to wooden shelves, all filled with books. The wall-to-wall dark brown carpet was cheap, but clean and unworn, and the cream-painted walls blended in with the woodwork. In one corner of the room was a small television set. In the centre, between a tobacco-coloured, cloth studio couch and matching chair, was a superb chess table which, from a distance, appeared to be made of ornate teak; it was on castors and the top was covered in green baize. Lying on this was a thick, leather chess-board and what looked like imitation ivory pieces.

'Come through to the kitchen,' said Calder. 'Coffee?'

'Thanks.'

The Englishman poured from a percolator into a mug, and pushed over a tin of sugar, a pint of milk and a spoon. Then he sat down and resumed munching his toast.

Striker helped himself to sugar, stirred, picked up the mug, noted the writing on the side which said, 'Coffee drinkers are sexier', took heart and sipped slowly. It was no good; he had to ask.

'Who *are* you?'

Calder finished his chewing, unhurriedly.

'A difficult question to answer,' he said, taking another bite. 'However, if you were to ask me, "*What* am I?" the answer would be easier. As you can perhaps surmise from this humble abode, I am a simple teacher.'

He twisted his mouth wryly before continuing. 'Temporarily unemployed.'

Striker sipped his coffee. 'With independent means?' he asked.

'You must be joking,' answered Calder immediately. 'You probably earn twice as much as I do. What makes you say that?'

Striker received the full glare of Calder's eyes as the man waited for an answer, and he suddenly felt out of his depth. His halfhearted attempt to impress Calder might go badly wrong.

'Mexico,' he said.

'Ah, the General said you were a good detective,' said Calder, but he didn't smile, in case Striker might think that he was being patronizing. 'As a matter of fact, I won a chess tournament and decided to blow the cash prize on a three-month holiday. Do I pass?'

Striker beamed.

'What did the General tell you?' asked Calder, leaning back in his chair, his face impassive.

'More or less everything, and that I was to do anything you asked.' He drummed his fingers on the table, lazily.

'How do you feel about that?' asked Calder. 'After all, you are the professional and I the amateur.'

Striker gazed into his coffee mug, then flashed his smile again.

'It does seem strange,' he answered, 'but there's one thing I've learnt about the General: he sure knows what he's doing.'

Calder stayed silent, waiting for Striker to continue, but he didn't, just kept gently tapping the table with his fingers.

'I'm going to need your advice,' said the Englishman.

He got up and leant against the sink.

'And if ever you think I'm wrong, lay into me hard, because we can't afford to make mistakes.'

He paused slightly.

'I'm travelling down to Surrey this morning to speak to a friend. He's an import/exporter, or something. Buys in one country and sells, for himself and other people, in another. He was once asked whether he could sell some enriched U-235.'

'What's that?' asked Striker quickly.

Calder bit his lip.

'It's a particular grade of uranium that has been through a re-processing plant. In that state it's the raw material for a nuclear bomb. It has very similar properties to the plutonium we're looking for. Also, if it *was* enriched 235, it had to be stolen and if it was being offered on the open market it could be for only one purpose, and that's to make a nuclear bomb.'

'You mean,' said Striker, 'they might have tried to get some plutonium by other means, before they decided on the hijack?'

'Spot on. In the meantime, I want you to find me the biggest criminal in London.'

Striker's fingers stopped drumming.

'The biggest criminal in London,' he intoned, as if repeating part of a shopping list.

Calder walked over to the table and picked up his coffee mug.

'I'll be perfectly honest with you,' he said. 'The General thinks it was a foreign terrorist group. I don't. He may be right, but even so, they needed some British help. It was a big operation and it all took place in the UK.'

Striker didn't say anything, just shifted uncomfortably on his chair.

'But,' continued Calder, 'they might be totally British. Either hired labour for some terrorist group or working for themselves. We've got to find that out by Monday.'

'We sure have,' said Striker, mimicking John Wayne and hunching his shoulders.

Calder looked at him hard. He liked Peter Striker. His manner was happy-go-lucky and he apparently saw life as one big joke. But Calder had realized on the trip from Mexico that his sarcasm and extrovert manner were part of a sophisticated sense of humour which helped him keep the world in perspective, a façade he hid behind. He'd told Calder that his family motto was going to be 'Carpe diem' and it wasn't just to demonstrate that he'd had a classical education. His philosophy was to live life to the full, as if each day was to be his last, but only sexually. He drank nothing but the occasional beer and had only a rare cigar. His major interest in life was, apparently, to have sex with as many pretty girls as possible. He was a man who was full of energy, finding difficulty in relaxing. When sitting, for example, he would prop his head up on alternate arms and move his fingers a lot. When standing, he shifted his weight constantly.

'Do you know where to get that information?' asked Calder.

'I have a few friends at the Yard,' replied Striker wistfully.

'Well,' said Calder with a smile, 'I see you've got your Dick Tracy suit on, so go out and super-detect.'

Striker stood up, clicked his heels and gave a perfect salute. Calder walked out into the hall and wrote on the telephone pad.

He returned to the living-room where he found Striker examining the chess set.

'Do you play?' asked Calder.

'Only if I can't avoid it,' replied Striker. 'What's this?' He took the slip of paper that Calder was holding out.

'My number here and where I shall be going this morning.'

Striker decided it was time for him to go. Calder may have asked for his advice, but all he wanted was his assistance. Also, although the blond had found that the traditional American image of the straight-laced Englishman was largely a myth, Calder certainly fitted the bill.

'Adios,' said Striker smilingly and left.

Ten minutes later Calder was in his Volkswagen Golf and heading for the A23 to the south. The 1600 engine had started after only the second turn, which wasn't bad after two months. It was good to be behind the wheel of a car again, especially since he was going outside London where he could do some real driving. The sky had clouded over and the wind was from the west, probably bringing some rain from the Atlantic. Incredible to think that, less than two days earlier, he had been sitting astride a horse under the hot sun of the Mexican desert. He sighed and, as the traffic was nearly stopped in front of him, pulled into a garage to check tyre pressure, oil and water.

Back on the road, he switched on the radio to take his mind off what he was doing. He didn't want to think too deeply about it at this stage. The ideas were really only embryonic. They could easily be questioned now. When they were followed through and things still didn't gel – that was the time to drop them.

Two and a half hours later, he was surrounded by the horse brasses and warming-pans of a pub in Bletchingley. It had taken some time to socialize with Julian's wife and four children in the garden of their eight-bedroomed Georgian house, but eventually they had got away and were one of the first groups in the pub.

Julian Foster was a big man in height and girth, without being fat. His facial features were rugged and dominated by one of the worst broken noses Calder had ever seen. Foster always claimed that it had happened in a rugger scrum and that he was so drunk for so long afterwards that he forgot to get it fixed. But for a number of reasons, not least of which was the fact that he was a teetotaller, no one believed a word of it. He had a mop of untidy, straight hair that was beginning to grey in various patches. Dressed in dark-blue cord trousers and scarred, blue crew-necked sweater, he was an imposing figure.

In terms of income he and Calder were worlds apart and, whilst their politics were not diametrically opposed, there were fundamental differences. But somehow they liked each other and had been firm friends for several years.

'Cheers,' said Foster, holding up his grapefruit juice. 'This is all very sudden. I take it this little jaunt down to the wilds of the stockbroker belt is not for social reasons?'

Calder sipped his pint and wondered how his friend was going to take it.

'You know of the plutonium hijacking, of course?' he asked.

'Of course,' replied Foster a little guardedly.

'Well, for some reason, the security services seem to think that I might be able to help them find it.'

Foster didn't react. He just sat looking at Calder. If he thought it strange that someone he'd believed for years was a polytechnic lecturer – someone who had told everyone in the rugby club the same story – should now be working for the security services, he certainly wasn't showing it.

'I am making an entirely unofficial approach to you,' Calder went on, 'because I think you may be able to help me find it.'

'How?'

'You were once offered some enriched U-235. You told me about it, remember?'

The big man nodded.

'I'm working on the assumption,' continued Calder, 'that some time before they decided on the hijack, the hijackers made inquiries about how to get hold of some reprocessed P-239, or enriched U-235, on the international market. We both know there's some about. If they did, then they might have spoken to your contact who offered you the uranium. He might be quite well known.'

'He was more likely working for a contact of a contact,' said Foster.

'OK, but at least he might know someone who knows someone. I know it's a long shot, but it's worth a try.'

Foster was looking down at the table.

'You must be really stuck for leads,' he said earnestly. Then he sucked on his lips. 'It might be difficult,' he said, looking up.

'I know,' said Calder, 'and I'm not asking you to get involved. All I want is a telephone number.'

'No,' replied Foster, 'that's not what I meant. I've met him. He's important. That means he will deny all knowledge and be able to summon help if necessary. He is not going to hand over a name and I doubt whether threatening him will make any difference. You could get into trouble. How far are you prepared to go?'

'I'm prepared to pull his fingernails out, one by one.'

Both men looked hard at each other. Foster drained his glass.

'Does that make you better than them?' he asked fiercely.

'Let's not moralize, Julian. Why do you think the plutonium was stolen? No one mounts that sort of operation for fun. Have you any idea how much damage a nuclear explosion would do in the middle of Tel Aviv, or Cairo, or London? If the wind was in this direction, the radiation would be so bad that growing vegetables in the gardens of Bletchingley would be out of the question unless the surface earth was removed. That's not to mention damage to the internal human organs from inhalation.'

Calder paused, leaving Foster alone with his thoughts, staring into his empty glass.'

'Can it be done?' asked the big man, with a frown. 'Made into a bomb, I mean?'

'Yes,' answered Calder, 'and so can enriched 235. If your man was trying to sell it, it must have been stolen and there is only one possible use for it.'

Foster looked at the table again. Calder picked up their glasses and walked over to the bar. When he returned, Foster looked as if he had made up his mind.

'All right,' he said, 'you win. But we'll have to do it my way. It will cause far less suspicion if I phone him myself. I'll tell him that if he still has the stuff – which of course he won't – I might have a buyer. Then you bug any calls he makes, or whatever it is you chaps do.'

Foster raised his glass with a smile. Calder smiled back in admiration.

'No, Julian. I appreciate the offer, but no. It would be too dangerous and you know it. Without wishing to sound melodramatic, you have a family.'

Foster gave a short laugh. 'With my insurances, Jane and the kids could live in luxury for the rest of their lives.'

Calder didn't laugh. 'That isn't what I meant. They could get at you *through* your family.'

Foster didn't laugh at that one.

'Why are you so bloody, damned clever?' he said angrily.

There was a small silence while Calder sipped his beer.

'So how are you going to get the information?' asked the big man.

Calder looked into his beer this time.

'I don't know yet, but I'll think of something.'

Striker was waiting inside Calder's flat when he returned, sitting in an easy chair reading *Winning Chess*, by Chernev and Reinfeld.

'I didn't think you'd mind, so I let myself in,' he said cheerfully. 'It would have looked suspicious, you know, me waiting outside your door.'

'A trick you picked up at Princeton?' asked Calder.

The blond man put on a look of amazement.

'Wow, how'd ya guess? No way one can survive there without being a whizz with a hairgrip or coathanger. But you really ought to get that lock changed, you know. Anyone could walk in here.' The American smiled blandly.

'Thanks for the tip,' said Calder in a voice which suggested he had no intention of taking the advice.

He sat wearily before speaking again.

'What did you find?'

Striker put the book down and reached inside his jacket pocket, extracting and unfolding a piece of crumpled A4 as if it contained the revelation of the century.

'You boys don't have the Mafia over here as you know, or anything like it, so organized crime is a fairly divergent business. I say,' he said, mocking a rather good home-counties accent, 'you couldn't put the kettle on, could you?'

Calder got up and walked through to the kitchen, amused that despite the American's forwardness he hadn't had the nerve to make himself a cup of coffee.

'However,' continued Striker as he followed, 'there are two or three large set-ups. My contact at the Met was reluctant to commit himself on who he thought was the strongest or biggest. Eventually, he decided on the least well-known of the big boys, working on the assumption that the more you stay out of trouble, the cleverer you are. George Cox. He's a legitimate businessman. Owns a chain of restaurants, as well as a chain of prostitutes, and has a couple of strip clubs. He's also a crook. We know he's been behind a number of bullion robberies, but there is no evidence. He's never even been in a court, let alone jail. The few of his men who have been caught in the act seem more afraid of him than of going down, and he'll reward them when they come out.'

Calder began to make some instant coffee.

'He's English and has a wife with whom he lives in a mansion in Bedfordshire. Surely you don't believe that he did it?'

'No,' said Calder. 'I don't know Mr Cox, but I don't think he could have the brainpower or the expertise to mount this sort of operation, to say nothing of the leadership and direction necessary to carry it out without leaving any clues.'

Striker winced as Calder continued.

'It was, in my view, if you'll excuse the pomposity, a military operation, not something that could have been done by your common criminal. I'm just hoping he is going to give me some information.'

The American was looking at him open-mouthed now.

'Has he ever dealt in drugs?' asked Calder.

'Er, it's not on his record,' answered Striker, looking at the paper. Then he looked up quickly before speaking again. 'You're not going to ask him for help?'

'As a matter of fact, I am,' said Calder as he switched off the kettle. 'Does his record say where he will be on a Saturday night?'

'No, but I asked, just in case. Saturday night is pay night. Apparently he always spends it in a suite of rooms behind a nightclub that he owns. Would you believe it's called The Blue Lady?'

'I believe it. Anything else?'

'Not really,' replied Striker coyly as he picked up the coffee mug with the sexy notation.

'As chance would have it,' he continued, 'I know The Blue Lady. Had to go there on business once or twice. You know the sort of thing that arises in our job – following someone or chatting them up.'

Calder laughed. It was the second time Striker had seen him laugh, yet he was a little surprised at how completely uninhibited it was.

'You know, your powers of extra-sensory perception are really extraordinarily good,' said the blond. 'But let's get things in proportion.'

He walked through to the comfortable chair in the living-room and Calder followed.

'It's a classy joint. Tuxedos and dicky-bows, and the artistes are only the very best, believe me.'

The last two words were said with some feeling and a glassy-eyed expression came over the blond man's face. Then he looked up as if the thought had just occurred to him.

'You wouldn't need any assistance, I suppose?'

'Well,' replied Calder with apparent reluctance, 'I guess I've got to keep the workers happy. Besides, if I've got to smell of mothballs tonight, I don't see why my able assistant shouldn't.'

Using Striker's membership, they managed to book a table for 8 o'clock and, shrugging off the attempts of two attractive ladies of doubtful virtue, were shown to seats just below the small stage. The atmosphere, Calder felt, was congenial, but cloyingly opulent. Most of the guests were of portly build and the small band of black musicians playing in the corner wore perpetual smiles.

To Calder's surprise they dined well. The dressed crab was delicious and the fillet steak even better. The out-of-season strawberries were a little crisp, but with the remains of a good red wine they went down smoothly. The meal was served throughout by a topless waitress who, although she didn't have a great deal to show, was extremely pretty. Calder felt somewhat uncomfortable, munching his steak while a bare-breasted female leaned over him to pour wine, but Striker appeared not to notice.

At 10 p.m. precisely, the low lights were dimmed even further and the footlamps shone purple. There was a roll of drums and two men, wearing nothing but G-strings, came out carrying a black girl. Completely naked, she was lowered to the floor on her knees, her back to the audience. The straight, muscled back gleamed in the light and her skin shone – covered in oil, Calder reasoned. Slowly, the two white men backed away into the shadows. The whole of the big room was silent and the girl remained motionless.

Then, a single bass drum began to beat and the girl's upper body began to writhe in time with the tone, her arms outstretched and her head still. Slowly she rolled over on to her stomach and pushed herself up on hands and knees, as if trying to resist the rhythm. Two of the most enormous breasts that Calder had ever seen dropped beneath her hard, compact frame.

Suddenly, she threw her head back, clenching her teeth, and her upper body moved again. Her breasts began to ripple obscenely as she straightened, running hands over nipples as they travelled to a point above her head. More drums entered, stepping up the rhythm, but the bass beat didn't falter. Calder knew that his pulse was probably keeping time to it.

The girl had her legs splayed now as she rose to her feet, her whole body undulating like a black sea. Then she stilled her upper body as her hips moved to the increased pulse. Calder marvelled at the way the huge breasts remained almost motionless, despite the sexual urgency of her stomach, hips and thighs.

The drums beat faster as her whole body began to pulsate, her breasts also vibrating now in pendulous tempo. Calder could see rivulets of sweat between them, clearing a path through the oil, and he became conscious of his hand grasping the stem of his wine glass too hard.

Then the girl opened her mouth and screamed as the drums thudded their complicated pernicious sound, and she lowered herself to the floor, side on to the audience, her knees bent and legs splayed, limbo style. Calder could hear her cries as she leant back, making her whole body bend, still moving to the rhythm. Hands crept across her belly and, suddenly, she thrust her body upwards in an arch as a long scream came from her throat. The drums stopped and the lights went out at exactly the same moment, but the scream continued, echoing around the darkness.

There were a few tentative claps and then the whole audience applauded loudly. When the restaurant lights went on, the two white men could be dimly discerned, carrying off the drooping body, an arm over each shoulder.

It had been an impressive display. It must have lasted at least ten minutes, yet the time seemed to go in no more than two. Calder was glad that he had finished his meal before it had begun. Striker was grinning at him.

'You know my one regret about tonight,' he said. 'After you've finished debagging Cox, I'm going to find it very difficult to renew my membership.'

Calder grinned back. He had temporarily forgotten why he was there. He turned to look for their waitress. She was snaking her way through a cordon of seemingly uninterested diners, some drinks balanced dexterously on a small tray above her head. Calder raised his arm and she saw him immediately. He watched her deliver the drinks to a party of laughing, sweating Germans and walk quickly over. She bent over slightly so as to hear what he had to say.

'Yes, sir?' she asked happily.

'I'd like to see the manager,' said Calder.

Worry showed immediately in her eyes. The gleaming smile disappeared. Calder quickly placed a hand on hers.

'Don't worry,' he smiled, 'it's not a complaint.'

He was relieved to see the teeth again as she let out a small laugh of pleasure and moved off.

'That was just a starter too,' chimed Striker, staring morosely at the stage. 'The others are even better.'

He turned back towards the table, extracted a packet of thin cigars and gave one to Calder before helping himself. As they lit up, Striker looked keenly at Calder.

'I don't know how you're planning to work this, but I suggest that we both go in together,' said Striker.

A man of about thirty, with oily hair and a bandito moustache, appeared at his elbow.

'Good evening. I'm the manager. Can I help you?'

The eyes were watchful. Calder stood up to find that he was looking quite a way down at the man.

'My name is Calder. This is Mr Striker,' gesturing with his hand.

The manager made no attempt to shake hands, but grinned condescendingly at Striker.

'Would you join us for a moment?' asked Calder.

The eyes were confident as the man looked up.

'Thank you, but I'm rather busy. Perhaps if you just tell me what it is that you require.'

'Your name is?' asked Calder.

The man hesitated slightly. 'Robinson.'

'Very well, Mr Robinson, perhaps you could ask Mr Cox if we could have an audience with him.'

The manager didn't falter.

'I beg your pardon? Did you say Mr Cox?'

'Yes,' said Calder politely.

'I am afraid I don't know what you are talking about,' said Robinson. 'There is no Mr Cox here,' and he began to walk away.

'Don't walk away from me, Mr Robinson,' said Calder.

Something in his voice made the man pause and turn. His eyes flickered over the bearded face.

'I suggest we stop playing around,' continued Calder. 'Mr Cox is at this moment not fifty yards from us. We are making a civil request to see him. Mr Striker and I are unarmed and our mission, I assure you, is a peaceful one.' He smiled.

The small man looked towards the door. When he turned back his expression had hardened.

'Why should Mr Cox see you? He, too, is a busy man.'

Calder hesitated and looked towards the stage. What he said was important. He hadn't told Striker, but he was prepared to force his way in if necessary and that would hardly be an ideal beginning to a request for help. Still looking at the stage, he said:

'Tell Mr Cox this. We do not come bearing gifts. Indeed, I think it's fair to say that he will not gain from our visit in any way that I can see. But if he does not see us, he stands to lose his whole empire. We want to help him stand still, but it is imperative that we see him now.'

He turned back to the manager, who was looking at him rather oddly. Then the man glanced pointedly at Striker and left.

'Well, of one thing I am sure,' said the American as he blew a smoke-ring at the ceiling. 'My membership *is* terminated.'

Calder smiled. 'Your membership is not the only thing you might lose tonight, if they don't let us in peacefully.'

Striker raised his eyebrows and glanced over at the exit. Two very big men, with necks like tree trunks, had stationed themselves by the stairs, looking in his direction. He swivelled his head to look at the door near the bar, where he found that a couple more had suddenly materialized. Slowly, he turned back, bent forward and casually flicked the ash off his cigar.

He looked at Calder, who was gazing into the distance above the stage, and wondered how he would manage. He knew from experience that in most circumstances he himself could handle two, but with three he generally needed help. Calder seemed to have no nerves at all, but surely he was too intelligent to attempt a forced entry without some probability of success?

Then the sheer force of Calder came across, as he sat there, perfectly relaxed, his mind on the problem in hand. He blinked slowly and looked at Striker, the eyes piercing and the corners of the mouth turned up. Suddenly, the blond man realized that although he wasn't frightened of the men at the door, he *was* afraid of Matthew Calder. It worried him that he didn't know why and, even more, that he realized he would follow him to Hell, without knowing the reason for that either.

The music changed from soft piano to something more sophisticated, as bright lights brought the stage alive. A girl, dressed in Victorian middle-class fashion, holding a parasol, waltzed on.

Striker was surprisingly looking the other way as he spoke.

'You won't believe what she does with that parasol. Especially since I don't think you're going to have time to find out.'

Calder looked round to see a heavily built man, whose function in The Blue Lady was fairly obvious, walking purposefully towards them. Calder stood up, waiting. The man stopped, confidently, like someone content in the knowledge of his own physical prowess.

'Mr Robinson will see ya now,' he said. The voice was East-End cockney.

He turned and they followed, through the bar door into a small ante-room, where two more men waited. They were roughly shoved against a wall and thoroughly searched. Then they went along a corridor, with only three doors leading off it. At the end they turned sharply right and walked to a door in an alcove. There a man knocked and they entered another ante-room. This one was decked out like an office, with filing cabinets, a typewriter and desk. Behind the last object sat a man of a smaller and different stature to the others. He raised his eyebrows quizzically, received a curt nod and closed the drawer in which his hand had been placed. He then stood up, walked over to the other door and knocked. In the silence which followed, Calder heard a muffled, 'Enter,' and they were ushered in.

The room was huge – at least thirty feet by fifty – and tastefully decorated, provided you could live with the colour scheme. A deep, red pile carpet accentuated the red and gold wallpaper. The wall-lighting shed pools of illumination on the many oil paintings. To the right was the glow of a real log fire surrounded by a marble fireplace. Near this were two comfortable, red leather, Chesterfield couches. At either side of the hearth stood a red and gold standard lamp. There were no windows and only one other door. The un-mistakable strains of Mozart filled the room.

Sitting in front of Calder, behind a desk, was a man who could only have been George Cox. Striker had not mentioned his age and Calder was surprised to see he was so young. He realized that he had subconsciously expected to see someone elderly, but this man was in his late thirties, even if his prematurely almost bald head made him look a little older. He had wide, flaring nostrils, hollow cheeks and a sensuous mouth, and the arms that leaned on the desk bulged with muscle under the dinner jacket. He looked as hard as nails.

In the middle of the room stood a Charles Atlas in blue T-shirt, and to Cox's right was the short Mr Robinson.

'Mr Cox?' asked Calder.

The man behind the desk did not answer, just sat back in his chair and gazed at the two newcomers. Then he rose and walked slowly over to the fireplace, where he warmed his hands with mock satisfaction. Calder wondered how much of it was for effect, to establish that his position of authority in the room was not just guaranteed by the muscle man. He felt Striker shift behind him.

'Who are you, Calder?' asked Cox, without turning from the fire. The accent was cosmopolitan.

Calder shot a glance at Striker and noted he was looking at the guard.

'I'm working for the government. So is Mr Striker.'

Mozart deepened in the room. Calder let himself surrender to it, sharing something with the man at the fire and sensing part of him. Cox retrieved a glass of what looked like brandy from the mantelpiece, and turned towards them.

'What part of the government, exactly?' he asked.

'The security services,' answered Calder.

Cox nodded. To Calder, it seemed that he was answering a question that he had already asked himself.

'You can prove it, of course?'

Calder looked at the roughneck.

'If your gorilla here won't jump to conclusions, my colleague has an identity wallet in the inside pocket of his jacket.'

Striker reached inside and gave it to the muscle man, who took it over to Cox. His boss examined it for some time before walking over to Calder and giving it to *him*.

'Very interesting,' said Cox. 'I've never seen one of those before.'

They were of a height and the man looked straight into Calder's eyes. Then he turned away uncomfortably and walked back towards the fire.

'Come and sit down and tell me what you want,' he said.

Calder glanced at Striker again. The blond man, for once, looked perfectly relaxed, feet slightly apart and hands at his sides. He was still looking at the heavy.

'I want your help,' said Calder, as he approached the hearth. 'But I must emphasize that this is a completely unofficial request.'

Cox suddenly burst out laughing. His whole body shook.

'I hardly think that MI5 would be asking me officially for help, Mr Calder.' He laughed again. 'It might soil their nice clean hands.'

His face hardened before he spoke again.

'But I'm sure your business is dirtier than mine, despite that.'

'In this case, Mr Cox, you're quite right. We know about your interests and we are not concerned with them – although I can't, of course, speak for the Metropolitan Police. But compared to what we are dealing with, you *are* the vestal virgin.'

Calder realized that he had almost gone too far as the man's face hardened again, so he pushed on quickly.

'You will have heard of the plutonium hijack?'

'Of course,' answered Cox and then he smiled. 'You don't think I did it?'

'No. But I'm asking you to help me find out who did.'

Cox burst into a fit of laughter. It was a long time before he stopped.

'I must confess, Calder,' he said, 'you take the cake for nerve. You come in here, as bold as brass, tell me that you represent the side of law and order and then you ask me to find the perpetrator of a hold-up.'

He walked towards Calder and stopped about a yard from him. His face was fierce but his voice was controlled.

'Give me one good reason why I should.'

Calder looked back into the brown eyes in his usual way. He saw hatred there and intelligence, but not fear. Cox was used to being on top and Calder did not want to alter that. Besides, he felt a strange liking for the man. He was more a product of society than the other way around. He probably had a resentment against the so-called legitimate world for producing him in the condition that it had, and the accusation had its point. What's more, he had risen to the top of his profession in a very tough environment. As did successful businessmen.

The music was reaching a crescendo. Calder turned to look at the guard.

'I'd prefer as few people to know as possible,' he said, looking back at Cox.

The latter glared at Calder until the sound died down, his nostrils flaring, before he signalled the guard to go.

'But Robinson stays,' he said forcefully.

Striker shifted his weight. Calder nodded and gathered his thoughts.

'I don't know whether you know, Mr Cox,' he said, 'but the

material that was stolen was reprocessed plutonium 239. With a certain chemical conversion – which is difficult, but can be done by a competent scientist – it is the raw material for a nuclear bomb.'

He walked over to the fire and stood in front of it.

'We don't know who stole it. It may have been a foreign power or terrorist group, or,' he paused slightly, 'it may have been a British group. We simply don't know. But we must eliminate possibilities. There would certainly need to have been British help for the job, even if it wasn't all British. A certain amount of recruiting might have gone on within the criminal fraternity. We thought that you, with your connections that are denied to us, might know something or be able to find it. Any clue would be useful.'

Cox shifted his position and scowled before he swigged at his brandy.

'Before I continue,' said Calder, 'please turn the concerto off. It would be a blasphemy to listen to it with what I am about to say.'

Cox remained perfectly still for several seconds, looking at Calder. Then his face visibly softened and he signalled Robinson. The short man bent to the desk and the room became silent, apart from the crackling fire. Calder felt that part of him had gone. So, he hoped, would Cox.

'Our fear is, Mr Cox, that if it was a British group, it can have only one object: nuclear blackmail. We don't know how much, as yet, was stolen, but assuming the bomb that may be built is about the smallest possible, it would contain about ten kilos of plutonium. In normal circumstances, that would produce an explosive power of about twenty thousand tons of TNT.'

Cox wasn't drinking his brandy now, Calder noticed. Striker was looking at him with a puzzled frown on his face and Robinson was impassive. He himself felt strangely calm.

'I'll spare you the technical details, but if such a bomb were exploded in Central London, let's say in the boot of a car in Horse Guards Parade, behind 10 Downing Street, the effect would be catastrophic.

'Most people and most things within a radius of one and three-quarter miles from that point can be expected to be destroyed by fire – from flash burns or simply burnt by fire – or crushed by falling masonry, or cut to ribbons by falling glass. The "blast wave" and the "fireball" would see to that. If anyone in that circle is lucky enough to survive the initial explosion and resulting firestorm, the gamma rays or neutrons – very intense and powerful initial radiation – that would be released at the same time, would probably finish them off. Almost everyone, and everything, within that three-and-a-half-mile circle would be destroyed and, of course, the effect would be greater the nearer one was to the centre.

'I needn't point out that Soho is well within that circle, and insurance companies don't pay out on nuclear explosions. This building would simply cease to exist. So would most things from the top of Tottenham Court Road in the north to the Oval cricket ground in the south, from Park Lane in the west to Southwark Bridge in the east.'

Cox was still not drinking his brandy. He was just staring at Calder. Striker was strangely immobile.

'Then,' continued Calder, 'the worst effect of all would still be to come. There would be residual radiation fall-out. Depending on the strength of the wind, it would fall in a cigar shape over a distance of about a hundred miles. I don't know whether you know the effects of radiation on the body. The main one is to cause cancers of various kinds, which are usually incurable.

'I don't know how many people live, or work, or visit within that circle – two hundred and fifty thousand? Five hundred thousand? A million? It would doubtless depend on the day and the time of day. Very few would survive and the eventual radiation, which would spread over a much larger area, would perhaps eventually kill even more. We are not just talking about your businessman in the Strand, but also a child playing in her garden in Bedfordshire.'

Calder moved to one side and noticed that Cox's gaze didn't alter. He was staring into the fire. Robinson hadn't moved and Striker was looking at Calder intensely.

Suddenly Cox drained his glass and looked Calder straight in the face. When he spoke he seemed perfectly calm.

'I'm going to have another brandy. Would you two gentlemen like one?'

Calder looked at Striker and said, 'No, thank you.'

Cox walked over to the decanter on the mantelpiece and began to pour.

'You have produced your reason, Mr Calder. I shall think about it and make some inquiries.'

Calder nodded, slightly surprised. Somehow, despite his confidence, he hadn't expected it to be so easy.

'We can't ask for more,' he said. It was time to go.

'Give your telephone number and address to Robinson on the way out,' said Cox. 'I'll call tomorrow evening.'

The quiet, watchful Mr Robinson was looking at Calder very carefully as they moved towards the door.

'Mr Calder?' called Cox from the fireplace.

They all paused and looked back.

'I suppose I'm a bit of a villain.' He was looking at the brandy in his glass. 'That's the main reason I've felt unable to have children.'

Then he looked into the fire.

The room was spacious and expensive. In the middle, covering most of the parquet flooring, was a large, greenish Persian carpet and, surrounding it, several pieces of chintz furniture. The space was lit by a single standard lamp and the glow of a colour television set that was perched in one corner. Six people sat in the room watching the late film: five bearded men and a woman. It was not quite midnight.

The atmosphere, Judy felt, was definitely unfriendly. Being virtually the only woman, and an extremely attractive one at that, you would think that she would be happy. But she knew that John wouldn't like her to get too friendly with the others. Yet he had hardly spoken to her since Monday. Once she had asked his permission to go for a walk, but that had been vetoed. She was a prisoner and she didn't like the feeling of oppression that had set in with the group since their return. Eighteen men enclosed in one house, with nowhere to go and nothing to do, was not a good recipe for congeniality, she knew. The daily exercise in the large enclosed garden was not enough to get rid of the excess energy, and there had been intense competition as to who went on the job with John and poor Vaisey the following night.

She looked down at her carelessly crossed legs, glanced up and saw Martin looking at her. She thought about what it would be like with Martin and, feeling beautifully mischievous, slowly drew her legs up underneath her on the soft chair, exposing the length of one thigh.

She looked up again and saw that John had just come in. He was looking at her. Had he seen and interpreted her movement? He had been giving her the same look now for a week. He had changed. He was colder. And she had to admit that the feeling was mutual. On the boat the distance between them had become even greater. But she still acted the part of faithful girlfriend. It saved a lot of friction. She didn't like the set-up now, but she knew how to survive.

John was signalling to her. Dutifully, she got up and followed him down the corridor and up the stairs to her room. There he locked the door and told her to strip. She did so. Then, without being asked, she bent over the bed with her rear in the air. She had found it rather animal at first and exciting, but it had now become a little monotonous.

He knew from experience that he could enter her immediately. She had four orgasms before his fingers pinched the flesh at the top of her thighs and he let out a long sigh.

Swiftly, he withdrew, zipped himself up, turned her around, smiled and kissed her. Then he walked out. It had been a relief of tension. Nothing more.

Chapter 10

Striker couldn't see out of the car windscreen, as the rain had distorted its translucence. It was coming down heavily now and there was a definite drumming on the roof. Condensation had been the major problem and he had had to have a side window continuously open to prevent the car steaming up. A small pool was beginning to form on the passenger carpet and the cloth seat looked as if it would never be the same again. But that couldn't be helped. He had to have clear vision to see out of his side window and he needed immediate forward sight if he had to move off quickly. The drumming got louder.

Keeping his breath away from his door window, he looked again at the solid gabled house, patches of it just discernible behind the newly-leafed beech trees. He had been there since 9 a.m. It was now nearly 11.00 and he had a thumping headache. Calder had insisted that he was up at 7.30, despite their late night. Not that Calder had slept much. He had been up even later, waking headquarters, arranging links with Special Branch, borrowing equipment and organizing a phone-tap of the house at which he was now looking. It was the residence of the man Calder's friend had put them on to, and by all accounts he was a legitimate businessman, completely unknown to the police. Not a thing had stirred since he had arrived, although, through binoculars, he had observed that curtains had been drawn about half an hour before.

On a wet, Sunday morning, Hampstead, it appeared, did not emerge from its lethargic affectation. Strange, Striker thought, how middle-class norms and values were so similar in all Western, industrialized societies – so exportable. Only the working-class were different. Hampstead did not differ markedly from the sort of area in which he had been brought up, in Los Angeles, where his father was a successful lawyer and his mother a society beauty. Only the weather, of course. Later on, about midday, he figured, one or two of the residents would drift along to the local or the golf-club bar, perhaps a little earlier than usual since gardening was obviously out.

A bedraggled dog – incongruously, yet somehow fittingly, a mongrel – cocked its leg at a gatepost for no more than two seconds, to mark its territory, before limping on home.

The car radio barked at him. 'Blue Wing. This is Red Wing.'

Striker unhooked the microphone.

'Receiving you loud and clear, Red Wing,' he answered, exaggerating his US accent.

'I'm going to call in exactly five minutes, Blue Wing.'

'Acknowledged, Red Wing. Anything else?'

'No. Out.'

A man of few words, Matthew Calder. God, what was he thinking? Striker started the engine and immediately put the heater and fan full on the windscreen. Then he switched on the wipers and reversed about a hundred yards up the road. This had been arranged beforehand. When Andrews received the call, he might get suspicious and look out of the window to see if he was being watched. A strange car parked just outside the front door would not look good. In his new position, Striker decided to keep the engine running. This enabled him to close the near-side window and keep the heater, fan and windscreen wipers on.

The inside of the car was now very noisy. He opened his window a little and watched the entrance to the house.

The plan was that Calder would phone Andrews and explain that he had acquired some P-239 and ask whether he knew of a buyer. Andrews, they had reasoned, would do one of three things. What they were hoping for was that he would phone his contacts to find out whether he could place the plutonium. In that case Calder would listen in. Alternatively, Andrews might make contact directly. That was what Striker was for. Alternatively also, he might decide to do nothing until Monday. After all, English Sundays were rather sacrosanct. But Calder was hoping to impress a sense of urgency upon him.

The next thirty minutes went by extremely slowly as Striker watched the end of the drive. He was about to call Calder for news when the car radio spoke again.

'This is Red Wing calling Blue Wing.'

'Blue Wing here. Anything?'

'No. Your end?'

'No.'

There was a pause.

'O K. Maintain surveillance. Out.'

Just then, a silver-metallic Mercedes swept out of the drive – if anything had been coming the driver would have been hard-pushed to stop – and accelerated away from Striker up the road.

'Red Wing. He's just emerged. Am in pursuit.'

With that, Striker dropped the receiver back on its rest, slammed the 2-litre Ford Cortina into first gear and sped off. He held it in each gear for a long time before he reached top and was hurtling after the speeding Mercedes. He saw its left indicator winking at the top of the road before it disappeared. Striker braked late and turned after it. He managed to close to within two hundred yards and grabbed the receiver.

'This is Blue Wing calling Red Wing.'

'Receiving you, Blue Wing.'

'Am coming towards you. He's heading south towards Central London.'

'O K. Out.'

Striker had to keep the pedal fairly well down to the floor to keep up with the Mercedes in the sparse traffic, but he managed without a great deal of trouble, although he had to shoot a red light to stay in sight. Finally, they entered Knightsbridge and turned into Princes Gardens. Andrews stopped outside a big Georgian terraced house and got out.

The blond man cruised by and stopped on the other side of the road. He looked back, saw Andrews reach the top of the steps and press a black bell that was set into the cream wall. Then he appeared to hesitate, push the door and walk in. Striker turned the car round and parked it right behind the Mercedes,

about nine feet from the bumper. Then he picked up the microphone.

'This is Blue Wing calling Red Wing.'

'Receiving you loud and clear, Blue Wing,' came the stronger
reply.

'Subject entered house in Princes Gardens, Knightsbridge.' He
gave the number. 'Request instructions.'

'Just follow and report, Blue Wing.'

Striker replaced the communicator with drawn lips. There was
something wrong. The front door had appeared to open as soon as
Andrews pushed the bell, or it was already open.

Suddenly, Andrews burst out of the door at a run. He stopped,
as if realizing that he was outside, and clambered down the steps to
his car. On reaching the street he glanced quickly, furtively, to left
and right. The front door of the house was still open.

On impulse, Striker decided to disobey orders and use his initiative. He left his car and began to walk towards Andrews. The
heavens seemed to choose that moment to rain even harder. The
older man saw him as he was opening his car door and just stood
there, a look of sheer horror on his pale face. The complexion
was whiter than it should have been, Striker decided, as if it had
been drained of blood. He was about sixty, with a full greased-
down head of straight white hair. The nose was long and thin,
the eyes a bloodshot blue and the lips also had a tinge of the
same colour. It was the face of a retired admiral, but Striker
knew that he probably didn't know one end of a ship from the
other. He was dressed in black overcoat with a beige scarf at his
throat.

'Mr Andrews,' said Striker in his best English accent, 'I want
you to shake hands and smile, as if we were old friends.'

Both the smile and the shake were pitifully weak, but adequate
in the circumstances.

'Now, I want you to slowly walk over to my car and get in the
passenger side. And be careful, Mr Andrews; I do have a gun under
my jacket.'

Andrews obeyed tamely, his arms hanging at his sides and his
head drooping. Striker managed to get in his side before Andrews
sat down. The latter appeared not to notice the wet seat.

'Good,' said the American. 'As you might have gathered, I'm a policeman. What went on in there?'

Andrews looked at Striker intently, as if he were relieved in some way. Then another thought appeared to cross his mind. He turned and stared through the windscreen. Striker waited.

'He's dead,' said the grey man absently. He turned to look at the blond again, fear in his eyes. 'But I didn't kill him. Honestly. He was dead when I arrived.'

Striker believed it.

'Anyone else in the house?' he asked.

'No. I didn't see anyone.' Andrews frowned. 'He has servants. But I didn't see any of them, and the door was open when I arrived.'

Striker unhooked the microphone.

'Blue Wing, calling Red Wing.'

'Go ahead.'

Striker took a deep breath and kept to the English accent.

'Have apprehended suspect as he ran from the address previously given. He says that there is a body inside, but no one else. Request assistance before proceeding.'

There was a pause.

'I'll be there in ten minutes.'

In that time Striker tried to prise some more information out of his captive, but he was now saying nothing. Striker strapped some handcuffs on him and waited for Calder. In the meantime he kept an eye on the house and tried to ignore his worsening headache.

Calder parked behind the Cortina and let himself in by one of the rear doors.

'Any life, from him or the house?' he asked Striker.

'None from neither, if that's grammatically correct. He wants to see his solicitor.'

'Does he?' answered Calder.

Striker had never seen Calder in this mood. He looked at the old man and almost felt sorry for him.

'If he doesn't co-operate,' said Calder, 'he'll be lucky if he *ever* sees his solicitor. Now, listen to me, Andrews. We are all going into that house to have a look at this body. Let's go.'

The anger, Striker realized, was only just under the surface. Calder had been almost deferential to Cox, but he treated this apparently respectable businessman with ill-disguised venom. He was being hauled out of his seat now by Calder, and Striker quickly followed, feeling uncomfortable.

They went down a dark corridor which led into a large, even darker room. The blinds were still down. Striker could just make out the wood-panelling and the big, empty fireplace. There was also a red and purple, patterned rug and, on it, right in the centre, a body, fully clothed. Andrews, he noticed, was staring at it with his mouth and eyes wide open.

Calder switched on the lights and Striker didn't have to go any closer to see that the man was an Arab of about middle age. He was also very dead. A pool of blood lay around his head and there was no doubt that his throat had been cut.

Calder pushed Andrews into a chair and bent over the body. So did Striker. It was very cold. He'd obviously been dead for hours. Certainly a long time before Andrews arrived. Calder was looking at him. Then he stood up and walked over to a telephone, on a small table to one side of the fireplace. Striker hadn't noticed it. Calder dialled a number and waited. The blond rose and looked over at Andrews. His strength appeared to have gone. He just sat, looking at the carpet, head in hands.

'Hello. This is Calder.'

A pause and then he gave the address.

'On following a suspect, we have found a murder victim. The man our suspect was going to see. He's an Arab. I don't know how you want to play it and I know it's a Sunday, but if it's possible, I suggest you send a small team round before we notify the police. There might be something of interest.'

Another pause.

'Yes.'

Then he put the phone down. Andrews, Striker noticed, had become attentive.

'If you're not the police,' said the grey man rather uncertainly, 'then who are you?'

'We'll stay here until they arrive,' said Calder to Striker.

Andrews was extremely nervous and glanced over at the blond American for assistance, having worked out that Calder was the danger man.

'Who is he?' asked Calder, pointing at the man on the floor.

'I'm not saying anything until I have seen my solicitor,' replied Andrews, looking at the door. But his voice was shaking and he was unsure of himself.

'Let me put you in the picture, Andrews,' said Calder. 'We know what you do and a lot of it comes under the Official Secrets Act. Do you know what that means? You come under the category of "spy" or "foreign agent", and if you're lucky enough to get a trial, it will be held *in camera*.'

'You can't prove anything,' interjected Andrews a little too confidently.

Calder, with hands hanging at his sides, was seemingly perfectly relaxed as he continued.

'Then, of course, there is the public trial for murder.'

The grey man stood up. 'You can't prove that either! He was dead before I arrived.'

'My assistant here observed you running from the house,' Calder went on. 'And this, immediately after receiving a phone call offering some plutonium for sale.'

Andrews looked away as the penny dropped.

'I don't think it would take the police long to make the connection between you and Mr X here, do you, Andrews? It looks very suspicious. Bound to be a trial.'

Calder paused for effect. Andrews had sat down again and was looking at the carpet.

'You may just get off the murder charge, if you're lucky, but the publicity would be ruinous,' continued Calder relentlessly. 'And I would make sure that you got it.'

Again he stopped momentarily.

'And there's one other thing, Andrews.'

He stepped purposefully over to the now dejected man, grasped him by the shirt and tie, and hauled him to his feet. Striker moved instinctively towards them, then stopped himself. Andrews's face was barely a foot away from Calder's. They both appeared to be shaking slightly, for different reasons. The words were not merely spoken, but spat.

'I hold little shits like you in nothing but contempt. Creatures who sell fuel for nuclear bombs on the open market are not people, they're the arsehole of humanity. If I had my way, I'd take you to the deepest hole I could find and let you starve to death. But even that's too good for you. As it is, I'd take the greatest delight in rearranging your face and believe me, I'd enjoy it.'

Andrews shivered. He was also clearly struggling, but Calder's grip was not allowing him any movement.

'As it is, you have precisely three seconds to start telling me all you know about that man and the rest of your filthy business, or I'll make a start on your teeth.'

A pause.

'Well?'

It was said with terrible portent and Andrews was not a man of courage. He cracked. Calder released his grip and his victim grovelled on the floor, staining the carpet some more with his vomit. He told all.

The dead man was a wealthy Arab named Khalid Aziz who owned the house they were in. Andrews had twice acted as a broker in selling him some enriched uranium 235, three years or so previously, and they had kept up a business and social relationship that did not involve nuclear elements. He had come to see him on three counts. On receiving the call that morning, he thought that Aziz had been the one to put the caller in contact, in which case he wanted to know who he was. Secondly, and if not, he thought he might be able to sell the plutonium to him. He also wanted to talk to him as a friend, because he was a little worried about his security.

'How many deals of this nature have you made?' asked Calder, while Striker took notes.

Just the twice with Aziz, it seemed. It was difficult material to come by.

'I've had one request for it recently, but was unable to find any,' concluded Andrews.

Striker stiffened and swapped glances with Calder.

'Why didn't you call that person – the one who wanted the U-235 – after I phoned this morning?' Calder wanted to know.

Andrews looked up pleadingly.

'I might have done, but I don't have his number or his address, or even his name. You've got to believe me. People are very cautious in this business. They hold back information about themselves until the last possible moment. He phoned one day, just like you, and refused to give his name and number. That's why I was suspicious about your call. He said he would phone again in a month.'

Andrews stopped.

'And did he?' asked Striker pleasantly.

The grey-haired man looked up, either surprised at the direction of the question or the change of accent. He nodded his head several times before speaking.

'Yes. But only once more. I never heard from him again.'

'How long ago was the last call?' asked Striker. 'Be absolutely sure, Mr Andrews.'

This time he shook his head.

'I can't be sure, I'm sorry, but it was around ... October or November of last year. I would not have made a note in my diary.'

Striker looked at Calder. The latter pushed his hand forward, encouraging him to continue. Striker looked back at the pathetic old man.

'We will be asking you to put down a transcript of the conversation, Mr Andrews, but can you remember anything about the man – any clue as to who he might be?'

Striker looked down at his writing pad before continuing.

'Needless to say, it will stand you in good stead if we can say that you were helpful.'

Andrews looked at Striker, then Calder, then back to Striker again.

'I don't know,' he said. 'What can you tell about a man from a telephone conversation?'

'Quite a lot,' answered Striker, but Andrews appeared to be thinking.

'It was such a long time ago.'

He paused and they waited.

'There was one thing. I remember thinking at the time that he had been in the Army.'

Striker and Calder swapped glances again.

'You know,' continued Andrews, 'officer type – used to giving orders. Had a way of saying things.'

He paused again.

'I was in the infantry, you know. Captain,' and with that he appeared to go into a trance.

A footfall sounded in the corridor.

'He'll have to be interrogated with a tape-recorder,' said Calder, 'but we'll let these boys handle that,' and he turned towards the door.

Striker was seated in one of Calder's comfortable chairs, drinking some of his dry ginger. Vaughan Williams was playing on the stereo. It was 7.30 p.m. and they were waiting for two things. Most importantly, George Cox was due to ring and they were also expecting a transcript of the interrogation of Andrews.

Calder was looking at the chess-board, deep in thought. The anger of midday had disappeared and he was almost his normal self, whatever that was. But Striker felt that their relationship had subtly changed. He wondered whether Calder was seeing the whole investigation in terms of a chess game. Would he, Calder, be the white queen or a knight? Andrews would probably be an expendable black pawn, or perhaps a white one.

He looked up to see Calder looking at him. Their eyes held.

'You disapprove of the way I handled Andrews, don't you, Peter?'

Striker looked down at his glass. This could get very heavy, he thought.

'I don't know how much of your anger was controlled or genuine,' he answered with a smile.

'A bit of both, I think,' said Calder. 'But I must admit, I was only just in control of myself.' He turned to look at Striker, a wry smile on his face. 'Does that make it better or worse?' he asked.

Striker hadn't lost his grin.

'I don't know,' he said, shrugging his shoulders in an attempt to lighten the atmosphere.

To himself he thought that it at least showed Calder was human. Out loud he said:

'It got what we wanted.'

Calder laughed before speaking.

'Since when did the ends justify the means in your philosophy?'

'Perhaps I was trying to ease your conscience,' smiled Striker.

Again Calder laughed.

'Come on,' he said, 'let's play chess. I want to think.'

'That's what I like about you,' said the blond man, 'the way you flatter your opponents.'

Calder signalled Striker to start with the white pieces as they moved over to the chess-board. Striker hesitated and picked up the white king. It was no use. He had to say it.

'There is one thing about you.'

The sudden seriousness in his voice made Calder look up.

'You make fundamental decisions for other people – moral decisions – that might affect them quite significantly. But you never seem to hesitate about making them. I'm not so sure that I could do that.'

Calder was looking at him intently now. Striker remembered their meeting in San Claro and how the eyes had bored into him then. It was the same look and he found it just as difficult to counter. The eyes told you nothing, yet they told you everything. They were neither hard nor soft, weak nor strong; just open. A gateway to *your* soul as well as his.

'Is that a question about me or you?' asked Calder.

To Striker's relief, the telephone rang. Calder merely blinked, hesitated until the second ring, then turned and moved into the hall.

'Hello ... yes, is this Mr Cox?'

There was a long pause. Then Calder turned and looked at him.

'I'm very grateful to you, Mr Cox. Would you write down the dates of those raids and send the information round to my address tonight ... Thank you ... Yes, it does ... Yes, I will. Again, thank you,' and he put the phone down.

He stood there for a moment and drained his glass. Then he picked up the receiver again and dialled a number.

'General? Matthew Calder. I think we ought to have a talk ... That will be fine. Good night.'

This time, after replacing the receiver, he walked through to the living-room.

'I'm seeing the General in his office at 9.30 tomorrow,' he said, walking over to the cocktail cabinet. He handed Striker the half-filled dry ginger bottle and tipped some more Scotch into his own glass before he spoke again. The American waited patiently.

'Cox has been making extensive inquiries. There have been a number of what he calls "recruiting drives" over the last two years or so, but he's not worried about them. Apparently the "recruits" were either petty villains who wouldn't be any use to our man – the fact that they are not permanently employed, he says, is testimony enough to their incompetence – or, he knows where the others went and, in his view, those groups would not be capable of this sort of operation.'

Calder took a swig before continuing.

'He also has some very interesting information about a number of bank raids in the last year or so that he and the rest of the criminal fraternity are very puzzled about. The perplexing factor, apparently, is that no one knows who committed them and that is extremely rare. What's more, no one connected with any of the raids has ever been caught. The word is, and Cox pointed out that this is only surmise, that the "gang" is not from your actual criminal fraternity at all, but that it is, and I quote, "an army group".'

'Ding dong,' said Striker.

'Yes,' answered Calder with a smile. 'Now let's start this game. I said I have to think and I do that best when I'm playing.'

Striker returned the white king to the board and advanced its pawn two squares.

'Do you know,' said Calder, 'some people actually believe that chess players imbue their pieces with life of their own, as if they were real men and women in a real-life situation? What these folk don't understand is that it's mainly the assumption that the pieces are lifeless and totally divorced from reality that provides the attraction of the game.'

Striker was, for once, completely lost for words. He advanced his queen's pawn one square to counter the attack of the black knight on his king's pawn. Already he was on the defensive. He knew that he was still afraid of Matthew Calder and he still didn't know why.

Felixstowe Docks are much like any other; dark, dank, dirty and wet might be a good description. But, lit gently by the lights of the moored ships that reflected in the black water, the place could, just possibly, have a fairy-land image for anyone romantically inclined. It did, paradoxically, have a kind of enchanting quality about it.

Romance, though, was the last thing on Brown's mind as he walked along the wharf, close to the wall. You needed the eyes of a cat to see him, dressed as he was all in black, with rubber-soled shoes and black cowl over his head. Most criminals, when engaged in skulduggery, dress in ordinary clothes; then, unless they are actually caught red-handed, they can claim innocence. However, Brown didn't want to be seen at all. If he *was* seen, it would be obvious that he was up to no good, but then the unfortunate person who saw him wouldn't live long enough to give the game away.

Brown stopped by a gate and listened. All he heard was the gentle slop of the slight swell against the wharf stanchions and the hum of distant traffic. The fresh, salty smell of the sea came to his nostrils. He was glad the rain had stopped.

The gate was strongly held by a padlock and chain, and along the top were several strands of barbed wire, as, indeed, there also were on the wall. Brown looked inside. There was a small square yard and to the left an equally small factory/workshop. He stood immobile for five minutes, watching and listening. Then he banged hard against the wall, twice.

Similarly dressed black figures began to emerge from the darkness. One detached itself from the others and bent down to the lock. Within ten seconds it was open. The chain took much longer to remove because silence was necessary. The gate made a small squeak as it was swung open. It had to be wide open because three men had to go through abreast, as Vaisey was carried to the side door of the workshop. When they had all passed through, the lock-picker, standing inside, reset the padlock on the outside. Two men stationed themselves on either side of the gate, in the shadows, just in case anyone unwisely decided to snoop.

Within minutes the side-door lock had been picked and Brown, Vaisey and the four remaining men entered the workshop. The place had been picked because the high, boundary wall would block out light from the side windows, but that left a couple of skylights. Brown gave a signal and three men, two with pre-cut sheets of dark plastic under their arms, disappeared outside.

Using a torch only, Vaisey moved to an impressive-looking lathe-type apparatus. He examined it closely and then moved on to another machine. The implosion assembly, into which the hollow hemispheres of P-239 had to fit, needed to be made of stainless steel and had to be exact. That meant the use of professional metal-spinning equipment and it was the one job in the construction of the bomb that he couldn't do in his own workshop.

He turned to see one of the men return and put a thumb up at Brown. The latter switched on the lights and looked around. Then he walked to a set of switches and pulled them. A soft hum arose as the power for the machinery came on.

Vaisey nodded at Brown and looked at his watch. 10.16 p.m. Brown wanted no trace left of their entry or their task. That meant that there needed to be enough time before dawn to clean up the equipment, sweep away excess material and remove the plastic sheets from the roof windows. He hefted his bag on to a near-by bench, and removed the raw material and a long list of mathematical calculations. It was going to be a long, hard night.

Chapter 11

As Calder pushed open the door to Stoddard's outer office Ann was sitting behind her desk smiling at him. With her clear eyes and fresh white blouse, she looked as bright as a new pin.

'Hey, you're too much for me on a Monday morning,' he said with a frowning smile.

She didn't laugh, just kept showing her teeth and said:

'You ought to try thinking good of people for a change. It helps one sleep at night.'

The barb was not lost on him. He wanted to walk round the desk and touch her.

'Tonight?' he asked.

' 'Fraid not. Evening class.'

'Political philosophy?' he ventured.

'Wine-making.'

'I want to kiss you.'

'I know.' She was still beaming.

He looked towards the door. 'Is he in?'

'No,' she replied between even teeth and let him stew for several seconds. His eyes shifted from side to side as he sought out the reason, though whether it was about the General's absence or her motives for not telling him why, she wasn't sure.

'He's at the zoo,' she said at last. 'He often goes there when he wants to think. There's a car waiting for you at the main entrance.'

She wondered whether he would work out that she could have got the doorman to tell him. He smiled thinly and walked towards the door.

'I always think it's the smell,' she said.

That *did* throw him. He stopped, looked back at her and creased his forehead.

'That helps him to think,' she added. 'Zoos always smell – haven't you noticed?'

He opened the door.

'I can make Tuesday,' she called.

He turned and laughed.

'Seven o'clock?'

She nodded, still smiling, as he left.

The black Rover 3-litre actually had one of those glass partitions which cut off the rear compartment from the driver. Calder had thought that they only existed in the imagination of writers of fiction. The car also smelt of tobacco. Perhaps Ann was right.

The driver said that Sir Giles would be by the polar bears, and Calder spotted him from a distance, an unlit pipe in his mouth and an Austin Reed mackintosh over his shoulders. When Calder was still forty yards away, he looked round, as if sensing that someone was coming. Behind him a huge white bear perched on a rock about twenty feet above a blue pond.

'Morning, Calder,' said the General brusquely and removed his pipe. 'I'm coming to believe your surmise was right. It *was* a British operation.'

The iron-grey hair looked darker in the morning light. The white bear slowly raised his head to the overcast sky, then looked down at the water as if to jump.

'I've finished here,' said Stoddard formally. 'Let's walk back to the car.'

Calder felt like a bridegroom who knew he was about to be told that he'd been left at the church.

'We've handed over the Arab to the Metropolitan Police. Andrews, we've let go.'

Stoddard glanced defiantly at Calder, expecting an argument. The younger man said nothing. The General was clearly in forceful mood and Calder decided that, on this occasion, discretion was the better part of valour. He kept step as they walked towards the entrance.

'Three of the servants have turned up,' continued Stoddard. 'They're all Arab. Apparently they fled when they got up in the morning and found their master sprawled in his own blood. I think they were expecting some sort of Islamic justice. Anyway, the police are handling it now and they will keep us informed if there are any connections with our little matter. Frankly I doubt it and I'd be surprised if they find the murderer. Probably some sort of Moslem feud.'

He stopped and looked up at Calder.

'The Navy have come up with the vital information, at last.'

Calder stiffened and looked back at the bear. He hadn't jumped.

'You were right again. The rods were missing from only one fuel assembly. The empty assembly is still there.'

They approached the car and Stoddard gestured for him to get in. No wonder the General was in a mood this morning, he thought. Enough plutonium oxide for ten kilos of plutonium had been stolen and there could only be one possible reason for that. When they were both settled on the large back seat, the car moved off smoothly. Stoddard began speaking again.

'It also tends to indicate that they are British. If it were a foreign group, why not ship the whole lot? Why just fourteen rods? The logistics of the actual operation were difficult enough to plan and accomplish. Surely they could have pinched the whole lot with a different kind of operation? Besides, MI6 have found nothing. There seem to be no foreign connections at the moment. Have you found any?'

'No. And there's something else,' said Calder, thinking he ought to say something.

'It's a military group,' said Stoddard.

Calder reminded himself never to underestimate the General.

'If they are British,' continued Stoddard, 'they have to be military, or rather, ex-Army.'

He examined his pipe as if viewing it for the first time.

'It was jumping the British hurdle that was important. After that, the assumption was almost inevitable. The criminal community don't have the organizational ability or discipline, not just to carry out the operation, which was difficult enough, but also to keep quiet about it afterwards. I should have seen it earlier. I should have recognized the style.'

He turned to the younger man and noticed that he was looking at him in an odd way. What's more, he'd hardly said a word.

'What do you think?' asked Stoddard.

Calder cleared his throat.

'I agree. Andrews mentioned something to Striker and me – before your boys arrived – that's not on the transcript. He received an inquiry for plutonium about October of last year. He had the feeling that the speaker had been an officer in the Army. He was one himself apparently.'

Stoddard was looking at him intently.

'In addition,' continued Calder, 'a contact of mine, from the criminal fraternity in London –' he hesitated and fingered his beard – 'by all accounts the biggest, informs me that, in his view, it is most unlikely that any of his partners in crime did it. Nor has there been any recruiting of specialist criminal personnel, that he knows of, that could be relevant.'

'This is rather speculative,' said Stoddard suspiciously.

Calder refrained from pointing out that the General's own surmise was hardly based on firm evidence. Instead, he said:

'Yes, but he also told me something else: that there have been a number of successful bank raids in the last year or so that no one in his business can fathom. He doesn't know who they are, nor have any of the robbers ever been caught.'

'I'm ahead of you,' said Stoddard, his eyes alive.

'My contact,' continued Calder, 'said there is a rumour, which he is very much inclined to believe, that they are an army group.'

Stoddard was nodding.

'Have you got the dates of the raids?' he asked, unable to keep a certain restrained excitement out of his voice.

Calder extracted a piece of paper from inside his jacket and handed it over. It was the page that Cox had sent. Stoddard placed pipe in mouth as he began to read.

'That was why I wanted to see you,' said Calder, feeling a bit like a spare part. 'If we can match up the dates in some way with people leaving from a particular regiment, we might be able to get a cross-reference of some sort on who the officer, or officers, are behind this. Clearly the "band" will have been hand-picked and all well known to the officer in charge. It's a huge job to trace them, but the Army must keep records.'

Stoddard was still looking at the piece of paper. The car seemed to travel at a constant speed, as if the traffic didn't exist, and they had nearly reached their destination.

'This is your line of country, General. You understand it. I don't. What's more, you can open doors in a moment, whereas it would take me months at the Ministry of Defence just to get permission for an investigation. You may have to check on the whereabouts of all those who left in, say, the last two years – perhaps three.'

Stoddard was still reading.

'Yes, I'll handle this,' he said absently. He was clearly thinking ahead.

The Rover pulled in at the kerb and they both stepped out. In the lift, Stoddard was silent, still looking at the sheet of paper. But as soon as he entered his office he came alive.

'Ann, the rest of my activities today – cancel them. If necessary, give them to Mr Jensen.' He looked at her and smiled. 'You know what to do.'

She nodded.

'All, that is, except the Fitch case,' said Stoddard. 'I'll deal with that in a moment.'

He paused.

'Thinking about it, you'd better cancel my business for tomorrow as well. I'll come and sort *that* out with you in a moment. Also, order my car for an hour's time. I'm going to be away for a couple of days.'

Stoddard was looking into the distance now.

'Will that be all, sir?' Ann asked.

Calder looked at her, thinking she was being sarcastic again, but her face was deadpan.

'Yes, thank you,' answered Stoddard and walked through into his own room.

Calder hesitated. Suddenly he realized what a vital person Ann was in the General's whole security set-up. The thought was strangely uncomfortable.

She stood up, lifted a tray on which was a percolator of coffee, cups, spoons, milk and sugar, walked over and handed it to him with a smile. He walked through and placed the tray on the General's desk. She was fascinating.

'Shall I do the honours?' he asked.

'Yes, help yourself,' answered Stoddard.

The pipe was now lying on the blotter. He flicked the piece of paper with the back of his hand and said:

'This is the best piece of news I've had all week.' He looked at his watch. 'Almost exactly a week,' he added, rather more bitterly.

Calder handed him his coffee and saw him help himself to milk only. He took a slow sip and looked at Calder steadily.

'This information is accurate?' asked the General.

Calder stirred his third black coffee of the morning, while he thought about the answer.

'As to the exactness of the dates, you'll see that my informant was a little unsure, but you can check that easily enough with the police, now you have the rough dates. With regard to the substance of the information, it's accurate.'

Calder sipped and glanced at the General. Stoddard was looking at him in that disarming way he had – pipe in mouth and calm, blue eyes. He was one of the very few people Calder had met who could gaze back at him without shifting. At length the General said:

'Forgive an old man's scepticism. Two questions. Why should the biggest criminal in London give you this sort of information, and how come he happens to be an acquaintance of yours in the first place?'

Calder didn't smile.

'I met him for the first time on Saturday night. He gave me the information because I described to him the effects of an explosion of ten kilos of plutonium in Horse Guards Parade.'

There was a pause while they continued to look at each other expressionlessly.

'He's a hard man,' continued Calder, 'but he became quite human towards the end.'

There was another small pause before Stoddard spoke.

'I had a feeling you would annihilate my brief moment of elation sooner or later.'

'Sorry,' said Calder, 'but if it is a British group, it has far-reaching consequences.'

Stoddard sat back in his chair, coffee cup in hand, ready to listen.

'To begin with, it increases the possibility of their making a bomb in this country. Indeed, I would say that it was a probability. Why else steal the stuff if not for nuclear blackmail? Besides, I keep thinking of the guard's wife and child at Windscale. Why take the chance of releasing them alive if they weren't going to use that piece of generosity as evidence that they keep their word? It also provides an additional explanation as to why they went to so much trouble to steal the stuff in the first place. If they had waited long enough they could possibly have picked up some U-235 or P-239 on the open market.'

'What do you mean?' asked Stoddard, looking genuinely puzzled.

'Well, if you got a threat tomorrow that there was a home-made nuclear bomb set to go off in, say, Central Manchester, unless you hand over, would you believe it?'

'Probably.'

'Why?' asked Calder.

'I see what you mean.' The General shook his head, his lips tight. 'No hijack and my natural scepticism might come to the fore. That doubt as to the bomb's authenticity might foil their whole plan. The hijack in itself provides evidence that the threat is real.'

Calder was looking out of the window.

'I should have thought of that,' said Stoddard, sipping his coffee.

'It's only just occurred to *me*,' said Calder. 'And anyway, I'm not too keen on it. As it happens, hijacking reprocessed plutonium seems to be easier than obtaining fissionable material elsewhere.'

Calder also sipped, unhappily. Stoddard did not exactly look bright either as he, too, gazed away to the window, his mind occupied. The younger man knew what the next question was going to be and was already thinking of his answer.

'You told me three days ago that a bomb could be made,' said Stoddard. 'Are you sure?'

Calder stood up, still holding his coffee. He moved to the window and spoke as he walked.

'Yes, I'm sure. It would need a highly competent scientist, one who isn't just an expert in physics and chemistry. He would have to be good with his hands and he would need considerable skill in electronics. Perhaps a team would be needed. But it could be done. Indeed, my guess is that it already is being done. They will have had enough time beforehand to prepare the basic connections. The chemical conversion and finishing touches wouldn't take long.'

Stoddard's cup returned to its saucer more loudly than it should have done. Calder turned to see the General standing up, his anger which had been simmering finally boiling over.

'But how would that be possible?' he demanded. 'Where would they get the information? Surely it's classified?'

Calder felt angry too, as if the other's ire had triggered off a chain reaction. He walked across to Stoddard and looked hard into the steel-blue eyes.

'Classified? All the information needed is available through legitimate bookshops. Most of it's American. On the inside cover of this declassified material there is a note of disclaimer, absolving the United States government of any responsibility for the use of any information enclosed within. I have the required volumes on one of my bookshelves at home. The only difficulty I had in obtaining them was finding the money.'

He placed cup and saucer on the tray and walked back to the window before continuing. He was still angry.

'The Flowers Commission in 1976 said that the equipment required might not be much more elaborate than that already being used by criminals in the manufacture of heroin.'

There was another long pause.

'What's more,' continued Calder, still looking unseeingly out of the window, 'this is just the beginning. The Fast Breeder Reactor Programme is in its infancy. The only FBR we have is the experimental one at Dounreay. The first commercial Fast Reactor is still at the planning stage. A public inquiry is being set up on its siting. We have, at the moment, about ten tons of plutonium in circulation in this country. In the year 2000, when the programme has really got going, it's estimated that there will be about 250 tons and the eventual, future total is ten times that. Can you imagine the security problem there, General?'

Stoddard said nothing.

'The new Pressurized Water Reactors that are being built at the moment are nothing but a short-term smokescreen. Any government that favours nuclear power must favour the Fast Breeder, because the fuel for conventional reactors, uranium, is running out, whereas the Fast Breeder, to a large extent, creates its own fuel, plutonium, as it goes along. Also, there are huge profits to be made in the export market for selling this sort of technology.'

Calder paused.

'The trouble is, plutonium is the deadliest substance known to man.'

Feeling suddenly guilty, Calder turned from the window and walked back to the desk, smiling apologetically.

'I'm sorry,' he said, 'I know you don't make energy policy.'

'I'm sorry too,' answered Stoddard, grinning. 'I just pick up the pieces.'

Calder nodded and sat down.

'Besides, we're wasting time,' he said.

'Yes,' said Stoddard. 'I'll have my work cut out finding the right bloody regiment. Once I've done that, finding the right man won't take long. With a man we get a name.'

Calder was looking at the ground and the older man got the distinct impression that he wasn't paying attention.

'What is it?' the General asked.

'Something has just occurred to me,' said Calder, getting up. 'If the bomb is being constructed, then there are certain specialized materials needed. They must have got them from somewhere. I'll write up a list and get Peter on to it.'

He reached the door. 'There's one other thing. Do you still believe it was a sea drop?'

'Yes.'

'And you've only checked the boats going out.'

Stoddard hit his forehead with the palm of his hand. Of course. Since they were now thinking it was a British operation, with Britain as the destination, he needed to check all the shipping that had come *in* over the past week.

'Remember that yacht you mentioned being in the Moray Firth?' asked Calder.

'Yes.'

'It would need to have special features to carry those twelve-foot rods. They weigh between a third and half a ton. Just above the keel would seem the only place. That way they might add to the stability instead of ruining it.'

Stoddard nodded, sombre-faced. Calder smiled and left.

The geiger-counter outside the basement door was still reading 'safe' as Vaisey entered. He was feeling good. The job last night had gone well. What's more, he had just consumed a superb chicken brunch on top of six wonderful hours' sleep. That Irma could cook. He waited for the fluorescent lights to struggle to full power before strong-arming his way down the steps. He was looking forward to the day.

The plutonium had now to be cut into two hemispheres. The sphericity of the moulds, moreover, needed to be just as exact as the implosion assembly. Then they had to be polished and lac-quered to avoid corrosion. When he had done that, the reflector, which had to be fitted to the inside of the assembly, had to be made. This would be done by melting high-tin-content solder into the assembly and the shape moulded to take the two plutonium hemispheres. When formed, the reflector would be removed and drilled to allow for the apertures for the plutonium assembly tube and the initiator.

Vaisey sat down at the workbench and glanced at the computer print-out. Then he lifted the implosion assembly and studied its beauty. He was sufficiently aware of his own motives to know that the whole project had now become a crusade, as well as a justifica-tion to other people of his existence. But he didn't care. He was enjoying it. At that moment, he had made up his mind. The bomb would be exploded, regardless of whether Brown gave his permis-sion or not.

He heard the door open, but did not look round. Caren, he knew, was coming to watch him work. He smiled to himself, glanced over at his glove tent and moved confidently off the stool.

Calder placed *The Plutonium Handbook* on the floor with the rest of the pile and looked at the list he had compiled of the materials required to make a home-made atom bomb. It was enor-mous because he had included everything, even the innocuous items, like solder. Striker would be arriving any minute to pick it up. He would have been sleeping that afternoon and evening, so that he could work through the night. Some of the stuff might have been stolen and hopefully the police would have a record of such thefts.

He needed an early night, but, although he felt physically tired, he knew that he wouldn't sleep until his mind relaxed. He stretched his limbs slowly and eased himself off the couch. Then he walked over to the television and switched on the 10 o'clock news.

As Brown slammed the door behind him, Judy burst into tears – not just tears of chagrin, but body-raking sobs of absolute despair. The knot in her stomach got worse and the remorse she felt would not go away. It was ten minutes before her body stopped shaking and she was able to think about her predicament.

It wasn't just the sex. Heaven knew, she was what is colloquially described as a nymphomaniac and had learnt to live with it. She had worked out how to use it to her advantage and enjoyed doing it.

It wasn't even that she hated John. Anyway, she wasn't really sure whether she did or not. This whole thing recently had changed him. She was secondary to it and always would be. Or perhaps she'd known that all along. Had he really changed that much?

She had also come to realize fully last night, while watching Irma cook dinner, what they were doing. Kevin had also let slip that the men in the hangar were dead. He had implored her not to let Brown know that he had told her. Once it had been a romantic dream with John but, now that the relationship had turned sour, the discovery of the reality of their deed became horribly oppressive.

But it wasn't even that that depressed her so much. Or perhaps it was. Was this what her life had become? She had no purpose again. The old neuroses, the old fears, had returned.

Feeling suddenly cold in her nakedness, she drew up her feet and burrowed down between the sheets. She drew them above her head until she was cocooned in darkness. Soon she felt warm, but not secure. Her body shook again at the blackness of her heart. There was only one thing, she knew, which would make her feel content, and her hands crept down to her middle.

Chapter 12

The Italian restaurant was already half-full when they walked in. Spring had suddenly and surprisingly burst upon the city, and the diners had been quick to dress appropriately. Some of the men wore open-necked shirts, the collar turned over the jacket, gigolo-style, but most of the others had removed their jackets. Flowing, lightweight summer dresses adorned the women, with baggy forearm-length sleeves and knee-length hems. They were coloured in numerous pastel shades, of which blue and green dominated. The candlelight was, as yet, superfluous, but the light from the street combined with it to make a sort of magical glow. The rich, aromatic smell of herbs beckoned.

'I can see why you chose this place,' said Ann, as she was helped into her chair by the head waiter.

'Its main advantage is yet to be revealed. It possesses the most delicious Italian house wine in the whole of the UK,' said Calder.

She laughed.

'And I thought that you were a sober individual.'

'I don't think the General would have employed me if I were that respectable.'

'True,' she answered coyly.

She picked up her napkin before continuing.

'He's terribly Byronic and I'm rather fond of him. In fact you have a lot in common.'

She looked up expectantly, but he changed tack.

'It occurred to me yesterday that you have a crucial position in his set-up. I haven't met any of the others, except Striker and Fox –

not even Jensen – but it seems to me that you are the central pin around which everything revolves.'

So much for romance, she thought.

'Actually, I'm probably even more important than you think. I'm not just executing decisions, you see. I also have to make quite a lot of them. Not major ones, but many of them are important enough to affect considerably the working of the Department if I made a mistake.'

'Does the General know that?' he asked.

She thought about it. 'He must do. Although we've never discussed it. I think he prefers not to, simply because it suits his purpose and, strangely enough, he does have confidence in me.'

'I see.'

'No, you don't,' she said cruelly. 'You see, he employed me for –' she hesitated briefly – 'three main reasons, in the following order of importance. First, because I'm quite intelligent and have a much better than average memory. He wasn't very impressed by my degree in English, or my previous administrative experience, but he *was* interested in my memory. One's creativity tends to suffer, but it can be a considerable advantage to a secretary.'

He nodded as she continued.

'I'm the sort that wins "Mastermind" competitions, but if you asked me to create some original prose, I'd struggle.'

She paused.

'Secondly, he places a great reliance on what he calls my honesty. I suppose he connects it with the fact that I'm a clergyman's daughter. At least, that's what he said at my interview – the fact that I was honest, I mean, not that I was a clergyman's daughter. He said he was impressed by the way in which I was completely open with him in my answers to every question.'

She frowned and felt suddenly flustered. She looked down at her lap.

'What's the third reason?' asked Calder.

'Ah, well, that's even more embarrassing,' she said, looking down at her napkin again. When she looked up her expression was set in mock arrogance.

'Being a typical male chauvinist pig like yourself, he prefers a secretary who is reasonably good-looking.' She hesitated. 'He likes my legs.'

Calder laughed out loud. Several people from near-by tables turned to look.

'Did he tell you that?' he asked.

'No,' she answered primly. 'That is my surmise.'

He couldn't help smiling. 'He's right though,' he said.

'About my legs?'

'No. About being open and honest.'

He smiled again and she stuck her tongue out.

Just then the waiter came over to take their order, already carrying the wine. By the time the coffee came they were into their second bottle.

'So,' he was saying, 'after graduating you became a career civil servant?'

She nodded.

'And how did you come to apply to be the General's secretary?'

'Oh, you don't apply for that sort of job. They pick you. I suppose I should consider myself lucky.'

She looked at the far side of the room. She wanted him to be unsure as to whether she was kidding or not, and she was getting that feeling again whenever he looked at her. But that was the second time he had brought the conversation round to the Department. It was almost as if he wanted to keep off any topic that recognized anything more than a sexual relationship between them. Well, perhaps he was right. She was acting like a schoolgirl again.

He was fondling his beard – a characteristic he had, she'd noticed, whenever a thought suddenly struck him.

'What is it?' she asked.

'You're going to think I'm very slow,' he said, 'but I've just realized why, in the two times we've been out together, you've never asked me about my past.'

She was smiling defensively.

'Why should that be of interest?'

'You already know,' he continued as if she hadn't spoken. 'You've read my file.'

'On the contrary,' she said, smiling genuinely to take the edge off her previous statement, 'most things – probably the most important things, in fact – are not on your file. You can't expect an official document to tell a great deal about a person's character.'

He could have used a lot of predictable lines at that point, but he didn't and she loved him for it. Instead, as she looked across, his mouth formed into an ironical smile and he turned his eyes away. It was a gesture that he performed often and she loved that too.

'I believe that you have rather taken my breath away,' he said, still smiling.

She linked into the role he expected of her.

'Don't say that. It could have disastrous consequences.'

They smiled conspiratorially across the table.

'You have a point,' he said. 'We're wasting time.'

'I thought that was all you could do until Sir Giles returned – wait.'

He was rescued by the waiter, who appeared silently at his elbow. His English was heavily accented.

'Excusa me, sir. Mr Calder?'

'Yes.'

'Telephone for you, sir.'

'It's Striker,' said Calder to Ann. 'I gave him this number.'

She smiled benignly. He walked over to the bar and picked up the phone.

'Matthew Calder here.'

'Matthew, Peter. Sorry to call you there, but I didn't know what time you'd be getting back.'

Calder felt a pang of guilt. Here he was, wining and dining, while his partner was flogging his guts out down at Scotland Yard.

'That's all right,' answered Calder innocently.

'Besides,' continued Striker, 'I thought it might be, you know, a bit difficult if I rang you at home later.'

'What have you got?' said Calder quickly.

'Well, according to the computer there have been very few thefts of the items on your list. Not much dough in them. There may have been some more but some of the items are so trivial that the theft might not have been reported. However, two I have unearthed, after considerable sweat and sandwiches.'

Calder felt that pang again. Striker really knew how to rub it in.

'What a lucky man I am to have an assistant who is so diligent.

Are you going to give me the information, or am I to bribe you for it with an Italian meal?'

Striker guffawed.

'No, thanks. Italian food's too fattening. I'll settle for a night out at The Blue Lady. Do you know, when this is all over, I might even get a discount on next year's membership.'

'You're on. Now, Peter – the information?'

'Oh, yeah. Well, a fairly large quantity of baratol went missing from an engineering firm in Peterborough about two and a half weeks ago and, the day before, so did a double-beam oscilloscope from Aston University in Birmingham. While they were there, they also filched some electrical circuitry.'

Calder's mind was racing.

'Incidentally,' continued Striker, 'a small firm specializing in metal-spinning was broken into, just as you suggested. Two nights ago. I've only just discovered it, as it's not yet on the computer. The oddest thing is that nothing was stolen. At least it was odd to the local cops. The only way the owner knew anyone had been inside was because he read the electricity meter before leaving on the Saturday and made a note of the numbers. Always does, apparently, God knows what for. Parsimony, I suppose. Anyway, the place was closed on Sunday, but when he came to check the meter on Monday morning, he was surprised to find that rather a lot of juice had been used. Especially since they had a lighter day than usual.

'He asked all his workers whether they had noticed anything odd in the morning. One operator said that he "felt" – I quote that word specifically from the police report – there was something different about his mechanism that morning. You know, the odd shaving in the corner and the blob of metal where he didn't usually let it fall. It had occurred to him that it might have been used, but he thought that he was being stupid, so he hadn't mentioned it. The owner phoned the police yesterday evening and that's all I know.'

Calder's heart was beating unnaturally quickly.

'Where was this, Peter?'

'Oh, sorry. Felixstowe. Ring any bells?'

'No.'

'Me neither.'

'Birmingham, Peterborough and Felixstowe,' said Calder. 'I

wonder whether they have anything in common. They must do. It's too much coincidence otherwise. I certainly feel that the Felixstowe thing is what we're after. It has their stamp about it. If it is them, it means they're not as far advanced in their construction as I thought. We need to know more.'

'I was wondering whether I should go down there and scout around, in my usual unobtrusive way,' said Striker.

'Yes, would you, Peter? Have a word with the owner especially. You've got the info' on the implosion assembly. Ask him whether this machine is capable of spinning that. If it is, put something under the local law and get them to do a thorough fingerprint job and search. I doubt whether they'll get anything, but it's worth a try.'

'OK, pardner,' said Striker in Western drawl.

'Do you think there will be anything more on that list?' asked Calder.

'Frankly, no, but I'll put one of my buddies on it while I'm away.'

Calder smiled to himself. 'If I were you, Peter, I shouldn't go till morning.'

'That's very gracious of you, sir. You mean I can actually get some sleep?'

'I think so,' said Calder grudgingly. 'Just enough to recharge the old batteries.'

'Yes, sir,' answered Striker, in true military style. Calder could imagine him standing to attention at the other end with hand tapping forehead.

'The General not back yet?'

'No,' said Calder a little too abruptly. 'Anyway, anything else?' 'No.'

'OK, then. Thanks for the information, get a good night's sleep and give me a ring from Felixstowe.'

Calder thanked the manager for the use of his phone and walked back to his table.

'I've paid the bill,' exclaimed Ann proudly.

'I must ask Peter to phone again at appropriate moments,' said Calder.

'It depends what appropriate moments you mean,' she replied and swept past him to the door.

Standing on the pavement, she asked whether Striker had had good news. He hesitated, as if struggling to focus on her question.

'Possibly,' he answered. Then his face came more alive. 'In fact,' he continued, 'it could be a very big lead.'

'You weren't thinking of that though, were you?' she asked perceptively.

He spotted a cruising taxi and pushed his arm out.

'No.'

She continued to look at him.

He turned to her and smiled. Then his face clouded over as he spoke.

'As you said, all we can do now is wait.'

The sun was halfway to its zenith before the mist finally cleared off the water, bathing the yacht station in its light. Dark glasses were imperative, as the river danced in sparkling brilliance. They were certainly necessary if you wanted to see the gulls and terns. These, now that the mist had gone, were coming in for a late breakfast on the rich pickings of the yacht basin.

It was the sort of morning that Tom Arkright liked. Cool at the beginning, then coming awake slowly, until the mist finally cleared and you could take your jacket off, revelling in the sun's warmth. It was like seeing the dawn without having to get up early. It had been a long, harsh winter and it was great to see the good weather setting in at last.

He was standing at the end of one of the many small, floating jetties in the marina, squinting at the birds feeding. The terns were always the most impressive, their acrobatic skill enabling them to judge their descent to the water so perfectly. Even the tiniest crust could be snatched from the surface by their sensitive bills.

He knew that he, too, was being watched. He'd been searching the boats since 8 o'clock that morning, which had caused a lot of indignant protests, especially when it was realized that he wasn't allowing anyone to leave, either on foot or by boat, until all vessels had been investigated. This Emergency Powers Act gave him more weight than he'd ever had before. If they protested, he could just slap them in jail, with no *habeas corpus* to worry about.

Well, he and his four-man team had completed about three-quarters of the boats and he wasn't having his lunch until they'd finished the lot. He knew what they'd be thinking as they stared at his back, but he didn't care. He even took a little sadistic pleasure in making them suffer a bit. Having been Sergeant of Police at the local station for eleven of his forty-four years, he was secure in that position. He knew that these people needed him more than he needed them.

He left the dipping terns and stepped across to the next yacht, on the other side of the jetty. It was a magnificent thing in dark blue called *Gorgon*. He looked at the checklist that the marina Superintendent had given him. Berth 95, *Gorgon*, owned by Mr D. Stephens, 13 Keit Road, Paddington, London. A young man, who had been coiling ropes on the foredeck, came along the side.

'Morning, Sergeant,' he called happily.

The accent, Tom noted, was just like that of the others – southern.

'Sorry to bother you, sir, but as you 'ave probably gathered, we're asking people if we can search their boats.'

'I'm not the owner,' said Jerry, 'but I'm sure he wouldn't mind. Come aboard. What are you looking for?'

Tom stepped on to the vessel carefully. He still hadn't got used to clomping about in Wellington boots on a boat. The owner of the first yacht had lent them to him so that he wouldn't mark the nice paintwork on the other boats, but they were too small and cramped his feet.

'I'd rather not say, if you don't mind, sir,' answered Tom seriously.

He stepped into the cockpit-well and looked into the main cabin. A special hollow compartment above the keel, they'd said. Even he knew what a keel was. He looked at the figure in T-shirt and denim shorts.

'I wonder whether you'd mind if I 'ad a look at your bilges?'

Not a flicker of anxiety crossed the young man's face.

'Sure,' he replied, and bent down to remove the wooden floor and duckboards.

Tom, too, bent down and examined the fibreglass. It was quite clear, from the stains and consistency of the worn appearance of the surface, that there were no joins and no hollow compartments.

In fact it looked just like every other bloody keel he had examined that morning, except the two where he had actually had to wait while they pumped the water out.

He stood up, surprised that he could rise to his full height of six foot four.

'That's fine, sir. Thank you very much. I'm afraid you won't be able to leave until we've checked everyone, though.'

He smiled for the first time.

'That's OK,' replied the young man merrily.

Tom, somewhat disappointed, levered himself out of the cabin and steadied himself in the well, preparatory to stepping on to the jetty. He could never sail on one of these things.

'Sergeant?' asked Jerry, who had silently appeared beside him: 'What would have happened if I had not invited you on board?'

His face was beaming innocently. Tom walked on to the gunwale and jumped from the boat before turning.

'You couldn't 'ave 'eard. Per'aps you've been away.'

Jerry said nothing.

'Don't you know there's been plutonium 'ijacking?'

'Yes, I did hear something about it,' answered Jerry with difficulty.

'Aye, well, Parliament passed Emergency Powers Act so we'd 'ave no trouble finding it. I can walk into any 'ouse, or boat, with or without owner's permission.'

Tom turned and walked up to the ketch moored alongside.

Jerry shrugged and moved back into the cabin. He'd done a good job on that keel, even if he did say so himself. Brown had insisted, in the weeks beforehand, that he develop a skill with fibreglass, and he could only now really appreciate why. Even if you got down on your hands and knees, the crack was totally undetectable, and he liked the work he had done wearing in the new glass so that it merged with the rest. Brown had inspected it. His respect for that man went up another notch.

He replaced the duckboards and flooring, then opened the door to the for'ard cabin. Judy, a sheet held to her throat, looked up, wide-eyed.

'It's all right,' he said, 'he was as thick as he was tall.'

She had arrived in the night and made him swear he wouldn't

tell Brown. He had agreed, then, and it would be a terrible shame when he did phone. But he knew where his priorities lay.

He looked at the shape under the thin sheet. There was no hurry. He couldn't leave the marina yet anyway. He'd phone this afternoon. All he could do now was wait.

Calder had spent all day reading on the construction of an atom bomb, plus Glasstone's book, *The Effects of Nuclear Weapons*. It was depressing and, although he had read it before, it frightened him more this time. Then, it had been theoretical; now it was a possibility.

Feeling the need for a return to sanity, he wanted to phone Ann and get her to come round. But he knew he couldn't. Not only was he expecting a call from Stoddard or Striker, but he had to be prepared to move immediately. He didn't think that Ann would be too happy at being interrupted in the middle of an embrace. She still hadn't forgiven him for letting Striker know the number of the restaurant. He smiled at a memory of the night before. That was better.

He was worried about the General, though. Two whole days and not a word. This waiting was making him pensive, but what else could he do?

As Brown drove to the marina, the sun was well down on the horizon. It had been a glorious day, with just a gentle breeze to prevent the air from becoming muggy. The leaves on the trees seemed to have grown greener and longer, just in one short day.

None of this was on Brown's mind, however. He treated the weather very philosophically. Since it was something over which he had no control, it was not worth bothering with. If it rained, it rained. If it was a fine day, then good, but since there had been no achievement in it for him, there was no real enjoyment. Harnessing the weather for one's own purposes, though, that was different. That was why he liked sailing so much. But he gained no pleasure from a fine day, as such, just as he didn't care whether England won the World Cup.

No, Brown was reflecting on the second and most difficult part of the operation so far: the period of the bomb's construction. It was the most difficult stage because the team was largely inactive and therefore fretful. What was more, he had tipped his hand with the hijacking, yet he could not move again until the bomb was completed.

Of course Vaisey had been right when he had said that most of the bomb's construction should have taken place before the hijack, to save time, and it was a pity that they'd had to commit themselves when they did. But it was unavoidable. Vaisey, being a scientist – albeit a very good one – couldn't understand the problem of keeping a team of men, already keyed-up, waiting around for six weeks or so until the next plutonium delivery, even if it might have been by road – rather easier to hijack. There had also been the problem of the security guard. There was always the risk of his making a slip; and the longer they were to hold on to the hostages, the greater the likelihood became.

Anyway, the construction had gone smoothly and quickly, and there was still no sign that the authorities had any mark on them, though they obviously had a smart boy on it. All yachts above the keel, Jerry had said. Perhaps they had already made the mental jump to 'non-foreign', which might cut the search time down. He must work on the assumption that they had.

However, he was sure, for a variety of reasons, that the bomb would be completed in time. Three to four days more had been Vaisey's last estimate earlier that day, for connecting up and final testing. Say another two days to allow for complications. That meant six days at the very outside, which would take them through to Tuesday.

He had kept out of the scientist's way and let him work at his own pace. A lesser man would have felt a compulsion to hurry him. But men like Vaisey formulated their own timetables, which were anyway horrendous. They worked as hard as they could because their work was their *raison d'être*. They had very little else to live for.

Vaisey had just completed what he had described as the 'trickiest' part of the whole construction, the shaping of the thirteen explosive lenses. He had designed them some time before apparently, when he and Caren had built the simultaneous detonation system. He'd had to use baratol, an explosive that could be cast very precisely, which was essential; but it was difficult to work with, especially since each lens had to be so finely shaped and identical to the others. But he had managed it, as Brown had known he would. He had been right about Vaisey.

His only real mistake was Judy. He had been more worried than he cared to show on discovering her missing. He knew why she had gone, and it wasn't to inform the authorities. But he had, nevertheless, been relieved when Jerry had rung. She might have blabbed to someone. He had called the search parties off, but she would have to be got rid of. Pity, she was such a good lay. Anyway, he couldn't do it yet. It would be bad for morale. He would have to keep her locked up for a week, though, while they waited for Vaisey. All he could do now was keep on waiting.

Chapter 13

Thursday, 15 May

The phone bell woke Calder immediately. He peered at his watch. 4.55 a.m. He'd found difficulty in sleeping and had only been under for about three hours. Quickly, he slipped out of bed, donned his dressing-gown, walked out of the bedroom, through the lounge and into the hall. The bell had rung ten times when he picked up the receiver.

'Hello,' he said, a little surprised at the huskiness in his voice.

The earpiece barked at him.

'Sorry to get you up so early. Can you come round?'

'General?' He suddenly felt very alert and realized that he hadn't stopped thinking about it, even when he was asleep.

'Yes.'

'Tell first.'

There was silence at the other end. Then:

'I've got him.'

Calder made himself relax. 'Your place?' he asked.

'Yes, do you know where it is?'

'No.'

Stoddard proceeded to give the address and directions.

'I'll be there in thirty minutes,' said Calder and put the phone down.

It was just getting light when he rang the General's door-bell. Stoddard, fully dressed in crumpled, grey suit and unshaven, opened the door wide. In the dim, overhead light from the hall he looked terribly tired. This impression was far from dispelled when Stoddard had ushered him into an immaculate and large room that was more brightly lit. He stared at the older man.

'If you'll forgive my saying so, General, you don't look too well.' Stoddard tried to smile.

'Thank you for your concern. I've only had a couple of hours' sleep since I last saw you, but I'm too much on tenterhooks to feel it at the moment.'

And it was true that there was a sort of faint ebullience about him, despite the large loops under his eyes and the general pallor of his skin.

'Coffee?' asked Stoddard, walking over to a mahogany bar.

Calder gave a soulful sigh, the meaning of which would have been apparent to anyone. Stoddard began to pour from the percolator.

'Help yourself to milk and sugar,' he said and walked over to a large, low, glass table set by a grey-brick fireplace.

'I'd only just got back when I called you,' he said and began to sip his coffee, gazing down at the mass of papers on the table.

Two things were clear to Calder as he spooned sugar into his cup. First, the General's mental powers were not up to par. He was behaving like a man in a dream. Besides, his pipe was nowhere to be seen. And, second, this in itself added to the sense of unreality he felt about the whole scene. The fact that it was so early didn't help. Was he really going to hear about the man who, in his imagination, had dominated his waking and sleeping thoughts for nearly a week? God, it was still only five and a half days. His attention was drawn to the table.

'John Brown,' said Stoddard suddenly. 'John Brown.' He looked up at Calder. 'Ironic, isn't it?' he said, then looked down again.

Calder felt unable to speak.

'Well, he isn't,' continued Stoddard absently.

The younger man thought that he ought to try and get in on the wavelength somewhere.

'Isn't what?' he asked, equally absently.

'Mouldering in his grave,' said the General. 'Far from it. Brilliant man.'

He looked up.

'That's what really made me certain about him. Sorry, I'm forgetting my manners. Please sit down.'

'I'm fine, thank you.'

'It was, I must confess, a difficult job,' continued Stoddard before Calder had finished speaking. 'I won't bore you with the technical problems I had in getting my hands on the records in the first place. I decided to go back three years and was prepared to go back further if necessary. I had the dates of the robberies, of course, which meant that it was pointless, working on the assumption that they were committed by our boys, to go any further forward. That gave me a period of about eighteen months, during which time a great many officers and men left the Army.'

Stoddard took another sip of his coffee, placed it on the fireplace and put both hands in his trouser pockets in a most unmilitary-like way.

'I concentrated on the enlisted men, to see if I could see a pattern in a particular regiment. I couldn't. Wasted a whole half-day. It wasn't until I began dissecting each regiment into its companies, and looking at that level, that I struck pay-dirt, so to speak.'

He looked up, as if surprised by his own use of the vernacular.

'A bit of luck really. It was fairly early on my list, but then I needed some luck at that stage. Examining this regiment,' he held up an insignia and Calder raised his eyebrows, 'I noticed that two companies had rather higher levels of leaving than the rest. That in itself is nothing unusual. Indeed, it's one of the things that is looked at anyway, as a check to find where the problem companies are. But one of them was particularly high around this period and not at any other time, whereas the other had a consistently high leaving record, stretching back over many years. What's more, the first company had a disproportionate number of "lifers" who bought themselves out.'

Stoddard was animated now.

'I didn't expect anything so obvious as their release money all coming from the same source, but I checked anyway. What I found was that some had paid cash. Since it amounts to a large sum of money, this would be unusual even for one, but when it turned out to be three within the space of six weeks I knew I was on to something.

'The key, though, was the officer, or officers. Once I'd found him, the rest would fall into place. Ignoring the others who had left and concentrating on the three cash-payers, I unearthed all the officers they had been associated with. Our man stood out a mile. I found him even before I learnt that he'd left about a year before the others. All three were under him for some time. Captain John Brown.'

He looked up.

'Actually, there was another possible: a lieutenant under Brown's command – Cosmo Binge.'

He shook his head.

'I later found that he died in a car accident two years ago. The Army is no place for a man with a name like that.'

He shook his head again.

'Sorry, being callous. Anyway,' he leant down to the table and picked up a buff folder, 'when I read this file, I became convinced that Brown was our man. I think I would have picked him out even if he hadn't had the connections.'

Stoddard waved his hand.

'I don't need to tell you,' he said, 'that we are not just looking for an average Sandhurst "hocker".'

He walked over to Calder and handed him the file. Calder put down his cup and glanced at the pages as the General continued.

'Although a little old-fashioned, Sandhurst is still one of the best military schools in the world. But I've always believed that leaders, like musicians, are more born than made and certainly before the tender age of sixteen. I was looking for someone who was not just good at his job, but very good, nay, brilliant. But more than that. He also had to be an outsider. This is a rogue elephant, don't forget.'

'A rare combination,' mused Calder.

Stoddard looked up quickly, clearly not expecting to be interrupted.

'What do you mean?' he demanded.

Calder regretted his interjection.

'Someone who is good at his job is usually acceptable by definition. To a large extent, you have to behave the way people above you expect in order to reach the top of the ladder yourself. There are exceptions, of course.' Calder smiled.

'Exactly,' replied Stoddard, who clearly thought he was one of the exceptions. 'Brown has both these . . . qualities. He was a brilliant officer. Of that there is no doubt. Cadet of the year at Sandhurst and he holds something of a regimental record from when he was a lieutenant, largely for the success of his platoons on manoeuvres. He is also, by the way, a crack shot.

'The rogue-elephant side of his nature doesn't come out in the report. I had to talk with some of his old chums for that. To say that he was unpopular with junior officers would be an understatement. Two showed open hostility when they realized that I was no longer serving and they could tell me the truth. One of them refused to say why he disliked him, even after I started to hint at dire threats.'

Stoddard looked at Calder with surprise on his face, as if he found it difficult to believe that a subordinate officer would openly defy him.

'Anyway, I decided to interview some enlisted men while I was there and it's a complete contrast. I could only find a few who were still about, but they all remembered him and spoke of him with affection. One of them, then a private, now a sergeant, said that he was the best officer he had ever served under.'

The General looked up again.

'A leader of men, Calder. And someone who does not suffer fools gladly. More coffee?'

The bearded man shook his head.

'Anyway, just to make sure I had the right man, I continued to check, in the other companies and regiments. I had a team of helpers by this time and it was easier. We came across a few possibilities, but they were all blind alleys. One of them turned out to be the manager of a Rochdale furniture store, with a wife and four children. It was pointless. As I've already said, there was only really one possibility. I was just being excessively careful. No, Brown's our man. I feel it.'

He stopped and looked intently at the man reading the file. Seeing no opposition, he continued.

'Being sure of that, I checked on all men serving in his company, in addition to those I already knew. As you can imagine, I came up with quite a list. I converted them into an "A" list and a "B" list, according to how long they served under Brown and how close they were to him. Only a small number of list "A", to say nothing of list "B", will be in his band, of course, working on the assumption that not every man who leaves the Army is a crook.'

He glanced wryly at Calder. This time the younger man looked up from Brown's file and smiled.

'So far I haven't checked any of them except Brown. Both his parents died when he was seven and his only known relative is an elderly rich aunt at Shrewsbury who brought him up. She's not there. None of the neighbours know where she is. Haven't seen her for months apparently. Brown, of course, is also nowhere to be found.'

Stoddard walked over to the mantelpiece and drained his coffee. Suddenly he felt very tired indeed. He took his cup over to the bar and refilled it.

'No photo, I'm afraid,' he said. 'It's at the Department being duplicated. So are the snaps of some of the others that I'm sure of. Within two hours they will be distributed to every police force in the country.'

His guest, he noticed, was not reading the file in front of him any more, but looking ahead without focusing.

'You're right,' said Calder. 'This is our man.'

Stoddard said nothing. Calder placed the file on the table and picked up his coffee before continuing.

'We'll have to handle the investigation and arrests ourselves.'

'Already being done,' interrupted Stoddard quickly. 'Sorry, I should have told you. No point in secrecy now. Jensen, my deputy, is setting up a team. I'm taking all these files round to the Department when we've finished.

Calder nodded. 'Who, or what, do you expect to find?'

'What do you mean?' intoned Stoddard, in a way that implied he knew the answer.

Calder fingered his beard.

'I hope this isn't deflating, General, and I hope I'm wrong, but I don't think that sort of investigation is guaranteed success.'

Calder drained his coffee and walked over to the percolator.

'I think,' he continued, 'that our man . . . Brown, will have foreseen this eventuality – that his identity might be discovered and, consequently, that of his men.'

Stoddard said nothing – just gazed myopically at Calder.

'He couldn't possibly risk dispersal after the hijack for that reason. Oh, we'll find plenty from your lists, but they won't be the ones we want.'

He paused for longer this time. Stoddard was nodding at the floor. Finally he spoke.

'I knew before I phoned you that you were going to say that. That's why I got you over.'

He grinned crookedly, before continuing.

'But I'm not as depressed about it as all that. His gang may be in hiding with him, but we might find some evidence – from their lodgings, a relative, a lover – as to where their hideaway may be.'

Calder hesitated again and sipped his coffee.

'I hope so,' he said, 'but I think Brown is far too clever to have allowed any of his men to know where they were going. On the other hand, he can't think of everything. You may be right. There could be some clues.'

He didn't sound hopeful. Then his right fist hit his left palm, the sound filling the room.

'Christ, Calder, be positive,' he said viciously to himself and began to pace up and down the long room.

Stoddard, despite the loud slap, felt that his brain had ceased to function. He saw Calder stop, place a bent forefinger into his mouth and bite on it. It was a gesture Stoddard would never have imagined him performing. Calder was speaking.

'Was there anything else – in your conversations with his friends in the mess? No clues as to where he spent his holidays or who he wrote to? Did he have a girlfriend, for example?'

Stoddard shook his head. He felt wretched.

'He kept very much to himself, apparently.'

He looked at Calder in sympathy. He remembered an officer – the only one who seemed to get on with Brown – saying that he used to feel sorry for him.

'One of his fellow officers said he never received any letters, even though he used to write quite a lot himself. Never said where he went on leave either. Always used to go to Paddington first, though, apparently.'

Stoddard paused, thinking.

'But the London station for Aldershot is Waterloo, isn't it?' he asked.

'Yes,' said Calder, whose brain was racing.

'Paddington,' he said. 'Paddington again. Didn't the security officer's wife say something about sending something to Paddington?'

'Yes,' answered Stoddard, suddenly alert.

'How did he know?' asked Calder absently.

'Who?'

'The officer.'

'Oh, I didn't ask. I can easily get in touch again.'

Calder was nodding, still pacing the room, his head bowed. Stoddard noticed that although he was clearly totally absorbed with his thoughts, the number of steps he took was the same in each direction, each leg turning at exactly the same spot every time.

'I think you may have something here, General. And why should he write a lot of letters and not get any back? Nobody's that unpopular.'

He stopped suddenly and appeared to look intently at the huge, copper chimney that rose from the kitchen area.

'It might not be the station at all,' he said. 'I wonder whether it's an accommodation address? Somewhere that Brown might use as a sort of clearing-house. It would certainly account for the fact that he received no letters.'

'It's a possibility,' said Stoddard, enthusiastically.

'He might not use his own name, of course,' continued Calder.

He turned from the chimney and looked at the General.

'But if we had his photograph . . . providing he didn't disguise himself.'

He punched his left palm again.

'We won't get anywhere worrying about it. I need to contact Striker. Can I use your phone?'

Stoddard held out his hand.

'There's an extension on the bar,' he said.

Calder walked over to it, but turned to the General before he lifted the receiver.

'Striker was in Felixstowe yesterday, interviewing people about a metal-spinning firm that was broken into. I'm certain it was used by Brown and whoever is making the bomb for him.'

He began to dial.

'I'm also hopeful that two important materials needed for the bomb's construction were stolen from Birmingham and Peterborough.'

Calder looked at Stoddard again as he waited for the connection. The grey-haired man was holding his coffee cup very limply and his expression of interest had gone. The bell began to ring at the other end. The General looked like what he was – a man on the brink of total mental exhaustion.

'I'll give you the details later,' said Calder and didn't think that he'd been heard.

A strangled voice answered.

'Peter? Will you get round to the Department as soon as you can? ... Yes, I know I am, but we may be on to something ... Because you're crazy about me ...'

Calder laughed out loud and replaced the receiver. As he walked towards Stoddard, the older man looked up quickly, as if awakening from a deep thought, or from sleep. He smiled crookedly again, waved at the mass of buff files on the table, and said:

'I'd better get these round to the Department.'

Then he turned to the door.

'No, General,' said Calder, stopping him in his tracks. 'You're not going anywhere except to bed.'

Stoddard's perplexed expression turned to one of hostility as he rounded on the younger man.

'Since when did you start giving me orders?'

Calder's face relaxed into a smile. His voice was gentle.

'Since now. You've worked miracles in coming up with this information in two days. You're dead on your feet and you know it. I'll be perfectly frank with you, General. You're no good to me at the moment. Your mind isn't working and it's not going to start up again until you get some sleep.'

Stoddard had softened a little, but Calder could still feel a sense of duty.

'Does Jensen know of me?' asked Calder.

'Yes, but only vaguely.'

Calder was still smiling, enjoying himself, as he spoke.

'Since my position is somewhat temporary, I don't need to worry about prospects of promotion. Your orders, General, are as follows. First, you pick up that phone and tell Jensen all about me and my status. He and I are going to have to work together today. Second, you leave the phone off the hook. I shall tell Jensen you are not to be disturbed except in an absolute emergency and I shall call on you when I need you. I shall then deliver these files to Jensen myself and we can get the investigation going. Third, you go to bed, don't set the alarm and sleep until you wake naturally.'

Stoddard finally relented. 'I suppose you're right.'

He looked at Calder fiercely, but there was no hostility in his eyes. The younger man merely grinned at him.

'You'd better get going then,' said Stoddard as he walked towards the telephone.

Calder grabbed the files and made to leave, hesitating in the doorway. Stoddard stopped dialling.

'Don't worry,' he said, trying not to smile. 'I'll go to bed.'

Calder grinned again and let himself out. The General continued to dial.

There were eleven known accommodation addresses in the Paddington area. Calder and Striker had drawn a blank at eight. It was 5.40 p.m. and they were stopped outside a TV rental store, watching the start of the BBC evening news. The manager always kept the shop open until 6 p.m., in hopes of catching the rush-hour pedestrian traffic, and he always kept some sets on to attract the cathode junkies after their harsh day of reality.

Brown's face suddenly appeared on the screen, then that of five others, who Jensen was by now fairly sure were his accomplices. Calder couldn't hear what was being said, but he didn't need to. Jensen had decided to release the names and photographs and claim that they were wanted in connection with the plutonium hijacking. It was a calculated gamble and there were good arguments against it.

To begin with, Jensen had had to seek the Minister's permission. The news of the hijacking was ten days old, and the newspapers and television (and consequently the public) had begun to forget about it. Advertising Brown and his cronies on TV would bring the whole thing back into public focus again. There was also the possibility that the advertising might force the hijackers underground, where it would be more difficult to find them. It had been argued by someone on Jensen's staff, moreover, that the advertising might make them more desperate, because it would indicate to them and, most importantly, to Brown, that they could never work in the country again. Calder had been impressed by that argument, even though he considered that Brown would already have worked it out.

But eventually he had come down in favour of the publicity. To begin with, someone *might* recognize them. And, it might panic them a little and slow them down. Brown might have worked out that he could never live in this country again, but the others might not have. They might, for example, decide to disperse. That might, paradoxically, make it easier to find one of them and therefore Brown as well, than if they all stayed hidden away in some retreat.

The picture switched back to Brown again and for the umpteenth time that day Calder reflected on how ordinary he looked. The only indications of the sort of man that lay behind this rather boring countenance were the eyes. They were brown and small, and gave just a hint of the mind lurking behind them. It was nothing that Calder could put his finger on, but he felt that they acted as a kind of calculated trigger for the rest of the face to come alive. Army photographs were not exactly known for their artistic qualities.

Calder jabbed Striker on the shoulder and they moved off along the grimy street. He wondered why it was that road-sweepers didn't seem to work as hard in inner London as they did in the suburbs. Perhaps it was just that people dropped more litter. Another one of the hidden effects of urban deprivation. The problem, he knew, was timeless; the absolute poverty of the late eighteenth and nineteenth centuries being replaced by the relative poverty of the twentieth. He also knew that there was no panacea, no sudden solution. Then he stopped in his tracks. He didn't like the way his thoughts were going, so he looked around for a street sign.

'This is it,' said Striker accommodatingly, looking up from his 'A–Z'.

Calder raised his head to the surprisingly bright sign plugged into the wall, set at right angles to their direction. It read 'Keit Road'.

'Yes,' said Calder. 'What number do we want?'

'Thirteen.'

They turned right, into the road, and saw the group of shops immediately, across and to the left. As they approached, Calder picked out number 13 – the first in line, beside the hairdressers. A rusted, red and yellow Goldflake sign was nailed to the side brickwork.

Any pretence the shop might once have had to being painted green had long since gone. There was more bare wood than paint and such of the latter that had survived was flaked and dull, although it was more green than any other colour. The sign on the frontispiece, in big black letters, said 'E M Powne' and, in smaller letters, from corner to corner, it had once read 'Newsagent, Confectioner and Tobacconist'. But the letters, in parts, had gone and some others were badly faded, so that it actually said '. . . . agent, .onfectioner and To. .c. .nist'. Magazines were pinned to boards in both windows. Behind one window some Ronson lighters, of incongruously modern design, were on display. In the other were pipes of numerous types, several maps and various bric-à-brac. The sign on the door said 'Open'. Striker pushed it and a real bell clattered above his head.

There were no customers inside the dingy shop – just a weasely-looking man standing behind the counter. Unless he was standing in a hole, he couldn't have been more than five feet two inches tall. He had a receding hairline, a thin face with large ears and a pointed nose. The eyes were anonymous. He was dressed in a studded, striped shirt, without the collar, and a far from clean, grey waistcoat, unbuttoned. The expression on his face was one of abject misery. He knew who they were and they couldn't be anything but bad news.

Calder looked around. The counter on his left was devoted wholly to tobacco, including brands that he thought had long since vacated the market. Powne had to be a bit of a specialist. To his right was the confectionery, the chocolate laid out on the counter, and the 'bullseyes' and 'candy twists' filling huge jars on the shelves behind. Calder had thought that this type of shop had long since gone out of business, but today had opened his mind. He wondered if Powne still weighed 'peardrops' by the quarter. Turning, he saw that the space behind each window, on either side of the door, was taken up with maps. There was quite a collection, including two full racks of Ordnance Surveys. The place had an order to it, although it could have done with a clean. He turned back to see Striker holding his false identification wallet across the newspapers and magazines.

'Special Branch,' he said.

The little man's face brightened a little. He now just looked miserable. Calder thought he probably knew that Special Branch were usually more gentle than the uniformed lot.

'Yus, guv, what can I do you for?'

The voice was moderately confident.

'We understand that you act as an accommodation address,' said Striker.

The man paused warily.

'What's a Yank doin' in Special Branch?'

'Answer the question,' said Calder quickly.

Powne blinked rapidly.

'Yes, I do do it,' he said, 'occasionally, for a few selected customers.'

'Ever been used by a man named Brown?' asked Striker.

The man hesitated again.

'Now look, fellas, this is private stuff, you know. I mean, people are intitled to their privacy, ain't they?'

As soon as he'd said it the little man appeared to realize his mistake. He looked down and began to fiddle with a large, leather-bound book in front of him. Then he looked up at Striker. The blond man took one deliberate step forward. Powne took one quick step back.

'I hope you're not going to give us any trouble, Powne,' said Striker, pausing for effect. 'You do realize, don't you, that I can throw you in jail and have my men ... *search* the place?'

The small man appeared to sigh. 'No Browns,' he said.

'Are you sure?'

'Positive, honest.'

'Show me your book,' said Striker.

Powne bit his lip. Calder noticed that his front teeth protruded.

'I don't keep one. I know I should, but I ain't never got round to it. I've got 'em all in me 'ead anyway. Honest.'

'Very well,' said Striker impatiently, 'ever get any from Aldershot? And don't tell me you never look at the postmark.'

The little man was thinking.

'I might 'ave 'ad,' he said dangerously.

Striker hesitated. Then he pulled out his wallet and extracted two £5 notes. He held them up between forefinger and thumb.

'This is just to demonstrate our good will,' said Striker. 'But it can rapidly disappear if we don't get the truth.'

Powne looked at the money and really did lick his lips. He appeared to make up his mind.

'Yus, I used to receive letters from Aldershot. Quite a lot at one time. None now though, that I can fink of.'

'How long ago would that be?' asked Striker carefully.

'Oh, about two, three, four year ago.'

Calder felt his heartbeat quicken. Just about the time when Brown would have been recruiting.

'And who were they addressed to?' continued Striker.

'A geezer named Stephens – D. Stephens, with a ph. Now, do I get the money?'

Striker turned to look at Calder. The latter was afraid to say anything, just in case he broke the spell and woke up. Instead, he extracted four more fivers of his own and passed them over to Striker. The little man watched this silent performance, licking his lips again and pulling his nose.

'I might have some more for you,' said Striker, smiling and fanning out what was now a set of six.

Just then the door-bell clanged. Calder and Striker swung round instinctively. A huddled figure in mottled pink coat and red slippers shuffled past them to the counter, head bowed. She could have been anything from forty to sixty-five years of age. Powne was quick to recover.

'Evenin', Mrs P,' he said, handing over an *Evening Standard*.

He took no money.

'Go carefully now,' he added.

She turned and walked out. The door clanged shut. She had

said nothing and appeared not even to have noticed the two extra men.

Striker realized that he was still holding up the six £5 notes and cleared his throat. The little man seemed to sense that, for the moment, he had the upper hand.

'You were saying?' he said to Striker rather carelessly.

Calder stepped forward and held out a photograph of Brown.

'That the man?' he asked.

Powne looked at it for several seconds, then at Calder. He then looked at the money, still held up in Striker's hand, and back to the photograph again. Finally, he looked at Calder and bit his lip.

'I take it you want me to tell the truth, like?' he asked.

'Yes.'

The little man took a deep breath.

'Well, I don't know is the truth. 'E always wore dark glasses – even in the winter. Yeh, 'e wore an 'at an' all. You know, one o' those floppy fishin' 'ats.'

He hesitated.

'I suppose it could be 'im,' he said finally.

'How big is he?' asked Calder, remembering that Brown was six feet two.

'About your size. Per'aps a bit taller. 'E was a big fella.'

Calder reasoned that anyone over five feet six inches was probably big to Powne. He also noticed that the little man was using the past tense.

'When was the last time Stephens came?' asked Calder.

'Oh, a long time ago now. In the last year or so someone else 'as collected 'is mail for 'im. 'E's much smaller than Stephens. 'E 'as dark glasses an' all, an' a bobble 'at. In fact, 'e came in last week. Can't remember what day. 'E 'ad a beard, I remember distinctly.'

'Why do you remember distinctly?' asked Calder.

' 'Cause 'e bought a map, didn't 'e?'

'He bought a map,' repeated Calder moronically.

He was going to look at Striker, then changed his mind.

'What map?' he said desperately.

Powne was looking perplexedly at the money, which now appeared to be clasped rather too firmly in the blond man's hand.

'Er, a map o' Norfolk,' said the little man, still staring at the money.

Calder felt his heart miss a beat and forced himself to keep his voice steady.

'Of all of Norfolk?' he asked.

'No, it was one of the Ordnance Surveys over there,' pointing.

'How do you know it was of Norfolk?' persisted Calder.

'Because I saw where 'e took it from, didn't I? – the top o' the second row on the right. That's Norfolk,' said Powne indignantly.

There was a silence while Striker turned and looked at Calder. Neither spoke, until Striker asked:

'Why did you happen to notice that he took that particular map?'

'Look, what is this, the Inquisition?' said Powne, rather too confidently. 'I've answered your questions, ain't I, and I ain't got no money yet?'

Calder stepped forward and fixed the little man with a long stare. The latter turned away eventually and his hand began to shake on the book.

'No offence meant,' said Powne, suddenly very defensive.

'My friend asked you a question,' asked Calder quietly.

'Well, if you'd bin takin' in letters an' parcels for a man for six years, who always took the trouble to disguise 'imself before 'e came in, wouldn't you take an interest in anyone who collected 'is mail for 'im?'

Calder nodded.

'I rather think I would,' he said.

'In fact,' continued Powne, 'I could tell you exactly which map it was, if you like.'

The little man was obviously trying to redeem himself. He glanced at the money, still firmly clasped in Striker's hand, and looked at Calder.

'I keep the complete set of OS maps, as you can see,' pointing again.

This time Calder turned to look at the maps he had already noticed. He thought that Powne probably took some pride in the mauve display.

'There were a few other gaps,' continued the now generous

Powne, 'so when this geezer bought this Norfolk map – I only keep one o' places like that – I decided to do some reorderin'. I wrote down the numbers o' the ones I needed on the order form. I've got a copy inside,' he added and turned.

He was nearly through the inner door when Calder stopped him.

'Just a minute,' he said, 'we'll come too. You *were* closing, weren't you?'

Calder looked at Striker, who got the message. He walked to the door and turned the sign over so that it showed 'Closed', then slipped the catch. Powne watched this procedure like a cornered animal, shrugged his shoulders and walked into the inner room.

In contrast to the shop itself it was very untidy. Cardboard boxes filled most of the space and were stacked against three walls. A large table, that Powne obviously used as a desk, was set to one side. It was piled high with various pieces of paper in, it seemed, no particular order. A grey filing cabinet, with the middle drawer open, stood alongside. In the far corner was a sink. The remains of a meal lay on the draining-board, together with an electric kettle, a mug with a spoon inside and plastic food containers. The room smelt heavily of tea leaves, although, as far as Calder could see, Powne didn't sell any tea.

' 'Ere's the order,' said the little man, holding up a large piece of paper. 'I ordered ten 176s – that covers this area – five 177s – that covers East London. One 198, one 89 and one 133. That must be it – 133.'

He looked at the chart on his desk.

'North-east Norfolk,' he said finally.

Striker looked at Calder, but he appeared to be looking into the distance. The blond man held out his hand and took the piece of A4.

'How can you be so sure that it was 133 that this man took?' he asked.

'I told you,' answered Powne more in frustration than anything else. 'I saw where 'e got it from on the rack. None o' the other numbers are anywhere near it.'

Suddenly, the sharp report of Calder's fist hitting the palm of his hand filled the room.

'My God, it's got to be,' he cried dramatically.

Striker looked at him, concerned.

'Peter – Felixstowe and Peterborough,' shouted Calder.

Both men looked at each other. Powne momentarily forgot his money and stared at Calder too.

'Of course,' said Striker, 'they're both close to Norfolk. In fact, if you put a compass point on Norwich and draw a circle, it probably falls through both towns. It's too much of a coincidence.'

He frowned before continuing.

'Birmingham doesn't fit though.'

'No,' said Calder, 'but Peterborough is in a straight line home from Birmingham to Norwich, and Peterborough was done the day after Birmingham.'

'You have an observer on Powne's shop, I take it?' asked Stoddard.

Both Calder and Striker nodded. The latter wasn't used to seeing his boss in pyjamas and dressing-gown, and for some inexplicable reason he felt embarrassed. What made it worse was that Calder didn't seem at all self-conscious. Striker felt himself in one of those environments where his personality was caged. He was also aware that he was jealous of Calder's self-assurance in any situation.

'Three, on eight-hour shifts,' said Striker a little nervously. 'They have orders to notify us and follow. We have a back-up team ready to take over the minute anyone shows.'

'Also,' interrupted Calder, 'Jensen has nothing on our suspects yet, except that a large number of them seem to be absent from their place of residence. The incident room has had a number of calls since the TV broadcast, but there's been nothing useful so far.'

Calder looked at Striker.

'It's early days yet, but I don't think that line of inquiry is going to be fruitful, for the reasons I mentioned this morning, certainly not in the short term, and we are running out of time.'

He hesitated.

'It's true that if it was them in Felixstowe, and I'm convinced now that it was, then they are not as far advanced in their construction of the bomb as I'd previously thought. But even so, there is really no way of accurately guessing when the thing will be finished. It could be two days, or a week or more.'

He looked hard at Stoddard.

'What I'm saying, General, is that I believe we must have an alternative strategy – now.'

It was Stoddard's turn to nod.

'Why do I get the feeling that you're going to ask me to do something unpleasant?' he said.

Striker noted Calder standing perfectly still, looking at the General. His friend had said that the old man had been exhausted this morning, but apparently he had slept for well over twelve hours and looked far from tired now. He was standing with his back to the fireplace, legs apart, hands in dressing-gown pockets. The eyes were as clear as Striker had ever seen them. They almost twinkled. Yet there was something different about him, something missing. Of course: no pipe. Perhaps he didn't smoke in his pyjamas.

He and Calder had discussed their tactics on the way over. There was only one thing to do, they knew. Actually, it was Calder who had suggested it. Striker had simply agreed. They were too close now to let Brown get away and were convinced that he was holed up in north-east Norfolk. It even fitted with the yacht theory and parachuting into the Moray Firth. Brown could have sailed straight down the east coast and there were plenty of deserted beaches up there to off-load a vessel. The fact that a massive, nationwide search had failed to find the yacht proved nothing. If anything, it could mean that he was simply extremely resourceful and they knew that anyway. Calder didn't hesitate any longer.

'I think you should organize a thorough search of the whole of the area covered by this map,' he said, pointing down at Ordnance Survey 133, already open on the low table, 'at dawn tomorrow.

'I don't know whether it's possible,' he continued, 'but I think it should be preceded by a complete seal-off. There are about ninety or a hundred roads leaving the area, as you'll see, which makes it difficult; and there are scores of tracks, which must also be covered, especially since Brown probably has a Landrover, or something like it. That also means that some could escape simply by driving through a ploughed field, which means that literally the whole border of the map has to be covered. That, in turn, means helicopters, continually patrolling the perimeter. That's difficult because the south, horizontal border is twenty-five miles long and the west, vertical border, twenty-three miles.'

Calder paused, apparently to assess Stoddard's reaction so far. The General bent down to look more closely at the map and Striker noticed that he was beginning to go a little thin on top.

'Yes,' said the older man, 'patrolling these three land borders is a major problem, but there are three others that also need thinking about. To begin with, we have this long coast to guard, which stretches for, what, twenty-five, thirty miles? That means boats and lots of them, not to mention more helicopters.'

He looked up at Calder.

'And don't forget that 'copters are useless for observation purposes at night.'

Calder bent down as well, looking puzzled. Only Striker remained standing.

'Then,' continued Stoddard, 'we have the fact that the top half of Norwich is also included on the map. Many roads there leading out of the area. Do we, therefore, go south of the map and seal off the whole of Norwich, which might be easier in the long run, or do we adhere strictly to the area on the map?'

It was a rhetorical question, but Calder interrupted anyway.

'I'm inclined to forget Norwich altogether. They won't be in the town. They must be away from prying eyes. That would make our seal-off easier.'

He paused and frowned.

'On the other hand, there's nothing nosier than a village community. You can be more alone in a town than you can in the country. Sorry, General, I don't know. Perhaps we should seal off the whole of Norwich.'

It was the first time Striker had known Calder unsure about anything. Stoddard seemed to look at him keenly before continuing.

'The fourth major problem is, of course, the sheer size of the operation. About five hundred square miles, I'd say, which must be totally isolated and searched meticulously.'

The General looked at Calder again. Striker screwed up his courage. He had to mention the Broads.

'Excuse me, sir,' he said, 'but I think there may be a fifth major problem.'

He squatted down to the map, feeling his heartbeat quicken and sensing Calder and Stoddard looking at each other over his head.

'I know part of this area,' said the American. 'I went sailing on some of these Broads last year.'

'Get to the point, man,' growled Stoddard.

'Yes, sir. The point is that this is a holiday area. It's called the Norfolk Broads. This whole south-east area here is a maze of interlocking rivers, dikes and lakes, and in the summer it teems with thousands of boats, some of them containing accommodation for up to ten people, or more.'

He looked up and saw Stoddard and Calder look at each other again as he continued.

'The problem is, of course, searching all those boats when they are continually moving about. I don't know how you intended to do it, sir – search in kilometre blocks I expect, as the map is set out that way – but unless you can find some way of preventing the boats from moving, you'll have a continuous, flowing transport system, moving into and out of areas which have already been searched.'

He looked up again. Calder and Stoddard were both looking at the map, so he went on.

'You can seal the boats off all right by simply blocking the junction where the rivers Thurne and Bure meet, here. You'll have a lot of unhappy holiday-makers, not to mention the commercial holiday operators, but you'll prevent boats moving out of the area. Also, of course, if the search goes over the weekend, the traffic will become a major headache. Being a popular vacation area, there is a continual stream of holiday-makers. Even though it's only May, you'll find it's still popular. I should think that a bulletin, telling people not to travel to the area, might help.'

Striker stood up and looked at the other two. He felt flushed.

'Thank you, Striker,' said Stoddard. 'I'm sure we could think of more problems as well, if we all thought hard enough.'

He moved off to the other side of the room and stopped in front of an oil-painting of a grand old house, set in extensive grounds. It had been done by a gifted amateur, Striker suspected, and he wondered whether it was connected with Stoddard's family. No one spoke for some time and Striker swayed nervously from foot to foot. Both younger men were looking at the older and the latter was gazing at the painting. He was still doing so when he began to speak.

'I take it you have thought about what this would mean? The social and economic upheaval that would be caused to the inhabitants by such an operation. And that's not to mention the question of life and death situations caused by the lack of mobility. It means completely immobilizing everyone within an area of five hundred square miles for . . . I don't know how long. This sort of thing has never been done before.'

He turned to look at them and spoke across the room.

'That is not to mention the cost and effort involved in diverting troops, civil police forces and equipment. One thing is certain, by the way; it couldn't be organized by dawn tomorrow. Dawn on Saturday is the earliest, if you're lucky.'

He looked down at the carpet and shook his head. Then he walked towards the two men and stopped very close to Calder. When he spoke, it was as if he were angry.

'Is that bomb in that area?' he demanded, pointing at the map.

'I believe so,' replied Calder woodenly.

'And you would recommend searching it?'

'There is no choice.'

Stoddard swung round on Striker.

'And what do *you* think, Peter?'

The blond man didn't know whether to be more surprised at being asked for his opinion or being called by his first name. But he was determined to remain impassive.

'I agree with Matthew,' he said after a little hesitation.

He felt Calder looking at him. Stoddard lifted his head to the ceiling, took a deep draught of air through his nose and smiled.

'In that case,' he said, 'since the top brains in my Department are unanimous, what else can I do?'

He looked at his watch.

'8.35. This decision will have to be taken by the PM himself, but I'll have to contact the Minister first. I hope they're not dining somewhere, because I'm going to disturb them.'

He paused and smiled again.

'On second thoughts, I hope they are dining somewhere. I want them in a good, pliable mood, because they are not going to like what I'm going to tell them.'

He looked at Calder seriously, then picked up his pipe from the mantelpiece and began to fill it. Striker realized then that some things never change.

'We'll just have to pray that they see things the way you do,' said Stoddard.

Then he winked and thrust the pipe into the side of his mouth.

'Don't worry. I'll scare the arses off them. They'll agree, eventually.'

He paused as the two younger men grinned.

'I'd better get dressed. This is going to be the biggest operation of its kind in British history, and I'm going to make sure that no one organizes it except me.'

Chapter 14

Wednesday, 21 May

All day the sun had shone from a cloudless sky and now it was evening as Calder pulled up outside the pub. It was still humid and he needed a long, cool drink. The beer garden was full of lounging soldiers in full camouflage, their packs and weapons back at their camp across the road. It reminded him of scenes during the First World War, although he was born well after the Second.

He left his car unlocked and walked through the garden, weaving his way through the smiling soldiers. They gave him strange looks, dressed as he was in casual jeans and shirt, but he had become used to that. Stoddard had given him a roving commission and he had moved around the area, sleeping in his car.

Some of the local pubs had run out of beer but this one had a brewery practically next door. The public bar was packed to the seams with soldiers and there was a sort of queue at the bar itself. Suddenly, as he began to muscle his way to the counter, he felt profoundly depressed. The operation had been delayed until dawn on Sunday, largely due to political reluctance. That meant that it had been going for four days, there were just forty square kilometres left and they hadn't found them. They'd found a few things that no one expected, but no Brown and no bomb. That meant, in turn, that either he had been wrong and the whole thing was a mistake, or they were here, but somehow they were cleverer than he had thought. They could still be in those forty square kilometres, of course, but somehow he wasn't hopeful.

Yet, he was sure he was right. They had to be here. And the police at Felixstowe had reported that the only fingerprints on the

186

metal-spinning mechanism were no more than a day or so old, the others having been completely erased.

The most likely possibility was that they had been by-passed. The major problem with an operation of this sort was making sure that everyone knew what they were looking for and he suspected that many didn't. It was inevitable really. He'd told Stoddard that communication might be a problem. No; that was unfair. Organization on the ground, if not the planning behind it, was in General Carey's lap and, anyway, if they didn't find that bomb it was everyone's problem. What's more, it looked as if they weren't going to find it and that meant that the number of choices open to them was becoming very limited indeed.

He reached the bar finally and realized that there was no choice of beverage either. The landlord was pulling pints continuously. You just took it and paid the robust barmaid beside him. So much for a civilized pint.

He forced his way out of the crush, his drink held high, and walked straight outside into the relative peace. He spotted an empty patch of grass and made a beeline for it. He sat down slowly and sipped his pint cautiously. It was surprisingly good. Then he focused his attention on a group of squaddies about five yards to his right. One of them was getting very excited. The cockney twang of London was clearly recognizable.

'An' I'm not jokin', I couldn't take my eyes off 'er. Showin' a leg, right up to 'ere she was.' His hand came down to point halfway up his left thigh. 'An' she didn't seem to mind neither. 'Arry 'ere,' he started to laugh, 'was pretendin' to examine the carpet – very studious like – but, all the time, 'e was tryin' to get a look up 'er skirt.'

The whole group guffawed and someone punched the blushing Harry on the shoulder.

'You dirty little bugger,' said someone else.

'I'm not jokin' though,' said the original speaker, 'she 'ad the most fantastic pair o' legs I've ever seen. Beautiful.'

Calder had the mug to his lips when something screamed at the back of his brain and he was back in Stoddard's office when he'd just got back from Mexico. His throat refused to swallow and he squirted beer all over the grass. The co-pilot of the Argosy had used exactly the same words, when he'd come round for a few seconds in the hangar – she had the most fantastic pair of legs he'd ever seen!

He found himself looking over at the small group. They had fallen silent and were returning his gaze. From the look on their faces they didn't think much of spitting good beer over the lawn. He could see their point. So she had good legs, just like hundreds of thousands of other women in the country. But they had both said *fantastic* legs. Oh, what the hell. He'd better say something intelligent anyway, before they thought he was mad.

'When was this, soldier,' he asked, 'when you saw the woman?'

The young man, not unnaturally, hesitated. He'd never seen Calder before and, dressed as he was, he didn't look like anyone in authority. None of his friends spoke. They just looked at Calder and then at the soldier who had spoken. Calder guessed that he was probably their leader and that he might get a little uppity, to demonstrate to his pals what a tough guy he was.

'What's it to do with you?' he replied.

Calder sighed audibly and fished in the top pocket of his open-necked shirt. He extracted his very high-powered pass and tossed it across to the group. They passed it to each other reverently. One or two began to look at their uniforms.

'I was hoping to avoid that bit of drama,' said Calder, holding out his hand.

The soldier who had spoken got up on to his knees and gave the pass back. He no longer looked recalcitrant.

'You ain't army or nothin', are ya?' he asked.

'No, I'm not army,' replied Calder.

The soldier looked even better.

'Now,' said Calder, 'when did you see the woman?'

'This mornin'. We was searchin' this 'ouse.'

'What time?'

'About ten.'

'How old was she?'

'Oo, about twenty-five I'd say.'

'How far is it – the house?'

The soldier turned away and thought. One of the others pointed a finger and answered.

'About two miles up that road, although you have to make a few turns.'

Calder followed the finger. The pub was on a crossroads.

'How many were there in the house, besides the woman?' asked Calder, hoping to keep up his own enthusiasm.

The original speaker got back in the act again.

'Just a crippled old man in a wheelchair. Oh, an' a butler. Now I think about it, 'e was rather odd. 'E 'ad a beard like. Whenever ya see 'em in films, they never 'ave beards, do they?'

Then he focused on the fact that Calder had a beard as well, but was quick to make amends.

'Not that I've got anyfing against beards like, but ya don't expect to see 'em on butlers, do ya'?'

No, you don't, thought Calder to himself.

'The old man,' he said. 'Did he have a beard as well?'

The soldier paused. One or two of the others answered in the affirmative.

'Yeah,' answered the soldier, ''e did, now I fink about it, but I didn't notice at the time. Grey it was.'

'And you searched the whole house?' questioned Calder.

'Yep, and – as far as I know, mind ya – we didn't find nothin', except those three.'

One of the others – the one who had directed him to the house – interrupted.

'A bearded butler, a beautiful bird and a crippled old man. Funny, isn't it?'

'Yes,' answered Calder thoughtfully, 'very funny.'

There was no reason why the butler shouldn't have a beard, nor the old man, come to that. But there were a lot of them about – the mail collector from Powne's shop, for example – and a beard made a natural disguise. And, of course, there was no reason why the women of Norfolk shouldn't have fantastic legs. There might even be a reason why a beautiful young woman should be living with a crippled old man. She could be his granddaughter. But even so. Somehow he *knew* Brown was in north-east Norfolk and it seemed that he'd been missed. Was it worth making a fuss about? Well, he knew he wouldn't sleep tonight unless he did something about it and, if he did, it was better to do it with fifty men armed with rifles at his back. He made up his mind, stood up and looked down at the small group.

'What's your officer's name?' he asked.

'Lieutenant Wellbeck.'

'And where can I find him?'

He'd noticed one or two of the group looking past him. Now they were looking over his left shoulder.

'I've no doubt you can find him in the saloon bar, sir.'

The voice came from above and behind him. He turned to find an enormous man, wearing sergeant's stripes, looking down at him. Calder was six foot and this man was at least a head taller. He was about thirty-five and running slightly to fat, but only slightly. He had shoulders like a gorilla. Calder looked into the face and decided he was intelligent too. He didn't flinch from the appraisal, which didn't surprise Calder at all.

'Thank you, Sergeant,' said Calder. 'If I were you, I'd advise my men to drink up quickly.'

He walked off in the general direction of the saloon, leaving the big man to look after him with a puzzled expression.

A temporary hand-written sign had been nailed to the saloon-bar door. It read: 'Officers, policemen and civilians only'. Calder's opinion of Lieutenant Wellbeck dived even before he'd met him. He pushed on the sign and searched the room. A group of three officers was standing at the bar to the left, a few nervous-looking regulars occupied a table in the centre and, scattered around the rest of the room, were half a dozen off-duty policemen. By comparison with the public bar, it was a haven of peace and quiet.

He noticed that all three officers were lieutenants as he approached them. One had already seen him as he had entered and the other two were now acknowledging the direction of his gaze. He stopped and stood for a few seconds, his eyes taking in the whole group. It was important that he make a good impression.

'I'm looking for Lieutenant Wellbeck,' he said to the group in general.

'That's me,' answered a wavy-haired young man in his early twenties. His uniform hung from his frame rather than fitted it. His face was pale and smooth, and surprisingly podgy. He held a glass of Scotch up in one hand and a cigarette in the other.

Calder removed his pass again and held it out for Wellbeck to see. His eyes widened and the other two leant forward to have a look.

'My dear chap,' said Wellbeck, 'even I haven't got one of those.'

Calder put it away as he spoke. His voice had an edge of urgency to it.

'I just heard one of your soldiers talking about a house that you searched at 10 o'clock this morning. It contained, according to him, a butler, a crippled old man and a woman.'

Wellbeck's face lit up.

'Oh, yes,' he said, 'she was a real cracker.'

One of the others laughed and Wellbeck sipped his Scotch.

'It may be nothing,' said Calder, 'but I'd like you and about fifty men to come with me now and search the place again.'

The atmosphere suddenly changed. No one spoke for a few moments while they all looked at Calder.

'What you showed me was a pass,' said Wellbeck. 'I cannot see that it gives you any authority.'

'Quite right, Freddie,' said the one who had laughed before. 'I think he's questioning your judgement.'

The third man turned away. Calder gave the last speaker a withering look and turned back to Wellbeck. The latter took a deep drag on his cigarette. Calder felt the door open behind him and Wellbeck looked over his shoulder.

'What is it, Sergeant?' he said irritably.

Calder didn't look round.

'The men are ready, sir.'

Calder recognized the big man's voice.

'Wh . . . what for?' stammered Wellbeck.

'To go wherever this gentleman wants them to, sir,' replied the sergeant.

Calder couldn't help grinning and half-turned to acknowledge the man at the door, who shouldn't really have been there anyway, according to the landlord. But then, Calder suspected, he'd probably got used to the fact that only maniacs tried to throw him out of pubs. Everyone focused on Wellbeck.

'Been ordering my troops about, have you?' said the lieutenant indignantly to Calder.

'No, sir,' came the immediate reply from the door. 'I did it on my own initiative.'

Wellbeck ignored his sergeant, just glared at Calder.

'I have no orders. I'd better get permission,' said the lieutenant, making no move at all.

'Where are your senior officers?' asked Calder.

'Not here,' answered Wellbeck sharply.

'Then there is no time to get them,' said Calder urgently. 'It'll be dark in about forty minutes. We must move now and quickly. I suggest you exercise some initiative, lieutenant.'

Wellbeck looked as if he was about to have a fit. He was torn between the prospect of a comfortable evening getting drunk in congenial company and that pass, which he'd noticed was signed by General Carey himself. The man in front of him might be connected with the big brass. He certainly had an air of authority about him. But, he wasn't in uniform, was he? Therefore, technically . . .

'You'd better go, Freddie,' said the officer who had so far remained silent.

He drained his glass and placed it down on the bar.

'I'll come as well,' he added and smiled genuinely.

Calder wondered what he was doing with the other two.

'Thank you, Lieutenant,' he said gratefully. 'What's your name?'

'Frobisher.'

Calder nodded.

'Oh, all right,' said Wellbeck suddenly.

Calder nodded again.

'How many men can you muster between you?' he asked.

Frobisher thought carefully. 'About forty-five,' he said.

'That'll do,' said Calder. 'Who's senior of you two?'

Since Wellbeck looked so young he was expecting Frobisher to answer.

'I am,' said Wellbeck forcefully.

Calder stopped himself from biting his lip.

'Fine,' he said, 'then let's go. I suggest that all the men are armed and we commandeer enough vehicles to get us there as quickly as possible.'

He turned away.

'I shall give the orders, if you don't mind,' said Wellbeck shrilly, still making no move from the bar.

Calder turned on him. He was angry now.

'No, Lieutenant Wellbeck. I shall be giving the orders. And if you question that, I should get on your field phone and call General Carey. With a bit of luck he might boot your arse from here right back to Sandhurst.'

Calder turned away again. Wellbeck opened his mouth to speak, then shut it. The bulky sergeant was still standing by the door. If ever a man was smiling without using the normal facial expressions, then that was what he was doing. Calder stopped about a yard from him and looked up.

'Thank you, Sergeant. What's your name?'

'Oakes, sir.'

Calder couldn't help smiling to himself, despite the situation.

'I should have guessed,' he said. 'Did you hear what I was saying just now?'

'Yes, sir. Enough vehicles for forty-five men, all armed. Two troop-carriers should do it, sir. Plus a Landrover for you and the officers?'

'Yes, Lieutenants Wellbeck, Frobisher and I will travel in the Landrover. You will drive.'

Oakes looked across at Wellbeck for confirmation or denial. The lieutenant was looking at him, but he wasn't saying anything.

'Yes, sir,' said Oakes, smiling.

'And, Sergeant,' added Calder. 'Make sure that you and each officer has a walkie-talkie and be as quick as you can. We must do this before it gets dark.'

'Yes, sir,' said Oakes and he strode off down the path, barking orders as he went.

Frobisher rushed past, presumably to organize his own men, and Wellbeck followed at a more leisurely pace. Calder suddenly centred on the possibility that he could be going off on a wild-goose chase. He might not have been so insistent had it not been for Wellbeck. Well, he was committed. He'd better be right, or one or two people would have a field day. But finding the bomb was more important than saving his dignity.

Within twelve minutes they were nearly there.

'How far is it down this lane?' asked Calder.

Wellbeck thought about it. Fortunately his sense of direction and distance were better than his ability to make decisions.

'About 450 yards, I'd say. On the left.'

'Stop,' said Calder and Oakes braked.

Calder took in the lie of the land. He had not time to reconnoitre. It was straight in now or nothing. The lane could barely take the width of two vehicles. There appeared to be a small track about twenty yards on the left, which hopefully led to somewhere round the back of the house. Anything past the entrance to the track though was screened by trees and shrubs. To the right of the lane was an old iron fence and a grazing pasture. It rose slightly and then disappeared over a hill after about two hundred yards. There were a few trees in the field and it had been heavily grazed, but there were no cows. Further down the lane – about a third of a mile it seemed – the field leant into a wood. The lane bent round to the left, but Calder guessed that the wood probably went right down to the road. That meant that it probably continued across the lane as well, along the side of the house.

He looked at the sky. The sun had already set, but there was still about twenty-five minutes of reasonable light left. It might not be enough. He turned to Frobisher.

'Lieutenant. Take your men up that track and see if you can come up to the rear of the house. I'm afraid I don't know what sort of terrain you'll find.'

He looked down at the map before continuing.

'The map doesn't make it clear. That wood down there is marked, but nothing else. It's important that you're not seen, so don't be afraid to stay back. Your job is merely to stop any rabbits bolting out of the back door.'

Frobisher nodded. Calder looked at his watch.

'I can only give you ten minutes to get into position,' he said. 'I'm sorry. I know it's not enough, but the light is fading rapidly.'

Frobisher nodded again and jumped down.

'Oh, Lieutenant,' called Calder.

The young man – no more than twenty-three, Calder estimated – looked back.

'Don't be afraid to shoot if you have to.'

Frobisher's eyebrows seemed to come closer together. Then he left.

'Lieutenant,' said Calder to Wellbeck. 'Set up a road-block, right here. If anyone breaks into that pasture you'll have a clear field of fire, for about a third of a mile, up to that wood. If anyone gets in there we've lost them. To avoid that, you'll take half your company along the lane, round the bend and past the house. There you'll set up another road-block this side of the wood. We'll just have to hope there are plenty of trees shielding you from the house, as there are here. If there aren't, you'll have to go into the wood. You must keep out of sight.'

Wellbeck nodded confidently. He had become accustomed to the situation now. He wasn't going to call Calder 'sir', but he'd carry out his orders. After all, that was what he'd been trained to do. He made to jump out, but Calder's voice stopped him.

'I suggest you and your men drop off while the driver continues some way past. If anyone is listening in the house he can hear the lorry receding into the distance. The driver can then turn the lorry and form a road-block.'

Wellbeck looked at him blankly, got out and called, 'Sergeant.'

The big man instinctively made to move. Calder gripped his arm.

'No,' he said, 'he stays with me.'

The lieutenant looked daggers at him and left. Frobisher and his men filed past at a trot. Then Wellbeck, shouting orders, caught his attention.

'I wish he'd keep his voice down,' said Calder absently.

The two men sat in silence for nearly a minute. Oakes looked over at Calder, who seemed to be deep in thought.

'And what do *we* do, sir?' asked Oakes politely.

At first Calder gave no indication that he had heard and spoke without looking at the burly driver.

'We walk up to the front door, Sergeant.'

'Yes, sir,' answered Oakes, as if Calder had asked him to pass a cigarette.

'Well, not quite like that,' continued Calder. 'First of all, you will open the bonnet of this vehicle and cut a slit in the top hose. Then we follow Wellbeck, at a discreet distance. By the time we reach the entrance to the house, we should be steaming like a Turkish bath. We then have a legitimate excuse to pull over and knock on their door.'

The big man nodded.

'We then play it by ear,' added Calder.

That was painfully true. He had no set plan for when they reached the house. He couldn't begin to doubt himself, but he was prepared to admit that he wasn't perfect. He turned to the professional sitting beside him.

'How am I doing, Sergeant?'

Oakes turned and looked Calder in the eye. He twitched his mouth and said:

'You're not army – that's obvious. But you're doing all right. I was right about you back in the beer garden.' He paused. 'When most people meet me for the first time, they're afraid – I can tell. You weren't.'

Calder didn't know what to say.

'Just one word of advice though, sir, if you don't mind.'

'Go on.'

'Lieutenant Wellbeck. I know him fairly well by now.' He stopped and frowned. 'The mood he's in, he's likely to go in, guns blazing at the slightest opportunity, just like he was leading the Seventh Cavalry. It might be worth having a word in his ear.'

Calder nodded and put his head out of the window. One lorry was already broadside across the road and men were in the ditch along his side. He jumped down and walked to the back of the Landrover. Wellbeck was just about to pull himself into the cab of the remaining lorry. Calder beckoned him over and he approached suspiciously.

'On no account break cover until you get a signal from me or Sergeant Oakes,' said Calder.

'Is that all?'

'Have you got your radio?'

'Yes.'

'Then that's all,' answered Calder and walked back to his vehicle.

He wondered whether he was being too hard on Wellbeck, especially since he was going to be quite angry when he discovered that Calder had no formal authority at all. Well, it was too late now. As he was settling himself in beside Oakes, the lorry eased itself narrowly past, then accelerated up the road.

'OK, Sergeant, the hose,' said Calder.

Like many big men, Oakes moved with surprising quickness. Within seconds he had jumped down and had the bonnet up. Calder hadn't even wondered how he was going to cut the hose. That a man like Oakes would have some sort of sharp instrument about his person, official or unofficial, he had no doubt. Almost immediately there was a hissing from the engine area and Oakes slammed down the bonnet. He leapt back into the driver's seat and put the vehicle into gear.

'We'd better get going,' he said, 'before this thing seizes up.'

He moved quickly up through the gears and in little more than a minute they were approaching the entrance to the drive of the house. Calder could see it now through the thinning hedge. Steam was definitely leaking out of the joints of the bonnet. Wellbeck had disappeared round the bend.

'There's no gate,' said Calder. 'Pull into the drive just a little and to one side.'

Oakes slowed down to walking pace, then did as Calder suggested.

'OK,' said Oakes, 'let's give them a show.'

He jumped down and threw the bonnet up, having to retreat swiftly as the suddenly released steam rose in a cloud.

Calder switched the engine off and jumped down. The house, about a hundred yards away, was half hidden by an enormous pine tree, about twenty yards from where the Landrover had come to rest. But he could see enough to know that it probably contained about a dozen or so bedrooms and probably had extensive grounds around the back. Some outbuildings to the right, that looked as if they had once been stables, formed an enclosed quadrangle.

He reached Oakes and, with him, bent over the engine, just like any motorist who had broken down and was examining the problem.

'If anyone comes and looks at this hose,' said Oakes, 'they're going to know it's a put-up job.'

'They won't get the chance,' said Calder, who turned round to look at the house again. 'We've given them as long as we can.'

He looked down at the walkie-talkie, nestling in a pocket on Oakes's thigh.

'I'll get my rifle,' said the big man.

Before long they were both moving up the tarmac drive towards the front door. Oakes, if it hadn't been for the automatic rifle slung casually over his shoulder, looked as if he was out for an evening stroll. Calder felt tense. He didn't know what he was going to do once he was inside, even if it was the right place. He had the glimmering of a few ideas, but right at that moment he did not want to follow them through. He consciously emptied his mind of all the immediate problems and just concentrated on putting one foot in front of the other. Slowly, the tension died and he let the evening creep in upon him as he heard a chaffinch and then another.

Thirty yards from the house he paused and stared up at it. It was old, covered in ivy and did not look well maintained. The piping needed a coat of paint and so did the window frames. The garden, though, was immaculate.

'Any movement?' he asked.

'I've been watching the windows, sir. Not a sign.'

They moved on and Calder felt a tightening in his belly as he approached the large wooden door, shadowed under a stone arch.

Ignoring the bell set into the stone, he walked up to the door, lifted the huge, carved-brass knocker and slammed it down twice on the woodwork. The sound echoed hollowly throughout the house and Calder felt immediately that it was empty. That told him nothing, of course, except that it was unusual for a house of this size to be completely deserted. You would expect at least one servant.

They waited for a full half-minute, then looked at each other. Calder waited a little more, then stepped up and knocked again. It sounded even more empty this time.

'The bell might go direct to a room at the back,' suggested Oakes.

Calder shook his head. 'Bells can be too easily booby-trapped,' he said.

When, after another minute, nothing had stirred, Calder came to a decision.

'There can't be anyone here. If there is, then they must be hiding, in which case we might as well break in anyway.'

He tried the handle on the door, but it was firmly locked.

'I'd ask you to put a burst through the lock,' he said, 'but Well-beck would probably charge up the drive. So let's go round the back and break in quietly.'

It took them far longer to walk round to the back garden, which was about three acres in area and ringed by trees, than it did to break a French window and walk in. There was no alarm.

The room appeared to be spacious and well decorated with chintz furniture, but no detail could be seen with clarity, as the light was fading rapidly. Calder crunched across broken glass to the light switch and flicked it on. Nothing happened. He moved out into a long, dark corridor and found the switch there, but that too produced no illumination.

That settled it. The house must be empty. The electricity supply had been turned off. That was odd, because big houses usually had freezers.

He caught sight of Oakes, framed against the remaining light, and said:

'Let's find the kitchen.'

They walked down the corridor, ignoring the many rooms leading off, and found themselves in the lobby at the front of the house. The inside of the house, in contrast to the outside, seemed to be well-maintained, clean and reasonably, if rather sparsely, decorated. By setting off down another corridor, Calder found the dining-room and hence the kitchen.

The light was too little to enable Calder to see very much at all, except a sink near the only, small window, a large table in the centre of the room and, at the far end of the large space, near the door, in the darkest corner, a long, low, chest freezer.

He walked over and lifted the lid. It was about a third full with what looked like meat, vegetables and bread, yet it was definitely not operating. He extracted a pre-packed chicken. It was still frozen. He must have stood there for some time, the chicken freezing his hand, before the burly sergeant walked in.

'Why turn off a freezer that's a third full of food, Sergeant? There must be at least two hundred quid's worth here. Answer – you don't need it any more.'

He suddenly felt angry. So near, yet so bloody far. Christ, it was pathetic. Oakes was about to walk over, but changed his mind as the light from the window caught Calder's face. He just held out his hand instead.

'I thought this might be interesting, sir. I found it in the waste-paper basket next door. It's a sort of study.'

Calder walked over, zombie-like, and took the crumpled, buff envelope. He turned it so that he could see in the light from the window. It was addressed to Mr D. Stephens, 13 Keit Road, Paddington, London.

He stared down at it, mesmerized. Then his anger rose again, this time uncontrollably. He turned and threw the frozen chicken into the freezer. The bird hit the underside of the lid with tremendous force and it slammed shut. He walked over to it and placed his hands on the surface, forcing himself to remain calm. Funny how he should throw the chicken *into* the freezer. He could have thrown it anywhere. He became conscious of the envelope, now crumpled in his left fist. Well, he could call off the guards on Powne's shop. If Brown was prepared to leave addressed envelopes about, he wouldn't be using that accommodation address again.

But why should they leave? The house had already been searched. It was clean. They could have stayed here indefinitely. It could have been that Brown just didn't want to push his luck and had decided to move on. But that wouldn't do. There was only one answer. They didn't need to stay any more, which again led to only one conclusion. Quite simply, the bomb was completed.

He lifted his head and looked unseeingly at the dark wall behind. As each piece of the map had been searched, so the security cordon had moved too, like a tightening noose. At least, that had been the idea. That was why there were a few surplus troops now. So, when the soldiers moved up, Brown and his cronies had simply hidden themselves and the evidence of a full house, put up a front of a woman, a crippled old man and a butler, waited for the place to be searched and for the cordon to pass by, gave it another three to four hours for safety, packed themselves into their cars and left at irregular intervals. The bomb was also, probably, in the boot of a big car and could now be almost anywhere in the UK. It was all so bloody simple. He'd missed them by about six hours. He didn't feel angry now, just empty.

'You still there, Sergeant?' he asked quietly.

'Sir,' said the big man, equally quietly.

'Get on that two-way radio of yours and call in the troops. I don't want them to come into the house or touch it though. Before anyone else comes in here I want to check it myself, with a geiger-counter.'

He turned to Oakes. 'You had yours on when you checked the house this morning, I take it?'

'Yes, sir, and it's still in the Landrover.'

Calder nodded.

'I'm puzzled as to why they didn't arrange to burn the place down before they left, Sergeant. They clearly didn't intend to return and it would destroy evidence. I'm probably being overly cautious, but I want an explosives expert to check this place over before anyone throws any more switches or turns on that electricity supply.'

'Sir.'

'Then go down to the Landrover and get on that field radio. Mention my name and ask General Carey to get here fast.'

'I'm afraid I didn't get your name, sir.'

'Calder.'

Oakes nodded. 'Anything else, sir?'

'That's enough for you to be getting on with,' said Calder, turning to look at the big man. His face was featureless in the near-dark.

'This is the place, is it, sir?'

'Yes,' answered Calder tonelessly.

'What put you on to it?' continued Oakes.

'You won't believe it, Sergeant, but it was a pair of beautiful legs.'

He clapped Oakes on the shoulder as he walked past.

'Thanks for your help,' he said.

It was becoming almost impossible to see and he stubbed his toe on the step. He left through the front door and walked slowly down to the Landrover. There, he searched for and found a battery-operated torch. It was big and powerful, as one would expect. With its assistance he then found the geiger-counter and returned to the house. He passed Oakes on the doorstep, still speaking into his hand-radio. Behind him he heard the sound of a lorry.

He switched on the geiger-counter on entering the house and noted that it showed no more than a normal reading. He went through to the kitchen again and searched for the cellar. With the aid of the torch he found it quickly and watched the counter carefully as he opened the door. Still normal.

His torch showed a fairly ordinary cellar, with prosaic-looking boxes, dusty sacks and various odds and ends. He descended the steps. Against the far wall was, however, a far from normal wine rack. It was nearly completely full with about two hundred bottles.

Calder shone the torch around the walls. It seemed a rather small cellar for such a large, old house. He moved over to the wall against which the wine rack was propped and shone his torch into the corner. Yes, that was it. The wall was built after the outside wall. The bricks were of a slightly different colour. He walked over to the corner and felt both walls. It was a different texture too, rough and dry, whereas the other was worn smooth by the mildew and damp of nearly a century. It didn't take a genius to work out that the new wall was probably a false one.

He spent fifteen minutes probing it, but there was clearly no entrance. There had to be one from another room, upstairs. He was a little concerned that Oakes was taking so long, but knew he was capable enough.

It took him another ten minutes to find it, although he should have seen it sooner. A wall stanchion in the huge forward lounge shouldn't have been there. True, it melded in with the rest of the woodwork, but there was just no reason for it to be in that particular spot. It took him a few seconds more to find the lever – a wooden knob, set low down in the wood. He turned it and heard a soft click. He pushed the wall and it moved silently, like an ordinary door on well-oiled hinges. There was still no sign of Oakes.

Calder shone the torch through. Immediately in front of him was a series of steps that would take him down about seven feet. At the bottom was a small, flat place and then a steel door. To one side of the door, set into the wall, was a geiger-counter. His own sounded a little more agitated but not appreciably so. It still read safe. The other almost certainly measured radioactivity within the cellar.

A little stunned, he descended the steps and looked at the dial. It didn't register anything and he realized that it wasn't switched on. He reached out to push the button, then arrested the movement as the realization struck him that it was the perfect booby-trap. Brown knew by now that they were on to him, which meant that he must also know that the authorities knew that he was making an atomic bomb. The natural thing to do, therefore, would be to press that button to discover the degree of radiation within. That triggers an explosion and, all at the same time, Brown destroys evidence, spreads radiation into the neighbourhood and demonstrates his earnest intent.

Calder would give anything to see inside that room, but he would have to wait until an expert checked out the geiger-counter. Anyway, he really knew what was inside: all the necessary equipment for making an atomic bomb. And the bomb would be gone – finished. He was almost certain, but he had to be sure, before the night was out.

He heard someone shouting his name up above.

'Down here,' he shouted back.

He was ascending the steep steps, which, extravagantly, had handholds on either side, when the unmistakable figure of Sergeant Oakes became framed in the entrance to the false wall-cavity. Calder was careful not to shine the torch directly into his eyes.

'Jesus,' said the big man, 'so this is where they were hiding.'

'Yes,' answered Calder, turning and pointing his torch at the cellar door. 'In there. And I'm not surprised your boys didn't find it. It took me half an hour and I was looking for it.'

He felt profoundly depressed.

'We had a little trouble with the radio, sir, but we've raised General Carey now. He was at Cromer and should be here in about five minutes or so.'

Oakes lowered his head.

'What's the problem?' asked Calder.

'It's Lieutenant Wellbeck,' answered Oakes immediately. 'He's been giving me some trouble and I'm finding it difficult to keep him out of the house. I think he feels that his authority is being questioned and he's threatened to demote me to private twice.'

'I'm sorry, Sergeant,' said Calder. 'I've caused you a lot of problems. I'll sort out Wellbeck.'

Just then some headlamps lit up the front of the house.

'Don't apologize, sir. I wouldn't have missed it for anything.'

Calder saw that the man was grinning as the sharp light reflected off his teeth and he smiled too.

'The radiation count is OK inside the house,' he said, 'but I can't guarantee that room. Pick two of your most reliable men and have them stand guard on the door. They must not touch anything. Also, no one, not even the General, is to pass without my permission. Then station some men around the house.'

'Already done, sir.'

Calder nodded.

'No one except those two guards is to set foot in this house until it's been checked by experts. Where is that explosives man, by the way?'

'We don't have anyone qualified enough here. Lieutenant Wellbeck mentioned it to General Carey.'

'Fine,' said Calder, 'then let's go and do battle with Wellbeck.'

They reached the front door. Oakes signalled to a group of men and left to give orders. Calder stood there on the doorstep for a moment, in the full glare of the headlights that someone had left on. He willed himself to think positively. All right, so he'd missed them this time. And, true, time was now running out fast. But he would simply have to build up again from square one. He could think of things that could be done now, but he had to get back to London and talk to Stoddard first.

The sound of a helicopter disturbed his thoughts and he allowed his mind to drift with it as it came closer. A powerful light stabbed down from the undercarriage, just forward of the vertical, and the machine landed. Calder continued to watch as the engine note dropped and two figures stepped out under the slowly flapping rotors. One of them was clearly in uniform. The other was smaller, with light-coloured hair and wearing a combat jacket. He looked familiar. Then he glanced Calder's way and stopped the uniformed man, who seemed bent on reaching the immaculate row of soldiers standing at attention by the pine tree. *He* carried on, but the man in the combat jacket started to walk towards Calder, and was no more than fifteen yards away before Calder saw that it was Stoddard. Calder also realized that he was never more glad to see anyone in his life.

3 THREAT

Chapter 15

Smokey Joe pushed his cart along the Horse Guards to the next pile of litter. He'd come by a few minutes before and brushed the discarded paper into little mounds along the curb, to make it easier for shovelling. As usual, he was in no hurry. There was always another lot of rubbish around the corner.

He became aware that his roll-up had gone out, so he stopped, propped his shovel against the cart and relit it. Then he extravagantly removed his pocket-watch and checked the time. Four minutes to ten. He would stay where he was now, watch in hand, until Big Ben's tenth chime. It was a ritual he never altered.

Smokey looked over at St James's Park and noticed two men, just leaving the park by the War Memorial, walking towards him. One was much older than the other and looked very distinguished. He was wearing a grey suit and his head was topped by short silver-grey hair. The other was bearded and dressed in a dark-brown corduroy jacket, brown trousers and tie, and white shirt.

They were in earnest conversation and appeared not to notice him as they headed directly for the cart. Then the younger man looked up and the other moved over slightly. As they approached the kerb the bearded man looked more closely at Smokey, who touched his cap and kept looking. The younger man smiled. To Smokey there was something strange about him. Then the troubled eyes moved away as he scanned the traffic and they crossed the road.

'You should have seen the PM's face when I told him about that booby-trapped geiger-counter,' said Stoddard as they entered Horse Guards Parade. 'I think it finally brought home to him that we're dealing with a man who is deadly serious and for that I think we ought to thank him – Brown, I mean.'

Calder looked puzzled. The older man caught the expression.

'Before that I was having all sorts of problems getting things done. But now,' he waved his arm dismissively, 'I seem to have no difficulty. When I told him about your conclusions he didn't say a word – just sat staring at the table. Finally, he came to his senses and said he wanted to know the effects of "this atomic device" if it were exploded and, taking advantage of my new-found influence, I suggested I had just the man for the job.'

Stoddard was grinning broadly. Calder felt uneasy.

'When he asked me about your qualifications I told him the truth. And I said that you had made a special study of the area in question.'

The General cleared his throat.

'I also told him that you had resigned your post at the Centre because you saw the dangers of nuclear proliferation through nuclear power and were frustrated when the people in control wouldn't listen. That pinned his ears back. What's more, I said that you could tell him what he wanted to know at 10 o'clock this morning, without the need for any preparation.'

Stoddard stopped at a black gate set into a high, brick wall. He looked down at the pipe in his hand.

'I rather built you up, I'm afraid.'

'Thanks, General,' said Calder crookedly. 'What I don't understand though is why. There must be scores of people who could do it. The Cabinet Office itself has nine scientific personnel on its payroll and that's to say nothing of the Prime Minister's Private Office. At least one of them must know something about nuclear explosions.'

Stoddard's smile had gone.

'Yes,' he said, 'and two of them will be there this morning – looking you over no doubt.'

Calder made no reaction at all, just gazed back at the older man, who, in turn, was looking him straight in the eye.

'I've already told you,' said Stoddard fiercely, 'that two weeks ago a very senior scientific adviser told me an atomic bomb could not be made from reprocessed plutonium oxide. Perhaps that will give you an answer.'

Stoddard's face showed pure aggression.

'I just hope he's not there this morning,' he added venomously.

With that he turned and placed the pipe in his jacket pocket. They were cleared by the policeman on duty and Stoddard opened the gate. It was the rear entrance to 10 Downing Street. Calder shut the gate behind him and followed Stoddard across the garden.

As he walked along the narrow path Calder felt apprehensive. After all, it's not every day you get to give a talk to the Prime Minister and some of his Cabinet colleagues. He was also a little tired, but then he'd been up all night. They hadn't left Norfolk until 3.30 a.m. and all he had had time for on his return was a bath and a sizeable breakfast. Stoddard had breakfasted with the PM at 8.00 and then phoned Calder as he was washing up. Come to think of it, the General should be tired too, but he looked like a man with eight solid hours behind him.

Big Ben began to chime.

'We're going to be late,' said Stoddard and quickened his step. Across the road, Smokey Joe looked from the gate where the men had disappeared, to his watch. He nodded ten times in extravagant satisfaction and returned to his daydream.

Within five minutes Calder was standing in what was obviously a briefing room. Two large windows at one end didn't quite shed enough light on the oblong space and fluorescent tubes were needed. Ostentatious wood surrounds were much in evidence along the borders around the cream walls. Along one long wall was a huge fireplace and, above it, hung an enormous, ornate mirror. A white screen stood at one end of the room and a film projector at the other. There were also a few TV monitors scattered about. On the floor was a plain, wine-red carpet over parquet wood and, in the centre, were sixteen straight-backed, leather-covered, red chairs around an elliptical table.

Seven men were seated there, some of whom were among the most powerful in Britain.

Calder was standing at one end. Halfway down, nearest to him on his right, sat Stoddard. Next to him and further down were two scientists, who had been introduced simply as Drs Crawford and Benavici. The former was about sixty-five, bald, diminutive and pale. A pair of bi-focals perched on the end of his nose and he was watching Calder suspiciously over the top of them. He looked like the stereotype of a nuclear physicist. Benavici, on the other hand, was young, large and dark, and clearly of Italian descent. The brown eyes had flashed at him briefly as they were introduced. They now looked at his own fingers, which fiddled nervously on the blotter. Calder wondered whether either of them was Stoddard's boffin.

Next to Benavici, near the end, was David MacPherson, the Home Secretary – known to his public simply as 'Mac' – a thickset man with curly, brown hair and a ruddy complexion which blended with his light-green check suit. By training he was a barrister and a man steeped in the belief of the freedom of the individual. It occurred to Calder that there must be a little worm working away inside his brain, due to the rather totalitarian measures he had been forced to adopt since the hijack and because of the even more Draconian actions that he must suspect would now be required to find the bomb. He appeared to have a headache – the forehead was wrinkled and the eyelids slightly closed. Calder didn't feel sorry for him. MacPherson was the member of a Cabinet which had allowed the Nuclear Power Programme and, while he wouldn't go so far as to say that the man deserved what he was getting, he wasn't going to hand him a handkerchief to cry into.

On the left of the smoothly polished table-top, nearest Calder, was Norman Stiles, Secretary of State for Energy. He was fifty-one years old and five feet five inches tall. This last feature, connected with the fact that he was somewhat overweight, made him a cartoonist's dream. To the press he was known as 'the Barrel' and was drawn in various guises – being filled up with some obnoxious substance, being rolled along the ground or, most commonly, bowling over the entire Cabinet or the House of Commons in a skittle alley. One way he did live up to his nickname was that he always seemed to be laughing. With his ubiquitous pipe continually turning up one corner of his mouth, he gave the impression that he was a little simple, but to Calder he had always had one of the sharpest brains in his party, even if at times his rebellious nature caused him to have a bad press. At times, too, he showed flashes of brilliance and it was well known that he was a potential rival for the party leadership. He was also the only man in the room, as far as Calder knew, who had spoken out publicly about the dangers of nuclear power, and for that Calder felt a rather biased affinity.

Next to him, further down, was the bespectacled John Corcorran, Minister of Defence. Calder suspected him of being one of the most influential members of the government – not because of his post, which is, on the whole, a relatively minor one in the late twentieth century, but because of his intelligence and personality. He was a hawk, or perhaps 'owl' would be a better word, and he had firm views on morality and the state of the nation. Calder knew that he was about fifty-five, although his wavy hair was completely black. He had piercing blue eyes behind the dark frames and a just perceptible scowl almost permanently on his long face. He was immaculately dressed in dark blue suit, white shirt and dark blue tie, and Calder knew that the black shoes would be spotless. Corcorran was not a man with whom he would care to deal on a one-to-one basis.

Finally, at the end of the table, in the middle of them all, sat the Prime Minister, Bernard Lecast. He was a big man in height and girth, who would have to have had his suits made to measure even if he couldn't afford it. Calder knew that he was nearly seventy, but he didn't look it, and although his hair was white, there was still plenty of it. His career in politics had been long and hard-fought, but he had been almost the natural choice for leader when his predecessor had resigned because of ill-health. He had made mistakes, but most of the time had been prepared to admit them and, although he was close to retirement, he showed a capacity for adaptation. The cynical called it pragmatism, his supporters flexibility. In any event, you couldn't run the first coalition in Britain's post-war history by being dogmatic.

Whatever was true, one thing was clear to Calder – something that could not be conveyed through a television screen. Lecast had a presence which dominated the table. Even if he were not sitting at its head, there would be no doubt as to who was in charge.

All the men looked cautious and tense, although there were no signs of fear, with the possible exception of Benavici. Well, thought Calder, that would soon change. His mind was suddenly crystal clear as he removed some notes from the inside pocket of his jacket. He looked at Stoddard to sense his mood but he was looking at his blotter.

'The floor is yours, Mr Calder,' said Lecast.

'Thank you.' Calder hesitated briefly while gathering his thoughts.

'I'm afraid,' he said, 'there is a bit of so-called "jargonistic" information that I must give you at the beginning. I'm sorry if I'm telling some of you what you already know, but it is important that all of you understand the whole situation.'

He turned to the white board standing beside him and lifted the felt-tipped pen that rested in the groove of the easel. He wrote at the top of the board, 'Effects of 20 Kiloton Nuclear Ground-Burst'. As he spoke, he summarized the main points on the board, throughout.

'As you probably know, in conventional terms, one kiloton is equivalent to the explosive power of one thousand tons of TNT. So, a twenty-kiloton bomb, which is what we have to face, is equivalent to twenty thousand tons of TNT. It's a very small nuclear bomb, but still extremely potent. Just to say that it represents that much explosive power in no way describes its capacity.'

He glanced around the table. Everyone except Benavici was looking at the board.

'We are fairly sure it's about a twenty-kiloton bomb,' continued Calder, 'because we know how much plutonium has been stolen.'

He paused.

'Actually, that's not, strictly speaking, true. We know how much plutonium oxide was stolen and we know how much plutonium 239 can be converted from it – about ten kilos. Now ten kilos represents two hundred kilotons, but we would expect only about ten per cent of the plutonium in our bomb to be involved in the nuclear reaction. I don't think it will be less then ten per cent but it could be greater. One has to make a calculated guess somewhere.'

Stiles was nodding and Calder felt encouraged.

'If you are looking for absolute accuracy in this talk, gentlemen, I'm afraid that I'm going to disappoint you. There are just too many variables. Ten per cent is, I think, a reasonable estimate, based on the state of our knowledge and the availability of that information.'

No one spoke. Calder looked at the two scientists and so did Lecast, but there was no reaction. Calder then glanced at Stoddard to gauge the General's mood but he was gazing at the blotter again.

'So,' he continued, 'we have about one kilo involved in the nuclear reaction – ten per cent of the total ten kilos – which is equivalent to twenty kilotons. That's very useful because Hiroshima and Nagasaki were both twenty-kiloton explosions, which means that we have considerable empirical evidence.'

He paused and looked at the listeners again, his eyes flickering back and forth. There didn't seem to be anyone obviously floundering.

'Fine,' said Calder. 'I can now move on to what you want to hear – the effects of a nuclear explosion of a bomb of this power. There are mainly four: thermal radiation, the blast or shock wave, initial radiation and residual radiation. These sound technical, but they're not difficult to understand really. The first three occur in all nuclear explosions and the last doesn't, but I'll explain that when I come to it.'

He turned to write on the board, hoping he wasn't sounding too patronizing. It was difficult to say it any other way.

'First, thermal radiation. This would be the first effect and although it's called "radiation", it isn't, in the normal sense in which we use the word. In fact it's non-radioactive heat that at one point reaches the sort of temperature achieved by the sun. It's in the form of a fireball that travels at the speed of light. Up to three seconds after the explosion it cools to an insignificant temperature, but in that short time the damage has been done. It causes two types of burns: flash-burns, caused directly by the fireball itself, and burns caused by the fire that the fireball creates.'

He paused and surveyed the table.

'I've got to make an assumption here, that, at the moment of explosion, average atmospheric conditions are prevailing and that the terrain is reasonably flat. That, of course, is a false assumption, because average atmospheric conditions, like all averages, are fictitious. I would ask you to appreciate that the effects may be more or less, depending on these conditions.'

He paused again, but no one spoke. *OK, here we go*, he thought. Looking at Stoddard, he said:

'Assuming these conditions, second-degree flash-burns can be expected at a distance of one and a quarter miles from "ground zero" – that's the point at which the explosion occurs.'

The General didn't react, but MacPherson sat up in his chair.

'A one-and-a-quarter-mile radius!' he exclaimed.

Everyone except Lecast and Stiles turned to look at him.

'That's right, Mr MacPherson,' answered Calder. 'In fact it could be worse,' he added cruelly. 'At Nagasaki, first-degree flash-burns were recorded at twice that distance, but that was an air-burst, where the flash-burn effect is greater. Twenty to thirty per cent of fatalities at Hiroshima and Nagasaki were due to flash-burns.'

He took a deep breath and let a silence develop. MacPherson was still sitting up in his chair and they were all staring at the board, transfixed – all, that is, except Benavici. His hands were moving more and he started blinking. Stoddard's expression was still annoyingly non-committal as Calder continued.

'But flash-burns are only part of the effect of thermal radiation. The other is "ordinary" burns caused by fire. In Hiroshima, everything combustible up to 2.2 miles from ground zero was completely destroyed by fire. In Nagasaki, it was only a quarter of this distance. But London, for various reasons which I won't bore you with, is more like Hiroshima in this respect.'

He paused.

'I mention London only because it seems to me the most likely target.'

MacPherson had already slumped back in his seat and was staring at the far wall. Everyone, including Benavici now, was immobile. If Lecast's secretary had walked in at that moment with no clothes on, he felt sure they wouldn't have noticed.

'Connected with this,' continued Calder, 'is the "fire-storm", which blows back into the area. The explosion causes a sort of vacuum, but the laws of physics tell us that the air must come back. In Hiroshima it was manifested by a wind that blew back in after twenty minutes, in varying strengths, for about six hours. It's good and bad news: it limits the range of the fire, but it also increases its intensity. My estimate is that, given average atmospheric conditions in London, the fire would consume everything combustible for up to one and three-quarter miles from ground zero.

Fifty per cent of the deaths in Japan were estimated to be by burns and two-thirds of those who died were badly burned.'

Lecast cleared his throat and swallowed heavily. The room was so silent that even the second sound was quite distinct. Calder sensed he was about to speak and waited.

'Let's get one thing absolutely straight,' the PM boomed eventually. 'You're talking about a circle, what, three and half miles across, totally consumed by fire?'

'That's correct.'

'My God,' said Corcorran slowly, 'and you said it was a small bomb!'

Calder knew he used to be a lay-preacher. Crawford interrupted unexpectedly.

'About the smallest it is possible to make and still be reasonably effective.'

All except Lecast and Stoddard looked at the elderly scientist, who was still looking at Calder. The latter caught his eye and decided it was friendly.

'And how would you reckon the survival rate of anyone within that circle?' persisted Lecast.

'It's very difficult to estimate,' answered Calder, 'but I'd rather do it at the end, if I may. I have so far only described the effect of thermal radiation. There are three other factors.'

The audience fidgeted nervously. Stoddard was still avoiding his eyes. He heard the Prime Minister take a deep breath before replying.

'Carry on,' he said flatly.

Calder nodded.

'The second effect, the shock or blast wave, would hit people within a second or so after the fireball. In ten seconds the blast would travel two and a half miles from ground zero and slow to about forty miles per hour. Its effect is similar to that experienced during an earthquake – basically, buildings collapsing and people being crushed. Indirectly, of course, it's another source of fire. In Nagasaki, buildings collapsed at 1.4 miles from ground zero and there was severe structural damage at 1.6 miles. I would expect that in London, severe structural damage would occur at up to one and a half miles, given average atmospheric conditions.'

Calder noticed that Crawford was plucking at his lower lip, but he didn't say anything. Neither did anyone else. They were just gazing at the board meekly. He got the impression that the politicians had finally begun to appreciate something of the scale of things, and the worst was yet to come.

'Thirdly,' continued Calder, trying to be matter-of-fact, 'initial radiation. To begin with, and to simplify it a little, two types of radiation are produced – Gamma rays and Neutrons. Gamma rays travel with the fireball at the speed of light and are effective for about a minute, when they decay to relative insignificance. Neutrons travel slightly slower, but are just as effective and last just as long. With a twenty-kiloton bomb, Gamma rays can be expected to travel for about two miles, but at that distance the effects are not very great, at least in the short term. With our bomb, and at a distance of half a mile, you would experience 1,000 roentgens of radiation, which produces hundred-per-cent fatalities. After this distance the Gamma rays would decay very quickly. At three-quarters of a mile, 300 roentgens would be experienced, which produces thirty-per-cent fatalities in two to six weeks. The effects for Neutrons would be similar.'

Calder paused. There was no reaction from his audience and there didn't look like being any. Stoddard just stared at the whiteness of his blotter. Calder must seem, to him, like an armed robot, churning out revolting information. Why the hell had he made a study of this subject anyway? He hated it. And the listeners hated listening, although they were compelled to do so. He took a deep breath.

'Depending on the atmospheric conditions and distance from ground zero,' he continued, 'anything from two to eight feet of concrete would be necessary for protection against Gamma rays. They can penetrate almost anything. Even this would be less effective for Neutrons, although wet soil more so.

'However, this in no way covers the total effects of initial radiation because of the various effects of relatively low doses of radiation on the human body. I'll deal with those in a moment. In Japan, up to fifteen per cent of initial fatalities were thought to be the result of initial radiation.'

Calder saw Lecast turn to Corcorran and the dark man returned his gaze. No expression passed between them that he could identify, but he knew what they were thinking. MacPherson looked sick. Stoddard could have given Calder a look of sympathy, but he didn't.

'The fourth and final effect is residual radiation. This is called "local fallout" and only occurs with a ground-burst. So, since Hiroshima and Nagasaki were both air-bursts, we have to rely on the evidence of American tests, although many countries, as you know, have exploded surface bombs.

'When a nuclear bomb is exploded in the air, all the residual radiation – usually Alpha and Beta particles – is taken straight up to the troposphere (fifty thousand feet) due to the updraft from the gigantic thermal. This is then carried by the wind and deposited in a few weeks, in very fine particles, over a wide area. It can even circle the globe in an easterly direction in four to seven weeks. Not enough is known about this tropospheric fallout, but it is thought to be so decayed and diluted as to be relatively harmless.'

Calder looked at Crawford before adding:

'I'm not sure about that in the long term.'

The elderly scientist made no reaction, but Benavici looked at him for the first and only time. Calder held his gaze for a few moments until he looked away. Then his hands began to move again.

'With a ground-burst, on the other hand,' Calder went on, 'which ours would almost certainly be, the residual radiation is taken up in the same way, but this time particles of earth and debris go with it and this is too heavy to remain in the air, let alone the troposphere, for very long. The Beta and Alpha particles become attached to this debris and fall back to earth in a steady shower. The rate at which they descend obviously depends on their weight and the strength of the wind, but they cause widespread contamination.'

Stoddard had raised his head and was now looking at Calder. The General looked down again and nodded, as if he had finally grasped something that had been eluding him.

'This is really the sting in the tail,' continued Calder, 'because, in my view, it is potentially, in the sense of long-term fatalities, more effective, if that's the right word, than the other three effects put together.'

Only the two scientists weren't staring at him now.

'With a fifteen-mile-per-hour wind, which is "normal", fifty per cent of the residual radiation would be expected to fall within two hundred miles of ground zero.'

He felt everyone stiffen. MacPherson leant forward in his chair again and this time so did Corcorran.

'Downwind, at a distance of 2.3 miles, given a wind strength of fifteen miles per hour, everyone exposed would die, at 5.3 miles thirty per cent would die and at fifty miles some would die over a much longer period. At its widest point the radiation band would be about five miles.'

Calder turned from writing the figures on the board. Benavici was still fidgeting, but everyone else was still. They weren't even blinking. He pushed on relentlessly.

'I am sure you know some of the long-term effects of a relatively small exposure to radiation, but I think it is worth mentioning them. Our knowledge here is rather shaky, but it is known that radiation causes death by leukaemia and other cancers. It can also cause cataracts, retardation of children, genetic mutations, bone defects and various other illnesses.'

Stoddard was looking at him again.

'Plutonium has a half-life of 24,000 years. That's the time it takes for the nuclei to reduce their radioactivity by decay to one half. So plutonium lasts for hundreds of thousands of years before it decays to relative insignificance. It also produces various isotopes, some of which can get into the human body through the food and drink chain, from contaminated ground. And that contamination, as I've already mentioned, would be a narrow band anything up to two hundred miles from ground zero, depending on the weather.

'The number of roentgens needed to cause cancer is not known exactly, but it is known that plutonium workers and people who have been exposed near test sites in the United States and elsewhere have suffered, in proportion, much more than the general population. Some of the cases are well documented, some not. You, of course, know this to be true because you have had access, and I have not, to the unofficial reports of the recent Aldermaston and Windscale scares.'

Again, Lecast and Corcorran looked at each other.

'Is there much more?' asked Lecast heavily.

'That's it,' replied Calder.

He had tried to present it objectively and unemotionally, but that was getting progressively more difficult.

'To give you some idea of what I'm talking about, Hiroshima had a population of 255,000. Of these people, 70,000 were killed and the same number injured, some very severely. I would expect the percentage casualty rate from our bomb to be greater.'

He paused, considering his next statement.

'I think it is also important to realize that I'm not just talking about the destruction of an area three and a half miles across, but also about the widespread contamination of a much larger area. In addition, if the wind is coming from the north, Alpha and Beta rays are going to cross the Channel and enter northern France.

'In my view,' said the relentless Calder, 'and this is an estimate based on many variables, no one in a circle a mile across would survive, two-thirds of those within a three-and-a-half-mile circle would be killed or injured, but I think that just as great a number would eventually die from cancer from the radiation, or be affected in some way by it. Central London would be uninhabitable for many years – perhaps for ever – and widespread decontamination would be necessary in an area about five miles wide and over a hundred miles long. Deep ploughing can do something, but you cannot completely decontaminate an area by human means. Time is the only healer. A very long time. It would certainly mean depopulation.

'Finally, I must say that terrain and weather can make a great deal of difference to my figures and it might not be London at all. It might not even explode, but personally I wouldn't count on it.'

With that he replaced the felt-tipped pen, returned the notes to his inside pocket and stood with his hands at his sides. The lecture was, at last, over.

No one spoke for at least ten seconds. Calder examined one of his hands and felt Stoddard looking at him. Finally, Crawford and Stiles looked to Lecast. The latter took another deep breath and scratched his forehead.

'Well,' he said, 'I don't know about anyone else but I could do with a cup of coffee.'

'A stiff whisky would be more to my liking,' said Corcorran. He turned to Calder. 'You tell a nasty tale.'

The Defence Minister was looking at him, Calder felt, rather as he would a creature that had crawled from under a rock. He looked back steadily and said nothing. Lecast pushed a button on the table intercom.

'Let's have some coffee in here,' he said simply, removed his finger and interlaced it with the others. Then he looked around the table. A sea-shore stone probably had more expression than he had on his face. He spoke very quietly.

'Shall we not concern ourselves with details, but with the overall concepts?' He paused. 'Dr Crawford. Is there anything you wish to say?'

The elderly scientist gathered his thoughts and looked at the table as he spoke.

'I wouldn't disagree fundamentally with anything that Mr Calder has said. However, there are one or two details . . .' He looked at Lecast and smiled. 'Scientists,' he said, 'are even more notorious than politicians for their lack of unanimity.'

Only Stiles laughed – a sort of short guffaw. It occurred to Calder that Crawford was only second to Stiles as the most relaxed man in the room.

'I wonder though,' continued Crawford, 'whether I can ask Mr Calder to bear in mind two points, if he will forgive my arrogance. As they are details, largely concerned with rainfall and humidity, I will send them to him rather than bore you all.'

He turned to Lecast before continuing and looked him straight in the eye.

'In relation to the overall catastrophe, Mr Calder is quite right. It would be the worst in British history, if we discount things like the Black Plague. What you do about it is up to you, of course, Prime Minister, but this bomb must not be exploded.'

Calder thought that his earlier estimate of Crawford's calmness might have been wrong. Moreover, no matter how he flowered his language, there was no doubt that he was telling Lecast what to do.

'Thank you, Dr Crawford,' said the P M. 'Dr Benavici?'

The nervous, dark man sat up as if someone had kicked him in the back. He moved his lips for a few seconds before anything came out.

'I have nothing to add,' he said eventually in an English public-school accent.

'Well, Doctors,' said Lecast, 'if there is nothing more . . .'

Both scientists moved their chairs back and stood up. Benavici turned and walked straight out. Crawford walked up to Calder with his arm outstretched. The latter shook it. The elderly scientist held on for a fraction longer than was normal and looked into Calder's face. He nodded very slightly, turned and left. Calder thought he had an ally and felt pleasantly surprised. Lecast motioned him to sit down and he began to wonder why he too hadn't been asked to leave.

'Now we have dealt with the accuracy of what Mr Calder said, we can decide what we are going to do,' stated Lecast firmly.

He looked down at the table suddenly.

'I'm sorry, Mr Calder. I am forgetting my manners. You have shocked me so much, I don't mind telling you, that I have not thanked you for explaining things, at such short notice. I don't know about the others, but I do feel that I now know what we could be in for. From what Sir Giles tells me, you found the process of telling it just as gruesome as we did listening.'

He glanced awkwardly at Corcorran.

'But it had to be done and for that I'm grateful.'

Stiles nodded. Stoddard had renewed his acquaintance with the blotter.

At this point there was a knock at the door and a coffee trolley was wheeled in, equipped with tea as well. Lecast stood up and so did the others. No one spoke as they helped themselves. It was almost as if the crisis didn't exist or had been relegated to second place, and Calder couldn't help wondering at this most English of habits. He tried to imagine it happening in the Oval Office or the Kremlin. The trolley was left where it was and they returned to the table.

'Of one thing I have absolutely no doubt,' said Lecast seriously. 'We must give in to them, whatever their demands. The sort of disaster we have just had described is too appalling to contemplate.'

'I agree,' said Stiles. 'Holding out to hijackers is one thing, but this is substantively different.'

MacPherson nodded.

'You are sure there is going to be a threat, Sir Giles?' asked Lecast.

Everyone looked at Stoddard. He hadn't said a word yet and his pipe was out of sight. Calder found that odd now he focused on it. The General looked up at Calder, then at Lecast.

'Yes, sir, I am. Probably in the next twenty-four hours.'

He paused.

'It may seem odd, but we have to be grateful for one thing. As you know, Prime Minister, we are pretty sure that they are not terrorists. If they were, the political demands they might make would be more difficult to meet, and might even be impossible to comply with if they involved a foreign power. And, even if terrorist demands were met, you could never be completely sure that they wouldn't explode the bomb anyway. We are almost certain that their leader, Brown, will be after one thing – money. And he won't come cheap.'

'So we have got to hand over to a gangster,' said Corcorran bitterly.

'Oh, you can be sure of one thing, sir,' answered Stoddard. 'Ruthless Brown may be, but he is not a gangster. He has one of the most calculating and brilliant minds I have ever come across.'

'Is this why your investigations have not found him?' persisted Corcorran.

Stoddard hesitated. Calder knew that Corcorran had some direct control over the foreign security services, like MI6 and the myriad of foreign off-shoots, but that Stoddard reported mainly to the Home Secretary and the P M.

'Since we found the workshop last night,' answered Stoddard, 'in which the device was made, we have lost all trace. We have a few ongoing investigations up our sleeve, but, to be frank, I'm not hopeful.'

Corcorran opened his mouth again, but Stiles got in before him. 'How would it be detonated?'

Stoddard immediately looked at Calder with a sort of priestly smile which the latter found a little disarming. He replaced his cup on its saucer, leant his forearms on the table and proceeded to answer the q .estion that he had already settled in his own mind.

'It could be done by a variety of means. It could be pre-set to detonate at a given time, but I think that's unlikely. Brown wouldn't have any flexibility and that wouldn't suit him at all. Alternatively, it could be plugged into the telephone system and exploded by dialling a certain number. But . . .'

Lecast interrupted.

'Just a minute. You mean it could be detonated by mistake, by someone simply dialling the wrong number?' he asked incredulously.

Calder nodded.

'It's possible,' he said. 'I don't think Brown will use that method though, partly because of the reason you mention, partly because it's subject to too many potential mechanical breakdowns.' His mouth twisted into a grin. 'Telephones are sometimes out of order. But the main reason is because it wouldn't be mobile. It would have to stay in a building, plugged into the telephone system, and Brown himself would have to stay near a phone. Mobility may be important to him, so he will probably use a radio signal. He can tune a receiver to a certain signal, at a certain pitch, on a certain frequency. The odds on that signal being made by accident are astronomical. With microtechnology the receiver need not be very big at all. Then all he would need is a powerful enough medium-frequency transmitter and he could send the vital signal over huge distances.'

'Good Lord,' said Lecast, 'he could be in another country.'

'Yes,' said Calder. 'He wouldn't even need to be by the transmitter. He could still keep his mobility. All he would need is a simple VHF transmitter, which would give him a fair distance and would fit into the palm of his hand. The tuner would be pre-set and locked on to the medium-frequency transmitter. All he would have to do would be to press a button, the VHF signal would be sent to the big transmitter, recognized and translated, then a medium-frequency signal would be sent to the receiver attached to the bomb. Within a second of him pressing the button the bomb would explode and he would be nowhere near it.'

Lecast silently drew his hands over his face, stretching the skin.

Corcorran still looked as if he wanted to kill someone. MacPherson looked sick. Stoddard merely looked at his blotter. Stiles, who was leaning back comfortably in his chair, switched his gaze from Calder.

'Sir Giles,' he said, 'what makes you think that Brown will not set off the bomb anyway?'

Calder looked at Stiles as he refilled his pipe from a tobacco pouch resting on the ample folds of his stomach. He could have been in his front room at home with his favourite slippers on.

'I don't think he is that type of man,' answered Stoddard.

He must have thought to himself that that sounded a bit lame.

'Besides, he has no reason to do so if he gets his money. But the truth is, I admit, we simply don't know for certain.'

He looked at Lecast and then back at Stiles before continuing. The confident smile was still there.

'We will continue to look for him and we may find him. But if we don't, as you said, we must pay up and hope. In the meantime there are measures which we can take. To begin with, we can seal off all the inner cities and search them thoroughly and meticulously. We can also check all traffic, in and out. Manpower might be a problem, but we still have the troops standing by in Norfolk.'

Lecast and Corcorran swapped glances as Stoddard continued.

'I agree with Mr Calder that London is the most likely target and, after that, other inner cities. Brown may choose to demolish a small town. We don't know. But we have to make a start somewhere. One thing is certain: he is not going to tell us what city it is in, even when we get his demands. That means, incidentally, that evacuation will be impossible.'

He paused to let that sink in. Calder noticed that Corcorran was glaring at the General.

'We may find it by searching every dwelling and building in the inner cities,' continued Stoddard, 'and we need to instigate a search of every sizeable vehicle in every part of the UK. I am told that it can fit into the boot of a big car.'

He looked at Calder, who wasn't surprised that there was no reaction to that statement. They'd had too many shocks. Even so, he *was* surprised that no one had asked about its size. Stiles lit his pipe.

'These measures, Sir Giles,' said Corcorran, his face like thunder, 'will totally disrupt the economy and social life of Britain. This will be much bigger even than your little affair in Norfolk, which eventually found the place too late. The country will literally come to a standstill. People will die from lack of mobility.'

Calder felt angry. And why was the hawk suddenly playing the dove? He glanced at Stoddard, whose face was still set in its relaxed smile. To a stranger it would look like a callous disregard for human dignity.

'Yes,' said Stoddard, 'they might, but that, in my view, is infinitely preferable to the loss of hundreds of thousands of lives.'

Stoddard, the General, weighing up human sacrifices, apparently without a care. Lecast came in quickly, glancing at his Defence Minister.

'I think you're being a little unfair, John. After all, it very nearly succeeded. We only missed them by about six hours and that in itself shows it was justified. But,' looking at Stoddard now, 'I also think John has a point here, Giles. If you feel that Brown is not going to use the bomb if we submit to his demands, why institute these terribly drastic measures, which have very little chance of success?'

It was a good question, that Calder knew he wouldn't like to answer. They all looked at the General, who seemed in no hurry to reply. Corcorran was leaning back and peering at him down his nose.

On the car journey from Norfolk, Calder had found out some more about Stoddard. He had a firm idea of his place in the order of things, having no hesitation about calling people 'sir' and expecting his subordinates to do the same with him. Calder, apparently, was one of the growing list of exceptions – 'a younger generation that has inherited a different and more confusing world'. Stoddard was English to the core and fiercely patriotic, believing in British-type 'democracy', the monarchy and public schools, and probably wore his considerable array of medals on Armistice Sunday. But he had far too robust an intellect to be fanatical and was aware that the system had flaws. Calder was mildly surprised to find that he understood the differences between Marx and the type of 'socialism' practised in the Soviet Union and Eastern

Europe, as well as the similarities. He also recognized that 'Communism' had many advantages over 'Capitalism', but, on balance, preferred Adam Smith to Lenin and, having made the decision, was prepared to defend it to the death.

Eventually, the General lifted his head from the blotter and placed his clasped hands upon it. When he spoke, it was with total confidence, as if he had just come down from Mount Sinai.

'Quite simply because we cannot afford to take the risk. We don't know what his demands are yet and, besides, until we know his set-up, we can never be *sure* that he won't explode it anyway. If he did, it would certainly take care of earnest pursuit.'

He paused and seemed to look at Corcorran.

'We cannot gamble with hundreds of thousands of lives. I realize that you have political responsibilities, but this is war. A rather warped war admittedly, but a war nonetheless, which has the classic symptom of killing the innocent rather than the guilty. And in war one has to make decisions which involve human lives. It's crude, calculated and barbaric, but it's necessary. You have to sacrifice some people so that more will live. In war, it is the one factor that makes a leader different from his subordinates and the main reason why he ages more quickly.'

Calder had never known Stoddard to be so profound, yet he was perfectly calm. It was emotive, but unemotional. The mild smile had not left his face the whole time. Lecast and MacPherson were looking at the General, and Corcorran at the table. Stiles, Calder noticed, was staring across at Stoddard, his mouth slightly open, his forgotten pipe going out as it lay in his palm on the table.

'I agree,' said the smoker suddenly.

Lecast looked at him and then at his Home Secretary. MacPherson took a long time before he nodded, his face deathly pale.

'What do *you* think, Mr Calder?' Lecast asked.

Calder felt that the PM hadn't yet made up his mind and that the question was more a breathing space, to allow him to do so, than because he really wanted his opinion. But then, he realized that he was appalled at the prospect of the totalitarian state that the General was advocating, however temporary it might be. And would it just be temporary, when the Plutonium Economy really arrived? The point was that they shouldn't be in the position now where they were forced to consider such measures. However, since they were, was it the lesser of two evils? Could he vote against Stoddard?

They were waiting for his reply. He felt Stoddard's eyes on him and he looked at him, in turn. Then he knew that his boss had perceived exactly what he was thinking.

'I agree with the General,' he said flatly, wondering whether he did or not.

They were expecting him to continue, but he had nothing more to say. Stiles flicked his lighter and relit his pipe. Lecast stretched the skin on his face again and glanced at Corcorran. The latter looked up and shook his head violently. Calder suddenly appreciated what a difficult job being Prime Minister was. The Premier blinked rapidly for several seconds, then turned to his Minister of Defence and spoke in a resigned tone.

'Sorry, John.' Then he looked up at Stoddard. 'Very well, Sir Giles. I shall have to inform the whole Cabinet, of course, and decide what to release to the press, but that's my problem.'

He paused, then said:

'I didn't think we'd be re-elected anyway.'

It took a few moments for that to sink in, but when it did, Calder flushed with anger. Then the PM smiled and Calder realized that it had been a joke. Stiles chuckled, removed his pipe and blew a smoke-ring at the ceiling.

'In that case,' he said, his mouth curling up at the edges, 'we can't do anything until we hear from our "gangster" friend.' And he winked slyly at Calder.

Chapter 16

Motorway service stations are much the same wherever you are and this one, on the M6, was no exception. The tarmac and concrete were littered with oil stains, the petrol was expensive, the toilets were just clean enough, but smelt occasionally, and the food was passably non-exciting. But then, what more could you do with a place where folks never stayed, just passed through?

For the four travellers, however, it was a welcome, lunchtime respite from the boredom of motorway travel. The cafeteria was about a third full and emptying as the diners finished their meals. Martin, Mac, Sash and Judy were taking their time over their second cup of coffee. They were in no hurry to get to their destination. None was noted as having a garrulous nature and conversation had died. Mac and Judy sat opposite each other, near the window, and gazed out. Martin and Sash beside them stared into their cups. The only notable thing about them was that all the men had beards.

Judy had thought about standing up and shouting rape, but that had no guarantee of success. They could simply inflict pain surreptitiously and tell anyone who inquired that she was drunk or insane. A man had arrived in a yellow sports car about half an hour earlier. She'd thought about chatting him up as he left, on the pretext of going to the loo. But that was even more risky. The timing was too exacting and, although he looked brave enough, you could never tell with men.

'This needs livening up a bit,' said Mac.

He reached inside his coat, extracting the familiar metal flask, and poured a generous helping into his cup.

'You'll get us arrested,' said Martin, but he didn't seem too concerned.

Finally, Judy had decided that it had to be done by going to the ladies' loo. Once inside she had a number of possibilities. The windows might be big enough for her to climb through, but she doubted it. Besides, they would probably check them. She had £150 in her purse. She could try and buy a disguise – an exchange of clothes – but again there were problems. Women were notoriously fussy about giving up their clothes and wearing others, even for £150. That, of course, was providing the clothes fitted in the first place and qualified as a disguise. It was a possibility, no more.

The most likely solution was to ask the first woman she came upon to call the police, on the grounds that she was being followed, then lock herself in a cubicle. What could Martin and co. do? It was a little primitive, but then John always said that the best plans were based on simple principles. It would serve him right if she took a leaf out of his book. Anyway, it was the only thing she could think of that might really work.

She willed herself to act naturally, stubbed out her cigarette and turned to Sash, sitting beside her.

'I take it I can go to the loo?' she asked sarcastically.

She hoped it wasn't too strong, but then she'd been locked up in her room for nearly a week and she was expected to be bad-tempered.

Sash looked at Martin, who nodded. The pilot stood up and watched Judy wriggle out of the booth. When she had left, Martin looked up.

'Don't sit down, Sash lad,' he said and tossed his head at the retreating figure in short, summer frock and matching shoes. 'Your turn, I believe,' he added. 'No need to check the windows – I've already done it.'

He smiled inanely and Sash did the same. He didn't like this thing with Judy, but then what could he do?

She stopped in the foyer, ostensibly to look for the toilet sign and saw that Sash was about twenty-five yards behind. She turned a corner and, for a fleeting moment, thought about dashing for the door. Her watchdog would think she had entered the Ladies. She would have at least five minutes' start and she knew she'd get a lift within minutes. But it was just too far. He would have turned the corner before she got to the entrance. No, there was only one place to go. She stopped at the door with the doll monogram and looked back. Sash was standing at the corner, watching. He looked slightly embarrassed and could not hold her gaze. She pushed the door and walked through.

A woman left as she entered and then she realized, in a moment of panic, that she was alone. There was no one in sight. She examined all the locks on the cubicle doors and they all read 'vacant', so she turned and looked at the entrance door. She would talk to the first person through.

Just then a small, round woman with short-cropped, mousy-coloured hair entered, opening her bag as she did so. Judy rushed up, making the woman retreat a few steps and leading her to drop her bag in the process. There was sheer terror in her eyes.

'Please, you must telephone the police. I'm being held prisoner. I don't know what they might do to me.'

The stricken woman hesitated, clearly torn between the apparently genuine agitation in the fair-haired woman and the thought that she might be mad. She looked down at her fallen bag. Judy bent down and picked it up.

'There's a man outside,' she said, 'with fair hair and a beard. He's one of them, and please, you must ring. Dial 999.'

The woman looked at her bag, still in Judy's hands, then at the cubicles. She bit her lower lip, snatched her bag, looked again at the frightened Judy and left quickly.

'Please hurry,' called Judy as the woman was halfway through the door, then looked at her own bag for her purse. She prayed that she had a two-pence piece, found one, let herself into a cubicle and locked it.

Outside, the woman looked round. Over by the entrance there *was* a man with fair hair and a beard and he did appear to be watching the Ladies. He was certainly watching her now. She looked around for a phone, then back again. He didn't look like a villain though. Rather a nice-looking man actually, with similar colouring to the woman. She'd ask her husband.

Sash had observed the woman exit the toilet rather swiftly and then stop. She'd only entered a few moments before. She began to stare at him, then glanced at the telephone and back at him again. He acted on impulse and walked up to the woman, smiling. She seemed rooted to the spot, her eyes wide. He put on his best public-school accent.

'Don't tell me,' he said, 'she gave you the man-following-her routine again and will-you-please-telephone-the-police. Am I right?'

The woman smiled too, relieved.

'Yes,' she answered and then, a little more carefully: 'You know her?'

Sash let out a short, polite laugh.

'I'm her brother,' he said. Then his face became serious. 'She has been in and out of hospital all her life. I had a feeling she was going to do something like this. That's why I stationed myself outside.'

He looked at the toilet door and sighed.

'She really believes it, you see. The last time was at Heathrow. We all spent the night in jail. Usually, when we travel, Mother comes now, but,' he lowered his head, 'that wasn't possible this time.'

Sash smiled again, bravely.

'How will you get her out?' asked the woman.

'Suppose I shall have to call the police myself and ask them to bring a policewoman along.'

His smile broadened.

'Perhaps they'll believe me if *I* phone *them*,' he added. 'Sorry you have been troubled.'

His face took on a new seriousness, he nodded his thanks and walked over to the public telephone. She turned and looked at the loo door. Well, she wasn't going back in there again. She'd just have to last until the next service stop. She walked back into the restaurant, passing the nice man as he was dialling.

Sash placed his finger on the bar just as someone said, 'Emergency, which service?' He suddenly realized that his heart was racing. He hadn't thought that he had it in him. It was because he did it without thinking, he supposed. He couldn't go in to tell the others about the problem, because it would look suspicious to the woman. But then he didn't have to move anyway. When neither he nor Judy returned, they'd come running soon enough.

He had waited about three minutes, still with the phone to his ear, when he noticed the woman returning. Beside her, incongruously, was a man as tall as Martin. Two kids followed in their wake. He saw her pointing at him out of the corner of his eye. His heart did a somersault and landed on its back. The man was looking at him suspiciously. Sash waved at the woman and began talking rubbish into the phone, putting on a look of frustration. To his immense relief they walked past.

He watched them go and replaced the phone, repositioning himself outside the Ladies. Within a minute, Martin and Mac arrived.

'What's up?' asked Martin knowingly.

He told him.

'Jesus Christ,' said Mac. 'That's all we need. If we had no' had to pick up that gear in Manchester we'd be there already.'

'Where's this woman now?' asked Martin.

'She's left with her family.'

'Good. We can't cause a fuss,' said the tall man, looking at the toilet door. 'But we've got to make an effort.'

Mac swore at the floor again.

'If we have to make the choice,' continued Martin, 'between leaving her here and being arrested ourselves, we leave her here. None of us has told her where we're going, have we?'

They both shook their heads.

'What's more, she doesn't know where the bomb is. Only three people know that: John, Wilson and Vaisey. He knows what he's doing, does John. Jeeze though, I wish he was here now.'

He bit his lip. He had to decide what to do.

'You did well, Sash,' he said. 'But you've got to have a final go.'

'What do you mean?' asked the fair-haired man suspiciously. 'What do you want me to do, walk in there and bring her out?'

'Judy's case is in the car,' said Martin. 'Go and get it and take it into the Gents. Lock yourself in a cubicle and . . .'

'You've got to be joking,' said Sash indignantly.

'It's got to be you, Sash. You're the only one who can get near her size and your blond beard doesn't show as much as ours. You should be all right if you keep your hands over your face.'

'And I suppose that is going to look perfectly natural,' said Sash. He crossed his arms in obstinate disobedience.

'I can't do it,' he said.

Martin closed in on one side and Mac on the other.

'Oh, yes, you will,' said Martin, 'because I'm telling you to.'

'Besides,' added Mac through broken teeth, 'you're prettier than we are.'

Martin pulled out the car keys. Then he had second thoughts and they disappeared back in his pocket.

'I'll walk over to the car with you,' he said. 'Mac will stay here and make sure she doesn't slip away. When you've got into something suitably feminine, bring the suitcase out with you, repacked with your clothes as well, and give it to me. When you go in, we'll be waiting over the far side, by the service exit, so that no one can read our number. If anything goes wrong, run for the car.'

Sash had become resolved to the idea.

'How do I know you won't just run without me?' he asked, suddenly seeing a picture of himself, dressed up in woman's clothes at a motorway service station and stuck without a car.

Martin sighed.

'For the same reason, stupid, that we're taking so much trouble to keep hold of Judy. You know even more than she does. Come on, let's go.'

Martin had been officer material in the Army. Brown had implied it. An ability to show initiative in tricky situations, he had said. Yes, he could have made lieutenant. The plan was excellent in the circumstances and, as he walked over to the car, he felt strangely elated. If he thought there was anything odd about being more pleased with the plan than he was disturbed at losing the reason for that plan, he didn't show it. He also hadn't considered one of the basic rules of command: that even the most brilliant scheme was only as good as the men who carried it out. Being officer material was not the same as being an officer.

Judy, meanwhile, was getting worried. She had lost count of how many minutes had passed since she had locked herself in the cubicle. Surely the police should be here by now? They had patrols going up and down the motorway all the time, didn't they? She had a minor heart-attack every time the door opened, which it did with amazing frequency. But surely Martin wouldn't come into the Ladies to get her?

She was fairly sure the place was temporarily empty when the door opened again. Almost immediately she felt her door being tried.

'Hello,' said a voice. 'This is the police. Was it you who called us?'

Relief flooded through Judy and she reached for the bolt. Then something stopped her. The voice sounded female, but there was something about it that she couldn't put her finger on. She stood back, her heart thumping in her chest. There was no harm in being cautious.

'How do I know you're police?' she asked defiantly.

There was a muffled expletive and a body slammed against her door. The bolt held. She heard the door of the next cubicle being tried, then *her* cubicle became dimmer as someone appeared over the door. There was the sound of material ripping. She looked up, terrified, unable to shout. It was Sash, his head in the hood of a cloak and one leg astride the door. Suddenly a woman screamed.

Sash had been wise enough to don long clothes. The dress reached the floor on Judy, but it didn't on him. His shoulders were scrunched up at an odd angle, although his hips were all right. Over this he had put a coarse, dark cloak he had found, and put the hood up. It hid a multitude of sins. Unfortunately, the one thing he could not get to fit him were Judy's shoes. She took a size five and, although Sash was not a particularly big man, there was no way his size eights could be squeezed in. So he had left his shoes and socks on, and hoped they wouldn't show under the cloak.

The woman had entered the room just as Sash lifted his leg up on top of the door. Her attention was immediately drawn by the sound of the dress ripping down the back, but she couldn't really have missed him anyway. What she saw was a muscular leg, covered in short, blond hairs, wearing a man's shoe and sock, half-way over a toilet cubicle. She did the thing that came naturally and screamed.

Sash realized, in that moment, that he had failed. He could, just possibly, have forced Judy out and to the car while they were perfectly anonymous, but with a hue-and-cry already instigated it was impossible. He, too, did what came naturally and ran – past the screaming lady at the door, past the staring, incredulous bystanders

234

in the foyer, into a startled, portly gentleman entering the building and sending him flying, past the petrol pumps and across the seventy or so yards of tarmac to the waiting car. A rear door opened as he approached and he dived in. The vehicle then accelerated away, past the 'No Entry' signs, up the ramp of the access road and away to the distant countryside. In the Ladies, the woman was still screaming.

Fifteen minutes later, Judy had become accustomed to the hum of voices on the other side of the door. One or two phrases she could hear distinctly, like, 'poor girl', and, 'the police have been called'. But she was still shaking.

The voices became hushed and there was a knock on the door.

'Open up now. This is the police.'

Judy was trying to concentrate. A woman's voice again. Fearfully, she repeated her last question.

'How do I know you're police?'

She heard someone sigh loudly, then:

'Anyone got 2p? . . . Ah, thanks, luv.'

A coin was placed in a lock meter and she heard the door of the cubicle next to hers being opened. Then someone stood on the toilet seat. She daren't look this time.

'What's the problem, luv?' came the voice from above.

Judy did look up. The black and white squares on the policewoman's hat were unmistakable and underneath them a friendly, chubby face smiled down.

''Ave ya got the runs?' it asked.

Judy burst into tears.

Calder emerged from his bedroom in underpants and switched on the television. He was just in time to hear the newscaster say, 'Good evening.'

'The government has announced,' continued the newsreader, 'that the inner city areas of nine major cities in England have been cordoned off and are at this moment being systematically searched. All traffic in and out of these areas is being checked and traffic on all roads is similarly being stopped.'

The picture switched from a studio to an outside broadcast unit, showing a long queue of traffic waiting to leave inner London.

'Large queues are already developing as motorists, caught unawares by the surprise decision, are waiting to drive home. Apparently public transport is not affected and motorists have been advised to use buses, the underground and trains tomorrow morning. All private vehicles should leave the inner city areas tonight though, if they usually do so, otherwise the boots of these cars are likely to be broken into. By the same token, motorists living within these inner city areas are advised not to stray too far from their vehicles until further notice.'

The newsreader came back on.

'The government have apologized for the inconvenience and say it is a training exercise.'

A picture of MacPherson, looking at least ten years younger than he had that morning, appeared and, alongside him, the typewritten government statement.

'According to an official statement from the Home Office: "The Government was taken by surprise by the plutonium hijacking on the 5th of this month and must be sure that they can handle a similar emergency again. Such security measures, by their very nature, must operate with surprise. Hence it was not possible to give any advance warning, even though it is only a training exercise. The Government apologizes for the obvious inconvenience, which will last three to four days, and hope that the necessity will be understood."

'Meanwhile,' went on the broadcaster, 'nine of England's major cities – London, Birmingham, Manchester, Liverpool, Sheffield, Leeds, Newcastle upon Tyne, Southampton and Bristol – are sealed off. Towns and cities in Wales and Scotland are unaffected, but they are subject to road-blocks.'

'They'll never get away with it,' said Ann.

He turned. She was leaning seductively against the door-jamb, wearing one of his best white shirts, the tails covering her front and back to a point about a third down her thighs. The side slit left a tantalizing strip of flesh up the hip and her nipples pushed proudly against the material, creating deep shadows. He forced his mind back to her statement.

'Probably not in the long term,' he said, 'but what else can Lecast say? That all those inner cities are in danger of being devastated by a nuclear bomb?'

She shrugged heavily. The shirt rode up and her breasts quivered.

'Coffee?' he asked, not taking his eyes off her.

She nodded and smiled.

He wandered into the kitchen. When he came out she was sitting primly on the couch, leaving just that little bit to the imagination. The screen showed the Queen opening a new hospital in North-ampton. They both watched moronically. The kettle boiled and Calder returned to the kitchen. *Nationwide* had begun when he got back. Ann made to speak, but he waved her to silence as he listened to their proposed programme.

'Sorry,' he said, placing a coffee in front of her. 'It would appear that they are not going to discuss it. Were there any announcements made about special programmes later on?'

'No,' she answered. 'That appears to be it.'

'Then the BBC and IBA and the press must be in on the cover-up. The Government must have come down really hard, or perhaps they simply let them in on the secret and they're doing their best to stop panic. They'd leap at the story otherwise. Infringements on individual liberty and all that. It's the only way they can hope to keep it from leaking out too soon. It doesn't take a great deal of grey matter to work out why these cities are being sealed off less than three weeks after a plutonium hijacking. Journalists must be eating their pencils in frustration and it would soon come out in a studio discussion.'

Ann frowned.

'Individuals up and down the country must be suspicious now,' continued Calder, 'especially after the "training exercise" in Nor-folk. You're right. They can't hope to get away with it in the long term, but they might just pull it off for three or four days, and that's all the time we shall need.'

He paused and grinned. She was glad when the telephone rang.

It was 10 p.m. when Striker pulled into the police station, which was not bad going. The traffic had been heavy from central London to the M1, but once on the motorway he had broken the speed limit the whole way, apart from two sections where there was only one lane open because of repairs. Two hours and five minutes later he was at the Stoke turn-off. There had been one cordon and two road-blocks on the way, but each time he had been able to use the police access lane and they had hardly held him up at all. The biggest problem had been finding the right police station. Stoke, it appeared, was not just Stoke. It consisted, in fact, of five towns, only one of which was Stoke, but all of which, together, went under the generic title of Stoke.

He noticed the desk-sergeant come involuntarily to attention as he walked in. Stoddard had obviously been on the phone to smooth his path. The sergeant put on his responsibility face.

'My name is Striker. I think you are expecting me.'

If the uniformed man was surprised at the American accent, he didn't show it.

'Yes, sir,' he answered, pushing a button on his desk. 'Super-intendent Bridges is in charge, sir.'

Striker looked round and took his bearings. It was interesting how police stations looked the same, wherever you were. Simi-larity of function he supposed. But he was not allowed to elaborate on these reflections, because a man came out of a side door. He was about forty, with fine, sandy hair and a clipped moustache.

'Bridges,' he said simply.

'Striker.'

They shook hands and the blond man showed his identification. Bridges nodded and ushered him through a different door. They walked down a corridor and Striker was told what had happened at the service station. Apparently there were no clues as to the identification of the vehicle or its subsequent journey.

'How is she?' asked Striker.

The Superintendent hesitated.

'Quite well, physically, although she won't eat anything – just drinks tea. She put up quite a fit of hysterics when the arresting WPC went off duty. Taken quite a liking to her. Only person she'd speak to, in fact. Hasn't said a word since she left.'

He stopped outside a door marked 'D' and lowered his voice.

'She refused to tell us at first who she was. It was when we told her that in that case we might as well release her that she told us some of the story. When she mentioned the name Brown, we at first didn't believe it. We questioned her a bit more.'

He lowered his head.

'I don't think we were too hard. Anyway, she said enough for us to realize that she was probably telling the truth, so we left it there and phoned you people.'

He looked unhappy, but whether it was about the girl, Striker wasn't sure.

'I'll go in alone if you don't mind?' said the American.

Bridges nodded and opened the door. It was an interrogation room, about fifteen feet square. The walls were off-white and totally bare. In the centre was a Formica-covered table and two canvas chairs. Sitting on one, facing the far wall, was the girl, her head held in her hands. She didn't stir as he came in. The woman police constable left.

Striker closed the door and walked round to the girl. She looked up at him. What he saw was a strained but attractive face. The skin under the eyes was a puffy red and a rather poor attempt had been made to repair the tear-stained make-up. The eyes themselves were bloodshot and frightened, and the tousled, fair hair could have done with a comb.

She put her hands on the table and sat back, her eyes not leaving him as he sat down.

'Hello,' he said, searching her face for a reaction.

She said nothing, just looked at him. He glanced at the table and back at her face. He spoke very softly.

'I'll lay it on the line for you. My name is Peter Striker and, as you can no doubt gather from my accent, I'm not with the police. At least, not exactly.'

She looked at the table.

'I've come from London,' continued Striker. 'I have a car outside and I'd like you to drive back with me tonight.'

She looked at him again.

'I'm going to ask you a few questions now, some of which you've already been asked. They won't last long and then I won't ask you any more. At least, not until you've had a good night's sleep. You can snooze in the car if you like. It's quite comfortable.'

He paused.

'They are very important questions. A lot of people's lives may depend on them. Do you understand?'

He saw the fear come back into her eyes again.

'Where did the hijack take place?' he asked quickly.

She hesitated a long time. Then her eyes flickered from side to side.

'Carlisle Airport,' she said.

It was a pleasant voice. He found placing British accents difficult, but hers sounded like what most southerners call 'northern'.

'How did you leave the plane?' he asked.

He saw the fear again – or was it terror?

'Parachute.' The voice was breathless. 'Into the sea.'

That almost settled it. He waited for a few moments, his eyes never leaving her.

'Do you know what we're looking for?'

'John Brown,' she answered plainly.

'Do you know where he is, or any of his gang?'

She shook her head. 'No. They didn't trust me.'

'So you have no idea where the bomb is either?'

'No,' she said immediately. 'I wish I did. Believe me, please.'

He smiled before answering. 'I do.'

He saw a window open in her face and, inextricably, felt himself blush. She seemed to smile.

'That's all for now,' he said quietly, looking down at the table, then up again. 'Will you come with me?'

'Yes,' she answered and stood up to reinforce it.

He followed suit.

'It's a three-hour journey,' he said. 'Perhaps you'd like to . . .'

'Yes, I would,' she said, still looking at him.

He walked past her to the door. Outside, the WPC was waiting patiently.

'Would you show this lady to the toilet? I'll meet her at the desk.'

Judy scrutinized him closely as she passed and he watched her walk carefully up the corridor. The final confirmation. He met with Bridges, signed her release papers and received a photocopy of the transcript of all her statements.

She looked different when she returned. Her hair was still in disarray, but the face was clean and some of the strain had gone. The desk-sergeant handed over her bag and Striker removed his anorak.

'You'd better put this on,' he said. 'It's cold outside.'

She looked at him closely again, then turned as he slipped it over her shoulders.

They walked out into the night. There was a fresh scent in the air. She stopped on the step for him and he placed an arm around her. He didn't consciously do it. It just seemed the most obvious thing to do.

Chapter 17

Friday, 23 May, a.m.

At 9.25 a.m., a man wearing dark glasses and a red and white bobble-hat walked through the front door of the *Daily Express* offices in Fleet Street. He headed straight for the porter's desk and handed over a small package, about two and a half inches by four, and half an inch in depth. It was wrapped in brown paper.

The porter took it suspiciously.

'For the Editor,' said the man and left.

The porter turned it over, weighed it in his hand and shook it. He shrugged his shoulders and put it to one side. Then he picked it up again. It was marked 'Urgent'. Well, the messenger would be back soon.

Along the street the man entered a phone box. He brought out a piece of paper from his coat pocket, lifted the phone and dialled. He replaced the paper and fished in his pocket for a coin. A 10p piece came between his fingers and he extracted it, pushing it into the slot as the pips sounded.

'News desk, please,' he said.

There was a short pause.

'Hello. A small package has just arrived at the porter's desk, addressed to "The Editor" and marked "Urgent". If I were you I wouldn't waste any time in opening it.'

Upstairs in the newspaper offices, the young reporter stared at the dead phone, replaced it, scratched his head, then headed for the stairs.

In the lobby, the porter was still waiting for the messenger to return when the journalist walked up.

'Have you just received a small package for the Editor?' asked the young man.

The porter picked it up. 'It seems all right.'

'I'll take it,' said the other.

The porter handed it over and watched the man depart. He shrugged his shoulders again and returned to his paperwork.

Upstairs, the reporter tore off the brown paper. He had no hesitation about opening it – the editor was in a meeting and so were the rest of the senior staff. And, after all, it *was* marked 'Urgent'. Inside was a cassette tape. He dragged over his own portable machine, slotted in the tape and switched on. Anyone observing him might have noticed him stiffen. They would certainly have seen his eyes get wider as he sat motionless.

After four or five minutes he stopped the machine and looked at the door marked 'Editor'. So they were in an important meeting, but he could interrupt them for this. It had to be the hottest thing he'd ever got his hands on. He grabbed his portable, walked briskly to the door, knocked and walked in without waiting for a reply.

The call came through for Striker at 10.50. A man entered the room where he was interviewing Judy with a colleague. The blond man looked up and switched off the tape-recorder. The man approached and placed a hand on his shoulder.

'The Old Man wants you. In his office.'

Striker looked across at Judy. They had arrived back in London in the early hours. She had slept most of the journey and, rather than take her to the Department, they had gone straight to his flat. She had had a bath and then a good night's sleep, while he had tossed fitfully on the sofa. In the morning they had showered and breakfasted slowly, then done a little shopping in order for Judy to buy some articles of clothing. They had arrived at the Department at 10 o'clock. He had insisted that he conduct the 'interrogation' and, to his surprise, found that he had no opposition. He was fairly sure she wasn't going to add to their knowledge in any vital area, but it had to be done none the less.

'I'll have to go now,' he said to her.

She nodded.

'I'll be back soon and we'll carry on.'

She nodded again.

'See if you can find some coffee, will you, Jim?' he said to the man sitting next to him. Then he left.

Ann was at her desk when he walked in. She smiled and flicked a switch.

'Mr Striker, sir,' she said.

'Fine,' answered Stoddard. 'Send him in and come yourself, will you? Route all the calls through to here.'

The General was being businesslike. She flicked a few switches, raised her eyebrows and followed Striker through. Bill Jensen was seated in front of the desk and Matthew was standing by the window, looking at the desk. He didn't move as they entered, or acknowledge them. The General was fiddling with a portable cassette recorder.

'Any luck with the girl, Peter?' he asked. 'Take a seat, Ann.'

It occurred to Striker that the Old Man had a professional set of priorities. And he had called him by his Christian name again. It was funny, but he didn't find him anything like so awesome now he was fully dressed and in his office, pipe in mouth. Then he noticed that Stoddard had broken a lifetime's habit as he saw smoke rising from the bole.

'I'm afraid not, sir,' he answered guardedly. 'I've asked all the important questions already and really there are only two: where is the bomb and where are the people who have hidden it? She has no more idea of the answers than we have. She's giving a lot of information that we wanted once, but it's really too late now.'

'You're sure about that?' asked Stoddard. 'She's not lying?'

Striker looked at him hard. 'No, sir. She's not lying.'

There was an awkward silence.

'She's innocent, sir. She's terrified of the whole business and she's also aware of the consequences. She'd tell me if she knew.'

He felt himself shift uncomfortably. Ann was looking at him, a faintly quizzical expression on her face. Stoddard was still touching the recorder, as if he had something else on his mind. Striker thought that he ought to be a little more helpful.

'The only possible hope is that she does know something but doesn't realize it. You know, the chance word or remark dropped in casual conversation that had no significance at the time.'

'Well,' said Stoddard, 'we didn't think it would be a breakthrough. Keep on it. As you say, something may show up. Send me a full transcript and have it on my desk by five.'

He sighed.

'We haven't had any luck with our other inquiries either, have we, Bill?'

'No,' said Jensen. 'I'm afraid . . .'

'Yes, I know,' interrupted Stoddard. 'It's no one's fault. I thought that we might get something useful out of all those names and addresses, but we haven't even got a lead to the house in Norfolk, let alone to where they are now.' He glanced at Calder. 'The Arab, Khalid Aziz, was a dead duck as well.'

Striker looked at Calder too. The bearded man's face was expressionless and he hadn't moved. He was still standing, hands at his sides, looking at the surface of the Old Man's desk.

'Anyway,' continued the General, 'the reason I have asked you all here is this,' pointing at the cassette recorder.

'This tape arrived, by hand, at the *Daily Express*, at 9.30 this morning. I've already sent someone round. He'll get a description of the delivery man and we'll put out an all-points bulletin, but I don't hold out any hopes there.'

He pressed a button.

'I've heard it,' he added and sucked vigorously on his pipe.

All of them, including Stoddard, stared at the machine. All they could hear at first was the rustling sound of the tape travelling through the amplifier. Then, a deep, well-modulated, yet somehow metallic voice began to speak.

'Good morning. This is John Brown. It seems immodest for me to say so, but I don't think I need an introduction. I am sending this tape to you, the editor of the *Daily Express*, for no particular reason, except that you will know the appropriate person to give it to. I advise you to do so immediately, not least because the longer you wait the greater the risk to human life, but also because the person you give it to may be annoyed at any delay.'

There was a pause while the tape crackled.

'To whom it may concern. As you no doubt know, I have built, from plutonium oxide hijacked on 5th May, an atomic bomb. I see no harm in telling you that it contains ten kilos of P-239. No doubt you have experts, as I have, who can tell you something of

245

the devastation that would be caused by the fission of that amount of plutonium. And devastation I assure you there will be, unless you meet my conditions. These are as follows.

'First, all road-blocks other than those around the inner cities will cease at 1200 hours on Saturday 24th. The reason for that will become apparent to you in a moment.

'Second, you have thirty-six hours from midday on Friday 23rd in which to deliver to me £25 million worth of the best quality, uncut diamonds.'

Striker looked at Calder as the voice went on. His face still had no expression.

'When I say the "best" quality, that is precisely what I mean. It seems almost pointless to say that I have an expert on my team who can tell the difference between "gem quality" and those things destined to drill people's teeth. They must be a mixture in terms of size, although there must be no small ones. In other words, they must be gems that, when cut, will be "Fine Blue-whites", "Top Crystals", "Capes" and so on, but they must not be flawed or of poor colour.'

There was a pause.

'I hope that is all understood, because if I find one poor-quality stone, I shall have no hesitation in exploding the bomb. I hope you believe that.'

Brown allowed another pause to develop. Striker could imagine him, sitting down recording it and seeing the people in this room looking at each other – which was precisely what they were doing. All except Calder, that is. He hadn't taken his eyes off the recorder.

'Thirdly, you will deliver these diamonds to the back of a lorry. In order to find it, take a robust vehicle along the M4 out of London. Make the Newbury turn-off and in Newbury take the A343 from the roundabout that also feeds the A34. Follow this road for precisely six and a half miles, until, nearly at the top of the hill, you will come to a left-hand fork directing you to Crux Easton, Woodcott and Egbury. Turn into this side road and stop immediately, waiting until exactly midnight. Then follow the road, without deviating, until you come to our first phosphorescent, orange arrow. Follow the arrows to the letter and you will come to the lorry. The tailgate will be down. Place the diamonds, which must be in twenty-kilo lots in transparent plastic bags, in the back of the lorry. Then leave the way you came.

'You will make no attempt to follow and there are to be no bugs. Also, don't be stupid enough to try and stake out the position beforehand. You won't know exactly where it is and if we spot you, I shall push the button.

'Fourth, you will initiate no search for myself or my men for a further forty-eight hours. You may continue to search for the bomb though, if you persist in wasting time. The road-blocks will, of course, have ceased as per my first instruction. In addition, all seaports, airports and coasts will be freed of all surveillance. If anyone tries to stop any of my men you know what will happen.

'That is all. Follow these instructions completely and exactly, and I give you my word that I will not explode the bomb. Also, within a few days, the *Express* will receive a letter giving its exact location. If, on the other hand, you do not follow these instructions, in any particular, the result will be catastrophic, and I'm not all that sure that history would blame me. This is the only communication there will be between us.'

There was a sharp click and the message was finished. Stoddard was the quickest to react. He reached forward out of the smoke and switched off the machine. Then he ejected the tape and held it in his hand.

'I'll get a copy made of this,' he said. 'Then I might as well go through the motions of giving it to the technical boys for some sort of clue.'

Striker saw Jensen nod.

'I'd like to hear it through again,' said Jensen, 'but it seems more or less what we expected.'

As he listened to the man continue, Striker focused on the fact that, to him, Jensen always seemed like a robot. His hair was the colour of wet rust, but he was sure that had nothing to do with it.

'It seems to be a good example of what we already know to be true, that Brown's *modus operandi* is simple, exact and faultless. I don't think we can complain about his demands. Indeed, they seem rather modest. I suppose the question is, do we play his game or don't we?'

Striker couldn't see his face, but he knew what the expression would be. Stoddard looked fierce.

'We have no choice,' he said. 'We have to play it his way. We simply cannot afford to do otherwise. I dread to think what will happen if we slip up.'

The phone rang and Ann picked it up. It gave an excuse for a comfortable pause, while the four men considered their acquiescence and accepted it into their being. Ann talked in low tones so that she did not disturb anyone. Striker looked at Calder. He still looked unconcerned, but there was tension in the voice as he spoke.

'Will there be any difficulty in getting diamonds of that quality and quantity in thirty-six hours?'

'Not really,' answered Jensen immediately. 'Oh, it will be difficult, but we can manage it. London is still the diamond capital of the world.'

'I thought it was Amsterdam,' said Striker without thinking.

Jensen seemed pleased by the comment, and looked round at the blond man with narrowed eyes and benign grin.

'That's where they are cut,' he said. 'Our friend wants uncut diamonds, because they are, to a very large extent, untraceable, and London is the place for uncut diamonds.'

He paused and looked at the ceiling, clearly gathering his thoughts before continuing. Most of the room now was quite thick with smoke.

'No, HMG will have to cough up to the diamond merchants, of course, at top-of-the-market prices, but there will almost certainly be that quantity available.'

'Exactly what would be the weight of that amount of diamonds of that quality?' asked Calder. He still hadn't moved.

Jensen's eyebrows came together as Ann replaced the phone.

'Difficult to say exactly,' he said. 'The last time I had to look into the diamond trade was not long ago, but with inflation and the pound changing all the time against the dollar – the US dollar is the major currency in the diamond trade – it's difficult.'

He bit his thumb delicately. Everyone there, except Calder, knew that he was going to come out with exactly the right answer.

'I would say,' he hesitated for five seconds, while he mumbled figures that no one could interpret, 'about 225 kilos, or nearly 500 pounds.'

'Jesus,' said Striker involuntarily.

'Yes,' continued Jensen, turning towards him, still with the grin on his face and his eyes screwed up. 'It is rather a lot. I can see why they need a lorry. We shall need something similar ourselves.'

To Striker it still seemed incredible.

'But how would they unload all that on the market without it being noticed?' he asked.

'They wouldn't,' answered Calder. 'Each member of the gang – we know already that there are about fifteen to twenty . . . Has the girl given you any clues there?'

Striker was taken off-guard.

'Um, eighteen she said, but she thought there might have been a few more in other places.'

'Let's say twenty,' continued Calder. 'Each one will get a share and then they'll go their own separate ways, to the four corners of the globe, with forty-eight hours' grace to get there. I expect Brown himself will take at least fifty per cent and he'll know how to get rid of them – slowly, over a period of time. Each member of his group wouldn't get more than half a million pounds' worth each – about five kilos or so. That's about, eleven pounds?'

He looked at Jensen, who nodded, smiling, so he continued. To Striker, he seemed to talk unnaturally.

'Provided each one doesn't try to unload all his share at one go, I imagine there are plenty of undercover operations that would be willing to take small amounts and possibly even large ones. Alternatively, they can simply put them into a safe-deposit box for years as a hedge against inflation. Diamonds are small, manageable and, above all, exchangeable. They're even better than gold in that respect.'

'Yes,' said Stoddard without looking at Calder. In fact he seemed uninterested in what was being said – just in his pipe.

'On the other hand,' continued Calder, 'I agree with you, Peter, in that it does seem rather crude and clumsy. Surely there are easier, although perhaps more complicated, ways of taking possession of an untraceable £25,000,000 sterling. Can't it be done through the banking system?'

Jensen pinched the bridge of his nose and looked at Stoddard.

'I believe it is possible,' he said, 'but it would be very difficult, in this situation, to keep it untraceable. Besides, I believe it requires a crooked banker.' He smiled thinly. 'I'm not saying there aren't any of those, but perhaps they are not within Brown's circle of acquaintances.'

The grin was broader than ever now.

'Nothing would surprise me about that man,' said Stoddard heavily. 'I'd like your girlfriend to hear this, Peter – to see whether it really is him.'

It was a casual, innocent colloquialism, Striker knew. The General simply had not known what to call her. Yet, Striker felt himself blush. He looked over at Ann, who was again looking at him. But Calder had not finished.

'It's a pretty foolproof plan. The instructions are clear and complete. There's just a little haziness around the drop, but that's deliberate, of course – so that we don't know exactly where it is. There are probably a number of tracks branching off that side road and they won't mark the route until just before midnight. They will almost certainly cover all the necessary radio wavebands as well, including VHF. And, of course, if we try anything, he has the ultimate form of retribution. I believe he'd do it too. The *Daily Express* won't publish yet, but you can bet your boots that the Editor has made a copy of this tape and will know exactly who to blame if things go wrong.'

He looked directly at Stoddard, who was looking absently at the tape and sucking even more vigorously, if that were possible, on his pipe. Then, having created an almost impenetrable cloud around himself, he started to speak in a manner that left no doubt about what would happen to anyone who disagreed with him.

'What I shall recommend to the PM is that we comply totally. And there is little doubt,' glancing at Calder, 'from what he said to Matthew and myself yesterday, that he will agree. What is £25 million against hundreds of thousands of lives? It's a paltry sum. Brown could have asked for much more. I should think the Prime Minister will be immensely relieved.'

Then he smiled broadly. They all felt the sense of relief and smiled too. All, except Calder. Striker wondered why.

Chapter 18

Calder had no trouble finding a space in the near-empty car park. The pub, on the bank of the Thames, was usually a very popular one at lunchtime. You could sit in the garden and watch the river traffic whilst eating good food. Above all, it was a 'Freehouse', which had a selection of fine brews.

'Where is everyone?' asked Ann.

Calder set the handbrake and switched off the engine.

'I'm not sure,' he answered, 'but I suspect most people decided not to come into town today, because of the congestion on public transport, which cuts out a lot of commuters, and perhaps the locals have their property to protect.'

'What do you mean?' she asked, getting out of the car.

He left it unlocked and walked round to her.

'I mean that a thorough search means just that. When the security forces come to an empty house, what do you think they do, leave a polite note saying they'll be back later?'

She looked at him, stunned.

'I never thought about it,' she said, 'but they can't just break in.'

'Of course they can. The search has to be done systematically, in blocks of roads and buildings. They can't miss houses out everywhere. It would defeat the object.'

She looked into his face.

'I can see the logic of that now, but it's monstrous.'

He controlled his rising anger, lest she think it directed at her. But he was very bitter when he spoke.

'It's a frightening infringement of civil liberties. Perhaps some good will come of it. Perhaps people will begin to realize, now, precisely what a Plutonium Economy means, but I doubt it.'

He put his arm round her and they began to walk towards the beer garden. He was still brooding.

'It means a police state, more or less,' he said.

'Oh, surely not? That's being a bit melodramatic, isn't it?'

'Why?'

She hesitated.

'Well, for one thing, at least in this country people can sue, even the government, for compensation for damage done to their property. In Eastern Europe that would not be possible.'

He couldn't help smiling at her traditional, blind-faith confidence in the infallibility of British liberal democracy. He shouldn't have smiled, because it wasn't funny.

'I'm sorry, Ann, but that's another thing. I don't think you realize, and neither do most people if it comes to that, exactly what an Emergency Powers Act means.

She looked at him. 'No compensation?'

He shook his head.

'I'd better not spend too much time drinking then and get back to my flat,' she said.

He looked down at her, knowing she was joking and glad she was with him.

'At least Peter's here,' she said, looking up into the raised garden.

At the far side of the nearly deserted beer garden, Striker was sitting talking to a woman. Calder knew who she was, because Peter had said he would bring her along. They were holding hands. Then Peter noticed them and stood up clumsily, jogging the table and showing his magnificent teeth.

'Hi,' he called, before they had really got within speaking distance.

'This is Judy,' he said. 'Ann and Matthew.'

She got up and shook their hands nervously, looking a little longer at Calder. He surmised that she probably felt more confident in men's company.

'Peter has told me about you,' she said.

'This is where I decide to go and get the drinks,' said Calder.

The sun felt warm on his shirt-covered shoulders as he carried the tray of drinks to the table. Why couldn't he believe it was all over? There was nothing now that he could do. Everyone else had accepted it. But he felt uneasy. Nothing he could put his finger on; just a feeling deep in his guts. Perhaps it was the security measures he was worried about and the increased militarism within London, or perhaps it was the 'them and us' syndrome that he felt would inevitably develop between the security forces and the citizenry. Or perhaps it was simply that he was a born worrier, and now that the major worry had been removed from his sphere of responsibility, he had to create another. Or perhaps, again, he was simply suffering from a sense of anti-climax. He smiled as he approached the table, to hide his thoughts. Ann was holding forth.

'. . . and I simply had no idea that that's what it meant – breaking into people's property and so on.'

Judy looked down at the table.

'I'm afraid I've caused you a lot of trouble,' she said.

'No way,' said Striker, rather too forcefully. 'From what you've told me, all that happened would have taken place whether you were there or not.'

There was an awkward silence while Calder distributed the drinks and sat down.

'That's true,' he said. 'You mustn't blame yourself.'

He held up his glass. Anyone who had befriended Peter Striker was good enough for him. Well, almost.

Just then, a military column rounded the bend and clattered past the pub. Apart from a few buses and the very occasional car, it was the first traffic for some time. They looked on in silence.

'I never thought I'd see tanks controlling the streets of London,' said Ann. 'And it's going on in eight other cities in the country,' she added as an afterthought.

Then she winced.

'Sorry,' she said, smiling at Judy. 'There I go again, opening my big mouth.'

'No, please,' said Judy, 'I want to talk about it – to get it out of my system. You and Matthew must be very wary of me. I would be in your place. You must ask me any question you like.'

The slight, probably Lancashire, accent was now unmistakable when pronouncing the letter 'u'. The rest she had mostly lost. Calder looked at her sitting up proudly. He lifted his beer and grinned.

'I never buy drinks for people I'm suspicious of,' he said.

They all laughed, including Judy.

'But,' continued Calder, 'there is one question that does intrigue me. At the risk of incurring Peter's wrath . . .'

'Go on,' interrupted Judy forcefully.

Calder looked at his friend, who was pretending to be unconcerned.

'Who made it – the bomb?'

'A man named Vaisey,' she answered immediately. 'I've never known anyone work so hard. He'd often been up all night when we got down to breakfast. We all ate at set times or it would have been impossible to organize meals. He used to look like death in the mornings. Actually, that's not very funny because, well, for one thing he nearly did die once, in a plane crash. I don't know where. He never talked about it. One of the others told me. His face is a terrible sight. I couldn't begin to describe it to you. He was mutilated in the crash, you see, and of course he's got no legs – just metal ones that he gets round on.'

She paused briefly from the stream of words. Calder had wanted to interrupt a few times but had decided against it.

'When I heard that tape this morning,' she continued, 'I thought of poor Vaisey. He used to talk to me quite a lot and I didn't mind. I suppose he wasn't afraid of me and I certainly had nothing to fear from him.'

She looked down nervously.

'He was gay, you see, and the others stayed away from him. I felt sorry for him. He was a nice man really, but very bitter about the world and how it had treated him. He . . . He . . .'

She lapsed into silence and stared at the wooden table. The others stayed quiet, looking at her. Ann thought she had gone into some sort of *post factum* trance – delayed shock or something. She looked to Matthew for his reaction. He was gazing at Judy rather intently and she felt a momentary pang of jealousy. She looked at her watch extravagantly.

'I'm famished,' she said brightly. 'Isn't it about time we ordered some food?'

No one moved – not a muscle. Judy uttered something incomprehensible, then turned to Striker, her eyes stricken.

'He's going to do it!' she breathed. 'Vaisey – he's going to do it!' She put her head on Striker's shoulder and began to shiver.

Calder, too, felt suddenly chill, as if a dark cloud had covered the sun. He looked over at the Thames, dull and deep on the ebb. On the far bank, sunlight reflected off a roof window. Why was it only now that he noticed there was no traffic on the river?

'She remembered something Vaisey had said to her in a private conversation once,' said Calder.

'Don't you think this is rather far-fetched – the mad scientist bit?' growled Stoddard.

The General was glaring at him under low brows, the pipe pointing like a gun. It made Calder feel as if he were confessing to raping his daughter. The birds continued to sing around him, though. They were walking on the grass to avoid being overheard and had just marched through some early sun-bathers. The fine weather had made the grass grow and it was long underfoot. Away to their right the normal traffic roar of the Mall was silent. It brought a strange solitude to the park, despite the fact that more people than usual were taking advantage of it. Stoddard started to walk again.

'He used to confide in her about many things apparently,' continued Calder. 'His homosexuality, his past life and recriminations. Anyway, they were talking about Brown at the time and Vaisey had had a few drinks. She said to him and I quote, "He won't set the bomb off, will he?" According to Judy, his mood completely changed and then he became, and again I quote, "sort of relaxed". Then he said, quote, "It doesn't matter whether he does or he doesn't. Things have a habit of happening, whoever is pulling the strings." Apparently he was always saying things like that and she didn't think anything of it at the time. Incidentally, she replied, "Of course it matters," and he said, quote, "You have a very naive view of life, young lady. What does it matter if a few of so-called mankind die?" He became rather angry then and the conversation ended by him walking away.'

Calder paused.

'As I said, she didn't think anything of it at the time. But she suddenly saw it, where we were, at the pub. Seen in a new context it had a completely new meaning to her.'

Stoddard stopped again and removed his pipe ominously.

'Is that all you've got to go on?' he shouted, as if Calder were a junior officer bothering him with trivia before he'd finished his dinner.

'It's enough, if you make the connections,' answered Calder calmly.

'Do you believe her?' demanded Stoddard loudly.

A strolling couple looked over.

'That she's telling the truth?' asked Calder. 'Yes. The situation, the conversation, her reaction, were not things she could have manufactured or acted. And anyway, why should she lie? What has she, or Brown, got to gain?'

He paused.

'I know you thought she might be a plant. That's why you invited Peter to hear the tape and our reaction to it – so that Brown would know we were playing the game. I thought she was too. That's why I sent Peter up to Stoke instead of going myself. I'm now convinced she's not.'

The General was silent for a few seconds, still glaring at Calder, his pipe held low in his hand. Then a string of obscenities came out of his mouth. Having got it off his chest he seemed to calm down a little. He ran his free hand through his hair and stretched his eyes.

'OK,' he said tiredly, beginning to walk. 'Tell me why you believe it.'

Calder got into the military step beside him and gathered his thoughts. They were heading for the bridge over the Serpentine.

'It all fits. An embittered man – a crippled homosexual, shunned by the scientific community. He would have something to prove. No, more than that. He would need to get back at them and the cruel society that rejected him as a leper.'

'Since when did you become the psychologist?' interrupted Stoddard, but he was noticeably less hostile.

'Then he gets the chance,' continued Calder, 'in one fell swoop, to prove to the scientific world his true talents and also get his own back, not just on them, but also on the world in general. Brown is something predictable. He's after one thing – money – and if everyone plays according to the rules, no one else is likely to get hurt. But Vaisey is different; he's a psychopath, which means that he's unpredictable and unreliable.'

Stoddard stopped again and both men looked at each other for some time. Eventually it was the General who spoke.

'All right. Let's suppose that you might, just possibly, be right. Would Brown necessarily be sorry about it?'

Calder fingered his beard.

'Difficult to say, but I think he would. It sounds strange, but I think he's a man of his word. Oh, I think he'll explode it himself all right, if we don't meet his demands. That's something that he could justify to himself – we didn't play the game and so on. But he might not be willing to explode it if we *do* go along with him. Also, I don't think he'd appreciate Vaisey going behind his back and doing the dirty without his permission. Anyone as brilliant and egotistical as Brown must take a tremendous pride in what he does – doing things correctly and being in control of events. He wouldn't like it if one of his subordinates upped and performed the *coup de grâce*, unnecessarily and without his OK.'

Stoddard was walking again, staring into space. Calder was looking past him at a girl, sunbathing topless – propped up on elbows and lying on her stomach, reading a book. The General appeared not to have noticed.

'Yes, I can see that,' he said dreamily, then stopped and looked at Calder.

'But how could Vaisey do it, without Brown's permission?'

'Piece of cake,' answered Calder. 'Whatever method of detonation they're employing, it was almost certainly fitted by Vaisey. He'd be just as capable of setting it off as Brown. If we assume, for the moment, that it would be by radio signal, Vaisey could quite easily have made a duplicate tuner.'

Stoddard ran hand through hair again.

'And no doubt,' he said, 'you've already thought of how we can stop him when we haven't a clue where he is. We can't even contact Brown for the same reason.'

'I must admit,' answered Calder, 'that did require a little thinking, but really there is only one way.'

Stoddard rolled his eyes at the sky.

'Frighten me again,' he said heavily.

'It is a risky plan,' said Calder seriously. 'I thought at first that we could try sending a broadcast, over the TV and radio waves, but dismissed that idea fairly quickly. To begin with there's no guarantee that Brown would hear it and, even if he did, we could hardly just say that Vaisey has a duplicate. Our mad scientist may be listening as well. And if we merely asked for a meeting, to discuss something of "compelling importance", Brown would simply ignore it, thinking we were trying to be tricky. No, the only way is to try and contact him at the drop. It's the only place we know he'll be.'

Stoddard was nodding.

'That's what I was afraid you were going to say. Rather risky, don't you think?'

'Yes.'

'He could just press the button himself because his conditions had been violated,' persisted Stoddard.

It occurred to Calder, then, that the General was going to arrive at the same conclusion as he. The older man was using him as a guide – a totem pole, which he danced around – striving for a less risky, more amenable alternative. But in the end he would return to the central point. It was a form of self-justification and it wasn't the first time he'd used it.

'Yes,' repeated Calder, 'but he might also be willing to talk. He'd have the diamonds. What would he have to lose?'

'Exactly. He might as well just shoot you before you can open your mouth.'

Stoddard stopped on the bridge, leaned over and gazed into the murky water. Then he lifted his eyes to the heavens.

'Lord, Matthew. You do pursue me with problems.'

'Your only problem,' said Calder, 'is pulling rank and getting Peter and me as the drivers of the delivery vehicle. When we get there, I shall have to play it by ear.'

He paused. Stoddard was still looking at the sky over the ministries.

'There is one thing I may be able to use to my advantage. Judy confirms that they've all grown beards. It's a perfectly natural disguise that helps to explain why none of them have been spotted. Brown thinks of everything – everything, that is, except Vaisey.'

Stoddard swung round on him.

'Perhaps he has thought of Vaisey,' he suggested.

Calder looked back.

'Perhaps,' he admitted. 'But do you want to take the chance?'

Stoddard looked down at the water again without saying anything. Calder let him think. There was nothing more he could say. Some fat ducks were converging on them, making arrowheads in the pool. A particularly noisy white one was creating figures of eight below Stoddard, who was now looking at it. The similarity between his behaviour and that of the duck was not lost on Calder. If it didn't shut up, it might cease to exist in a few days' time, he thought callously. Eventually, the General spoke without turning.

'There is another problem.'

He grimaced.

'The PM. He won't agree. To begin with, he won't see your story the way I do. I believe you because I know you. I have a certain trust in your powers of reasoning and,' he turned slightly, a thin smile on his face, 'your intuition. Past experience tells me that and it tips the balance. For the PM it will be different. He's the one who has to make the decision, and there is, inevitably, a tendency towards conservatism with a small "c". Also, he knows that if anything goes wrong, it's he who takes the can back. At least if he does nothing, he can claim that he abided by the terms of the agreement.'

Calder thought that that didn't sound like a description of the man he had met the previous morning, but he didn't argue – Stoddard knew him far better. The General looked him full in the face as he spoke, a very faint smile on his lips.

'He might agree. But can we afford to take the chance of him refusing? The answer is clearly, no. So, I simply don't tell him. He need never know. Neither must anyone else. To everyone else – that is, everyone except you and me, Bill and Peter, and I think, Ann – everything is proceeding normally. Meantime, I'll wangle it so that you and Peter are the drivers. It's a perfectly natural request.'

Stoddard never ceased to amaze Calder. He knew him to be a

man with a deep sense of morality, yet here he was, talking of deception of the utmost gravity. He hadn't thought it possible that his admiration for the General was capable of going up any more notches. He didn't know whether to thank the duck or not.

'You know, Matthew, I thought that the decision I came to in Number 10 yesterday would be the most difficult I ever made. I was wrong.'

With that he inserted his pipe and strode off again in true Army style. Calder smiled at the broad back. He'd already decided what he was going to do, whether the General had agreed or not.

'What did he say?' asked Ann.

She was sitting rather stiffly on the couch in her living-room, an untouched sherry in her glass.

'He's in a difficult position,' answered Calder. 'He feels that the PM won't give permission, so he's not going to tell him, just in case he refuses.'

'So he agrees with you,' she said unbelievingly.

'He came round to it in the end.'

'But it's madness.'

Calder could sense the strain and desperation in her voice as she went on. It wasn't difficult.

'He'll probably just kill you and set the bomb off anyway, and you'll have gained nothing.'

Her voice trembled. He smiled.

'I don't think he'll kill me.'

'Why not?' she shouted. 'He killed the two security guards and that pilot.'

He drained his Scotch, then walked over and knelt down in front of her.

'It's got to be done, Ann. It's the only chance we've got.'

'But you could even be wrong about Vaisey. He could be perfectly innocent. You could be causing more problems than you're attempting to solve.'

'Do you really believe that?' he asked quietly.

'Yes, I do,' she shouted angrily.

There was a small silence.

'You can help,' he said patronizingly.

To her credit she didn't throw the sherry over him. Instead, she drank it in one gulp and hurled the empty glass across the room to shatter against the far wall. Then she crossed her arms, pursed her lips and glared at him. His eyes didn't leave her the whole time.

'So that we don't compromise the General – he's needed in his job – we devise a plan of which we think he would approve, but which he doesn't know about. Besides, if he knows, he might get pangs of guilt and tell someone and that could be dangerous.'

She remained immobile, still glaring down at him defiantly.

'I'm going to need a back-up team – just in case. I might need to move quickly, or Vaisey might not even be there. It can't be Striker, because he's got to drive the truck back to London, and since the only other person who's supposed to know, apart from Jensen, is you, you're it.'

He didn't really think he'd need her, but he might and it should make her feel better. Besides, it would get her out of London. She wasn't glaring now, just staring.

'Newbury seems to be the nearest big town and I shouldn't think they'd be holed up too far from the drop. So, we pick up the phone and book you into an hotel in Newbury. Then, early tomorrow morning, you take my car and drive up, settle yourself in and wait for my call. You'd better phone me when you get there and give me a number where you can be reached at all times of the day and night.'

She seemed to realize then that there was nothing she could do that would stop him and he could see a tear creeping out of the corner of one eye. He reached out to wipe it, but she pushed him away angrily. She was beginning to sob.

'Make love to me,' she said.

He parted her legs and inserted his hand between them, feeling her body move towards it.

In the centre of London, within the rectangle bordered on three sides by Green Park, Piccadilly and Pall Mall, are some very fashionable and extremely expensive dwellings. The maze of streets has names like Crown Place, Apple Tree Yard and the Duke of York.

Near the end of one of these places stood a tall, elegant house. From the outside it looked smart and on the inside it was fit for a king. In fact, it was owned by someone connected with royalty, but he didn't live there now. Instead, he had left it in the hands of a rental agency which charged a large commission for managing the property. The substantial rent was, at that moment, fully paid up till the end of the month. An American millionaire, who found hotels too public, was using it as a temporary home during his month's stay in England.

For a couple of weeks, a North American visitor had indeed been resident there – or rather an actor pretending to be an American millionaire. But since the night of Wednesday 21st the house had been empty. The only sound now, in the whole building, was the intermittent whirr of the deep freeze in the kitchen and the steady drip of water in the large, deep water tank in the loft.

If anyone were so inclined as to lift the lid of this tank, he would have seen nothing within but dark water. But if, for some obscure reason, he were to have inserted a long stick, he would have found that the water level stopped about two and a half feet from the base of the tank. After some time, he might be able to work out that the water was, in fact, in a tank within a tank, and that the inner skin was only half as deep as the outer one. If he were even more inquisitive and scrutinized the base of the green metal, he might be able to find the wire that snaked under the felt insulation and up through one of the rafters, under the TV aerial.

But it's unlikely that he would have done all these things. Even a man conducting a search would see a perfectly ordinary water tank in a far from ordinary house. Why should it be anything else? How was he to know that death lurked in the centre of London, a third of a mile from 10 Downing Street?

Chapter 19

Saturday, 24 May

Geoffrey Torrington, a director in the oil business, was steering his new motor-cruiser down the Thames towards Putney Bridge. It was about five to eight in the morning.

The boat had been moored outside his house near Windsor all winter and he had spent every available minute preparing her for this, her maiden voyage. He planned on mooring the coming night in the Thames Estuary and then cruising round the South Coast harbours for a fortnight.

He was going a fair lick because he had just realized that he had made his first mistake. He was moving against the tide and he knew it would get worse. He'd already decided that he would try and moor until the ebb tide, just after midday, but he wanted to make as much progress as possible now, while the current wasn't too strong.

The Army had set up the westerly edge of their security ring on Putney Bridge, and river traffic was just as much subject to scrutiny as road vehicles. There were only two routes through that were not cordoned off – the second arch in on each side of the bridge – the right arch for down-river traffic and the opposite arch if you were going up river. Engineers had erected stout, floating jetties leading from the bridge stanchions, pointing up and down river, on which boats could moor while being searched. A makeshift plastic boom, that parted in the middle, spanned the stretch of water under the two arches as a warning that boats must stop.

Torrington and his wife Gillian had been so busy in the last few days, provisioning their craft, that they hadn't heard anything of the 'security exercise' that was taking place throughout the country.

Their eldest daughter, Miranda, had mentioned something about it, but she didn't really understand and they hadn't really listened to her. She was only seven and always repeating what she saw on TV.

As he approached the bridge, Torrington noticed a large arrow directing him to the right passage, so he got himself into position for a straight run through. He noticed the jetty, completely bare of boats, and also a large, white on red 'Stop' sign. This was puzzling, but didn't worry him unduly. He thought vaguely that it was probably the legacy of some sort of regatta that someone had forgotten to take down.

Then, at about seventy-five yards out, his stomach turned over as he saw the boom. He hadn't noticed it before because it was under the shadow of the bridge. It was then that it happened.

Before his hand could reach the throttle lever, he caught sight, out of the corner of his eye, of his twenty-month-old daughter Stephanie, climbing over the steering-well gunwale. He knew, in an instant, that it was a position from which she could not possibly recover and that she would be over the side in a second.

It was one of those moments when you don't decide on your priorities – they are decided for you. The decision has to be made faster than the rate at which the human brain normally works. It's almost as if it realizes that and allows something else to cut in – an emotion or feeling. The mind, rid of the normal societal encumbrances, is so minutely focused that in that flash of a second it becomes crystal clear.

Without thinking, Geoffrey Torrington left the wheel and ran for his daughter. Before he could reach her, her hand slipped and she toppled back towards the water. Again, the man did not hesitate. Without checking, he dived over after her, shouted for his wife, grabbed the child's sweater as they disappeared below the surface and kicked out to avoid being dragged towards the thrashing twin propellers. As the boat was new, the rudder was a little stiff and the craft ploughed on, at twelve knots, straight towards the boom.

Gillian Torrington, meanwhile, was making breakfast in the galley. She hadn't heard her husband's cry, but Miranda suddenly screamed down from above.

'Mummy! Mummy! Daddy's just dived overboard!'

Miranda was prone to playing practical jokes, but there was something in her voice. Gillian sprang up the steps and, looking back at their wake, she saw a man in the water, holding up Stephanie. She knew it was her because of the red, white and blue, striped sweater that they had bought her especially for the trip, to keep her warm. Instantly, she knew what must have happened and, her heart thumping against her ribs, she turned to the boat and saw the bridge.

If she had been a lesser woman she would have panicked then and swung the steering-wheel. But it was already too late for that. Instead she steered the craft straight for the centre of the gap. She didn't see the boom, now hidden by the rising foredeck and pushpit, but it wouldn't have mattered if she had, because her husband hadn't had time to show her how to work the controls.

'Mummy, what about Daddy?' shouted Miranda.

'He can swim like a fish,' said her mother breathlessly. 'We'll get under the bridge first, then go back.'

She looked down at the mass of dials and levers.

'When I've worked out how this thing works,' she added.

Ned Sheen was busy conversing with his relief guard as the latter descended the ladder. It had been a long, cold night, perched above the river under the bridge arch. Although he'd noticed the craft when it was some way off, he didn't want to have to deal with the first boat of the day before he'd even had his breakfast. The lazy sod on the opposite arch had already ascended his ladder, without waiting to be relieved. That left muggins Ned holding the fort. Anxiously, he watched the corporal descend, in the hope that he wouldn't notice the boat before he officially relieved him.

Then, through his numbed and far from large brain, something struck him as odd about the boat's engine note. It wasn't slowing. He swung round and it was fully three seconds before he realized that it wasn't going to stop. Stunned, he watched it pass through the floating boom, its engines loud under the bridge. Then it was through and speeding away.

Ned raised his automatic rifle and set it to fire. He had direct orders to stop anyone who tried to run the boom, but he'd never shot anyone in his life. He hesitated.

'What the hell are you playing at, Sheen?' cried Corporal Bellows from behind him and fear of recrimination for not stopping the boat almost made him pull the trigger. But still, something stopped him. Then the engine note deepened and the craft rose up in the water, accelerating away.

On getting under the bridge, Gillian decided she'd have to experiment with the levers. She pushed one down and the craft speeded up. It was the last thing she ever did.

The soldier fired a burst that cut the woman down. Too late he saw the child and too late he heard Bellows's further anguished cry.

'What the . . .'

Then one of the bullets punctured a petrol tank and the boat disintegrated in a mammoth explosion. No one stood a chance — not even poor Ned Sheen and Corporal Bellows.

The Prime Minister heard about the Putney incident too late to keep it out of the midday news, but it was doubtful whether he would have been successful anyway. A frustrated mass-media jumped on it, like dogs at a bone. Up and down the country the populace were told about it on their radios and watched it on their television screens, and their mood became more hostile.

Wilf and Joan Painter heard of it on the TV in the bedroom of their St John's Wood house. Joan had been ill for some weeks with her back and, since she was seventy-three she took longer to recover than she used to. Wilf had insisted that she stay in bed as long as she liked. They'd just eaten a sardine lunch that he'd prepared as they listened to an interview with the tear-stained Torrington.

'Bastards!' said Wilf suddenly.

'Wilf!' reprimanded his wife, but he would not be placated.

'A man jumps overboard to save his daughter from drowning and sees his wife and daughter get blown to bits for his pains. Anyone'd think we were at war. For Christ's sake, what's it all about? None of the bastards had better knock at my door, that's all.'

Joan knew that there was nothing she could say or do when he was in this mood.

'To think I was in the Navy during the war, fighting with bastards like that.'

She let him mumble on. Eventually, he picked up the lunch things and walked downstairs. She heard him washing up and, soon after, the back door slammed as he went out to do some gardening. Then she heard the key turn in the lock. That was something he'd never done before. He was not only angry at those soldiers, he was worried as well. He was probably going down to the vegetable patch. It was at the bottom of their long garden and screened by trees, and he clearly didn't want any soldiers walking in while he wasn't around. She smiled to herself and let her neck relax on the pillow. Soon she was asleep.

When the first of the five soldiers knocked on the door, he received no reply. Joan woke on the second knock, but by that time there was so much noise going on that her feeble cries couldn't be heard. A soldier returned.

'All locked up round the back, Sarge,' he said.

'Very well,' said the sergeant. 'Stand back.'

He fired a small number of bullets into the lock of the thick wooden door.

On hearing the automatic rifle fire, Wilf, who had in fact been a Chief Petty Officer in the Navy, knew exactly what it was. He grabbed a near-by shovel and ran for the house, as fast as his seventy-one-year-old legs could carry him. He paused, frustratingly, to unlock the back door and entered the house just as a young soldier stepped into the kitchen.

'You Nazi bastards!' shouted Wilf and hefted his shovel.

The young man fell heavily, a gaping wound in his neck. Wilf charged on into the hall, laying about with the shovel and shouting. Caught completely by surprise, two more had fallen before their sergeant, leaving the living-room, put out the raging man with the butt of his rifle.

Another young soldier came rushing down the stairs, from the room where he had discovered the nervous old lady in bed. He stopped and stared in stupefaction at the blood and devastation.

'Christ, Sarge,' he said. 'I don't understand.'

The sergeant was very angry.

'Neither do I, lad. Called us Nazis. But I got the bastard,' he said, holding up his rifle proudly. 'Bloody Commie. Now, get on that phone and get an ambulance here. Our boys are hurt.'

*

Judy felt the tension fall from her body. She kept hold of the man though, because she didn't want to break the tie just yet and also because she wanted to give him some security. She always felt that men were more vulnerable in these post-coital moments than women. She didn't know why, but there was definitely something ungainly about them – like seals out of water.

She held on for another reason too: because she knew what she was going to do. It had been taking shape at the back of her mind ever since the pub, but now she was clear about it. She stroked his hair and he stirred.

'Sorry, am I too heavy?' he said, lifting his weight off her and on to his arms.

She felt tears welling up at the back of her eyes and pulled him back down so that he wouldn't see.

'No, you're fine,' she said, stroking his hair again.

She waited a while, until she had controlled her emotions.

'What happens when you get there tonight?' she asked.

'I'm not sure. All I know is that Matthew wants me to drive our vehicle away and leave him there – after delivering the diamonds, of course – so that he can tell Brown about Vaisey.'

His voice told her that he was not confident of success.

'What do you think will happen?' she asked, trying to keep her tone matter-of-fact.

He got up and rolled on to his side. When he spoke, his voice was empty of expression.

'I think they'll either shoot him on the spot before he can get a word out, or they'll explode the bomb – perhaps both.'

'So do I,' said Judy, still lying on her back and looking at the ceiling.

Then she rolled off the bed and searched for his bath robe. Striker examined the perfection of her body in the afternoon light. Her modesty restored, she turned and looked at him, and he realized, in that moment, what she was going to do.

'Don't do it,' he said desperately.

'I must, Peter.'

'Why?' It was a cry from the depths.

She sat down beside him and held his hand. The words were surprisingly easy.

'Because they will recognize me and they won't shoot. Perhaps that will give me just enough time to talk to them and perhaps John will believe me. After all, why else would I go back to him if I weren't telling the truth?'

She paused.

'Because Matthew's life and thousands of others depend on it, and because I love you. I'm not a brave woman and I can't explain it very well, but I want to live with you for the rest of my life and I couldn't do that if I didn't go with you tonight.'

He made to speak, but she covered his mouth with her hand and smiled.

'For years I've been searching for a purpose in my life,' she said. 'Now I've found it. It's funny, but I wouldn't have done this two days ago. I'd be with you under false pretences, don't you see?'

She continued to look at him and saw that he did understand, but that he wasn't going to admit it. It occurred to her that it was odd how two people so closely attuned could almost read each other's thoughts.

'You know what they might do?' he said. 'You deserted them, don't forget.'

'Yes, but I don't think so. I don't think John is a vindictive person.'

'You couldn't have known him very well if you're not sure about that.'

'I didn't,' she said without hesitation. 'I thought I did, but I didn't.'

He stood up and put his pants and trousers on. She felt a sense of hostility in him.

'You're not going to give me any trouble, are you, Peter?'

He shook his head. 'I don't know,' he answered.

Then he turned and looked down at her still kneeling by the bed. She stood up and threw herself into his arms, the tears coming uncontrollably now.

'Come back, Judy,' he said urgently.

She smiled to herself. How contradictory love was. You wanted to be with a man forever, yet you'd also be willing to die for him. For the only time in her life, the first love-making had been a bond. She hoped it wasn't a farewell as well.

'I promise,' she said.

Chapter 20

Calder looked at his watch for the fifth time in that many minutes. Midnight.

They had reached the turn-off without any trouble about forty-five minutes earlier and had been stationary ever since, just as Brown had said they should be. It had been the hardest and most uncomfortable forty-five minutes Calder had ever spent.

The worst thing had been the silence in the cab of the small one-and-a-half tonner. They had driven in silence and waited in silence, until, half an hour earlier, he had got out of the vehicle and left them alone. He had walked round the back of the lorry, leant against it and waited. He'd watched the cars moving past on the main road – moving as quickly up the hill as down – and was glad that the predicted rain had not come from the dark sky.

He had been amazed when Judy had offered her services. For one, brief moment he had considered refusing, but had realized immediately that there was too much at stake. So had Stoddard. Calder had pointed out the dangers, but she had been adamant.

No, the problem was Striker. Calder had been surprised too about the way in which she had explained her relationship with the blond man. She had told him, as well, that Striker had argued against her going and of the feeling she had that he might try to prevent her. Calder had interrupted then and said that it was too much of a risk for him to come along. She had smiled and explained, as if he were a child, that he didn't quite understand – that replacing Peter would not be an answer, because she would simply refuse to go. Her feeling for Peter, she said, was just as important as her motivation to help Calder. Indeed, it was the very reason she was doing it at all. It was imperative that he come along and make the decision for himself. He might try to prevent her from leaving the vehicle, but that was one of the chances Calder had to take, if he wanted her along. And, anyway, wouldn't he prefer Peter to be where he could see him?

When he had returned to the cab at 11.55, they were both still staring out of the windscreen into the blackness, in precisely the same poses as when he had left them.

Midnight. They must be going. He sensed Striker turn his head towards him and Calder looked in his direction. But Judy was squeezed in between them and he could not see his face.

'Let's go,' said Calder.

Striker started the engine, put it into gear, released the handbrake and they started off down the country lane. Calder put his hands in the pockets of his anorak, sat back in his seat and tried to relax. It didn't work. He still felt tense, as he watched himself descending into the tunnel of their headlamps.

They followed the road faithfully. It was pretty well deserted, with just the odd house. The occasional rabbit faltered in their glare but, apart from that, nothing disturbed their passage, not even another vehicle.

After about four or five minutes there appeared to be a thick, unbordered wood to their right and then they came to the orange arrow. They could see it clearly from a distance, caught in their lights, pointing straight into the wood. When they got closer they saw that it was perched on a long stake and that what had seemed like impenetrable foilage was, in fact, a sort of track through the trees.

Calder noted that Striker turned the wheel without hesitation and they travelled down a green tunnel. They heard the sound of the undergrowth brushing the sides and the occasional low branch touching the roof. The track had clearly not been used regularly for some time, as the grass was thick under the wheels. But, from its flattened appearance, a vehicle had been down the path recently.

Then, no more than fifteen seconds after they had turned, they rounded a bend and saw the rear lights of what had to be Brown's lorry. As they closed, Calder noticed that it was parked just the other side of where another path crossed their own, almost at right-angles. Brown had made sure that they could turn round after unloading without too much difficulty. Reversing back the way they had come would have been almost impossible in the dark.

'Pull over into there,' said Calder, indicating the right branch of the intersecting path.

He jumped out and walked round to the back of the vehicle. The engine died, and he stood and looked and listened. There wasn't a sound – not even a breeze to rustle the branches. It was also nearly pitch dark, the roof of trees blanketing out any light. It was only the red glow from the tail-lights of both vehicles which allowed Calder to see at all. It would have been useful, for the transfer of the diamonds, to back the vehicle up and shine the headlamps on the scene, but he wasn't going to do that. The darkness suited his purpose perfectly.

He flicked a torch as Striker trudged round to join him. Together they unlocked the rear door and transferred ten twenty-kilo bags. It only took a few minutes. That left one bag which was heavier than the rest. The plan was that Calder would take it over with Judy and they would both stay there while Striker drove off.

Calder felt a grip on his arm.

'You drive, Matthew. Let me go?' whispered Striker.

Calder held the other's arm in turn. He'd known it was coming and knew also that he couldn't comply with the request. The American was too emotionally involved. Besides, the blond man had been right about one thing: he, Calder, did make important, moral decisions for other people and Striker couldn't. The Englishman didn't care whether that was arrogant or not. It was simply something that had to be done.

'Sorry, Peter,' he said and prayed that the friendship between them would be enough. He was heavier, but the American was quicker, fitter and more skilled, and, frankly, he didn't fancy his chances. He held on to the arm, waiting for the tightening of the muscles that would signal a blow. But to his immense relief the grip on his own arm was released and Striker walked back to the cab. Calder was glad he had not been able to see the face and wondered whether his friend had registered that he had not promised to take care of the girl.

He waited again, not sure what he would do if Striker tried to restrain her.

She appeared suddenly at his elbow from the other side of the vehicle. He tossed the torch in the back, hefted the remaining bag of diamonds, in itself worth about £3,000,000, and closed the rear doors. Then, together, they walked across to the other lorry.

They waited for Striker to start his engine and then Calder lifted the bag and Judy into the truck in the same movement. He got up too, being as quiet as he possibly could. Striker ran the engine for a further twenty seconds, opened and slammed his passenger door, then backed up and drove away. Within half a minute Calder could hear the vehicle accelerating up the road into the distance and, soon, silence again descended upon the wood. The only sound was the thump of his heart in his ear-drums.

It was the moment, he knew, that was crucial. If Brown shot them on sight, that would be that. It occurred to him that if he had been a historian it would have made him realize how inadequate his usual long-term analyses were. That, ultimately, momentous events were determined by brief moments in time and space that tended to be ignored, but which were in themselves of overwhelming importance.

He reached for Judy's hand. It was steady but cold. Together they waited in the dark.

A minute stretched to five and then ten. He could no longer hear the beat in his chest. Still nothing happened. A pheasant called in alarm, very close by, and his pulse began to race again, all his senses straining. He bent down to where he thought Judy's head would be and whispered, as softly as he could:

'Whatever you do, don't move a muscle.'

Without a doubt, Brown himself was out there – had been since their arrival – and was now making sure that no one had been left behind. The pheasant shouted his alarm again and then the stillness was back – a silence so deep that a rustle of clothing or the creak of a bone would have sounded loud in the clearing. That would tell Brown what he wanted to know and he would shoot them before they had opened their mouths. At the same time he had to admire the man's coolness. There was £25,000,000 worth of diamonds in the lorry, but he was content to wait.

Calder's finely tuned senses picked up a car a long way off. Eventually it went by on the near-by road and so did another five minutes.

Then someone spoke right beside the vehicle and he heard someone else approach the rear of the lorry. Suddenly they were dazzled by a powerful torch beam and a man shouted. Calder put up his hands. There wasn't time to be afraid.

'Don't shoot!' shouted his companion. 'It's me, Judy!'

'Hey! It *is* Judy. John . . .'

'Yes, I can see.'

The voice was unmistakable.

'The diamonds are here, John,' said Judy breathlessly, 'just as you asked, and everything will be done as you instructed. But there is something you don't know about, about the bomb, that we must tell you.'

Calder could see nothing through the blinding light, so he averted his eyes and looked at Judy. Her face, in the harsh glare, looked stricken as she waited for a reply. She waited for some time and Calder suddenly realized how brave she really was. He'd been thinking of her as a means to an end and not as a person. He'd committed the same appalling sin that he had accused the nuclear power lobby of many times.

'For God's sake, John,' she cried. 'Would we risk our lives and those of other people if it wasn't important?'

She turned to Calder.

'This man knows all about it.'

Brown hesitated a few moments more before Calder heard whispering. Then he heard Brown say:

'Let's get moving. We've been here long enough.'

Calder felt relief flood through him. The suspension creaked as men jumped inside. The light never left his face, though.

'Who are you?' he heard Brown say from close by.

'My name is Calder.'

'And why shouldn't I shoot you right now, Mr Calder?'

'Hey! Will you look at these diamonds,' someone interrupted excitedly, but he was quickly hushed.

'Because you're curious,' replied Calder. 'Curious to know what the message is that's important enough to risk nuclear devastation and because you're also curious to know where I fit in.'

He heard the sound of a rope fall near him.

'Tie him up – by his hands,' said Brown and Calder heard him moving off to the back. He also heard the tailgate being fixed up and then the engine started. The light left his face and centred on his hands, as he was roughly turned round and the knot tied behind his back. The vehicle was already moving. The light returned to his face again momentarily and then it was extinguished.

For at least a minute, Calder could see absolutely nothing as his retina retained the image of the glare. Even when his vision began to return and adjust to the darkness he could still see virtually nothing. The lorry bounced along the track for about ten minutes in second gear and all he saw were indistinct shapes. Then it met a road and speeded up. He was able to see a little more then, but only the hazy silhouette of men in the back of the truck. It turned numerous corners and negotiated scores of bends, and it was impossible for him to memorize the route in the gloom. He thought they were heading in a general south-westerly direction, but he couldn't be sure. No one spoke. After about half an hour, they pulled off the road on to a gravel drive and stopped.

Calder was pushed out and, when he looked up, saw an ordinary-looking gabled, country house, with fields beyond. No attempt was made to blindfold him as he was shoved through the front door into a bare hallway and then into a room on the left.

A light came on and two men came in, stationing themselves on either side of the door. One was tall and well-muscled, and the other was small, but looked equally fit. Their size was the only difference between them, though. They were both bearded, dressed in full combat gear, and they both held machine carbines that were pointing straight at his stomach. He didn't know what the weapons were, but he had no doubt that they could both use them. The way they stood, with a wide stance, connected with the seemingly casual way in which they grasped the weapons and the expressionless yet watchful faces, gave off a general air of competence that he didn't doubt. Not that he'd expected anything else.

While he examined them they looked at each other. The bigger man shifted his position. The smaller merely grinned. Calder walked over to the far wall, where the brown paper was peeling off with the damp, and used it to prop himself up. He waited – for fifteen minutes or more. Then Brown walked in.

The two guards didn't exactly jump to attention, but they did involuntarily stiffen. Brown moved away from the door so as not to interfere with the field of fire. Calder pushed himself off the wall and both men stood examining each other.

What Calder saw was a man about two inches taller than himself and darker, in full, unmarked combat gear, no different from that which the others were wearing. It occurred to him that photographs could indeed be deceptive. The resemblance to the snap was there, but only just. If he hadn't known he was looking at Brown he wouldn't have recognized him. The beard and receding hairline made him look a completely different person. No wonder there hadn't been a positive identification. There was also something else that photographs couldn't portray. Calder felt an inner dynamism in the man that didn't have to be expressed in action. He stood perfectly still, hands in pockets, in the middle of the room, the brown eyes examining Calder's face.

'Judy has been telling me a great deal,' said Brown. 'Apparently you think Vaisey is going to explode the bomb without my permission.'

It seemed, to Calder, to be said with gentle inquisitiveness.

'Yes.'

'Persuade me.'

Calder shook his head. 'I don't have to. Judy must have told you.' He paused. 'Besides, you believe it yourself – now.'

The eyes never left him.

'Then why you?' asked Brown.

'I was going to come on my own. Judy only joined later.'

Calder shrugged his shoulders before continuing.

'I suppose I'm here to tell you that for the time being we're on your side. We violated your conditions because, unlike you, we value human lives and there was no other way of getting in touch with you. That bomb must not explode. You've got your diamonds and you have your forty-eight hours. Just give us Vaisey. We won't inquire of him where the bomb is until the forty-eight hours are up. You have my word.'

Brown looked back at him calmly. Calder had expected him to

smile at the last sentence. Yes, there was definitely a gentleness there.

'You haven't answered my question. Why you?'

Calder understood then and, in so doing, understood a great deal about why Brown was so successful at what he did.

'Because I happen to have been involved in trying to catch you from the beginning. I was the natural person to come.'

'Again, why? Judy tells me that you are not permanently employed by MI5, or whatever they call themselves – that you are, how shall I put it, temporarily co-opted.'

Calder looked straight back into the other's eyes. The dark man didn't flinch. There was no harm in telling the truth.

'Because I have a special interest and special knowledge in your particular activity: plutonium hijacking and the manufacture of home-made atom bombs.'

Brown nodded for the first time and the traces of a smile could be detected at the corners of his mouth. He walked towards Calder and stopped about a yard from him, his hands now at his sides. The two men examined each other in silence for a second time. Calder decided that he had been mistaken. It wasn't dynamism that lurked beneath the surface, but a calmness – a satisfaction, a competence, an awareness, a total confidence in how to solve problems.

'You're my opposite number,' said Brown suddenly.

'I am part of a team that . . .'

'No,' said Brown emphatically. 'You're the one. I feel it. Just as I have felt you breathing down my neck from time to time, Calder, I don't mind telling you. I think it is that which has allowed me to stay one jump ahead of you.'

Calder held his gaze before speaking.

'It must have been pure luck in Norfolk rather than second sight. I missed you by six hours.'

Brown flicked his eyes away and then back again. He nodded.

'What put you on to Norfolk?' he asked.

'Your pick-up boy at Powne's shop bought an Ordnance Survey of the area.'

'Did he, by God?!' laughed Brown.

He didn't seem at all concerned.

'And what put you on to Powne?'

Calder shrugged his shoulders again.

'A number of things. The Windscale security officer's wife overheard one of your men talking about getting something off to Paddington and one of your ex-fellow officers remembered that you were always going to Paddington straight from the barracks. We put two and two together and figured that an accommodation address would be useful to you. The rest was just legwork.'

Brown was smiling fully now.

'That was very good,' he said. 'It seems to me, though, that you made five, not four.'

He turned away before continuing, then walked back to his previous position, putting his hands back in his pockets.

'Isn't it interesting,' he said, 'the way in which seemingly innocuous pieces of information can be put together to provide a clue? The permutations are endless.'

Brown was clearly enjoying himself.

'But that doesn't explain how you knew it was that particular house. It was searched in the morning. I was sure we fooled those sappers and that idiot officer.'

Calder hesitated. He didn't want to implicate Judy any more than he had to.

'Oh, you did,' he said. 'I overheard a conversation of a description of the search. I was suspicious and we checked again.'

Brown was looking at him intently.

'And just to put your mind at rest,' said Calder, 'because I can see that you're worried, I didn't trip your crude little explosive device.'

Brown laughed fully this time.

'A worthy opponent,' he said. 'But it seems to me that you had your own little piece of luck there.'

Calder said nothing.

'You're quite wrong though,' continued Brown, 'about my luck, that is. You make your own. I have made numerous mistakes, but then I recognized in advance that I would, or that those who work for me would. Therefore I planned for that contingency. The secret is to stay one jump ahead – to keep moving, so to speak – so that your mistakes don't catch up with you. I knew you'd work out who I was eventually.'

He paused and looked up.

'How did you, by the way?'

'You can't expect me to give away all my secrets,' answered Calder.

Brown nodded unconcernedly.

'It doesn't matter. I know I would have worked it out if I'd been in your shoes and, although I'm arrogant, I'm not so egotistical that I don't recognize that there are others who can think like me.'

Calder let that one go. He thought he had better get back to the reason he was there.

'Your biggest mistake was in choice of personnel,' he said.

Brown raised his eyebrows.

'Judy you mean?' he asked absentmindedly. 'Yes, you're quite right there. But she didn't do any harm and, in the end, she's proved to be an advantage, hasn't she? She's told us about my other failure in personnel – our mad scientist.'

He gazed abstractedly at the wall behind Calder.

'A bit of an unfair accusation of myself, though. Vaisey is quite brilliant, make no mistake, and he did the job I asked of him in double-quick time. What's more, I think you will appreciate that my field of choice was rather limited. Nuclear physicists with enough brains and no scruples don't exactly advertise in the *New Scientist*.'

He looked at Calder consideringly.

'But you're right. He will explode it. I can see that now. What's more, I should have seen it before. I should have known that that combination would not just be interested in money.'

He paused.

'You see, Vaisey isn't here. He went to a little hideaway he's got, after we set the bomb, asking me to send his share on. I should have wondered why he should trust me so much. Then I would have seen that the bomb itself had become more important than the two million I promised him.'

Calder continued to say nothing as Brown looked at him.

'As you have no doubt surmised, it does bother me that one of my team should act in such a manner.' He didn't look bothered at all. 'I have given my word and, strange as it may seem, my word I keep.'

He paused again. Then his eyes flickered and a faint smile appeared.

'The problem is that, as again I'm sure you can appreciate, I cannot spare the time to go looking for him myself and I can't exactly deactivate the bomb, because *my* legs would be knocked from under me.'

He stared at Calder.

'It must remain where it is for forty-eight hours, while we make our escape, and it will. Vaisey won't explode it before then. He has some loyalty to me and the boys. Besides, he knows that I'd kill him if he did set it off before the two days had elapsed. But,' he shrugged very slightly, 'after forty-eight hours, he might think he can escape my wrath.'

He was looking keenly and amusedly at Calder.

'It will be interesting to see if *you* can stop him. I think you could. Indeed, I think the personal approach will be the only way and I would seriously advise you not to inform your superiors. Send in the troops and he'll explode it immediately and then neither of us wins. He's afraid of me, but not that afraid.'

Brown removed a small black box from his trouser pocket. It was no bigger than a matchbox. He held it up so that Calder could see. It had two buttons on the face: a red and a green.

'This is what you'll be looking for. He's no doubt made a duplicate. The buttons must both be fully depressed, three times, in sequence, to avoid the bomb being exploded by accident. A radio signal goes to a transmitter near by, which sends a signal to the bomb and explodes it. He will almost certainly have one in his house, but it could be anywhere. He is very shrewd.' He hesitated and smiled thinly. 'Mine, by the way, will travel with me.'

He looked Calder up and down.

'I'll leave his address somewhere prominent, but I can't have you rushing up to Scotland just yet. So you'll be unconscious for about twelve hours. It will take you several more hours to get organized, get up there and talk him out of it. But I don't think you'll manage to get him to tell you where it is. Why should he? Physical torture won't work on Vaisey. Oh, you might get it out of him, eventually, using drugs, but by that time I think my forty-eight hours will be up and you'll still have to work out how to deactivate the thing.'

He walked towards the door. The two guards were like statues, but Calder had been too absorbed by Brown to have noticed whether they had been like that throughout their conversation.

'What about Judy?' he asked.

Brown was looking at the door.

'Like I said, Calder, I always keep my word.'

His voice was expressionless. He opened the door and looked back. The calmness was still there, like a sleeping man awake. After some time he said:

'You know, I think there is only one major difference between us two.'

With that he closed the door behind him. Calder reflected on the conversation. The most puzzling thing was what he had said about Judy. The Vaisey thing might work. And Brown was right; he had to do it alone. Provided he was left enough time.

He turned away from his two guards and surreptitiously examined the windows. There were two and they were both covered with a thick blanket. He walked slowly over to one and tried to peer round the edge of the material without appearing to do so. With both hands tied behind his back it wasn't easy. He couldn't see a thing.

'Get away from there,' said the bigger guard.

Then the door opened and a man with red hair and a moustache entered. Unlike the others he was wearing civilian clothes, dominated by a large overcoat. He seemed slightly older. He was also carrying a syringe. He placed this in his pocket, walked round Calder and began to untie his hands. They were both facing the guards, who seemed particularly alert. Calder decided that to try anything would be suicide and, anyway, stupid.

The prisoner's hands untied, the newcomer stepped to one side.

'Take off your anorak and pull up your sleeve,' he said.

The rrrs were rolled in a Scottish accent. Calder obeyed.

'How long will it put me out for?' he asked.

He felt fairly sure that it would not be fatal, but he didn't trust Brown too much.

'Aboat twelve hours, give or take an hour or two,' said the Scot, grinning. 'And ye'll wake up with a wee man in your head, laying aboat with a sledgehammer.'

'Thanks a lot,' said Calder as he felt the crude insertion of the needle and the pain as the drug was forced into the vein. The syringe fully depressed, the needle was removed and the man walked to the door.

'Whatever happened to cotton wool and TCP?' asked Calder.

The man turned and grinned again. 'Sorry,' he said, 'we ran out.'

After a pause, he added:

'If I were you I'd put that thing back on,' pointing to Calder's anorak. 'You haven't much consciousness left and it's going to get a wee bit cold in here.'

Then he turned to the two guards, who had been watching this interplay with interest.

'He should be on the floor soon. Give it five minutes to be sure, then you can leave him.'

They both nodded and smiled. Calder reckoned that they'd be glad to finish what must be a rather boring duty. The bigger one called out of the door.

'Hey, Mac! You don't need whisky when you've got that stuff,' and he laughed at his own joke.

Calder heard the words, 'Sassenach ignoramus,' but that was all. The smaller of the two had not taken his eyes off him.

He was grateful to the Scotsman for his advice and reached down for his anorak. At least it indicated that he hadn't been given a fatal dose. The Scot wouldn't be worried about him getting cold if it had been and he didn't believe it had been double-bluff.

Already he was beginning to feel weak and groggy and, suddenly, dizzy. He zipped up his anorak and decided to sit down before he fell. But he couldn't reach the wooden floor. He kept bending down, but his hands wouldn't touch. He fell, consciously, with his hands out in front, but he still didn't reach the wood, just kept falling. Then he disappeared into a black hole. He was falling down it and at the bottom he could see Judy's face, but she never seemed to get any closer.

In another part of the house, Brown was watching Max Liden examining the diamonds. He was taking about ten from each bag at random and so far he had checked eight bags. After each one he exclaimed their authenticity with a certain mad glee and dipped his hand into the next bag so that the stones ran over it and through his fingers. Then he would extract one and examine it with his eyeglass. Strange animal sounds kept coming from his throat and his eyes sparkled like the gems the now dull diamonds would later become. Brown could understand Max's emotion. He supposed it was rather like a sex maniac waking up in a harem.

Brown turned and absentmindedly examined the Schmeisser, cradled in his hand. They would be genuine. The government wouldn't take the chance of throwing in some duds. What would be the point? He had never had any doubt that they would be prepared to give away a measly £25 million for the safety of London. It would cost the country a lot more, just in terms of money, to rebuild the place. Nor would they have planted a listening device in any of the bags or on Calder. The risk was too great to them.

He also felt that Calder might do it. He had made a mistake with Vaisey; not in employing him in the first place – that had been inspired – but in not seeing his real motivation and taking care of it. It was poetic justice to let Calder try to stop him. He was sure he would come close – probably succeed. He might not be able to understand men like Vaisey very much, but he knew men like Calder. They were more dangerous than a dozen heavies. Those eyes.

He looked across the room at where Judy was huddled in the corner. She was being ignored by the men, as if somehow they knew her fate and didn't want to be tainted by her. They were all watching Max. Occasionally, the door would open as men came down from changing into civvies.

Within the hour they would all be gone, with their share. The operation was finally over. He had made mistakes, but it had worked, just as, lying in that cold hangar at Carlisle, he had known it would. And he had enjoyed every minute of it. Indeed, he regretted that it was now over. He felt a deep sense of satisfaction and pride as he looked at his men. He wondered how many of them would be caught. Most. But *he* would survive. He had made arrangements.

It was then he noticed that Wilson was looking at him and not at the diamonds.

Chapter 21

Sunday, 25 May, p.m.

The face at the end of the tunnel opened its mouth for the first time. Calder strained to hear the jumbled whisper of words. That was odd. The face was relaxed and beautiful, but the words were hissed, as if she were out of breath or in pain. The voice seemed to be coming from beside him, not from the face at all. He felt a weight on his back and consciousness returned. He involuntarily opened his eyes. Then he remembered.

He remembered because of the pain. The Scotsman's description had been spot on. He saw the note, about two feet from his head, pinned to the floor with a bayonet. Then he tried to push himself up, but the heaviness of his back held him to the floor. He pushed more strongly and wriggled to escape. The weight slipped off him and there was a dull thud. Turning on to his side, he saw Judy beside him, face down, seemingly unconscious and completely naked.

His head reeled as he saw the blood on the floor and knew that he had to roll her over. He got into a kneeling position and turned her, as gently as he could. The handle of a knife protruded from her belly, in the centre of a crimson stain. The rest of her body was covered in abrasions. His head was forgotten as he sat back on his haunches and took it in.

He knew nothing of medicine, but he knew that the wound must be terrible. It also occurred to him that Brown was the most vindictive bastard he'd ever come across, to stab this innocent girl so that she died slowly. He also knew, in that instant, without a shadow of doubt, that if he ever came across him again, he would kill him with his bare hands and feel the better for doing it.

He felt for her pulse. His senses weren't too good, but he felt it – weak, but there. The red stain stretched to the door. She had obviously been stabbed some time before, in another room, and had dragged herself in here to find him. He didn't wish to think how long it had taken her. He lifted his hand and looked at his watch. 1.30!

Unzipping his anorak he shrugged out of it. His limbs felt very heavy. Leaving the knife where it was, he placed the anorak over her, as much to cover her nakedness as to keep her warm. The blue material was smeared in blood from where she had lain on him. He knew that he had to get an ambulance quickly if there was to be any chance at all of saving her life. Then he thought of Peter.

He stumbled to his feet and nearly fell over as the pain flooded through his head again and life came back to his stiff limbs. He remembered the note and lowered himself carefully to his knees so that he could keep his head upright. He removed the bayonet and slid the note from its blade. It was an address in the Trossachs, Scotland. He pushed it into his trouser pocket and rose to his feet. It was slightly less painful this time. Then he negotiated the door and lurched out of the room to look for a telephone, still clutching the bayonet.

There was nothing in the hall so he searched the other ground-floor rooms. A trail of blood led from almost every one. It *had* taken her a long time to find him. All the rooms were as bare as the one he'd been in for over twelve hours. Blankets covered all the windows, but there was enough light to see by.

He was just leaving one room when he noticed an odd-looking bundle in a corner. On drawing closer he saw that it was a man, in army combat gear, with a small, red circle in his back. It looked like Brown, but he knew it couldn't be. He bent down tentatively – more out of deference for his head than from fear of attack – and turned the man over. He had a crimson circle in the front too, but there was hardly any blood and this hole was directly over the heart. The bullet, Calder surmised, had passed right through and he had died instantly. Not exactly a brilliant deduction, but then he wasn't feeling all that bright.

The face was vaguely familiar. He searched his memory. It was difficult, but he came up with an image from the small gallery of snapshots they had sent over the air on the evening they had found Powne. The fellow's name was Wilson and by all accounts he was a pretty big fish in Brown's set-up. Well, now he was dead. There was no remorse.

He thought of Judy and decided that he would have to speculate later. He rose to his feet again, feeling steadier this time. But now a queasy stomach had joined his head and he was glad he hadn't eaten for nearly twenty hours. He walked to the front door. It opened immediately and he ran out into the bright sunshine. He squinted up at the house and, after about half a minute of adjusting his eyes and scanning the wall, decided that there was no telephone wire. That meant a run to a public telephone, or a near-by house. It would be a risk, knocking at someone's door, but Judy was the immediate problem. Well, at least his brain was working again. There was no point in going back inside to search the upper rooms, so he turned to the road. He hesitated, deciding which way the nearest village would be, chose and began to run, slowly; it could be a long way.

After some time and a number of bends and turns, but no houses with phones, he found himself running down a long, steep hill. The view to his left, down into the valley, was breathtaking and at any other time he might have stopped to admire it. The descent seemed endless and more punishing on his legs than running on the flat. He realized at one point that he was going too fast and slowed, getting into a rhythm. It was a long time since he had done this sort of exercise and a stabbing pain rode in his side with every breath. It was some compensation that it took attention away from the ache inside his skull. But he was fit and he knew he could keep up the same pace for miles.

Finally, he reached the bottom and a junction. A sign read: Vernham Dean ½. There were some cottages on the corner, but since he was so close to the village, where there would almost certainly be a public phone, he turned and kept running.

He was soon entering the cluster of houses and slowed to a walking pace so that he wouldn't call attention to himself. In the centre, he spotted the telephone box, opposite the pub. He walked a small way past it and examined a large signpost, getting some breath back.

Then he entered the still empty phone box and looked at his watch. It was nearly 2 p.m. He picked up the receiver and began to dial 999. It was only then that he noticed his hands were covered in dried blood. Well, that would have to wait till later too.

He asked for an ambulance and was immediately asked for his name and phone number. He refused to give them, but instead, described the route from the village back to the house.

'There is a woman there who has been stabbed in the stomach,' he finished. 'I would recommend that a doctor travels with the ambulance. Have you got all that?'

'Yes, but what is your name and number?' came the reply.

He replaced the receiver and dialled the Department. The phone was answered after three rings.

'This is Matthew Calder. I want to speak to the General immediately.'

'I'll switch you through, sir.'

Stoddard answered within a few seconds. 'Hello?'

'This is Matthew. I . . .'

'Matthew! What's happened?' came the urgent voice.

'I'm afraid Judy's been stabbed. She's still alive, but barely. I've called an ambulance. Tell Peter, would you?'

'I take it he listened to you?' said Stoddard.

Calder could almost feel the tension at the other end of the line, but he kept the General waiting as he gave him the same directions as he had given to the 999 call.

'Did he listen to you?' repeated Stoddard.

Then the pips went. He fumbled in his pocket for another tenpence coin and managed to insert it before the line went dead.

'Yes,' he answered finally. 'I'm sorry I haven't been on before now, but Brown put me out for twelve hours.'

He hesitated.

'Vaisey wasn't there. But I have an address. I'm going after him.'

He was about to replace the receiver.

'Matthew! You're not going alone?'

'No. Your secretary is coming with me. I'm sorry, General, but it's the only way.'

This time he did replace the receiver, lifted it again immediately and dialled a Newbury number which he had committed to memory. It rang fourteen times. He counted.

'May I speak to Miss Ann Stuart, please? She is staying with you.'

'Just a moment,' said an officious female voice.

Ann would know it was him. No one else knew she was there. He wouldn't tell her about Judy, yet.

There was a two-minute delay. He began to imagine ambulances and police cars zooming through the village any minute. He felt in his pocket for another ten-pence piece, but there wasn't one. He'd forgotten how long you got for local calls at weekends.

'I'm putting you through now,' said the voice.

'Matthew! I've been frantic. Are you all right?'

He hadn't heard the click.

'I'm fine, but I wish busybodies wouldn't listen in on private conversations.'

There was an audible click this time as the telephonist went off the line.

'She's gone,' said Ann.

'Yes. Listen. Take down this number in case my money runs out.' He gave it. 'I'm at a village called Vernham Dean. I've no idea how far it is from Newbury, but there's a signpost here which says: Hungerford, 10 miles, to the west; Upton, 1¾ miles, to the east; and Linkenholt, 2¼ miles, to the north.'

'Hang on while I write that down,' she said.

He repeated it.

'It can't be too far from Newbury,' he continued. 'If I had to make a guess, I'd say south-west, but I can't be sure. I'm not hanging about here. It's too public. So I'll walk along the road that leads to Linkenholt. And I hope your sense of direction is better than that of other women I've known.'

He regretted saying it, instantly. You can't soften seemingly harsh words on the telephone by facial expression. There was a small silence.

'I'll be there as soon as I can,' she said. 'Anything else?'

He sensed a certain reticence.

'Yes,' he answered. 'First, don't check out of your hotel, secondly, don't contact the Department or Stoddard, and thirdly, I don't know what I'd do without you.'

'This is no time for light-hearted banter, Matthew Calder,' she scolded.

'I've never been more serious in my life,' he said.

She paused. 'I'll be there even sooner.'

Then the phone went dead.

He replaced the receiver and left the phone booth, looking around. A couple of people were leaving the pub rather noisily, but no one else was about. It *was* Sunday lunchtime after all, to people who live normally, that is.

He crossed the wide street and began to walk, slowly, up the road that led north to Linkenholt. A picture of Judy flashed across his mind and he forced it away. Dwelling on her wouldn't do any good at all. As he paced, some of the tension left him and he focused on his head once more. The pain had become a dull ache centred over his left eye, but it was getting better. He had to make plans.

If a vehicle came he would get off the road quickly. It could be from the Department. The General might have had vehicles stationed in Newbury for just such a contingency, although he would almost certainly have mentioned it in the planning stage. More likely, he would have sent cars to Newbury on receiving no word from Calder.

He didn't like crossing Stoddard, but it had to be done. He had finally found something that was more important to him. Calder believed he could do better with Vaisey than a posse from the Department. He knew that he might be gambling with countless lives, but he believed he could succeed, whereas he wasn't sure about anyone else. It was as simple as that. It was supremely arrogant, but necessary. It never occurred to him to doubt his own ability, or to wonder whether he could cope with the terrible responsibility and guilt if he failed. As far as he was concerned, what he was doing was the logical and correct thing to do in the circumstances. But failure was, anyway, unthinkable.

When he found a suitable spot along the road, where he could see in both directions, without being seen himself, he would stop and wait. He estimated that Ann would be there within the hour. That would be about 3 p.m. or so.

When she arrived, they would go straight back to her hotel, and he could get cleaned up and changed. Then they would eat. Food was the last thing he felt like at the moment, but he might later. If he didn't, he would force himself to eat it. Then he would phone through and book them into an hotel in Carlisle for the night – ironically, where it had all begun. The route was through Oxford and Banbury, joining the M6 just east of Birmingham. Then it was motorway all the way to the border. If they left straight after the meal, he was sure they could reach Carlisle before midnight, providing there weren't too many lanes closed on the M6.

It was important that they get a good night's sleep. After a hearty breakfast they would buy hiking gear. The address in Scotland sounded very countrified and hiking would be a good cover. They should be in the Trossachs by early afternoon.

There was no real hurry. As Brown had said, Vaisey wouldn't push the buttons until midnight the next day. The image of Brown made him think of Judy, but fortunately he couldn't dwell on it, as he heard a car approaching. He swivelled round, couldn't see it and jumped behind a near-by tree. His head caught a low branch and he decided then that his priorities had been all wrong; the first thing he was going to do was buy some aspirin.

Chapter 22

Monday, 26 May

Ann felt the butterflies start up in her chest as Calder turned the Volkswagen off the A821 and on to the B829. She looked down at the Ordnance Survey on her lap. Matthew had marked the spot where he thought Vaisey's house would be. They needed to follow this road for a number of miles and then turn off right, on to what seemed like some sort of track. It was well past midday but she wasn't hungry. She turned to Calder.

'Sandwich?' she ventured.

'No, thanks.'

Her mind returned to Judy again and what must be going through Peter Striker's mind. She also couldn't help thinking that Matthew shouldn't have let Judy go with him. God, they didn't even know whether she was alive or dead. Matthew had refused to phone Newbury hospital. It was that really which had made her phone Stoddard again, at least that's what she kept telling herself. She had done it after breakfast that morning, while Matthew was settling the bill. To her huge relief the General had approved of Matthew's plan and told her to play along. It didn't make her feel that it was any less of a betrayal, though. She would tell him, but not yet – not until after Vaisey.

He sensed her looking at him and flashed a smile.

'I wouldn't mind some of that coffee, though,' he said.

She half-filled the lid of the flask with the still steaming black liquid and handed it over. She had filled the thermos that morning at the hotel. She didn't like black coffee but had suggested to him that she could always add milk. He had agreed that that was the best way to do it, but his mind had been on something else. Besides, she knew it wasn't quite as simple as that. He took sugar and she didn't. To pour milk into one mug and sugar into another, in a moving car, was no joke and, quite frankly, she couldn't be bothered. She had made black coffee with sugar, just as he liked it. This was his second cup and he hadn't noticed. Her butterflies had stopped flapping.

'Are *you* hungry?' he asked suddenly.

'No.'

'Have some coffee anyway,' he said, handing over the now empty lid.

She bit her lip. 'I'm all right,' she said.

Well, *he* was driving.

They sat in further silence for a mile or two. Something had occurred to her in the night, while she was lying awake. She was sure there had to be a good argument against it and had said nothing. But now they were nearly there . . .

'Matthew?'

'Ya?'

'Can't we just jam the radio waves or something, so that the signal can't be sent to trigger the thing?'

'Yes, the Department could probably do that. But I'm afraid it's not a very safe proposition.'

'Why?'

'Well, to begin with, Vaisey might have a back-up trigger system.'

'That's unlikely, surely?' she exclaimed, thinking he was creating difficulties.

'It's not a chance I'd like to take. Besides, there's another major problem. Since we don't know where the bomb is we can't jam the radio waves. It's not logistically possible to do it for every major city in England and, even then, it might be elsewhere. Also, Vaisey's transmitter may be mobile, or it may not be where we think it is at all. We just don't know. We think it's going to be down the road, but do you realize that Brown could be wrong? Vaisey may not be there either.'

Well, she'd known there had to be a reason.

'I wouldn't like to play chess with Brown,' he said suddenly.

'Why not?'

'Because I'd probably lose.'

She decided there was no answer to that and they travelled on in heavy silence. She was torn between leaving him alone with his thoughts, so that he could plan his strategy, and her desire to hug him – to feel a part of him. Most of the feeling of guilt had gone now. The rising fear had pushed it out and she felt the butterflies again.

In a short while, Calder swung off the road on to a mud track, which fortunately was fairly dry. The names of the residences were listed. This was the way, he confirmed. The fine weather had followed them north and the sun shone from a blue and white sky. Calder had been thinking about the information which Crawford had sent him on the added problems of atomic explosions in fine weather. There was clear space to the left so he pulled on to the grass.

'It can't be far up here,' he said, 'so we'll get out and walk. We don't want to drive up to his front door.'

It wasn't as hot outside the car, but it was still shirt-sleeve weather. He opened the hatchback and fitted the rucksacks on their backs. Then he picked up the map, locked the car, walked over to Ann and kissed her full on the lips.

'You choose the most awkward moments to give me the first real kiss of the day,' she said.

'When we get this little problem over I'll kiss you all the time,' he enjoined confidently.

'Not with that beard you won't,' she answered and pulled his hand, adding: 'Come on. As you said, it can't be far.'

But they were both wrong. They had been walking for over an hour and the sweat was pouring down Calder's back. They had already investigated two lodges and now there was another, showing yellow through the trees. It was an ordinary-looking wooden hunting lodge, with one floor and rather cramped conditions. The garden, if that is what it was, was overgrown and looked more unkempt than the hillside beyond. By high summer it would be a jungle. He could see no aerials, but thought that they would be at the back of the house, if anywhere at all, and that was screened by trees. A battered Landrover stood to one side. The embossed, faded name on the gate thrust out at him like a challenge. 'The Grecian Urn'.

Ann grasped his arm.

'Are you sure this is the place?' she whispered.

'Yes,' he said, but he could see what she meant. A blackbird was chirping in a near-by bush and the soothing hum of bees could be heard. Shadows on the hill sketched buttercups against deep green. The path that led to the house was covered in splashes of sunlight as the glare penetrated the shade of the silver birches that filled the garden in apparently haphazard fashion.

The scene was so peaceful that for a moment he himself began to doubt that a man in that picturesque little house could destroy Central Manchester in a few seconds.

He unclipped the gate and paint flaked off in his hand.

'Don't forget,' he said, 'at the appropriate moment, look ill.'

They walked towards the lodge. It was strange how, in moments like these, he could make himself feel relaxed. His heart was beating a little faster and the adrenalin was probably beginning to flow, but that was all to the good. His mind felt content. Ann still held his arm, but more tightly now. He looked down at her and smiled.

'There's nothing to worry about,' he said.

There was no bell or knocker on the door, so he rapped with his knuckles on the wood. He felt the skin cut on some flaky paint. Nothing happened. He knocked again and waited. He didn't think it was possible for Ann to grip his arm more tightly, but suddenly she did.

'The curtain twitched,' she hissed.

They heard a strange, shuffling sound through the thin walls and he sensed there was someone behind the door. Then it opened, quickly.

Neither had seen Vaisey before – not even a photograph – but Judy had described him and his appearance was not something you were likely to forget. It was Vaisey.

Calder's first feeling was one of relief that the man was here. Then it seemed to him that he had been standing, staring, for a number of seconds, which was probably not true. Anyway, it flashed through his mind that Vaisey must have got used to people staring at him a long time ago.

'Hello,' said Calder, smiling. 'Look, I'm terribly sorry to bother you, but we're, well, we're lost. I wonder whether you can help us? Yours is the first house we've come to for ages.'

He held out the map and looked into the thick lenses. It was impossible to see behind them and the man's expression said nothing. It was almost as if he hadn't heard and it occurred to Calder that he could try grabbing him now.

Suddenly, without warning, the scientist threw the door closed with such force that the whole front of the building shook. Calder didn't hesitate. He threw his shoulder against the door. The lock tore away from the rotting wood and he jumped through.

At first he couldn't see Vaisey, because he was looking at the wrong level and it took a few moments for his eyes to adjust to the comparative dark. Then he saw him, moving with incredible speed along the floor, using his arms as legs, the latter dragging behind like useless baggage.

Calder jumped after him, but the crippled scientist was too fast. He was through the door at the far side of the room and had reached up to a kitchen worktop before Calder was across the room. He stopped immediately as he saw what Vaisey was holding. It was a duplicate of the buttoned panel which Brown had shown him. The lips of the man on the floor were drawn back in a snarl and he was panting heavily.

'I knew I was right,' he gasped. 'You know exactly what this is, don't you?'

As he looked down at Vaisey, it came to Calder how slim the margins of history could be between totally different events. If a speck of dust had caused the gun to misfire at Sarajevo, would the First World War have started at all? Possibly. If the weather and an error of judgement had not caused the German pilot to lose his way, so that he released his bombs over London instead of over open fields, as he had intended, would the bombing of German cities in retaliation and hence British cities as well have occurred during the Second World War? Possibly. If he had grabbed Vaisey at the door, when he was within feet of him, if he had been a little quicker across the room, if he had not been hampered by the rucksack, if he had made different decisions earlier, would he have saved countless lives and the total destruction of Central London, or Birmingham, or Bristol?

'Matthew?' came the tentative call from the door.

Another man in the circumstances might have given up. He would certainly have allowed himself an inward groan of anguish. But Calder was already adjusting his method. So plan 'A' had failed. He would just have to try another. He turned to see Ann framed in the doorway.

'Come in, darling,' he said. 'It seems that Mr Vaisey has us by the short-and-curlies.'

He made to move.

'Stay where you are,' said Vaisey.

The scientist had recovered a little and his voice was now firm.

'Tell the young lady to come in here and sit in that corner,' he said, pointing, his eyes apparently not leaving Calder's face. 'You too,' he added.

Ann was already by Calder's side.

'May we remove our packs first?' he asked.

'Be very careful,' said Vaisey.

They helped each other.

'Just let hers slip off on to the floor,' said the scientist. 'Don't make any attempt to grasp it.'

Calder did as he was told.

'Fine,' continued Vaisey. 'Now kick them to the side of the room so that they are resting against the wall.'

It occurred to Calder that Vaisey must have watched some good thriller movies, as he negotiated the packs to the side of the room. Then he and Ann sat down on the two pink, cane chairs indicated.

Calder forced himself to relax again by examining the inside of the house. In complete contrast to the outside, it was neat and tidy. There was an old-fashioned fireplace in the central wall, with logs stacked alongside. The oak table beside Ann was polished bright and the Persian-looking carpet was spotless. Light shone in columns through the two small front windows and the open door. It was light without being bright in the room. Vaisey was still lying on the floor in the kitchen.

'Who are you?' he asked.

'My name is Calder. This is Miss Stuart. We both work for MI5. Judy told us that you were going to explode the bomb and . . .'

'*The* bomb? *My* bomb!' interrupted Vaisey fiercely. 'And you were going to stop me.'

A strange wheezing sound came from his throat, as if he were choking and fighting for breath. Ann and Calder looked at each other. The latter decided that he was laughing. He stopped suddenly.

'How did you know where to find me?'

'With great difficulty, but once we found out who you were, things got easier. A nationwide checking system connected you with this place. You're not exactly Mr Average. People remember you.'

The last thing he wanted to do was tell Vaisey that Brown had told him. The scientist was looking at him, considering. He found it disconcerting that the lenses of the man's spectacles made it impossible for him to see the eyes. It was his tuning stick as well as his weapon. Vaisey was not the one who was virtually blind.

'Please do not move, Mr Calder. One press of these buttons and you know what will happen.'

He put the little box down on the worktop and proceeded to lever himself up. He was about fifteen feet from Calder. Three presses, Brown had said, in sequence. Could he reach him in time? After all, Vaisey had now to pick it up first before he could press it three times. Surely he could cover the distance before that happened? But, as he thought it, he knew that he couldn't. He had already seen how quickly the man could move when he wanted to. It just wasn't worth the risk.

Vaisey picked up the buttoned box and moved over to the door. He glanced outside and back again at Calder. This he did very swiftly a number of times. Then he closed the door as best he could and moved to the centre of the room. Calder spoke.

'I see your incapacity doesn't hinder your mobility a great deal.'

Vaisey wheezed again before answering.

'Flattery will get you nowhere.'

'How did you know,' asked Calder, changing tack, 'when we were at the door?'

The scientist sighed.

'You people. I didn't for certain, but you gave yourself away. You see, when people see me for the first time they behave oddly. I'm such a ghastly sight that they usually do one of three things:

297

give a terrified grin and turn away; smile patronizingly; or they stare, as you did, wondering how to talk to me. I've got used to it now and I don't notice it. What I do notice is when someone reacts differently, however minutely. You didn't show enough surprised horror and you didn't stare for quite long enough. You knew what to expect. I also saw something in your eyes. I sensed something.'

He seemed quite pleased with himself, but Calder couldn't tell from his countenance, just his voice.

'Your arriving is a nuisance though. I shall have to explode it earlier now. Unless I can keep you like that for nine hours. Actually, why can't I do just that? You'll wait, thinking that my concentration might slip at some stage and fancying that you can take this off me.'

Calder saw the teeth again, paradoxically perfect, and thought he caught a gleam behind the lenses. The scientist seemed to have made an error of judgement. As far as he knew, if Calder and Ann didn't show, a back-up team would come in. Vaisey wasn't to know that no one else knew of the place.

'But why?' asked Calder, to occupy the man's mind with something else. 'Why kill hundreds of thousands of innocent people? Is that so corny that –'

'Innocent!?' The word was almost screamed. 'If you had looked like me from your early teens, Calder, with a reasonably intelligent brain on your shoulders, you would not ask such an absurd question. People treat me like dirt. The only parts of me that are not scarred in some way are my hair – that grew again – and my testes. I have feelings like everyone else. I can even reproduce the species.'

He laughed for a long time before continuing.

'However, women do not interest me. Instead, I have to . . .'

He broke off and snarled, then quietened down. When he began again he was calm.

'Only two people have shown me any respect recently. One is Judy and the other is John Brown, who, I take it, you know about. Oh, yes, Brown used me, but not like the others. He respected my work.'

Ann couldn't remain quiet any longer.

'But you can't blame everyone,' she said. 'Those who die will not have known you. Surely *they* are innocent?'

Vaisey seemed to look at her for the first time.

'I don't think you understand,' he said. 'Everyone is the same. The fact that they have not met me is irrelevant. They would react the same way if they ever did. They are part of the same shameful, corrupt system. Why should I not destroy it?'

He lifted his head and appeared to be looking above Ann as he continued.

'The race needs a shock to the system. Only good can come of it in the end.'

Ann was silent.

'And what about Judy?' asked Calder.

The scientist was slow to react, as if coming out of some sort of daydream.

'What about her?' he asked eventually.

'Brown has stabbed her.'

'I don't believe it,' said Vaisey.

'She escaped and came to us. She told us that you would explode the bomb and came with me to see Brown, to find out where you were. She did it because she cared about people. She risked her life to save those lives that you are dismissing as so much rubbish. And Brown stabbed her in the stomach.'

Vaisey was silent for a while.

'Is this true?' he asked shortly.

It was impossible to see exactly where he was looking and Ann didn't realize for a few moments that the question was directed at her.

'Yes,' came the eventual reply.

Calder reasoned that Vaisey would be used to that sort of delay and would not read anything more into Ann's hesitation. The cripple lifted his head and appeared to gaze over her head again.

Calder realized then that he had made an unforgivable, fatal error. What felt like a black crow flapped its wings in his chest.

'Is she dead?' asked Vaisey.

'I don't know,' answered Calder carefully.

'Where is she now?' persisted the scientist.

'Newbury General, I expect.'

'I believe you,' said Vaisey. 'And in that case I have no need to wait until midnight. If I am going to get caught, then so can Brown.'

Calder felt Ann look at him. He knew exactly what she was thinking. The bird felt as if it was about to take off.

'What *do* you believe in, Vaisey?' he asked desperately.

'Myself,' came the immediate reply. 'And very soon, so will those ignorant pigs who spurned my brilliance because they couldn't bear to look at me.'

For the first time for as long as Calder could remember, he felt totally lost. He'd known before he came why Vaisey was doing it, but now he was here he couldn't stop him. The crow had apparently changed its mind and was now just flapping its wings slowly.

'You know they'll probably kill you,' said Calder absently.

The wheezing started up again.

'You really don't understand, do you Calder? Don't you see? I don't care. It sounds pathetic, but I really do have nothing to live for. If I didn't press these buttons I would not be being fair to myself.'

Ann made to speak.

'And please, young lady,' said Vaisey, 'spare me your sympathetic platitudes. I don't need them.'

He looked at the deadly, black box in his right palm. Then he looked up and spoke.

'If there is a real sinner in all this, it's not me. Nor is it Brown. He was merely showing an entrepreneurial spirit that has been lacking in this country for many years. Perhaps it is your fault for not stopping me,' he said unforgivably. 'After all, that is your job.'

He looked at the little box again and so did Calder. There was no outward manifestation that the decision had been made, but Calder leapt off his seat in the same instant that Vaisey's left hand began to move.

The next few moments appeared to occur in slow motion. He seemed to float through the air as he watched the index finger travel across the tiny box – one green, one red, one green. Then things speeded up as he cannoned into Vaisey, knocking him down and sending his spectacles flying.

He knew he was too late. He knew it by the sublime look on the scientist's face. The now completely blind man began to laugh.

Calder levered himself up into a sitting position and looked at Ann. Her mouth was open and she was staring at the cripple. The fireball was reaching its limit now and the blast wave was following. Soon, most people within that three-and-a-half-mile circle would be either crushed or destroyed by burns, if not already. More would die or suffer, terrifyingly, from radiation. How many tens of thousands had already died because he had not covered that short distance across the room more quickly; because he had been so arrogant as to believe that he could sort out everything on his own; because he had been so moronically stupid? He didn't even know what city he had destroyed, but was in no hurry to ask.

He became conscious of the absolute silence. Vaisey had ceased to laugh and even the birds seemed to have stopped singing. The crow had died. Ann was staring at *him* now.

Then a shadow appeared in the room and he looked up to see Peter Striker standing in the kitchen doorway, his face like death. Calder, already numb, failed to react – just gazed at his friend. Striker was looking at Vaisey, but the scientist couldn't see him. The blond man said:

'She told me where to find you. Before she died.'

Vaisey stirred and looked in the direction of the voice.

'I decided to come up and give you a hand,' said Striker hollowly.

Still no one else spoke. Striker was looking at Calder now.

'Don't worry, pardner,' he said, his face still empty of expression. 'I disabled his transmitter a couple of minutes ago. It's in a shed with a generator out in the field. Everything's OK now.'

With that he turned and walked out the way he had come. Calder and Ann watched him go. They still said nothing. There was nothing to say.

MORE ABOUT PENGUINS, PELICANS AND PUFFINS

For further information about books available from Penguins please write to Dept EP, Penguin Books Ltd, Harmondsworth, Middlesex UB7 ODA.

In the U.S.A.: For a complete list of books available from Penguins in the United States write to Dept DG, Penguin Books, 299 Murray Hill Parkway, East Rutherford, New Jersey 07073.

In Canada: For a complete list of books available from Penguins in Canada write to Penguin Books Canada Ltd, 2801 John Street, Markham, Ontario L3R 1B4.

In Australia: For a complete list of books available from Penguins in Australia write to the Marketing Department, Penguin Books Australia Ltd, P.O. Box 257, Ringwood, Victoria 3134.

In New Zealand: For a complete list of books available from Penguins in New Zealand write to the Marketing Department, Penguin Books (N.Z.) Ltd, P.O. Box 4019, Auckland 10.

In India: For a complete list of books available from Penguins in India write to Penguin Overseas Ltd, 706 Eros Apartments, 56 Nehru Place, New Delhi 110019.

Transforming Business

Transforming Business

Big Data, Mobility, and Globalization

Allison Cerra

Kevin Easterwood

Jerry Power

WILEY

John Wiley & Sons, Inc.

Transforming Business: Big Data, Mobility, and Globalization

Published by
John Wiley & Sons, Inc.
10475 Crosspoint Boulevard
Indianapolis, IN 46256
www.wiley.com

Published by John Wiley & Sons, Inc., Indianapolis, Indiana

Published simultaneously in Canada

ISBN: 978-1-118-51968-4

ISBN: 978-1-118-51972-1 (ebk)

ISBN: 978-1-118-58323-4 (ebk)

ISBN: 978-1-118-58303-6 (ebk)

Manufactured in the United States of America

10 9 8 7 6 5 4 3 2 1

For general information on our other products and services please contact our Customer Care Department within the United States at (877) 762-2974, outside the United States at (317) 572-3993 or fax (317) 572-4002.

Wiley publishes in a variety of print and electronic formats and by print-on-demand. Some material included with standard print versions of this book may not be included in e-books or in print-on-demand. If this book refers to media such as a CD or DVD that is not included in the version you purchased, you may download this material at http://booksupport.wiley.com. For more information about Wiley products, visit www.wiley.com.

Library of Congress Control Number: 2012950505

ABOUT THE AUTHORS

ALLISON CERRA has more than 15 years experience in the telecommunications industry, working in both the service provider and equipment vendor categories. She has led the marketing, sales, and product strategy efforts for several new technologies including broadband, mobile, and video services. She holds two bachelor's degrees from the University of South Florida and master's degrees in Business Administration and Telecommunications from Southern Methodist University. In addition to *Transforming Business*, Allison is also the co-author of *The Shift: The Evolving Market, Players and Business Models in a 2.0 World* and *Identity Shift: Where Identity Meets Technology in the Networked-Community Age* and has published multiple whitepapers and articles about emerging user broadband trends and market potential for next-generation services. She was recognized as the Outstanding Young Alumna from Southern Methodist University in 2011, honored by the Dallas/Fort Worth chapter of the American Marketing Association as CMO of the Year for 2011, and named to the Global Telecoms Business and *Dallas Business Journal*'s lists of the top 40 under 40 in 2012. She serves on the boards of the World Affairs Council of Dallas/Fort Worth and the Telecommunications Industry Association.

KEVIN EASTERWOOD has more than 19 years experience in both the consumer electronics and telecommunications industries. He has led marketing teams focused on the definition, launch, and ongoing support of advanced communications and technology solutions in business-to-business and business-to-consumer environments. Kevin holds two bachelor's degrees from Southern Illinois University and a Master of Business Administration in International Marketing Management from the University of Texas at Dallas. In addition to being a co-author of *Transforming Business*, Kevin was also a principal researcher on the team behind both *The Shift: The Evolving Market, Players and Business Models in a 2.0 World* and *Identity Shift: Where Identity Meets Technology in the Networked-Community Age*.

JERRY POWER has over 30 years experience in strategic marketing and business analysis in the telecommunications industry. With extensive expertise in the areas of mobility, optics, IP/data networking, and network management, Jerry has published numerous articles describing the impact of technology on business models and practices, network architectures, operational procedures, and users. His research efforts have been discussed in both *The Shift: The Evolving Market, Players and Business Models in a 2.0 World* and *Identity Shift: Where Identity Meets Technology in the Networked-Community Age*. His research on *Identity Shift* was recognized with the Outstanding Market Research award in 2012 by the Dallas/Fort Worth chapter of the American Marketing Association. Jerry holds a Master of Science in Computer Science from Pennsylvania State University and has served on multiple industry committees and boards focused on improving the telecommunications industry and uncovering new, sustainable business models across the ecosystem.

CREDITS

CONTENTS

Prologue:
The Crystal Ball

→ *He who lives by the crystal ball soon learns to eat ground glass.*

EDGAR R. FIEDLER, ECONOMIST

I n 1980, at an otherwise ordinary industry conference, William Synott, then Senior Vice President of the First National Bank of Boston, approached the microphone and boldly asserted a prediction for the future of his profession. The event was the Information Management Exposition and Conference, and Synott would create a moniker, redefine the IT function, and invent a new career aspiration for the budding professionals in attendance. He stated:

> *The manager of information systems in the 1980s has to be Superman— retaining his technology cape, but doffing the technical suit for a business suit and becoming one of the chief executives of the firm. The job of the chief information officer (CIO)—equal in rank to chief executive and chief financial officers—does not exist today, but the CIO will identify, collect and manage information as a resource, set corporate information policy and affect all office and distributed systems.[1]*

With that, a new title and role for information managers was born. The goal of their craft was no longer merely to be a technical expert but to combine this know-how with business proficiency to advance the goals of the enterprise.

That same year, the largest IPO in nearly 25 years was offered, creating more millionaires than any company in history. Apple would grow to become the largest technology company in the world as measured by revenue and profit, topping Google and Microsoft combined, but its origins were a bit volatile. After several unsuccessful runs at conquering the enterprise user, Apple stuck to its niche in creating elegant devices with superior intuitive capabilities and providing them to a committed base of zealots in the consumer market. By the mid nineties, the company fully embraced its consumer identity and held fast to creating cooler computers with better capabilities. By the turn of the century, the niche player succeeded where so many before it had failed in devising a commerce platform through its iTunes storefront that finally made an MP3 player worth owning. Not long after, it took the same design and commerce principles and redefined the smartphone market—one previously reserved for the serious Blackberry enterprise user, with the launch of iPhone. iPad soon followed, generating more revenues in the first quarter of its debut than the entire company had just 10 years prior.

It is fitting, if not fate, that Apple's success would be predicated on consumer acceptance of its better mousetraps. The same year the company went public marks the genesis of a generation that would grow up as the most connected in history. Millennials would mature during the age of the Internet, mobile ubiquity, and Facebook, hardly living a moment of their lives unconnected to the virtual world surrounding them. Their rabid appetite for all things digital spawned the growth of new forms of communication and content and upended traditional business models for companies attempting to woo a multitasking generation on steroids.

As these examples illustrate, every so often, the confluence of multiple trends creates seismic shifts that even the most visionary futurists would have failed to predict given their seemingly unrelated origins. The year 1980 illustrates how disparate movements can originate in isolation, only to drift together decades later with tectonic force. Those technology-insatiable Millennials are now storming the enterprise gates and will represent roughly one-third of the workforce by 2014.[2] Apple is a seemingly unstoppable juggernaut launching ever-cooler new devices to a now insatiable base of consumers that goes well beyond the niche fringes. In an ironic twist, these enthusiastic consumers have given Apple entrée to the enterprise market that once eluded it as they increasingly use their iPhones and iPads in the work environment—in some cases, without their company's consent. And, the CIO, once a position conceived by a visionary speaker at an industry conference and now an essential role within most private enterprises, finds himself in the eye of a perfect storm—a changing workforce with radically different work habits colliding with consumer companies that have become the gold standard in shaping how technology is used. The result some

decades later is perhaps the most profound shift to ripple through enterprises since
the advent of the personal computer.

Fueling this transformation are employees and the expectations they bring to the
workplace as by-products of behaviors first adopted in the home. The way employees
work is fundamentally changing. Buoyed by the plethora of technology options surrounding them and the marriage of previously distinct personal and professional
personas, employees (and the land grab by companies to attract and retain the most
attractive of them) are at the center of this change. Of course, there are also external
forces in play accelerating the momentum and creating an environment conducive
to the transformation:

- **Mobility**—Mobility has changed work from a place employees go to a thing
  they do. More people have access to mobile technology worldwide than they
  do drinking water.[3] The year 2011 marked the milestone when smartphone
  shipments exceeded those of PCs (including desktops, netbooks, and laptops)
  worldwide.[4] Mobility has altered the landscape beyond simply connecting
  people on the go. It has reshaped expectations as to what they presume should
  be available from any remote corner of the globe. Although the phenomenon
  started in the consumer market, consumers are employees too. They expect
  to be just as productive (if not more so) with a smartphone, laptop, or tablet
  as they are from a traditional office. That's a seismic shift for the historically
  brick-and-mortar, 9-to-5 enterprise attempting to address an insatiable mobile
  appetite among employees who crave to work when and where they want.
- **Cloud**—The cloud is changing the economics of scarcity. Capital is often among
  the scarcest resources for a firm (particularly in recessionary times or among
  smaller enterprises). The historic model for procuring technology within an
  enterprise required just that—procurement of capital-intensive devices, servers, and network infrastructure along with the retention of trained staff able
  to manage the complexity that so often accompanies technology (think of all
  those aspiring IT professionals at that conference in 1980). To balance the risk
  of obsolescence with the scarcity of capital, enterprises often made do with
  technology that wasn't always the latest or state-of-the-art. After all, employees
  were afforded little other alternative given that the most advanced technology
  options were often reserved for those with serious needs—in other words,
  businesses. But, somewhere around the turn of the millennium, broadband

and advanced devices began proliferating. Households and enterprises soon found their technology options lagging those made widely available to consumers. No longer able to mollify tech-savvy employees with yesterday's dated technology and unable to keep pace with the significant capital investments required to do so, pioneering enterprises began turning to cloud alternatives to bridge the gap. The cloud allows companies to parse out and pay for technology on an as-needed basis. However, it also introduces new complexities for enterprises straddling the line between creating a culture of flexibility and protecting the physical borders of their assets and intellectual property.

- **Big data**—Big data is changing the way decisions are made. In an enterprise with countless mouse clicks, updates, phone calls, e-mails, instant messages, and meetings occurring each day, remaining shrewd despite the deluge of data can be an overwhelming challenge for managers and employees. The opportunities for enterprises to mine their own coffers of data to make smarter decisions are real and revolutionary. Yet, such an approach requires different skill sets and cultural enablers, both difficult to effect overnight. However, firms embracing the challenge and boldly moving forward to translate big data into big information stand to gain in an always-on culture inhabited by employees and consumers.

- **Collaboration**—Collaboration is changing the tone and the accessibility of conversations. Gone are the days when work product was relegated to teams of individuals who could interact directly and often in a collocated space. Social networking, the rage that enthralled college students seeking a virtual stage on which to share their latest stories and conquests, has seeped into the fabric of the enterprise as a viable means of getting the right people connected and interacting without the organizational friction that is often prevalent in traditional hierarchical structures. Conversations are asynchronous, multiparty, and perpetually evolving. The way employees interact is changing and creating additional pressures for company managers attempting to harness the output while not stifling the creative process.

Although these external forces are playing out in shaping how employees work, they are also having an impact on how enterprises compete. Almost since the arrival of Michael Porter's seminal work in studying the forces of competition, debates have raged about whether technology is sufficient in creating sustainable competitive advantage for a firm. We side with the school of thought that it is not. To find sustainable competitive advantage, a firm must generate something valuable, heterogeneous (meaning that it is composed of multiple elements such that the whole is greater than the sum of the parts), and highly immobile (meaning that other firms would find great difficulty in attempting to replicate said advantage to equalize the playing field). Technology on its own is subject to commoditization, making it difficult for companies to leverage it for sustainable competitive advantage. However, although technology alone is insufficient for this cause, it is an essential ingredient in other aspects of how enterprises function.

Among the most important intangible elements affected by technology is a company's culture. A firm's ability to create sustainable competitive advantage by affecting the heterogeneous, invisible activities surrounding its culture can be significantly hampered or enabled with its technology mind-set. This reality is also changing the definition of critical roles within the enterprise:

- **Employees**—Employees, led by technology-addicted Millennials, are the precipitating force driving new functional requirements for traditional roles in the enterprise. Furthermore, a new breed of talent yet to enter the market (those graduating with advanced degrees within the next two years) works and thinks differently than even the most advanced Millennials currently in the workforce today. They will bring with them even more change to the enterprise and impose their requirements for how technology serves to enable cultural reform. Furthermore, the elite of this crop (those graduating from the top 100 colleges nationwide, who also maintain a superior grade point average and engage in a range of extracurricular and leadership activities) will have a significant say in how readily recruiters attempting to attract them advance their company's technology agenda. Back in 1980, job perks included the front-row parking space and the corner office—physical amenities during an era when time and space were measured. Today, they represent the borderless, timeless realm that work represents—things like flexible technology and work policies that embrace this segment's penchant for individualism and connectivity. This new generation of knowledge worker represents the sweeping changes yet to transform the enterprise and will commence a new era of change made possible, in part, by the technology orientation of the firm.

- **HR managers**—Human resource leaders are typically ambassadors of cultural change. Historically, these individuals did not need to invest time or energy in contemplating how technology could be used in the enterprise. That was for the IT department to determine. HR was just another recipient of technology made available by an IT function that enjoyed a monopoly position in making such decisions. However, HR managers must now address the new work habits of employees. From internal social networking spaces to flexible work-at-home arrangements to mobility options for the road warrior, the HR manager's arsenal of attractive policies is critically dependent on the technology available in the enterprise. Increasingly, these technology options are having a significant impact on attracting and retaining talented employees. In addition, they bear equal weight in helping or hindering productivity and throughput for today's knowledge worker. As such, HR is gaining a louder voice at the table in evangelizing the key part that technology plays in influencing a healthy culture.

- **Marketers**—Marketers, once lauded for creativity, now find a very different skill set in demand for their profession, one that activates the truckloads of data generated by hyperconnected consumers. The thousands of mouse clicks, location updates, and channel changes taken by a user each day present an interesting constellation of behaviors and preferences among prospects and consumers. The result can be a marketer's dream come true—the ability to use predictive analytics to intercept the consumer with the right message and right offer at precisely the right time to compel purchase or action. However, these relatively uncharted waters are fraught with challenges as marketers struggle to walk the fine line between consumer exploitation and empowerment. Adding complexity to the profession is the fundamental shift from broadcast, one-way media (such as television, radio, and print) that once dominated marketing spend to the two-way media propelled by the web and mobile technologies increasingly entering the scene. Marketers can no longer simply be creative, and they certainly are no longer the owners of their message in a market consumed by social media. They must be able to translate data into propensity models, do so without compromising consumer privacy, and harness new two-way technologies that are constantly evolving to reach an ever-changing marketplace. How companies invest in and embrace new technologies to answer the marketer's challenge will separate the leaders from the laggards.

- **CFOs**—CFOs are the consummate resource allocators for their firms. In a sluggish economy, every line item is under intense scrutiny. Yet, CFOs increasingly realize they can't *shrink* their companies to greatness. Escalating cost-cutting measures are reaching a point of diminishing returns. CFOs are desperate to find the next growth engine or breakthrough. However, those looking within conventional research and development teams to find it may miss it outright. In a time of scarce resources, CFOs are getting more creative about how to tap new sources of internal and external innovation. An innovation-based approach requires a venture capitalist mind-set supported by metrics, rewards, and technologies that grease the gears of hierarchical organizations and harness the talents of multiple third parties. While balancing the ongoing needs of the business through compliance oversight and reporting measures, CFOs are also evolving as the most effective and credible leaders of their companies to champion an innovation culture.

- **CIOs**—Beyond donning a business suit, the CIO is facing the most unprecedented role change in her short life span. Once the technical gatekeepers of a firm, these decision makers increasingly find themselves losing relevance among a new crop of tech-savvy employees. With familiar consumer brands now encroaching on the enterprise, CIOs also face complete disintermediation by their employees in favor of quicker, easier ways to get things done. For example, if an employee needs storage on a server to deposit a large file, he may go to his IT department or provider for support. Or, he could just go to Dropbox instead for free storage available in a fraction of the time. Of course, this employee is often not concerned with the potential security ramifications of doing so. That's for the CIO to worry about, even though her team may never have been consulted in the first place. CIOs are often the first, last, and only line of defense against attacks targeting the firm's network or intellectual property. Yet, they must also address the insatiable needs of employees influenced by technology options that are perfectly well suited to the consumer market, even if those alternatives carry some measure of risk when taxed for an enterprise purpose. Indeed, the role of the CIO, even as defined by Synott, is an endangered species. She must reinvent her role within the organization's value chain or risk disintermediation by the very employees she is paid to support.

In short, the external forces of mobility, cloud, data analytics, and collaboration are creating seismic shifts in the role of employees at all levels of the organization. The result can mean the difference between success and failure for the employee or the company itself. In fact, although politicians for years have stressed the urgency behind a "digital divide" in the United States—one where more populous areas are the beneficiaries of more advanced technology options (such as broadband), leading to increased growth potential—there is, in fact, a less popular digital divide remaining in this country, because it is not among consumer households. Indeed, the digital divide still plaguing the nation's opportunity for growth falls between the more advanced enterprises that use technology as a strategic asset and those that still view technology as a necessary evil. As economists have demonstrated with numerous studies, consumer broadband penetration alone is a leading indicator of economic growth for a nation. Imagine the national growth potential when broadband and associated technologies are examined within the context of private enterprises responsible for jobs, goods, and services. It is this last digital divide and the contrast between successful and unsuccessful companies that will be explored in this book.

The journey begins with a closer analysis of the sweeping technology trends affecting enterprises of all sizes, including employees' increasing appetite for mobility, the role of the cloud in transforming business economics, the significant opportunities and challenges precipitated by seemingly infinite data, and the dynamic pace of workflow brought forth by collaboration. Next, the associated change occurring for various roles within the company, including next-generation knowledge workers, human resource professionals, marketers, finance heads, and information technology leaders will be explored. This analysis will be reconciled against the impact on company culture with an assessment of how technology can play a part in a firm's financial success. Finally, broader technology implications will be discussed in the context of economic advantage—whether in leveling the playing field between large and small enterprises or competing for growth on a global stage between national superpowers. Each chapter will be accompanied by prescriptive actions for businesses wrestling with these knotty issues, if not pointed observations of how the landscape is poised for change in the not-too-distant future.

To examine the topic from multiple angles requires a review of some of the more provocative insights over the past few decades from leading researchers and analysts. Those commentaries are included throughout the book. At the same time, these findings are augmented by multiple primary research studies commissioned by the global telecommunications leader Alcatel-Lucent. One study in particular represents more than 2,800 respondents across every walk of life in the U.S. enterprise—including frontline knowledge workers and HR, IT, and business decision makers. It includes representation from the very small (between five and 19 employees) to the largest of companies (more than 1,000 employees). It is augmented by a separate questionnaire covering more than 300 elite upcoming graduates from the top 100 universities in the United States. Throughout this book, the results of this study offer perspective to the broader trends discussed. Hereafter, the results derived from this research will be referred to as the "2012 Alcatel-Lucent study," and they specifically cover findings among U.S. respondents, unless otherwise noted. In particular, this research informs the analysis to address the following questions:

- How are company culture and the role of various functions being affected by the changing appetites and work patterns of employees?
- How is the "consumerization" of IT transforming the role of technology within the enterprise?
- How and where can technology be used as a means toward sustainable competitive advantage, and what separates companies that are perceived as leaders in their space from their laggard peers (the "Enterprise Digital Divide")?
- How can technology be leveraged among small enterprises, often the subjects of greater cash and resource constraints than their large enterprise counterparts?
- What are the untapped business models and opportunities that may usher in a new wave of technology adoption similar to that witnessed in the consumer market?

Although the most prophetic soothsayer would have been hard pressed to recognize the relationship between an emerging IT function, the rise of consumer technology juggernauts, and the birth of an always-on connected generation in 1980, the confluence of these trends in our current year is undeniable. There are likely numerous "unrelated" trends currently happening that will not reach fruition of intersection for multiple decades hence. We the authors won't be so bold as to connect these yet-unrelated dots, but this book will inform you how the current landscape is poised for future transformation in the next couple of years. In doing so, it offers prescriptive advice to companies struggling with their own digital divide and employees angling to compete in a workplace increasingly transformed by habits first adopted in the home. Although it is true that there is no crystal ball to indicate where the road will lead decades from now, research and analysis will illuminate the possibilities of the path. The destination 30 years hence remains unclear, but the journey begins now.

1 The Technology Trends

In This Part

The Mobile Movement

→ *According to iPass, 92 percent of today's mobile workers believe their smartphones should be enabled for both work and personal use.*[1]

Merriam-Webster defines *phobia* as "an exaggerated usually inexplicable and illogical fear of a particular object, class of objects, or situation."[2] Some phobias are fairly well known by name, if not association. There's arachnophobia, the fear of spiders, tormenting 55 percent of females and 18 percent of males.[3] Glossophobia may not be in one's common vernacular, yet with approximately 75 percent of the population afflicted by a fear of public speaking, it is certainly well-known, nonetheless.[4] And, in 2008, a new phobia entered the scene, one that has yet to be officially recognized as a disorder but plagues two-thirds of people regardless.[5] These *nomophobes* are terrified of being without their cell phones. Although critics may be quick to dismiss this latest phobia as silly, the case for mobility's indispensability is compelling. There is no device more personal than the mobile phone. It knows your location and preferences. It holds your pictures, e-mail, text messages, calendars, and contacts. It's no surprise, therefore, that such a large percentage of the population report that they can't live without their phones. However, despite the dependence that people have on these devices, they still lose them. According to a study by the mobile security firm Lookout, 9 million smartphones tracked by the company in 2011 were lost[6]—at a cost of more than $30 billion. Per consumer, that works out to about $250 each, and for the nomophobes among them, countless sleepless nights.

Although the negative impact of a personal mobile phone falling into the wrong hands can be high, the impact of losing a business-connected device can be devastating. To demonstrate the risk that a lost device can create for a business, the security firm Symantec conducted what it calls the Smartphone Honey Stick Project. This project involved the "loss" of 50 mobile phones across five U.S. cities. These phones were preloaded with a combination of well-labeled personal and corporate applications and data files—some of which featured a simulated login page with the username and password prepopulated. From an enterprise point of view, the results were sobering. The study found that when a lost business-connected mobile device is discovered, there is an 83 percent chance that the person who found it will attempt to access corporate data or the corporate network. A file titled "HR Cases" was accessed on 40 percent of the devices, and attempted access to a "Remote Admin" application was recorded on 49 percent of the devices. Of the 50 phones, there was an attempt to return only half—despite the fact that the "owner's" name and contact information were easily available.[7]

The advent of mobile broadband networks has driven a pervasive, always-on connectivity and mentality. The rise of smartphones, tablets, and ultrabook computers gives employees the ability to leverage a constellation of applications and functionality to remain productive and get things done no matter where they are. The consumer market has wholeheartedly embraced this technology to manage both personal and family lives. Applications for personal finance, time management, information gathering, and even entertainment have become essential tools for a wide section of the population. The potential is even greater in the enterprise. Mobile technologies allow today's workforce the ability to work effectively from anywhere, to collaborate with others across geographies and time zones, and to realize productivity benefits by working smarter. However, the ultimate responsibility for the safety and integrity of company data and workflow lies with the company's Information Technology or Information Security Office. As the Smartphone Honey Stick Project so dramatically illustrates, the benefits of a mobile workplace are not without their risks. Despite the concerns and potential pitfalls, enterprises find themselves in the throes of one of the most significant workforce trends since the dawn of the personal computer, with an evolution as profound to match.

As with most evolutions, the path to true mobility in the workplace has been developed over many years. Researcher and professor Jack Nilles is credited with first using the term *telecommuting* in 1973, while he was the Director for Interdisciplinary Research at the University of Southern California. According to Garrett and Danziger,[8] "telecommuting" or "telework" is characterized by the following four dimensions:

- **Work location**—Which refers to any location other than a centralized organizational work space;

- **The usage of information and communication technologies**—Which indicates the technical infrastructure and support required;
- **The time distribution**—Which compares the replacement of working time out of the traditional office versus in the traditional office; and
- **The type of contractual agreement between employer and employee**.

In simpler terms, *telework* can be described as a work arrangement between employee and manager that allows the employee to leverage technology to gain flexibility in terms of where and when they work. As the oft-repeated mantra says, "Work is something you do, not where you go."

Needless to say, at the time of its inception in the early 1970s, telecommuting was much more concept than widespread practice. Using the technology of the time, satellite offices were linked to mainframe computers that were centralized at the company headquarters using telephone lines as the network bridge. This was a rather expensive proposition and, although it did provide some degree of flexibility to a specific segment of the employee base, the freedoms they enjoyed were somewhat limited. With the introduction of the personal computer in the early 1980s, however, employees could connect to these mainframes through terminal emulation. Given that one would consider this access slow and cumbersome by today's standards, this technology allowed a larger segment of the workforce to begin to realize the benefits of working from their homes.

The early 1990s through the early 2000s is often referred to as the "Digital Age." Characterized by the ubiquity of the personal computer and the connections that allowed these computers to interact with a larger network, the Digital Age represented the first glimpse of true workplace flexibility. With the rise of the "Information Age" in the early to mid 2000s, individuals were no longer limited to primarily performing localized tasks but could take advantage of the world of information available with the click of a mouse. Beyond just access to information, the Information Age also introduced high-speed Internet access to the home. Once only accessible in the workplace, these broadband connections in the home introduced a flood of new applications and technologies designed to give the employee a greater degree of freedom than ever before. Advanced Virtual Private Network (VPN) capabilities to allow secure access to company data, Voice-over-IP to allow inexpensive voice communications over a home broadband connection, and videoconferencing applications to encourage face-to-face interactions from the comfort of the home office, all served to make the modern teleworker more productive than ever before.

Personal computers and high-speed Internet access allowed employees to replicate the office experience in their homes like never before. The Digital and Information Ages provided the employee with the access and tools to work away from a centralized company workplace productively, but she was still shackled to a desk. Enter the most current step in the evolution. In *Identity Shift: Where Identity Meets Technology in the Networked-Community Age* (Wiley, 2011), authors Allison Cerra and Christina James introduced the "Networked-Community Age." Characterized by pervasive, always-on connections to a virtual world, in the Networked-Community Age individuals are no longer tethered to PCs and their fixed broadband connections. Mobile devices, such as smartphones and tablet computers, now provide ubiquitous high-speed connectivity. And while the Digital and Information Ages saw a transition of office-based technologies—such as e-mail and broadband—to the home, the Networked-Community Age has turned that model on its head. It is now the technologies, devices, and applications that consumers enjoy in their personal lives that are being driven into the workplace. These advanced devices and the applications that they enable are creating the most mobile workforce in history. Today's employee can work productively and efficiently from home, while waiting at the doctor's office, from his son's soccer game, from almost anywhere. And although the benefits of a mobile, always-on workforce are clear, there are a fair share of challenges and complexities—both for employees and organizations.

The introduction of the original Apple iPhone clearly illustrates the benefits and challenges this Networked-Community Age imposes on the workplace. When it was released in June of 2007, there was no doubt that the iPhone would be popular. "Popular" turned out to be somewhat of an understatement. According to market research firm Gartner, within the first year of its release, the original iPhone captured 20 percent of the smartphone market.[9] At the time, the iPhone was second only to Blackberry, the enterprise workhorse that was a constant on the hip of workers around the world. Consumers loved their iPhones—they loved the sleek design, they loved the interface, and they loved the apps. It finally seemed that someone had put the "smart" into the smartphone, allowing the consumer to realize a world of additional benefit from his device beyond voice, e-mail, and text.

Apple originally designed and marketed the iPhone as a consumer-specific product. As a result, the device did not include many features and functionalities required for widespread enterprise adoption. It offered limited Exchange support for e-mail, calendar, and contacts. It didn't have a physical keyboard or 3G support. In the event one of the phones was lost or stolen, there was no way for the IT department to wipe or disable the missing phone. Of course, this didn't stop then–Apple COO Tim Cook (now CEO) from telegraphing their intentions in 2007:

> We've said many times that we're providing a solution in iPhone that many businesses love.... [C]learly, there are some businesses buying them and very much enjoying them.[10]

It also didn't stop enamored consumers from bringing these devices to work and using them for work purposes—often against internal IT policies. As more and more consumers began to use their iPhones in the workplace, it became clear to CIOs that something would have to give. As Apple began addressing key enterprise management and security functions, their market share in the enterprise began to grow. According to mobility management provider Visage Mobile, in the third quarter of 2011, the iPhone broke Blackberry's grip to become the most-used device in the enterprise mobility space with a 45 percent market share.[11]

The term *BYOD*, or "Bring Your Own Device," has become commonplace in the lexicon of IT departments around the country. Although the BYOD phenomenon encompasses multiple types of devices, including tablets and laptop computers, the smartphone is easily the most visible example of the trend. As the story of the original iPhone illustrates, devices that capture the imagination of the consumer and provide the features and functionalities that allow her to be more productive will find their way into the workplace—with or without the support of IT. According to the 2012 Alcatel-Lucent study (described in the prologue to this book), BYOD is rapidly becoming less of a trend and more standard operating procedure. Half of frontline workers use their personal devices to help them get their work done.

The increasing reliance on personal devices for work purposes is a key contributor to the rise of an incredibly mobile workforce. According to the 2012 Alcatel-Lucent study, 83 percent of respondents identify themselves as "mobile capable," meaning that they already have all the tools in place to work effectively away from an office environment. More than 90 percent of surveyed enterprises already allow some employees to leverage the technology at their disposal to work remotely. Such a high number is not surprising because the benefit to the business can be significant. In an effort to accommodate their growing mobile workforce, pharmaceutical giant GlaxoSmithKline reconfigured their Research Triangle Park, N.C. office to an unassigned seating scheme. Should any of the 1,200 employees at that location decide to come into the office to work, they set up their laptop at a workstation enabled with an

Internet phone and—voilà—instant office. The company says that it has saved nearly $10 million a year in real estate costs alone. This transition has been so effective that the company has adopted the plan in 20 other offices around the world.[12]

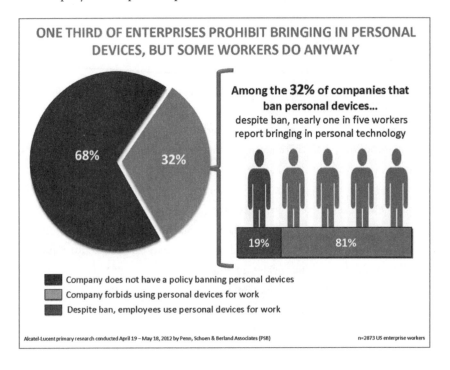

If the financial benefits to the company of encouraging and supporting a growing mobile workforce are clear, what about the appetite of the employee base for an increasingly mobile work life? Despite the overall success of GlaxoSmithKline's program, it was not immediately popular with every employee. Some workers felt the scheme was too cold and impersonal because they had no permanent space to make their own. Others felt unorganized and had a harder time adapting to the idea of unpacking and packing up their belongings every time they came into the office.[13] In addition to losing a connection to a permanent office space, the shift to a more mobile approach to work also means that one's work is with him all the time, no matter where he goes. To better understand the feelings of enterprise workers around these possible tension points, the 2012 Alcatel-Lucent study asked respondents to make a choice between two options: (1) The technology at my disposal gives me the freedom to work when I want, where I want; or (2) I can't escape from work demands. More than three in four indicated the former.

When it comes to more flexible working arrangements, it is clear that these enterprise workers want, and value, the responsibility and freedom that mobility gives them.

Of course, just because something is technically possible does not mean it should be pursued. When evaluating the appropriateness of a mobile workforce, the obvious question of employee productivity must be asked. With the number of potential diversions and distractions outside of the office, how productive does an employee expect to be if provided with the opportunity to adopt a mobile work life? According to enterprise workers in the 2012 Alcatel-Lucent study, the "greatest benefits to more employees working remotely" are increased productivity (26%) and increased morale (21%). Of those enterprise workers who already work remotely, the vast majority say that this mobility makes them more productive. Despite the notion that focusing on work tasks is more difficult given other distractions surrounding the mobile worker, nearly half indicate that they are more productive because there are actually fewer distractions than in a traditional office setting. Half are more productive simply because they are more comfortable, and nearly the same number indicate that spreading their work out over more hours allows them to better focus on their work on their terms.

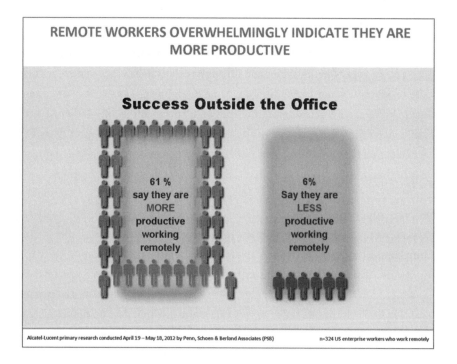

REMOTE WORKERS OVERWHELMINGLY INDICATE THEY ARE MORE PRODUCTIVE

Success Outside the Office

61 % say they are MORE productive working remotely

6% Say they are LESS productive working remotely

Alcatel-Lucent primary research conducted April 19 – May 18, 2012 by Penn, Schoen & Berland Associates (PSB)   n=324 US enterprise workers who work remotely

Although more flexible working arrangements may positively impact employee productivity, there are some negative aspects to working and managing others in a mobile-centric environment. When asked to identify the "greatest drawbacks to more employees working remotely," respondents in the 2012 Alcatel-Lucent study highlighted the increased challenges in coordination and monitoring of work (29%), the difficulty in managing employees (16%), and the difficulty in developing relationships with coworkers (15%). Perhaps these challenges help explain why only 15 percent of entry-level employees are trusted to work remotely, whereas 42 percent of experienced employees are afforded the opportunity. Given the managerial challenges associated with a mobile workforce, a certain degree of personal productivity and managerial trust needs to be developed before such flexibility is provided. The difficulty in developing relationships and working with coworkers is also reflected by the enterprise workers who already work remotely. As stated above, 61 percent of this population say that their mobile work life has increased their personal productivity. Yet, although individual productivity is gained, the jury is still out when it comes to how a virtual workforce affects team output. On this point, the sample is divided, with 51 percent of this same cohort agreeing that working from outside the office reduces team productivity because people do not see each other as often.

Still, despite the questionable effects that a mobile workforce has on team productivity, the myriad benefits evidenced through real estate savings and increased employee productivity, not to mention the surge in employee satisfaction, are often sufficient to compel enterprises forward. From an IT perspective, the challenges are formidable. According to a recent report by enterprise mobility services firm iPass, IT managers feel that they are losing control of the mobile landscape in their organizations. More than two in five believe that they have less control over the employee's choice of device than a year earlier. Of greatest frustration to these IT professionals is in properly supporting their internal customers, despite lacking the authority to govern a fragmented device ecosystem in the enterprise. They cite the challenges in providing support for nonprovisioned devices and in onboarding them to the corporate network, as the top frustrations expressed.[14] It is telling that two issues related to the introduction of personal devices into the workplace rank higher as a source of consternation for IT managers than the veritable mainstays that have beleaguered this profession since its inception, that of data encryption, loss or recovery, and network security. And, not surprisingly, for those IT departments that do retain a degree of control over the selection of devices in the workplace, the 2012 Alcatel-Lucent study found that security and data protection are the primary reason that 59 percent of IT decision makers restrict personal devices.

The security concerns shared by the more cautious IT departments who are not rushing toward the BYOD trend are not unfounded. If the Honey Stick experiment isn't sufficient to demonstrate the potential harm that is created when a mobile device is lost or stolen, perhaps the exponential increase in mobile threats capable of seeping through the virtual door is cause to keep an IT manager awake at night. The security firm Securelist found only 153 families of mobile malicious programs and more than 1,000 modifications of mobile threats at the end of 2010. By 2011, the company says, those figures grew by 178 new families and more than 5,000 new modifications. Nearly 37 percent of the mobile malware in 2011 came in the form of seemingly innocuous SMS messages.[15] A global study by (ISC)[2] confirms the same. In it, 56 percent of respondents indicate an increase in security risks in 2011, with 38 percent attributing the cause to mobile devices.[16]

Although legitimate concerns remain, it's clear that the mobility trend in the enterprise is not going away. A recent report from the global telecommunications service provider BT shows that 84 percent of IT decision makers believe that companies that allow their employees to use their personal devices for work enjoy a competitive advantage.[17] When coupled with increased employee productivity and satisfaction, the benefit to the enterprise of a mobile-enabled workforce, powered by their own devices, becomes hard to ignore.

The following are some practical considerations that may help more conservative enterprises get over the mobility hump, if not improve the situation for those who have already embraced the trend:

- **Quarantine the disease, not the patients**—One of the most counterproductive measures enterprises can take is to treat mobility demand among employees as a contagion deserving of quarantine. These enterprises often impose a stranglehold on procedures and policies in an attempt to suppress mobile appetite.

  Unfortunately, the opposite is often experienced. Studies by the Aberdeen Group and others show that such inflexible control increases costs and risks as employees simply bypass corporate-sanctioned systems.[18] Still, there is inherent complexity in supporting an average of eight mobile platforms per company in 2011 (according to Sybase research surveying 250 IT managers).[19]

Risks such as provisioning complexity across multiple devices, data security, device loss, and increased data usage costs cannot be ignored.

Mobile device management platforms and cloud-based containerization technologies that allow for the partitioning of users' professional and personal profiles can help address these technical dilemmas.

- **Clarify the prescription**—Addressing technical challenges is one matter, but how should organizations go about executing an effective mobile strategy? In a research note written in collaboration with BT, Gartner identifies three best practices for organizations that are allowing their mobile workers to equip themselves.

  First, support agreements are essential in clarifying the expectations between employees and management. Included is the arrangement that specifies accountability—such as who is responsible for backing up the device, in what scenario can the IT department wipe the device, and what are the acceptable use policies—to remove as much ambiguity from the BYOD equation as possible.

  Second, the involvement of Human Resources, auditors, insurance providers, and legal staff in the development of any BYOD program ensures that their requirements (such as device wiping or retrieving devices to satisfy possible e-disclosure demands) are accommodated.

  Finally, contingency plans and support teams need to be identified in the event that external events, such as legal rulings, require rapid changes to the BYOD policy.[20]

- **Monitor health without compromising trust**—Beyond the IT implementation of BYOD and telecommuting policies designed to enable an adaptable workforce, the management of these remote workers is also a key consideration for enterprises hoping to realize the benefits such flexible organizations promise. As previously discussed, employees must first demonstrate a certain degree of productivity before being afforded the trust to work remotely. However, even the most productive and responsive remote workers require some specific care and feeding from their management.

  From an employee management perspective, it can be difficult to keep track of what is going on in the field and how remote employees are performing. Of course, technology can provide some level of oversight for managers of a remote workforce. Smartphones can be monitored and configured to report on location, usage, and activity to provide a degree of worker oversight for managers wanting to monitor specific performance metrics. More than one in four business decision makers and one in three IT decision makers in the 2012 Alcatel-Lucent study indicate that managers have the right to use such technology to monitor their employees at all times. However, the acceptable oversight of employee behavior is not necessarily shared by the subjects in question, the frontline employees themselves. In a working arrangement that is built on trust, such an approach needs to be handled openly, above board, and with full disclosure to the employee.

Before implementing such a practice to remote worker management, perhaps a more old-school approach would be more appropriate. *Fast Company* magazine recently identified three specific ways to encourage and get the most out of a virtual team.

First, make sure the right tools are in place. Especially in an age when people are using their own devices and applications, work collaboration can suffer in a remote working environment. Half the employees in the 2012 Alcatel-Lucent study indicate that team productivity is negatively impacted in remote working situations. By coalescing around a common set of tools, a team can establish a simple and easy way for a manager and team to keep track of progress against objectives and work together.

Second, managers need to remember to recognize and reward remote workers as they would ones in the office. Making sure that the mobile workforce is acknowledged in a similar fashion to office workers reinforces the fact that the company is one team and part of the same culture.

Finally, managers should never discount the in-person connection. Day-to-day work may take place from separate locations, but the occasional onsite meeting or monthly face-to-face lunch can help eliminate the potential feeling of isolation.[21]

The mobile workforce has proven itself to be a productive and contributing force in today's enterprise. Enabled by new and emerging technologies, mobile employees are leveraging the flexibility and power of an always-connected world to get their jobs done regardless of the time of day or their physical location. Successful organizations with established remote working arrangements continue to see cost and employee satisfaction benefits. As the workforce becomes more virtual and continues to bring their personal technology into the workplace, today's companies are at a crossroads: Continue to restrict their employees to a set of formally approved tools, or fully embrace the newer BYOD trend and the older telecommuting movement before it and the benefits both can bring to the organization? Those enterprises that conscientiously support technologies to address the needs of an increasingly fluid workforce and implement demonstrated best practices may find themselves the beneficiaries of lower costs with higher employee throughput and satisfaction—a goal upon which both business leaders and frontline employees can agree.

FREEING THE "SCREEN SLAVES"

As companies have responded to the economic climate of the past several years by laying off employees and closing company facilities, many workers have responded by working longer hours and forgoing vacation time. Smartphones and tablet computers have allowed these employees the ability to maintain constant contact with what is going on at work and remain productive at all hours of the day. In her book *Sleeping with Your Smartphone: How to Break the 24/7 Habit and Change the Way You Work* (Harvard Business Review Press, 2012), Harvard Business School Professor Leslie Perlow found that 70 percent of professionals check their smartphones each day within an hour of waking up in the morning. More than 55 percent of these same professionals do the same within an hour of going to bed each night. Perlow found that, even while on vacation, more than half continuously checked in while they were supposed to be getting away from work.[22] It's true that the devices around us help employees stay in touch and be more responsive and productive—but at what cost? It used to only be medical professionals that were on call 24 hours a day. Now, in an always-on world, more frontline knowledge workers are connected and in touch all day, every day. According to the Chartered Society of Physiotherapy, this is not such a good thing. In an online survey of 2,010 office workers, the Society found that employees have become "screen slaves," working on average two or more extra hours of screen time every day. Society chairwoman Dr. Helena Johnson says that these findings are of "huge concern." She reflected, "If it becomes a regular part of your evening routine then it can lead to...stress-related illnesses."[23]

As part of her overall study for her book, Perlow questioned the notion that staying connected 24 hours a day, seven days a week is essential for success. To test her ideas, she worked with the global consulting firm The Boston Consulting Group (BCG). BCG prides itself on being available to their clients day or night and is a prime example of an always-on culture. Working with a small group of consultants at BCG, Perlow mandated that each person on the team take a night off each week from work—no e-mails, no calls, nothing. They would power down and rely on their coworkers to handle any issues that might arise. As part of the test, the team was required to check in as a group once a week to discuss their feelings about how it was going. After some initial resistance, Perlow found that communication had improved and the overall quality of the team's work had increased. "The equation increases the level of teamwork," Perlow said. "People are covering for each other with a collective goal in mind. The team knows more about what's going on, so it creates an openness and builds a deeper sense of trust." Today, BCG has adopted the model company-wide, ensuring that the highly mobile and connected workforce is even more productive and satisfied with their delicate work/life balance.

The Cloud Conundrum

→ *The world created and replicated enough data in 2011 to fill over 50 billion iPads—a cost equivalent to the GDP of the United States, Japan, China, Germany, France, the United Kingdom and Italy combined.*[1]

When Jeff Bezos, CEO of Amazon.com, introduced the company's latest breakthrough, the Kindle Fire, in late 2011, the visionary declared it "the culmination of the many things we've [Amazon.com] been doing for 15 years."[2] With the Fire, Amazon planned to take on the 800-pound gorilla in the tablet category, the Apple iPad. Although the two devices may have appeared similar in form factor and functionality to the general public, the strategy behind each product couldn't have been more different. Apple had earned the coveted position as the most valued company in the world, with a $465 billion market capitalization that exceeded Exxon's $400 billion in early 2012,[3] based on a strategy of delivering better machines (91% of its revenues are device sales, compared with just 6% from iTunes).[4] In contrast, Amazon survived the web bubble burst to rise as the most successful online retailer based on a content approach—with almost half of its revenues derived from sales of media like books, movies, music, and television shows.[5] With Apple emphasizing a download approach to its devices (thereby placing a premium on storage and memory performance), Amazon challenged this notion with a streaming strategy intended to disrupt the tablet category. As such, Amazon boldly entered the market with a retail price for its new Fire far below any established by Apple. The debate surrounding which was better—a cloud-based approach à la Amazon or a device-led strategy as espoused by Apple—was on.

The Fire was just the latest manifestation of an ongoing strategy years in the making. And, while Amazon's tablet relied on the cloud to serve insatiable consumers the latest streamed content on demand, the company had already established itself as a cloud provider to business customers with its Amazon Web Services portfolio. In an interview with *Wired*, Bezos recalled the genesis of the new venture for the company:

> *Approximately nine years ago we were wasting a lot of time internally because, to do their jobs, our applications engineers had to have daily detailed conversations with our networking infrastructure engineers. Instead of having this fine-grained coordination about every detail, we wanted the data-center guys to give the apps guys a set of dependable tools, a reliable infrastructure that they could build products on top of.*
>
> *The problem was obvious. We didn't have that infrastructure. So we started building it for our own internal use. Then we realized, "Whoa, everybody who wants to build web-scale applications is going to need this." We figured with a little bit of extra work we could make it available to everybody. We're going to make it anyway—let's sell it.[6]*

And with the same pioneering spirit that became synonymous with Amazon's culture, the company allowed capital-constrained enterprises of all sizes to purchase IT services as easily as standard utilities. Rather than invest in costly servers for storage capacity or computing horsepower, businesses could simply choose to rent such capabilities from Amazon, leading the provider soon to generate more traffic through its cloud computing services than from its established global websites. In essence, those uncongested lanes on the virtual highway Amazon created to accelerate its own development cycles were monetized and consumed by companies needing an on-ramp—and quick exit—from an otherwise considerable investment in computer hardware that was often underutilized itself during their nonseasonal periods. And, true to Amazon's heritage of offering premium products at nonpremium prices (as Bezos told *Wired*, the company had become "very accustomed to operating at low margins"[7]), enterprises were afforded access to Amazon's on-ramp of cloud capabilities at extremely competitive rates. A win–win partnership was created in the marketplace, and Amazon quickly catapulted to annual revenues exceeding $500 million from the new line of business.[8] But it was a well-publicized outage in April of 2011 that stole the headlines and overshadowed the success generated by the company in such a short period of time.

On April 21, 2011, in a series of events triggered by a mistake in redirecting existing traffic to a lower-capacity, rather than higher-capacity, redundant network while performing a routine network upgrade, the company soon found itself the victim of automated intelligence gone haywire. As any reputable cloud provider would, Amazon established redundancy algorithms throughout its network, whereby storage nodes were replicated to back up data. However, when it inadvertently directed traffic from a primary network route to a lower-capacity backup route, some affected storage nodes were unable to find their replicas. This triggered a re-mirroring storm, in which a large volume of storage nodes attempted replication concurrently, exhausting available capacity in one of Amazon's main serving areas. This chain reaction led to a customer outage of key Amazon cloud capabilities lasting approximately four days. At a cost of $5,000 per minute during an IT outage, as estimated by Emerson Network Power,[9] the resulting implications to businesses most affected by the Amazon interruption were devastating. For one customer, in particular, the consequences were potentially life-threatening, as evidenced by his desperate blog posted to Amazon's site, which soon earned notoriety as it propagated virally as an example of what not to do in the cloud:

> *Life of our patients is at stake—I am desperately asking you to contact ...*
>
> *Sorry, I could not get through in any other way.*
>
> *We are a monitoring company and are monitoring hundreds of cardiac patients at home.*
>
> *We were unable to see their ECG signals since 21st of April.*
>
> *Could you please contact us? ...*
>
> *Or please let me know how can I contact you more ditectly [sic].*
>
> *Thank you*

Although the post drew the criticism of dozens of IT professionals perplexed by this customer's ignorance, the following response by a fellow IT professional sums up the consensus quite nicely:

> *Oh this is not good. Man mission critical systems should never be ran [sic] in the cloud. Just because AWS is HIPPA [healthcare] certified doesn't mean it won't go down for 48+ hours in a row.*

And in less than 50 words, the opinion of one IT professional speaking on behalf of many in his community punctuated the point that makes the cloud in the enterprise so tricky. Although consumers may become *irritated* if a cloud outage disrupts their ability to stream the latest content to their Kindle Fire, a business with a "mission-critical" need facing such an interruption risks loss of productivity, data, or—even worse—customers. IT downtime costs businesses more than 127 million person-hours per year—an average of 545 person-hours per company—according to research among IT and business executives by CA Technologies. In the study, 35 percent of respondents indicated that IT downtime harms customer loyalty, and 44 percent stated that it damages staff morale. What's more, 87 percent of respondents said that failure to recover data would be damaging to their business, with 23 percent labeling such inability "disastrous." [10] When control over IT resources is abdicated to a third-party provider like Amazon, enterprises must consciously weigh the benefits of shifting the upfront capital investment burden to said provider versus the potential risk of outages should the infrastructure that is outside of the enterprise's jurisdiction fail. In addition, although many large companies, including Netflix, successfully weathered the Amazon storm because of their premeditated cloud redundancy planning, several others found themselves dead in the water.

Although the Amazon outage was journalistic fodder for days after the event, perhaps the bigger story resided in the fact that Amazon never violated its service level agreement (SLA) with its customers. In industry parlance, an SLA is a written arrangement between a supplier and a customer that defines critical aspects of a service, such as uptime and other performance metrics. If the SLA is violated, there is generally some form of compensation exchanged between supplier and customer to remunerate the latter for his or her losses. In Amazon's case, the company offers its cloud platform in multiple regions, with multiple availability zones within a region. According to the company's website at the time, customers who launched server instances in multiple availability zones could "protect [their] applications from failure of a single location." [11] At the time of the outage, Amazon's SLA committed to a 99.5 percent uptime for customers with deployments in more than one availability zone within a specific region. However, those who scrutinized the language of this SLA would have discovered that it applied only to the commitment of connecting and provisioning instances. In fact, the outage didn't have a negative impact on customers in this regard. Still, that left many customers exposed and unprotected when the outage affected other cloud activities not covered by the SLA and disabled by the interruption.

The cloud represents an interesting conundrum for enterprises. As the Amazon experience demonstrates, there is still much to be learned in this emerging space. Of course, "the cloud" itself is not a new concept. Its origination can be traced back to the 1960s, when John McCarthy suggested that "computation may someday be organized as a public utility." [12] Since then, the market has been flooded with seemingly unending variations of the concept delivered by multiple vendors, each with different capabilities and SLAs. The cloud has suffered a bit from its own success, leading to more providers hopping on the bandwagon and fragmenting the definition of "cloud" even further. A simple Google search on the term "cloud computing" renders more than 100 million hits. For definitional purposes, this chapter explores a very specific category within cloud computing, that of infrastructure as a service (IaaS). In nontechnical terms, IaaS allows users to purchase computer horsepower virtually. These virtual machines (VMs), as they are known in the industry, can be dynamically instantiated and extinguished based on the needs of the end user. In other words, rather than purchase hardware that is equipped with more storage or processing power needed for an immediate, although temporary, task, users may instead rent these capabilities from the cloud using just about any terminal at the endpoint as a "dumb device" or "thin client."

Under the IaaS scenario, the user requires a network connection through which cloud resources are accessed. Here is where the fragmentation of cloud offerings by unique providers has created untapped opportunity in the market. Anyone who has a high-speed broadband connection at home can relate to the following example: When attempting to download bandwidth-hungry content from a site, the speed of one's connection becomes increasingly important. The slower the speed, the more frustrating is the experience. In reverse, the upstream speed becomes more critical when attempting to interact with the network, such as when uploading a large file or engaging in other "high-twitch" activities. Ask a hard-core gamer how important a highly responsive network connection (termed low "latency" in industry terms) is to her online passion, especially in fast-paced first-person shooter gaming varieties, and she will likely offer an enthusiastic response. In business terms, latency translates into far more than simply failing to fire a shot before one's enemy does in an online game; latency can deteriorate business value and revenues. In an Amazon study, the cloud provider found that an additional 500 milliseconds in completing a Google search results in 20 percent less traffic for the search engine. An additional 100-millisecond delay on the provider's own retail site converts to a 1 percent decrease in sales.[13] In other words, the speed and latency of the network have a profound impact on one's experience (a concept well understood by consumers) and one's business value (a fact recognized by companies).

Now imagine a business user attempting to access greater compute or storage resources on demand. Historically, these IT-related infrastructure components were the domain of data center companies—providers with significant computing platforms capable of renting their unused IT capacity on demand to interested buyers. It isn't far-fetched to suggest that, when one is in need of greater storage capacity and/or higher computing processing power, the network is affected in the exchange. Yet many of these companies ignored the network element completely, forcing enterprise users to understand the implications of renting IT resources and the associated impact to network demand. Even more confounding, those important SLAs that establish the covenant between buyer and seller often partitioned the cloud into distinct stovepipes—with IT SLAs provided by data center companies and network SLAs offered by service providers. In essence, buyers were forced to stitch together a cloud value proposition from multiple parties and do so while keeping an end-to-end view of SLA requirements. Perhaps this challenge helps explain why, in a 2011 IDC study among CIOs, the top two factors inhibiting adoption of cloud services among respondents were (1) bandwidth and latency needs for specific applications (mentioned by 44% of respondents) and (2) service level guarantees (cited by 40% of respondents). Even more revealing, these concerns topped conventional cloud criticisms like security and data ownership, privacy, and compliance.

Although performance and SLAs topped the list of concerns in the IDC study, there are those persistent security questions that still hold sway. In a global study of 573 business and technology executives commissioned by IT services provider Avanade in 2011, 51 percent of respondents cited security concerns as the top reason deterring their company's move to the cloud. There appeared more to the concern than simple paranoia at play. Nearly one-fourth of respondents reported that their company had experienced a security breach with a cloud service. Putting their money where their mouth is, 20 percent of respondents admitted to turning off a cloud service in their organization and returning to on-premise services, with security concerns the biggest driver of this move.[14]

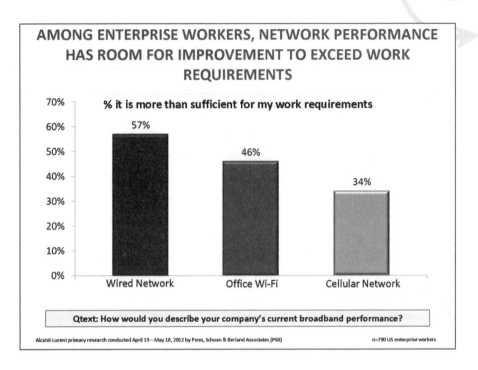

AMONG ENTERPRISE WORKERS, NETWORK PERFORMANCE HAS ROOM FOR IMPROVEMENT TO EXCEED WORK REQUIREMENTS

% it is more than sufficient for my work requirements

Wired Network — 57%
Office Wi-Fi — 46%
Cellular Network — 34%

Qtext: How would you describe your company's current broadband performance?

Alcatel-Lucent primary research conducted April 19 – May 18, 2012 by Penn, Schoen & Berland Associates (PSB)   n=790 US enterprise workers

If performance and security weren't enough, there's always the dreaded outcome of cloud sprawl to dissuade otherwise eager prospects from jumping on the cloud bandwagon. The fragmentation in the industry that has done so much to complicate the definition of *cloud* has a more practical consequence in the enterprise. In the same Avanade study, 60 percent of respondents were worried about unmanaged cloud sprawl—the use of multiple cloud platforms by multiple vendors with little to no management in how these clouds interoperate, if at all. To this point, more than one in four respondents reported not having a centralized system to identify and track their IT cloud service providers.[15] The problem of cloud sprawl is further exacerbated when one mixes private and public clouds in the soup. Public clouds are just that—they are offered by service providers (like Amazon) that lease "public" facilities to buyers with a temporary need or looking to conserve cash up-front. In contrast, private clouds are built using an enterprise's own resources in its data center and leveraged across its key internal constituents, leaving the company in control but also shouldering the overhead costs. There are pros and cons to both approaches, leading many enterprises to pursue a mix of private and public clouds. Although private clouds offer greater control and reuse of infrastructure (enterprises using private clouds have been shown to increase utilization of their existing assets from about 40% to 75% or more, with detailed insight of exactly how their infrastructure is being used across their organization),[16] they don't offer the same speed or agility offered by their public competitors. All of this complexity often results in multiple clouds being used for different purposes or organizations, leading to the unenviable cloud sprawl position in which enterprises increasingly find themselves.

Despite the cautious attitude of many IT professionals, it isn't stopping the average enterprise employee from adopting cloud alternatives with enthusiasm. In the 2012 Alcatel-Lucent study, 35 percent of workers admit to using Dropbox (a cloud-based storage service) for work purposes. One-third of respondents confess to using Amazon's web-based services, apparently undeterred by the well-publicized outage of 2011. In addition, although two in five large enterprises in the study have policies that restrict web applications or personal technologies (largely because of concerns for data protection and the infiltration of viruses and malware to the corporate network), as evidenced by the research, even these rules are no match against an employee's tenacity in using such services.

The confluence of all these factors—the fragmentation of cloud offerings with unique SLAs, the balancing act of protecting corporate assets while securing IT services on tap, and the unencumbered will of increasingly tech-savvy employees—makes the cloud a huge source of consternation for IT professionals. In the 2012 Alcatel-Lucent study, the cloud ranked as the biggest concern among IT managers and professionals, with 25 percent of respondents ranking it their top issue, even above the consumerization of IT trend and the strategic role of the IT function. Still, the promise of the cloud is hard to resist, even among enterprise leaders who arguably bear the most responsibility in protecting the firm's prized assets. As one respondent in a related Alcatel-Lucent study of more than 200 enterprise professionals in the United States put it:

> **Moderator:** *Anything else that's intriguing to you that you're not ready to bring into the firm?*
>
> **Respondent:** *Cloud. I think Cloud is probably the latest thing on everyone's mind. You look at it, and in theory it's a great idea, but just like everything that first comes out it needs some time to be developed and to be beneficial. But sure, think of the storage you would save, and think of how you can just go in and get what you need from this one area. It's just a matter of how could you protect it?*

It's this constant tug-of-war that leaves the cloud market open to even more oppor-tunity than the exponential growth seen in the category to date. The reality is that enterprises are still proceeding very cautiously into the cloud. Some are outright retreat-ing because of poor experiences. Despite a market that is conservatively estimated to exceed $20 billion worldwide by 2014 according to analyst IDC (and that's just for the IaaS cloud flavor discussed in this chapter),[17] an industry more than 50 years in the making still appears to be in its infancy. To back up this controversial claim, in 2011, Alcatel-Lucent commissioned research covering more than 1,000 IT decision makers in the United States to explore specifically the issues and opportunities still existing in the cloud landscape. Whereas more than 80 percent of respondents reported using the cloud for at least one need (for the technophiles reading this, these cloud alternatives may also have included software-as-a-service ([SaaS] or platform-as-a-service [PaaS] varieties), only one in four report relying on the cloud for at least one "mission-critical" application. This finding is corroborated by another research study commissioned by the IT Governance Institute, which polled more than 800 executives around the world and found only 18 percent of those who currently outsource considering the cloud for mission-critical services (helping to explain how the aforementioned Amazon customer could be so excoriated by his IT peers for trusting his "mission-critical" application to a cloud). Yet, according to the 2011 Alcatel-Lucent study, if the performance, latency, and security considerations could be sufficiently addressed, 95 percent of respondents who could be convinced to migrate at least one mission-critical application to the cloud would also transfer an additional five to six applications. The result is a tsunami of new opportunities not yet tapped by cloud providers, anchored by mission-critical applica-tions that stimulate the movement of other IT needs to a cloud environment. The result, based on Alcatel-Lucent analysis from the 2011 study, is a fivefold potential increase in addressable market opportunity not yet served by today's cloud alternatives.

The attractive market up for grabs by cloud providers does little to alleviate the concerns faced by the enterprises they hope to serve. For these companies, the trade-off is an unenviable one—does one cede control of its IT infrastructure to gain capi-tal and speed advantages, or retain control at the risk of competitive disadvantage? Unfortunately, the answer is not as black-or-white as the question. There are several implications that enterprises must consider when evaluating if a move to the cloud is right for their company:

- **Don't silo the cloud**—Although many companies specialize in one aspect of the cloud (such as storage, computing power, or network resources), the reality is that an effective cloud solution requires both IT *and* network resources to work effectively. Focusing on one domain at the expense of the other (IT vs. network connectivity) can yield damaging consequences to well-intentioned enterprises eager to dabble in the cloud. Of the enterprises that use the cloud in the 2011 Alcatel-Lucent study, 28 percent indicated that cloud performance was the single attribute that needed the most improvement (including response time and end-to-end performance). This was the most popular option cited by these cloud users, beating out strong contenders like security, ease of use, and price in the debate. Harmonizing IT and network components gives these enterprises what they crave and fills a void that largely remains in today's market—an end-to-end cloud solution that seamlessly adapts when greater bandwidth, storage, and/or compute pressures are applied by users.

- **Don't underestimate SLAs**—SLAs are the written covenant between provider and customer, and they are often the latter's only course of action when something goes wrong. If there is one given with the cloud (or any technology, for that matter), one can expect that things will go wrong. In the 2011 Alcatel-Lucent study, nearly two in five respondents indicated that they have experienced cloud outages ranging from frequent interruptions that are short in duration to infrequent disruptions with longer staying power. Nearly the same number report that their current cloud latency spans from uncomfortable to intolerable response times. Despite this, more than one in five enterprises are forced to monitor their SLA performance themselves, and more than one-third have no remediation when said SLAs are not met. SLAs may be common in the cloud market today, however, as the Amazon case illustrates, one must examine these contracts carefully to ensure understanding of the risks and benefits. Otherwise, it's Buyer Beware.

- **Don't ignore new business models**—The cloud is certainly a technology, but it is more importantly a new business model. For the first time, small enterprises have a viable means to compete against their larger counterparts, who have previously been the sole beneficiaries of dedicated IT staff and resources and the resulting advantages. Although the cloud itself is a new business model for pay-as-you-go IT infrastructure and support, there are more business models yet untapped in this market. As the last chapter discussed, more employees are bringing their own devices to the enterprise with an expectation that these devices will function for work. In essence, these employees are subsidizing the costs of IT by procuring the device themselves and using it for work purposes. Alcatel-Lucent was curious to see if the same phenomenon might hold true for network-based services offered through the enterprise. Specifically, would cloud-based solutions, like a virtual desktop service that allows the user access to corporate resources through any device, be compelling enough that employees might be willing to help subsidize their costs? In the 2012 Alcatel-Lucent study, the answer was clear. One in four frontline workers was very likely to pay \$5.00 per month to their company—taken as a paycheck deduction, for example—in exchange for such a service. Although \$5.00 per month per employee may not seem huge at face value, the figure adds up quickly as the size of the enterprise grows. Furthermore, this treasure chest is in addition to the amount of money willing to be paid, in a more traditional sense, by business and IT decision makers allocating organizational budgets to cover the costs of the service. In other words, just as the cloud has morphed into several hybrid implementations (from public to private to hybrid clouds), the potential business models for funding different cloud-based services are equally diverse.

- **Don't overestimate policy**—Companies are quick to respond to potential abuse by instituting policies. As previously discussed, policies are essential to establish the written code between employer and employee. But moving from definition to alteration of behavior requires policies that are accompanied by employee understanding and management enforcement. Ignoring these critical elements in effective policy execution exposes enterprises to risks thought to be contained simply because a "policy" exists. A report from Application Security found that 28 percent of enterprise data breaches are due to "management complacency or a lack of awareness." [18] If lack of knowledge or enforcement isn't the culprit, perhaps employee apathy is to blame. A Cisco study found that 56 percent of employees don't always comply with IT policies even though they are fully aware of them.[19] Even if the communication or enforcement of policy is sufficient, sometimes the policy itself is misguided. Particularly when employees are fully informed of the potential consequences of a policy decision, management may find a different attitude among those they are most interested in influencing. The BYOD phenomenon is one such example. Based on the 2012 Alcatel-Lucent study, nearly three in five frontline workers prefer a policy that permits an employee to connect to the corporate network to access company resources (cloud) as opposed to allowing the company access to personal devices that may attempt to store such assets (BYOD). This percent is more interesting when one considers that the majority prefer the former despite potential network latency or performance issues. In fact, only one in four would accept a policy that allows employees to download corporate information to personal devices at the expense of also granting authority to the company to monitor the device's contents. Policies are a necessary evil to mitigate lawsuits and establish written rules between management and employees. That said, relying exclusively on policy to dictate acceptable technology behaviors may result in a blindside to the company or the employees it attempts to influence.

- **Don't miscalculate security**—When important corporate assets and data are virtualized in the network, one must take precautions to ensure that such resources are protected, such as seeking multitenancy options that partition data from multiple customers in a cloud environment. In addition, although security will remain a top concern for enterprises considering the cloud, there is an argument to be made that suggests that the cloud may offer better security advantages in some cases, particularly when protecting the firm from its own employees. It's not necessarily the case that employees are malicious (although according to the book *Essentials of Business Ethics*, 75% of employees have stolen something from work in the course of their careers),[20] but all too often, employees are simply careless. The increasingly mobile workforce simply compounds the risk that corporate information or assets will be left exposed. A Symantec MessageLabs Report indicates that mobile employees are 5.4 times more likely to access dangerous content than those in the office.[21] Protecting corporate assets behind the perimeter of a cloud that is either bordered by multitenancy (in the case of a public cloud) or its own firewall (in the case of a private cloud) also mitigates the risk of such assets being exposed by innocent employees polluting the corporate waters by infecting or losing connected devices. Security is a double-edged sword, and the risks and benefits of both cloud- and client-based alternatives should be considered.

Although Amazon took it on the chin during the media hype surrounding its cloud outage, the company responded with a detailed post-mortem that established a new level of transparency for cloud and other service providers to emulate. The misstep itself was an anathema to the company's vigilant obsession with error avoidance, as Bezos remarked to *Wired*: "We really obsess over small defects. That's what drives up costs. Because the most expensive thing you can do is make a mistake." [22] Yet mistakes will be made, and cloud providers are no exception to the rule. Lew Moorman, chief strategy officer of Rackspace, another cloud service provider, compared the Amazon outage to an airplane crash—a major event with widespread damage. As Moorman astutely points out, however, airline travel is still safer than driving in a car—the metaphorical comparison of the cloud to privately owned infrastructure. [23] No matter how much journalistic fodder such crashes may generate, it isn't doing much to temper the enthusiasm of eager passengers willing to get on the plane and take to the clouds, as demonstrated by the Amazon customer who trusted the cloud for his mission-critical healthcare service. Although ridiculed by his community for what many considered an ignorant move, perhaps the sentiment of an IT executive, a respondent in the 2012 Alcatel-Lucent study who also happens to be in the healthcare field, sheds some perspective on why the cloud will be significant for possibly another 50 years to come:

> *The healthcare industry is amazing evolving and changing on a daily basis. IT has to be able to keep up with this evolution. Our customers rely on us not just for a product but sometimes for a life or death solution. There is much more at stake than just revenue and we have to be successful at all things. The introduction of cloud computing will become the norm eventually in our business. No longer will we need to continue to purchase large storage servers, nor will we have to worry about running out of space. Our doctors can log from anywhere and access patient files or lab reports. Hospitals have to increase their customer base just as any business does. If we don't have cutting edge technology or meet the customers' needs they will go somewhere else. And not just down the street, they will go across the country or around the world to get the most effective healthcare that they need. We have to manage these customers' needs efficiently and financially effectively. This can't be done without highly effective technology.*

Whether embraced by all functions of the enterprise or not, the cloud offers one such technology option to level the competitive playing field. What's more, it represents a new business model that will transform the way enterprises run on IT, thereby changing the complexion of the IT function and releasing new opportunities for an insatiably connected workforce. The terrain is not without its risks, although educated enterprises and the trustworthy providers that serve them have only scratched the surface of potential rewards.

MAKE HISTORY

In April of 2012, mobile history was made. That month, an application only 50 days in the making managed to break 50 million downloads and set a new record as the fastest-growing original mobile game of all time (even displacing "Angry Birds" as the top-paid application in Apple's App Store). "Draw Something," the addictive Pictionary-esque mobile game in which users engage in a social gaming platform and guess each other's drawings while separated by space and time, grew from three drawings per second when the game launched to 3,000 drawings per second at the time of its record.[24] Even the most adept soothsayers would have been hard pressed to predict such growth (even if they had, few would have given credence to the prognostication). A company confined to internal IT infrastructure would be even more challenged to rise to the capacity demands created by such explosive growth. In fact, if a company like Draw Something had been confined to its own infrastructure to support its users, the capital pressures would only have been exceeded by the time crunch itself in building such capacity. Thankfully, for Draw Something, such an outcome never had to be entertained. The company could scale up and down with cloud-based solutions as quickly as their demand ebbed and flowed (or, in this case, continued to ebb) to meet the insatiable appetites of its Picassos in the making. Luckily for the millions of rabid fans now addicted to the application, there's no shortage of drawings to be encountered anytime soon.

The Data Deluge

→ *According to IDC, the amount of data in the world is doubling every two years.*[1]

Anywhere from 5 to 20 percent of the nation's population contract the flu each year, a cause of roughly 36,000 deaths annually.[2] Those numbers were sufficient to earn the common flu a place among the top 10 killers in the United States in 2010—beating suicide, homicide, and other lethal forces in the process.[3] As with any epidemic, early detection and warning are critical to contain contagion. Enter the Centers for Disease Control and Prevention (CDC), part of the U.S. Department of Health and Human Services, and responsible, in part, for notifying the public of potential epidemics. They do so by monitoring data collected and compiled from thousands of health care providers, laboratories, and other sources. But, in 2008, there arrived another alternative to the CDC—one that relied not on medical records from esteemed sources but the seemingly banal keyboard searches from millions of everyday consumers. That year, Google debuted its Google Flu Trends service, designed to mine and analyze the millions of search terms entered through its engine in an attempt to predict the threat of an epidemic. Even more boldly, the company suggested that it may have the ability to detect regional outbreaks a week to 10 days before the authority on epidemics, the CDC. As evidence to the claim, the company pointed to February of that year, when the CDC reported a spike in flu cases in the mid-Atlantic states, yet Google's search analytics revealed an increase in flu-related search terms fully two weeks before the CDC's release.

In 2010, Southeastern Louisiana University released data confirming that popular microblogging site Twitter was also capable of beating the CDC. Aron Culotta, assistant professor of computer science, and two student assistants analyzed more than

500 million Twitter messages over an eight-month period in 2009. By using a small number of keywords to track rates of flu-related messages on the site, the team was able to forecast future flu rates with a 95 percent correlation to the national health statistics compiled by the CDC. According to Culotta, the predictive nature of Twitter not only beat the CDC in speed but in cost as well:

> A micro-blogging service such as Twitter is a promising new data source for Internet-based surveillance because of the volume of messages, their frequency and public availability. This approach is much cheaper and faster than having thousands of hospitals and health care providers fill out forms each week.... The Centers for Disease Control produces weekly estimates, but those reports typically lag a week or two behind. This approach produces estimates daily.[4]

The potential opportunities associated with how existing data could be mined and exploited were sufficient to capture the attention of the United Nations, which established its Global Pulse initiative in 2009. The program is designed "to explore opportunities for using real-time data to gain a more accurate understanding of population wellbeing, especially related to the impacts of global crises."[5] Apparently, the data extracted from social media updates can go much further than predicting the latest disease epidemic—as incredible as that outcome may be on its own. As it turns out, social media can help prognosticate *economic* epidemics as well. As part of a joint engagement between the United Nations and SAS, the organizations monitored two years worth of social media data, comprising half a million blogs, forums, and news sites, from the United States and Ireland. The organizations sought to correlate the mood of social chatter with official unemployment figures to determine if the former could prophesy the latter. In a fascinating conclusion, the analysis concluded that increased chatter about cutting back on groceries, downgrading one's automobile, and increasing use of public transportation carried tangible value in predicting an unemployment spike. Even by assessing the subtle changes in the tone of conversations, the organizations were able to predict the amount of time preceding an unemployment surge. For example, in the United States, a rise in "hostile" or "depressed" mood occurred four months before the unemployment increase. In Ireland, increases in "anxious" unemployment chatter preceded an unemployment spike by five months. Increased "confused" chatter came three months before the unemployment gain, whereas "confident" chatter significantly decreased two months out.[6]

If harnessing existing data is sufficient for predicting major health and well-being trends, what does that suggest for an enterprise seeking the same simply to make better decisions? The digital trail composed of millions of keystrokes, social networking and location updates, channel changes, user-generated and surveillance photographs, and inventory movements creates a staggering amount of data for enterprises potentially to exploit each year. In fact, the precipitous growth in data has become both opportunity and challenge for businesses in recent years, with more and more data becoming digitalized—from a paltry 0.8 percent of data being digitalized in 1986 to a staggering 94 percent by 2007. Today, 99.9 percent of all new information is digital, adding to the data treasure trove that can be mined and monetized by resourceful enterprises.[7] In fact, there is growing evidence to suggest that companies can work smarter by harnessing data to make informed and actionable decisions. In 2011, a study by MIT and the University of Pennsylvania determined that "big data"–driven decision making can be associated with a 5 percent to 6 percent rise in productivity, after studying the success of 179 large publicly traded firms. In addition, the benefits went beyond mere productivity to include other financial performance indicators, such as asset utilization, return on equity, and market value.[8] The data is validated by an Economist Intelligence Unit study commissioned by Capgemini in 2012, which surveyed more than 600 executives from across the globe on the topic. They found nine in 10 respondents agreeing that data is now an essential factor of production, gaining parity with land, labor, and capital. On average, they agree that big data has improved their organizations' performance in the past three years by 26 percent, and they are bullish that it will do so by an average of 41 percent in the next three years.[9]

Yet, for all its hype and potential, "big data" has failed to produce big results in the majority of enterprises. More than half the respondents in the Capgemini study say that big data management is not viewed strategically at senior levels of the organization.[10] In addition, when Alcatel-Lucent took the pulse of a solution that would analyze the digital footprint of an enterprise and its customers to assist in better decision making, the reaction ran the gamut of optimism to apathy among the 200 respondents, representing a variety of functions in large and small U.S. firms:

> *A big data customer-facing solution will save man hours and will make the workplace more efficient. This is a brilliant idea to make the workplace more efficient and profitable. I think it will help for sure for customers to*

get manager attention with their needs and problems. Time saving and improving productivity is what retailers need. I like it. [Retail employee]

I don't think this would help my business. I can see how this would be a big help for large business. For a large organization, this sounds like a great tool to manage and make information and data more useful. [Small business owner]

Helping to explain the volatility of responses is the dilemma of big data itself. That is, although there are real opportunities facing companies capable of mining their digital data reserves, the challenges are simply too overwhelming for many to succeed. According to McKinsey, 15 out of 17 sectors in the United States have more data stored per company than the U.S. Library of Congress. They project a 40 percent increase in global data generated each year compared with only a 5 percent growth in global IT spending.[11] And, although nearly all of the new data produced is digital, thereby making it more available for rapid decision-making capabilities, the reality is that most of it is unstructured—with documents, images, videos, and e-mail comprising the majority of existing data in most organizations and contributing most of the growth.[12] According to the Capgemini study, 40 percent of executives complain they have too much unstructured data.[13]

Despite the challenges, enterprising companies are forging ahead, spurred by the promise of superhuman decision-making capabilities. Once a concept reserved for the wild imaginations of sci-fi authors, the notion of computers outsmarting human beings has made real headlines, most notably when Watson, an artificial intelligence system developed by IBM on 90 distributed computers, defeated returning champions Ken Jennings and Brad Rutter on the popular game show *Jeopardy!* It's not altogether impressive that a computer can sift through millions of algorithms to render answers to questions for well-indexed data sets. However, what made Watson so unique and revolutionary was its ability to do the same for unstructured data—the very bane of organizations attempting to make their growing loads of dirty data actionable. As such, Watson's victory was sufficient to capture the attention of couch potatoes and business decision makers alike. Watson's fame earned it more than a place in game show record books; it also secured it employment at Citigroup as the company's newest sales "recruit." By using the scores of data available in the company's coffers, Watson will make intelligent recommendations as to what products or services (including loans and credit cards) should be offered to customers.[14] As it so happens, product recommendations are a boon to other businesses that rely on such data manipulation to make informed suggestions to customers. As an example, at one point, Amazon reported that 30 percent of its sales resulted from its recommendation engine.[15] In addition, for organizations capable of converting structured and unstructured data into meaningful information, the results can yield far more than revenue growth. Partners HealthCare, the largest healthcare provider in Massachusetts, is reusing medical data originally collected for clinical purposes, encompassing structured and unstructured formats, to accelerate medical research dramatically. As former CIO John Glaser explained, "We can cut the cost of research by a factor of five, and the time required by a factor of 10. This is a big deal. And even if those [improvements] are halved, this is still a really big deal."[16] Perhaps these early pioneers give hope to other companies aspiring to the same superhuman results, leading at least one analyst to project that the big data technology and services market will grow to roughly $17 billion by 2015, seven times the growth rate of the overall IT category.[17]

But although the big data movement is not without its success stories, these examples are currently more the exception than the rule. For struggling organizations wondering what to make of this latest craze, history can be an interesting precursor to future events. McKinsey charts four waves of IT adoption, each with varying degrees of impact to productivity growth, in the United States. Within each tranche, the firm estimates the productivity gains associated with IT improvements versus managerial innovation. In the "mainframe" era (from 1959 to 1973), although annual U.S. productivity growth overall was high at 2.82 percent, IT's contribution to output was rather modest, along with its share of overall capital expenditure. During the era of "minicomputers and PCs" (from 1973 to 1995), the U.S.'s overall productivity decreased to 1.49 percent, but IT's contribution grew significantly to more than 40 percent of the measured output. The era of "Internet and Web 1.0" (from 1995 to 2000) was characterized by deepening IT spend and significant managerial innovations that leveraged previous IT investments. During this period, overall U.S. productivity burgeoned to 2.7 percent, with IT's contribution ballooning to nearly 60 percent of the reported output. The fourth and final era, what McKinsey terms that of "mobile devices and Web 2.0," shows a slight decrease in overall productivity (at 2.5%), with the contribution from managerial innovation again taking the lion's share of credit (at more than 60%). McKinsey's assessment reveals a time lag between increased IT expenditures and the associated return on these investments in the form of managerial innovation. The result is higher levels of overall productivity for firms able to leverage their technology infrastructure. The analyst uses this rationale to help explain, in part, the lack of significant empirical evidence between data intensity or capital spend in data investments and productivity in specific sectors. McKinsey suggests that the evidentiary void is not due to a lack of causality but is merely the result of the same time delay seen in the previous waves of IT adoption.[18] However, what companies can learn from this history lesson is that, to make big data pay off in a big way, they will require both IT expertise and managerial innovation. Although intuitive at face value, there is probably no greater example of IT investment requiring managerial buy-in and collaboration with IT than that mandated by the big data phenomenon.

Unfortunately, for the many organizations where functional silos reign supreme, fostering collaboration between business leaders and the IT unit is complicated at best. Marketing, Finance, Human Resources, Operations, Sales, and IT may be aligned to overarching company strategy, but each department typically owns specific metrics for getting there. In the case of IT, these individuals have traditionally been the stewards of managing the technology infrastructure of the firm, including the data centers and computing horsepower therein. After all, IT professionals have the technical expertise required to solve appropriately for how a company's data assets are processed, stored, and retrieved. But the staggering data load on its own is sufficient to stretch IT's technical skills to new extremes. According to IDC, users created and replicated 1.8 trillion gigabytes (GB) of data in 2011, equivalent to filling more than 57 billion 32 GB Apple iPads—sufficient to build a structure equal in distance to the Great Wall of China and twice its height. The study asserts:

> Over the next decade (by 2020), IT departments worldwide will experience [growth of] 10 times the number of servers (virtual and physical), 50 times the amount of information to be managed, [and] 75 times the number of files or containers that encapsulate the information in the digital universe, which is growing even faster than the information itself as more and more embedded systems, such as sensors in clothing, in bridges, or medical devices [proliferate].[19]

Yet, for the vast increase in technology infrastructure required, the growth in IT personnel to manage this data tsunami is nowhere near keeping pace. IDC expects to see growth of only 1.5 times the number of IT professionals over the same period of time.[20]

But, beyond the technical gymnastics required to move and store bits and bytes securely and efficiently at a torrid pace, the promise of big data requires understanding what data is useful and how it can be interpreted to produce action. As capable as IT professionals may be in addressing the nontrivial technical challenges, they lack the know-how of separating the wheat from the chaff in data interpretation and analysis—such proficiency is the dominion of those business leaders residing in their functional silos. Not only does this new paradigm require closer collaboration between IT and business leaders than perhaps ever before, the burden itself may prove too great for passionate teamwork to address. McKinsey foretells of a creeping labor shortage that may leave many organizations paralyzed by an inability to turn data into insights. Unfortunately, this gap is neither the exclusive problem of IT nor the functional leaders they support. By 2018, McKinsey warns that the United States alone could face a shortage of 140,000 to 190,000 people with deep analytical skills—in addition to the 1.5 million managers and analysts with the expertise to use such data to make effective decisions.[21]

Even if blessed with the right number of people possessing the right skills who work across functional silos effectively, companies also risk falling victim to making bad decisions—using big data as their crutch—all the same. Whether manifesting itself in statistical scourges (such as multicollinearity, whereby highly correlated variables may yield invalid results as to the predictive value of said inputs) or simple human bias in interpreting the data, the field is littered with potential landmines. Using big data as their sword, firms may enter battle with erroneous conclusions based on a flawed assumption that patterns in a data set, such as correlation, on their own suggest causation. Consider some of the more ridiculous examples demonstrating that correlation does not imply causation: Shark attacks and the sale of ice cream have been positively correlated (not because sharks have a penchant for ice cream but, rather, because the two variables exhibit a common response to the warmer season); the number of cavities in children and the size of their vocabularies have been positively correlated (with neither having anything to do with the other but with both being associated with the maturing age of the child in question); or the confounding mystery of rising skirt hemlines with corresponding increases in the stock market. In some cases, these correlations can appear very strong, further compounding the risk of faulty interpretation. For example, Google Correlate is a tool that helps identify best-fit correlations between two sets of terms in online search patterns. Since 2004, there has been a 0.9 correlation (90% fit) between the terms "weight gain" and "apartments for rent" in the United States, although it is a mystery how one variable could cause the other.[22]

Although big data is not without big problems, there are some early lessons that may prove useful to companies hoping to turn big data into bigger results:

- **Create a culture of data-driven actions**—In the 2012 Alcatel-Lucent study, nearly two-thirds of the most successful companies in the study (as measured by self-reported feedback on a variety of financial metrics, including sales, profitability, growth, and employee retention) are also those that respond well to changes in the market environment, according to their employees (compared with only 39% of failing companies whose employees stated the same). Paradoxically, these successful companies are also much more likely to involve multiple people in decision making (50% of successful companies vs. 30% of their failing counterparts). Typically, the more heads involved in decision making, the slower is the speed to market for the firm—the classic result of bureaucratically laden organizations. However, these successful firms are somehow managing to respond well to changes in their environment while enlisting multiple inputs. They also manage to do it without working much harder than their counterparts, as measured by respondents' answers to the average hours worked per week at their companies—employees in top-performing enterprises report working an average of 44 hours per week, compared with 42.5 hours for employees in failing firms.

  A culture focused on data insights and powered by automated and guided decision making may be, in part, to credit. In the Capgemini study, two-thirds of executives agree that there is not enough of a "big data culture" in their organizations. According to nearly 60 percent of them, the biggest impediment to cultural transformation is the resolute bastions of organizational silos that are still the mainstay of so many cultures. Culture is a concern for every employee of a company, and, to pull this objective off, senior business leaders and IT decision makers must create deeper and more creative linkages between their teams than ever before. It will require IT to become more business-savvy and business leaders to up their technical knowledge. For those organizations able to crack the culture code, the sustainable competitive advantage can be lasting and meaningful, precisely because this is not a problem that will be easily solved by most enterprises.

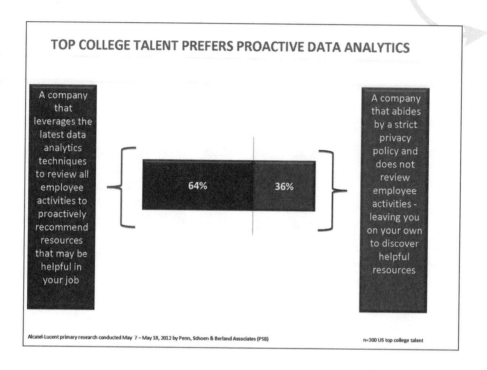

TOP COLLEGE TALENT PREFERS PROACTIVE DATA ANALYTICS

A company that leverages the latest data analytics techniques to review all employee activities to proactively recommend resources that may be helpful in your job

64%   **36%**

A company that abides by a strict privacy policy and does not review employee activities - leaving you on your own to discover helpful resources

Alcatel-Lucent primary research conducted May 7 – May 18, 2012 by Penn, Schoen & Berland Associates (PSB)   n=300 US top college talent

- **Prepare for a recruitment war**—Second only to the cultural challenge is the clear dearth of professionals capable of analyzing and activating corporate data—a problem that will only be exacerbated in coming years as data growth continues at exploding rates. According to the 2012 Alcatel-Lucent study, a minority of upcoming college graduates have taken more than a few statistics courses, reflecting a deficit in qualified talent able to process volumes of data with business insight.

  Resourceful companies are facing the challenge head-on, engaging their recruitment forces for an all-out war and gunning for talent at a very young age. For example, SAS created Curriculum Pathways, a web-based tool for teaching data analytics to high school students, a target woefully underrepresented in the United States as measured by those interested in a career in science, technology, engineering, or math (STEM). The course has been running for 12 years across 18,000 American schools. The company has also developed analytics courses with several universities to seed the next generation of data analysts.[23] In the big data game, there's no such thing as starting too early in building a talent pipeline capable of being converted to human resources.

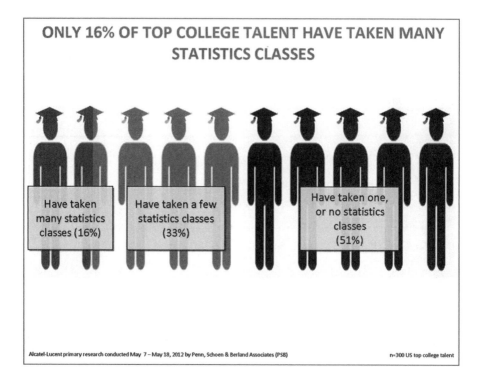

ONLY 16% OF TOP COLLEGE TALENT HAVE TAKEN MANY STATISTICS CLASSES

Have taken many statistics classes (16%)

Have taken a few statistics classes (33%)

Have taken one, or no statistics classes (51%)

Alcatel-Lucent primary research conducted May 7 – May 18, 2012 by Penn, Schoen & Berland Associates (PSB)   n=300 US top college talent

- **Determine your risk quotient**—There's a wide chasm between using data to automate, versus support, decision making. In the Capgemini study, on average, big data is used to support decision making 58 percent of the time, whereas it is applied to automate decisions 29 percent of the time.[24] A company's approach to its own data philosophy will depend on its risk tolerance in making a poor decision versus the speed it loses in not making decisions automatically.

  For Citi, the risk assessment varies to properly reflect the costs of making a poor decision. A "false positive" by an automation error where the system inaccurately rejects a loan based on various set parameters can be corrected with a simple phone call to the consumer in question. However, with corporate clients, the stakes and risks increase considerably, thereby decreasing the tolerance for making bad decisions. According to Michael Knorr, head of integration and data services at Citi, "Suppose that a ship cannot leave a port due to late payment, and suddenly all the bananas go rotten; from a commercial perspective, this involves a much higher risk because the amounts are much larger. The human element and review by somebody for larger amounts of money won't go away."[25] Companies must establish the risk parameters for various decision rules within the organization, automate decisions where possible, and oversee system-generated recommendations where necessary.

- **Structure processes to structure data**—Just because the volumes of data being generated are increasingly unstructured in nature does not mean that processes should follow suit. In fact, the opposite is the case. The more unstructured the data, the more structured the workflows around it must be to maximize its value. A team of university researchers that has explored the risks, opportunities, and case studies in this space recommend using manual or automated processes for using metadata—tags that allow unstructured data to be categorized or manipulated, thereby taking on more of the desirable characteristics associated with structured data. Once the business has defined how unstructured data should be tagged and used, the IT function can respond in kind with the right tools to implement those decisions.[26]

- **Demystify storage and network costs**—Technically storing and transporting the volumes of data created each day by employees and customers create challenges that would make an IT veteran weep. For this reason, the vast majority of data created within an enterprise is not stored or used—largely because of a deficit of storage facilities globally, what some call the case of "the leaky corporation."[27] Companies would be wise to take a page from traditional service providers—particularly video service providers—that have made big business out of efficiently transporting and storing lots of data.

In the most basic of explanations, a network architecture is composed of three main components—a content asset in question, the cost of storing the asset in a data warehouse, and the cost of transporting the asset to a user in need. In general, the closer the stored asset is to the user, the lower are the transport costs to freight it and the better response time afforded the user (termed *latency*, a concept covered in Chapter 2). Conversely, the data asset may be centralized in a large data warehouse that is located further from the end user, but one in which the efficiency gains in storing the content more than make up for the higher costs in backhauling the traffic across a longer network route.

This concept is important when considering video on demand, a popular service offered by many video providers. In a typical video on demand library, there are popular releases and niche content. Based on the basics of network architecture, it typically makes more economic sense to store the more popular fare closer to the consumer, because this will yield a better quality of experience at a lower overall cost. Niche content, on the other hand, is better stored in centralized data centers, where the savings in storage can more than compensate for higher delivery costs. Enterprises can adopt the same principles when considering their own data sets.

More mission-critical or time-sensitive data, especially that which is accessed on a regular basis, should be prioritized and stored accordingly. Less popular data sets can take advantage of better storage rates and a lower quality of experience given the infrequency with which this data is needed. In either case, the IT unit would do well to demystify and communicate the actual storage and transport costs for each business unit, such that decisions can be made about how much and which data to expunge, relocate, or capture.[28]

- **Understand context; establish governance**—Even when data is accurately predictive in modeling phenomena, it still may lead to faulty conclusions if context is not properly understood. In the case of Google Flu Trends, a team of medical experts compared data from the service with data from two surveillance networks and found that, although it did a very good job at predicting nonspecific respiratory illnesses that closely resemble the flu, it did not predict the actual flu very well. According to one of the researchers, "this year, up to 40 percent of people with pandemic flu did not have 'influenza-like illness' because they did not have a fever.... Influenza-like illness is neither sensitive nor specific for influenza virus activity—it's a good proxy, it's a very useful public-health surveillance system, but it is not as accurate as actual nationwide specimens positive for influenza virus." In response, Google addressed its critics by reiterating that a person searching symptoms would have no way of knowing if he or she was the victim of flu, although "it's just as important to monitor symptoms as it is to monitor specific information." [29] Both sides of the argument are correct. It's a matter of understanding the context of the data being analyzed before drawing conclusions about its meaning.

Big data is often accompanied by a bigger debate—that of privacy for those being studied. In 2011, Alcatel-Lucent asked more than 5,000 U.S. consumers about their definition of privacy in today's networked age. When asked to choose which statement came closest to their view: (a) Privacy is the right to be left alone; or (b) Privacy is the right to control and manage what information about oneself is available to others; an overwhelming 78 percent of respondents selected the latter option. Boundaries are being redefined and contracts are in flux between customers and companies, and employers and employees. Making use of data without compromising ethical standards or violating a coveted trust position with key stakeholders will be central to companies attempting to monetize their data assets. Once governance in how an enterprise plans on using its own data is established, there is also the matter of determining if sharing such information with others may provide a buoy to the broader market collective. The more variables shared between firms, the more interesting are the insights that may be derived. In response to this unfulfilled need, the United Nations' Global Pulse is championing its concept of "data philanthropy," whereby "corporations [would] take the initiative to anonymize (strip out all personal information) their data sets and provide this data to social innovators to mine the data for insights, patterns and trends in realtime or near realtime." [30] Firms may be slow to embrace such a program, being preoccupied initially with managing their own data flood. Still, the United Nations' proactive and visionary approach will be there for companies, when and if their data needs mature to such a point.

There is no shortage of data. Any organization—large or small—has within it a digital footprint capable of revealing the path to better and faster decisions. What is in short supply, however, is the ingenuity in considering how the data might be used differently, experimentation in measuring if hypotheses are warranted, and a perseverance to drive cultural change where information is revered, not feared. But, in perhaps the best example of how these forces can create the perfect environment for aspiring companies, look no further than Billy Beane, general manager of the baseball franchise Oakland A's and the subject of the Hollywood movie *Moneyball*. Beane and team revolutionized the way big data was used in baseball, arguably one of the most data-intensive sports. Rather than relying solely on the batting average or earned run average as the critical criteria in assessing a player's performance, Beane began looking at different metrics to predict the efficiency of the player, including base runs, on-base plus slugging percentage, and fielding independent pitching. [31] These variables were available to any of Beane's competitors, although they remained under-utilized until he identified the meaningful pattern that made such data an actionable precursor to a team's success. As the amount of data produced and consumed by private enterprises and their customers continues unabated, the opportunity for the next Beane to generate the next "moneyball" remains the territory of the most resourceful and data-driven companies.

ATTACK OF THE MACHINES

Since the beginning of automation, early prognosticators have warned of a cataclysmic outcome in which machines cannibalize the jobs of humans. In many cases, the foreboding was justified—consider the steep decline in manufacturing jobs with the advent of assembly automation. Yet, these jobs have typically been the domain of highly repetitive, mundane tasks, wherein robotic machinery provides speed and accuracy while relieving the human to higher-order cognitive functions. After all, computers were the manufactured products of human beings, giving the creators the benefit of the doubt in being considered the smarter "race." Although this is a straightforward argument, it doesn't necessarily bear true. Andrew McAfee, principle research scientist at MIT and author of *Race Against the Machine*, looked at a group of 136 man-versus-machine studies and found humans on the winning side just eight times. The irony is that this may be the *best* outcome humans can hope for, given that the tests were run in an era preceding big data. In all likelihood, the reason the machines didn't do even better is that they didn't have enough data—a problem being rectified every day with more data being added to the equation. According to McAfee, "I kind of see our robot overlords and computer overlords getting smarter and smarter."

Rather than retreat in a coward's stance in the corner, McAfee recommends that enterprises and employees embrace the challenge to race with the machines humans have created. And, for now, there are still problems that are better served by human beings (such as scientific research that depends on complex understanding about human proteins).[32] Although big data may present a big threat to the average knowledge worker, it is more likely a case in which the skills of the American worker will evolve—those with a strong analytical foundation who are able to link data to more fundamental business implications will be in high demand. Increasingly, they will be joined by Watson and his ilk, more than capable of crunching volumes of structured and unstructured data in such a way that a better decision—whether on the part of a human or machine—is more likely to be made.

4 The Collaboration Craze

67% of employees say they feel powerless to control email and meeting overload.[1]

When Brian Uzzi, a sociologist at Northwestern University, endeavored to find the recipe to successful teams, he turned his attention to Broadway musicals. According to Uzzi, pulling off these theatrical productions requires the epitome of teamwork: "Nobody creates a Broadway musical by themselves. The production requires too many different kinds of talent." Indeed, a musical is delivered through a diverse cast and crew—including the performers, choreographers, composers, musicians, producers, stagehands, and director, to name but a few. Having dedicated his career to discovering the ideal composition of a team, Uzzi wondered if groups consisting of those with preexisting relationships perform better than those composed largely of strangers. To answer the question, he studied the teams behind 474 musicals produced between 1945 and 1989 and charted the degree of extant relationships among collaborators with the success of the show. He devised a formula to measure the relative density of previous relationships on a team, a factor he called Q. His hypothesis was that those teams with a history of working together would yield more winning ventures. Indeed, his data proved Q to be a reliable predictor of a show's success. On a scale from 1 to 5, with 1 being lowest and 5 being highest, those shows with a Q below 1.7 were most likely to fail. "This wasn't so surprising," Uzzi says. "It takes time to develop a successful collaboration."

However, in an interesting revelation, his data concluded that shows for which Q was too high—above 3.2—also had weak results. In a case of diminishing returns, deeply embedded and familiar relationships led to productions that failed to deliver. As evidence to this claim, Uzzi points to shows produced in the 1920s—commonly filled with big-name talents, although 90 percent flopped nonetheless. As he opines, "Broadway had some of the biggest names ever. But the shows were too full of repeat relationships, and that stifled creativity." Uzzi and his team calculated what they termed the "bliss point" for Q—between 2.4 and 2.6—representative of teams with a mix of social intimacy. According to Uzzi,

> *The best Broadway teams, by far, were those with a mix of relationships. These teams had some old friends, but they also had newbies. This mixture meant that the artists could interact efficiently—they had a familiar structure to fall back on—but they also managed to incorporate some new ideas. They were comfortable with each other, but they weren't too comfortable.*

This interesting team dynamic of familiar and new relationships translated to box office results. A show with a Q in the bliss point range was three times more likely to be a commercial success than those at either end of the scale. It was also three times more likely to win the praise of critics.[2]

Hoping to stumble into their own *bliss point*, companies are deploying tools to connect employees like never before, creating a new social dynamic where relationships are created and nurtured. Spurred by a technologically ravenous employee population and convinced of the veracity of the old adage "multiple heads are better than one," companies are jumping headlong into a new category of collaboration and socialization tools. The passion to find more valuable avenues for employee engagement is legitimate given how much time employees spend with one another—time that is often deemed unproductive. According to a 2011 study by GetControl.net, 60 percent of the average workday is spent on e-mails and meetings, of which one-third is considered "wasted" by employees. More than half of professionals are frustrated by the hyperactive multitasking of their peers, particularly annoyed by those coworkers distracted by their mobile devices during important meetings. What's worse, nearly half of meetings are arranged quickly, without a clear purpose or agenda. In addition, the amount of time consumed by these nonproductive activities adds up quickly, with the study estimating that companies spend $12,000 in annual waste per employee as a result of e-mail and meeting distractions.[3] At an average employee salary of $45,000 in the United States, that equates to about a quarter of an enterprise's payroll burned.

The fascination with getting more out of these team interactions can be traced at least as far back as 1948, when advertising executive Alex Osborn released his bestseller, *Your Creative Power* (Charles Scribner's Sons, 1948). The book gave Osborn's prescription for unlocking creative genius based on his experience in doing the same for advertising agency BBDO. Perhaps the most eternal idea to emerge from the book was found in Chapter 33, "How to Organize a Squad to Create Ideas," in which Osborn introduced the concept known as *brainstorming*, which, by his definition meant, "using the brain to storm a creative problem—and doing so in commando fashion, with each stormer attacking the same objective." Osborn heralded brainstorming as key to his success at BBDO, pointing to incredible examples of a team's ability to tackle a problem more quickly and comprehensively than any individual on his own. In one, he reflected on a group consisting of 10 BBDO employees crafting 87 ideas for a new drugstore in 90 minutes.[4] At roughly one idea per minute, the potential output of brainstorming was hard to deny, and companies enthusiastically embraced the concept, along with Osborn's prescriptive rules for running effective brainstorming sessions, in their own organizations.

Among Osborn's most important cardinal rules of brainstorming is the pursuit of quantity over quality. In other words, members are explicitly instructed not to criticize an idea during the brainstorming process. The idea is to get as many ideas on the board as possible before worrying about the merits of any. Criticism is kryptonite to the creative process. If people on the team are concerned about rebuke by their peers, they are less likely to offer ideas, bringing the entire brainstorming process to a grinding halt.

Since Osborn's brainchild, there have been numerous experiments measuring the collective wisdom of groups. In the case of brainstorming, the evidence suggests that individuals almost always outperform groups in both quality and quantity of solutions. In one of the early experiments at Yale University in the 1950s, 48 male students were divided into groups of four and asked to solve creative puzzles. Simultaneously, 48 individuals in a control group were given the same objective. Not only did the individuals working alone come up with roughly twice as many solutions as those working in groups, but also the viability of their responses were deemed more "feasible" and "effective" by a panel of judges. Many follow-up studies have reached a similar conclusion. According to Keith Sawyer, a psychologist at Washington University, "Decades of research have consistently shown that brainstorming groups think of far fewer ideas than the same number of people who work alone and later pool their ideas."[5]

Rather than generating more or better ideas, group collaboration can have the opposite effect, as brainstorming experiments through the ages have demonstrated.

Some attribute the outcome to lower individual accountability for each member of the team (meaning that each individual suppresses his or her output in anticipation that the collective team will pull the weight). Others cite a psychological reflex triggered by the amygdala in our brains—a primitive response function that serves as the body's danger center and kicks into high gear when humans feel threatened, a common reaction to conflict. To avoid the uncomfortable sensation the amygdala creates when one is at odds with many, an individual in a group may simply choose not to dissent and instead follow the crowd. In still other cases, the result may be a situation in which collaboration isn't warranted in the first place. For example, in one study of more than 100 experienced sales teams at a large information technology consulting firm bidding for multimillion dollar contracts, researchers found that the greater the cross-team collaboration (measured by hours of help a team received from another more experienced team), the worse is the result (measured by success in winning contracts). The researchers discovered that teams did not learn as much from one another as first anticipated, and whatever information was gained was more than offset by a loss in productivity in completing the proposal. They attributed the finding to a case in which collaboration was simply the wrong tool for the job.[6]

Or, perhaps the reason that individuals tend to perform better than groups has something to do with those sacred rules first established by Osborn. In 2003, in yet another brainstorming experiment, University of California at Berkeley Professor Charlan Nemeth divided 265 female undergraduates into teams of five. She assigned each team 20 minutes to solve the same problem: how to alleviate traffic congestion in the San Francisco Bay Area. Teams were assigned one of three conditions. The first set of teams received the standard no-critique rule as prescribed by Osborn. The second set of teams was encouraged to share ideas freely but to critique and debate suggestions openly. The rest were part of the control group and given no ground rules on how to behave. Although the traditional brainstorming teams outperformed the control groups in the number of ideas generated, those assigned the debate condition were the most prolific, generating nearly 20 percent more ideas. After the exercise was completed, researchers asked each respondent if she had any more individual ideas to solve the problem. Those in the brainstorming and control groups produced, on average, three more ideas each; those in the debate group generated seven more ideas per individual.[7]

It appears that brainstorming itself is not the problem, but the way in which it is applied in organizations. And, for all the inherent challenges of collaborating with others, the growing complexity of problems facing organizations creates a situation in which teamwork is important, if not essential. Academic journals are increasingly littered with research studies born of a group of collaborators, not of lone rangers. In analyzing nearly 20 million peer-reviewed papers and 2.1 million patents over the past 50 years, Northwestern University Professor Ben Jones discovered that the levels of teamwork have increased in more than 95 percent of scientific subfields, with the average team size increasing roughly 20 percent each decade.[8] With the glut of collaboration tools entering the enterprise, there's no shortage of technology available to a company looking to pool resources in solving a complicated problem of its own.

As evidence to the hot technology trend, consider recent efforts by Microsoft to take its share of the collaboration market. Long the mainstay of office software, Microsoft has made some bold moves to ensure that its place in the enterprise environment is not ceded to disruptive competitors eager to define the emerging collaboration space. In 2011, it made its largest acquisition in company history when it acquired Skype, the online voice and video service, for $8.5 billion. When Microsoft announced its purchase, questions abounded as to the reasoning and value of the deal. The prior year, Skype had a small loss of $7 million and had accumulated $686 million in long-term debt. Microsoft's own software had considerable overlap with Skype, with three times the number of active users.[9]

In June of 2012, Microsoft announced another purchase when it acquired Yammer, the social networking equivalent of Facebook for the enterprise, for $1.2 billion. In an effort to retain its share of the $280 billion global enterprise software market (roughly comparable to the GDP of Greece),[10] Microsoft signaled its intentions of adding Yammer to its growing portfolio of enterprise collaboration solutions (alongside existing Microsoft solutions and Skype).[11] The latest acquisition again spawned criticism for its seemingly exorbitant purchase price. According to Aaron Fulkerson, founder and CEO of MindTouch, "Microsoft acquiring Yammer will make them relevant in the social space, but their lack of execution is forcing them to pay a premium." [12]

Even if Microsoft is indicted in the court of public opinion for paying a premium for its latest acquisitions, it does so to remain meaningful to a changing enterprise market it once dominated. If not Microsoft, there are scores of other software providers willing and able to offer the latest collaboration solutions sure to fit the bill for just about any enterprise need. In addition, just as they welcomed brainstorming when it entered the scene, enterprises are embracing new technologies hoping such tools will lead to the desired bliss point for employee collaboration, helping to explain why Microsoft and other providers are plunging headfirst in an attempt to deliver.

Yet, just as organizations had to learn how and when to apply brainstorming concepts effectively, the same is true when assessing the purpose and fit of collaborative technologies. As an example, businesses plunk down nearly $3 billion in videoconferencing solutions each year,[13] in part to reduce the time and costs of travel, but also to facilitate long-distance relationships. Despite the investment, the technology has not alleviated the problem of nonproductive meetings in the first place. According to analyst Ovum,

> *Meetings intermediated by video screens are still meetings, and once the novelty wears off have the potential to be just as frustrating as face-to-face meetings in conference rooms. That is provided users can get the videoconferencing system to work properly in the first place.*[14]

But, when an organization has a clear purpose for using the technology, collaborative tools can help nurture healthy cultures—making investments in technologies like videoconferencing worthwhile. In the 2012 Alcatel-Lucent study, 71 percent of the top-performing companies (as self-reported based on several financial indicators) use videoconferencing compared with slightly more than half of companies, on average. An identical 71 percent of companies with forward-leaning cultures also use collaborative technology, compared with 58 percent of all companies. With an ever-growing mobile workforce, the challenges in creating collaborative environments will only intensify for enterprises. In the 2012 Alcatel-Lucent study, the top concern mentioned by employees when considering the greatest drawback to those working remotely was the increased challenge in coordination of work (cited by close to one in three respondents). Although videoconferencing, in particular, has suffered a prolonged gestation period, there is evidence to suggest that it may have finally earned its place as a viable enterprise technology. More than 60 percent of all employees (including frontline workers and decision makers) in the 2012 Alcatel-Lucent study (discussed in the preface to this book) prefer videoconferencing to audioconferencing because nonverbal communication is not sacrificed and richer interactions can result.

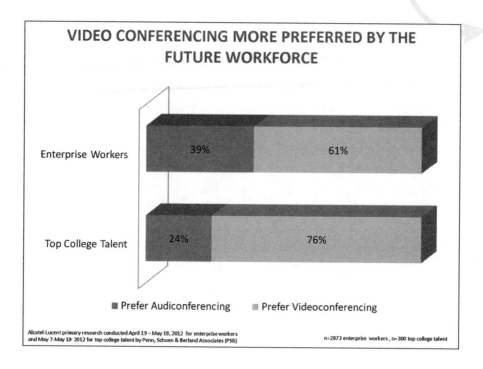

It is precisely the complex recipe involved with collaboration that makes the current craze so confounding. On one end, individuals working alone often produce better results than those in teams, and enterprises would be wise not to stifle the creative genius that may just spark the next major breakthrough. At the same time, the very complexion of a mobile and virtualized workforce is demanding a toolset capable of addressing the challenges created by time and space. As such, there are several implications that companies should consider before blindly deploying collaboration alternatives:

- **Don't fake it**—In a 2001 article in the *Journal of Educational Administration*, researcher Megan Tschannen-Moran contemplates the challenge of the time in fostering collaborative relationships between administrators, teachers, and parents. She posits that the tepid progress in doing so has something to do with intentions. She cites studies of schools in which shared decision making was undertaken in order to increase the satisfaction, loyalty, and decision acceptance of teachers and parents. However, success was stunted because of teachers and parents complaining of not being given any real influence over the outcome of decisions—a condition Tschannen-Moran calls "contrived collaboration."[15] The same result is awaiting enterprises with disingenuous intentions. Managers may encourage a spirit of collaboration while at the same time deliberately withholding necessary information to employees or ignoring suggestions entirely. Under this scenario, employees will resent the time they invested working in good faith toward a solution and will likely suppress creative contributions in future contrived exercises. In other cases, a lack of intention is sufficient to derail progress, with many companies launching the latest collaboration tool expecting that employees will simply use it, despite the fact that there may be no reason to engage with one another in the first place. As evidenced by the study of experienced sales teams in the information technology consulting market, sometimes collaboration is not just unnecessary, it's counterproductive.

Tschannen-Moran submits that trust and collaboration are intertwined concepts. She names multiple examples in which trust has an accretive effect to an organization's effectiveness, transparency, employee commitment, and team cooperation. At the same time, distrust has negative consequences, with organizations turning to onerous rules and regulations as an ineffectual substitute for trust.[16] If a collaborative approach is not in accordance with the management philosophy of the company, business leaders should realize that investing in associated technologies will only amplify this point. Collaboration technologies serve as a magnifying glass on a company's existing culture. Organizations faking a collaborative approach by masquerading behind the latest technology advancements are often left underwhelmed by the results, with 75 percent of companies deploying such tools, considering them fair at best.[17] Enterprises must start first with behavioral and structural factors before tackling technologies and tools.

In addition, although collaborative tools magnify a company's culture, there is also evidence to support the idea that greater collaboration holds the possibility of fostering greater trust. That is, once individuals have the opportunity to prove their intentions by working honestly and transparently with others over time, trust is accumulated. Researchers call this accumulation of collective trust *social capital* and argue that it is a tangible asset to communities that earn it.[18] Yet, to do so requires an authentic foundation through which such genuine interactions can occur. Even when management provides an open culture, there is the element of human behavior that can thwart the success of teams (as seen through the scores of brainstorming experiments proving that individuals perform better than groups, based, at least in part, on the human tendency of following crowds). Here again is where the outlook is encouraging for technology-based collaboration tools. As it so happens, electronic brainstorming is the notable exception to the concept's anemic track record—because groups participating in electronic brainstorming outperform individuals. Not only do large groups do better in this case, but the larger the group, the better are the results. It appears that the protection of the computer screen enables groups to overcome brainstorming's traditional challenges—in essence, allowing large groups to collaborate while maintaining the individualistic contribution of each person.[19]

- **Respect lone geniuses**—In a *New York Times* blog, author Susan Cain laments, "Solitude is out of fashion…. Lone geniuses are out. Collaboration is in." She points to compelling evidence suggesting that some of the most creative people in many fields are introverted by nature. One popular example is the Apple success story. With the passing of Steve Jobs, much has been written about Apple's meteoric rise as the most valued company in the world. Jobs was certainly at the heart of Apple's success, and his charismatic presence was a force in the industry. Yet, at the origin of the Apple story was another genius, not known for a magnetic personality, but one whose quiet introversion led to the birth of the world's first user-friendly computer. Steve Wozniak was the yin to the yang of Steve Jobs. It was Wozniak who developed the first Apple prototype, whereas Jobs commercialized it. Introverts like Wozniak walk the virtual and physical corridors of enterprises each day. Indeed, addressing aspiring inventors in his memoir, Wozniak offers the following controversial advice: "Most inventors and engineers I've met are like me…. they live in their heads. They're almost like artists. In fact, the very best of them are artists. And artists work best alone…. I'm going to give you some advice that might be hard to take. That advice is: Work alone … Not on a committee. Not on a team."[20]

Yet, in a rush to be all things collaborative, many enterprises are turning a deaf ear to the potential of individual genius, literally knocking down walls with open and unassigned floor plans (a trend fueled by the increasingly mobile workforce, as discussed in Chapter 1). These pursuits, although well-intentioned, ignore the creative genius lurking in the introvert. Collaboration can harness the output of many, but privacy can fuel the production of individuals. In a study covering 600 computer programmers at 92 companies, researchers found that the performance gap between successful and unsuccessful organizations was not the result of better pay or greater experience. In this case, those in the top-performing companies were much more likely to benefit from increased privacy, personal work space, and freedom from interruption.[21] Organizations should respect the need for employees to get away and be alone with their own thoughts, an option certainly enabled by online collaboration tools that allow employees to work together, yet still on their own. It's this sense of individualism that Cain says has attributed to the success of the Internet in the first place, leading to many of its "wondrous collective creations." She writes, "[The Internet]'s a place where we can be alone together—and this is precisely what gives it power."[22]

• **Embrace the horizontal hierarchy**—In 2010, CNBC released its list of the six coolest places to work. The list featured a beer company that offers employees two free cases of beer each month, an online retailer that allows employees to burn off stress with an onsite arcade, and a web giant featuring offices with everything from giant slides to climbing walls. Also making the list was Ning, a Palo Alto–based company that specializes in custom-branded social networks. But, it wasn't free food, beer, or recreational activities that earned the company top honors. Instead, it was what employees called its "horizontal hierarchy," meaning that all levels of the company collaborate with one another. As one employee commented, "I like that, at age 25, I work alongside the executive team and the CEO. They literally sit across from me, they know who I am and what I'm working on."[23]

In a culture in which collaborative values live, the tools that nurture a collaborative spirit do far more than increase collective output. In fact, they change the boundaries of the organization, whether in unifying employees across distance or time or in collapsing the vertical silos and layers prevalent in many companies. Indeed, such tools engage managers and employees in new ways, reducing organizational friction and allowing for the generation of new ideas. To this point, as a means of preventing some of the negative outcomes associated with brainstorming, experts recommend building as widely a diverse team as possible to tackle a problem. Doing so avoids the potential for *groupthink*, a psychological phenomenon that occurs within groups of people when the desire for harmony overrides a realistic appraisal of alternatives. It also reduces the chance of generating a group with an excessive Q—as Uzzi found in the Broadway study—a condition commonly associated to entrenched organizations with well-defined relationships. The key to getting the most out of collaborative efforts is to harness the input of multiple stakeholders from various levels and functions of the organization, thereby increasing the likelihood of finding the coveted bliss point in a frictionless horizontal hierarchy.

- **Underestimate security**—With the movement toward more collaborative and open work spaces has come the debate of whether such an approach increases the risk of theft or leakage of a firm's intellectual property. As a result of the current networked age, privacy is more difficult to maintain, whether as consumers attempting to reduce the digital breadcrumbs behind them or enterprises seeking to keep sacred information secret. The challenge is especially prevalent in high-tech companies relying on technology to remain ahead of their competitors, but littered with examples of cases in which employees absconded with the idea only to execute it better somewhere else. According to Internet security firm Symantec, 65 percent of employees who steal intellectual property from their employer have already accepted positions with a competitor or started their own company. More than half of these individuals commit their crimes within a month of leaving their job."[24]

The threat is sufficient to cause some to ignore the collaboration trend outright in an attempt to secure the firm's assets. Yet, these companies simply risk being outmaneuvered by resourceful, tech-savvy employees who will increasingly find ways of bypassing organizational blockages to collaborate using their own bootstrapped solutions. Other organizations place an emphasis on firewall protection measures. Although a necessary component of any collaboration solution, firewalls and other security technologies are not sufficient to stop leaks (whether intentional or accidental). Employees are still capable of stealing assets or exposing information. Therefore, although companies should consider security as any part of a viable technology solution, just as collaboration tools on their own will not change culture, security mechanisms will not be solely sufficient in protecting the organization from the carelessness or malice of its own employees.

For all the hype surrounding collaboration, very few companies get it right. Technology is certainly an enabler, but it is ill equipped against a dogmatic culture that does not first embrace the principles of collaborative teamwork. Even when the most forward-leaning companies endeavor to create an environment in which ideas flourish and knowledge is transferred, they can only do so when employees themselves accept the opportunity. One of the most collaborative geniuses of our time, Steve Jobs, discovered this reality when attempting to design a collaborative environment for Pixar's headquarters in 1999. He arranged the building around a central atrium, such that Pixar's diverse staff of artists, writers, and computer scientists might have the opportunity to collide more often. When building the space wasn't sufficient, Jobs realized that he needed to create a reason for people to go there. He moved mailboxes, meeting rooms, the cafeteria, coffee bar, and even bathrooms around the central location, increasing the chances of such collisions. As Brad Bird, the director of *The Incredibles* and *Ratatouille* stated, "[Jobs] made it impossible for you not to run into the rest of the company."[25] And, while companies hustle to create the same cosmic energy in their workplaces, some are either missing the point or applying the wrong formula to the problem. Collaboration is not the be-all, end-all to every issue. It doesn't obviate the need for individualistic thinking on the part of creative geniuses. However, when executed in an environment that espouses and walks the virtues of collaborative decision making, technology can reduce organizational friction and harness the true power of collective wisdom among introverts and extroverts alike.

THE HIVE MIND

In recent years, much has been written about the hive mind—a visual representation of the power of collective thinking made possible through the Internet and other online tools. The analogy is taken from that of bees. Interestingly, there are many similarities that can be drawn between organizational design and bee colonies. First, bees learn from one another. Younger bees are consistently paired with older ones throughout life and in various stages of work progression to learn the ways of the colony. Next, bees are empowered. Individual bees are able to make decisions based on local cues and information and, to mitigate the risk of a bad decision, they share an extensive communication system by which information is shared and on display for all to see. Additionally, bees value diversity. Evidence shows that bees literally use a voting process when making a big decision in the hive. Through an iterative process, they assemble information and vote independently until a quorum is reached. Honeybees have an undeniable track record of productivity and growth—more than 100 million years, to be exact—by using some of the basic tenets of successful collaboration: respecting individual viewpoints, revering diversity, and sharing knowledge and expertise. Companies looking to reap the honey in their own organizations need look no further than the hive for the blueprint.

2 The New Workforce

In This Part

The Architects

→ *According to MTV, 92% of Millennials think their company is lucky to have them as an employee.*[1]

Companies are always on the hunt for the best talent. Despite the difficult economic environment of the past several years, top talent is always in high demand, and those who have the skills, drive, and determination are in the best position to reap the rewards. In industries in which there are shortages of essential skills, creative companies are going after that top talent in new and aggressive ways. The technology sector has been especially active in its pursuit of the next generation of talent, those that will design and build the future of their industry. Facing an acute shortage of software developers and engineers, these companies are offering their top candidates starting salaries that range anywhere from $75,000 to $100,000 and signing and relocation bonuses valued from $5,000 to $15,000. In addition to generous salary packages, these new hires are also being offered additional cash bonuses or equity grants—sometimes worth as much as 1 percent of the company.[2] Of course, showering a desirable candidate with monetary incentives is nothing new in a highly competitive job market. What is new is the field of candidates being wooed. According to the *Wall Street Journal*, in an effort to address the ongoing shortage of professional and qualified candidates, these companies are following the model set by professional sports. High-tech companies are identifying the top students, putting on the full-court press, and encouraging them to leave their education behind to join the workforce. On-campus recruiting events, paying other students to help identify the best talent, and routinely wining and dining prospects in an effort to encourage them to forgo the rest of their education is not at all uncommon in this competitive environment. As you would expect, this doesn't always sit well with school administrators. According to Mark Stehlik, the Assistant Dean of the School of Computer Science at Carnegie Mellon, most students would be better off getting their degrees: "Students get a little starry eyed. For many of them they are better off finishing." [3]

And it's not just companies encouraging students to leave their academic days behind them. In 2011, billionaire venture capitalist Peter Thiel founded the "20 Under 20" Fellowship Program to identify and pay selected students to abandon their studies and focus on their ideas and inventions. Needless to say, both Thiel and his foundation have come under serious fire for asserting that college can be a distraction. Thiel, however, points to Bill Gates and Mark Zuckerberg to illustrate his point that credentials are not really what matters when it comes to success.[4] Of course, no one is more familiar with the stories of Bill Gates and Mark Zuckerberg than today's college students. These successful entrepreneurs both famously dropped out of Harvard to go on to found Microsoft and Facebook, respectively. But for every Gates or Zuckerberg who abandons his education and goes on to find success, fame, and fortune, there are countless others who do not find the same. Most experts agree that, for most students, finishing a degree is the best path to take to ensure future success. The Bureau of Labor Statistics reported in the first quarter of 2012 that college graduates command more earning power than non-college graduates—earning a full $505 more per week.[5] In addition, despite the fact that his story often influences young entrepreneurs to leave school and forge their own path, Bill Gates himself is a strong proponent of a college education:

> I'm very glad I went to college. I only stayed three years, but in terms of growing up, meeting other smart people, meeting Steve Ballmer, who I later hired to help build Microsoft. I would counsel people to go to college, because it's one of the best times in your life in terms of who you meet and develop a broad set of intellectual skills.[6]

Those students who go on to complete their degrees also see the overall benefit in completing their degrees. Four-year college graduates who responded to a Pew Research Center survey weighed in on the advantages that they received from their college education. Nearly 80 percent say that their college education helped them grow intellectually, 69 percent say it helped them mature as a person, and 55 percent indicated that their college experience helped prepare them for their future job or career.[7]

Seton Hall University, located near New York City, prides itself on providing each of the advantages identified by the previously mentioned Pew Research Center survey.

According to their university mission statement, academic development and ethical development are key components of the Seton Hall experience. In addition to these aspects, the school also places a focus on preparing their students "to be leaders in their professional and community lives in ... an evolving technologically advanced setting." To support this mission statement, the University's IT organization developed their own technology mandate in 1997 to "support the university's mission of providing state of the art technology tools to enhance the student experience and prepare students for success in a rapidly changing world." [8] To help meet this goal, the University has augmented its existing program that equips students with free laptops by providing the incoming class of 2016 with new Nokia Windows smartphones along with an AT&T service plan. These phones come loaded with customized applications that provide the students with housing information and tools to allow them to connect with their peers and academic advisors. Beyond information related to campus life, the University also expects the devices to be used in the classroom to further prepare students to use mobile computing in their future careers. Although the vast majority of students already have their own cellular devices, school officials decided to provide equal access to the same smartphone, regardless of income level, to ensure learning equity.

Whereas the distribution of smartphones to the incoming class of freshman at Seton Hall University is sure to excite the already well-connected students, the University is set to benefit as well. Officials plan to use a data-gathering feature to survey students on how they are using the devices in an effort to understand better how technology is changing the way that today's student works and learns—and how the administration should adapt the way they approach the overall university experience. According to Michael Taylor, the Director of Seton Hall's Center for Mobile Research and Innovation, "Mobile technology has become ubiquitous and pervasive, but we are just beginning to understand the breadth and impact across campus." [9]

This trend isn't a new one, because as early in the age of the smartphone as 2009, Abilene Christian University began offering incoming freshmen iPhones and iPod Touches and is now considering offering iPads. The use of advanced mobile devices has sparked users to a range of uses from the expected (in-class surveys and collaboration) to the unexpected (using the devices to map and block stage productions in the arts school). What Seton Hall has done is leverage not only the use of the technology but also the data created by its use to transform the way they teach and develop curriculum.

Seton Hall, Abilene Christian University, and their progressive ilk get it. This generation of students has always been connected. They have never known a world without the Internet. The answer to just about any question they might have has always been just a mouse click away. They have likely never owned a CD. Any music they might want to listen to has always been readily available online. Social networking is a constant in their lives—so much so that they are rarely out of synch with friends, both close and distant. This confluence of technology in their lives has impacted everything, from the way they think, the way they work together, to the way they learn. It stands to reason that, in order to remain relevant, the approach that a university takes to educating their students would need to change as well.

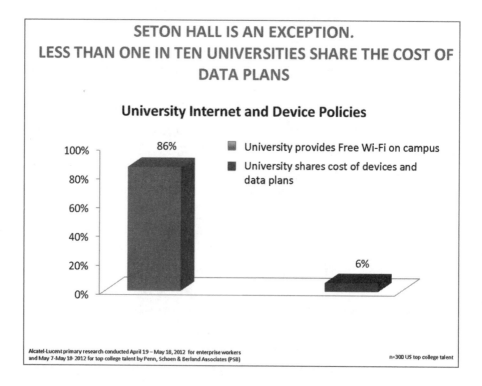

SETON HALL IS AN EXCEPTION.
LESS THAN ONE IN TEN UNIVERSITIES SHARE THE COST OF DATA PLANS

University Internet and Device Policies

- University provides Free Wi-Fi on campus
- University shares cost of devices and data plans

86%

6%

Alcatel-Lucent primary research conducted April 19 – May 18, 2012 for enterprise workers
and May 7-May 18 2012 for top college talent by Penn, Schoen & Berland Associates (PSB)   n=300 US top college talent

The same goes for enterprises. The habits and experiences of the future workforce are set to turn the long-established state of business on its head. The up-and-coming employees of tomorrow have a different set of skills, a different way of working with others, and a different set of expectations of what their work life will look like.

Today's enterprises have already felt the tremors of the first wave of employees who were essentially born connected to the network. Internal company social networking sites, widespread use of Instant Messaging and collaboration tools, fewer solitary offices in favor of more collaborative work spaces—all have been implemented in direct response to a workforce that demands that the enterprise accommodate their working style and not the other way around. As today's students graduate and join those who preceded them in tomorrow's professional world, the initial tremors will grow into a powerful earthquake—demanding that their employers take notice. The organizations that will be successful in the future are those that, like Seton Hall, anticipate the shaking and embrace and accommodate that which can harness the potential and productivity of their future employees—those that don't risk losing their business in the storm.

They are called many things—Millennials, The Net Generation, or Digital Natives. Regardless of the label that is thrust upon them, this generation of young people, born between 1980 and 2000, approaches life, school, and work in vastly different ways than those who came before them. Smartphones, computers, tablets, gaming consoles, and a world of different applications and social networking platforms are more than tools to these young people but, rather, extensions of who they are at a fundamental level.

The human brain is an amazing organ. It is constantly changing and evolving based on our own personal experiences. Scientists studying the brains of these children and young adults have discovered that it is much more than habits and tools that differentiate the digital natives from the digital immigrants—there are actual physical differences as well. The folds in the brains of this younger generation are different from those who didn't grow up in a hyperconnected world. [10] The devices and applications that these young people surround themselves with every day are literally woven into their brains. Thanks to these physiological differences, digital natives have very different cognitive skills. They have stronger multitasking abilities, they can process information much faster than the adults around them, and they thrive in an environment of instant gratification.

In an effort to illustrate how the working styles of these Millennials differ from older workers, the CEO of a marketing services agency ran an experiment at a seminar he was giving. The room was divided, with the older generation on one side and the younger participants on the other. Each group was told that they could take notes however they wished in order to keep track of the seminar and prepare for a quiz on the content. During the seminar, the older workers were busy scribbling notes into their notebooks while maintaining eye contact at all times with the speaker. On the other side of the room, the youngsters had powered up their laptop computers, iPads, and smartphones and rarely, if ever, looked up from their devices to try to connect with the speaker. At the end of the session, the speaker administered a quiz on the content, and the young workers in the room scored a full 20 percent higher than their older counterparts. Although this group rarely looked up from their devices, they were not only paying attention but also sharing and discussing what they were learning with their counterparts in the room in real time.[11]

However, despite their ability to multitask and quickly process and absorb information, experts agree that this generation does suffer some deficiencies. One respondent to a survey of educators conducted by the Pew Research Center in conjunction with Elon University best articulated these downsides:

> *I have seen a general decline in higher-order thinking skills in my students over the past decade. What I generally see is an over-dependence on technology, an emphasis on social technologies as opposed to what I'll call "comprehension technologies," and a general disconnect from deeper thinking.*[12]

It is no wonder that teachers and managers have difficulty connecting with them—they are wired differently, both physically and mentally.[13]

Although understanding the differences between the work and learning styles of different generations may not seem to be a mission-critical aspect of conducting business in today's society, a closer look at the changing complexion of the workforce in America underscores the urgency. Most estimates put the number of Millennials in America at about 80 million. They outnumber baby boomers by 4 million. Half of these Millennials are already part of the professional workforce, and approximately 10,000 of them turn 21 every day.[14] This generation is already reshaping the workforce, and their impact is only going to increase as they continue to join the professional ranks—bringing their different work styles, habits, and expectations with them into the office place. As part of the 2012 Alcatel-Lucent study, 300 top students at prestigious universities across the United States were polled to understand the way they work, the way they use technology, and the way that these combine to influence the expectations they hold for their future careers.

For this cohort, technology is ingrained into their everyday lives. It allows them to get the things they want, find the information they need, and connect to the people they value. This connectedness is reflected in the way that these individuals approach everything they do, including their future work lives. As they enter the workforce, these current college students will bring with them, not only their personal devices, but also the ambitions and expectations forged in a Networked-Community Age. As you would expect, this is a remarkably connected group of people. Beyond just staying connected to others, a full 96 percent of these future workers use a laptop and 71 percent use a cellular device, specifically for school purposes.

This group also holds strong opinions when it comes to the use of technology and flexibility in the workplace. Almost nine in 10—88 percent—say that "the technology at my disposal gives me the freedom to work when I want, where I want," compared with 74 percent of the current enterprise workforce. When asked if a dynamic work schedule and the ability to work from any location are significant benefits for a potential employer to use to woo worthy candidates, a full 96 percent and 87 percent, respectively, either strongly or somewhat agreed. Furthermore, when asked what benefits they would most value when evaluating a potential employment offer, good technology and workplace flexibility were almost as important as salary considerations. This preference for working remotely is even evident in the way that they currently approach their school work. When faced with a group project, a full 40 percent never meet face-to-face as a group when completing their tasks. Instead, they rely on free services such as Skype, Dropbox, or Google Docs to coordinate with team members. Of those that do meet face-to-face, 59 percent only meet once in order to assign responsibilities before relying on other means to collaborate to project completion.

However, just because they are not meeting face-to-face doesn't mean that they don't value the collaborative process. To a generation steeped in social networking and always-on communication, the collaborative process is not just valued, it is preferred. A full 86 percent of respondents find that working on a team with a high degree of cooperation, in which team members work toward a common goal, is the most productive way to get things done. When a similar question was asked of 2,873 current enterprise employees in the 2012 Alcatel-Lucent study, 63 percent reported that their organizations approach work in this manner—revealing a clear chasm that could impact the productivity of the future workforce.

Although this generation is immersed in technology and the social networking that is enabled by their devices, they do have a good understanding of how this immersion can impact their productivity when it comes to their working lives. Having grown up steeped in an increasingly connected Internet culture, today's college student knows when to say when. Compared with current enterprise workers, today's top college talent is more likely to view surfing the web and social networking activities as a distraction that negatively impacts their ability to get things done.

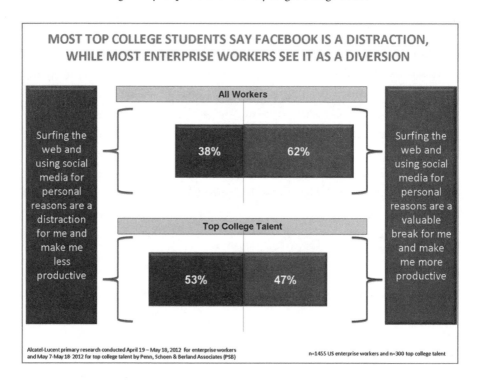

MOST TOP COLLEGE STUDENTS SAY FACEBOOK IS A DISTRACTION, WHILE MOST ENTERPRISE WORKERS SEE IT AS A DIVERSION

Surfing the web and using social media for personal reasons are a distraction for me and make me less productive

All Workers

38%   62%

Top College Talent

53%   47%

Surfing the web and using social media for personal reasons are a valuable break for me and make me more productive

Alcatel-Lucent primary research conducted April 19 – May 18, 2012 for enterprise workers and May 7-May 18 2012 for top college talent by Penn, Schoen & Berland Associates (PSB)   n=1455 US enterprise workers and n=300 top college talent

In addition to being remarkably savvy users of technology, the emerging workforce is also very capable when it comes to providing their own support should some sort of issue arise with their devices or applications. Given the pervasive nature of smartphones, tablets, and computers in their daily lives, it only makes sense that they would develop a high degree of competence when it comes to troubleshooting technical problems. The same Alcatel-Lucent study found that 89 percent of respondents report having outstanding to strong expertise with their technology. Only one in five, or 19 percent, report a reliance on their campus IT support. When an issue presents itself, 67 percent report having the capability to fix it solo or with the help of a peer. Typically, according to a *GigaOM* report, this often involves "Googling" the problem—with 71 percent identifying this as their primary troubleshooting method.[15]

By 2025, Millennials will make up an estimated 75 percent of the workforce.[16] Their utilization of, and comfort with, technology of different types and their preference for a collaborative and team-based environment are raising the bar on what this future workforce expects from their prospective employers. To attract the best talent and remain competitive in this hyperconnected world, it is clear that successful companies must continue to evolve to satisfy these demands. And although established organizations can't change their ways overnight, there are some fundamental actions that can be implemented in the workplace to support this generation in reaching their full potential:

- **Let them multitask**—No doubt you have seen this behavior before—a young person is listening to music while surfing the web and engaging in a text message conversation with a group of friends at the same time. This behavior easily translates to an office environment as well and is one of the characteristics that makes this generation as productive as they are. It would be easy as a manager to counsel a young employee to focus and tackle one activity at a time. However, this is not how they operate. Growing up connected to the network has literally wired the employee's brain differently than the rest of ours.
- **Allow some flexibility**—According to *Time* magazine, research shows that 81 percent of Millennials believe that they should be allowed to work when they want, from wherever they wish.[17] As previously discussed, this generation sees the opportunity to set their own hours and work from wherever they like as an important incentive for employers looking to hire the best talent. This is an incredibly active and mobile group of people. They are always connected and rarely out of touch. A strong work–life balance is of significant importance, and a flexible working arrangement allows them to feel that they have achieved this balance. Of course, just because they want something doesn't mean that they should get it right off the bat. As previously discussed, Alcatel-Lucent found that only 15 percent of entry-level workers are trusted to work remotely in today's enterprise. This number rises to 43 percent as employees become more experienced—illustrating a significant managerial trust gap between inexperienced and experienced workers. However, in today's fast-paced corporate world, the enterprise only stands to gain by reducing the amount of time required to build that trust. Today's technology can provide tools to shorten this gap in the form of monitoring applications that offer

managers a degree of unobtrusive oversight. As you would expect, today's top college talent is wary of such monitoring, with only 37 percent agreeing that managers have a right to monitor employees during work hours. However, by establishing clear guidelines in the spirit of full transparency, such objections can likely be overcome. Once a certain degree of trust has been established and a measurable level of productivity has been maintained, loosening the reigns on these employees will go a long way toward establishing a fruitful and productive working relationship.

- **Foster a collaborative environment**—Born into the ways of the social network, these employees are connected to each other like no generation before them. They are the generation of the viral video, the Twitter feed, and of Kickstarter campaigns. Working as a part of a team toward a common goal is second nature to them. Giving them the tools they need to collaborate virtually and providing physical spaces for them to work with others will help them flourish in an office environment. Additionally, providing the opportunity to work with others across the organization is the best way to integrate them into the culture of the company and to encourage them to share their ways with the rest of the enterprise. However, although nurturing a collaborative environment is an important means to engage this generation, companies should also take care to respect lone geniuses lurking in the virtual hallways (as discussed in the last chapter).

- **Let them use their tools and give them the support they need**—As discussed in an earlier chapter, BYOD has become a significant issue for IT organizations as workers continue to leverage their personal smartphones, computers, and tablet computers for work purposes. In addition to these specific devices, employees are also going around their IT organizations to use often unauthorized applications and services such as Dropbox and Skype to get their work done. Despite the obvious security risks, no group feels more strongly about using their preferred tools than this emerging workforce. According to a recent report by the security firm Fortinet, 55 percent of workers aged 20–29 believe that using their own device for work is a "right" versus a "privilege." [18] By respecting their choice of tools, organizations can increase overall employee satisfaction and boost productivity by allowing them to work with the devices and applications with which they are most familiar.

Given this generation's comfort level with technology and their do-it-your-self approach to troubleshooting issues, organizational IT departments have a unique opportunity to support and engage with these tech-savvy employees. The development and maintenance of self-help portals, troubleshooting communities and discussion groups, and specific device and application training allow the IT organization to fill a real need for those employees who prefer to find the answer to a problem on their own terms. By engaging in this way, the IT department becomes a partner in their success and eliminates the risk of complete disintermediation by a growing workforce demographic.

- **Give regular feedback**—A recent poll discussed in *Forbes* magazine indicates that 80 percent of Millennials want regular, ongoing feedback from their managers.[19] Millennial employees have grown up in an environment of instant gratification. The Internet and all its associated services and applications have conditioned this generation to expect the information they need and the answers they want without hesitation. Beyond the instant availability of data, these young people are accustomed to the immediate feedback of loving, doting parents who scheduled their lives around their children's events and activities. Waiting for the traditional semiannual review of their performance is a constant source of frustration—they want to know how they are doing now. In addition, despite their preferences for all things virtual, this cohort strongly prefers face-to-face contact with management. The 2012 Alcatel-Lucent study found that 71 percent of these employees prefer to work in an environment where their management engages in direct contact with employees, despite the fact that virtual contact could allow for more frequent interactions. Millennial employees want to learn, they want to understand the big picture, and they want to understand how their efforts are positively contributing to the goals of the organization. Spending time providing feedback and coaching to these employees may take some extra effort on the part of the manager but will pay dividends from an employee development perspective.

- **Provide structure, demand accountability**—This generation of workers approaches their work life much differently than the traditional enterprise employee. Like their older counterparts, they want to excel in their professional lives and provide value to the organization, but they want to do so on their terms. However, accommodating these specific wants and needs doesn't mean that projects don't have due dates, meetings don't need to be attended, and goals don't need to be met. Setting expectations and getting agreement on clear objectives are essential components for effective management of any employee group—doubly so with members of this generation. This is the generation whose parents inspired the term *helicopter parent*. These overinvolved parents were involved in every aspect of their child's life—setting high expectations and encouraging them every step of the way. The 2012 Alcatel-Lucent study found that 58 percent of these respondents prefer to work in an environment where management sets objectives and provides frequent direction. *Frequent direction* is key. Millennials flourish when engaged by participatory leadership. By providing clear objectives and personally investing in their quest for success, the enterprise will enable these employees to thrive and exceed expectations.

The 2012 Alcatel-Lucent study found that 61 percent of top college students prefer to work in an organization that is constantly changing and provides new challenges for employees. Luckily, these Millennials are entering the workforce at just the right time. Today's fast-paced and constantly changing world is custom-made for a generation that thrives on new challenges. In an economy that demands that organizations continuously innovate to remain competitive, this younger generation has the skills and abilities that today's companies so desperately need. Comfortable with all types of technology, connected and collaborative, these innovative employees appreciate an environment that allows them to make an immediate impact on the success of an organization. To help them live up to their potential, today's enterprise needs to adjust and adapt the way they approach their employees and their way of doing business. As more and more Millennials enter the workforce, the successful enterprise will be the one that realizes the need for a new contract between employer and employee—a contract not based on command and control but, rather, one based on transparency, collaboration, innovation, and flexibility. Whether an organization chooses to respond or not, there is no denying that this emerging workforce is redrafting the very design of the modern enterprise. In today's rapidly changing and competitive environment, the organizations that understand, respect, and accept the blueprint of these new architects are the ones best poised for sustainable future growth. Those that don't should prepare for demolition.

I WANT MY MILLENNIALTV

Founded in 1981, MTV strives to keep its finger on the pulse of youth culture. From the creation of the music video as an art form to their pioneering work in reality TV with the creation of shows like "The Real World," MTV is consistently reinventing itself to remain useful and relevant to its core demographic. However, by 2008, MTV realized that its focus on reality shows like "The Hills" and "My Super Sweet 16" were no longer resonating with their audience as the national economy was struggling, banks were failing, and people were losing their jobs. MTV had failed to notice that their emerging audience had different tastes and sensibilities from their original Generation X target demographic. President Stephen Friedman realized that the network needed a total reinvention, stating, "This was a real opportunity to transform MTV once again. But we needed to let go of Generation X so we could own the Millennials." [20]

To better connect with their emerging Millennial audience, MTV embarked on an in-depth study designed to understand the way they think, work, and live. Nick Shore, Senior Vice President of Strategic Insights and Research at MTV, says that, despite common perceptions to the contrary, this generation has a strong work ethic and does a better job of integrating their work and personal lives than previous generations.

> They're really different in the workplace. If there are distinctions between things—if you put things into boxes of black and white— Millennials are really good at melting those boundaries, at creating a smoothification of things. [21]

It's exactly this *smoothification* that MTV is after within its own organization. Embracing its own horizontal hierarchy of sorts, MTV seeks to leverage the innovative and creative approach that this generation brings to the workforce to transform products and services. To this end, the executive management team has set up what they call a *reverse mentoring* program in which the youngest members of the organization act as actual advisors to the leaders of the company. The program has had immediate impact. According to Shore, Friedman's Millennial advisor came up with a new category for the popular MTV Video Music Awards show. Their ideas are also starting to influence programming itself at the network, especially the series "Underemployed"—which focuses squarely on the Millennial generation. In addition, although MTV is also sharing this research with their partners and clients, the biggest impacts have been internal to their own organization as they continue to seek to remain relevant to their constantly changing audience and their own employees.

The Tightrope Walkers

→ *According to the Hay Group, only 8% of senior managers believe that Human Resources provides a significant strategic contribution to their company.*[1]

It was raining and gloomy outside, and the mood inside the social-buying startup BuyWithMe was no better. A group of employees sat around a table having drinks and working their way through a stack of pizzas. The feeling of dread in the room was compounded by the fact that the number of pizzas ordered was in no way sufficient to feed all 200 employees waiting to discover their fate. The past couple of months had seemed bright for this promising young organization. Companies such as Groupon and LivingSocial had defined an effective business model in the social buying space, and BuyWithMe executives liked to emphasize that it held a strong number three position to those competitors. The organization had been hiring staff, and the new Chief Marketing Officer had been heard discussing plans to advertise the company during the Super Bowl. However, the optimism and enthusiasm of this young organization were replaced with feelings of fear and dread just two weeks before the rainy day pizza party. An e-mail, intended for the executive team, that outlined the names, salaries, and proposed termination dates of a large number of workers was mistakenly sent to a group of employees. Needless to say, the rumor mill kicked into high gear as the unwitting workforce waited for some kind of explanation. The management team took an entire day before addressing the mistake and announcing that, because of the lack of capital, layoffs would indeed take place, hiring was frozen, and that terminated employees would not receive any severance. Two weeks later the axe fell, and BuyWithMe immediately showed more than half of its employees the door.[2]

Layoffs of this kind are not uncommon in the startup world characterized by small groups of people, banded together in a fast-paced environment, working together for long hours in an effort to achieve a common goal. Oftentimes, that common goal is meeting certain milestones to secure the next round of funding that is needed to keep the lights on—that, or attract the attention of a larger, more successful company interested in a purchase. Both of these objectives were in play at BuyWithMe, so perhaps it is not surprising that mistakes were made as the leaders of the company desperately searched for a solution to their problem.

Surely a larger, more established organization would have clearly defined processes and procedures in place to avoid such blunders.

Aviva Investors was experiencing a slowdown in sales. The European debt crisis and the worsening economy were taking a toll on the organization. In an effort to balance their business, the asset management arm of the United Kingdom's second largest insurance company had just announced a reshuffling of their board and the replacement of several corporate executives. The company was also in the all too familiar position of having to reduce their staff. And although employees were aware of the ongoing restructuring, more than 1,300 global staff were shocked to receive an e-mail from the Human Resources Department asking them to return all company property and hand over their security badges on their way out of the building. The e-mail read, in part:

> *I am required to remind you of your contractual obligations to the company you are leaving. You have an obligation to retain any confidential information pertaining to Aviva Investors operations, systems and clients.... I would like to take this opportunity to thank you and wish you all the best for the future.*

Thankfully, shock turned to relief a few moments later when the staff received another e-mail apologizing and explaining that it was a mistake. Paul Lockstone, a spokesperson for Aviva explained:

> *It was intended that this e-mail should have gone to one single person. Unfortunately, as a result of a clerical error, it was sent to all of the Investors staff worldwide. From time to time, things go wrong.[3]*

The poor economic environment of the past several years has been difficult for organizations around the world. Mistakes like the ones illustrated above do little to bolster the security or enthusiasm of employees in today's business environment. Reductions in force, elimination of benefits, and teams struggling to do more work with fewer resources are common refrains in today's enterprise and are impacting the relationship that companies have with their employees. A human resources and leadership consulting company recently published a study that illustrates the decline in this employer/employee relationship. According to Interaction Associates, of the 440 workers polled from a variety of industries, only 27 percent of respondents said that they have a "high level of trust in management and the organization." That is down a full 39 percent from just three years ago.[4] Additionally, Maritz Research found that only 14 percent of employees believe that their company leaders are ethical and honest. Only 10 percent indicated that they trust their management to make the right decisions in times of uncertainty. And just 7 percent believed that senior management actions were consistent with what they told employees. These 1,857 employee respondents cited poor communication, lack of perceived caring, inconsistent behavior, and perceptions of favoritism as the largest contributors to the overall lack of trust in their organizations.[5]

Unfortunately, in a tough economic climate, the human resource function is often seen solely as the organizational hatchet man—trimming and cutting a workforce to satisfy a management team that is neither trusted nor respected by the workforce. The perception couldn't be further from reality. Charged with everything from the selection and onboarding of employees, the training of the workforce, the oversight of organizational leadership, and employee and labor law compliance, today's human resources (HR) organization finds itself in the difficult position of trying to serve two masters. As the primary recruiting arm for the organization, HR is responsible for ensuring that the company is attracting the best talent—allowing the organization to grow and remain healthy and competitive. They are also the primary arbiter in ensuring that both the company and its employees are protected from a policy and workforce and labor law perspective—ensuring that clear policies are in place to protect companies from legal action and employees from exploitation. Finally, as the cultural steward of the enterprise, HR is tasked with maintaining a healthy and productive work environment—ensuring that current employees are properly prepared, engaged, and satisfied in their work lives. Unfortunately, this organizational department often finds itself at cross-purposes as it struggles to balance its role as an advocate for both employees and the company it serves.

In a rapidly changing and hyperconnected world, human resource departments are faced with new issues and challenges every day. Building an effective organization in a shifting business environment and ensuring that productivity, culture, and retention rates remain positive, present daily obstacles that must be overcome for an enterprise to achieve its goals. In addition, although some of the most significant challenges faced by today's organizations are specifically people-related, finding the right candidate for the right job goes a long way toward mitigating some of the issues that might arise. Bad hires are much more common than one might think. According to a report by CareerBuilder, more than two-thirds of employers were impacted by a bad hire in 2011. This impact can be significant. Of the 2,700 employers surveyed, 41 percent estimate that the cost of a single bad hire to the organization was $25,000. An additional 25 percent of the respondents estimated that bringing in the wrong talent costs their organization $50,000 or more.[6]

Human resources has a significant role to play in the reduction of poor hiring decisions; however, evidence suggests that there are areas for improvement. There are few groups within an organization that touch as many other departments as human resources. One would expect that no other group would be in a better position to understand the strategy, direction, and business needs of the company it represents. But this doesn't seem to be the case. In a survey of more than 1,400 HR professionals and senior management from around the world, the global management consultancy firm Hay Group found that only 34 percent believe that HR provides some strategic contribution to their organization. Furthermore, only 36 percent of respondents indicate that talent management and organizational effectiveness are closely aligned.[7] It seems that the C-Suite would agree. In the fall of 2010, the Human Resources Professionals Association and the human capital consultancy firm Knightsbridge Human Capital Solutions conducted a series of interviews with CEOs from companies across a variety of industries. Virtually across the board, the CEOs they spoke with stressed the need for HR managers to understand the challenges and business needs of their internal customers better. One CEO said:

If HR is not embedded in the organization, it is not successful. It needs to be visible. It needs to understand the business better in order to bring greater value to the table. HR can become too narrow, too specialized—it needs to be broader in its approach to the business.[8]

A broad approach to the business is essential to the hiring manager in avoiding a bad hire. Beyond just understanding the checklist of required qualifications and experience for a specific role, a deeper understanding of the internal team's goals, challenges, and culture will ensure more accurate identification and successful hiring of the best talent for the team.

In addition, securing top talent is no easy task, because regardless of larger market conditions, top talent is always in high demand. In the ongoing battle to secure the best resources, it's the role of the HR department to model and communicate why an external candidate should consider their organization over another. Job seekers are often counseled to develop and present their own personal value propositions to separate themselves from other candidates. The same holds true for employers as well. Developing a compelling story to demonstrate to a candidate why she should invest her future with the organization makes it far easier to attract and retain the best candidate in a market where the best talent is always coveted. Southwest Airlines is a great example. Known for its unique and fun-loving culture, Southwest has created a high-performing environment focused on teamwork. Those who have flown Southwest have no doubt noticed that the entire flight crew, including the pilots, helps to clean and prepare planes for their next flight. Core expectations, such as efficient operations and superior customer service, are clearly articulated to employees, and they are rewarded with an environment that encourages them to "bring their personality to work." [9] As a result of this employee-centric culture, the airline has three times lower turnover than the industry average and has won numerous awards, including *Fortune*'s America's Top Ten Admired Companies.[10]

Given the view that the HR department has across the breadth of their organization, no other internal department is better suited to develop an organization's employer value proposition. This differentiator could be based on company culture, opportunity for advancement or learning, or even the technology resources that are provided to employees. For example, forward-leaning companies have already realized the connection between a positive company culture, technology, and company success. In the 2012 Alcatel-Lucent study described in the preface of this book, nearly 79 percent of those in high-earning and successful companies (as self-reported based on a series of company financial metrics) indicate that HR has more influence over organizational technology decisions than they did just three years ago. Three in five, 61 percent, of HR decision makers say that their influence on technology decisions is continuing to increase. In an always-on world, successful organizations are using every asset at their disposal to create an environment that will attract the best and brightest. Understanding what sets the business apart from the competition allows for the creation of a compelling proposition designed to sell the organization to the best talent in the market.

In addition to ensuring that the organization is staffed with the best possible personnel, human resource professionals are also responsible for setting the policies and procedures that govern all facets of organizational life. From policies surrounding drug use to workplace harassment, records management, disciplinary procedures, and technology usage, these guidelines are designed to provide a safe, professional, and empowering workplace environment for all employees. Policies surrounding technology usage have proven to be especially challenging as today's HR organizations strive to maintain pace with a rapidly changing workforce and the ever-changing innovations that are brought into the workplace. According to Josh Bersin, President and CEO of HR industry researcher Bersin & Associates:

> We're in a complete revolution of technology in general, to mobile devices, cloud computing and consumer-user interfaces. They're affecting our everyday lives, so they're affecting HR. HR just can't afford to ignore it.[11]

Policies that address technological innovations in the workplace will continue to evolve as more and more employees bring their own devices with them to work, access third-party applications, and leverage all of these tools to take their work mobile. Issues such as technology usage, monitoring, privacy, and data protection have now taken on a higher degree of importance as HR strives to protect both the employee and the organization itself. Beyond technology distracting workers and negatively impacting their productivity, more serious risks to the organization abound. The loss of a device that contains company information can be devastating to an organization if it falls into the wrong hands. E-mail and other company communications need to be retained and made available in case of litigation against the company. Improper use of technology in the workplace could expose the organization to lawsuits by harassed employees. As the primary functional department responsible for developing the policies and procedures that protect the organization, HR needs to consider all possible contingencies.

However, as stewards of company culture, the HR department also needs to balance the requirements of the organization with the needs of the employees. In addition to keeping employees in contact with others and making a world of information available to them wherever they may be, the technology that surrounds the workplace also offers up significant opportunities for worker exploitation. RFID and GPS technologies allow managers to monitor and track employees whenever they like. Every keystroke, every phone number called, and every text message sent can be archived and retrieved to maintain a constant eye on employee activity. And while federal law gives employers the legal right to monitor an employee's activity, the tracking and monitoring of every move an employee makes don't do much for morale. Only 28 percent of current employees surveyed in the 2012 Alcatel-Lucent study found it acceptable for managers to monitor the current location and availability status of employees during work hours. Although the United States lags behind other nations in the adoption of regulations addressing workplace privacy concerns, effective workplace technology policies need to address the evolving implications of an always-connected workforce. Flexible and clear guidelines related to the use of technology in the office will only become more important in the coming years as the next generation of workers enters the ranks. This next generation of workers lives their lives through their devices. It is up to the HR department to ensure that organizational guidelines and policies both protect the company and empower and support the worker in his quest to be a successful and productive employee.

Perhaps one of the more challenging roles that HR is expected to fill is the effective "care and feeding" of an increasingly disenfranchised workforce. According to the *Gallup Employee Engagement Index*, a full 71 percent of American workers are "not engaged" or are "actively disengaged" from their work.[12] Based on a random sample of 2,341 employed adults, this survey paints a sobering picture of the state of the American workforce. Over the past several decades, Gallup and other researchers have identified a strong connection between employees' workplace engagement and their company's overall financial performance. The data indicates that businesses in the United States, and as a result the U.S. economy, are likely not reaching their full potential because disengaged workers are less productive than their more engaged counterparts. Gallup estimates the cost of this lost productivity to be more than $300 billion.[13] In addition to being less productive, the less engaged an employee is with his or her work, the more likely he or she is to leave the company—adding further costs to the equation. As the cultural stewards of the organization, today's HR department plays a significant role in ensuring that employees are engaged in their work, invested in their company, and contributing from a productivity standpoint.

Human resource professionals understand that employee engagement affects everything they do. From recruiting the best talent, to developing policies to protect the organization and the employee, to preventing employee churn, HR needs to engage the employee's head, heart, and hands (commonly referred to as the *3-H principle* in HR parlance). Engaged employees understand what they need to do to add value to a company, have a feeling of connection to the organization, and are willing to put those thoughts and feelings into action. Some could argue that the manager is in the best position to support her employees and ensure that they are properly engaged with their work. It is a logical assumption. However, Teresa Amabile, a professor of management at Harvard Business School, found that leaders frequently misunderstand what drives their employees. Amabile asked 600 managers to rank the factors that they felt most contributed to an engaged workforce. "Recognition for good work" was number one with "Progress" coming in last. She then compared that feedback to the results of a multiyear study tracking the day-to-day activities and motivations of knowledge workers and found that "Progress" ranked as the primary engagement mechanism. After analyzing 120,000 journal entries, Amabile uncovered a significant disconnect in the perception of managers and the needs of their employees.[14] Managers clearly need a partner. By working across the organization to understand the needs and desires of an increasingly disengaged workforce and properly equipping company leadership with the insights and tools they need, human resources is in the best position to make a significant impact on employee morale and retention.

In addition to partnering with individual managers to understand and improve engagement across the organization, HR professionals have an opportunity to look across the organization as a whole and work with leaders in other functional areas to reduce organizational churn and satisfy the needs of the employee base. The IT department is a perfect example. The 2012 Alcatel-Lucent study found that one-half of HR decision makers drive technical requirements or cooperate with IT in considering new technology solutions that will have a positive effect on the culture of the enterprise. Further to this, when company decision makers were asked how the introduction of advanced technology solutions would impact their desire to stay with the enterprise, almost 50 percent indicated that having access to several of the specific services would entice them to stay. Beyond just engaging these established leaders, enticement of the future workforce also depends on the technological environment in the workplace. When these upcoming college graduates were asked what approach to technology they preferred in a future employer, 57 percent indicated their prefer- ence to work for an organization that offers them the latest tools. In addition, good technology, training on that technology, and the ability to use those technological tools to realize flexibility in where and when they work ranked almost as high as sal- ary as key consideration factors when evaluating a job with a prospective employer.

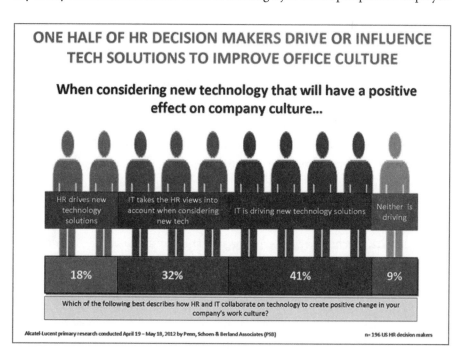

ONE HALF OF HR DECISION MAKERS DRIVE OR INFLUENCE TECH SOLUTIONS TO IMPROVE OFFICE CULTURE

When considering new technology that will have a positive effect on company culture...

HR drives new technology solutions

IT takes the HR views into account when considering new tech

IT is driving new technology solutions

Neither is driving

18%   32%   41%   9%

Which of the following best describes how HR and IT collaborate on technology to create positive change in your company's work culture?

Alcatel-Lucent primary research conducted April 19 – May 18, 2012 by Penn, Schoen & Berland Associates (PSB)   n= 196 US HR decision makers

Employee engagement is no simple matter. And while some may scoff at the appar- ent *softness* of an approach that engages the head, hands, and heart of an employee, organizations ignore engagement at their peril. An engaged employee is a productive employee. Productive employees add value to the business and are much less likely to leave one organization for another. In a highly competitive world, working to build a positive and engaged company culture is not "soft"—it is essential for success.

As HR departments struggle to find the appropriate balance between protecting the interests of the organization and advocating for the employee, the challenges they face in a competitive business environment continue to evolve. Many in the organiza- tion may only see HR through the lens of a singular function, but the opportunity to make positive lasting impacts on the success of the enterprise has never been more real. The following actions will likely elevate the standing of the HR professional in the boardroom and in the eyes of the employees he or she serves:

- **Build partnerships**—More than anything else an HR professional can do to establish credibility and have a positive impact on the success of the company is to better understand the strategic direction of the organization and market forces surrounding the business. Understanding these forces and the challenges faced by individual groups within the company allows HR professionals to respond more effectively to the needs of their internal customers. Comprehension of the challenges and issues faced by a specific line of business allows hiring managers to identify and recruit the best talent for the organization—ensuring ongoing success and productivity. Beyond just recruiting and hiring, partnering with internal lines of business means developing an ongoing working relationship with specific organizations within the enterprise. These working relationships facilitate a more effective approach to staff training, workforce management, and long-term resource planning. Given that HR touches every internal organization in some way, the opportunity to deliver real value and economies of scale across the organization is a significant strength.

  This may be more easily said than done. Survey evidence points to the challenges that HR is having in achieving this ambition. A global 2003 study by the consulting firm Mercer found that, despite their best intentions, HR professionals only spend 15 percent of their time strategically partnering across lines of business.[15] Finding themselves more frequently concerned with the *how* than the *why* often diminishes HR's role from a strategic effort to a second-order activity. This lack of attention to strategic detail also affects the perceptions of their internal partners. The Chartered Institute of Personnel and Development reports that, although HR professionals may rate themselves "good" at partnering with line-of-business management, these managers have an opposite view—reporting HR performance as "below average."[16] Chris Brewster, Professor of International HR at the Henley Management School, points to three key problems that HR professionals have in effectively partnering across their organizations: The role that HR hoped to take in strategically supporting the business was not sufficiently defined; the desires of the internal customer were not taken into account; or HR suffered from a lack of appropriately skilled leaders to gain and maintain credibility in the role.[17]

Forward-leaning organizations that value benefits derived from effective HR/business partnerships are looking at new ways of approaching the issues above. Becton, Dickinson and Company, a medical technology company, restructured its global organization to better support its global business strategy. Faced with cultural and managerial difficulties in implementing the structure, the company's CEO turned to HR for help. The recently hired Vice President of Human Resources had earned the company several industry and functional accolades for his implementation of multiple innovative HR programs and processes, such as a new education and training initiative and a cafeteria-style approach to employee benefits. Unfortunately, however, the CEO discovered that, internally, the HR function lacked the ability or credibility to influence the needed organizational transformation effectively. Thinking out-of-the-box, the CEO responded by asking his head of strategy to take control of the HR organization. The merger of these two functions led to a new approach to HR—one that was based on the foundation of the alignment of behavior, strategy, and aspirations across the business.[18]

- **Police the policy**—As the organization charged with defining, creating, and communicating the policies that govern the workforce, HR is responsible for setting the stage for what activities are appropriate, useful, and legal in the workplace. A consequence of a litigious society is the burden HR professionals face in navigating the shifting sands of policy direction. Comprehensive policies are often seen as too complicated. At best, they lead to confusion, and, at worst, they are completely ignored by a workforce that doesn't see value in taking the time to understand the intricacies of the complicated documents. A recent study by the UK-based office services provider Business Environments found that less than a third of the 1,000 UK office workers they surveyed (27%) were aware of their firm's policies related to dealing with suppliers and clients. Only half of those surveyed (53%) had any knowledge of their employers' general HR guidelines, and a full 24 percent reported no knowledge at all of any workplace policies. A basic lack of understanding, or even awareness, of such HR policies puts the organization at significant risk for organizational confusion, lost business, and even lawsuits.

Although they may be comprehensive, complicated and difficult-to-understand policies don't benefit the employees, and they certainly don't benefit the organization. To gain maximum compliance and acceptance of workplace policies, HR leaders should simplify language to explain the policy and its reasoning. The legal team can still provide the required legalese, but only after they have partnered with HR to craft a sensible, easily understood summary of the policy and its guidelines and ramifications.

- **Get to know technology**—By their own admission, HR leaders don't consider themselves to be experts when it comes to technology. The 2012 Alcatel-Lucent study found that only 29 percent of HR decision makers consider themselves outstanding in terms of technology expertise. In this age of smartphones, social networking, and always-on connections, understanding the tools and applications that the workforce is using, both in and out of the office, allows HR to be relevant to the employees and a successful partner to the IT organization. The consumerization of IT, the emergence of BYOD in the workplace, and the demands of workers to enjoy a more flexible working arrangement all require ongoing adjustments to existing company policies. Only by understanding the technologies that workers are using every day can HR accurately reflect the appropriate policies and procedures to govern their use.

Embracing technology also allows the HR professional to increase the amount of focus put on strategic endeavors. In a 2005 keynote presentation addressing the 10 HR trends that are changing the face of business, Dave Mackay, the Chief Operating Officer of the human resources services organization Ceridian, pointed specifically to the importance of understanding emerging technology and the benefit to the HR function:

> Employees can self-manage activities previously handled by human resource professionals. This is a cost-saving and time-saving benefit to organizations and it frees the HR practitioners to focus on more strategic issues. But more importantly, it is a fundamental expectation of Gen Y's and Gen X's.... It's important that we continue to embrace technology and keep our eyes on new advances that may bring even better communications and collaboration tools. Technology helps people connect within the work environment regardless of time and place.[19]

- **Bridge the skills gap**—The global economic crisis of the past several years has delayed the impending retirement of those workers that are part of the baby boom generation. These workers, born between 1946 and 1964, represent a full third of today's workforce. Financial uncertainty, family obligations, and, in many cases, a desire to keep working have all converged to keep these workers on the payroll lending their skills to the organization. However, as this cohort continues to age and their 401(k) values continue to rise, today's enterprise is facing an unprecedented mass exodus in talent. Such a rapid and abrupt dissolution of knowledge capital from within the enterprise could spell significant difficulty for the organization that fails to respond. According to Jackie Greaner, Talent Management and Organization Alignment Practice Leader for North America at the human resource consultancy firm Towers Watson:

  > *Organizations are running much leaner than ever before, and there are not a lot of extra people to pick up the slack when someone exits. Companies need to do a better job of identifying critical skills and planning for their inevitable loss.*[20]

  North Carolina-based Duke Energy understands the issue and is working quickly to respond. More than 60 percent of employees at the company are considered baby boomers, with more than half of their workforce becoming eligible for retirement in the next five years.[21] Realizing that traditional mentoring programs can require many years to begin having a significant impact, Duke Energy is using software and scenario-planning tools to capture institutional knowledge and facilitate its dissemination across the organization. By leveraging these advanced tools, the organization has developed a knowledge database of manuals, drawings, and other informational assets about its stable of power plants. This repository of information is augmented by the inclusion of audionarration recorded by the most senior engineers at the company. According to Arnold Fry, Manager of Substation Engineering Standards and Power Delivery Engineering at Duke Energy:

  > *In the old days, a younger worker would shadow an older one, who stood over his or her shoulder and said this piece is rated at that voltage. This type of mentoring is fine when you have the time, but now there are too many older workers ready to retire, and far fewer younger ones to come up the ranks. Now when people retire, their*

experience is preserved and can be passed on to future generations.
And you are able to access knowledge from multiple people.[22]

Leveraging their knowledge and experience within the organization to identify critical skill sets and pockets of essential know-how, HR is an essential player in the development of strategies designed to address future deficiencies. Accelerated learning programs that leverage big data analytics in the enterprise, collaborative-based mentoring assignments that pair more experienced workers with their younger counterparts, and even flexible working arrangements with retired boomers who still have the desire to participate in the workforce can all be employed to ensure that the organization effectively maintains the level of impact required from its human capital. Although preparing the organization for the habits, desires, and expectations of the next generation of employees is important, the HR professional must also ensure that these workers are ready to walk in the shoes of those who came before.

There is no denying that HR is a challenging job. Responsible for managing the human capital that an organization needs to function, HR professionals often find themselves relegated to the backseat when strategic organizational decisions are made. The HR professional walks the delicate line of implementing and enforcing company policies and procedures designed to protect the organization, while also striving to create a positive and inclusive company culture that attracts new talent and satisfies the existing employee base. Worsening economic conditions have required that organizations around the world reduce staff, freeze hiring, and mandate that their employees do much more with much less. Often seen as the mouthpiece of an uncaring and out-of-touch management team, the human resource professional is the one left to communicate these unfortunate realities to an increasingly disenchanted workforce.

However, despite the bleak outlook faced by many companies, there is an opportunity for forward-thinking organizations to break down internal silos, work across the aisle, and prepare for a brighter future. The human resource department is in the best position to take up this mantle and lead the charge. No other internal organization understands the state of the workers better than HR. No other internal organization has as wide a view across the internal silos of a business than HR. No other internal organization is as prepared to get the most out of the oncoming throngs of digital natives just beginning to enter the workforce. Although the function does have areas in which to improve, it has a strong foundation on which to build. As cultural stewards of the enterprise, no other department is as well equipped to walk the tightrope of dual advocacy for both the employer and the employee.

TEXTUAL HARASSMENT

One of the more visible functions of today's HR department is putting the policies and procedures in place that facilitate a safe working environment for all employees. We've all seen the headlines—companies forced to pay hundreds of thousands of dollars to employees who have been verbally, physically, or sexually harassed in the workplace. We've likely all taken the training classes that outline which workplace behaviors are appropriate and which are not, as HR works to communicate the costs and mitigate any possible damage to the company or its workers. Unfortunately, the very technologies that empower and enable the workforce are now forcing HR departments around the world to revisit their long-standing workplace harassment policies.

Ralph Espinoza worked as a correctional officer at a juvenile facility in California. Born with a deformed left hand, Espinoza was self-conscious and often kept his afflicted hand in his pocket to hide it from view. Several of his coworkers took to mocking Espinoza by putting their hands in their pockets in the same way and scrawling "the claw" around his personal work space. Things got even worse when these coworkers set up a blog and began posting comments such as:

> I will give anyone 100 bucks if you get a picture of the claw. Just take your hand out of your pocket already!!!

and

> Espinoza is useless even with his good hand. Can we have staff that at least have two hands (sic).

When discovered by management, an e-mail was sent to all employees stating that these blog posts violated organizational policy. Despite the fact that management knew the names of several of the blogs' authors and that HR had been notified of their identities, the harassment never stopped, and no one was held accountable. In the end, as a result of *Espinoza* v. *County of Orange*, the County was ordered to pay Espinoza $820,000 for failing to stop the harassment.[23]

continued

TEXTUAL HARASSMENT *(CONTINUED)*

A recent government report found that 23 percent of harassment victims were targeted through some form of technology—be it text, e-mail, or social networking platforms.[24] Human resource professionals tasked with investigating claims of such behavior often listen to the accused individuals explain that they used their own phones or their own personal computers on their own time to conduct their misdeeds. It doesn't matter. Harassment is harassment—regardless of the form, regardless of the location, and regardless of the tool used to harass. According to the judge in the case of *Espinoza* v. *County of Orange:*

> Employers have...a duty to take effective measure to stop co-employee harassment when the employer knows or has a reason to know that such (actions are) taking place...in settings related to the workplace.[25]

In other words, when looking to protect employees from such issues, the responsibility of the organization extends well beyond the physical workplace.

The Storytellers

→ *According to Gartner, by 2017, CMOs will spend more on IT than CIOs.[1]*

Imagine 300 people donned in their finest gala attire gathered at the most celebrated awards ceremony in their professional field. The big night starts with a bit of a hiccup. Several ticket holders are left holding the bag and out in the cold as their prepaid $125 tickets go missing at the admission office. Inside, things are a bit stranger. The program begins hours behind schedule because the emcee is also missing in action. Adding to the weirdness of the situation, the caterer steps on the stage and attempts to assuage an increasingly hostile crowd by commencing with the evening's ceremony. But, there's no script. Winners are forced to identify their prized work—projected in an out-of-focus slide show—to claim their coveted statuette as an everlasting symbol of a momentous and proud occasion. Just when things can't get any worse, they do. There is no winners' list for a key category, provoking the most exasperated in the audience to bum-rush the stage and claim any idle trophy as their own. The night ends in a cacophony of boos, hisses, and slurs as the curtain falls on the most prestigious event of the year.[2]

This incredible circus actually happened. But, because the statuettes in such high demand were not Oscars, Emmys, Tonys, or Grammys, many never heard about it. However, the spectacularly disastrous occasion is well known among those in the advertising community. Indeed, the 1991 Clio Awards have been appropriately labeled the "most bizarre event in advertising history." [3]

The Clio is the advertising world's prestigious nod to creative excellence in the field. Although it is deeply coveted among advertisers as validation of their work, it seems that there is more to the Clio than just pomp and circumstance. In a world once dominated by physical media, the advertising game was twofold: (1) Expose one's message as often as possible to capture attention, generate preference, and stimulate action among one's target prospects before diminishing returns set in; and (2) create a compelling advertisement that has the potential to "break through" the clutter generated by advertisers. Referring to the latter, in 2007, Yankelovich, a market research firm, estimated that a person living 30 years earlier saw up to 2,000 ad messages a day, compared with up to 5,000 in 2007.[4] And this was before the tsunami of new digital media options ushered in by online and mobile technologies had yet fully developed. Advertisers are the victims of a cluttered marketplace that they helped spawn—one in which creativity and ubiquity hold sway—explaining, in part, why an esteemed crowd would devolve into an angry mob for a trophy. Indeed, evidence suggests that creative ads are more successful in capturing the elusive attention of consumers in an increasingly cluttered market.[5]

Marketers are the consummate storytellers. They must create a more compelling narrative than their competition does and deliver it to their intended audience in a more effective way—helping to explain the tremendous importance placed on well-executed advertising. Today's technologies serve new opportunities to accomplish these goals. They also result in a catch-22 for marketers, who often find themselves breathless in keeping lockstep with, if not slightly ahead of, an increasingly savvy marketplace that changes its behavior as quickly as it adopts the latest technology. As consumers embrace new technologies, they fragment their time and attention across an increasing spectrum of options, and marketers must follow suit or risk being abandoned by those they intend to woo. The CMO of today must be more than just fluent in the stories that will resonate with her target customer. She must understand how to apply her message across a wide variety of new platforms, how to share ownership of her brand with the community she serves, how to apply rich data analytics that expose offers to prospects at precisely the right time without exploiting them in the process, and how to navigate a sea of evolving regulations surrounding consumer privacy. The result is a fundamental shift in the skills and metrics that define success for the enterprise's modern storytellers.

To understand the challenges facing marketers, one must first understand the nature of the field and how it has changed over time, particularly in the discipline of advertising. Advertising is as dated an art form as selling itself, but the industry came into its own with the advent of print in the early eighteenth century. Some 200 years later, radio entered the scene, leaving doomsayers to question the value of print against the new broadcast kid on the block. But it was the television boom of the 1950s that lifted the advertising industry to new heights with its compelling visual medium. Between 1949 and 1953, the number of households owning a television soared from just under 1 million to 20 million.[6] Advertisers enthusiastically followed. In 1948, the number of sponsors of television programs increased to 993, an exponential increase of 515 percent over the previous year.[7] In the early years, television had no playbook or official means of measurement, leaving many critics to scoff at an unproven medium some saw as merely a passing fad among simpletons. As radio began losing followers and advertisers, its long-standing institutions saw their demise. Among the most legendary programs to fall victim to the television trend was *The Fred Allen Show*, which had been a radio fixture in most American homes since 1931. Allen reacted bitterly to the downfall, mocking television as "a device that permits people who haven't anything better to do to watch people who can't do anything." Taking a jab at Ed Sullivan, one of television's early talking heads who would dominate the medium for an impressive 23 years, Allen remarked, "Sullivan will stay on television as long as other people have talent."[8] Despite the naysayers, it was hard to ignore the television juggernaut. Whereas it took radio 38 years to reach 50 million users, television was able to accomplish the same in roughly one-third the time.[9] Early shows dominated and set records for ratings. At one point, Milton Berle had an unprecedented 86.7 percent share of the available audience—a feat never to be matched.[10]

Fast forward to the present day, and things seem strangely familiar. Online and social media are now the darlings on the block, leaving some critics to prophesy the death of traditional alternatives, including print, radio, and television. Although there is some validity to the claims (consider that print advertising, once a $60 billion market at the turn of the millennium, eroded in value to $20 billion by 2011—a precipitous drop attributed to online advertising alternatives[11]), there is also a fair degree of hyperbole in the mix. A marketer's success now requires the ability to distinguish such hype from reality. Take the demise of television as one such example. Although the death of the television spot has been predicted for years at the hand of competing online alternatives if not the ad-skipping threat fueled by DVR households, the reality paints a very different picture. It turns out that the traditional television advertising market is still alive, well, and booming, reaching a record-setting $72 billion market in 2011.[12]

Despite the sustainability of television as a media powerhouse, significant challenges for marketers linger. It is true that television measurement has come a long way since its inception, yet there remains a void in understanding exactly how attention—not just time—is spent in a household with proliferating distractions. Unlike online, there are no ubiquitous click-through capabilities on television to measure attention and behavior, at least not yet. And, in a space cluttered with hundreds of channels, the television advertising market has become congested and fragmented, making it all the more difficult for a marketer to determine where to invest precious dollars in the medium itself, not to mention how to spread those dollars across multiple platforms. Although some may view the fragmentation paradigm opportunistically by accessing a very targeted demographic on a specific channel or show, gone also are the days of ubiquitous reach and frequency on the medium itself. Milton Berle once commanded nearly 90 percent of the viewing eyeballs, but today's top show attracts just over 10 percent of the viewing population.[13]

Competing for the consumer's attention is a plethora of new options, and, whereas marketers once eagerly followed consumers down the uncharted television path, there appears to be some reluctance or inability to give new media its due. Despite the strange reality that more people worldwide have a mobile phone than a toothbrush and 91 percent have said mobile device within arm's reach 24×7,[14] the mobile advertising market has only recently eclipsed $1 billion.[15] Compare that with the $70 billion television advertising market. In fact, although the media time consumers spend with mobile devices is now at 10 percent, the advertising industry's investment in the platform has yet to reach 1 percent.[16]

So, why is the same industry that once demonstrated such unbridled enthusiasm for a yet-unproven medium in television not following as whole-heartedly down the paths of mobile and online alternatives? Some may argue that it is the lack of measurement provided across these new media. Social media, in particular, have suffered a black eye by not sufficiently proving its ROI to companies fixated on profitability. However, compared with the early days of television when measurement was nonexistent, online, social media, and mobile options provide a wealth of information that can be used to measure and, in some cases, predict consumer behavior. One cannot also make the argument that television was more popular in its formative years in drawing an audience than either online or mobile, hence explaining the reason that advertisers eagerly followed their consumers by blindly investing in the new platform. The Internet had a much more aggressive adoption curve—reaching the 50 million user mark at roughly one-third the time of television.[17] In comparing the adoption rate of television to mobility, one has to change the axis of the latter to even be relevant in measuring its exponential growth—the iPhone marketplace hit 1 billion applications in less than a year.

If not lack of measurement or slower adoption rates, what else can explain the tempered enthusiasm for new media platforms? It seems that the more tepid response among advertisers has more to do with the sheer volume of platforms available than a lack of interest in any one media alternative itself. At MediaPost's recent Mobile Summit, media guru Patrick Quinn reflected on how the number of media alternatives available to an advertising agency has grown over the years: "In the 1970s, there were eight choices. Today, there are more than 100, and 17 from mobile alone."[18] Adding to the complexity of the equation is the dependency of platforms on one another. Consumers rarely invest undivided attention into one medium at a time. Multitasking is commonplace, with youth spreading their coveted attention even more thinly than older generations. According to the Kaiser Family Foundation, 8- to 18-year-olds manage to pack an astounding 10 hours and 45 minutes of media into just over 7.5 hours of entertainment time by consuming more than one medium simultaneously.[19] Marketers must not only determine how and where to invest dollars across more than 100 platforms, they must also construct a plan of attack to use media synergistically across platforms—all the while devising creative concepts and executions that work across multiple device and experience environments.

It seems that just as marketers gain traction in balancing multiple platforms, a new media alternative enters the ring vying for their scarce resources. In an ironic twist of events, online video is now emulating traditional television in more ways than one. YouTube has announced its intention of offering more than 100 channels of original programming, sponsored by the likes of significant brands, and has backed this commitment with a $100 million investment.[20] It and fellow online cohorts AOL, Hulu, and Yahoo are looking for a piece of the advertising spend still dominated by traditional television and have devised a new commercial industry—the *NewFront*—to sell their wares. For those familiar with advertising, the "upfront" market has been the mainstay of traditional television advertising sales for some time. This is the time when television executives shop around their upcoming programming lineup in hopes of selling advertising inventory for the forthcoming season. Before the upfront market had an opportunity to open for business in the spring of 2012, online media companies promoted their programming options in the NewFronts, making a case that their content is complementary, if not cannibalistic, to the television time invested by today's multitasking consumer.

If that weren't enough to make marketers' heads spin, perhaps the new family of augmented reality possibilities will do the trick. Just as QR Codes, those funny-looking schematic designs that are increasingly found on print advertisements and publications and can be read by a smartphone to push content (such as a web page or video) to the consumer, become more mainstream, they are being displaced by newer forms of augmented reality in which conspicuous codes are no longer necessary. With the latest technologies, the "code" still exists, although it is invisible to the user. Whether using an audio fingerprint that identifies a particular sound (such as *shazaming* a commercial) or an image recognition software that can automatically identify an object (such as the object-driven capabilities of HP's Aurasma), the user need not scan a "code" to get more information or content. Of course, the challenges for advertisers remain because they must extol the virtues of this new media technology to their consumers while also designating the capabilities existing in a particular advertising format, at least until *augmented* reality becomes the *expected* reality on the part of mainstream consumers. Of course, when this day comes, advertisers who have not embedded the latest visual and audio cues may find themselves at a disadvantage as opposed to those that do, in much the same way that companies were forced to hop aboard the Internet bullet train with a website and e-commerce platform to remain competitive a few years back.

With so many choices present, and more entering the market each day, marketers are confounded with how to keep up. A 2010 survey from the staffing firm The Creative Group found 65 percent of marketing executives considering it at least somewhat challenging to stay current on social media trends.[21] The problem reaches across enterprises of all sizes. A Forrester study concluded that less than a quarter of Fortune 500 companies had effectively integrated interactive marketing teams.[22] The vast majority had maintained artificial silos between traditional and interactive marketing efforts, despite the fact that the majority of their consumers no longer partitioned their time and attention as such. Because more and more of a consumer's time is spent through these interactive media, they also represent a breeding ground for rich consumer feedback and insights. But, like the challenges in using such media for promoting a company's message, marketers encounter similar difficulties when mining the treasure trove of consumer data available through online options. A 2011 study by IBM found that, although marketers believe such data is important, they find themselves ill equipped to harness it, with more than 80 percent of CMOs still relying on traditional marketing research to build market strategies.[23]

New alternatives are not only changing the way marketers promote their brand, they are also changing the discourse of the brand itself. In the good old days of one-way broadcast media, marketers owned their brand. The most brand-conscious of them took painstaking caution to ensure that the integrity of their image remained true to the personality and promise of the identity they attempted to create and solidify in their consumer's mind. Feedback was controlled, often through channels as dated as toll-free numbers or snail mail correspondence. Word of mouth was limited to those individuals within a consumer's close circle over whom he had direct influence—a positive outcome for brand missteps but one that also limited the positive referrals coveted as the crown jewel of "advertising." The two-way world in which consumers now dwell significantly alters the paradigm for marketers. In a 2010 study by KRC Research among company owners, executives, brand managers, and marketers, 40 percent of respondents agreed that social media created new challenges for protecting a brand's integrity.[24] With a few keystrokes, consumers can opine about their personal experience with the brand and share those thoughts with millions of strangers around the virtual world. But marketers attempting to put a lid on such feedback may find themselves the scorn of the population they attempt to influence.

And, in a media category in which instantaneous action goes both ways, marketers are prone to mistakes not common in other media in which checking and rechecking are the norm. Those who do not fess up to such errors find themselves ridiculed by a savvy consumer market unforgiving of attempted cover-ups, as Chrysler learned the hard way. In 2011, the author of the ChryslerAutos Twitter account inadvertently tweeted, "I find it ironic that Detroit is know [sic] as the #motorcity and yet no one here knows how to f***ing drive." The company deleted the tweet and claimed it was the product of a hacker, only to admit later that the tweet was the opinion of an employee at the company's social media agency, "who had since been terminated." But the damage was done for Chrysler, who suffered a black eye in the court of social opinion for attempting to bury the offense.[25]

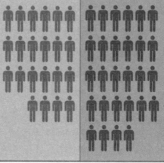

EMPLOYEES DIVIDED AS TO HOW MUCH OWNERSHIP THEY HAVE OVER THEIR COMPANY'S BRAND

Which statement do you agree with more?

44% said "as representatives of a company, employees have a right to speak about the company's products or services in forums like Facebook and Twitter, as long as confidential information is protected."

56% said "companies must maintain a certain image in the market and it is dangerous to allow employees to speak about the company in forums like Facebook and Twitter, regardless if confidential information is not leaked."

Alcatel-Lucent primary research conducted April 19 – May 18, 2012 by Penn, Schoen & Berland Associates (PSB)   n=2873 US enterprise workers

If the changing landscape in how one creates, maintains, and promotes a brand is insufficient in throwing marketers off balance, there's always the altered selling process itself to keep them unsteady. In 2011, the average U.S. shopper consulted 10.4 sources before making a purchase, twice as many as the year before.[26] The fact-checking is no longer relegated to research done at home through a stationary broadband connection. More consumers are using the ubiquitous computers attached to their hips—smartphones—to do comparison shopping while in the field. Seventy percent of these smartphone consumers use their device while shopping in-store.[27] For retailers, that behavior presents an interesting set of unique challenges. *Showrooming*—the use of a mobile device to comparison shop for cheaper or better alternatives for a product while in a store—is entering the consumer mainstream. The problem is particularly daunting for big-box retailers, who increasingly find themselves the victims of merchandising the physical product for curious consumers to investigate, only to have said consumers increasingly opt to purchase the product from an online retailer capable of offering cheaper prices. In response, these retailers are turning to sophisticated data collection mechanisms, using technology often embedded in the store, such as Wi-Fi and surveillance cameras, to serve up special targeted offers to consumers about to vacate the premises and likely to purchase the merchandise from another retailer based on showrooming behavior. For companies vying for limited space within major retailers, they may find themselves coerced into offering exclusive promotional pricing or products to earn their slot on the shelf. Advanced negotiation tactics are yet one more way retailers are addressing the showrooming trend, attempting to secure some measure of exclusivity to counter competitive offers, and challenging the traditional rules of channel marketing in the process.

Of course, building a brand, promoting a message, and selling a product presume some understanding of a target market in the first place, bringing the discussion to how a marketer now finds his ideal consumer or prospect. It is perhaps the best of times and the worst of times for marketers in this regard. No longer are they relegated entirely to buying expensive media time through broadcast channels based on broad demographic cohorts. On the contrary, the hundreds of mouse clicks, IPTV channel changes, and location-based updates that consumers make each day reflect a dazzling constellation of preferences, patterns, and intentions. However, effectively mining this data without crossing a fine line into "creepy" territory becomes the new battlefield for marketers. The public narrative had been fairly clear on this debate. Marketers were given considerable free reign in mining their own company's data in an attempt to offer more targeted or discounted products to their consumers (think of the targeting schemes popularized by grocery stores and large e-commerce retailers as examples).

Marketers had to proceed cautiously when attempting to sell or use their consumer data with third parties. These unwritten, although well understood, rules of the road existed before Target making national headlines. The retailer used its own shopping data and a complex statistical algorithm to serve up targeted offers to consumers based on transaction history and patterns. In 2012, the retailer sent a direct mailer with specific offers for expecting mothers to a household where the matriarch was not pregnant. Outraged, the patriarch called the retailer, excoriating the company for a clear miscalculation in their targeting attempts. That was, until a few weeks later, when the same father made another call to the retailer sheepishly admitting that his teenage daughter was pregnant, unbeknownst to him at the time of his initial complaint. The creep factor of a retailer using advanced statistical data-mining capabilities on its own shopping transactions to target an expecting teenage mother before her parents were even aware heightened the sensitivity of using such big data for a marketer's efforts—whether the data was in the clear perimeter of said marketer's consumer database or not.

Those supposedly well-understood guidelines were upended overnight, leaving marketers questioning, if not gun-shy about, the implications of using their own data for sophisticated targeting efforts. Any lack of clarity on the topic is rich fodder for regulators or journalists seeking their next poster child of a company crossing the line. Despite the trouble spots awaiting pioneers, innovative marketers continue to test the limits of this largely uncharted terrain. Perhaps it's because the payoff is big for those who succeed. Among the more than 1,200 U.S. advertisers in a 2010 Alcatel-Lucent study in which various potential media options were tested, the most universally popular among company marketers and advertising agencies alike was one that generated targeted lists based on rich profile data of consumer activities across multiple digital platforms (including online, mobile, and IP television)—the likely outcome among a base of respondents in which more than one in three strongly agree that digital media offer a high ROI.

Although challenges abound for professionals in this field who find themselves at the cross roads where marketing and technology intersect, there is hope, and some prescriptive guidelines, that can help when navigating the goldmines from the land-mines. Among them are:

- **Earn trust**—Marketers have long been accused of being tone-deaf to the needs of their company by focusing on "squishy" metrics (things like share of voice, qualified leads, brand preference, social buzz, etc.) that are often difficult to correlate to the most important metric favored by CFOs and CEOs—profitability. However, a 2011 Alcatel-Lucent study covering more than 5,000 consumers (from teens to empty nesters) challenged the conventional wisdom of money as the most valued currency exchanged in a market where consumer data is up for grabs. In the study, Alcatel-Lucent tested 10 brands from across the service, web, and consumer equipment provider industries. Respondents were asked to measure each brand on a variety of scales, including things like how much the consumer loved or hated the brand or how much he trusted the brand to keep his information safe and secure. Those attributes were then correlated with how much money consumers were willing to pay for a service offered by each brand. The results showed a more than 60 percent correlation between trust and willingness to pay; that is, the more respondents trusted a brand, the more likely they were to pay for a service offered by the company. Although that may seem intuitive, consider that other metrics, such as how much a respondent loved or hated a brand, had virtually no impact on the same. As it turns out, trust can be converted into dollars. In addition, when consumers willingly trade information about themselves in exchange for free, better, or discounted goods and services (the fuel driving the big data phenomenon), there is an implicit understanding that they themselves are the product for sale, making trust an all the more coveted currency for brands attempting to cash in.

- **Build clarity**—Contrary to legal counsel that marketers may receive from within their companies, privacy policies do not engender trust. They mitigate lawsuits, admittedly an important objective in a highly litigious society; but, to build trust, marketers must go the extra mile in ensuring that the only privacy policy that exists in their company to sufficiently inform consumers about how and when their personal data may be used is not one written in convoluted legalese unintelligible to the average person. According to the same 2011 Alcatel-Lucent study, attributes associated with low trust are (not surprisingly) those concerned with how a company goes about informing consumers of its data-collection procedures. Companies that are perceived as not respecting their customers' privacy, not being upfront or honest in how they use customer information or collecting "too much" information about their customers, suffer a lower trust score and consequently a lower willingness for customers to pay. In an era of big data, privacy policies are simply too important to be left exclusively to a company's legal department or outside counsel. Marketing must take an active role in ensuring that said policy is clearly written (such that one with a junior high school education can easily understand it), conspicuously available (such that one without a detective's license can easily find it), and readily controllable (such that one may opt in and opt out of sharing data in a temporal manner based on contextual or preferential changes).

- **Lose control**—Perhaps the most difficult aspect for any professional is in letting go of some of the controls once afforded him or her. This couldn't be truer than for marketers zealous to create and maintain an appropriate image of their company in the marketplace. However, the rules have changed in a two-way market in which conversations, not monologues, are expected. This new environment requires marketers to cede some control of their brand to the consumers who helped create it. Although this may be a scary proposition, new evidence suggests that letting go may yield significant dividends in shaping consumer perception—a key objective of a successful branding strategy. This includes allowing vocal consumers to opine about a brand's attributes—both positive and negative. According to Reevoo.com, 68 percent of consumers trust reviews more when they see both good and bad scores. Furthermore, shoppers who actively look for bad reviews convert 67 percent more than the average consumer.[28]

- **Retain purpose**—Losing control is not to be conflated with abandoning strategy outright. Marketers have a responsibility to put forth a strategy that equips their company for success. But, with new media alternatives beckoning the attention of company executives, marketers have fallen victim to losing purpose in favor of trying a new medium just because they can. The social media highway is littered with the carnage of companies who dabbled in the medium with no sense of purpose or objective, only to be left deflated and bewildered by the consequential lackluster success. This is, in part, due to the cost-effectiveness of this medium against more traditional alternatives—like television, print, and radio—where production costs can run high. As such, social media tend to favor the pointless, and marketers have proven susceptible to the hype of their market and/or executives with blind experimentation in this space. Any media tactic, including the latest varieties, must be used in concert with others to execute a purposeful strategy within a market. Anything less will result in a disjointed set of activities seeking a mission and leaving marketers and company executives alike confused and underwhelmed.

- **Fail fast**—Although appearing contradictory to the earlier point, failing fast is not the same as lacking purpose. Marketers are entering the age of experimentation, in which empirical testing can be executed fairly quickly and cost-effectively, yielding the most reliable and affordable market research that money can buy. Google runs hundreds of experiments per day to optimize clickthrough rates and results. Amazon is able to test the impact of relocating its shopping cart upon the user experience—and can improve conversion rates within hours, not months or years. Marketers have a bevy of new media alternatives that come with sophisticated measurement capabilities. By having a purposeful testing strategy, they can determine the impacts of precise variables on the consumer's shopping experience and convert more sales as a result. Although these leading indicators can predict and influence purchase intent, marketers must resist the temptation to be seduced by their allure at the CEO's table. For the CEO and key executive stakeholders (including the

CFO), it comes down to ROI. Experimenting quickly, failing fast, and course-correcting are important marketing activities, but only to the extent that their effects can be translated to ROI.

- **Recruit reinforcements**—Traditional marketing has seen its facelift, and it's time the complexion of the marketing department reflects the change. Although it is beneficial to recruit tried-and-true marketing talent, CMOs must now augment their organizations with additional skills to address the changing needs of their consumer base. Statisticians will command a premium in an environment in which big data must be translated into propensity models that yield actionable insights. Engineers and other technologists will earn their respect among marketers by demystifying the dizzying array of innovative media platforms entering the scene. Last, but certainly not least, marketers will find themselves increasingly reliant on an IT organization to support a single customer view across multiple inputs and data-mining capabilities. Fences surrounding these previously distinct organizations will be replaced by bridges among the more innovative firms that embrace the synergies imposed by a hyperconnected market.

There's no doubt that the landscape for marketers has changed dramatically. But not all the changes have been negative, nor should they be met with trepidation. Consider how different the world is for marketers since 2007. Aside from the vast technology changes that have occurred since then, 2007 was also the year when *Businessweek* penned an article that called the CMO position "radioactive." At the time, CMOs had the shortest tenure (just 26 months, on average) among any of their executive counterparts (including CEOs, CFOs, and CIOs). Among the reasons hypothesized by a *Businessweek* source at the time was the fact that 70 percent of companies did not know what to look for in recruiting a CMO.[29] The startling statistic left *AdvertisingAge*— one of the more influential voices in the marketing community—to editorialize why CMOs existed in the first place: "Perhaps we should just call for the end of the CMO position. Put the job out of its misery. It's not really working anyway, is it?" Since then, the "radioactivity" of the CMO position appears to have been contained, with CMO average tenure hitting 42 months in 2010 (still below the average tenure of CEOs, but a marked improvement since executive recruiting firm Spencer Stuart began measuring the statistic in 2004).[30] Although less radioactive, the job has never been more mercurial. Those who adapt to their new surroundings will find new relevance for their hard-earned stories—both in the boardroom and the market they serve.

SEX SELLS

It's among the oldest storylines in the marketing book: Sex sells. The story began in 1911, when Woodbury Soap introduced its "The skin you love to touch" campaign in the *Ladies' Home Journal*. The provocative tagline sufficiently caught the attention of consumers to compel other advertisers to jump on board with sizzling campaigns that continue to push morality limits to this day. Few categories tell the story as well as the apparel industry (remember a teenaged Brooke Shields professing that "Nothing comes between me and my Calvins" in a racy, yet memorable, 1980s commercial?). But it was American Apparel that decimated any socially acceptable boundaries in 2007 with its series of provocative ads. The company gained infamy for featuring scantily clad young girls—some who were even topless—in its racy campaigns. One outdoor treatment attracted attention in Lower Manhattan. There, what one critic described as a "pre-pubescent" young woman was sprawled on a larger-than-life outdoor board, bent over, posterior in the air, and wearing American Apparel tights. Of course, she was also topless. The provocation was not ignored. One vandal defaced the billboard with the musing, "Gee, I wonder why women get raped." [31]

To avoid being the next poster child that attempts to up the provocative ante set by American Apparel, there's a new narrative in the works by creative marketers: Targeting sells. In many ways, targeting is much easier than constantly pushing the creative limits on what the public will find morally acceptable. It eliminates the need to consistently one-up one's competitors with ever more titillating campaigns. Then again, targeting is much more contentious than sex. After all, consumers can simply turn a blind eye to a campaign that offends them. It's much more difficult to escape the trappings of shrewd marketers who seem to know what consumers will do before they do it. In addition, public headlines are riddled with examples of companies that misstep across the dangerous boundary between empowering consumers and exploiting them in the process.

As with any good story, the ending of this one is far from certain, and there are bound to be more cliffhangers and twists ahead. Only the next breed of marketers and the consumers willing to accept their narrative will pen its conclusion. Until then, the public will be mesmerized by provocation, if not outright controversy, as marketers draft the next storyline in their playbook.

The Venture Capitalists

8

→ *The Boston Consulting group found that 22% of senior finance leaders say they are the driving force of innovation at their company. Only 3% of non-CFO executives agree.[1]*

When Norman Macrae died at the age of 89 in 2010, the world lost a visionary. Although *The Economist* journalist was hardly a household name, he was oracle to some of the most sweeping trends of the last century. It was Macrae who predicted the collapse of the Soviet Union when Westerners feared the growing superpower, who prophesied the rise of Japan as an industrial powerhouse when others dismissed it as a purveyor of tchotchkes, and who imagined a world of "terminals" connecting users to giant databases (a primitive foretelling of what would become the Internet). And, long before today's progressive technology darlings entered the scene, it was Macrae who envisaged a world in which *innovation*, not bureaucratic management, would become the primary driver of sustained growth.[2]

In 1976, big business was in fashion. Spurred by the boom of the manufacturing age, companies relied on increasing layers of management to extract as much productivity from line workers as possible. Hence, when Macrae published his seminal article, "The Coming Entrepreneurial Revolution," it was undoubtedly met with a fair degree of skepticism and resistance among large company bureaucrats. In it, Macrae outlined the two fundamental problems with the hierarchically managed companies in vogue at the time:

> *During the Henry Ford manufacturing age about 40 of the world's 159 countries have grown rich because they were temporarily able to increase productivity efficiently by organisational action from the top.... This method of growing rich has now run into two rather fundamental difficulties: a*

"people problem" because educated workers in rich countries do not like to be organised from the top; and an "enterprise problem" because, now that much of manufacturing of most of simple white collar tasks can be gradually automated so that more workers can become brainworkers, it will be nonsense to sit in hierarchical offices trying to arrange what the workers in the offices below do with their imaginations.[3]

In a radical departure from conventional thinking of the time, Macrae offered his prescription to the looming challenges, rebuking the popularity of monolithic hierarchies in favor of greater employee freedom. He imagined a future in which employees harmonize work style with lifestyle and companies thrive off internal competition by harnessing the talents and energy of individuals "who are part-entrepreneurial sub-contractors and part-salaried staff but wholly neither." With a stroke of the pen from arguably one of the brightest futurists of the time, *intrapreneurship* was defined as Macrae predicted: a coming marketplace in which big corporations devolved into "confederations of entrepreneurs."[4]

It took a few years for businesses to catch on to Macrae's vision, but, by 1985, intrapreneurship was in. A *New York Times* article of the time captured the sentiment in its headline, "Now 'Intrapreneurship' is Hot," and trumpeted the arrival of intrapreneuring as evidenced by its appearance in the *Sloan Management Review* and *Harvard Business Review*, its inclusion in a government report on industrial competitiveness, and a best-selling book of the same name.[5] Yet, just over a year later, enthusiasm had chilled for the radical managerial concept, with a few too many companies bearing witness to failed attempts. A 1986 *New York Times* article dubbed the new attitude with its headline, " 'Intrapreneurship' Raising Doubts." The unfettered enthusiasm had waned, and the accolades behind intrapreneurship along with it, because the *Harvard Business Review* was now scattered with foreboding tales of intrapreneurship gone haywire. According to Hollister B. Sykes, former Exxon executive quoted by the scholarly journal at the time, "It is impossible to preserve completely an independent entrepreneurial environment within a large, multiproduct corporate setting."[6] Disillusionment crept into the social narrative, as analysts joined Sykes' way of thinking, positing that large enterprises were simply ill equipped to offer the reward structure, personal autonomy, or risk-taking culture necessary to stimulate and channel the entrepreneurial spirit of employees. Even among the success stories of the time, doubts lingered. During a conference that paraded the best examples of intrapreneurship in action, one such poster child was asked how his company tolerated the failure of an entrepreneurial idea generated by one of its employees. In response, he sheepishly admitted, "That is a very good question. I must confess that we have not yet developed a way to deal with that situation. It does seem clear however, that once a manager's project has failed, it will be difficult to promote him in the future."[7]

But for all of its challenges, intrapreneurship was simply too alluring for some companies to resist. Macrae offered an alternative to big-business bureaucracy and hope to struggling companies seeking to tap an innovation faucet of fresh money-making ideas right from their own reservoir. It is this potential that has given intrapreneurship many spurts in the hallways of businesses for the better part of four decades—each striving to catch lightning in a bottle with that one creative spark. It was intrapreneurial spirit, not bureaucratic dogma, that led to the creation of 3M's wildly successful Post-It note. An intrapreneur, not an executive, conceived the Sony Playstation. It was a Sun employee, not a manager, who ignited a rallying cry that ultimately led to the development of the Java programming language and shifted the course of the company.[8]

Innovation begets growth—an elusive goal as investors reluctantly celebrate the one-year anniversary of the most tumultuous market period since the depths of the financial crisis.[9] At the same time, austere times call for intense budget scrutiny, forcing companies to become more resourceful. In addition, although a near-double-digit unemployment rate may paralyze many employed from considering alternatives, the risk-taking attitude of entrepreneurial employees will not be tamed, leaving many businesses struggling with how to retain restless innovators. Intrapreneurship is again making headlines as companies seek to grow in a tough economy by harnessing the ideas of the most creative and entrepreneurial geniuses from within their organizational charts.

Yet, many are loath to repeat the mistakes of their predecessors. The road is littered with the carnage of intrapreneurial ventures suffocated under the weight of traditional bureaucracies lacking the measurement or reward systems necessary for idea germination. Enter the Chief Financial Officer. The CFO is second only to the CEO in appropriating how resources are allocated in a company (in fact, roughly 30% of Fortune 500 CEOs spent the first few years of their careers developing a strong foundation in finance).[10] CFOs have a reputation for being the *bean counters* of an organization, a pejorative that undermines a far more important strategic contribution they bring to their firms. If intrapreneurs are the budding whiz kids within a company's ranks, CFOs are the enterprising venture capitalists doling out the resources for the projects they believe most worthy.

It's a role that CFOs accept, if not covet. In a gathering of big-company CFOs at a *Wall Street Journal* conference in 2012, attendees longed to drive innovation through incentives or funding. However, because organizational hierarchy runs counter to entrepreneurial risk-taking, a CFO's priority of protecting cash during challenging times opposes a desire to invest, leading skeptics to question if venture capitalism is a mindset that CFOs can afford to embrace. At the *Wall Street Journal* event, Martin Sorrell, CEO of WPP Group PLC and a former CFO himself, challenged the attendees' ability to grow their companies' revenues and expand their function in a cash-constrained economy, acknowledging the innovative desire within CFOs but doubting "whether they are allowed in the straitjacket that we operate in."[11]

The dilemma is not lost upon CFOs. According to a 2012 Deloitte study, CFOs acknowledge that cost-cutting efforts, while important, are yielding diminishing returns, making growth strategies all the more imperative. Given capital constraints, organic growth remains in favor with these cost-conscious leaders, with the focus overwhelmingly on generating scale and efficiencies. And, beyond worrying about the right growth strategies to pursue, CFOs keep a critical eye on delivery, with 85 percent worried about their company's ability to execute.[12] Increasingly, these executives are turning to technology as yet another resource in their coffers to address such issues. Indeed, according to Gartner, roughly half of CFOs play a major role in authorizing IT investment, with nearly the same number indicating that their influence has increased over the past year.[13] In addition, in terms of where technology investment can be of most use to these internal venture capitalists, CFOs align their top three priorities around creating an environment conducive to information sharing, facilitating analysis and decision making, and improving the quality of data used for business information[14]—all of which can relate to a framework that more accurately measures risk against potential rewards and unlocks the potential of intrapreneurship as Macrae envisioned.

To get CFOs one step closer to an information-sharing environment conducive to intrapreneurial pursuits, hierarchical structures must be greased. Collaboration has already been discussed as a means of reducing hierarchical friction in an enterprise and collapsing vertical or functional silos. However, according to a global study by MIT Sloan Management Review and Deloitte, pragmatic CFOs need more convincing when it comes to internal social media technologies, with just 14 percent of them seeing these tools as important (compared with more than half of all corporate leaders).[15] The finding is not altogether surprising assuming that CFOs conflate social media with frivolous conversation or otherwise squishy employee networking benefits. Perhaps a more utilitarian use of social media tools is in order to convince a function bent on maximizing efficiencies and improving decision making. In an ironic twist, CFOs are perhaps the most attuned function in the enterprise that understands the power of collective wisdom—a potential benefit of collaboration-based tools so undervalued by these very executives. After all, the stock market itself is an output of the collective wisdom of millions of shareholders buying and selling options based on their best prediction of a company's future performance. Using internal collaboration tools in the same way can place the CFO in comfortable territory while increasing the accuracy of decision making for these venture capitalists.

Google was among the first notable companies to use one such internal prediction market. The company is no stranger to harnessing the wisdom of crowds as its algorithm quickly made it an online juggernaut by prioritizing the most popular pages in search results. It has also been on Macrae's intrapreneuring bandwagon from the start, allowing engineers to spend as much as 20 percent of their time on projects of interest to the company that are not directly related to their jobs. In 2005, the company launched its Google Prediction Markets, an application conceived and developed by a group of Google employees during their 20 percent intrapreneuring time. The GPM, as it was internally termed, provided a virtual stock market of ideas whereby Google employees could place their bets on which outcomes they believed had the greatest probability. Although employees used fictitious "Goobles" as a currency to trade on the ideas or decisions with the greatest merit, there was very real prize money at stake for those employees who participated—up to $1,000 per winner. In its first quarter of operation, the GPM offered employees 24 markets (questions) and 95 total securities (answers) upon which to trade Goobles. A total of 7,685 trades were made, and 436,843 shares changed hands among employees from all walks of life. Analysis revealed that, even as much as 10 weeks away from the closing date of a market, the outcome with the highest valuation was the one most likely to actually occur, demonstrating the ability of employees to predict likely results with speed and accuracy. Google was able to tap into this collective wisdom with prize money amounting to $10,000 per quarter[16]—an easily justifiable ROI for even the most conservative CFO.

With GPM, Google was able to leverage its existing resources to accelerate and improve decision making. Although a large company in its own right, it proved skeptics wrong by overcoming hierarchical or functional constraints with an open tool backed by a rewards structure to motivate employee participation. And, if such a tool were not sufficiently valuable in predicting the accuracy of decisions, perhaps CFOs may appreciate the role that collaboration can play in solving problems. As discussed in an earlier chapter, heterogeneous teams are more successful than homogeneous ones. The finding is perhaps truer when tackling a difficult problem. CFOs relying exclusively on engineering teams for research and development may find themselves missing the opportunity for exponential growth breakthroughs, as history has shown. Case in point: When the British government offered a prize of £20,000 to the person who found a way to accurately determine a ship's longitude, the legendary Isaac Newton had predicted the answer would come from astronomy. Imagine the surprise when it came from a clockmaker instead.[17] Solutions to problems may not rest with the obvious group, hence the reason Google's GPM and others like it are successful—they organize the chaos of multiple viewpoints into informed opinions and coordinated actions, thereby appealing to CFOs focused on execution.

It's this very diversity of opinion that is leading the most innovative companies to move beyond intrapreneurship and seek ideas from external partners in co-creation and open innovation ventures. Harvard Business School studied hundreds of scientific problems posted on InnoCentive, a virtual marketplace where problems are displayed and ideas are for sale. The problems in the Harvard study were those that the laboratories of science-driven companies had mostly failed to solve. The InnoCentive network of crowds solved nearly 30 percent of them. According to the researchers, the more diverse the interest base of solvers, the more likely the problem was to be solved. In fact, having expertise in the field of the problem actually *hurt* the solver's chances. According to the authors, "The further the problem from the solver's expertise, the more likely they are to solve it." In fact, when the problem fell completely outside of the solver's area of expertise, the chance of success increased by 10 percent.[18]

Such findings are causing CFOs to rethink their company's approach to research, development, and growth—one where diversity trumps expertise and future solutions beat past achievements. To this latter point, McKinsey reports that, before 1991,

97 percent of prize money offered rewarded past achievements (such as the Nobel Prize). Since then, 78 percent of new prize money has been dedicated to the future solution of problems, backed by governments, nonprofit groups, and even capital-constrained corporations.[19]

Yet, as CFOs yearn to tap into more innovative sources for growth both internally and externally, that pesky straitjacket tightens its grip. Beyond bearing the responsibility of preserving cash and using resources efficiently, CFOs often carry the burden of ensuring compliance with a host of regulations. As such, technology trends take on new meaning. For the CFO, the cloud is as much about jurisdiction as it is security, lest the company wants to find itself out of compliance in its next audit, because where data is physically stored in the cloud has a bearing on which local laws and regulations apply. Beyond jurisdiction, some industries go so far as to mandate data preservation for a minimum length of time, a particularly tricky requirement in a digital era when a file can be erased with the simple click of a mouse. In many cases, the financial punishments are sufficient to make cash-conscious CFOs swoon. Piper Jaffray was fined $700,000 by the Financial Industry Regulatory Authority (FINRA) for failing to retain approximately 4.3 million e-mails from November 2002 through December 2008. The fine was the result of an investigation triggered by a single e-mail—one that FINRA investigators had already been provided in hard copy but that the investment bank was unable to produce in soft copy after the investigation commenced.[20]

There's the rub for today's CFO. Although she may aspire to unleash her inner venture capitalist and spend more time in the innovation cycle, she cannot escape the financial and regulatory requirements that bind her. Technology is both contributor and ameliorator to these issues, depending on if the CFO is able to harness it effectively. There is no panacea, although there are a few actions that CFOs can take to bridge the divide between venture capitalist and compliance officer:

- **Align rewards; monitor innovation**—A primary reason for early intrapreneurial failings was the lack of a reward structure conducive to fostering creative talents. At the same time, although an internal employee may not suffer a lack of imagination, he may not be able to say the same when it comes to sound financial judgment. CFOs are in a unique position to align reward structures with business metrics to increase the chances that innovation yields commercialization. Consider prediction markets as an example. When the wrong reward structures are applied, collective folly ensues—something political analysts have learned the hard way. Before prediction markets were embraced by innovative companies, they were the domain of politics. The Iowa Electronic Markets launched in 1988 as a means of predicting races and, through the years, has been found to be more accurate than traditional polling at least 75 percent of the time. But, in January 2008, prediction markets took a credibility hit when they gave Barack Obama a 91 percent chance of beating Hilary Clinton in the New Hampshire primary election. Clinton won. *New York Times* columnist Paul Krugman opined in his blog, "Nobody Knows Anything," the next day: "But to be more specific, the prediction markets—which you see, again and again, touted as having some mystical power to aggregate information—know no more than the conventional wisdom."[21]

As it turns out, the reason for the blatant miss had a whole lot to do with the reward structure in place. When the stakes are low, participants can recklessly gamble on wild guesses, spurring a type of groupthink if others begin to mimic the voting behavior of the crowd. The Google intrapreneurs knew that the proper reward structure would be paramount to the accuracy of their prediction market. Although the Goobles exchanged were fictitious, they wanted to incentivize participation with tangible rewards. Yet, if they simply distributed cash prizes to the most successful traders at the end of the quarter, they feared some employees might attempt to game the system and behave counterproductively. For example, they could bet big on a low-probability outcome in the hopes of it materializing (the equivalent of playing against the odds in a high-stakes game). To prevent such reckless gambling from poisoning the accuracy of the market, Google established a lottery system, whereby employees earned tickets based on their final Gooble balance at the close of the market. To increase the chances of winning the lottery, employees relied on the accuracy of their predictions. The reward structure was aligned to the needs of Google in establishing a prediction market in the first place.

Beyond aligning rewards, CFOs can establish dashboards to measure the effectiveness of innovation pursuits. Of course, CFOs are familiar with ROI as the gold standard in measuring the value of an investment. However, relying exclusively on ROI undervalues the process needed to stimulate and nurture growth ideas. CFOs can (and should) still use estimated ROI when determining which projects are most worthy of funding and resource. However, they should also demand a new set of metrics within their companies to monitor the health of the enterprise's innovation practice. Measurements like the number of ideas developed, the number contributed from staff versus those of outside partners, and the number of concepts that make it through to launch (or not) are useful leading indicators to monitor the performance of the innovation cycle. Just as CFOs monitor the sales funnel process to identify the status of opportunities through all stages of the buying cycle, an innovation funnel can do the same to monitor the success of the company in accelerating ideas to market.

- **Raise the ratio of innovators**—It is not sufficient for CFOs simply to allow innovation in their companies. They must radically champion the freeing of innovators, using internal and external sources, if they hope to discover the next growth engine in a stagnating economy. Beyond tapping their internal source of intrapreneurs, there are a host of external options available to CFOs, each with varying degrees of potential risk and reward. *Forbes* demystifies the potential sources of open innovation available to CFOs anxious for the next growth curve:[22]

  - They may take a page from Threadless, a company that asks designers to design t-shirts they would buy, gets opinions about which designs are the best, and then manufactures the t-shirts and sells them to the community that developed them. In this innovative model, the company harnesses the innovation and talents of its own prospect base to reduce development risk.

  - Those CFOs with a greater appetite for complexity may consider leveraging their own ecosystem for development. Although certainly more challenging, the potential rewards are commensurate. This is the playbook espoused by innovators like Apple and Google, companies that build a platform surrounding their products and create new value chains of developers and advertisers eager for their piece of the pie.

  - If ecosystems are too unwieldy, CFOs can always turn to co-development partners and short-term non-equity alliances. In this model, companies collaborate on a joint project with most of the risk being in the coordination of people, processes, and ideas from two or more often bureaucratic enterprises.

- CFOs can turn to innovation contests and tournaments and award prizes for the most viable concept. As mentioned earlier, InnoCentive and other crowdsourcing pioneers allow companies to tap into large groups of customers, partners, and other thinkers around the globe to tackle the knottiest of problems.

The key in using any or all of these concepts is to raise the ratio of innovators available to the company to increase the chance of a breakthrough dramatically. In addition, some of these breakthroughs can come cheap. Linux was developed by an army of volunteers that contributed more than 30 million lines of code, representing roughly 8,000 person-years of development time. Had a conventional software company attempted to invest in a more traditional way by paying its own engineers for the same, the cost would have come to roughly $1 billion.[23]

- **Leverage data analytics for compliance**—As discussed in an earlier chapter, unstructured data is on the rise, making it all the more difficult to those charged with monitoring compliance at their company. At the same time, forensic data reviews preceding and during investigations can be costly. Piper Jaffray certainly experienced this firsthand. According to Kon Leong, CEO of ZL Technologies, "The Securities and Exchange Commission, healthcare regulations, [and] the Federal Rules on Civil Procedure that weigh digital evidence equally with physical evidence are all requiring that everything be kept forever."[24]

Yet, some are using the digital wasteland of data to their advantage. Carter Malone, Vice President of Compliance at investment bank Crews & Associates, uses trigger words to alert him to potential compliance issues.

> *For me, a [bad] keyword is* guarantee. *I don't want to see that word. I can't have a salesperson, a stock broker, use* guarantee *in a communication. The other big bad word is* complaint. *If we receive a complaint from a customer, the salesperson is not supposed to communicate with that customer. The rule says the complaint has to go to the salesperson's supervisor and escalate to the compliance department.*[25]

Therefore, Malone uses specialized software from ZL Technologies proactively to find these keywords in e-mail communication at his firm. Beyond simple keyword searching, the software performs *concept searching*—looking for patterns that could signal fraudulent intent, such as the misspellings spammers use to confound spam filters. With data analytics on his side, Malone is able to review 8,000 e-mails per day, monitoring around 80 percent of his company's communications, far greater than the 20 percent requirement set by FINRA.[26] If burdened with the mandate of preserving data, CFOs can at least use analytics proactively to inspect their own digital landfills.

Since Macrae published his vision of confederations of entrepreneurs, businesses have certainly experimented with the concept with varying degrees of success. Many simply got it wrong—either attempting to shoehorn entrepreneurial spirit within a bureaucratic structure or misaligning reward structures behind counterproductive behaviors. All the while, CFOs sat in an unenviable position of measuring company performance and ensuring compliance while watching growth prospects slip away as markets constricted. But a new day is dawning for these leaders. The most progressive of them recognize their indispensible value in appropriating resources behind growth prospects. They also realize that continued cost cutting is increasingly less sustainable. Traditional models of discovering growth prospects are giving way to more progressive alternatives made possible in a connected workplace and marketplace. CFOs have the opportunity to harness internal and external resources more efficiently, thereby sweating the assets already within their control. However, if they attempt to overregulate the innovation process by exclusively holding to traditional financial metrics, they will fare no better than the many firms that failed to find Macrae's destination on their outdated roadmaps. Although CFOs may still be burdened by the reality of a "straitjacket" confining them, these new sources of innovation can at least free the inner venture capitalist. And, that may just be sufficient to unlock the next major growth market, making the CFO a major player in plotting his or her company's *destiny*, not just success.

THE INNOVATOR

One of the first things John Varvaris did when appointed CFO of Best Doctors, a network of leading doctors and specialists, was to put in place a process to support widespread company innovation. Led by Varvaris, a decision-making team made up of the company's executive team and other relevant senior leaders assemble once a month to listen to employees present their ideas for improving the company. Nothing is off limits in these meetings. According to Varvaris:

> We have a culture of experimentation; we like to try new markets, extensions of products, new distribution partners, etc., though to do it in a risk-balanced way is a challenge.[27]

The company's decision makers face this challenge head on. Given that many of these new ideas have legal or finance implications, projects that are approved to move forward are handed off to a dedicated team of project managers who involve other internal stakeholders to develop the business plan further. Varvaris says these decision gates are critical:

> It's really a series of go/no go decisions. We first look at "What do we have to do to deliver the project with low to moderate risk?" Then, if it's working, we build resources around it. That allows us to say keep going, build bigger, or stop, as the case may be.[28]

This collaborative approach to innovation is reaping benefits for the rapidly growing company. According to Varvaris, around 70 percent of pitched ideas make it to the second phase, with 20 percent of those going further. To date, some 30 projects, such as selling health insurance in Canada and the implementation of a global CRM, have gone through the committee. Looking differently at how innovation can translate to real company growth is important to Varvaris: "The goal for me is to build a dynamic infrastructure so we can tell the businesspeople to bring it on."[29]

The Endangered Species

→ *According to Korn-Ferry, 98% of executives say innovation is important for top-line growth, yet over half are less than satisfied with the level of innovation in their companies.*[1]

In his provocative 2003 article, "IT Doesn't Matter," Nicholas Carr presents a compelling case for the diminishment of IT funding and the function itself. Through a series of examples that compare IT with popular and ubiquitous infrastructural technologies like water, telephone, and power utilities, Carr makes the argument that IT rarely generates sustainable competitive advantage. In fact, the very ubiquity of IT resources renders the function inadequate as a strategic asset, given that scarcity, not ubiquity, is what sets up a firm's opportunity to generate a sustainable competitive advantage. As an example, consider the proliferation of cloud-based alternatives mentioned in an earlier chapter and how these providers now offer a viable option to an otherwise expensive IT proposition. In essence, the democratization of IT resources and the leveling of the playing field it creates remove a significant barrier to entry for firms and thereby eliminate a source of competitive advantage for the privileged few once able to attain it.

To address the new environment of IT ubiquity and commoditization, Carr offers a cogent playbook that encourages enterprises to think differently of their IT investment and resources. He encourages them to spend less on IT, citing evidence from the consulting firm Alinean comparing IT expenditures with the financial performance of 7,500 large companies with sobering results: The most conservative spenders on

IT were also the most successful. He tells companies to follow, not lead, and allow impatient competitors to experiment with new IT solutions and bear the burden of higher costs and buggier implementations as a consequence. Finally, he asserts that companies are better served focusing on defense as opposed to offense where IT is concerned. The function is best viewed through the mundane lens of mitigating risks rather than the rose-colored glasses of generating opportunities for the enterprise. Carr crisply summarizes his article as prescriptive advice to an audience of eager readers still left reeling by the devastating bubble burst of the time:

> IT management should, frankly, become boring. The key to success, for
> the vast majority of companies, is no longer to seek advantage aggressively
> but to manage costs and risks meticulously. If, like many executives, you've
> begun to take a more defensive posture toward IT in the last two years,
> spending more frugally and thinking more pragmatically, you're already
> on the right course. The challenge will be to maintain that discipline when
> the business cycle strengthens and the chorus of hype about IT's strategic
> value rises anew.[2]

In fact, Carr was prescient in his assessment of IT. For a variety of factors unforeseen at the time of his writing, including the outright disintermediation of IT to third-party providers by the very employees the function is paid to support, the CIO and his corps increasingly find themselves the endangered species of the enterprise. But, warm up the chorus, for it is the very extinction of the function that may secure its reinvented future as strategic to the enterprise.

The CIO's road to strategic relevance has been rocky at best. To Carr's point, enterprises became enamored with IT around the dawn of the personal computer in the 1980s. As Carr cites numbers from the U.S. Department of Commerce's Bureau of Economic Analysis, in 1965, less than 5 percent of the capital expenditures of American companies went to information technology. By the early 1980s, that figure had increased to 15 percent. In the early 1990s, it was at more than 30 percent. By the end of the decade, information technology comprised nearly 50 percent of a firm's capital expenditures.[3] The CIO function was lauded by self-proclaimed pioneering firms who suggested that the IT function was critical to their strategic objectives.

Yet, for all the hype, many in the IT department found themselves unable to rise in rank to the coveted executive corner office. According to a 2011 study by the Chally

Group, which surveyed top executives worldwide to better understand the leadership characteristics required for the C-Suite, just 12.8 percent of C-level executives came from the IT department. In contrast, other departments far outperformed the function in providing fertile farming ground for tomorrow's top leaders, including two functions that often suffer credibility challenges themselves: 34 percent and 24 percent of C-levels were sourced from Marketing and Human Resources, respectively.[4] It appears that the outcome has something to do with how the IT function—once eulogized as critically strategic and showered with exponential increases in company resources over several decades—has diminished in capacity and influence. The same Chally Group study found less than one-third of respondents agreeing that "developing an accurate and comprehensive overview of the business" is an essential function of the CIO. Even fewer respondents, just 22 percent, said that "creating a strategic vision" is a key role for CIOs.[5]

In stark contrast to the IT love affair and associated spending frenzy at the turn of the millennium, today's CIO finds her department the subject of relentless scrutiny—often the target of budget cuts and outsourcing plans—which is only exacerbated in a stagnating economy. According to a 2010 study by PA Consulting Group and Harvey Nash, more than 60 percent of CIOs had experienced a salary freeze since the start of the recession. One in 10 suffered a pay cut. Nearly three-fourths had been asked to cut costs to ensure organizational survival, while the same number had been asked to increase operational efficiency (the tired cliché of doing more with less). Nearly 90 percent planned to maintain or increase investments in outsourcing projects. And, the realities of the constant pressures generated a kind of death spiral to the strategic value of the function itself—more than half of respondents admitted to not setting innovation targets.[6] Carr's prescription in 2003 appeared to be reality by 2010 and the chorus was in harmony with him. In 2012, Alcatel-Lucent asked more than 200 executives if the time was finally right to reinvest in information technology, and received the following response from a small business non-IT executive, almost as if taken from Carr's playbook verbatim:

> *I do not see the need to spend the money, in these tough economic times. Besides, if you can wait, there will be a new version of Windows out, plus smartphones, tablets and cloud services are just going to get better, faster and less expensive, over time.*

Although just about every enterprise function finds itself the victim of budget pressures in today's recessionary times, the CIO and his or her team are a bit more unique. On the one hand, they must answer the call of increasingly demanding employees who view technology as indispensable to their work productivity. On the other, they must justify their very existence as they compete against external providers for the right to perform the IT function. In the heyday of the 1980s, when the CIO moniker first came into the corporate narrative, the IT department was the sole arbiter of determining how and when technology decisions were made in the enterprise. Of course, all that changed when a more adept and tech-savvy generation of workers, propelled by advanced technology options adopted in the household, demanded equal or better alternatives in the enterprise. The CIO who does not respond may find his team completely circumvented by the employees he is paid to support. All the while, budget pressures persist. While the consumerization trend has increased the burden experienced by IT managers, with nearly one in three IT employees indicating that personal technology in the workplace has led to an increase in support needs (according to the 2012 Alcatel-Lucent study), the IT operational budget per employee is at its lowest in six years, based on a 2011 assessment conducted in the Computer Economics IT Spending and Staffing Benchmarks study.[7] In an ironic twist, the people most influential in assigning budget cuts to the IT department, the CFO and his guild, are equally difficult in their expectations as internal customers of the function. A 2011 KPMG study of 444 CFOs from around the world found 52 percent of U.S. CFOs blaming their IT department for being "out of date and inflexible" when they experience less-than-ideal finance functions. Perhaps more interestingly, 73 percent of U.S. CFOs said that issues with finance-related technology and systems are the biggest reason they can't achieve their objectives.[8]

Beyond these challenges, it appears that IT departments risk being tone-deaf to the organizations they support. In the 2012 Alcatel-Lucent study, there are several cases in which IT appears out-of-sync with the rest of the business. As noted above, roughly one-third of IT personnel indicate that the support needs of the enterprise have increased with the advent of personal technology in the workplace. However, this opinion is not shared by the frontline workers they support. In fact, among that audience, only 7 percent report that they contact their IT department or provider more as a result of the consumerization trend. IT employees also hold a higher opinion of themselves than warranted as perceived by the rest of employees. In the study,

76 percent of IT employees said their department "equips employees with innovative tools, services or capabilities that foster a healthy culture." The sentiment was shared by only 45 percent of frontline employees, with another 13 percent admitting, "IT is a frustration, often a source of employee aggravation due to inferior tools, services or capabilities." Finally, in one of the bigger disconnects discovered in the study, more than one in three IT decision makers agree that managers have a right to monitor their employees at all times, compared with only 16 percent of frontline employees who find this approach acceptable.

Before being overly critical of an IT function appearing out-of-tune with the rest of its company, consider the potential reasons for the gap. It's not entirely surprising that IT decision makers would perceive an increase in support demands due to the consumerization trend or find it necessary—even a right—to keep an eye on employees at all times. After all, IT shoulders the burden of defending the enterprise's information assets. With more and more personal devices and technology making their way into the enterprise, the threat of attack rises commensurately. A 2011 global study of 250 IT decision makers by Evault found 95 percent of US respondents indicating that at least some of their company's data is on mobile devices.[9] In addition, Symantec's annual 2011 *Internet Security Threat Report* showed a 93 percent increase in mobile malware over 2010 levels.[10]

All too often, breaches occur at the hands of current or former employees or even their families, given the accessibility of information far beyond the enterprise's walls. Pfizer made unenviable headlines for three distinct security breaches occurring over a few months. In one instance, an employee had two laptops stolen from his car. In another, an employee's spouse illegally downloaded information from the company compromising the security of 17,000 employees. In yet another, a former employee stole confidential information, including names, Social Security numbers, birthdates, and banking information for 34,000 employees, former employees, and healthcare professionals.[11]

Of course, IT professionals are human too and are subject to making mistakes that, in many ways, are even more dangerous than those of the average employee. In late 2010, the Mesa County Sheriff's Department in Colorado found itself in a public relations nightmare when an IT employee inadvertently posted thousands of internal, computerized records collected over 20 years. The mistake came when the employee attempted to park files from the sheriff's records-management system on a server the man thought to be secure. Contained in the exposed files were names of confidential informants to the drug unit, e-mails between officers about crime victims, and personal information for the County's employees. Turning the situation from bad to unbelievable, the security breach was not discovered for some seven months, leaving the information exposed to being accessed "multiple" times by unauthorized parties.[12]

In addition, if not current or former employees deliberately or unintentionally exposing corporate assets for the world to discover, there's always the matter of policing employee activities that may appear harmless at face value. The consumerization trend is far more sweeping than employees simply wishing to connect personal mobile devices. Employees are transferring technology habits of all kinds from the home to the workplace. Surfing the web and engaging in personal social media comprise the metaphorical smoke break of the twenty-first century worker. In the 2012 Alcatel-Lucent study, 61 percent of frontline workers agree that taking breaks through the workday to peruse social media and personal websites makes them more productive. Most enterprises in the study share the sentiment, with more than two in three not blocking access to these leisure sites. However, such a cavalier attitude toward permissive technology usage will prove dangerous if Amit Klein is remotely accurate in his prediction of the top cybercrime trends in 2012. Klein is the CTO of the security company Trusteer and has a unique perspective given that his company is in the business of scanning for malware, spyware, and viruses across 26 million agents installed on devices in the field. He predicts that the corporate raiders of 2012 will increasingly enter the enterprise border by surreptitiously duping unsuspecting employees—those who freely engage in social media activities at all times of the day—into downloading harmful links while connected to recreational websites via the corporate network. Those links can monitor keystrokes, among other insidious activities. And, contrary to conventional wisdom that the target of these attacks is likely sitting in the corner office, Verizon reported that 80 percent of those victimized in this way are regular employees.[13]

IT employees are often the first, last, and only line of defense against attacks or leaks, a hat they may unwillingly wear, but one that helps explain, in part, the disconnect between their reality and that of the employees they support. Additionally, they are also the go-to department for enabling an increasingly mobile workforce while addressing the concerns shared by the very frontline employees asking for the flexibility. As discussed in an earlier chapter, enterprise workers in the 2012 Alcatel-Lucent study ranked the three greatest drawbacks to a mobile workforce as being increased challenges in coordination and monitoring of work (cited by 29% of respondents), difficulty of developing work relationships with coworkers (16%), and difficulty of managing employees (15%). The IT department must simultaneously create a non-invasive border surrounding the enterprise's assets while creating a permeable internal membrane that facilitates real-time interaction in complex organizations where speed is the currency.

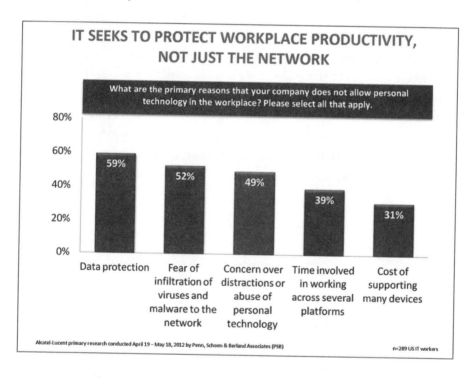

To Carr's potential dismay, IT management today is anything but boring. Quite the contrary, those finding themselves in this function today are stuck in a quandary. They can't ignore the technology appetite of a changing workforce any more than they can a new string of malicious threats crouched at their virtual threshold. They likely lack the budget to do their job effectively, yet external competitive pressures are forcing them to compete at market rates. They yearn for a more strategic focus within the enterprise, yet they can't escape the trappings of daily fire drills.

Despite the seemingly insurmountable challenges, there is at least one reason to be excited about the future of IT—not despite, but because of, the role's current metamorphosis. When asking the more than 2,500 enterprise employees in the 2012 Alcatel-Lucent study a battery of questions surrounding their perception of company success and the perception of IT within the company, some interesting correlations may be fodder for boardroom and water cooler discussion. Specifically, 74 percent of employees in companies with rapidly increasing profits, rising employee populations, and superior revenue growth agree that their IT function equips employees with innovative tools, services, or capabilities to foster a healthy culture. Only 30 percent of employees in companies on the other end of the spectrum of financial performance could say the same. Not to contradict Carr's evidence of a negative correlation between IT spend and company profitability, this is not merely about IT investment. It is much more about IT's role within the enterprise as a strategic enabler (or inhibitor) to cultural transformation and the subsequent advantage that may be gained by companies as a result.

As an alternative to Carr's prescription, we offer the following remedy for CIOs struggling to find their place in today's consumerized workplace:

- **Let your people go, but don't leave them feral**—Although it may be difficult to accept, the technology emancipation of employees has already occurred. CIOs must fundamentally rethink their position in the new value chain in which employee opinion increasingly holds sway. To do this effectively, they must redefine the current parental role occupied by many IT organizations to one of trusted business partner. The consumerization trend does not suggest that CIOs will be less relevant. However, it does require the IT function to behave in a way that showcases unique value to those it serves. For example, IT may accelerate the consumerization trend by aggregating its purchasing power to negotiate better rates or terms of service for its employees. IT managers old enough to remember the first consumerization trend in the enterprise—that of the personal computer in the 1980s—may find comfort in a strangely familiar place today. Just as the personal computer craze left many organizations spinning in a sea of fragmented platforms, the current consumerization trend has even farther-reaching consequences. IT professionals learning from past mistakes can proactively address the current trends by focusing on streamlined management capabilities that simplify internal architectures. To avoid being sucked into a less valuable tactical role, these management systems should also consider workforce monitoring capabilities (using caution so as not to be seen as surreptitiously snooping on employees) to address the very real concerns shared by employees and management as the workforce becomes more virtualized. Finally, not to understate the importance of security in this unending story, CIOs must occupy the role of guardian of corporate assets without becoming so difficult to work with as to actually encourage employees to bypass their department entirely. According to PwC, doing so requires a paradigmatic shift in defining the jurisdiction of the CIO—one from control of all things (such as business processes, compliance, security) to control over those assets most meaningful or required under law.[14] Of course, this presupposes a renegotiation with business leaders throughout the enterprise, not the least of whom is the CEO, to properly align expectations and objectives for the evolved CIO position.

However, liberating employees should not be conflated with allowing them to roam wild in the enterprise wasteland. Security issues and business process concerns notwithstanding, there is evidence to suggest that such wildly unconventional organizations perform at a lower standard compared with those with IT oversight and partnership. Specifically, in the 2012 Alcatel-Lucent study, those companies that embrace a culture where IT acts as a partner to business units represent 40 percent of the top-performing companies in the study. In contrast, those unrestricted cultures where IT policies are largely void account for only 21 percent of the elite performers.

- **Focus on your differentiation**—The latest souped-up devices in the enterprise are worth little more than paperweights if not connected to an equally high-performing network. Luckily for IT professionals, this is one technical bastion of their former role still within their grip. Although it may be relatively easy for an employee to bring her device into the workplace and bootstrap it until it works, manipulating the performance of the corporate network itself is much more difficult. Not only is IT well equipped to address the need, but also doing so will add immediate and tangible benefit to those they support. In the 2012 Alcatel-Lucent study, respondents were asked a series of questions regarding network performance in the enterprise (whether while downloading or uploading files over a fixed or wireless network). More than one out of three respondents indicated that current network performance in a variety of situations was either merely sufficient or inadequate to get their work done. Faster devices require faster networks, as the more than one in five respondents who pay for their own mobile or fixed broadband connections out-of-pocket and use them primarily for work purposes will attest. Even resourceful employees looking to cloud-based alternatives to satisfy their demand will require a more intimate understanding of how network and IT performance are linked (as mentioned in Chapter 2). By equipping employees with better network performance backed by robust SLAs to mitigate delivery or security risk, IT departments and providers will reinsert themselves into the consumerization value chain.

- **Get more political**—IT is an integral function to the operation of the enterprise. Yet, the function itself is not perceived by many of its peers as being particularly engaging, nor with a need to be. The role of IT is still largely relegated to tactical implementation, perhaps a case of the "urgent" pushing out the "important." In the Chally Group study, 70 percent of respondents indicate that staying on top of technical and business competencies is a key function for CIOs. More than half believe that performing timely and effective execution is a primary role of CIOs. In contrast, less than half say that being collaborative is a main duty for CIOs, and only 16 percent of respondents believe that these executives must inspire others and maintain leadership responsibilities. Finally, only about 10 percent say that CIOs must be politically astute.[15]

At the same time, IT decision makers tend to have an inflated view of their capabilities when it comes to collaboration. Many believe that they are working the political angle of the business to remain relevant and engaged with senior decision makers. Unfortunately, their peers aren't likely to feel the same way. In the 2012 Alcatel-Lucent study, 41 percent of business decision makers indicate a great amount of communication between the IT department and business leaders in their enterprise pertaining to how IT can help their company fulfill its goals. In contrast, 65 percent of IT decision makers feel the same. Perhaps more concerning, nearly 20 percent of business leaders say that there is at best some communication (many indicate little to none) between IT and business leaders. This compares with only 1 percent of IT decision makers rating their communication efforts so deplorably.

It goes without saying that IT needs to forge tight partnerships with senior business leaders who are indirect arbiters of if and how IT funds are authorized and distributed. However, IT has a more strategic role to play in influencing major cultural touchstones within the enterprise. To do this effectively, IT should consider new bedfellows in the organization that have an increasing dependency on the IT function—human resources, legal, and marketing. Human resources are the change agents of an organization, and, in order to attract and retain the right talent, IT policies and capabilities have a role to play. Of the more culturally progressive companies canvassed in the 2012 Alcatel-Lucent study, more than two-thirds agree that there is a connection between IT tools, services, and policies and employee recruitment and retention. This compares with only 13 percent of cultural laggards admitting the same.

Of course, policy is a necessary, although insufficient, means of influencing employee behavior. Simply having a policy is not enough and, in fact, could be dangerous if assumed as such. In a 2011 IDC study, only 40 percent of IT decision makers indicated that policy allowed workers to access non-work-related websites, yet 70 percent of workers polled admitted to doing so at work.[16] That said, there are bridges to be established between IT and Legal that can help establish new or modify fallible policies in the workplace. According to Gartner, only about half of Chief Legal Officers report having a dialogue with the CIO at least once a month. Of those who do, 76 percent reported changing their legal strategies related to IT, and more than 80 percent said they changed their corporate policies to benefit IT (compared with less than half of respondents who admitted to less frequent communication).[17] Finally, to avoid the trap of creating policies written by lawyers, for lawyers, IT departments should consult the consummate storytellers of the organization, the Marketing department, to increase the chance such policies will be readily understood by the average employee. What's more, marketers will come to rely on CIOs more than ever before for their own success, given the momentum to more effectively target prospects and customers using rich analytics across a broad range of new digital channels. Although CIOs may feel a bit out of their comfort zone with becoming more politically astute, the benefits to their organization and the cultural health of the company at large should not be underestimated.

- **Eat your own young**—The IT function is evolving, yet the old guard largely remains. CIOs must focus more than ever in attracting employees with a passion not just for technology but in how it empowers the internal customers who ultimately justify their existence. The consumerization trend can be traced to a dissatisfaction among employees of their IT's department inability or unwillingness to keep pace with ever-growing needs. Yet, many IT employees find themselves disconnected from company strategy, leaving them vulnerable to irrelevance. In the 2012 Alcatel-Lucent study, IT workers are still primarily implementers, a fact that is to be expected no matter the function as one delves into the working levels of an organization. Yet, despite the imminent threat of disintermediation facing them, more than three in five are unsure what functions of the IT department will be outsourced in the next couple of years. Although this uncertainty may be understandable given the torrid pace of change facing the function, it is disconcerting nonetheless that these implementers may find themselves the victims of blindsided displacement. The reality paints a picture in which CIOs must either upgrade the talent of their existing organizations or deliberately outsource functions to a provider with better capabilities. In either case, CIOs must "eat their own young" of established IT professionals to address the new needs of today's workforce.

  Upgrading talent involves more than competitive compensation. There are intangible rewards for which many IT professionals hunger to increase their own abilities and relevance in a dynamic workplace. According to a 2011 Forrester study among 125 top IT professionals, nearly 80 percent report that having interesting work to do is a significant motivator—the most-cited factor. Base compensation came in fourth on the list behind autonomy and work/life balance. Among those younger than 45, employee development carries greater importance, reflecting an opportunity for CIOs to nurture an enthusiastic population of IT professionals eager to up their game.[18]

  Yet, outsourcing cannot be eliminated from the equation. If not to quickly scale capabilities to a third party better able to deliver, the challenge in recruiting the next wave of IT employees may make outsourcing the only option for enterprises. According to a group backed by luminaries including Microsoft's Steve Ballmer, JP Morgan Chase's Jamie Dimon, and New York City Mayor

Michael Bloomberg, "US companies are hungry for talent with degrees in STEM (Science, Technology, Engineering and Math)—these jobs are increasing three times faster than jobs in the rest of the economy. However, these positions are the hardest to fill because of the dearth of native-born Americans with these degrees." The group estimates a shortage of 224,000 hi-tech workers in the United States by 2018 and is calling on Congress to enforce some changes in immigration policy that will place the country on an even footing with its global peers.[19] Until then, CIOs and company executives may find outsourcing one practical solution to an immediate and growing problem.

Regardless of how the IT function is reinvented—through internal development programs, outsourcing alternatives, or a combination of both—the approach is insignificant compared with the outcome. That is, as discovered in the 2012 Alcatel-Lucent study, the top-performing companies are neither more nor less likely to outsource compared with their counterparts. Where they did separate from their failing peers is in their overall satisfaction with the IT service—whether outsourced or insourced.

The road ahead for IT employees is unpaved and winding. More interestingly, it is riddled with fissures that create the next chasm within the IT profession itself—a type of digital divide in how the function is perceived by those who occupy it. In *CIO Magazine*'s 2012 "State of the CIO" survey among 596 IT leaders, more than 80 percent expect that the global recession will have a negative impact on their organization within the next three years. However, CIOs operating as strategic business partners (a minority of the sample) are more likely to predict a good year ahead, confident in their abilities to mitigate risks and commanding a higher salary compared with their tactical counterparts. The most business-savvy CIOs in the population are significantly more likely to report to the CEO (60% vs. 38%), sit on the business executive committee (85% vs. 66%), and lead a non-IT area (68% vs. 57%). For these executives, they have secured their seat in the C-Suite and are acknowledged as primary drivers of the enterprise's competitive future.[20] In a 2011 study with comparable findings by Deloitte among 1,000 IT executives asking how they perceive their role in the enterprise: 45 percent of respondents view the CIO as an IT steward, responsible for mundane (although necessary) activities like keeping the lights on and leveraging existing IT assets. The same number see the CIO as a strategist who translates business needs into IT action and ensures that IT is relevant and keeps pace with business leaders. Most interestingly, a very small minority (just 10%) view the CIO as a revolutionary, who uncovers new markets and revenue streams, translates IT momentum into business action, and interacts with C-level executives.[21]

And, in a move that would likely not please Carr, Gartner finds that despite fears in the economy, by more than 2:1, CEOs say that they will increase IT investment in 2012, rather than cut it.[22] While more head honchos of the enterprise are reinvesting in a function that has suffered whiplash between praise and criticism in recent decades, the CIO may find his true strategic value displaced by the boss himself. That is, when CIOs focus on the wrong side of the digital divide—consumed by distracting fire drills at the expense of connecting their role to the strategic outcomes of their companies—the CEO steps in to fill the void. According to Gartner, one-third of CEOs say that they are their company's innovation leader. Only 4 percent would give the same credit to the CIO.

CIOs are the organization's endangered species, subject to complete bypass by their own internal customers or marginalized to tactical activities by their peers and leaders. Although CIOs are challenged, there is evidence that a reinvention of the role is in order. In fact, there is a fairly clear divide among CIOs who have already shed their purely technical skin to evolve as business leaders capable of effecting tangible cultural change, often a precursor to financial success. Perhaps the richest irony of all is that those who embrace the extinction of their role will finally be free to evolve their purpose and relevance within the enterprise.

CHIEF IDLE OFFICER

LinkedIn, the social media platform designed for professionals, reported a security breach in which a hacker absconded with at least 6.5 million passwords in June 2012. The company aggressively responded with a series of initiatives, including the disabling of suspected compromised accounts and conspicuous notification on its website encouraging members to reset their passwords. As with any breach of this magnitude, LinkedIn found itself the subject of headlines for days following the episode. In one such follow-up story, it was uncovered that the company, whose very existence trades on the secure information of its members, itself lacked a Chief Information Officer or Chief Information Security Officer. When asked, a LinkedIn spokesperson replied, "We don't currently have executives with those specific titles, but David Henke, senior vice president, operations, oversees the functions." [23]

It seems that the CIO function is perhaps more endangered than originally thought, with some companies (even those that would appear to have the greatest need) choosing to forego the position entirely. Perhaps LinkedIn is rethinking its approach given the attack. If so, let's hope that it designs the function to be as innovative as the company it represents.

3

The New Face of Business and Industry

The Culture Recipe

→ *According to Bain & Company, fewer than 15% of companies succeed in building high-performance cultures.*[1]

In February of 2012, more than 2 million Americans quit their jobs, the most since November of 2008. The vast majority simply gave perfunctory notice to their employers before moving quietly to their next ambition.[2] In more than a few cases, the real reasons for departure may never have been disclosed, because employees are often loath to burn bridges with former employers, especially in a job market still recovering from the recession. But, in March, one U.S. employee resigned his post in a decidedly noticeable way. In a *New York Times* Op-Ed piece entitled, "Why I Am Leaving Goldman Sachs," Greg Smith, the firm's Executive Director and head of the United States equity derivatives business in Europe, the Middle East, and Africa, offered more than 1,000 copious words as to his reasons for leaving his employer of nearly 12 years. Smith could hardly be described as an average employee, or human being, for that matter. He attained a full scholarship to go from South Africa to Stanford University, was a Rhodes Scholar national finalist, and a bronze medalist at the Maccabiah Games in Israel (known to fans as the "Jewish Olympics"). At Goldman Sachs, Smith's accomplishments were equally impressive. He spent more than a decade recruiting and mentoring employees. He was one of only 10 employees (out of the company's more than 30,000) selected to represent the company in its recruiting video, played on every college campus visited around the world. He managed the firm's summer internship program in sales and trading in New York for the 80 college students selected out of the thousands who applied. In short, by all appearances, Smith was a model employee, one loyal to his company and passionate about recruiting and training the next crop of leaders.

To compel such a dedicated employee to quit, yet alone broadcast his reasons to a world of strangers, is significant, to say the least. Yet, Goldman Sachs managed to instigate one of its most fervent supporters to extreme measures nonetheless. As Smith opined, the reason for his departure had nothing to do with compensation or even a better opportunity at a place promising greener pastures. The reason for his disgust and ultimate departure came down to Goldman Sachs's culture. He wrote:

> It might sound surprising to a skeptical public, but culture was always a vital part of Goldman Sachs's success. It revolved around teamwork, integrity, a spirit of humility, and always doing right by our clients. The culture was the secret sauce that made this place great and allowed us to earn our clients' trust for 143 years. It wasn't just about making money; this alone will not sustain a firm for so long. It had something to do with pride and belief in the organization. I am sad to say that I look around today and see virtually no trace of the culture that made me love working for this firm for many years. I no longer have the pride, or the belief.[3]

If any leaders in the business community were themselves skeptical about the role of culture in affecting company performance, Smith's piece—and its immediate negative $2.15 billion effect on Goldman Sachs's market value[4]—gave them reason to pause. In a study of more than 100 business leaders and human resources (HR) professionals administered a few months following the public Op-Ed resignation, three out of four respondents believed corporate reputation to be substantially driven by internal corporate culture, yet only 5 percent thought their organization's culture strong enough to preclude reputational crisis, like the one experienced by Goldman Sachs. Of the sample, more than three-fourths believed that Smith's letter had a negative impact on Goldman Sachs' reputation, only 3 percent attributed it to an isolated incident on the part of a single disgruntled employee at the company, and two-thirds expected to see more of the same for other companies in the future (a sobering possibility given that only 74 percent believed their own employees were committed to their company's culture).[5] Indeed, there are more Greg Smiths walking the halls of businesses who have also lost their pride in their companies. According to the 2010 General Social Survey, nearly 10 percent of people are not proud of their employers.[6]

If such an event is likely to be repeated, companies should learn a lesson from Smith and Goldman Sachs before finding themselves the next potential target of an Op-Ed excoriation. According to Smith, the defining moment when he realized his time was up was when, "I realized I could no longer look students in the eye and tell them what a great place this was to work." [7] Indeed, finding that special *je ne sais quois* that makes a company special has been the Holy Grail eluding firms for decades. One organization, in particular, has a unique perspective on demystifying what makes a company great. Since 1980, the Great Place to Work Institute has made it its mission to build a better society by helping companies transform their workplaces. Committed to this goal, the Institute has studied thousands of businesses and surveyed millions of employees to find the recipe that defines a great workplace. Each year, it publishes its results in a stack ranking of the top businesses to work for in the United States and many other countries. The list includes small and large enterprises across a wide range of industries experiencing different degrees of growth. On it are companies that pay top dollar for talent, share their profits with employees, and offer some of the most sensational perks imaginable (including onsite day cares, gymnasiums, café bars, and concierge services). But, although any of these benefits would be desirable to the average employee, the Institute has determined that none really matters when it comes to determining what makes a workplace great. As it turns out, the complicated recipe in creating a work environment worthy of being considered among the top in the country comes down to one essential ingredient—trust. According to the Institute:

> We know that trust is the single most important ingredient in making a workplace great. Our data show that building workplace trust is the best investment your company can make, leading to better recruitment, lower turnover, greater innovation, higher productivity, more loyal customers and higher profits. [8]

Trust is a currency. It is traded, accrued, and lost. In Smith's case, he lamented Goldman Sachs's erosion of trust among its client base. In the Institute's findings, internal trust yields dividends to companies in other performance categories. However, when contemplating esoteric terms like *trust*, the challenges in measuring exactly what a company gets in return can be difficult at best. Fortunately, the

Institute's decades of research provide an arsenal of results whereby intangible cultural characteristics, like trust, can be quantified. Furthermore, to satiate critics quick to dismiss such fluffy terms as irrelevant to a firm's going concern, the Institute and others have measured the financial impacts associated with healthy cultures. Researchers at the Wharton School of Business compared the stock performance of companies making the Institute's list against their peers over a period of 25 years. Even when controlling for mitigating factors like industry performance, risk, outliers, and firm characteristics, the study found that companies on the Institute's list generated statistically significantly higher stock returns (2.4%–3.7% per year) than their counterparts—an outcome based on the cultures of these great places to work.[9] At the same time, other esteemed lists of companies that use more socially acceptable business criteria, like financial metrics, cannot claim the benefit of longitudinal performance discovered in the Wharton analysis. In fact, even the seemingly indomitable monoliths on the Fortune 1000 list have not benefited from the same success, with approximately 70 percent of companies expected to be replaced within a decade.[10] Although surprising, it appears that soft cultural metrics are actually the leading, lasting, and predictive indicators to financial performance.

Yet, despite its importance, culture is easily one of the most misunderstood aspects of a firm. Academic definitions suggest that it is a collective framework of attitudes, beliefs, behavioral norms, and expectations. Still others put it in simpler terms. Bain & Company succinctly define culture in this way: "A company's culture is essentially the organization's soul, shaped through success and setback." They attribute it to the way employees behave in an organization when they think no one is watching. They metaphorically describe it as the company's fingerprint—something unique to every firm and the singular quality protected from competitive duplication. As Herb Kelleher, founder of Southwest Airlines, once said, "Everything [in our strategy] our competitors could copy tomorrow. But they can't copy the culture—and they know it." [11]

Still, the vast majority of firms fail in building high-performance cultures, perhaps by underestimating the role that culture plays, relegating it as the exclusive domain of a human resources team or miscalculating the route to getting there. The perceptual gap between employees and management is sufficient to throw well-intentioned companies off the track of cultural success. As an example, in a 2012 Deloitte study of more than 1,000 employees and 300 managers, the latter cohort ranked competitive compensation and financial performance as the top factors influencing work culture. In contrast, regular communication and accessibility to management topped the list of most important cultural building blocks for employees.[12] Employees get that the thousands of horizontal and vertical connections made each day form the prism through which culture is refracted. As the Deloitte study shows, they value these interactions. And, as discussed in Chapter 4, relationships built and nurtured over time have the propensity to build *trust*, the critical ingredient to a healthy culture, per the Institute's battery of research.

Technology is playing a part in determining how these interactions are created, nurtured, or thwarted. However, technology no more defines culture than do the ostentatious amenities and top compensation packages from the Institute's greatest places to work. The trouble is that some leaders are turning to technology as a poor substitute for a rich foundation of cultural values, relying on its usefulness in building connections that are rendered meaningless without broader company context. Consider that 41 percent of executives in the Deloitte study believed social media to be important in building and maintaining workplace culture, yet only 21 percent of employees felt the same way.[13]

If technology is not eulogized for its capacity to build connections effortlessly, it is otherwise vilified for enabling an always-on work culture that never rests. In 2006, Columbia University economist Sylvia Ann Hewlett looked at "extreme jobs," those that required 73 hours a week or more of work. She found that nearly half of the managers in top multinational companies had them, and she blamed technology, at least in part, for enslaving a population of work drones, "Driven by globalization and always-on technology, increasing amounts of upper-echelon workers are giving huge amounts of their hearts and minds to the job." And, despite the increased hours, multiple studies have failed to find a positive correlation between labor input and output.[14]

Inspired to understand the complexities associated with technology's role (or lack thereof) in facilitating culture—by reducing organizational friction, increasing workplace flexibility, or disrupting the delicate work-life balance—the 2012 Alcatel-Lucent study canvassed more than 2,800 U.S. employees and decision makers. It asked a series of questions about the cultural attributes of the respondent's company (including, but not limited to, how decisions are made, rewards are dispensed, communication flows, values are modeled, strategy is clarified, and technology is embraced) and clustered the responses into behavioral segments that define organizational culture as follows:

- **Dinosaur organizations**—These represent 15 percent of the population and are characterized by uncommunicative upper management, a lack of strategic planning, non-established company values, and a very unhelpful IT organization that is viewed as a cost center with little to no interaction with other departments.

- **Stodgy and strict organizations**—These comprise nearly 23 percent of the population and have strictly defined hierarchies that address issues ahead of time and with lots of management and peer oversight. These companies have very established values and primarily use an analytic approach to decision making. Employees are afforded very little technology or web freedoms, such as those associated with personal devices or applications in the workplace or flexible work arrangements offered through telecommuting benefits.

- **Top-heavy bureaucracies**—These represent more than 9 percent of companies and are depicted by free-flowing hierarchies with no entrenched values or ways of doing things. They are characterized by considerable internal competition between employees and departments with commensurate oversight. In these companies, IT is fairly isolated from other departments but is also seen as helpful.

- **Unrestricted companies**—These are companies with relaxed hierarchies, risk-taking cultures, and unrestricted web and technology policies. They comprise more than 27 percent of the population, and their employees consider their cultures to be fairly healthy.

- **Cultural gurus**—These represent more than 25 percent of the population. Employees at these companies evaluate their cultures as healthy. Upper management is communicative, the companies address issues with strategic planning, and IT is an extremely engaged and helpful strategic asset to the firm.

Beyond measuring the intangible qualities comprising a company's culture, the study also evaluated the financial success of firms. Although respondents were selected from a variety of functions and levels in the organization, all had to be familiar with their company's financial performance (including directional trends in revenue, profitability, and employee growth). When mapping the impact of cultural characteristics on financial results, the 2012 Alcatel-Lucent study validates the work done by the Institute, Wharton, and others in confirming culture as an essential component of success. Specifically, 50 percent of failing companies (those characterized by poor performance across a wide range of financial indicators) are dinosaurs. This compares to just 8 percent of cultural gurus finding themselves in a comparably abysmal financial situation. In contrast, 40 percent of the top-performing financial companies are cultural gurus compared with only 7 percent of dinosaurs finding themselves in such fortune. Clearly, although culture is a predictive value for success, it does not render an organization bulletproof to external pressures. As the Alcatel-Lucent data demonstrates, any organization can find itself the victim (or beneficiary) of market conditions. However, the Wharton data takes a longitudinal view of company success over time to compensate for such variability and again proves the critical role of culture. Where the 2012 Alcatel-Lucent study is potentially helpful is in going beyond correlating cultural attributes with financial success to determine the habits of highly successful companies and their approach in adopting technology. Although trust is the essential ingredient for any successful culture, the top-performing companies in the 2012 Alcatel-Lucent study appeared to be using it as part of the following recipe:

- **Successful companies place high-end mobile technology in the hands of their employees**—Employees at successful companies are much more likely to use mobile technology for work purposes. In particular, they have a greater propensity to use 4G LTE devices (4th Generation, Long Term Evolution—the next generation of mobile broadband services) and tablets. Such a technology philosophy is particularly attractive among younger workers and those about to enter the workforce ranks, the digital natives who have never known a life without mobility. Beyond simply being more inclined to encourage wireless in the workplace, successful companies are more likely to pay for such services on behalf of their employees. As such, these companies are characterized by a more mobile workforce, with nearly one in three employees classified as heavy telecommuters, based on a set of criteria evaluating how much time is spent away from a traditional office. But one cannot infer causality from correlation (in other words: Do companies with a more mobile workforce pay for these services out of need? or Does equipping the workforce with these services free them to be more mobile?). However, although correlation does not imply causation, there is evidence to support that leading companies are more optimistic about the opportunities that a mobile workforce affords. Specifically, nearly two in five dinosaurs indicate that more people working remotely would have a negative impact on company culture, compared with just one in five gurus. Furthermore, employees at these culturally advanced companies are more likely to feel liberated, rather than enslaved, by the technology that surrounds them. Nearly nine in 10 of those employed by gurus agree that technology gives them the freedom to work when and where they want. In contrast, just over 60 percent of employees at dinosaurs feel the same.

- **Employees at successful firms are leveraging personal technology**—Employees at successful firms are much more likely to use web solutions offered by Dropbox, Amazon, and others. They are also more likely to use cloud-based services (50% frequently use the cloud compared with 39% of the average). And, rather than retaliate against or resist the consumerization trend, the IT departments of these firms are willingly embracing it—60 percent of IT professionals in successful firms indicate that the migration of personal technologies into the workplace has allowed them to be more strategic, because they are no longer consumed with purchasing and maintaining hardware for employees in the company (compared with 45% of average IT professionals who feel the same way).

- **IT departments at successful companies equip employees with innovative tools to help foster a healthy culture**—Nearly three in four successful companies consider IT essential in enabling culture, as opposed to just 30 percent of those in failing companies—a noble cause given that employees at successful firms are almost four times more likely to say they have a very healthy corporate culture than those at failing companies. Nearly 70 percent of IT departments at successful companies saw budget increases in the past year compared with 42 percent in other companies. Again, although causation cannot be inferred, it is not farfetched to believe that these increases have at least something to do with IT's esteemed value in the company. In fact, nearly three in five top-performing companies indicate that senior management is very involved in adopting new IT solutions, compared with less than one in three failing companies.

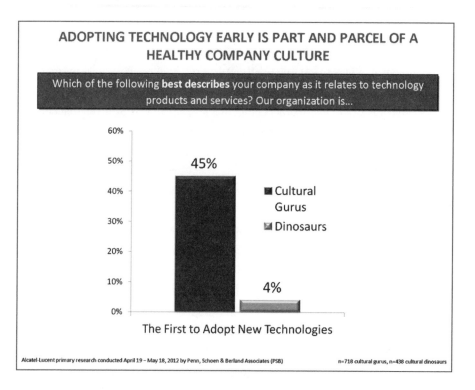

three in five top-performing companies indicate that senior management is

- **Successful companies seek out leaders with poise, not drones**—There are considerable differences between attributes that are considered attractive by successful and failing companies when evaluating candidates for employment. Whereas successful companies find confidence (cited by 29% of these respondents) and leadership (28%) desirable employee characteristics, in failing companies, neither quality is highly valued (confidence was mentioned by 5% of respondents and leadership by 18%). Respondents in failing enterprises value people capable of following direction, with nearly two in five indicating this as the most desirable quality in a new recruit. These struggling companies are more likely to offer technology to senior leaders, rather than equip their front line with the tools and technology that may be needed.

- **In successful companies, HR and IT communicate to improve the culture as well as employee recruitment and retention**—Almost three in five HR decision makers in successful cultures say that there is a connection between themselves and IT to work at improving the culture (compared with less than half of all HR decision makers, on average, who state the same). Beyond culture, HR leaders at successful companies also recognize the role that technology can play in helping to attract and retain employees. Two in three HR decision makers from the most successful companies recognize this connection; only two in five at other companies see the same. And, given that culture, recruitment, and retention are too important to be relegated merely to IT and HR, business decision makers in successful companies also see the linkage. Nearly two in three business decision makers in successful companies admit to a great deal of communication with IT, compared with less than one-half in other companies.

- **Successful companies have employees who know when to take a break**—Almost seven in 10 employees at the most successful companies use social media and other web activities as a valuable break to make them more productive. In addition, as an indirect gauge of internal trust, seven in 10 also agree that allowing their coworkers to do the same provides a deserved breather. Trust is bidirectional between management and employees as well, with 80 percent of cultural gurus affording some technology and web freedom to employees, compared with less than two out of three dinosaurs.

- **Successful companies have forward-leaning cultures that break from the norm**—These companies respond well to changes in their market environment and involve many people in the decision-making process, thereby increasing the likelihood of diverse viewpoints and mitigating the risk of poor decisions more typical of homogeneous, entrenched organizations (as discussed in Chapter 4). They encourage employees to take calculated risks without fear of reprimand in the event of failure. They dispense rewards based on clearly defined measurements of employee performance, not subjective management evaluations. They use a deliberate planning process to anticipate future needs. Finally, they view IT as a strategic asset, capable of delivering competitive advantage, and offer employees the flexibility to work from wherever and whenever they choose. In addition, to relieve the concern expressed by Hewlett and her ilk, it appears that these companies have employees who are indeed working smarter with the technology, not harder. Employees at successful companies in the sample indicate working an average of 44 hours per week, compared with 42.5 hours for the average employee at a failing enterprise.

There is much to be learned by watching successful companies. Despite the uniqueness of culture in the mix, there is no doubt that this intangible quality has a very meaningful and enduring impact on a company's success. Inherent in successful cultures is trust, and, although technology can be the channel through which it is bestowed vertically and horizontally within an organization, it is merely that—a channel. Culture is much bigger than technology, although the latter certainly plays a part as the walls of the enterprise are increasingly virtualized. Although the forward-leaning companies in the Alcatel-Lucent study provide a recipe of sorts for those interested in mimicking their success, any attempt to do so is futile if the primary ingredient of trust is missing.

Even when trust is present, cultural recipes are not tweaked overnight. It takes time and fortitude to reverse deeply entrenched beliefs, attitudes, and ways of an organization—something consultants in the field attempting to assist companies longing for healthier cultures know all too well. Peter Bregman is one such advisor to companies. He points to a study in the late 1970s by University of Illinois researcher Leann Lipps Birch, in which she conducted a series of experiments on children to see what would get them to eat vegetables they disliked. Explanations as to why these vegetables were healthy for the child were inconsistent in getting results. The same goes for proper modeling by an adult to encourage the child to consume the distasteful foods. As Bregman explains, there was one consistent way in which Birch was able to attain success in her goal:

> Birch found one thing that worked predictably. She put a child who didn't like peas at a table with several other children who did. Within a meal or two, the pea-hater was eating peas like the pea-lovers. Peer pressure. We tend to conform to the behavior of the people around us. Which is what makes culture change particularly challenging because everyone is conforming to the current culture.[15]

Indeed, culture is a reflection of the human beings comprising it. And, although peer pressure is yet one more ingredient in the cultural soup of a firm, a winning recipe is possible and profitable for those committed to success.

RETAILING CULTURE

Zappos, the online retailer that has captivated fans with its extraordinary approach to customer service, has also generated rabid interest for its innovative culture. CEO Tony Hsieh offers his philosophical approach to management, "It's about giving employees permission and encouraging them to just be themselves." His company walks the talk, documenting 10 core values that are not management lip service for a corporate plaque but are paramount tenets to the way employees are recruited and retained by the company. Each recruit goes through at least two rounds of interviews—one with the hiring manager to determine technical qualifications and another by the HR team to assess cultural fit. As Hsieh states, "Basically what we're looking for are peoples [sic] whose personal values match our corporate values. They're just naturally living the brand. Wherever they are whether they're in the office or off the clock."[16] The company is so passionate about finding folks who embody its cultural values, it actually offers new trainees an incentive to quit—just one more example of a radical approach by an unorthodox leader.

Zappos is relying on its culture to deliver bottom-line results in more ways than one. Taking another unconventional page from his management playbook, Hsieh actually offers seminars and other training curricula to companies looking to replicate Zappos's not-so-secret recipe. The company offers other firms, including competitors, the opportunity to learn from its unique management principles. In a customer service environment where turnover is a constant challenge, Hsieh has managed to attract and retain some of the best professionals in the industry. He has done so without exorbitant compensation packages, learning that employees value freedom more than paychecks. Zappos employees may chat for hours with customers, write thank you notes, send flowers, or even direct customers to competitive websites in the event that an item is out of stock. As such, the company has been able to weather the economic turbulence better than its competitors.[17] It's generous enough to offer them a page from the cookbook that has made it so successful.

The Small Business Dream

→ *According to Citibank, 73% of small business owners would start their business again and 64% would recommend entrepreneurship as a career to their children.*[1]

Benjamin Franklin famously said, "In this world nothing can be said to be certain, except death and taxes." In Washington, DC these days, there is one more certainty to add to the list—government gridlock. In 2011, as the world watched, the U.S. government took the global stage in a spectacular display of dysfunctional stalemate, as Democrats and Republicans publicly squabbled about the right way forward to increase the country's debt limit and prevent the superpower from defaulting on its loans. Not surprisingly, citizen confidence in and approval for government politicians seemed to be in a freefall. According to a *USA TODAY*/Gallup Poll, approval for Republican congressional members had sunk to 28 percent; Democratic congressional approval wasn't much better at 33 percent; and Obama himself was not immune to the damage, with just 45 percent of Americans approving of the President's performance at the time. As one self-described Republican voter from Utah so eloquently put it, "They're [the Government] screwing up right and left.... All they're doing is arguing among themselves and not getting anything done." [2]

Alas, although political impasses have consumed politicians in unending discord, there is one economic objective it seems both Democrats and Republicans can rally behind—that of preserving the growth of small businesses in the United States. According to President Obama, "Small businesses create two out of every three jobs in this economy, so our recovery depends on them." Republican Presidential candidate Mitt Romney couldn't agree more, stating on the stump, "My job, if I'm President, among other things, is to make sure that we are the best country in the world for small business."[3] Indeed, even big businesses are joining the crusade. In announcing a program that would offer $10 million in credits to small business advertisers on Facebook, Chief Operating Officer Sheryl Sandberg said, "Small businesses are the backbone of the American economy."[4]

Small businesses are about as American as motherhood and apple pie. Aside from owning a home, starting a small business is the epitome of the American dream. Politicians, eager to reflect the ideals of the constituency that elected them, idolize small businesses as the engine behind economic growth and, in particular, job creation. The phrase "small business" appeared in the Congressional Record more than 10,000 times in the past two years, outranking references made to the very public debt limit debacle by comparison. It appears that Congress's fascination with the topic is warranted, at least insofar as the phrase "small business" is sufficient on its own to evoke emotion. According to Frank Luntz, GOP pollster and language specialist,

> I've tested language. I've tested "small-business owner," "job creator," "innovator," "entrepreneur" and nothing tests better than "small-business owner" because it represents all of those. It represents someone willing to take a risk. It represents hard work and perseverance.[5]

Indeed, small businesses are known for their sweat equity, with a majority of Americans (59%) believing it difficult for people like them to start a company, compared with only 36 percent who thought otherwise.[6]

If starting a business is difficult, staying in business is even more so, according to data from the Small Business Administration (SBA). Half of startups fail within the first five years. Less than one in five make it 10 years. Indeed, in the 2012 Alcatel-Lucent study of more than 2,500 enterprise respondents, small businesses (five to 99 employees) made up nearly half of the failing companies, as self-reported through a battery of financial metrics covering revenue, profitability, and employee growth. In contrast, they represented less than one in five of the top-performing companies by way of financial success. Proving that these top performers are the exception and not the rule, two in five business "exits" in 2009 were the result of bankruptcies, rather than successful acquisitions or initial public offerings, according to a report by the Center for Venture Research at the University of New Hampshire's Whittemore School of Business and Economics. The trend is even more sobering, because just 27 percent of exits suffered the same misfortune in 2007.[7]

Still, some 600,000 new businesses are founded each year,[8] despite the challenging odds. According to research by Yahoo! and Ipsos, entrepreneurs shoulder significant risk to pursue a personal passion. Twice as many small business owners than non-business owners say they are doing their dream job. Nearly 80 percent say the best thing about owning their own business is a flexible work schedule. Even among those who have not yet started a business, 61 percent say they want to do so such that they can earn a living while fueling personal passions.[9] In addition, government lauds these indomitable risk takers for being the economic engine behind job creation—that is, until new data surfaces that challenges the veracity of this claim and, accordingly, the government's love affair with small businesses.

It's not that small businesses don't create two out of three jobs as President Obama claimed; it's what's behind those numbers that reveals a different story. According to Kelly Edmiston, a senior economist at the Federal Reserve Bank of Kansas City, the claim "masks a huge amount of people being hired and let go." He asserts that small-business jobs are far less stable than those within large enterprises precisely because of those high failure rates facing startups in their initial years.[10] According to Edmiston, 22 percent of staff in companies with fewer than 100 employees quit or are fired, compared with only 8 percent of those with 2,000 or more workers. Hourly wages are also more lucrative in larger enterprises, earning employees $27 per hour, on average, compared with $16 per hour for employees in companies of less than 100 employees. Companies with more than 100 employees are also more likely to offer superior benefits to their workforce when compared with smaller enterprises.[11]

Part of the challenge facing small companies is their lack of productivity efficiencies—more common in larger firms able to acquire economies of scale. In fact, most small businesses occupy the services sector, such as restaurants, skilled craftsmen, independent retailers, and personal service providers—areas where economies of scale are typically not realized as the size of the firm grows. According to an analysis of Census data by Erik Hurst and Ben Pugsley of the University of Chicago, in the United States there were roughly 6 million companies with workers on the payroll in 2007—90 percent of which employed fewer than 20 people. Collectively, this lion's share of companies accounted for just 20 percent of all jobs. And, according to Hurst and Pugsley, these firms had no intention of growing their payroll in the first place. Eight in 10 small businesses that remained in business from 2000 to 2003—the most recent data for Hurst and Pugsley's analysis—did not add a single employee.[12] Their data is corroborated by economist Scott Shane at Case Western Reserve University, who found that, among small businesses in their second year of business, more jobs were lost to bankruptcy than were added by those still operating. The same held true in years three, four, and five.[13]

But, perhaps the most damning evidence to cast doubt on small business as an employment engine comes from the agency that purported the two-in-three job creation claim in the first place—the Bureau of Labor Statistics. In February of 2012, the agency released figures that challenged its original and longstanding assertion. "The most growth in employment has been in large firms," said Nathan Clausen, the Bureau's economist in charge of the development of new statistics. In looking at data spanning April 1990 through March 2011, large company employment (at those companies with at least 500 employees) rose 29 percent, while employment at smaller companies increased by less than half as much. The data was released by a separate unit of the Bureau of Labor Statistics than the one founding the original two-in-three job creation claim, a discrepancy the agency attributes to the way businesses are classified by each division. Even for the incongruities of the claims, both groups agree that the proportion of private sector employees working for large companies has been steadily rising in recent decades—at a much faster growth than that experienced by small companies—tarnishing, in part, the lustrous image of small businesses as the backbone of employment growth.[14]

Before casting aspersions on these entrepreneurs for failing to create as many jobs as once thought, consider the risks they incur for doing so. Nearly 80 percent of small companies (those with annual incomes between $10,000 and $10 million) have no payroll at all.[15] They represent sole proprietorships of committed individuals resolute in following their passion or destined to pursue an entrepreneurial path for lack of any other viable employment option in a tough economy. To this latter point, a 2011 survey among 1,700 small business owners by the company Webs found nearly two in five respondents to be unwitting entrepreneurs forced to start their own business because of a layoff or inability to find full-time employment.[16] Whatever accidental or deliberate causes behind these ventures, many small business owners have no intention or desire to hire employees. Even among those who do have such aspirations for growth, a soured economy is forcing other plans. Although the same Webs study revealed nearly half of respondents believing the economy would bounce back in the next few quarters, virtually the same number admitted delaying hiring someone because of the recession.[17]

Perhaps there is no single function more complicated to a small business owner than that of IT. If the vast majority of small business owners will not or cannot hire staff, they are certainly not keen to inflate their payroll with IT professionals who may prove indispensable one moment and extraneous the next. Kevin Kay, owner of a South Carolina healthcare company with 53 employees, expresses the sentiment shared by his entrepreneurial ilk: "I don't have an IT department. It's not a luxury I can afford." [18] Yet, these same small businesses also can't afford to ignore the significant disadvantage they carry against their larger competitors when it comes to employee productivity. According to a study by economists Rafael La Porta of Dartmouth College and Harvard University's Andrei Schleifer, in developing countries, large companies are far more productive—with value added per worker an average of 59 percent higher.[19]

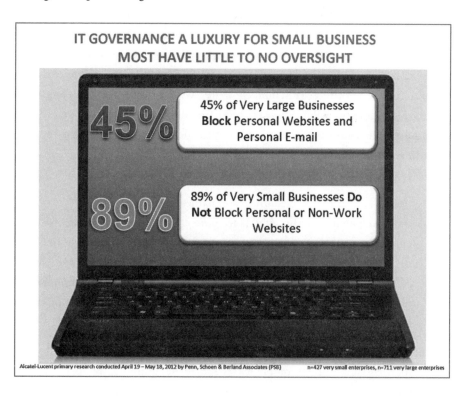

IT GOVERNANCE A LUXURY FOR SMALL BUSINESS
MOST HAVE LITTLE TO NO OVERSIGHT

45%
45% of Very Large Businesses **Block** Personal Websites and Personal E-mail

89%
89% of Very Small Businesses **Do Not** Block Personal or Non-Work Websites

Alcatel-Lucent primary research conducted April 19 – May 18, 2012 by Penn, Schoen & Berland Associates (PSB)   n=427 very small enterprises, n=711 very large enterprises

Luckily for small enterprises, technology offers advantages to help narrow La Porta and Schleifer's productivity gap. Beyond the technology, a vibrant IT services market consisting of some 300,000 independent IT consultants and another 114,000 small IT companies[20] stands ready to support entrepreneurs who would rather save their payroll dollars for other needs. IT outsourcing is a trend that is creeping into mid-sized businesses as well. According to the research firm IDC, U.S. businesses with fewer than 500 employees spent roughly $23.5 billion on IT services in 2011, a figure that is expected to grow to $27.2 billion by 2015. As proof that outsourcing is more than just a passing trend or one simply relegated to small and medium companies, spending on IT services by U.S. companies of all sizes now exceeds $300 billion, has been growing an average of more than 3 percent in the past five years, and is 55 percent more than these companies spend on computer hardware and software combined, according to Gartner.[21] Whereas this is an impressive market for companies of all sizes, the pressure among very small enterprises to compete on a level playing field with their larger counterparts is readily ameliorated in a booming IT services market. The 2012 Alcatel-Lucent study finds very small companies with a payroll (those between five and 19 employees) having the highest incidence of IT outsourcing. Specifically, nearly three in 10 of these very small companies admit to currently outsourcing their entire IT function, compared with just 11 percent of companies composed of more than 100 employees reporting the same. And, the complexity of selecting and managing these outsourced IT providers is outweighed by the benefits, according to the majority of subjects in the 2012 Alcatel-Lucent study. When asked to choose which statement came closer to their view:

- Access to IT through outsourced companies has increased the opportunities for my company by allowing us to more effectively compete against large enterprises without requiring us to maintain significant IT staff or technology; or
- Access to IT through outsourced companies has introduced new complexities for my company since we must closely manage a third party and don't have as much control over our IT resources or support,

roughly 60 percent of very small firms (five to 19 employees) selected the first statement. Not surprisingly, these companies recognize that technology, once a "luxury" reserved for the most highly efficient and scalable large enterprises, is increasingly being democratized with a glut of IT options available for outsourcing—the very outcome that Carr predicted and that led to his assertion that IT would soon be irrelevant because it alone is incapable of yielding sustainable competitive advantage. Yet, if the technology on its own cannot provide sustainable advantage, it can at least be leveraged to neutralize a disadvantage faced by smaller enterprises. For too long, these companies have been unable to influence the market price or quantity of IT services. They have been unable to lock in suppliers and could not overcome the barriers to entry set by their larger counterparts. All the while, they have been saddled with significant odds against their favor in seeing their five-year anniversary, complicated by scarce human and financial resources and a productivity deficit that would seem insurmountable at best. Of course, the complexion is radically different once technology and the resources needed to support it become democratized in the market. Among the most significant trends that level the playing field are the following:

- **Cloud services inoculate the weakness**—Among other outsourced areas, these small companies are turning to cloud services to afford them the elasticity they desperately crave in both resources and capital costs. Even if a startup were able to invest in the necessary human resources to staff its own IT department, maintaining a sophisticated team of professionals is in itself too much for many to bear. According to Rich Rodgers, cofounder of Tesaro Inc., a two-year-old biopharmaceutical company based in Massachusetts, "The minute you bring them [IT professionals] in, unless you spend a tremendous amount on training and keeping them up-to-date, their skills deteriorate." Instead, Rodgers turned to Mindshift Technologies Inc., a Massachusetts-based provider of IT services to more than 5,400 small and mid-sized businesses nation-wide and a recent acquisition target of national big-box retailer Best Buy. Best Buy led the trend of full-service IT for the consumer market with its Geek Squad–branded suite of in-home technical support services. It is now hoping to be an early front runner for small and mid-sized businesses with Mindshift. However, Best Buy does not plan on allocating retail space for Mindshift as it has with its Geek Squad line. It's apparently not worried that foregoing a retail presence for Mindshift will harm its ability to compete against those hundreds of thousands of consultants and smaller IT providers eager to amplify their highly localized capabilities. That's, in part, due to the lower provisioning and support costs associated with the cloud-based model. "We can do 99 percent of the work remotely," says Paul Chisholm,

Mindshift CEO. "More and more customers want to go to the cloud, and the independents and small regional providers don't have the financial capital and expertise to develop scalable cloud offerings." Scalability matters to small businesses unable to sink the same resources to match the economies set by their larger counterparts. In Rodgers' case, he was able to pay Mindshift about $40,000 for all of Tesaro's 2011 IT needs.[22] The same budget could hardly have afforded even one dedicated and competent IT professional on staff.

Although the cloud is not without its challenges, including the most often mentioned security issues likely to capture headlines and cause many a sleepless night, in a paradoxical twist, small businesses are sometimes finding it *more* secure to turn to a cloud provider rather than attempt a do-it-yourself alternative. When San Antonio Food Bank's Eric Cooper wanted to secure the nonprofit's donor list and supplier network, he needed a solution that went "well above our technological and intellectual capacity." He outsourced Food Bank's IT needs to a cloud provider, stating, "It was a no-brainer. I can't be worried about whether there's someone hacking our system."[23]

It appears that more small and mid-sized businesses are coming around to Cooper's point of view. In 2008, when research group IDC asked what factors were most likely to dissuade company usage of cloud services, 72 percent of small businesses (those with less than 100 employees) and 63 percent of mid-sized companies (100–999 employees) cited security as their chief worry. However, the trend shows that cloud security solutions, if not the way small and mid-sized businesses think of them, are evolving. By mid 2011, the numbers had dropped to 50 percent of small and 47 percent of mid-sized companies indicating security as their top concern. At the beginning of 2010, roughly 7 percent of small companies and 17 percent of mid-sized businesses had some cloud activity. In just 18 months, the numbers had doubled to 13 percent and 36 percent, respectively.[24] In the 2012 Alcatel-Lucent study, more than one in three small enterprises (those between five and 99 employees) were very likely to use a cloud service that dynamically offered network, storage, or compute resources on demand. Nearly two in five mid-sized companies (100–999 employees) indicated the same. When combining a cloud-based service with a mobile application through a virtualized desktop solution (one that gives employees access to enterprise files and programs from any device), the appetite soared to more than 40 percent of small enterprises and nearly 50 percent of mid-sized companies being very likely to use such a capability.

- **Mobile services accentuate the strength**—It's no surprise that a solution leveraging both mobility and the cloud scored so well among small companies in the 2012 Alcatel-Lucent study. Small businesses were on the mobility bandwagon even before consumers caught on to the trend. In late 2010, when only 17 percent of Americans had smartphones, Forrester found a whopping 49 percent of small business owners using the gadgets for work.[25] For these early adopters, mobility has proven an indispensable resource in helping narrow the productivity advantages of the large enterprise. A study by the Small Business and Entrepreneur Council found that small businesses that use mobile applications to help manage their business are saving more than 370 million of their own hours and more than 725 million employee hours annually. The study showed nearly one in three very small firms (fewer than 20 employees) to be using mobile applications, with owners estimating saving an average of 5.6 hours per week. By reducing the amount of nonproductive time associated with onerous administrative tasks and processes, nearly half of these very small businesses are able to spend more time increasing sales and chasing new revenue streams[26] (important, because nearly 40 percent of small business owners in the Webs survey were most concerned with generating new leads and acquiring new customers[27]). These benefits add up to an indispensable technology for these small enterprises. A 2011 AT&T study among businesses with two to 50 employees found nearly three-fourths using mobile applications in their business, with roughly four in 10 reporting they could not survive—or it would be a major challenge to survive—without the applications.[28] Indeed, it seems that very small enterprises are jumping head-long into the newest flavor of wireless technology, 4G LTE, as evidenced by the 2012 Alcatel-Lucent study, which found nearly one in five respondents from very small businesses (five to 19 employees) currently using the technology for work and home purposes, compared with less than 15 percent of respondents from very large enterprises (more than 1,000 employees) stating the same.

Catalyzing the continued adoption for advanced mobility services are the productivity benefits that small businesses seek to attain. However, there is perhaps an even more powerful reason one will find an advanced mobile device on the hips of so many small business owners and their employees—mobility plays to a small business's customer service advantage. A 2011 American Express survey reported that more than eight in 10 consumers believed small businesses deliver better service than their large competitors. What's more interesting, the same study found seven in 10 Americans willing to pay an average of 13 percent more with companies they believe provide excellent customer service. In comparison, in 2010, just six in 10 Americans indicated that they would be willing to spend an average of 9 percent more with such exemplary companies.[29] Perhaps it's a function of more nimble capabilities, a more localized touch, or the halo effect of consumers rewarding the Americana of the entrepreneurial spirit, but, whatever the case, small businesses consistently outmatch larger behemoths when it comes to servicing customers. And, given that many small businesses are inherently service-oriented by their very nature, mobility allows these companies to forage for their customers in the field, rather than be tethered to an office or desk. One such service company, C&C Landscaping in Salt Lake City, was able to use mobile technology to connect the owner with five of his top employees to share multimedia messages of clients' sites before determining how best to serve them. For just $720 per year, the company's use of the mobile application has resulted in it being able to reduce mistakes in the field by 75 percent, cut driving time in half, shed overhead by about 6 percent, and maintain annual sales despite the economic downturn.[30] Of course, none of this would have been possible even five years ago if not for the burgeoning mobile application market and the ever robust mobile broadband networks and devices accompanying it.

- **Big data evens the score**—Although small businesses are known for delivering superior customer service, larger companies are known for having a wealth of data about their existing customers. Incumbents that are able to mine the history of customer purchases and contact transactions can leverage this resource to build propensity models that help attract or retain clients—in a way, using this data as a means to improve customer service and defend against smaller challengers that tend to fare better in caring for customers. Small companies (or any new challenger, for that matter) are at a significant disadvantage when attempting to steal market share from established incumbents that have amassed a wealth of information about their customers. Historically, these small challengers have been forced to rely on guerrilla marketing tactics and word-of-mouth referrals to lure customers away. But statisticians offer a new approach using readily available data that can yield interesting propensity models to rival the proprietary knowledge earned by incumbents over time. Big data has altered the landscape and democratized market knowledge once reserved for large enterprises.

As an example, consider a specialty retailer that provides goods to expecting mothers. Among notable large-scale retailers also capable of serving this demographic is Target. As discussed in an earlier chapter, Target has quite advanced statistical models capable of using past purchase history for its customers to predict future needs. Its accuracy in using these models is uncanny, because, by comparing the combination of purchases in a particular household, the retailer was able to inform an unsuspecting father of his teenage daughter's pregnancy before he was even made aware of the fact. For any independent retailer attempting to grab a slice of the expecting mother market, facing giants like Target that are capable of sending premeditated and targeted offers to buyers before the prospects in question even realize they have such a need is daunting, to say the least. Yet, here is where big data from publicly available sources evens the score. According to Kurt Jetta, CEO of the TABS Group, a consumer analytics company in Connecticut, there's no shortage of data available that can be used to create propensity models for small and large enterprises alike. In addition, because the data in question is readily available, there are also fewer opt-in concerns associated with using what already exists in the public domain. For the independent retailer specializing in maternity goods interested in combating a statistical powerhouse like Target, consider Jetta's solution that offers its own propensity model:

If I took the voter roles and census data for a neighborhood, I could go to Google Earth and look at how many houses have jungle gyms and overlay census income data and identify the average square footage of the houses, and I could identify which houses have kids. I could identify when they were born and understand the probability that within the next three years another one's going to be born. The combinations are infinite. Those are publicly available sources of information that you can't shut down, and there will always be a statistician like me to figure it out.[31]

For small enterprises willing to dedicate a portion of their marketing budget to hire a statistician like Jetta on an as-needed basis, the return on investment will more than likely justify the expense. Of course, whereas small enterprises are fighting fire with fire to know more about the prospects they want to woo, large enterprises are using big data to even the score in their own way. That is, in addition to combating small business's superior customer service capabilities with more intimate customer knowledge, large businesses are using big data combined with collaboration tools to accelerate decision making within their enterprises. Indeed, one advantage of small companies is the velocity with which they are able to maneuver dynamically and respond to changing market conditions. Consider that small-company employment seems to be more stable in good times and bad, growing and receding more predictably. When large companies shed employees during the recession of 2001, the number of people working for small companies actually rose. At economic turning points, these smaller businesses are better able to respond to headwinds and tailwinds. In June 2007, at the first signs of economic recession, small companies began to reduce employment, seven months before larger ones did. At the first inkling of economic stability, small companies began to add workers in November 2009, four months before larger ones responded.[32] Whether because of a lack of bureaucracy, scarcer resources, a more sensitive tuning to market dynamics, or a combination of all factors, small businesses are faster than their larger counterparts. However, the more successful companies among the latter are increasingly using data-driven decision making to recognize harbingers sooner and accelerate their response to market turbulence.

Although small businesses may not actually create the wealth of jobs ascribed to them by politicians, it is difficult to impugn a category of entrepreneurs for an objective most never had in the first place. However, some are calling for government's love affair with small businesses to come to an end, or at least be tempered. As economist Scott Shane concludes, after studying the economic data, "Because the average existing firm is more productive than the average new firm, we would be better off economically if we got rid of policies that encouraged a lot of people to start businesses instead of taking jobs working for others." [33] Yet, before doing so, politicians may want to reevaluate the real economic value provided by entrepreneurs. That is, although job creation may be a bit spurious, based on how it is measured and defined, the economic development offered by small businesses cannot be denied by the communities they support. According to Edmiston, although one might think that a large firm would spur economic growth by yielding significant gains in employment and personal income, the *indirect* effects carry greater weight when evaluating net economic impact. He cites evidence of new-firm locations and expansions in Georgia that suggests that the location of a new large firm (greater than 300 employees) often retards the growth of the existing enterprises or discourages the establishment of enterprises that would otherwise have located to the area. He advises communities to forego aggressive attempts at recruiting large enterprises to their area and instead invest those same resources in creating a more conducive business environment for existing firms—both large and small.[34]

America's fascination with the unwavering spirit of today's entrepreneur will not falter any time soon. As Dieter Ibielski, international small business counselor and senior advisor at large of the World Association for Small and Medium Enterprises, poetically offered in 1997:

> *Small businesses are mighty minnows, reflecting the competitive spirit that a market economy needs for efficiency; they provide an outlet for entrepreneurial talents, a wider range of consumer goods and services, a check to monopoly inefficiency, a source of innovation and a seedbed for new industries; they allow an economy to be more adaptable to structural change through continuous initiatives embodying new technologies, skills, processes, or products.[35]*

Small business owners are the consummate risk takers, fighting for a piece of the American dream, and increasingly relying on technology solutions to level a historically uneven playing field. And, as entrepreneurial contributions to economic growth continue to evolve with the latest numbers, the love affair shared by Americans and politicians is sure to remain timeless. Perhaps this is yet one more certainty to add to Franklin's list.

MIDDLE AMERICA

For all the recent numbers from competing sources about where job growth is ultimately created in America, it's no wonder that there is confusion on the topic. If small businesses aren't the high-growth job engine responsible for creating long-term jobs as once thought, then what sector of the economy is? It turns out that middle market companies might be the unsung heroes of the story. According to a study from the Ohio State University Fisher College of Business and GE Capital, companies with between $10 million and $1 billion in sales create 34 percent of all the jobs. They represent a tiny slice of the U.S. economy composed of just 200,000 companies. Unlike their bigger or smaller counterparts, these mid-sized firms are not typically concentrated in one geographic region, industry, or ownership structure. As such, they are more resilient to forces affecting any of these factors singularly. The study reports that, from 2007 to 2010, these mid-market companies added 2.2 million employees, while their large business counterparts cut 3.7 million jobs.[36] Of course, perhaps Americans don't hear much about this slice of the market because these firms don't have the same lobbying resources as their larger competitors or the American idealism bestowed on small business owners. Assuming that politicians did begin to give these enterprises their due, it certainly would give new meaning to the term *Middle America*.

The New Civil War

→ *In 1964, American 13-year-olds took the First International Math Study, ranking eleventh on a list of twelve countries.*[1]

"**O**ur Nation is at risk. Our once unchallenged preeminence in commerce, industry, science, and technological innovation is being overtaken by competitors throughout the world."[2] Those words were written in 1983 by an independent commission tasked with evaluating the current landscape of education in the United States and recommending a prescriptive path forward. The 65-page report gave a blistering account of America's eroding position in the global education race. The opus was laced with incendiary language, intended to provoke response and action:

> *What was unimaginable a generation ago has begun to occur—others are matching and surpassing our educational attainments. If an unfriendly foreign power had attempted to impose on America the mediocre educational performance that exists today, we might well have viewed it as an act of war. As it stands, we have allowed this to happen to ourselves.... We have, in effect, been committing an act of unthinking, unilateral educational disarmament.*[3]

At the time, this might have been perceived as a commission's flair for the dramatic (or a well-crafted piece of propaganda designed to convince then President Ronald Reagan to jettison his plans of abolishing the federal U.S. Education Department[4]), however according to a recent nonpartisan assessment of the topic, the "war" metaphor may have proven more prophecy than hyperbole. A 2012 Council on Foreign Relations report on U.S. Education Reform and National Security warns that the country's anemic educational performance is a threat to its national security, stating,

"Educational failure puts the United States' future economic prosperity, global position, and physical safety at risk."[5]

Despite the fact that the United States spends more in K-12 public education than many other countries, its results are not commensurate. The country ranks fourteenth in reading, twenty-fifth in math, and seventeenth in science, when comparing the performance of American 15-year-olds to that of their peers in other industrialized countries. More than one-quarter of U.S. high school students fail to graduate in four years, a number that approaches 40 percent among minorities. Less than a quarter of U.S. high school students meet college-ready standards. Even among college-bound seniors, less than half meet these standards, forcing more college students to take remedial classes. Adding to the problem, three-fourths of U.S. citizens aged 17–24 cannot pass military entrance exams because they are physically unfit, have criminal records, or lack critical skills needed in modern warfare (including basic world geography knowledge). The report goes on to say that such lack of preparedness threatens the United States on five national security fronts: economic growth and competitiveness, physical safety, intellectual property, U.S. global awareness, and U.S. unity and cohesion.[6] Considering that the United States spends more than 5 percent of its GDP[7] to ready tomorrow's workforce, one expects better than mediocrity.

For healthcare, a sector that exceeds 15 percent of the GDP (making it the single largest component of the U.S. GDP) and more than $7,000 per capita—the highest for both metrics of any country in the world[8]—one expects excellence. However, *excellent* is hardly a word to describe the current U.S. healthcare system, with expenses at nearly 2.5 times the health spending, yet with fewer practicing physicians, nurses, and acute-care bed days per capita of the median country in the Organization for Economic Cooperation and Development (OECD).[9] The point is further accentuated when one considers that comparable healthcare costs in almost all other advanced industrial countries cover virtually everyone, yet the United States leaves nearly 50 million people uninsured.[10] The trend shows no signs of abating, because U.S. healthcare costs are expected to double over the next decade.[11] A key contributor to spiraling healthcare costs is the American lifestyle, rendering at least one in three Americans obese, a condition that spawns other chronic diseases. According to David Squires, primary author of a Commonwealth Fund study on U.S. healthcare, the United States suffers from "a failure to effectively manage these chronic conditions that make up an increasing share of the disease burden."[12] With chronic diseases estimated to afflict more than six in 10 Baby Boomers by 2030, one can expect healthcare costs to continue to soar accordingly. The situation is exacerbated by a shortage of registered nurses that is projected to exceed 250,000 by 2025,[13] the result of an equally aging nursing population combined with a deficit of qualified candidates entering the employment ranks (partly a response to a lagging educational system that is failing to generate the next crop of employees).

Despite the obvious differences between education and healthcare as independent sectors of the economy, the similarities are compelling. Both critically serve the public at large. Both are significant beneficiaries of national investment and discourse. Both have characteristics similar to enterprises, yet they also serve the private market in unique ways—either by preparing tomorrow's employees or caring for today's workforce. Yet, neither is attaining the level of performance one would expect despite the level of spending and focus. What's more, both sectors possess long-term implications for the nation's ability to compete and cooperate on a world stage.

As it has for the private sector, evidence suggests that technology (or lack thereof) is already playing a role in enabling the current situation in the public sector. A 2006 study by authors at Johns Hopkins found the United States lagging as much as a dozen years behind other industrialized countries in healthcare information technology, a cornerstone of which is the electronic health record (EHR).[14] Although the EHR can reduce costly errors and duplications, the United States trails its counterparts in usage, an issue given the Commonwealth Fund's findings that Americans are more likely than people in other advanced nations to experience medical problems with uncoordinated care.[15] In education, the outlook isn't better, with the United States falling behind other countries in equipping classrooms for twenty-first century skill development. South Korea, which has the highest college attainment rate in the world, will phase out physical textbooks and replace them with digital versions by 2015. Even Uruguay, a developing country in comparison, provides a computer for every student.[16]

However, technology is hardly a panacea for the considerable issues facing citizens of this country. In fact, it also imposes consequences on today's grim landscape. The Commonwealth Fund points to excessive use of high-priced technology (including MRIs and CT scans) as a major contributing factor to the United States' escalating healthcare costs. In education, the jury is still out on technology's impact on classroom learning, driven largely by how instructors incorporate such technology into an integrated curriculum. When this point is underestimated, the results can backfire. For example, a national study in the 1990s found a negative relationship between the frequency of use of school computers and scholastic achievement.[17]

Yet, despite the extenuating circumstances surrounding the positive or negative contributions of technology to these public sectors, technology is being adopted nonetheless. Students and patients in households are using it to further their academic pursuits or manage complex healthcare conditions, respectively. Academics and clinicians are bringing personalized technology into the workplace to serve their stakeholders. Institutions are leveraging the latest technology trends to address increasingly formidable challenges. Fortunately, there is much to be learned from these trailblazers in how to apply technology to help solve some of the country's most daunting problems. As an example, consider how the healthcare field is tackling opportunities associated with big data. It turns out that Watson, IBM's supercomputer of artificial intelligence, is capable of more than just beating the toughest *Jeopardy!* champions or becoming the latest employee of financial services giant Citigroup—it is starting to make waves in healthcare. WellPoint Inc. plans to use Watson to monitor patients and offer support to physicians. According to WellPoint's CIO Andrew Lang, "We're the first to bring the Watson solution to the market, and our first focus is on a diagnosis and treatment for oncology. Then, we're moving both vertically and horizontally from that space to explore other partnerships with Watson and IBM."[18] Some of the potential adjacencies for Watson include helping manage those complex and chronic conditions that have become the bane of the country's healthcare system. By ingesting a patient's progress over a period of time, Watson can leverage the history to drive continuity of care. As Lang states, "It would dramatically improve the health of our patients and improve the quality of physician treatments and diagnoses. Ultimately, through Watson, we want to reduce costs and promote best practices around diagnoses. We want to get better results while spending less money."[19]

Indeed, big data in healthcare far surpasses even the most interesting applications for Watson. According to IDC, the big data market is expected to grow from $30 billion in 2011 to close to $34 billion in 2012, in part because of increased use in the healthcare industry.[20] This investment is more than offset by the potential benefits in reducing healthcare overhead, with administrative inefficiencies estimated to cost providers $100–$150 billion annually.[21] The EHR is the centerpiece of the transformation, although it will be augmented over time with medical activities that

overwhelmingly occur outside the doctor's office. For example, of particular importance in managing disease is compliance in taking prescriptions. Unfortunately,
studies show that less than half of Americans take their medications as prescribed.
Noncompliance in doing so is attributed to 30–40 percent of hospital admissions for
seniors over 65, roughly 125,000 deaths per year, and a healthcare tab of $290 billion
annually.[22] To address the need, a new category of pill bottle caps has entered the
scene, complete with digital intelligence to detect the length of time since the pill
bottle has been opened, alert patients with reminders that medication is due, and
send weekly progress reports of compliance to physicians over a wireless network.
In independent studies in which such caps have been deployed, patients using the
technology had nearly a 34 percent increase in compliance with dosage instructions.[23]
Such ongoing data can be used to monitor and chart a patient's progress in managing stubborn chronic diseases while going about daily life, thereby creating a more
holistic and accurate view of one's unique medical history.

In education, big data is endowing academics with similar visibility as it pertains
to a student's distinctive learning approach. In 2011, Stanford University placed three
computer science courses online and embarked on an unprecedented study to understand how students learn. Although other studies have certainly tackled the knotty
topic, they have done so by using small groups of students and comparing results
in different classrooms, leading to uncertain and delayed research conclusions. The
Stanford experiment is revolutionizing the approach by studying the real-time mouse
clicks and interactions of 20,000 online students. According to Daphne Koller, a
professor at the Stanford Artificial Intelligence Laboratory, "If 5,000 people had the
same wrong answer, it's obvious a concept is not getting through, and you have a
clear path that shows where students went wrong." [24]

Beyond merely detecting where curriculum may be missing its objective, such
big data can be used to tailor educational content to the specific learning needs of
the student. In 2011, the Bill and Melinda Gates Foundation endowed $1 million to
launch an ongoing data mining effort involving a half dozen online universities. The
project has led to the development of a database measuring 33 variables for the online
coursework of 640,000 students to track student performance and retention across a
broad range of demographic factors. In a surprising break from conventional wisdom,
early findings suggest that at-risk students do better if they ease into online education
with a small number of courses, as opposed to the full-course immersive load required

for maximum federal aid. The data set has the potential to give tremendous insights into the learning patterns for small subsets of groups, such as targeted minorities. Although the study is far from complete, it is already being heralded as a potential Match.com for aspiring college students. According to Sebastian Diaz, the project's senior statistician, "Rather than just going on rankings done by a particular news agency, [students and parents] could really look at tailoring which institution provides the best fit for a particular individual student." [25] Lest one believe that big data's role in education is limited to these higher education examples where online coursework is the norm, consider that 40 states have virtual schools or state-led initiatives. In fact, 30 states and Washington, DC are home to statewide full-time online schools, comprising millions of mouse clicks and interactions on which to study how younger students learn and modify or personalize curriculum accordingly. [26]

Yet, big data is only as useful as it is available. In both healthcare and education, the data tsunami is fueled by Internet-connected devices and the clouds connecting them. According to CompTIA's 2011 Third Annual Healthcare IT Insights and Opportunities study, the prevalence of mobile technology among practitioners is rivaled only by its adoption by their patients. One-quarter of healthcare providers currently use tablets in their practice. Another 21 percent expect to do so in the next year. More than half already use a smartphone for work purposes. Perhaps most telling, two-thirds of healthcare providers say that implementing or improving their use of mobile technologies ranks as a high- or mid-level priority over the next 12 months. [27]

These numbers point to additional opportunities for cloud-based solutions, where the demand for immediate and simple access to data stimulates appetite for centralized IT services. They are also introducing a bevy of new challenges for healthcare providers. Whereas more than eight in 10 healthcare providers use mobile devices to collect, store, and/or transmit some form of personal health information (PHI), nearly half admit to not taking proper steps to secure their devices. [28] Some industry experts predict an increase in the number of class-action lawsuits in 2012 as a result of PHI violations. As such, although mobile technology is on the rise, many healthcare providers remain cautious about BYOD policies. In the 2012 Alcatel-Lucent study, healthcare organizations were among the most aggressive in outright rejecting a BYOD policy—with two in five healthcare organizations precluding the use of personal technology in the workplace, compared with just one in five educational respondents stating the same. Among the top reasons cited for a more cautious BYOD approach was the fear of infiltration of viruses and malware to the network—of particular importance given electronic protected health information (EPHI) security concerns. According to at least one expert, "With EPHI being accessed from a multitude of mobile devices, risks of contamination of systems by a virus introduced from a mobile device used to transmit EPHI significantly increase. Mobile devices and BYOD policies leave a healthcare organization open to potential data breaches."[29] And, the concerns are sufficient to create additional pressures on the IT function for healthcare organizations, regardless if a policy outright denies the use of personal technology in the workplace or not. According to the 2012 Alcatel-Lucent study, more than two in five healthcare IT respondents admit to being contacted more by their internal customers, as a result of employees bringing personal technology into the workplace and experiencing issues in using it for work purposes (compared with just one in five education IT respondents).

Although educators are far more permissive with BYOD than their healthcare counterparts, they face a different set of challenges that are unenviable on their own merits. Mobile technology is certainly popular among educators. In the 2012 Alcatel-Lucent study, educators are more likely to own tablets (61%), use a personal 4G/LTE mobile device for work purposes (31%), and pay for cellular data services (3G/4G) for work purposes out of their own pocket (21%). Although the educator's fervent adoption of mobility can best be explained by the changing complexion of her students, most of whom come equipped with a sophisticated mobile device perennially attached to their hips, mobility in the classroom suffers from a lack of compelling evidence as to its effective use in the curriculum. Compounding the problem is the length of time required to form an informed opinion regarding a technology's impact on learning juxtaposed with the speed with which technology itself is evolving. Soon after the iPad was introduced, enthusiastic schools began permitting the device in classrooms and learning environments, despite the lack of evidence on which to justify its acceptance. Interestingly, schools rallied behind laptops in much the same way just a few years earlier. In fact, a 2010 study by Project RED, a research initiative linked with the One-to-One Institute (which supports one-to-one laptop initiatives in K-12 schools), found that most schools that had integrated laptops and other digital learning tools into learning were not maximizing the use of the technology to get the most benefit from its potential.[30] But despite the challenges, there is hope for educators overwhelmed by technology options that seem to germinate daily. That is, as more sophisticated data analysis accompanies the deluge of mouse clicks and keyboard entries inside and outside the classroom, the more educators' understanding about technology's role in the learning process can catch up with the pace of technological change itself. Until then, educators will rely on increasingly sophisticated mobile device management capabilities that can be incorporated in the classroom to at least provide instrumentation to instructors as to how such devices are aiding or deterring a legitimate learning environment.

These advanced mobile and cloud management tools are not far from availability, if collaboration solutions in the classroom are any indicator. Just a few years ago, teachers were struggling with whether to incorporate social networking tools in their instruction. Although Facebook is the seemingly unstoppable social networking juggernaut among consumers, it lacks the management oversight required for coursework completion. Enter a new range of collaboration tools purpose-built for teachers striving to incorporate interactive learning while protecting the integrity of their curriculum. One such solution is Gaggle, which allows students to join only at the invitation of teachers, does not allow students to have private conversations, and has filters to detect inappropriate language, bullying references, and pornography. The options offered by Gaggle and its ilk address the relatively recent concerns plaguing teachers since social networking became unavoidable in the classroom. Nancy Willard, the executive director of the Center for Safe and Responsible Internet Use, comments that, although these academic interactive environments look and feel reminiscent of Facebook, "... the emphasis is different. You're not trying to pick someone up for a date. This is where you're trying to focus on 'Romeo and Juliet.'"[31]

As such, many of these academically tailored solutions are capable of far more than simple collaboration, including cloud-based storage and multimedia capabilities. In addition, for teachers interested in having students collaborate with experts and instructors across the globe, Skype offers its classroom-tailored service to answer the call. Through a variety of educational partnerships, Skype offers a search-and-retrieval method connecting instructors and experts with classrooms around the world. Penguin Young Readers Group connects authors with students for discussions about books and writing, whereas the New York Philharmonic offers interactions with esteemed musicians.[32] Indeed, Skype has permeated the classroom, with educators in the 2012 Alcatel-Lucent study among its heaviest users. Educators' appreciation of videoconferencing has also seeped into their nonclassroom instruction time as a valuable tool when interacting with their peers. In the 2012 Alcatel-Lucent study, when educators were asked to choose which statement came closer to their view:

- Videoconferencing is better than audioconferencing since nonverbal communication is not sacrificed and richer interactions can result;
  or
- Audioconferencing is better than videoconferencing because it allows employees to multitask through otherwise mundane meetings;

more than two-thirds selected the first option, the highest of any professional segment tested.

In contrast, healthcare providers had among the lowest preferences for videoconferencing, with only a slight majority (59%) preferring it to audioconferencing. Perhaps the lower appetite has something to do with the nascent condition of telemedicine, especially when measured against the relatively booming online education market in comparison. According to the CompTIA study, only 14 percent of healthcare professionals report actively following news and trends in telemedicine, for which patient consultation via videoconferencing is seen as a primary benefit. Only one in 10 healthcare providers intends to use videoconferencing for patient interaction in the next 12 months,[33] helping to explain how the technology could be evaluated so poorly as a means of employee engagement in the 2012 Alcatel-Lucent study. Yet, the suppressed interest may be more a function of onerous or ill-fitted videoconferencing solutions on the market today as opposed to a lack of demand. When asked about a service that would seamlessly engage multiple individuals in a high-definition video and collaboration conference through any device—one in which participants control their virtual environment with simple hand gestures and are unbothered by otherwise annoying background noises, which are effortlessly muted—healthcare professionals were the most enthusiastic cohort to respond. Specifically, more than three in 10 indicated that they would be very likely to use such a service if it were made available. With $1 billion in annual federal support to study telemedicine and its benefits and nearly one-fifth of Americans living in areas where primary care physicians are scarce, telemedicine may finally be due for a surge. Still, critics question whether doctors will be able to detect subtle cues via a remote, albeit high-definition, connection that sacrifices tactile capabilities.[34] In yet another demonstration of how these technology trends are intertwined, perhaps this sensory void is more than handled with a wealth of big data statistics that can track a patient's progress unlike ever before.

Indeed, whether exploring big data, cloud, mobility, or collaboration, the inextricable connection among these technologies yields an effect in which the whole is greater than the sum of the parts. When dealing with some of the most formidable challenges facing the nation, such synergies are welcome ammunition in a metaphorical war. However, despite the similarities of both healthcare and education in taking their respective shots in the court of public opinion, there are profound differences in how each sector will embrace technology's role in addressing its unique challenges:

- **A new power relationship is emerging in healthcare, with technology at the center**—Advanced technology has been a leading contributor to exorbitant healthcare costs. However, the emerging healthcare consumerism trend seeks to redefine the relationships between patients, clinicians, and insurance providers. Among other items, the movement seeks to put more information in the hands of patients to help them make informed decisions about providers, insurance coverage, and treatment. It seeks to provide full transparency of a patient's medical records within his or her hands to allow for the quick resolution of errors, omissions, or derogatory information. At its most advanced stage, healthcare consumerism seeks to empower patients with personalized development plans and corresponding incentives designed to change lifestyle, another major contributing factor to escalating healthcare expenditures. The result of this power shift, one that transforms a patient from a passive observer in his healthcare plan to an active partner with those who serve him, will be enabled by affordable and pervasive technology options (including telemedicine and remote monitoring capabilities) that have a long-term impact on lifestyle alteration. When coupled with financial incentives, the potential to reduce bloated healthcare costs is profound. In a six-month experiment involving 139 patients suffering from hypertension, researchers measured the effectiveness of rewards linked to a connected pill bottle cap. Respondents in the experimental group received up to $90 if they adhered to their medication schedule at least 80 percent of the time. The difference in behavioral compliance between this cohort and the control group (which was offered neither the connected pill bottle cap nor an incentive) was significant. Those in the control group were compliant 71 percent of the time, whereas those in the experimental group met their schedules 99 percent of the time.

Such a variation could yield significant healthcare savings when extrapolated to the broader population of chronic disease sufferers.

Beyond the potential cost savings, patients are ready to be empowered. According to a 2012 Deloitte study among 4,000 consumers, 44 percent report being very interested in videoconferencing capabilities for follow-up visits, and 41 percent are eager to try self-monitoring devices that send electronic readings to doctors via the network.[35] Despite the enthusiasm among early adopters, the same primary issue plagues both consumers and clinicians unwilling to experiment with such innovative technologies: that of protecting the security of personal health information. However, given the surprising number of clinicians failing to protect this information when currently using mobile devices, security issues will likely not be the impediment to adoption. Instead, advanced mobile data management and cloud-based solutions will increasingly be relied on to mitigate data risks created by these security-minded clinicians themselves.

- **Educators will experiment, demanding a new relationship between IT and HR**—Led primarily by administrators, technology will play an increasingly important role in creating new learning environments. Instructors are following suit, driven by the need to adapt to changing student expectations. However, a lack of instruction for instructors will continue to challenge the effectiveness of technology in and beyond the classroom, leading to results that do not fully maximize the potential benefits. This is, at least in part, due to the velocity of technology adoption, driven by newer crops of more advanced digital natives entering the classroom. Academics will impose greater expectations on IT professionals as a result. In the 2012 Alcatel-Lucent study, only 35 percent of education respondents indicate that the level of training provided to them when new technologies are introduced by their organization is more than adequate or sufficient (compared with half of healthcare respondents). One in five educators rates their training as subpar or poor.

  At the same time, IT professionals in this sector are challenged with keeping up with the pace of technology while keeping an eye on essential IT concerns. Among them, nearly one-third cite their biggest challenge as being the move toward cloud-based services, which creates new security, reliability, and performance challenges for IT to manage (the highest percentage of IT respondents out of any industry tested). However, IT is also stepping up their response and embracing other trends in their organization, including consumerization, with a welcoming attitude. Nearly half agree that the movement by employees in bringing personal technology into the workplace has allowed the IT function in their organization to become more strategic, no longer encumbered with purchasing and maintaining hardware for employees in the company. In addition, their internal customers agree, because 60 percent of educators indicate that IT equips them with innovative tools, services, or capabilities that foster a healthy culture—particularly important given that one in five educators is likely to state their organizational culture is due for serious changes, making them the most eager cohort in support of cultural reform.

Finally, while there appears to be a respect among educators as to the importance of technology within their organizations (with nearly half of executives driving deployment decisions, compared with less than one-third, on average for all industries, in the Alcatel-Lucent study), much work remains to be done in tightening the critical HR and IT connection. Teachers are increasingly accepting technology's role in curriculum and professional development. According to a 2011 Project Tomorrow study of more than 36,000 K-12 teachers nationwide, one-third of teachers are involved in an online professional learning community (compared with just one in five in 2007). Nearly two-thirds of instructors regularly download music for classroom use (up from less than 40% in 2007). However, many still crave resources and training for how to incorporate digital resources in the classroom more effectively. More than half of teachers desire access to an online collection of vetted content-specific courses to assist them in incorporating digital content within their learning environment. Nearly 40 percent want face-to-face professional development for the same.[36] Despite the accelerating adoption of teachers and the gaps that still remain in making them fully comfortable with new learning environments, HR professionals appear to be underestimating their value. According to the 2012 Alcatel-Lucent study, more than 50 percent of HR professionals in the education sector admit that their influence over technology decisions has not changed in the past three years. Close to 10 percent shockingly admit that their influence has actually *decreased* in that period of time. To ensure that technology is not underutilized in and beyond the classroom, IT and HR must work cooperatively to equip instructors with both tools and training.

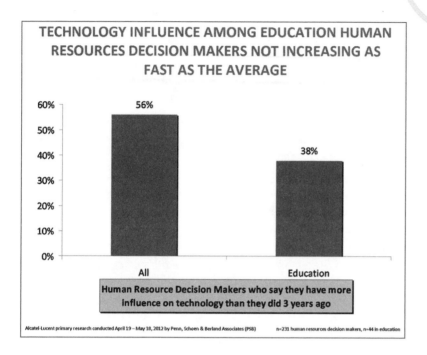

TECHNOLOGY INFLUENCE AMONG EDUCATION HUMAN RESOURCES DECISION MAKERS NOT INCREASING AS FAST AS THE AVERAGE

Human Resource Decision Makers who say they have more influence on technology than they did 3 years ago

Alcatel-Lucent primary research conducted April 19 – May 18, 2012 by Penn, Schoen & Berland Associates (PSB)   n=231 human resources decision makers, n=44 in education

Education and healthcare are the critical engines of citizen welfare in this country. And, for all that has changed in each of these sectors over the past several decades, much remains the same. Each institution finds itself the subject of discourse, even criticism, as the beneficiaries of significant taxpayer investment. Each is struggling to prove its value as the United States continues to be outranked by other countries that are getting better results with less money. Yet, the United States isn't so much competing with other countries as it is competing with itself. Take those mediocre scores in education as an example. According to Andreas Schleicher, the head of education indicators and analysis for the Organization for Economic Cooperation and Development, from a statistical perspective, "There is no decline on any measure that we have for the United States." Instead, he cites the issue as "the rate of improvement in other countries, in terms of getting more people into school and educating them well, is steeper."[37] Other countries are raising their game, and there is much the United States can learn from their success, while not underestimating unique cultural nuances that must be acknowledged. However, becoming infatuated with the latest ratings and rankings—whether in education, healthcare, or other global indicators—can have counterproductive results if one assumes that those other countries are the competition, when, in fact, the battle begins at home.

THE NEXT ARMS RACE

Education and healthcare are not the only sectors in the spotlight when comparing the United States against its global peers. A 2011 report by the Information Technology and Innovation Foundation ranked countries on the basis of their innovation. It states, "It is worth reiterating that in 2000 the United States ranked first, a position it likely held for the majority of the post-war period, but in a decade it has fallen to fourth. At this rate, where will the United States rank at the end of the next decade?" Such findings are likely to provoke response, as President Obama issued a challenge in a 2011 State of the Union address, "We need to out-innovate, out-educate, and out-build the rest of the world." [38]

Yet, this new arms race is not without its critics—those quick to point out that the United States operates as part of a global economy, not an island deserving of wartime preservation. In fact, they cite evidence supporting a slightly negative correlation between R&D investment and GDP growth. They create a case for a rising tide lifting all boats, indicating that the United States will benefit from developments made abroad. In his article, "No One Can Win the Future," Konstantin Kakaes argues that, although Democrats and Republicans agree on the question, "How can America compete with the rest of the world, especially China?" it's the wrong question to start. He submits:

> Imagine that someone in a lab in China cured cancer tomorrow. Technology spreads quickly—that cancer cure would be applied in the United States (and throughout the world) with tremendous benefit for human welfare. In no way would we be worse off. Sure, a Chinese pharmaceutical company would make money. But so would the pharmacist who sold the drug in the United States and the doctor who prescribed it. American researchers would build on the Chinese discovery. American workers would be more productive, and American families would have their sarcoma-ridden loved ones futures restored to them. The money made by the notional Chinese pharmaceutical firm is inconsequential compared with the worldwide effect of the miracle cure.[39]

So, although the United States will continue to fight to regain its status as a globally recognized innovative bellwether, perhaps there is relief, rather than anxiety, in knowing that other countries are seeking the same.

The Global Race

→ *There are 220 million "surplus workers" in China's central and western regions. The number of people working in the United States is about 140 million.*[1]

Modern technologists like to trace the beginnings of the "social network" back to the late 1970s when the first electronic bulletin board systems were brought online. These small servers, powered by personal computers, were linked to telephone modems and allowed users to engage in discussions, file sharing, and online games with like-minded peers. The early 1990s saw the rise of more mass-market friendly platforms such as Prodigy, Compuserve, and AOL capture the public's imagination as they linked far-flung friends and acquaintances around the world. As the World Wide Web began to grow and the personal computer became ubiquitous, new platforms designed to connect us socially took root. Early pioneers in the social networking arena such as Napster, MySpace, and Friendster made headlines as they allowed us to share, connect, and maintain relationships in a digital world. Although, in most cases, these early innovators have seen their popularity and relevance all but disappear, their influence has been profound. Without their early contributions, you could argue, there would be no Facebook. With more than 900 million active user accounts, Facebook boasts the largest online community in history[2]—connecting people to those they care about, those that share their interests, and the brands they love like never before. The very concept of *social networking* has become one of the hottest trends in the consumer market, and the business world, always looking for the best way to connect with customers, is starting to take notice. The past five years has seen a whole new industry emerge to help organizations navigate the world of social networks. And while Western companies engage with consulting firms and perform countless ROI studies to determine if the social network can in some way benefit their bottom lines—they only need to look East to understand the impact and importance of the social network in a business context.

With apologies to the modern technologists referenced above, the idea of the "social network" dates back much further than the 1970s. Dating back thousands of years, *guanxi* is an essential component of getting anything done in China. It's the original "social network." Commonly translated as "connections" and "relationships,"[3] *guanxi* refers to an individual's personal network of family, friends, classmates, coworkers, military peers, and other personal contacts with which the individual has formed some kind of relationship. When combined with the networks of those in your immediate circle, *guanxi* provides a complex web of connections and contacts much greater than the sum of a single individual's reach. Whereas the West wrestles with new platforms such as Facebook or LinkedIn to develop, nurture, and leverage a network of connections to our own personal or professional benefit, *guanxi* is ingrained in the very fabric of Chinese society and culture.

Taking the phrase "It's not what you know, but who you know" to a whole new level, *guanxi* traces its roots to Confucianism, which emphasizes group identity and long-term personal alliances. Essentially a system of mutual obligation,*guanxi* is based on long-lasting individual relationships that require the exchange of personal favors.[4] As these ongoing interactions are nurtured through the reciprocation of these favors, the personal network grows stronger and more effective for the individual who maintains a state of "good" *guanxi*. But to the outsider, *guanxi* can look a lot like corruption or cronyism. According to Andrew Hupert, a consultant to Western companies looking to do business in China, this is true to an extent:

> But Guanxi also has a lot of positive aspects. These include the networking effect, where you are expanding your range of resources. What I've been talking about a lot lately is the due diligence aspect to Guanxi. When Americans think of due diligence, we think of financial statements and we look at rating agencies. This is definitely part of the picture. But when a Chinese negotiator thinks about...what we call due diligence, he looks at character, commitment, maturity, and the other party's attitude toward risk. And when you build a long-term partnership, these are extremely important.[5]

New technologies and services, which have introduced the West to the concept of social networking, are also being leveraged in China to further augment *guanxi*. Researchers have pointed to the impact that the spread of advanced IT technologies and services has had on encouraging and improving this unique Chinese practice.[6] According to the China Internet Network Information Center, China boasted 513 million Internet users at the end of 2011, with 356 million of these getting online via a mobile device. Although Facebook may be prohibited from operating in China, there is no shortage of social networking activity on home-grown Chinese language sites. According to the consulting firm TNS, 265 million Chinese participate in social networking via these sites for 5.6 hours per week on average. More than half (54%) of these users engage with these sites on a daily basis.[7] In the United States, the same social networking activity is primarily just that—social. In China, the activity is much more. According to Hupert:

> The Chinese social media tools are developing much faster and more broad-ly than American social media systems, which is more for entertainment and younger people. In China, you see a lot more social media that are more serious and designed to develop business networks. The positive aspect of guanxi—about broadening your network, or knowing who you do business with, about meeting the friend of a friend—really lends itself to some new technologies coming up.[8]

There is no doubt that things are done differently in China. Custom and tradition dictate a certain set of social rules that regulate the interactions that people have with one another in both their personal and professional lives. Beyond these traditional social norms, the emergence of new technologies and services in the workplace is changing the complexion of how this global powerhouse goes to market. Instead of upending long-established organizational culture, Chinese workers are integrating new technologies into their work lives and embracing the opportunity to augment and strengthen their competitive efforts.

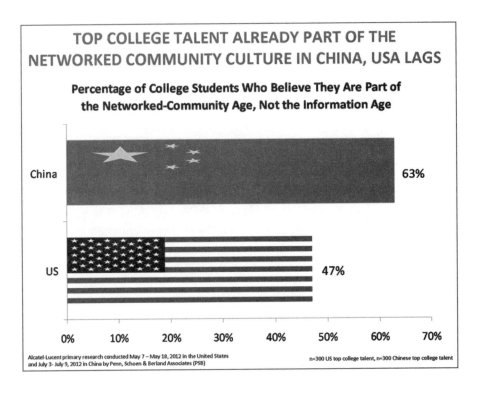

TOP COLLEGE TALENT ALREADY PART OF THE
NETWORKED COMMUNITY CULTURE IN CHINA, USA LAGS

Percentage of College Students Who Believe They Are Part of
the Networked-Community Age, Not the Information Age

China — 63%

US — 47%

0% 10% 20% 30% 40% 50% 60% 70%

Alcatel-Lucent primary research conducted May 7 – May 18, 2012 in the United States
and July 3- July 9, 2012 in China by Penn, Schoen & Berland Associates (PSB)

n=300 US top college talent, n=300 Chinese top college talent

It is clear that China is no longer an "emerging" economic superpower. Since the late 1970s, China has focused on shifting its national economic focus from a closed, centrally planned system to a more open market-oriented economy. A careful and gradual approach to opening to foreign trade and investment, fiscal decentralization, and the encouragement of private sector growth saw China stand as the second largest economy in the world by 2010. With an estimated 2011 GDP of $11.29 trillion, China ranks number three just behind the United States and the European Union, respectively. With a total population of 1.3 billion and a workforce estimated at 796 million, China boasts the number one position in each category.[9]

In an effort to understand the impact that new and emerging network-based technologies are having on the productivity, culture, and competitiveness of this immense workforce, in 2012, Alcatel-Lucent engaged in a comprehensive qualitative and quantitative primary research study to compare and contrast adoption and integration of these technologies between Chinese and American firms. This study on the future of the enterprise comprised more than 3,000 frontline workers and decision makers from a variety of Chinese industries whose responses were analyzed alongside those of their American counterparts. The results paint an interesting and informative picture of two cultures leveraging technology to enhance and improve their go-to-market efforts:

- **The Chinese worker is personally connected to the professional workplace**— Along with rapid urbanization and a growing middle class, China is becoming much more than a manufacturer and supplier of goods to the world, but a nation of consumers as well. This is especially true when it comes to technology. According to the *2012 Accenture Consumer Electronics Products and Services Usage Report*, Chinese consumers spend the largest percentage of their income (4.5%) on consumer electronics—especially mobile computing devices such as smartphones and tablet computers—when compared with the rest of the world.[10] This rapid adoption of smartphone and mobile technology is having an impact on all aspects of Chinese life. A study by the consulting firm KPMG found that China leads the world in terms of mobile shopping and payments. Consider that 79 percent of those Chinese surveyed by KPMG prefer to leverage their devices to purchase goods online. A full 84 percent indicated that they are willing to use their mobile device as a wallet—compared with 66 percent globally. According to KPMG, such widespread use and adoption of advanced mobile technologies signals a significant trend for the global market place:

  > *Asia seems set to leapfrog the rest of the world when it comes to the use of new technologies. This Asian-led revolution will have a dramatic impact on the global market and will largely influence the future design and sales of new technology products.[11]*

  This widespread adoption of mobile computing technologies is by no means confined to the consumer space. As discussed in previous chapters, BYOD has emerged as a significant trend in today's workplace. Looking to increase their productivity, workers around the world are leveraging their personal devices to get their work done—often in direct defiance of established company IT policies. China is certainly no exception. Alcatel-Lucent found that of the almost 1,300 frontline Chinese workers surveyed, a full 72 percent indicate that they are using their personal devices to help them get their work done—compared with 48 percent of their American counterparts. Almost two in five (38%) of those same Chinese frontline workers bring their own device to work despite specific organizational restrictions on such a practice.

According to Patrice Perche, Senior Vice President of International Sales and Support at the Internet security firm Fortinet, the rapid adoption of BYOD by Chinese employees, even in the face of corporate restrictions, is due to several factors:

> *The widespread broadband availability, Asians strong commitment to work, and rapid urbanization drive more young people to work in cities. Their growing affluence also enables young workers to afford smartphones and handset manufacturers have successfully positioned high-end gadgets as status symbols. Compared to their counterparts in the U.S., Europe and Middle East, young workers here are significantly more attached to their mobile devices. This is not surprising, due to the rapid mobile device and social networking adoption in Asia.[12]*

These forces have combined to create a remarkably connected workforce that is prepared to leverage the technology available to them to further increase their productivity for the benefit of the enterprise. When the same Alcatel-Lucent study asked Chinese frontline workers to make a choice between two options:

- The technology at my disposal gives me the freedom to work when I want, where I want;

   or

- I can't escape from work demands;

nearly three in four selected the former. And although 92 percent of these same workers indicate that they are "mobile capable"—nine points higher than American workers—the majority of them (76%) are more likely to be office-bound. Despite the fact that 71 percent of those Chinese workers who do work remotely report that telecommuting makes them more productive, deeply ingrained cultural issues are slowing the mass adoption of mobile work in the Chinese enterprise.

Renowned researcher Geert Hofstede is well known for his work in developing a framework for assessing national and organizational cultures. Characterized by Hofstede as a high-power distance culture, Chinese workers accept more autocratic and paternalistic management. Power is granted to others simply based on where they fall in the organizational structure. The result is a much more centralized and directive style of management. Regardless of the capability and the desire of the workforce, researchers have found that, because telecommuting provides greater autonomy to the workforce and decentralizes authority, the long-term development of a mobile workforce in China is questionable.[13]

Cultural issues aside, the influx of Western organizations and business practices combined with a remarkably "mobile-capable" workforce could trump tradition—especially if a mobile workforce can show itself to be more productive. Researchers at Stanford University set out to determine the impact that telecommuting would have on the productivity of Chinese workers. Partnering with a Chinese travel agency, these researchers asked for volunteers to participate in a study that would find them working from home as opposed to working in the physical office. Volunteers were screened to ensure that each had adequate work space in his home and that each had the trust of his manager based on a personal track record of performance. Once selected, 255 volunteers began to telecommute. In the end, it was clear that the telecommuters were outperforming their peers back in the office. The telecommuters took more calls, worked more hours, and experienced fewer sick days. As a result, the company found that these telecommuters contributed more profit to the bottom line and immediately began to implement a wider telecommuting policy.[14] Unfortunately, despite the overall success of the program, previously discussed cultural complications reared their head during the course of the wider rollout. Slate.com performed a deeper investigation of the results and found that:

> Surprisingly, only about one-half of the employees agreed to the deal, and many of those involved in the original experiment decided that they'd had enough, preferring the hours in commute in exchange for the human interaction of office life and a fixed beginning and end to each work day.[15]

But even if the Chinese workforce is slow to embrace the concept of a more flexible workplace, this increasingly "mobile-capable" segment has wholeheartedly embraced the connectivity provided by their mobile devices. Alcatel-Lucent found that Chinese enterprise workers depend on their mobile phones and/or tablets much more than their American peers. More than 70 percent of frontline Chinese report that they use their mobile phone or tablet computer at least several times per day, compared with only 57 percent of American workers. Despite this increased level of interaction with their technology, enterprise workers in China report that they are less tech-savvy than their counterparts in the United States—with only 25 percent indicating that they have "outstanding" technical skills compared with 39 percent of American frontline workers.

- **As a result, the Chinese worker holds his or her IT staff in high regard**—When the Chinese employee encounters some sort of issue with her personal technology, she is much more likely to contact her IT department for help than a peer in the United States is. In China, it would appear that the enterprise IT organization is under less threat of disintermediation than they are in the United States. Alcatel-Lucent found that 60 percent of non-IT personnel and 74 percent of IT personnel agree that the influx of personal devices into the workplace has increased the amount of contact that workers are having with their IT departments. As discussed in an earlier chapter, only 7 percent of American frontline workers report that they are contacting their IT department more often as a result of the consumerization trend. There are three primary reasons for this disconnect. At a fundamental level, as previously discussed, Chinese workers report being less tech-savvy than their American counterparts—they simply realize they need the help. Second, Chinese IT departments have been more open to embracing the BYOD trend in the workplace—with 78 percent of Chinese IT respondents indicating that their organization encourages employees to leverage their personal technology in the workplace. Finally, as a high-power distance culture, the Chinese worker is more culturally inclined to grant power to a person or department based on where they fall in the organization. To the Chinese worker, it is the obligation of IT personnel to help them solve their technical issues. This openness on behalf of IT and the willingness of employees to leverage their expertise are positively affecting the perception of the IT department in the Chinese enterprise. A full 67 percent of Chinese frontline workers agree that their IT department "equips employees with innovative tools, services, or capabilities that foster a healthy culture," with only 1 percent indicating that "IT is a frustration, often a source of employee aggravation due to inferior tools, services, or capabilities." Contrast this with only 45 percent of American workers agreeing that IT provides innovative tools and services and 13 percent agreeing that IT is a source of frustration, and the cultural differences become clear.

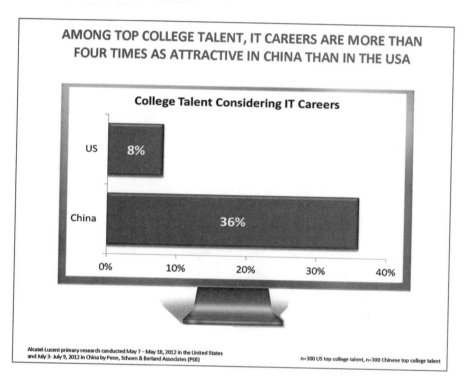

AMONG TOP COLLEGE TALENT, IT CAREERS ARE MORE THAN FOUR TIMES AS ATTRACTIVE IN CHINA THAN IN THE USA

College Talent Considering IT Careers

US 8%

China 36%

0%   10%   20%   30%   40%

Alcatel-Lucent primary research conducted May 7 – May 18, 2012 in the United States and July 3- July 9, 2012 in China by Penn, Schoen & Berland Associates (PSB)   n=300 US top college talent, n=300 Chinese top college talent

Beyond the positive relationship that the Chinese worker has with his IT department, the BYOD trend is also changing the face of enterprise IT in China. More than half (56%) of Chinese IT personnel surveyed by Alcatel-Lucent indicate that consumerization has "allowed IT to become more strategic, since we are no longer consumed with purchasing and maintaining hardware for employees in the company." These Chinese IT organizations are taking full advantage of the BYOD trend to refashion themselves into strategic organizational partners aimed at improving employee productivity through the implementation of advanced technologies.

* **A more strategic view of IT finds China leading the new technology-adoption curve to its own competitive advantage**—Chinese enterprises are

more quickly adopting and integrating technological innovations into the fabric of their organizations. Alcatel-Lucent found that 59 percent of Chinese enterprises report that they are generally among the first to try new technological solutions compared with only 25 percent of American companies that would prefer to wait. For example, face-to-face meetings are an important part of Chinese business culture. However, not unlike the way that Chinese workers are leveraging social networking platforms to improve their *guanxi*, videoconferencing has emerged as a significant force in today's Chinese enterprise. Four in five (83%) enterprise workers surveyed by Alcatel-Lucent indicate that they use videoconferencing on a weekly basis—compared with slightly more than half of their American counterparts. This desire is reinforced by the fact that 75 percent of these same respondents preferred videoconferencing to audio-conferencing given that nonverbal communication cues are not sacrificed and richer interactions can result. Surprisingly, these "richer interactions" that are gained through videoconferencing are not being delivered via the latest and greatest, high-definition videoconferencing systems. As part of the same survey, Alcatel-Lucent found that Chinese enterprise broadband speeds are slower, on average, than in the United States. Two in three (66%) Chinese enterprises have broadband connections slower than 20 Mbps—less bandwidth than is typically required to effectively deliver high-definition videoconferencing. In contrast, only two in five (38%) U.S. companies reported having speeds that slow. Regardless of the lack of quality, Chinese workers find significant benefit in interacting with internal and external stakeholders via videoconferencing.

Cloud technology presents yet another example of Chinese IT rapidly embracing an emerging technology for the benefit of the organization. Morgan Stanley reports that companies in China represent the heaviest users of the public cloud, at more than 73 percent—almost twice the level found of companies in Europe or the United States. This integration of the cloud into the workplace is happening despite the fact that 33 percent of IT personnel say that the move toward cloud-based services, which creates new security, reliability, and performance concerns, is a key challenge for their organization. These IT organizations understand the benefits that the cloud can offer their organization from a cost and productivity perspective and are trying to stay ahead of the demand. Their workforce is already embracing the flexibility that the cloud provides. Alcatel-Lucent found that a full 63 percent of Chinese workers surveyed indicate that they use Amazon, or some other cloud-based service, to help them get their work done. More than 20 percent of these workers do so in direct violation of company IT policies. In contrast, only 32 percent of American workers reported using these services in their ongoing work life.

Far from being bypassed in the Chinese enterprise, these IT departments are supporting employee needs for technological flexibility and working to stay ahead of the curve in reaping the benefits that new and emerging solutions can provide the organization. As discussed in an earlier chapter, Nicholas Carr famously proclaimed in 2003 that "IT doesn't matter" and companies should follow, not lead, when adopting IT solutions, treating the function more as necessary defense than opportunistic offense. With respect to Carr and his theories, it would appear that the Chinese enterprise has cracked the code on implementing technology to realize a competitive advantage. Alcatel-Lucent found that the most successful Chinese companies (as self-reported based on various financial metrics) were the ones most willing to adopt and deploy the latest technological solutions. A full 75 percent of companies identified as "Top Earners" and 71 percent of "Tier 2 Earners" indicate that their organization is generally among the first to adopt a new technology product or solution. When contrasted with the fact that 65 percent of the least successful companies tend to lag their competitors in implementing new technology, a causal relationship between technology adoption and organizational success may be responsible. Further to this evidence, 69 percent of these top-earning companies report wider usage of more advanced technological devices (such as tablet computers and smartphones) in the workplace versus only 35 percent of less successful enterprises. By providing the tools, support, and services that the employee base demands, the Chinese organization is creating a productive working environment that influences organizational competitive advantage. As part of the same Alcatel-Lucent study, 82 Chinese enterprise workers were interviewed to provide their perceptions of technology and IT in the workplace. According to one interviewee, the link between IT and competitive advantage is obvious:

> *IT spending is seen as a cost that can bring strategic advantages of investing in today's era of science and technology by constantly updating. If they lose the advantages of information technology, we will lose the company's development potential and the company's survival will encounter great difficulties.*

Successful, top-earning organizations in the United States are also finding success in proactively implementing new technologies across the workplace—just not at the pace seen in China. Alcatel-Lucent found that 35 percent of the most successful American companies were generally among the first to implement new technologies. The differences between American and Chinese enterprises don't stop there. Despite the global economic difficulties of the past several years, more than half (53%) of Chinese enterprises report that they are "very profitable," with profits of at least 8 percent. In contrast, only two in five, 38 percent, report the same in the United States. This Chinese profitability shows no sign of falling off. More than 15 percent of Chinese enterprises report that their profits have increased significantly, and a full 66 percent report at least modest growth. Enterprises in the United States are starting to recover from the economic downturn, but, with 16 percent reporting significant profit growth and 43 percent reporting modest growth, they still lag the performance of the Chinese enterprise. The Chinese workforce is reaping the benefits of this ongoing success. A full 99 percent of these employers provide bonuses on an annual basis. Additionally, three in five (58%) Chinese companies report giving out more bonuses than last year. The combination of all these factors has resulted in a thriving and expanding workforce. Despite the job worries faced by the rest of the world, 62 percent of Chinese enterprises are growing their workforce, compared to 45 percent of American companies.

- **China is keeping its eye on the ball when it comes to instilling a culture focused on doing what works**—When Chinese workers were asked to identity what they saw as their biggest advantages when competing in the global marketplace, innovation (27%), technology (26%), and the ability to adapt (23%) ranked the highest overall. Surprisingly, these same factors were again identified when these respondents were asked to identify the areas that need to be improved to increase global competitiveness—technology (28%), innovation (23%), and the ability to adapt (20%). This alignment signals a clear understanding by the Chinese enterprise that current actions are working, and fostering a culture of continuous improvement in these areas will only serve to benefit the economic health of the enterprise.

In an effort to better understand how the introduction and implementation of new technologies are affecting the organizational culture of the modern

Chinese enterprise, Alcatel-Lucent asked nearly 3,000 Chinese employees and decision makers to respond to a series of cultural attributes that best described their company. These attributes probed areas such as organizational decision making, strategy development, communication flow, and how technology is embraced. These responses were used to segment Chinese organizational cultures into the following categories:

- **Cultural laggards**—These represent almost 17 percent of the population and are characterized by a risk-averse environment, a dearth of employee training and assistance, and an unhelpful IT department that is primarily viewed as a cost center across the organization. On the whole, employees of cultural laggards understand and readily admit that their organizational culture is not very healthy.
- **Traditionalist** —These organizations comprise nearly 38 percent of the population and represent the common assumption of the culture of a Chinese enterprise. These organizations are distinguished by a strictly defined organizational hierarchy, a high degree of managerial oversight, and a lack of interconnectedness among the employees.
- **Decentralized leadership**—These are those organizations that feature a more relaxed hierarchy and a very uncommunicative management team. At 8.4 percent of the population, these organizations tend to severely restrict web and technology usage among employees and impose considerable managerial oversight of activities while demonstrating a low ability to adapt to change.
- **Cultural gurus**—These represent just more than 37 percent of the sampled companies and feature an overly communicative upper-management team and a proactive approach to addressing business issues. The IT department is considered very helpful and is widely regarded as a strategic resource for the enterprise.

In addition to measuring these qualitative attributes that comprise a company's culture, the study went one step further to evaluate the financial success (or failure) of each of the different types of firms. As previously stated, all respondents were screened for a competent degree of knowledge related to the financial metrics of their organization and self-reported these metrics for their own enterprise. When comparing the impact of cultural characteristics to financial results, a clear picture of the impact that culture has on success begins to emerge. Specifically, a full 66 percent of those least-successful Chinese companies are classified as cultural laggards. This compares with just 6 percent of cultural gurus who find themselves in a similar position. On the other hand, 58 percent of the top-earning companies find themselves classified as cultural gurus compared with only 4 percent of cultural laggards enjoying a top-earning position. Although they can clearly influence the ongoing success of an enterprise in a competitive marketplace, cultural aspects alone aren't sufficient to predict the future health of an enterprise effectively. However, when that culture places a focus on the integration of technology across the workplace, a more open, flexible, and communicative organization culture will find itself best poised for success in a highly competitive and rapidly changing marketplace.

As the second largest economy in the world, China has done a remarkable job of insulating itself from the storms of the recent global economic downturn. Since opening up its internal markets in the late 1970s, the Chinese have been methodically working to merge the most effective business practices of the West with those of its own culture to great benefit. Armed with an understanding of how technological advances can help increase productivity in the enterprise and staffed by the largest workforce in the world, China is flexing its muscles in the global market more than ever before. By encouraging the use of personal technologies across the enterprise, the Chinese company is freeing its IT organization to focus on developing and implementing the most cutting-edge solutions for their employees. As a result, the Chinese CIO is seen as a significant strategic contributor to the business with a full 91 percent of Chinese business decision makers indicating that IT is an effective and strategic tool. While the American enterprise continues to struggle with the strategic value of IT and technology in the business world, the Chinese seem to have figured it out. By continuing to focus on those factors that have already made them a success—innovation, technology, and adaptability—the Chinese are signaling their intention to further stretch their capabilities and remain successful in a highly competitive business environment.

THE NEXT SILICON VALLEY?

The United States holds a long and proud tradition of entrepreneurialism and technological innovation. Some argue that this innovative and entrepreneurial spirit is one of the key traits that make America the successful and prosperous nation that it is. Nowhere is this spirit more alive then in Silicon Valley. Located in the southern part of the San Francisco Bay area of Northern California, Silicon Valley is home to some of the largest and most innovative technology companies in the world. Companies such as Apple, Google, and Hewlett-Packard were born into an environment steeped in technological know-how and emboldened by an entrepreneurial culture to become some of the most influential and successful companies in the world.

That spirit, however, seems to be on the move. According to a survey of 668 global technology business executives at large companies, startups, and virtual capital firms around the world, Silicon Valley's days as the world's innovation center appear to be numbered. Forty-four percent of those surveyed indicated that they believe that the "technology innovation center of the world"—currently located in Silicon Valley—will move to another country within four years. The same respondents indicated China as the most likely location for the next wave of disruptive innovation.[16]

China's growing clout in the world of technology has become a major issue in Washington, DC. At a recent hearing on the country's innovation efforts by the U.S.–China Economic and Security Review Commission, Robert Atkinson, President of the Information Technology Innovation Foundation, testified that the Chinese:

> ...no longer want to dominate just cost-based commodity production and let us be the innovators. They also want to win in innovation-based economic competition.... They want to make virtually everything, especially advanced technology products and services.[17]

And while the sponsors of the KPMG study are quick to highlight that the results don't necessarily mean that Silicon Valley will disappear, they are quick to point out that other regions of the world, especially China, are beginning to focus more of their efforts on the practice of innovation. If history is any indication, Washington is right to be concerned.

Epilogue:
The Next
Decade

→ *We always overestimate the change that will occur in the next two years and underestimate the change that will occur in the next ten. Don't let yourself be lulled into inaction.*

BILL GATES

Although even the most astute forecasters would have likely underestimated the impact from the intersecting generational, technological, and enterprise forces that originated in the 1980s, today's enterprises can hopefully learn from the lessons of their counterparts, based on the primary and secondary evidence offered throughout this book. It would be foolhardy to consider what the next 30 years may reveal, but we the authors are prepared to make the following predictions as to how enterprises will continue to be reshaped over the next decade:

- **Employee subsidization of IT costs will be common**—It is impossible for IT budgets or resources to increase commensurately with demand, as evidenced by the unending trajectory of data and mobile traffic in the enterprise. To attempt to meet the demand, enterprises will increasingly turn to innovative business models whereby employees help subsidize the costs for innovative enterprise services. These services have tangible value, and, according to the 2012 Alcatel-Lucent study, employees are willing to help pay for their deployment. Service providers with an interest in both consumer and enterprise markets will increasingly innovate to offer hybrid consumer/employee-based service plans that combine billing, offer discounts, or otherwise manage services across the dual personas between work and home.

- **IT is too important to be left solely to IT**—As forward-leaning enterprises begin to recognize the cultural benefits enabled by the right IT ingredients, they will engage a much broader effort in approving and deploying technology in their companies. Particularly, Human Resources will have an increasingly louder voice at the technology table as further evidence is accumulated pertaining to technology's role in attracting and retaining employees. Far more creative career paths within the enterprise will emerge, with IT professionals being sourced from HR, Marketing, and other lines of business.

- **The recruitment war will intensify, and intangible perks will be ammunition**—There is no question that enterprises face a dearth of qualified talent, whether in the IT function itself or among the rank-and-file business population capable of applying statistical muscle to business problems. These candidates will be in short supply. Although some companies are already responding with lucrative compensation packages and outrageous physical amenities within their corporate premises, others will fight the battle with the intangible perks that technology provides. Mainly, new candidates will increasingly be offered dynamic and flexible working arrangements to appeal to their mobile lifestyle. The current landscape involves new recruits having to earn such managerial trust over time, but the future will be a workplace where trust is assumed, until either employee or employer violates it.

- **Machines will enter the workforce**—Just as the advent of the assembly line transformed the complexion of factory workers, machines with big data analytic capabilities will transform the knowledge worker of the twenty-first century. Employees will not suffer a deficit of data, although interpreting it into accurate and actionable prescriptions will separate corporate winners from losers. At the same time, machines will increasingly help employees engage with one another. Whereas today's social networks are those derived from a consumer curiosity to know *who knows whom*, semantic intelligence in the enterprise will connect employees by answering the more important question, *who knows what*. The result of machines either processing volumes of structured and unstructured data seamlessly to provide statistical results or simply directing employees to knowledge experts within their own companies will yield better and faster decision-making capabilities.

- **IT will continue to be commoditized, although not underestimated as an ingredient toward sustainable competitive advantage**—Technology will continue to be commoditized, much as it has been for the past several decades. However, although IT by itself will fail to yield sustainable competitive advantage, it will neutralize barriers to entry, thereby allowing smaller firms to intensify the competitive landscape. And, as a key component of healthy cultures, IT's role in helping a company generate sustainable competitive advantage through a more functional cultural dynamic will earn the function greater esteem.

Even if only one of the above predictions becomes common practice in the next 10 years, the impact on enterprises will be significant. Those enterprises capable of riding the technological waves currently cresting will find themselves well positioned to compete and cooperate on a global stage. Those that resist the changes may find themselves holding fast to relics from the past, philosophies that are outdated and irrelevant in an enterprise increasingly without borders. In either case, the digital divide between enterprises will become clearer and will serve as yet one more predictive variable in determining the success of a company, industry, and nation.

Citations

Prologue: The Crystal Ball

[1]Allan Alter, "The Changing role of the CIO," *CIO Insight* (5 April 2005). http://www.cioinsight.com/c/a/Research/The-Changing-Role-of-the-CIO/.

[2]Terry Heick, "How the Workforce Is Changing," *Edudemic* (1 July 2012). http://edudemic.com/2012/07/23507/.

[3]Jay Yarow, "More People Have Mobile Phones Than Electricity or Drinking Water," *Business Insider* (30 April 2012). http://articles.businessinsider.com/2012-04-30/tech/31488477_1_electricity-phones-twitter.

[4]Trevor Mogg, "Smartphone Sales Exceed Those of PCs for First Time, Apple Smashes Record," *Digital Trends* (3 February 2012). http://www.digitaltrends.com/mobile/smartphone-sales-exceed-those-of-pcs-for-first-time-apple-smashes-record/.

Chapter 1: The Mobile Movement

[1]"Mobile Darwinism: The iPass Mobile Enterprise Report," *iPass* (6 March 2012). http://mobile-workforce-project.ipass.com/reports/q1-report-2012.

[2]http://www.merriam-webster.com/dictionary/phobia.

[3]G.C.L. Davey, "Characteristics of Individuals with Fear of Spiders," *Anxiety Research* 4 (1992): 299–314.

[4]A. Swenson, "You Make My Heart Beat Faster: A Quantitative Study of the Relationship between Instructor Immediacy, Classroom Community, and Public Speaking Anxiety," *UW-L Journal of Undergraduate Research* XIV (2011): 1.

[5]"Nomophobia: 66 Percent Are Afraid To Be Separated From Cell Phones, Survey Shows," huffingtonpost.com (8 May 2012). http://www.huffingtonpost.com/2012/05/08/nomophobia-cell-phone-addictio_n_1500670.html.

[6]"Lookout: Lost and Stolen Smartphones Will Cost Consumers Over $30B in 2012," *Techcrunch.com* (22 March 2012). http://techcrunch.com/2012/03/22/

`lookout-lost-and-stolen-smartphones-will-cost-consumers-over-`
`30b-in-2012/`.

[7]Kevin Haley, "Introducing the Symantec Smartphone Honey Stick Project," *Symantec* (9 March 2012). `http://www.symantec.com/connect/blogs/introducing-`
`symantec-smartphone-honey-stick-project`.

[8]R. Kelly Garrett and James N. Danziger, "Which Telework? Defining and Testing a Taxonomy of Technology-Mediated Work at a Distance," *Social Science Computer Review* 25, no. 1 (1997): 27–47.

[9]Jacqui Cheng, "The Truth about the iPhone's Sales Numbers," *ars technica* (23 January 2008). `http://arstechnica.com/apple/2008/01/the-truth-about-the-iphones-`
`sales-numbers/`.

[10]Erik Kennedy, "iPhone Making Inroads in the Corporate World," *ars technica* (7 December 2007). `http://arstechnica.com/apple/2007/12/`
`iphone-making-inroads-in-the-corporate-world/`.

[11]"iPhone Surpasses BlackBerry among Enterprise Users, Finally," *Visage Mobile* (17 November 2011). `http://visagemobile.com/2011/11/17/`
`iphone-surpasses-blackberry-among-enterprise-users-finally/`.

[12]Rachel Emma Silverman and Robin Sidel, "Warming Up to the Officeless Office," *The Wall Street Journal* (17 April 2012). `http://online.wsj.com/article/SB1000142405270`
`2304818404577349783161465976.html`.

[13]Ibid.

[14]"The iPass Mobile Enterprise Report," *iPass* (2011). `http://mobile-workforce-`
`project.ipass.com/reports/mer`.

[15]Don Reisinger, "Security Slideshow: Mobile Security: Why It's Your Biggest Threat," *cioinsight.com* (14 March 2012). `http://www.cioinsight.com/c/a/Security/`
`Mobile-Security-Why-its-Your-Biggest-Threat-875401/`.

[16]Don Reisinger, "Security Slideshow: Information Security Professionals Are in Demand," *cioinsight.com* (7 March 2012). `http://www.cioinsight.com/c/a/Security/`
`Information-Security-Professionals-Are-in-Demand-333921/`.

[17]"Rethink the Risk," *BT Assure* (April 2012). `http://globalservices.bt.com/static/`
`assets/pdf/campaign/security_that_matters/BT_Assure_Rethink_the_`
`Risk_summary.pdf`.

[18]Galen Gruman, "Mobile BYOD Strategy Reveals if Your CIO Is Good or Bad," *InfoWorld* (17 May 2011). `http://www.infoworld.com/d/mobile-technology/`
`mobile-byod-strategy-reveals-if-your-cio-good-or-bad-246`.

[19]Don Reisinger, "Mobile & Wireless Slideshow: What IT Leaders Really Think about Mobility in the Enterprise," *cioinsight.com* (20 January 2011). `http://www.cioinsight.com/`
`c/a/Mobile-and-Wireless/What-IT-Leaders-Really-Think-About-Mobility-`
`in-the-Enterprise-290422/`.

[20]"Rethink the Risk (Featuring Research from Gartner)," *BT and Gartner* (2012). http://
www.globalservices.bt.com/static/assets/pdf/campaign/security_that_
matters/rethinktherisk.pdf.

[21]Cari Sommer, "3 Tips for Managing a Virtual Work Force," *Fast Company* (4 May 2012).
http://www.fastcompany.com/1836332/3-tips-for-managing-a-virtual-
work-force.

[22]Leslie Perlow, "Turning Off Your Smartphone: More Stress or Less," *huffingtonpost.com* (18
April 2012). http://www.huffingtonpost.com/leslie-perlow/
work-stress_b_1429692.html.

[23]"Smartphone Users 'Risking Health' with Extra Work," *4rfv.co.uk* (19 June 2012).
http://www.4rfv.co.uk/nationalnews.asp?id=146048.

Chapter 2: The Cloud Conundrum

[1]Josh Catone, "How Much Data Will Humans Create & Store This Year?" *mashable.com* (27
June 27 2011). http://mashable.com/2011/06/28/data-infographic/.

[2]Steven Levy, "Jeff Bezos Owns the Web in More Ways Than You Think," *Wired* (13
November 2011). http://www.wired.com/magazine/2011/11/ff_bezos/all/1.

[3]Robert Passikoff, "The Most Valuable Company in the World," *forbes.com* (16
February 2012). http://www.forbes.com/sites/marketshare/2012/02/16/
the-most-valuable-company-in-the-world/.

[4]See Note 2.

[5]Ibid.

[6]Ibid.

[7]Ibid.

[8]Andrew R. Hickey, "Amazon Q3 Cloud Revenue Skyrockets," *CRN* (26 October 2011).
http://www.crn.com/news/cloud/231901724/amazon-q3-cloud-revenue-
skyrockets.htm.

[9]Chris Preimesberger, "Unplanned IT Downtime Can Cost $5K per Minute: Report,"
eWeek.com (13 May 2011). http://www.eweek.com/c/a/IT-Infrastructure/
Unplanned-IT-Downtime-Can-Cost-5K-Per-Minute-Report-549007/.

[10]Bob Violino, "Infrastructure Slideshow: IT Downtime Carries a High Price Tag," *cioinsight
.com* (25 May 2011). http://www.cioinsight.com/c/a/Infrastructure/
IT-Downtime-Carries-a-High-Pricetag-448122/.

[11]"Why Amazon's Cloud Computing Outage Didn't Violate Its SLA," *Cloud Computing
Today* (24 April 2011). http://cloud-computing-today.com/2011/04/24/
why-amazons-cloud-computing-outage-didnt-violate-its-sla/.

[12]*Wikipedia* (19 June 2012). http://en.wikipedia.org/wiki/Cloud_computing.

[13]Greg Linden, "Make Data Useful," *Amazon.com.* `http://www.scribd.com/doc/4970486/Make-Data-Useful-by-Greg-Linden-Amazoncom`.

[14]Bob Violino, "IT Management Slideshow: Data Security, Cloud Sprawl Are Top IT Concerns," *cioinsight.com* (10 June 2011). `http://www.cioinsight.com/c/a/IT-Management/Data-Security-Cloud-Sprawl-Are-Top-IT-Concerns-545487/`.

[15]Ibid.

[16]Dave Malcolm, "Tech Debate: Cloud: Public or Private?" *NetworkWorld.* `http://www.networkworld.com/community/tech-debate-private-public-cloud`.

[17]IDC Cloud Services Forecast, 2009–2014, April 2011.

[18]Don Reisinger, "Security Slideshow: 10 Reasons You Can't Trust Employees," *cioinsight.com* (10 March 2011). `http://www.cioinsight.com/c/a/Security/10-Reasons-You-Cant-Trust-Employees-699652/`.

[19]Ibid.

[20]Ibid.

[21]Ibid.

[22]See Note 2.

[23]Steve Lohr, "Amazon's Trouble Raises Cloud Computing Doubts," *The New York Times* (22 April 2011). `http://www.nytimes.com/2011/04/23/technology/23cloud.html`.

[24]Mark Raby, "Zynga's Draw Something Makes Mobile Gaming History," *slashgear.com* (4 April 2012). `http://www.slashgear.com/zyngas-draw-something-makes-mobile-gaming-history-04221613/`.

Chapter 3: The Data Deluge

[1]Stuart J. Johnston, "World's Data Doubling Every Two Years," *InfoStor* (28 June 2011). `http://www.infostor.com/storage-management/worlds-data-doubling-every-two-years-.html`.

[2]Miguel Helft, "Google Uses Search to Track Flu's Spread," *The New York Times* (11 November 2008). `http://www.nytimes.com/2008/11/12/technology/internet/12flu.html`.

[3]Sherry L. Murphy, Jiaquan Xu, and Kenneth D. Kochanek, "Deaths: Preliminary Data for 2010," *National Vital Statistics Reports* 60, no. 4 (11 January 2012). `http://www.cdc.gov/nchs/data/nvsr/nvsr60/nvsr60_04.pdf`.

[4]"Twitter Used to Predict Flu Outbreaks," *ScienceDaily* (28 September 2010). `http://www.sciencedaily.com/releases/2010/09/100928153809.htm`.

[5]*Global Pulse.* `http://unglobalpulse.org`.

[6]"Can a Country's Online 'Mood' Predict Unemployment Spikes?" *Global Pulse* (15 March 2012). http://www.unglobalpulse.org/socialmediaandunemployment.

[7]Martin Hilbert and Priscila López, "The World's Technological Capacity to Store, Communicate, and Compute Information," *Science* 332, no. 6025 (1 April 2011): 60–65.

[8]Erik Brynjolfsson, Lorin M. Hitt, and Heekyung Hellen Kim, "Strength in Numbers: How Does Data-Driven Decisionmaking Affect Firm Performance?" (22 April 2011). http://papers.ssrn.com/sol3/papers.cfm?abstract_id=1819486.

[9]Economist Intelligence Unit, "The Deciding Factor: Big Data & Decision Making," *Capgemini* (June 2012). http://www.capgemini.com/insights-and-resources/by-publication/the-deciding-factor-big-data-decision-making/.

[10]Ibid.

[11]McKinsey Global Institute, "Big Data: The Next Frontier for Innovation, Competition and Productivity" (May 2011). http://www.mckinsey.com/insights/mgi/research/technology_and_innovation/big_data_the_next_frontier_for_innovation.

[12]Cynthia Beath, Irma Becerra-Fernandez, Jeanne Ross, and James Short, "Finding Value in the Information Explosion," *MITSloan Management Review* (19 June 2012). http://sloanreview.mit.edu/the-magazine/2012-summer/53409/finding-value-in-the-information-explosion/.

[13]See Note 9.

[14]"Crunching the Numbers," *The Economist* (19 May 2012). http://www.economist.com/node/21554743.

[15]See Note 11.

[16]See Note 12.

[17]David Rosenbaum, "When Big Data Gets Small, It Gets Useful," *CFO.com* (27 March 2012). http://www3.cfo.com/article/2012/3/analytics_big-data-applications-business-execution.

[18]See Note 11.

[19]See Note 1.

[20]Ibid.

[21]See Note 11.

[22]"Big Data for Development: Challenges & Opportunities" *Global Pulse* (May 2012). http://unglobalpulse.org/BigDataforDevWhitePaper.

[23]See Note 9.

[24]Ibid.

[25]Ibid.

[26]See Note 12.

[27]See Note 22.

[28]Ibid.

[29]Ibid.

[30]Ibid.

[31]Stuart Rose, "Data Discoveries and Analytics Unite to Ignite Innovative Thinking in Financial Services" *Insurance & Technology* (8 June 2012). http://www.insurancetech.com/blogs/240001751.

[32]Laurianne McLaughlin, "Enterprise 2.0: Uncomfortable Truths About Big Data," *InformationWeek* (20 June 2012). http://www.informationweek.com/thebrainyard/news/social_analytics/enterprise-20-uncomfortable-truths-about/240002413.

Chapter 4: The Collaboration Craze

[1]Dennis McCafferty, "10 Reasons You Can't Get Anything Done at Work," *Baseline* (6 October 2011). http://www.baselinemag.com/c/a/IT-Management/10-Reasons-You-Cant-Get-Anything-Done-at-Work-435516/?kc=BLBLBEMNL06272012STR2.

[2]Jonah Lehrer, "Groupthink: The Brainstorming Myth," *The New Yorker* (30 January 2012). http://www.newyorker.com/reporting/2012/01/30/120130fa_fact_lehrer?currentPage=1.

[3]See Note 1.

[4]See Note 2.

[5]Ibid.

[6]Morten T. Hansen, "When Internal Collaboration Is Bad for Your Company," *Harvard Business Review* (April 2009). http://hbr.org/2009/04/when-internal-collaboration-is-bad-for-your-company/ar/1.

[7]See Note 2.

[8]Ibid.

[9]Peter Bright, "Microsoft Buys Skype for $8.5 Billion. Why, Exactly?" *Wired* (10 May 2011). http://www.wired.com/business/2011/05/microsoft-buys-skype-2/.

[10]Ryan Holmes, "Behind Microsoft's Yammer acquisition," *CNN Money* (26 June 2012). http://tech.fortune.cnn.com/2012/06/26/behind-microsofts-yammer-acquisition/.

[11]Kelly Clay, "Microsoft Confirms Yammer Acquisition for $1.2 Billion," *Forbes* (25 June 2012). http://www.forbes.com/sites/kellyclay/2012/06/25/microsoft-confirms-yammer-acquisition-for-1-2-billion/.

[12]Barb Mosher Zinck, "It's Official: Microsoft to Acquire Yammer for US$1.2 billion Cash," *CMS Wire* (25 June 2012). `http://www.cmswire.com/cms/social-business/its-official-microsoft-to-acquire-yammer-for-us12-billion-cash-016251.php`.

[13]Richard Thurston, "The Future of Video Conferencing (OT0084-005)," *Ovum* (April 2011).

[14]Ian Jacobs, "Videoconferencing with a Collaboration Wrapper (OT00141-009)," *Ovum* (April 2012).

[15]Megan Tschannen-Moran, "Collaboration and the Need for Trust," *Journal of Educational Administration* 39, no. 4 (2001): 308–331.

[16]Ibid.

[17]The Staff of the Corporate Executive Board, "The Technology-Collaboration Disconnect," *Bloomberg Businessweek* (12 February 2010). `http://www.businessweek.com/managing/content/feb2010/ca20100211_233652.htm`.

[18]See Note 15.

[19]Susan Cain, "The Rise of the New Groupthink," *The New York Times* (13 January 2012). `http://www.nytimes.com/2012/01/15/opinion/sunday/the-rise-of-the-new-groupthink.html?pagewanted=all`.

[20]See Note 19.

[21]Ibid.

[22]Ibid.

[23]Cindy Perman, "Six Cool Companies to Work For," *CNBC* (8 October 2010). `http://www.cnbc.com/id/39573304/Six_Cool_Companies_to_Work_For?slide=1`.

[24]Eric D. Shaw, Harley V. Stock, "Behavioral Risk of Indicators of Malicious Insider Theft of Intellectual Property: Misreading the Writing on the Wall," *Symantec* (Dec. 7 2011). `http://www.symantec.com/about/news/release/article.jsp?prid=20111207_01`.

[25]See Note 2.

Chapter 5 The Architects

[1]Joe Mandese, "MTV Studies Millennials in the Workplace: Uses It to Transform Its Own, Maybe Even Yours," *MediaPostNews* (15 March 2012). `http://www.mediapost.com/publications/article/169980/mtv-studies-millennials-in-the-workplace-uses-it.html`.

[2]Spencer Ante, "Revenge of the Nerds: Tech Firms Scour College Campuses for Talent," *The Wall Street Journal* (31 May 2012).

[3]Ibid.

4 "Dropping Out: Is College Worth the Cost?" *60 Minutes* (20 May 2012). http://www.cbsnews.com/8301-18560_162-57436775/dropping-out-is-college-worth-the-cost/.

5 "Usual Weekly Earnings of Wage and Salary Workers, First Quarter 2012," Bureau of Labor Statistics, U.S. Department of Labor (17 April 2012). http://www.bls.gov/news.release/pdf/wkyeng.pdf.

6 "Bill Gates on the Facebook IPO, and His Idea of Happiness: Full Transcript," *NDTV* (1 June 2012). http://www.ndtv.com/article/india/bill-gates-on-the-facebook-ipo-and-his-idea-of-happiness-full-transcript-221053.

7 Cheryl Issac, "Stop Telling Millennials That College Is Bad," *Forbes* (8 May 2012). http://www.forbes.com/sites/worldviews/2012/05/08/stop-telling-millennials-that-college-is-bad/.

8 Eric Zeman, "Seton Hall Gives Nokia Windows Phones to Freshmen," *Information Week* (12 June 2012). http://www.informationweek.com/news/mobility/smart_phones/240001927.

9 Ed Oswald, "Nokia Lumia 900 Phones Appear in One College's Freshman Packet," *PC World* (11 June 2012). http://www.pcworld.com/article/257369/nokia_lumia_900_phones_appear_in_one_colleges_freshman_packet.html.

10 Paula Quam, "Millennial Minds: The effects of Digital Stimulus on Today's Youth," *suite101* (12 October 2010). http://suite101.com/article/millennial-minds-the-effects-of-digital-stimulus-on-todays-youth-a296016.

11 Michelle Stinson Ross, "Social Media and the Millennial Brain," *Search Engine Journal* (21 February 2012). http://www.searchenginejournal.com/social-media-and-the-millennial-brain/40424/.

12 Janna Anderson and Lee Rainie, "Millennials Will Benefit and Suffer Due to Their Hyperconnected Lives," *Pew Research Center* (29 February 2012). http://pewinternet.org/Reports/2012/Hyperconnected-lives.aspx.

13 Paula Quam, "Millennial Minds: The Effects of Digital Stimulus on Today's Youth," *Suite101.com* (12 October 2010). http://suite101.com/article/millennial-minds-the-effects-of-digital-stimulus-on-todays-youth-a296016.

14 Dan Schawbel, "Millennials vs. Baby Boomers: Who Would You Rather Hire?" *Time* (29 March 2012). http://moneyland.time.com/2012/03/29/millennials-vs-baby-boomers-who-would-you-rather-hire/.

15 Simon Mackie, "Supporting Millennials in the Workplace," *GigaOM.com* (11 July 2011). http://gigaom.com/collaboration/supporting-millenials-in-the-workplace/.

16 Erica Dhawan, "Gen-Y Workforce and Workplace Are Out of Synch," *Forbes* (23 January 2012). http://www.forbes.com/sites/85broads/2012/01/23/gen-y-workforce-and-workplace-are-out-of-sync/.

[17]See Note 13.

[18]Ned Smith, "Why Gen Y and BYOD Can Be a Security Nightmare," *Business News Daily* (19 June 2012). http://www.businessnewsdaily.com/2713-millennial-byod-ignore-security-policies.html.

[19]Ty Kiisel, "Gimmie, Gimmie, Gimmie—Millennials in the Workplace," *Forbes* (16 May 2012). http://www.forbes.com/sites/tykiisel/2012/05/16/gimme-gimme-gimme-millennials-in-the-workplace/.

[20]Meg James, "MTV Aims to Capture the Spirit of Millennials," *TDN.com* (9 October 2012). http://tdn.com/lifestyles/article_614f2710-f2c5-11e0-ada9-001cc4c03286.html.

[21]Joe Mandese, "MTV Studies Millennials in the Workplace: Uses It to Transform Its Own, Maybe Even Yours," *MediaPostNews* (15 March 2012). http://www.mediapost.com/publications/article/169980/mtv-studies-millennials-in-the-workplace-uses-it.html.

Chapter 6: The Tightrope Walkers

[1]"Human Resource Professionals Are Struggling as Strategic Business Partners, Global Study Finds," *HayGroup.com* (March-April 2012). http://www.haygroup.com/ww/Press/Details.aspx?ID=33887.

[2]Peter D'Amato, "LaidOffWithMe: The Day the Axe Fell at BuyWithMe," *TechCrunch* (28 October 2011). http://techcrunch.com/2011/10/28/laidoffwithme-buywithme/.

[3]Dan Beucke, "Aviva Fires Everyone: Great Moments in Employee Motivation," *BloombergBusinessweek* (20 April 2012). http://www.businessweek.com/articles/2012-04-20/aviva-fires-everyone-great-moments-in-employee-motivation.

[4]Susan Adams, "Trust in Business Falls Off a Cliff," *Forbes* (13 June 2012). http://www.forbes.com/sites/susanadams/2012/06/13/trust-in-business-falls-off-a-cliff/.

[5]Barbara Richman, "Maritz Research Poll Shows Employees Don't Trust Management," *Memphis Business Journal* (30 March 2012). http://www.bizjournals.com/memphis/print-edition/2012/03/30/maritz-research-poll-shows-employees.html?page=all.

[6]David K. Williams, "Seven Non-Negotiables to Prevent a Bad Hire," *Harvard Business Review* (31 May 2012). http://blogs.hbr.org/cs/2012/05/7_non-negotiables_to_prevent_a.html.

[7]See Note 1.

[8]"The Role and Future of HR: The CEO's Perspective," *HRPA and Knightsbridge* (2011). http://www.hrpa.ca/Documents/HRPA_KB_CEO_Perspective_Research_Highlight.pdf.

[9]Jim Kochanski and J.P. Elliot, "Improving Performance through the Employee Value Exchange," *Sibson.com* (13 October 2010). http://www.sibson.com/publications-and-resources/articles/Improving-Performance-Employee-Value-Exchange.pdf.

[10]Gabriela Santamaria, "The 4 P's of an HR Brand: People, Pay, Process & Promotion," *Helios HR* (23 March 2012). http://www.helioshr.com/blog/category/communication/.

[11]Michelle V. Rafter, "2012 Technology Forecast," *Workforce* (10 January 2012). http://www.workforce.com/article/20120110/NEWS02/120119996/2012-hr-technology-forecast.

[12]Nikki Blacksmith and Jim Harter, "Majority of American Workers Not Engaged in Their Jobs," *Gallup.com* (28 October 2011). http://www.gallup.com/poll/150383/majority-american-workers-not-engaged-jobs.aspx.

[13]"Employee Engagement Overview," *Gallup.com* (2011). http://www.gallup.com/consulting/121535/employee-engagement-overview-brochure.aspx.

[14]Society for Human Resource Management, "Raising Engagement," *HR Magazine* 55, no. 5 (1 May 2010). http://www.shrm.org/Publications/hrmagazine/EditorialContent/2010/0510/Pages/0510fox.aspx.

[15]Chartered Institute for Personnel and Development, "The Changing HR Function: The Key Questions," *CIPD* (2006). http://www.cipd.co.uk/hr-resources/research/changing-hr-function.aspx.

[16]Ibid.

[17]Ibid.

[18]Michael Beer, "The Transformation of the Human Resource Function: Resolving the Tension between a Traditional Administrative and a New Strategic Role," *Human Resource Management* 36 (Spring 1997): 49–56. http://onlinelibrary.wiley.com/doi/10.1002/(SICI)1099-050X(199721)36:1%3C49::AID-HRM9%3E3.0.CO;2-W/abstract.

[19]Dave MacKay, "10 HR Trends That Are Changing the Face of Business," *Keynote* (2005). www.Ceridian.ca/en/news/2005/10trends.pdf.

[20]Russ Banham, "When the Boomers Go," *CFO.com* (15 June 2012). http://www.cfo.com/article.cfm/14644365/c_14644972?f=magazine_featured.

[21]Duke Energy, "2012 Sustainability Report" (2012). http://sustainabilityreport.duke-energy.com/downloads/files/10-quality-workforce.pdf.

[22]Russ Banham, "When the Boomers Go," *CFO.com* (15 June 2012). `http://www.cfo.com/article.cfm/14644365/c_14644972?f=magazine_featured`.

[23]Jared Bilski, "Firm Didn't Protect Staffer from Cyber-Bullying, Owes $820K," *CFO Daily News* (1 June 2012). `http://www.cfodailynews.com/firm-didnt-protect-staffer-from-cyber-bullying-owes-820k/`.

[24]Mark Geary, "Textual Harassment in the Workplace Becoming More Common," *Digitriad .com* (18 June 2012). `http://www.digtriad.com/news/local/article/232739/57/OMG-Thats-Textual-Harassment`.

[25]Ibid.

Chapter 7: The Storytellers

[1]Lisa Arthur, "Five Years From Now, CMOs Will Spend More on IT Than CIOs Do,"*Forbes .com* (8 February 2012). `http://www.forbes.com/sites/lisaarthur/2012/02/08/five-years-from-now-cmos-will-spend-more-on-it-than-cios-do/`.

[2]"Advertising the Collapse of Clio," *Time* Magazine (1 July 1991). `http://www.time.com/time/magazine/article/0,9171,973271,00.html`.

[3]"Clio Awards, " Wikipedia.org., `http://en.wikipedia.org/wiki/Clio_awards`.

[4]Louise Story, "Anywhere the Eye Can See, It's Likely to See an Ad," *The New York Times* (15 January 2007). `http://www.nytimes.com/2007/01/15/business/media/15everywhere.html?pagewanted=all`.

[5]Rik Pieters, Luk Warlop, and Michel Wedel, "Breaking through the Clutter: Benefits of Advertisement Originality and Familiarity for Brand Attention and Memory," *Management Science* 48, no. 6 (June 2002): 765–781.

[6]History.com, "Radio and Television." `http://www.history.com/topics/radio-and-television/page2`.

[7]Kevin Mitchell, *Jacobs Beach: The Mob, the Fights, the Fifties.* (Cambridge, UK: Pegasus, 2012).

[8]See Note 6.

[9]United Nations Cyberschoolbus, "Information and Communications Technology (ICT)." `http://www.un.org/cyberschoolbus/briefing/technology/tech.pdf`.

[10]See Note 6.

[11]Derek Thompson, "The Collapse of Print Media in 1 Graph," *The Atlantic* (28 February 2012). `http://www.theatlantic.com/business/archive/2012/02/the-collapse-of-print-advertising-in-1-graph/253736/`.

[12]Stuart Elliott, "YouTube and Kin Woo Marketers, Seeking to Siphon Dollars From TV," *The New York Times* (2 May 2012). `http://www.nytimes.com/2012/05/03/business/media/youtube-channels-court-advertisers-at-newfronts.html`.

[13]Nielsen Prime Broadcast Network Television Ratings—United States, Week of May 21, 2012. `http://www.nielsen.com/us/en/insights/top10s/television.html`.

[14]Kaitlyn Ytterberg, "Mobile Phones More Popular than Toothbrushes?" *Officite* (24 May 2012). `http://www.officite.com/blog/mobile-phones-more-popular-toothbrushes`.

[15]"Smartphones, Mobile Internet Set Stage for Increased Mobile Ad Spend," *eMarketer* (4 October 2011). `http://www.emarketer.com/Article.aspx?R=1008622`.

[16]"Mobile Passes Print in Time-Spent Among US Adults," *eMarketer* (12 December 2011). `http://www.emarketer.com/PressRelease.aspx?R=1008732`.

[17]See Note 8.

[18]Joe Mandese, "Quick How Many Media Platforms Currently Exist for Advertisers to Use? (Hint: It's More than 100)," *MediaPost Raw* (26 January 2012). `http://www.mediapost.com/publications/article/166592/quick-how-many-media-platforms-currently-exist-for.html`.

[19]Kaiser Family Foundation, "Daily Media Use Among Children and Teens Up Dramatically from Five Years Ago" (20 January 2010). `http://www.kff.org/entmedia/entmedia012010nr.cfm`.

[20]Daniel Frankel, "The Plan by Yahoo, Hulu, Other Big Video Firms to Grab Upfront TV Ad Money," *paidContent* (24 February 2012). `http://paidcontent.org/2012/02/24/419-the-plan-by-yahoo-hulu-other-big-video-firms-to-grab-upfront-tv-ad-mone/`.

[21]"Are Marketers Struggling to Keep Up with Social Trends?" *eMarketer* (20 August 2010). `http://www.emarketer.com/Mobile/Article.aspx?R=1007878`.

[22]Jennifer Rooney, "Marketers Failing Interactive Part of Interactive Marketing," *AdvertisingAge* (4 April 2011). `http://adage.com/article/cmo-strategy/marketers-failing-interactive-part-interactive-marketing/149711/`.

[23]"Marketers Overwhelmed by Customer Data in Social Media: IBM Survey," *media.cbronline.com* (11 October 2011). `http://media.cbronline.com/news/marketers-overwhelmed-by-customer-data-in-social-media-ibm-survey-111011`.

[24]Mires+Ball, KRC Research, "Building Buzz. Building Brands: State of the Brand Report, August 2010." `http://www.krcresearch.com/pdfs/StateBrandReport.pdf`.

[25]"Flawsome: Why Brands That Behave More Humanly, Including Showing Their Flaws, Will Be Awesome," *Trendwatching.com* (April 2012). `http://trendwatching.com/trends/12trends2012/?flawsome`.

[26]Think with Google, Google/Shopper Sciences, "The Zero Moment of Truth Macro Study US" (April 2011). `http://www.thinkwithgoogle.com/insights/library/studies/the-zero-moment-of-truth-macro-study/`.

[27]Think with Google, Google/OTX, "The Mobile Movement US," (April 2011). `http://www.thinkwithgoogle.com/insights/library/studies/the-mobile-movement/`.

[28]See Note 24.

[29]David Kiley and Burt Helm, "The Short Life of the Chief Marketing Officer," *Businessweek* (28 November 2007). `http://www.businessweek.com/stories/2007-11-28/the-short-life-of-the-chief-marketing-officer`.

[30]"Average Chief Marketing Officer Tenure Hits New High: 42 Months," *SpencerStuart* (24 May 2011). `http://www.spencerstuart.com/about/media/65/`.

[31]Emily Friedman, "Sex May Sell, But Some Say Ads Go too Far," *abcnews.go.com* (26 October 2007). `http://abcnews.go.com/Business/story?id=3778073&page=1`.

Chapter 8: The Venture Capitalists

[1]Kate O'Sullivan, "In Search of the New," CFO.com (19 April 2010). `http://www.cfo.com/article.cfm/14491395/c_14492952`.

[2]"The Unacknowledged Giant," *The Economist* (17 June 2010). `http://www.economist.com/node/16374404`.

[3]Norman Macrae, "The Coming Entrepreneurial Revolution: A Survey," *The Economist* 261, no. 6956 (25 December 1976): 41–65.

[4]Ibid.

[5]Eric N. Berg, "Now 'Intrapreneurship' is Hot," *The New York Times* (4 April 1985).

[6]Steven Prokesch, "'Intrapreneurship' Raising Doubts," *The New York Times* (28 July 1986).

[7]C. Wesley Morse, "The Delusion of Intrapreneurship," *Long Range Planning.* 19, no. 6 (1986): 92–95.

[8]Jake Swearingen, "Great Intrapreneurs in Business History," *CBS Money Watch* (10 April 2008). `http://www.cbsnews.com/8301-505125_162-51196888/great-intrapreneurs-in-business-history/`.

[9]Tom Lauricella, "Markets Regain Footing, Not Faith," *The Wall Street Journal* (30 July 2012). `http://professional.wsj.com/article/SB10000872396390444130304577556971056345342.html?mod=wsjcfo_hp_midLatest`.

[10]Eric Savitz, "The Path to Becoming a Fortune 500 CEO," *Forbes* (5 December 2011). `http://www.forbes.com/sites/ciocentral/2011/12/05/the-path-to-becoming-a-fortune-500-ceo/`.

[11]Matthew Quinn, "CFO's Wish List," *The Wall Street Journal* (29 June 2012). `http://professional.wsj.com/article/SB1000142405270230356150457749315341293554.html?mg=reno64-wsj`.

[12]"CFO Insights: What Is Keeping CFOs Up at Night?" *Deloitte* (2012). http://www
.deloitte.com/assets/Dcom-UnitedStates/Local%20Assets/Documents/
CFO_Center_FT/us_cfo_CFO-Insights_CFOupatnight_060612.pdf.

[13]Bill Gemeglia, "The CFO's Increased Focus on IT Spending," *MyITView*
(20 July 2012). http://www.myitview.com/it-management/
the-cfos-increased-focus-on-it-spending.

[14]John Van Decker and Bill Overell, "The CFO's Impact on Technology Investment Decisions:
2011 Gartner FEI Technology Study," Gartner and Financial Executives. http://www
.google.com/url?sa=t&rct=j&q=gartner%20fei%
20technology%20study&source=web&cd=5&sqi=2&ved=0CFIQFjAE&url=
http%3A%2F%2Fwww.financialexecutives.org%2Feweb%2Fupload%2FFEI%2F20
11%2520Gartner%2520FEI%2520Technology%2520Study.pptx&ei=
NKwaULOtNOSU0QWSkYHoDQ&usg=AFQjCNFrcaWQ0jPgZcN9SnODFoSg9aI7GA.

[15]"C-Suite Has Difference of Opinion on Importance of Social Business," *TechJournal* (31
May 2012). http://www.techjournal.org/tag/cfos/.

[16]Peter A. Coles, Karim R. Lakhani, and Andrew P. McAfee, *Prediction Markets at Google*
(Boston: Harvard Business School, 2007).

[17]Tina Rosenberg, "Prizes with an Eye Toward the Future," *The New York Times* (29
February 2012). http://opinionator.blogs.nytimes.com/2012/02/29/
prizes-with-an-eye-toward-the-future/.

[18]Ibid.

[19]Ibid.

[20]"FINRA Fines Piper Jaffray $700,000 for Email Retention Violations, Related Disclosure,
Supervisory and Reporting Violations," *FINRA News Release* (24 May 2010). http://
www.finra.org/newsroom/newsreleases/2010/p121506.

[21]John McQuaid, "Prediction Markets Are Hot, But Here's Why They Can Be So
Wrong," *Wired Magazine* (19 May 2008). http://www.wired.com/techbiz/it/
magazine/16-06/st_essay.

[22]Raul Chao, "The Ins and Outs of Open Innovation," *Forbes* (6 May
2012). http://www.forbes.com/sites/darden/2012/05/06/
the-ins-and-outs-of-open-innovation-3/.

[23]Gary Hamel and Gary Getz, "Funding Growth in an Age of Austerity," *Harvard Business
Review* (July–August 2004): 76–84.

[24]David Rosenbaum, "Digging Out from Big Data," *CFO Magazine* (1 August 2012). http://
www.cfo.com/article.cfm/14652726.

[25]Ibid.

[26]Ibid.

[27]Alix Stuart, "Teaming Up on Innovation," *CFO.com* (25 January 2012). `http://www3`
`.cfo.com/article/2012/1/growth-strategies_best-doctors-varvaris-`
`ernst-falchuk`.

[28]Ibid.

[29]Ibid.

Chapter 9: The Endangered Species

[1]Dennis McCafferty, "IT Management Slideshow: Corporate Innovation Is in Short Supply,"
cioinsight.com (22 June 2011). `http://www.cioinsight.com/c/a/IT-Management/`
`Corporate-Innovation-Is-in-Short-Supply-280294/`.

[2]Nicholas G. Carr, "IT Doesn't Matter," *Harvard Business Review* (May 2003): 41–49.

[3]Ibid.

[4]Dennis McCafferty, "IT Management Slideshow: CIO Job Description:
Which Skills Really Matter?" *cioinsight.com* (17 April 2011).
`http://www.cioinsight.com/c/a/IT-Management/`
`CIO-Job-Description-Which-Skills-Really-Matter-842565/`.

[5]Ibid.

[6]Dennis McCafferty, "Careers Slideshow: State of the CIO Survey," *cioinsight*
.com (2 June 2010). `http://www.cioinsight.com/c/a/Careers/`
`State-of-the-CIO-Survey-557604/`.

[7]Tom Sheehan, "5 IT Spending and Staffing Trends for 2011 to 2012," *ciozone.com* (22 June
2011). `http://www.ciozone.com/index.php/IT-Services/5-IT-Spending-and-`
`Staffing-Trends-for-2011-to-2012.html`.

[8]Don Reisinger, "IT Management Slideshow: CFO and CIO: A Love–Hate Relationship,"
cioinsight.com (14 April 2011). `http://www.cioinsight.com/c/a/IT-Management/`
`CFO-and-CIO-A-LoveHate-Relationship-860443/`.

[9]Don Reisinger, "Security Slideshow: Data Protection: The Secret Expense You Don't Want to
Face?" *cioinsight.com* (9 May 2012). `http://www.cioinsight.com/c/a/Security/`
`Data-Protection-The-Secret-Expense-You-Dont-Want-to-Face-837847/`.

[10]Jennifer Lawinski, "Security Slideshow: Malicious Attacks
Skyrocket as Hackers Explore New Targets," *cioinsight.com* (7
May 2012). `http://www.cioinsight.com/c/a/Security/`
`Malicious-Attacks-Skyrocket-As-Hackers-Explore-New-Targets-356545/`.

[11]"Pfizer's Third Security Breach Occurs as Former Employee Steals 34,000 Records," *Media
Health Leaders* (20 June 2012). `http://www.healthleadersmedia.com/content/`
`HOM-76228/Pfizers-third-security-breach-occurs-as-former-employee-`
`steals-34000-records`.

[12]Paul Shockley, "County Posts Classified Info," *The Daily Sentinel*, Grand Junction, Colorado (2 December 2010). http://www.gjsentinel.com/news/articles/county_posts_classified_info/.

[13]Linda Musthaler, "Social Engineering Attacks on the Enterprise Are Trending Upward," *NetworkWorld* (5 January 2012). http://www.networkworld.com/newsletters/techexec/2012/010612bestpractices.html.

[14]"The Consumerization of IT: The Next-Generation CIO," Center for Technology and Innovation, *pWc* (November 2011). http://www.pwc.com/us/en/technology-innovation-center/consumerization-information-technology-transforming-cio-role.jhtml.

[15]See Note 4.

[16]Ibid.

[17]Don Reisinger, "IT Management Slideshow: CIOs and Lawyers: A Match Made in Heaven or Hell?" *cioinsight.com* (23 May 2012). http://www.cioinsight.com/c/a/IT-Management/CIOs-and-Lawyers-A-Match-Made-in-Heaven-or-Hell-590181/.

[18]Dennis McCafferty, "IT Management Slideshow: What Motivates Your Top IT Employees?" *cioinsight.com* (23 February 2011). http://www.cioinsight.com/c/a/IT-Management/What-Motivates-Your-Top-IT-Employees-615817/.

[19]Paul McDougall, "U.S. Tech Worker Shortage Looms, Study Warns," *InformationWeek* (23 May 2012). http://www.informationweek.com/news/global-cio/outsourcing/240000853.

[20]"2012 State of the CIO Survey," *CIO Magazine* (January 2012). http://mkting.cio.com/pdf/2012_stateofthecio_highlights-FINAL.pdf.

[21]Tony Kontzer, "Are You a Revolutionary CIO?", *cioinsight.com* (20 September 2011). http://www.cioinsight.com/c/a/IT-Management/Are-You-a-Revolutionary-CIO-548120/.

[22]Jennifer Lawinski, "IT Management Slideshow: CEOs Plan to Invest in IT, Innovation in 2012," *cioinsight.com* (20 April 2012). http://www.cioinsight.com/c/a/IT-Management/CEOs-Plan-to-Invest-in-IT-Innovation-in-2012-487188/.

[23]Eric Chabrow, "LinkedIn Has Neither CIO nor CISO," *Bank Info Security* (8 June 2012). http://www.bankinfosecurity.com/blogs/linkedin-has-neither-cio-nor-ciso-p-1289.

Chapter 10: The Culture Recipe

[1]Paul Meehan, Orit Gadiesh, and Shintaro Hori, "Culture as Competitive Advantage," *Leader to Leader* 2006, no. 39 (Winter 2006): 55–61.

[2]Ben Casselman, "Good Jobs News: More People Are Quitting," *The Wall Street Journal* (11 April 2012). `http://blogs.wsj.com/economics/2012/04/11/good-jobs-news-more-people-are-quitting/?KEYWORDS=BEN%20CASSELMAN`.

[3]Greg Smith, "Why I Am Leaving Goldman Sachs," *The New York Times* (14 March 2012). `http://www.nytimes.com/2012/03/14/opinion/why-i-am-leaving-goldman-sachs.html?pagewanted=all`.

[4]Christine Harper, "Goldman Roiled by Op-Ed Loses $2.2 Billion," *Bloomberg* (15 March 2012). `http://www.bloomberg.com/news/2012-03-15/goldman-stunned-by-op-ed-loses-2-2-billion-for-shareholders.html?mrefid=twitter`.

[5]"MWW Survey: 3 Out Of 4 Business Leaders Believe Corporate Reputation Is Substantially Driven By Internal Culture," *PRNewswire* (31 May 2012). `http://www.prnewswire.com/news-releases/mww-survey-3-out-of-4-business-leaders-believe-corporate-reputation-is-substantially-driven-by-internal-culture-155975085.html`.

[6]NORC, *GSS General Social Survey*. `http://www3.norc.org/gss+website/`.

[7]See Note 3.

[8]Great Place to Work, "About Us." `http://www.greatplacetowork.com/about-us/about-us#ixzz1zC8rbyeH`.

[9]Alex Edmans, "The Link between Job Satisfaction and Firm Value, with Implications for Corporate Social Responsibility," Wharton, NBER, and ECGI (26 May 2012). *Academy of Management Perspectives* (in press). `http://amp.aom.org/content/early/2012/09/02/amp.2012.0046.full.pdf+html`.

[10]Nathan Furr, "Big Business ... The End Is Near: Why 70% of the Fortune 1000 Will Be Replaced in a Few Years," *Forbes* (21 April 2011). `http://www.forbes.com/sites/nathanfurr/2011/04/21/big-business-the-end-is-near/`.

[11]See Note 1.

[12]David Mielach, "Surprise! Bosses Value Social Media More Than Employees," *FOXBusiness* (14 June 2012). `http://smallbusiness.foxbusiness.com/technology-web/2012/06/14/surprise-bosses-value-social-media-more-than-employees/#ixzz1zCOlBpCt`.

[13]Ibid.

[14]Rana Foroohar, "Can't Have It All? Blame Our Extreme Work Culture," *Time Ideas* (25 June 2012). `http://ideas.time.com/2012/06/25/cant-have-it-all-blame-our-extreme-work-culture/#ixzz1zCUlwfYK`.

[15]Peter Bregman, "A Good Way to Change a Corporate Culture," *Harvard Business Review Blog Network* (25 June 2009). `http://blogs.hbr.org/bregman/2009/06/the-best-way-to-change-a-corpo.html`.

[16]Steven Rosenbaum, "The Happiness Culture: Zappos Isn't a Company—It's a Mission," *Fast Company* (6 June 2010). http://www.fastcompany.com/1657030/the-happiness-culture-zappos-isn-t-a-company-it-s-a-mission.

[17]Christopher Palmeri, "Zappos Retails Its Culture," *Bloomberg BusinessWeek* (30 December 2009). http://www.businessweek.com/magazine/content/10_02/b4162057120453.htm.

Chapter 11: The Small Business Dream

[1]Steve Strauss, "What's Better: Working for a Big Company or a Small One?" *USA TODAY* (20 February 2011). http://www.usatoday.com/money/smallbusiness/columnist/strauss/2011-02-20-small-businesses-big-challenges_N.htm.

[2]Mimi Hall, "Americans Fed Up with Constant Political Gridlock," *USA TODAY* (19 July 2011). http://www.usatoday.com/news/washington/2011-07-18-poll-politicians-approval_n.htm.

[3]Tamara Keith, "Small Businesses Get Big Political Hype. What's the Reality?" *NPR* (2 July 2012). http://www.npr.org/blogs/itsallpolitics/2012/04/18/150822919/small-businesses-get-big-political-hype-whats-the-reality.

[4]Charles Kenny, "Rethinking the Boosterism about Small Business," *Bloomberg BusinessWeek* (28 September 2011). http://www.businessweek.com/magazine/rethinking-the-boosterism-about-small-business-09282011.html.

[5]See Note 3.

[6]Scott Shane, "Most People Think Starting a Business Is Difficult," *Forbes* (14 August 2011). http://www.forbes.com/sites/scottshane/2011/08/14/most-people-think-starting-a-business-is-difficult/.

[7]Sarah Morgan, "10 Things Start-Ups Won't Tell You," *SmartMoney* (6 February 2012). http://www.smartmoney.com/small-business/small-business/10-things-startups-wont-tell-you-1328313304334/.

[8]Darren Dahl, "Top 10 Reasons to Run Your Own Business," *Inc.* (21 January 2011). http://www.inc.com/guides/201101/top-10-reasons-to-run-your-own-business.html.

[9]Mike Sachoff, "Yahoo Looks at Why People Start a Small Business," *Small Business Newz* (3 February 2011). http://www.smallbusinessnewz.com/yahoo-looks-at-why-people-start-a-small-business-2011-02.

[10]See Note 3.

[11]See Note 4.

[12]Ibid.

[13]Ibid.

[14]Floyd Norris, "Small Companies Create More Jobs? Maybe Not," *The New York Times* (24 February 2012). http://www.nytimes.com/2012/02/25/business/data-challenges-idea-that-small-companies-create-more-jobs.html.

[15]Felix Salmon, "The Unhelpful Lionization of Small Business," *Reuters Opinion* (24 October 2011). http://blogs.reuters.com/felix-salmon/2011/10/24/the-unhelpful-lionization-of-small-business/.

[16]"Webs Survey Reveals Small Business Owners Attitudes towards Economy," *PRWeb* (1 December 2011). http://www.prweb.com/releases/2011/12/prweb9005153.htm.

[17]Ibid.

[18]Sarah E. Needleman, "'Small' IT Market Attracts Big Companies," *The Wall Street Journal* (26 January 2012). http://online.wsj.com/article/SB10001424052970203806504577183052169000964.html.

[19]See Note 4.

[20]See Note 18.

[21]Ibid.

[22]Ibid.

[23]John Bussey, "Seeking Safety in Clouds," *The Wall Street Journal* (15 September 2011). http://online.wsj.com/article/SB10001424053111904060604576572930344327162.html.

[24]Ibid.

[25]Erica Swallow, "49% of Small Business Owners Use Smartphones," *Mashable Business* (21 October 2010). http://mashable.com/2010/10/21/small-business-smartphones/.

[26]Alicia Ciccone, "Mobile Apps Save Small Businesses Time and Money, Study Finds," *The Huffington Post* (10 February 2012). http://www.huffingtonpost.com/2012/02/10/mobile-apps-save-small-businesses-time-and-money_n_1269049.html.

[27]See Note 16.

[28]AT&T News, "AT&T Survey Shows Mobile Apps Integral to Small Business Operations, Remote Workers on the Rise, Facebook Use Growing Rapidly" (15 March 2011). http://www.att.com/gen/press-room?pid=19326&cdvn=news&newsarticleid=31689.

[29]*BusinessNewsDaily* Staff, "Small Business Gives Best Customer Service," *BusinessNewsDaily* (4 May 2011). http://www.businessnewsdaily.com/928-small-business-customer-service.html.

[30]Jennifer Alsever, "A $10 App Saves Hours of Commuting," *CNNMoney* (3 May 2010). http://money.cnn.com/2010/05/03/smallbusiness/pixetell/index.htm.

[31]Minda Zetlin, "The Latest Privacy Invasion: Retailer Tracking," *Fox Business* (16 May 2012). http://www.foxbusiness.com/personal-finance/2012/05/14/latest-privacy-invasion-retailer-tracking/.

[32]See Note 14.

[33]See Note 4.

[34]Kelly Edmiston, "The Role of Small and Large Businesses in Economic Development," Federal Reserve Bank of Kansas City, *Economic Review, Second Quarter 2007*, pp. 73–97. http://www.kc.frb.org/publicat/econrev/PDF/2q07edmi.pdf.

[35]Dieter Ibielski, "So What about Small Business Productivity?" *National Productivity Review* 17, no. 1 (Winter 1997): 1–4.

[36]Carol Tice, "Are Small Businesses Really Big Job Creators?" *Entrepreneur* (28 October 2011). http://www.entrepreneur.com/blog/220616.

Chapter 12: The New Civil War

[1]Liz Dwyer, "Debunking Education Myths: America's Never Been Number One in Math," *Good Education* (10 February 2011). http://www.good.is/post/debunking-education-myths-america-s-never-been-number-one-in-math/.

[2]"A Nation at Risk: The Imperative for Educational Reform," A Report to the Nation and the Secretary of Education, United States Department of Education by The National Commission on Excellence in Education, April 1983, http://teachertenure.procon.org/sourcefiles/a-nation-at-risk-tenure-april-1983.pdf.

[3]Ibid.

[4]Greg Toppo, "'Nation at Risk': The Best Thing or the Worst Thing for Education?" *USA TODAY* (1 August 2008). http://www.usatoday.com/news/education/2008-04-22-nation-at-risk_N.htm.

[5]Joel I. Klein and Condoleezza Rice, "U.S. Education Reform and National Security," Independent Task Force Report No. 68 (New York: Council on Foreign Relations, 2012). http://www.cfr.org/united-states/us-education-reform-national-security/p27618.

[6]Ibid.

[7]CIA, *The World Factbook*. https://www.cia.gov/library/publications/the-world-factbook/rankorder/2206rank.html.

[8]World Health Organization, "World Health Statistics 2011." http://www.who.int/gho/publications/world_health_statistics/EN_WHS2011_Full.pdf.

[9]Gerard F. Anderson, Bianca K. Frogner, Roger A. Johns, and Uwe E. Reinhardt, "Health Care Spending and Use of Information Technology in OECD Countries,"

Health Affairs 25, no. 3 (2006): 819–831. http://content.healthaffairs.org/content/25/3/819.full.pdf+html.

[10]Philip M. Boffey, "The Money Traps in U.S. Health Care," *The New York Times* (21 January 2012). http://www.nytimes.com/2012/01/22/opinion/sunday/the-money-traps-in-us-health-care.html.

[11]"Healthcare Is Huge," *CompTIA*. http://enews.comptia.org/blog/comptia_hit_infographic.png.

[12]Kathryn Smith, "U.S. Health Care Spending 'Dwarfs' That of Other Countries," *Politico* (3 May 2012). http://www.politico.com/news/stories/0512/75851.html.

[13]Vanderbilt University Medical Center, "Recession Temporarily Easing Nursing Shortage" (12 June 2009). http://www.mc.vanderbilt.edu/news/releases.php?release=901.

[14]See Note 9.

[15]See Note 10.

[16]Arne Duncan and Reed Hastings, "A Digital Promise to Our Nation's Children," *The Wall Street Journal* (19 September 2011). http://online.wsj.com/article/SB10001424053111903927204576575101438816300.html.

[17]Robert B. Kozma, "Technology and Classroom Practices: An International Study," *Journal of Research on Technology in Education* 36, no. 1 (Fall 2003): 1–14. http://robertkozma.com/images/kozma_jrte.pdf.

[18]Michelle McNickle, "5 Things to Know about Watson's Role in Healthcare," *Healthcare IT News* (7 November 2011). http://www.healthcareitnews.com/news/5-things-know-about-watsons-role-healthcare.

[19]Ibid.

[20]Jordan Robertson, "The Health-Care Industry Turns to Big Data," *Bloomberg BusinessWeek* (17 May 2012). http://www.businessweek.com/articles/2012-05-17/the-health-care-industry-turns-to-big-data.

[21]Roger Foster, "Reducing Healthcare Administrative Inefficiencies with Big Data," *Government Health IT* (22 May 2012). http://www.govhealthit.com/news/reducing-healthcare-inefficiencies-big-data.

[22]Elizabeth Carey, "High Tech Way to Remember Your Meds," *Buffalo Business First* (10 January 2012). http://www.bizjournals.com/buffalo/blog/stay_tuned/2012/01/high-tech-way-to-remember-your-meds.html?page=all.

[23]Ibid.

[24]Steve Lohr, "New U.S. Research Will Aim at Flood of Digital Data," *The New York Times* (29 March 2012). http://www.nytimes.com/2012/03/29/technology/new-us-research-will-aim-at-flood-of-digital-data.html.

[25]Paul Fain, "Big Data's Arrival," *Inside Higher Ed* (1 February 2012).
http://www.insidehighered.com/news/2012/02/01/
using-big-data-predict-online-student-success.

[26]John Watson, Amy Murin, Lauren Vashaw, Butch Gemin, and Chris Rapp. "Keeping
Pace with K-12 Online Learning: An Annual Review of Policy and Practice," *Evergreen
Education Group* (2011). http://kpk12.com/cms/wp-content/uploads/
KeepingPace2011.pdf.

[27]"Healthcare Practices Embrace Mobile Technologies, New CompTIA Research
Reveals," *CompTIA* (16 November 2011). http://www.comptia.org/news/
pressreleases/11-11-16/Healthcare_Practices_Embrace_Mobile_
Technologies_New_CompTIA_Research_Reveals.aspx.

[28]Michelle McNickle, "11 Healthcare Data Trends in 2012," *Healthcare
IT News* (6 January 2012). http://www.healthcareitnews.com/
news/11-healthcare-data-trends-2012?page=0,0.

[29]Michelle McNickle, "13 Tips for Fighting Mobile Device Threats," *Healthcare
IT News* (19 June 2012). http://www.healthcareitnews.com/
news/13-tips-fighting-mobile-device-threats.

[30]"Technology in Education," *Education Week* (1 September 2011). http://www.edweek
.org/ew/issues/technology-in-education/.

[31]Michelle R. Davis, "'Safe' Social Networking Tailored for K-12 Schools," *Education Week*
(13 June 2011). http://www.edweek.org/ew/articles/2011/06/15/
35mm-social.h30.html.

[32] "New Resources Help with Using Skype in the Classroom," *eSchool News*
(23 May 2012). http://www.eschoolnews.com/2012/05/23/
new-resources-help-with-using-skype-in-the-classroom/.

[33]See Note 27.

[34]Milt Freudenheim, "The Doctor Will See You Now. Please Log On," *The New York Times* (29
May 2010). http://www.nytimes.com/2010/05/30/business/30telemed
.html?pagewanted=all.

[35]Deloitte Center for Health Solutions, "Deloitte 2012 Survey of U.S. Health Care Consumers:
The performance of the health care system and health care reform." http://www
.deloitte.com/assets/Dcom-UnitedStates/Local%20Assets/Documents/
Health%20Reform%20Issues%20Briefs/us_chs_IssueBrief_
2012ConsumerSurvey_061212.pdf.

[36]Project Tomorrow Speak Up, "Speak Up 2011: National Findings K-12 Teachers, Librarians
& Administrators" (May 2012). http://www.tomorrow.org/speakup/pdfs/SU11_
PersonalizedLearning_Educators.pdf.

[37]Sean Cavanagh, "U.S. Education Pressured by International Comparisons," *Education Week* (9 January 2012). http://www.edweek.org/ew/articles/2012/01/12/16overview.h31.html.

[38]Konstantin Kakaes, "No One Can Win the Future," *slate.com* (9 January 2012). http://www.slate.com/articles/technology/future_tense/2012/01/u_s_scientists_are_not_competing_with_china_or_any_other_country_.html.

[39]Ibid.

Chapter 13: The Global Race

[1]Ted C. Fishman, China, Inc.: How the Rise of the Next Superpower Challenges America and the World (New York: Simon & Schuster, 2005).

[2] Nicholas Carlson, "Facebook Now Has 901 Million Monthly Users, with 526 Million Coming Back Every Day," *San Francisco Times* (24 April 2012). http://www.sfgate.com/cgi-bin/article.cgi?f=/g/a/2012/04/23/businessinsiderfacebook-now-has-900.DTL.

[3]Wikipedia, "Guanxi." http://en.wikipedia.org/wiki/Guanxi.

[4]Fang Yang, "The Importance of Guanxi to Multinational Companies in China," Asian Social Science 7, no. 7 (July 2011). http://www.ccsenet.org/journal/index.php/ass/article/view/9446.

[5]Jackson Zhang, "Andrew Hupert, a Master in Chinese Guanxi Relationship, Discusses Aspects of Negotiation in China and Other Important Skills to Succeed in China," Rensselaer in China (1 May 2012). http://gcbc.union.rpi.edu/stories/andrew-hupert-a-master-in-chinese-guanxi-relationship-explains-aspects-of-negotiation/.

[6]See Note 4.

[7]"Five Myths about Business in China," *The Wall Street Journal* (19 June 2011). http://blogs.wsj.com/source/2011/06/19/five-myths-about-business-in-china/.

[8]Jackson Zhang, "Andrew Hupert, a Master in Chinese Guanxi Relationship, Discusses Aspects of Negotiation in China and Other Important Skills to Succeed in China," *Rensselaer in China* (1 May 2012). http://gcbc.union.rpi.edu/stories/andrew-hupert-a-master-in-chinese-guanxi-relationship-explains-aspects-of-negotiation/.

[9]CIA, *World Fact Book* (20 June 2012). https://www.cia.gov/library/publications/the-world-factbook/geos/ch.html.

[10]"Always On, Always Connected: Finding Growth Opportunities in an Era of Hypermobile Consumers," *The 2012 Accenture Consumer Electronics Products and Services Usage*

Report (2012). http://www.accenture.com/SiteCollectionDocuments/PDF/ Accenture_EHT_Research_2012_Consumer_Technology_Report.pdf#zoom=50.

[11]"China's Tech-Savy Consumers Have Highest Take-Up of E-Commerce and Mobile Technologies, Says KPMG Survey," *KPGM* (17 April 2012). http://www.kpmg.com/ cn/en/pressroom/pressreleases/pages/press-20120417-consumers-convergence.aspx.

[12]Ellyne Phneah, "Asians More Dependent on BYOD," *ZDNet* (2 July 2012). http:// www.zdnet.com/asians-more-dependent-on-byod-7000000104/.

[13]Sumita Raghuram and Dong Fang, "Telecommuting in China: Supervisory Power as a Determinant of Its Use," Penn State (2011). http://www.industrystudies.pitt .edu/pittsburgh11/documents/Presentations/PDF%20Presentations/ 5-6%20Raghuram.pdf.

[14]Jessica Stillman, "Scientists Prove Telecommuting Is Awesome," *GigaOM* (14 November 2011). http://gigaom.com/collaboration/ scientists-prove-telecommuting-is-awesome/.

[15]Ray Fishman, "Is Telecommuting a Good Idea?" *Slate.com* (9 November 2011). http:// www.slate.com/articles/business/the_dismal_science/2011/11/is_ working_from_home_a_good_idea_.html.

[16]Patrick Thibodeau, "Silicon Valley's Top Threat Is China, Survey Finds," *Computerworld* (28 June 2012). http://www.computerworld.com/s/article/9228619/ Silicon_Valley_s_top_threat_is_China_survey_finds.

[17]Ibid.

Index

Index